SHADOW
OF THE TITAN

Alan Fenton

COLLINS
8 Grafton Street, London W1
1989

William Collins Sons and Co. Ltd
London · Glasgow · Sydney · Auckland
Toronto · Johannesburg

First published 1989
Copyright © Alan Fenton 1989

BRITISH LIBRARY CATALOGUING IN PUBLICATION DATA

Fenton, Alan
Shadow of the titan.
I. Title
823'.914[F]

ISBN 0-00-223526-9

Photoset in Linotron Trump Mediaeval by
Rowland Phototypesetting Ltd,
Bury St Edmunds, Suffolk
Printed and bound in Great Britain by
Mackays of Chatham PLC, Chatham, Kent

FOR PRISCILLA

CONTENTS

BOOK ONE

Exodus

Jack Greenberg did not bother to knock. He ambled into Mortimer King's office, dumped his ample backside in a chair and laid his heels on the desk. He was too insensitive to notice, or too indifferent to care, that he was irritating his colleague.

'We would make a great team – you and me,' he said. 'The best.'

Mort contemplated the soles of Jack's shoes. There was a hole in one of them and the heel was worn. Jack would be mortified if he knew. Down at heel was not his image. Absolutely not. Down at heel was a lead weight on the upwardly mobile and Jack was as upwardly mobile as they came. It was how he saw himself – born to climb. He had started the process the moment the midwife dangled the ten pounds of slippery flesh and bone by the heels and slapped the shrivelled ass. At that instant Jack shrieked his protest and his scarlet face swelled to bursting. He was telling anyone who was there to listen that no one would ever do that to him again.

'Team?'

'You and me,' Jack repeated. 'That's what I said.'

'What did you have in mind?'

Jack eased his legs off the desk and leaned forward, lowering his voice conspiratorially.

'You're a winner, Mort. Everyone knows that. You might even make it on your own. You might, but why take the chance? The two of us . . . I tell you – with me you'd be unstoppable. Let's do it, Mort,' he urged.

'What are you talking about? Do what?'

'Force E.M. into retirement. You can be President of the Oil Corporation. I'll be number two. Just as long as my financial needs are taken care of – and I'm sure you'll organize that – I'll be happy.' Jack smiled ingratiatingly, sighed and looked up at the ceiling, as if his buoyant ambition were beaming him right up to E.M.'s office on the thirty-fifth floor.

'I have nothing against E.M.,' said Mort. 'On the contrary, I like the guy.'

'Sure you do. I hear you like his job too. I hear you like it a lot.' His expression conveyed that Jack Greenberg knew a thing or two.

Mort considered what he was about to say, like he always did. 'I have no interest in starting a Palace Revolution. All I want is what's due to me.'

'And if you don't get it?'

Mort stared at Jack impassively.

'What will you do? Quit?'

Mort was silent.

Jack persisted. 'Start your own company?'

'Whatever.' Mort moved a bunch of telexes from one end of his desk to the other as if he were pushing aside an uncomfortable question.

'You're crazy. It's all here in our hands. Don't you see? We hold all the cards. If you and I threatened to leave and take the best traders with us, it would be the end for E.M. What could he do? He'd have no company to run – nothing to sell.'

Mort was staring out of the window. What was he thinking?

'Face it, Mort – the thirty-fourth floor is great – it really is. I'd like to be here myself.' He looked around enviously. Mort's office was bigger than his, a whole lot bigger. The pile of the pure wool honey-brown carpet was thicker. And the desk – that damned pretentious desk. It was glowing now in the evening sun, brass-bound, deep shiny blue lacquer, while his . . . ? Well his was US Steel's standard 'don't look at me I'm just an employee' assembly-line

12

product, sprayed metallic grey. Mort's walls were lined with lemon-coloured wild silk, his were painted off-white. Off-white! Jesus!

'You've done great. But the thirty-fifth floor, Mort, now that's something else. That's the ultimate. It's as close to heaven as either of us will ever get. And you could be up there. You and me both.'

Mort nodded thoughtfully and crossed the room to the bronze-tinted plate glass. He looked down at Park Avenue, thirty-four floors down. It was the rush hour. Two million commuters were fighting their way home – most of them, it seemed, via Grand Central Station. Up here, the loudest sound was the hush of the air-conditioning. Down there was bedlam. A man could be knocked down and trampled in the panic.

The howl of a car horn drifted up like a distant cry for help ... some poor bastard, some cab driver no doubt, with a two-day growth and disillusioned eyes cursing his despairing way through yet another Manhattan evening ritual.

'Think about it, Mort. We could be up there.' Jack was beaming up again.

Mort settled in his chair and studied the only photograph on his desk. Jack followed his gaze. Julie – black hair, hazel eyes, lively, intelligent. A dish. Lucky bastard. How long had they been married? A long time. No children, though. He had often wondered why.

He was waiting for Mort to speak, but the guy never said a word. He just sat there, looking at Jack, calm and relaxed as ever. Mort and his silence – brooding, disturbing. You never knew what the hell he was thinking.

He leaned forward again, straining to capture Mort's attention, talking insistently, chopping the air with his hands, intense, persuasive.

'Listen to me, Mort. We put it to him. Sell us the shares of the Oil Corporation at a real good price, or else. He'd have no option. He would beg us to buy the company. On his hands and knees he'd beg us. Think of it. To own

13

the Oil Corporation. The biggest trading company in the whole goddam world. Is that what you always wanted or isn't it? Isn't that your dream? Be honest, Mort. Well, it doesn't have to be a dream any more. Don't you see? We could run the place our way, pay ourselves whatever we liked and, one day, when it's five times as big as it is now – because it will be, that's for sure – we could sell it and live in luxury. Or,' he added hastily, seeing the look on Mort's face, 'you could keep your shares and I could sell mine – to you, of course. Naturally.'

'Naturally,' said Mort.

Jack was trembling with excitement. 'Wouldn't it be great? Wouldn't it just? What do you say?'

Mort's face was impassive. He considered Jack – the blue eyes, the neat little nose and ears, the self-indulgent mouth and the fleshy, shiny face. Did he polish and buff it every morning before he left for the office? He considered him coolly, concealing his distaste.

'I have to tell you something, Jack . . .' He left a pause.

Jack nosed the air apprehensively, like a wild animal suspecting a trap but too hungry to resist the bait.

'Go ahead.'

'If I needed help, you'd be the last man I'd turn to.'

Jack flushed angrily. 'What are you saying, for Chrissake?'

'I don't trust you. I never did. Not since I caught you with those busy little hands in the till. Remember, Jack? Making out phoney charter parties at inflated freight rates and pocketing the difference? Bad for the company. Good for Jack. Remember?'

'That was a long time ago,' Jack muttered sulkily. 'I was just a kid.'

'Sure you were. Just a kid. A kid of twenty-six. I wonder what E.M. would have said if I'd told him?'

Suddenly Jack was grappling with hysteria. 'You gave me your word.' His face was shinier than ever and two thin rivulets of sweat trickled down the plump cheeks

14

towards the chin. 'You swore you'd never tell him. It would finish him if you did.'

'What you mean is it would finish you,' said Mort contemptuously. 'Don't worry. As long as you behave yourself, I'll keep my word.'

Jack glared at him sullenly. 'Don't threaten me. It makes me nervous. Besides . . .' He was looking a touch more cheerful. 'You gave me the file. Maybe you forgot?'

'No,' said Mort, 'I hadn't forgotten.' He had given Jack the file, but he had kept his own copy. Only Jack did not know that.

'You're making a mistake.' Jack stood by the door, reluctant to leave, still hoping for a change of heart. 'I made you a fair offer. You shouldn't have thrown it back in my face.'

Mort was already picking up a telex, seeming to ignore him.

'Jack.'

Was that a half smile on Mort's face?

A glimmer of hope. 'What is it?' Petulant – like a scolded child.

'You have a hole in your shoe,' said Mort, not looking up.

Jack's mouth gaped. 'What?'

'The sole of your shoe. There's a hole in it. I thought you'd like to know.'

Standing there, his mouth twisting, Jack tried to articulate his resentment, but it was no use. The words were not there.

'Asshole,' he muttered as he slammed the door.

It was a moot point, Mort reflected, whether it was more dangerous to have Jack Greenberg as a friend or an enemy.

Edmund Meyer was a big man, big in every sense of the word. His head was big, with its crop of white hair contrasting so dramatically with the bushy black eyebrows; his shrewd brown eyes were big; his nose, too, the dominant feature and focus of his face, its proud curve asserting his Jewish ancestry. He would sooner have eaten a side of ham than have a nose job. Either one would have been a betrayal of everything he believed in, of his allegiance to his ethnic background, his commitment to his religious upbringing, his unquestioning acceptance of his destiny. A man with a big reputation, dwarfing his competitors, Brobdingnagian in Lilliput, at the age of fifty-eight boss and majority shareholder of the Oil Corporation, the largest, most dynamic oil trading organization in the world, he weighed in at around two hundred pounds and forty or fifty million dollars. Maybe more. He had not counted his money recently. Not bad for the son of a Czechoslovakian cobbler.

He believed in three things: the Oil Corporation, survival and Edmund Meyer. His baby – his life's work – was the company. His employees were his family and he was their father. He demanded absolute devotion and loyalty from everyone who worked for him and, in return, he gave them a sense of belonging, the feeling that they were involved in a community that cared. Whether it did, or not, was beside the point. Working for Edmund Meyer was sufficient reward. Everyone knew him. He was a face and a force around town, respected for his fairness, admired for his success.

Unfortunately, the admiration lavished on him by his staff did not seem to be shared by his family. It was something he could never understand. After all, did he not treat them with exactly the same consideration and generosity with which he treated his employees? And yet, despite the attention he gave them, for all the care and concern he bestowed on them, they were a disappointment to him. Life, for sure, was too short and business too time-consuming to get over-involved, but he had the humiliating sense of being less important at home than he was at the office, and so, not unnaturally, as time passed, he devoted more and more of his efforts where they appeared to be most productive and most profitable.

Why his daughter should be so different from him he

16

could never understand. Was she not his own flesh and blood? Could she not at least have humoured her father by showing some interest in the business? But no, it seemed that rebellion was endemic in the young and yet another indication of the modern generation's lack of love and respect for their parents. He had given her everything money could buy, including the best psychiatrist in New York, but it was all futile. She was fat, lazy and oversexed. Her all-consuming interests – and consuming was the word – were Hershey bars, rocky-road ice cream and hot fudge sauce. And boys. It was sad. Sadder still for E.M. that he had no son to carry on the family name and, more important, the family business.

And so, Edmund Meyer consoled himself for these domestic shortcomings with the compensations of life thirty-five floors above Park Avenue. Here, he was someone. More than someone. He was it.

He hooked his thumbs in his blood-red suspenders and drummed his fingers complacently on his chest. In the office he rarely wore a tie and never a jacket. He liked to present the image of a worker to his employees. Of course God help any of them who schlepped round the office looking like he did. There were certain standards that had to be maintained. Tolerance was fine, but it was no use pretending that you were the same as everyone else. You were not. How could you be? You had made it. They hadn't. Not that he had ever forgotten where his roots lay. He knew about life down there in the canyons of Manhattan. He knew where he came from. He had not always been one of the immortals. That was why, from time to time, he made a conscious effort to recall – hard as it might be – what it had once been like to be just another ordinary guy.

Jack Greenberg knew where his duty lay. Duty, after all, was not such a hard taskmaster when you discovered – as Jack had long ago – that duty coincided with self-interest. What he lacked in intellect, he made up for in guile, diplomacy and an infallible instinct for being in the right place at the right time, that place, in Jack's estimation, being as close to Edmund Meyer's asshole as it was possible to get. Whenever he was in the vicinity, his cerebral Geiger counter crackled as joyfully as if E.M.'s fundament had been stuffed with enriched uranium.

A wise man, Jack had learned, remained as near to the source of power as he could. Proximity was ninety per cent of the battle.

When other executives were floundering, when they found themselves cornered, savaged and shredded by E.M.'s tongue at the morning meeting in the pine-panelled boardroom, Jack sat back and smiled inwardly, congratulating himself on his cleverness. Those poor creeps. They thought they were smart. They were too, some of them. They knew about tankers, they knew about charter parties, they knew about sources of supply and they knew about outlets. They knew all there was to know about the oil industry, but he – he knew something far more important: he knew what Edmund Meyer was thinking. Moreover, he had perfected the knack of repeating what E.M. had told him an hour or two before in such a way that it sounded like his own idea. He was so convincing, he often had the Titan fooled. E.M. would nod and smile and look round the boardroom when Jack was speaking as if to say, 'Why couldn't you schlemiels have thought of that?'

Jack, the faithful dog, followed his master everywhere he went. He rode to the office with him in the stretch Cadillac; he lunched with him in the executive dining room; he stood by him in the urinals, sighing when he sighed, shaking when he shook; he sat in the next cubicle and held his nose, tempted sometimes to make a dash for it, but restrained – always restrained by the inseparable Siamese twin obligations of duty and self-interest. Day after day, month after month, year after year, Jack trailed his master's rear end, crackling away.

E.M. found these attentions flattering. He was by no means blind to their hidden purpose, but he appreciated them none the less. They demonstrated not only admirable respect, but a grasp of priorities that was, in his view, praiseworthy.

Dedicated self-interest was a motive he could readily relate to, though not, perhaps, something he could ever admire. For all that, he was fond of Jack, and Jack responded by being protective, available and servile.

'I hate to tell you this, E.M.,' he said. 'As you know it's not in my nature to stab a colleague in the back. I'd sooner cut off my right arm.'

E.M.'s big eyes grew even bigger at this piece of gratuitous bullshit. He wondered what was coming next.

'It's just that – for me – the company comes first. In my book loyalty takes precedence over . . . well, over any damn thing. Even friendship.'

Jack paused, feigning deep emotion, but really checking E.M.'s reaction. Then, satisfied that his master was listening approvingly, he went on.

'That guy is going to make trouble if we're not very careful.'

E.M. was not sure he appreciated the use of the word 'we' in this context. It implied an identity of interest that was almost irreverent, but he let it go.

'That guy?'

Jack paused again, seemingly tormented, as if he were taking the strain, roped by his feet and hands between the stallions of duty and friendship, and E.M. were standing over him with a six-shooter in his hand.

'What guy?' E.M. could not have sounded less sympathetic to Jack in his apparent predicament.

It was time.

'Mort.' He was galled to note that E.M.'s brown eyes softened momentarily at the mention of the name. But the expression soon passed.

'What's with Mort?'

'He wants more money and he wants a promotion.'

'Promotion. What promotion?' Edmund Meyer's voice was scornful, incredulous, and it riled Jack. 'Mort is already number two man in the company. One day he'll be number one. What more can he want? What's with this promotion?' E.M. laid his huge hands palms up on the desk and showed Jack the New York Jewish shrug.

Jack Greenberg flinched. He hated to be reminded that Mortimer King was senior to him and he loathed the way E.M. invariably spoke about Mort as if he were some kind of young god.

E.M. flashed his perfect crowns in a sardonic grin. 'How many presidents can a company have?'

Jack paused to enhance the dramatic effect of his words. 'That's what Mort says.'

He watched the big face glow red, then drain white.

'What . . . what are you saying?'

'I'm saying,' said Jack, 'that Mort is telling everyone he should be President. Not you.' He sat back and watched the show.

'Not me.' E.M.'s throat seemed to be closing up. He could scarcely squeeze out the words. 'What is supposed to happen to me?'

'You, E.M.,' said Jack, plunging in the knife, the mortal blow at the back of the neck that dispatches the bull, 'you are going to be an ex-president.' He recognized too well the signs of an imminent storm to hang around when he had better things to do. His work was accomplished. He closed the door quietly, respectfully, behind him and strolled off down the corridor humming to himself.

Jack lay on his back, panting slightly, and concentrated on lighting up a long fat Monte Cristo cigar. He was satisfied that he had earned it. At this moment he was a happy man. He had never understood the Latin phrase . . . what was it? Post coitum something something something . . . triste . . . Whatever. What the hell was there to feel sad about? He had never felt low after a good screw. Fatigued, sometimes. Depressed, never.

Maybe he should take more exercise. Apart from screwing, that is. He touched the mounds of fat under his chin

20

where his jawline used to be. Diets . . . he had tried them all. Who cared anyway? When he held his head up, no one could see he had a double chin.

He felt good. This time, Mortimer King was surely overreaching. When a man was off balance, a sharp finger-prod in the back – a Jack Greenberg special – was really all that was needed. He had seen this Western once. The baddie had slipped and fallen, screaming, all the way down into the depths of the Grand Canyon. That was how it would be. Only this canyon was not the Grand one; it was Park Avenue, and the baddie was Mortimer King. How he hated the cocky, confident bastard . . . Fade on Jack Greenberg's face, smiling through the window of his office. Music up and over. Roll credits . . . And he would get them all. What a dream. Only it was not a dream any more. It was about to happen.

He puffed at his cigar contentedly and patted the large white breast squashed against his chest. One for the road, he thought. His batteries still recharged pretty damn fast. Thirty-three was not that old, after all.

Rachel was counting on her fingers.

'I'll be sixteen in exactly a hundred and twenty-three days,' she cooed, 'the anniversary of our first screw.'

Jack's batteries suddenly went flat.

'Jesus, honey. Must you keep reminding me you're underage?'

'I thought it excited you.'

'Sure, honey,' he said. 'Sure it excites me. If it excites me any more, I'll have a cardiac arrest.'

'You're funny, Jack. When I'm sixteen, you can ask me to marry you.'

'And you can turn me down.'

Rachel pouted. He had forgotten that girls still pouted.

He looked down at her. Marriage to Rachel Meyer? The idea had certainly occurred to him. The Boss's daughter. Heiress to a fortune but, what was more important, heiress to the Oil Corporation.

He looked at her again as she lay there, fifteen, fat and

21

silly, and decided it was a temptation he could resist. Besides, E.M. would never accept him as a son-in-law.

Rachel began to stroke the hairs on his chest.

'You know what Rachel means in Hebrew?'

'No,' he said indifferently. 'Should I?'

She giggled. 'Naive and innocent.'

'Your father should only know,' said Jack gloomily.

'There's a lot of things he should know,' said Rachel.

'For instance?'

'I'm pregnant,' she said.

Jack choked on his cigar. He felt that stabbing pain in his chest again.

'Jesus Christ. Don't make jokes like that.'

But it was not a joke.

The Oil Corporation was a company rich in many things but, above all, in vice-presidents. It had executive vice-presidents, junior vice-presidents, senior vice-presidents, trading vice-presidents, administrative vice-presidents, area vice-presidents, group vice-presidents, financial vice-presidents and many others. E.M. invented the titles when he had nothing better to do. It was his equivalent of the British New Year Honours' List and, every year, one or two more devoted employees were rewarded. None of the titles meant a damn thing, nothing more than an ego massage, or a substitute for an increase in bonus.

The real status of an employee of the Oil Corporation was measured not by his title, but by the manner in which he was received on entering Edmund Meyer's office. Most merited no more than a twitch of the eyebrows, or an indifferent wave of the hand. They were rarely invited to take a seat. A successful executive – one, for example, who had recently pulled off a lucrative trading coup – might earn from E.M. a half crouch, a brief contortion in which the President raised a reluctant butt three inches from his chair, shook hands swiftly with his flushed and flattered employee and, virtually simultaneously, sank down again.

Jack Greenberg was special.

He normally received an invitation to sit coupled with a smile or a wave, even, on particularly good days, a fractional uplift of the presidential ass.

Mortimer King, on the other hand, received the kind of greeting any other VP of the Oil Corporation would have killed for.

When he entered the presidential suite, Edmund Meyer stood up instantly, beamed, walked briskly round his desk to greet Mort and, towering over his favourite, opened wide his arms and embraced him. Crossing to the group of armchairs in the corner of the room reserved for distinguished visitors, he lowered his massive frame into one of them and beckoned to Mort. So low was the chair that when he leaned back, his great head with its thick white crop of hair was barely higher than his knees. Mort took his time. He selected the chair by E.M.'s desk – an open-ended Sheraton-style piece of great pretensions and little worth – carried it over to the corner, sat by his boss and looked down at him.

E.M. waved to the armchair opposite him.

'Make yourself comfortable,' he said expansively.

'This'll do fine,' said Mort, the inflexion of his voice suggesting that he was not worthy of an armchair.

E.M. tried to push himself up from floor level, but, struggle as he might, he was unable to prevent himself from slipping back again. For a moment it troubled him – the feeling that he had been outmanoeuvred – but he quickly dismissed it. There was, after all, no doubt in anyone's mind who was the boss.

He glowed approvingly at his protégé.

Mortimer King was thirty-eight. What you noticed first were his catlike green eyes, bright, predatory. There was about him an air of confidence, of absolute conviction and resolution. He knew what he was doing. He knew where he was going.

As always, he came straight to the point.

'I have some figures for you, E.M. Don't read them now,

but when you do, you'll see they confirm an interesting fact. Over the last seven years, I have consistently generated more than sixty per cent of the Oil Corporation's profits.'

E.M. struggled to lever his body a few inches higher in his chair.

'No one can say that,' he said. 'This is a team. Decisions are made by the team. Profits are generated by the team. We're like a family. Each member of the family makes his special and unique contribution.' He spread his arms wide and smiled benevolently.

Mort had heard the speech before. He laid a file of papers on the low table in front of Edmund Meyer.

'I had an accountant go over the figures,' he said.

E.M. looked at the neat pile of papers and began to tap the table nervously with his thick fingers. What was it about Mort that was different? The man was so goddam self-contained. Look at the way he had simply ignored his best speech. There was always the sense that he knew more than he said. It was disturbing. Disrespectful even. He decided to show a glint of the iron hand.

'This is really not necessary, Mort. You know how I trust my employees.'

Just to set the record straight, E.M. liked to remind people on occasions where they stood in relation to him. An employee was an employee. Even the best.

'Yes, E.M.,' said Mort, 'I know how you trust your employees.'

Was there not just a hint of irony in his voice? E.M. hastily pulled on the velvet glove. He would have to tread cautiously.

'Mort, my boy, you're like a son to me.' His voice broke. It was painful to reflect that he had no son. 'Sure you've made a unique contribution to this company. No doubt about it and I'm grateful to you. We're all grateful. But think, Mort . . . we all benefit from the company's success . . . you, me, everyone. We rejoice in each other's success.'

24

He flipped through the pages in front of him without seeing the figures.

'After all,' he said expansively, spreading wide his arms again, as if to embrace the whole building, 'this is our company, Mort.' He liked the phrase. 'This is our company,' he repeated.

'No it's not. It's yours,' said Mort.

'What?' For a moment E.M. was confused, distracted by his own rhetoric. Mort was never distracted.

'I said it's your company, not mine.'

'So? Who cares who owns it?' Edmund Meyer decided to rip off the velvet glove, to exercise his authority. For the first time, he raised his voice. Any other man would have been cowed, but not Mort. He was completely indifferent to E.M.'s rages, impervious to his autocratic manner.

'I care,' he said.

Edmund Meyer wagged an imperious forefinger at his favourite son. 'Be careful,' he said. 'Don't kill the goose that lays the golden eggs.'

He sat back, looking like a man who has just made an original, not to say inspired, statement. His eyes gleamed and his expression had an inference of 'checkmate' about it.

'I don't want to kill the goose,' said Mort. 'I just want more eggs.'

E.M. glared at Mort, drawing down his black brows menacingly. He was beginning to feel that things were not completely in his control: not an experience he was accustomed to. Mort stared back at him with his clear green eyes, expressionless, unwavering.

'We'll talk about it,' said E.M. He was playing for time and they both knew it.

'When?'

'Soon.'

'When?'

'Next week.'

'Tomorrow would be better,' said Mort coolly.

E.M. hesitated, then he raised his hands, showing Mort the giant palms. It was a gesture of surrender.

'Tomorrow,' he agreed. 'We'll talk tomorrow.'

'I'd like you to know what I have in mind, so you can prepare yourself,' said Mort.

It sounded ominous. But there had to be a way out. There always was. He could not afford to lose Mort. Who would run the company when he was gone? Who would carry on his life's work? He had no son of his own. Who would take on the burden? Not Jack Greenberg, that was for sure.

'I wish I had a son like you,' he said quietly. 'I wish you were my son.'

Emotional blackmail. 'Please, E.M. . . .'

E.M. raised a hand once more, this time to turn aside the protest.

'No, I mean it. I created a great company and you've helped me make it the best in the world. I salute you. But don't ask too much of me. Don't ask me more than I can give. Don't forget loyalty, Mort.' E.M. wagged his forefinger again. 'Doesn't the company deserve loyalty? Don't I?'

'Who knows, E.M.? Who knows what any of us deserves?'

Edmund Meyer felt cold, afraid almost, for the first time in his life. He realized that before he met Mort, he had never really known what single-mindedness was.

'What do you want from me?'

'More money.'

'What else?'

Mort considered his boss. At fifty-eight he looked younger than his years. A big man. A Titan. He had strength and vitality. He could still work harder, still outthink and outsmart anyone in the oil business. The company was his life. Mort knew that. He was almost sorry for him.

'I want your job,' he said.

E.M.'s reaction was surprisingly restrained, perhaps

26

because he was not unprepared. There was no outrage, no temper tantrum, not even a comment. He simply pushed himself up and, shoulders hunched, walked slowly across the room to his desk. There he stood for a few moments, looking bewildered, as though he had forgotten where he was. Picking up a silver-framed photograph of his family he looked at it for a long time, wishing that it could have given him more pleasure. The greatest satisfaction he had in his life was here in this room. And now this youngster wanted to take it all away from him. Suddenly he was infinitely depressed. He felt so wretched, it was almost unbearable.

'I never thought I would hear that from anyone, least of all from you, Mort,' he said sadly. In that moment he looked his age. More than his age. He looked an old man. 'No one understands the meaning of the word "loyalty" any more,' he muttered.

Reuben King stared at his half-brother as if he were crazy.

'What's wrong with the Oil Corporation?'

'Nothing.'

'So why quit?'

'It's not my company.'

'You want your own company? No problem. Take this one. I give it to you for nothing. You'd be doing me a favour.'

'It's not your company I want,' said Mort. 'It's you.' He looked around Ruby's office. The floor was stacked with files. Somewhere, under the heaps of papers, legal tomes, documents and ashtrays, was a desk. Through the open door he could hear Ruby's secretary screaming down the phone and the clients in the waiting room complaining loudly to each other about life in general and their spouses in particular. The words drifted down the corridor ... 'How can you live with a man who never leaves you alone? The moment he comes home from the office ... I swear on the Bible. I hear his key in the door and I want to run ... the man's a sexual pervert. Three times a night ...

27

the only time he puts his pants on is when he goes down to the deli . . .'

'Three times a night?'

'Sometimes four.'

'You've got to be joking.' Enviously.

'What do you think? I'm inventing it? You should see the size of it. You think I could invent that. I can't take any more . . . at my age, noch .'

'So what will you do?'

'Sue for divorce. What else can I do?'

'On what grounds?'

'Impotence.'

'Are you crazy? Three times a night, sometimes four, and you sue him for impotence?'

'It's what he wants. He says if I tell the truth about him all the women on the Upper West Side will be after him. All he wants is a quiet life. Don't we all?'

Ruby shrugged apologetically. 'That's how it is to be a Midtown Manhattan lawyer.'

'How do you stand it?'

'What can I tell you? It's tough sometimes. The money's lousy. Even if those guys out there paid their bills – which they don't – I wouldn't exactly be setting the world on fire. But then who wants to be the richest Jew on the Upper West Side? It would complicate my life and the neighbours would talk. I'm a simple guy. What do I need with money?'

'Who said anything about need?'

'What can you do with it? You buy clothes and more clothes. How many suits can you wear? How many houses can you live in? How many vacations can you take? OK, so I'd buy Sarah a diamond necklace and a mink. What then?'

'Would you believe I'm not in it for the money?'

'You're going into business on your own and you're not in it for the money? You've got to be kidding.'

'I don't kid, Ruby.'

'So tell me – what are you doing it for?'

28

Mort looked into the middle distance with those catlike eyes of his.

'What can I tell you, Ruby? I was never the greatest at self-analysis. I guess I'm programmed, that's all. When I see Pop and what life has done to him, I'd like to do things differently. I'm going to make it up to him for all those things he wanted and never had.'

'What are you talking about? Life never did anything to him. He just never made it big. Millions of guys don't make it big and they learn to live with it. He never did. Well, that's his bag – not yours, not mine. Have an eclair,' said Ruby. He reached into the top right-hand drawer of his desk and pulled out a deli bag. Producing a fat chocolate eclair, he waved it under Mort's nose.

Mort shuddered. 'No thanks. I'll pass.'

'You had breakfast?'

'A cup of coffee.'

Ruby attacked the eclair. The cream blossomed on his face. 'You don't eat right,' he said. 'You're too thin.'

'You're overweight.'

Ruby grinned and patted his stomach. 'I'm into greed,' he said. 'It's the latest thing.'

Words floated into the office, a man's voice this time, heavily sarcastic . . . 'Would it be too much trouble. . . ? Your being his secretary and all. Could you maybe ask Mr King to grant me an audience? It's Shabbath tomorrow, the day I make out with my wife. It looks like I'll still be waiting here, so maybe you should phone her and tell her to start without me?'

Followed by prolonged high-pitched shrieking . . . presumably Ruby's secretary . . .

The man was laughing. 'Ugly fat bitch.'

Hysterical wailing and heavy sobs . . .

Mort raised an eyebrow.

Ruby looked embarrassed. 'My secretary is full of complexes. She has this thing about her looks. I don't know why, but she's convinced she's ugly.'

'That's not a complex. She's right. She *is* ugly.'

'She's a great secretary. What can you do?'

Mort waved at the chaos. 'Better than this.'

Ruby moved some cigarette ash around his filthy shirt-front and scratched his unshaven face.

'When did you last shave?' said Mort.

'Who knows?' said Ruby. 'Yesterday. The day before. I don't remember.'

'You're letting yourself go,' said Mort sourly. 'A two-day growth in the office. That's not good.'

Ruby slammed his hands on the desk. He was beginning to lose patience with his brother. 'What do you want of me? I'm a lawyer. I'm a Talmudic scholar. I'm no businessman. If you want to know what I really am – I'm a frustrated rabbi. You want clean-shaven? You want Ivy League? This is the wrong address. Try Fiftieth Street.'

'I want smart. That's what you are, Ruby.'

Ruby assumed his tormented expression. 'Listen to me, Mort. I'm not your man. I smoke. I eat chopped liver and schmalz every day. I'm addicted to chocolate eclairs. If there was such a thing as an eclairoholic, that's what I'd be. My flesh oozes cholesterol. I'm thinking of leaving my arteries to science as a warning to others. You understand what I'm saying? I'm saturated, man. I'm not what you want. You want healthy? You want unsaturated? Do me a favour. Try Fiftieth. Try anywhere you like – only leave me in peace.'

'When can you start?' said Mort.

'Don't you ever give up?'

'You know me better than that.'

Ruby bridled. 'What, in God's name, makes you think you can railroad everyone in the world into doing what you want them to do? Forget it. I like what I'm doing. I don't want to change. See yourself out.'

Mort picked up his coat – the same undistinguished dark blue belted raincoat he had worn for the last ten years . . . maybe more.

'How many times you reckon the average guy screws

30

his wife?' he said, as if he were asking Ruby the time. 'Forgetting the one out there.'

Ruby removed his glasses and rubbed his shrewd brown eyes. Then he put them on again and directed a hostile glare at Mort.

'What the fuck are you talking about?'

'Twice a week? Three times? . . . Let's say three times shall we?'

'Why not?' said Ruby nervously, now convinced that his brother had lost his marbles.

'You know anything about sperm counts. . . ? OK, you know nothing about sperm counts. Well, I'll tell you. Every time a guy lets loose . . . Pow! About three hundred million spermatozoa are launched into space, if you know what I mean by space . . .'

Ruby disdained to answer.

'And out of those three hundred million, give or take a few million, only one, just one little fellow hits the jackpot. Or does he? . . . Maybe he's trapped in a rubber chamber. Maybe he dies in a sea of spermicidal cream. Maybe he swims all that way and finds nothing. No egg. Wrong time of the month. Whatever.'

'Mort, I'm busy. I know about sex. I watch television.'

'And what about all the billions, the billions and billions of spermatozoa that never even get the chance . . . what happens to them, Ruby?'

'What the hell. . . ?'

'You don't know, do you? Nor do I. But I tell you something, Ruby. Every one of those little guys, every one of them, is a potential human being, a potential Reuben King . . . only they never make it. Right?'

'I made it,' said Ruby.

Mort was putting on his coat. 'Lucky you.'

'So?'

'You have any idea what the chances are of being born?'

'No one can answer that.'

'A billion to one? Ten billion? A trillion? A hundred trillion?'

31

'What are you saying, Mort? For Chrissake, what are you saying?'

'What am I saying? Life's a long shot, Ruby – a real long shot. That's all I'm saying. Don't waste it.'

He closed the door quietly behind him.

Edmund Meyer greeted Mort affectionately, but also with foreboding. This was one deal he could not afford to blow. This was the big one. He was ready to give up a whole lot to keep Mortimer King in the fold.

Nothing, nothing in the world was more important to him right now.

'Tell me what's in your heart, Mort,' he said. He smiled a big smile. He felt kindly, well disposed to his protégé, and he intended to keep the discussion on the same level: intimate and gracious.

Mort had other ideas.

'This one's strictly in my head, E.M.'

When he said that, E.M. knew he had lost. He fought hard, because that was the only way he understood, but he knew it was hopeless.

'I want the salary and bonus I deserve – not what you think you can get away with paying me.'

'I'll make you an offer you can't refuse,' E.M. said jocularly. He paused for dramatic effect. 'You can have a salary of a million dollars. Your bonus at the end of the year will be another million.'

He sat back, thrusting out his jaw like an exclamation mark, as if daring Mort to complain.

Mort made no comment. It was a generous offer – more, much more than he would have asked for.

'And the presidency?'

'You can have that, too,' said E.M.

Mort let out a breath, a deep sigh of satisfaction. And yet . . . It was not like E.M. to give in without a fight, not his style. Was there a catch?

'When?'

'When I'm sixty-five,' said E.M. 'I guess that's reasonable.'

Mort frowned. So, there it was. The catch.

'I'm not waiting seven years. I want it now.'

E.M. soothed the air with his hands. 'Take it easy,' he said. 'Now is too soon. I know what's best for you.'

E.M. always knew what was best for everyone.

'I'm ready now. The company's ready. You can be Chairman – the nominal boss. You can stay as long as you like. You don't have to retire when you're sixty-five – not ever. Name your salary. Name your terms. Whatever you want. But I won't accept anything less than the job of Chief Executive – the President.'

Edmund Meyer spoke softly, but there was menace in his voice.

'Haven't you forgotten something?'

'I don't think so.'

'No? Haven't you forgotten I own the stock? It's my company. Like you said.'

Mort nodded. 'That would be part of the deal. I want you to sell me fifty-one per cent of the Oil Corporation – at a fair price of course.'

To Edmund Meyer it was the ultimate intolerable arrogance. It was the end. He raised a huge hand as though about to strike Mort. His brown eyes glowered with rage. His black brows bunched.

He thundered the words. Angry Titan. 'You're crazy. You're obsessed with power and money. You lust after it. It's unnatural. God help you. I'll make you a prophecy . . . One day it will destroy you. One day you'll regret you ever spoke to me the way you just did. What you want, you can't have. No one can. Get out of here. You're through. Get out! You disloyal goddam bastard! You arrogant son-ofabitch!'

Edmund Meyer's mouth hung open as he fought for breath. His hands were shaking like an old man's and his fleshy face was streaked with sweat. He shuffled across the room with small hesitant steps and collapsed into the high-backed leather chair behind his desk, clutching its arms for security, as if he would fall out of it if he let go. The meaning was clear. It was his desk, his chair, his room.

And it was his company.

'All this,' he panted. 'Who do you think did all this? Look around you, boy. Not you. Not any of those assholes out there.'

'You did,' said Mort quietly. 'No one can take that away from you.'

Edmund Meyer leaned across his desk and hissed the words: 'No one's ever going to take it away from me, my friend.'

'I only want what's due to me,' said Mort.

'When I think ... when I think what I've done for you ...' Loyalty. Forgotten word.

'I know what you've done and I'm grateful.'

'You're nothing without me. Wait and see.'

'At least let me leave decently,' said Mort. 'I'll stay on three months, hand over to Jack. It'll be good for the company.'

'So you can steal my secrets? You must really think I'm crazy.'

'I never stole anything in fifteen years. Why should I now?'

'Where will you go?' E.M.'s voice was low, like a man defeated.

Mort did not answer.

'What will you do?'

'Start my own company – maybe.'

'That was what you wanted all the time. I warn you – stay out of the oil business.'

'I wouldn't count on it,' said Mort.

Edmund Meyer's face was deathly white. His hand trembled as he pressed the intercom.

'Send in Greenberg. Get him in here, right away.'

'I'm sorry, E.M.,' said Mort. 'I'm truly sorry.'

Edmund Meyer sat at his desk, his chest heaving. No

34

longer Brobdingnagian in Lilliput, he looked shrunken, boneless, like a rag doll in an oversized chair.

Jack Greenberg rushed in. E.M. stood up, erect, autocratic, in control again.

'Mortimer King is leaving the company,' he said. 'Have him out of the building in fifteen minutes. He can take his private possessions, but no papers – absolutely no papers – and don't let him out of your sight. I want every lock in the office changed by tomorrow morning.'

'Not like this,' Mort said. 'Not after all these years.'

The Titan loomed over him. 'You want me to make it easy for you, Mort? You betray me and you want me to make it easy for you? You make me vomit. You've broken faith. You've sold out to the enemy. You're nothing but a goddam renegade.'

BOOK TWO

---◆◆◆---

The Renegades

Sarah was upright and angular. Before she married Ruby she might even have been described as severe, but eleven years of marriage had blunted the sharp edges and softened the outlines. There was not a trace of subtlety or deviousness about her. She was what you saw and what you saw was a woman whose simplicity was her strength, whose emotions were honest and direct and whose intellect was neither troubled by doubts nor exercised by curiosity.

She had never left the Upper West Side, except once to go to Lincoln Center to see a ballet which she had not enjoyed – an adventure that only strengthened her stubborn conviction that she was happiest at home. That was where her duty and her pleasure blended in perfect measure. It was where she felt fulfilled, comfortable.

Ruby was her contact with the outside world, the only contact she needed. She, in return, was his prop and his security. She had done her duty in bed and eight-year-old Saul and seven-year-old Ruth bore witness to that. Ruby's jovial interest in sex was something she tolerated but never understood. For her, the regular weekly upheavals of the sheets were to be endured for Ruby's sake. Sex was an uncontrollable urge, a quirk of the male hormones, less disgusting perhaps than comic, but for all that not a significant part of life and not relevant to her relationship with her husband.

These things were never mentioned by her; they were simply not included on her list of subjects acceptable for family discussion, with the reservation that anything that Ruby chose to say, or do for that matter, was sacrosanct.

39

In her eyes, the sun rose and set with her husband – not to mention the moon and the outer planets. Her approval was fundamental, unquestioning and uncompromising.

Ruby knew exactly what he had got and he appreciated it; not that he had ever, or would ever, give up hoping that his wife would grow to understand that physical passion was an essential ingredient of marriage – even of marriage. But it was not at the top of his list and he had largely sublimated this most natural of impulses in favour of work and food.

'Do you think I need a change, Sarah?' he asked her.

'If you think so,' said Sarah reasonably.

'I like familiar things,' said Ruby. 'You know what the word "familiar" means? It means things that relate to the family.'

At heart, Ruby was a scholar, never happier than when he was exchanging views on some abstruse interpretation of an obscure phrase in the Talmud with his Chassidic friends.

'That's what I am. A family man. That's what I live for – my wife, my kids, my home. What do I need with change? What do I need with money? What do I need with success?'

'You're right, dear,' said Sarah.

'I know what I want. I guess you do, too.'

'You want to be a rabbi, dear.'

'Two years . . . three at the most . . . I always promised myself I'd give up the law practice some day.'

'Yes, dear,' said Sarah patiently.

'I'm an intellectual. Business is not for me. Mort is different. He always hankered after adventure. He was always the ambitious one. It's right for him to start up on his own. That's what he needs to do. He'll do great. He'll make a fortune and he doesn't need me to help him do it.'

'No, dear.'

'He's my brother and I love him, but I tell you, sometimes I think the guy's a screwball. You know what he wants me to do? He wants me to drop everything – close down the practice in a couple of weeks and join him. Just like that. Can you imagine?'

'No dear.'

Ruby was meditating. She knew the signs. His eyes were blank, his face drained of all expression. What was he thinking about? The Talmud? The kids? A case he was working on? Maybe that poor woman who was suing her husband for divorce because he . . . he . . . how many times a night had Ruby said? Men were animals. Thank God Ruby was not obsessed with . . . all that.

'Sarah?'

'Uhuh?'

'How many spermatozoa do you think there are in one ejaculation?'

Sarah blushed to the roots of her hair – every root of every hair in every part of her body.

'I – uh – I really don't know . . . dear.' She cleared her throat.

'Guess.'

'I really couldn't say.'

'Three hundred million.'

'Is that a fact?'

'You only get one chance, Sarah. Life's a real long shot.'

'So, when are you joining Mort?'

'In a couple of weeks.' Ruby grinned. It was good to have a wife who understood you.

'It happened,' said Mort. 'I never thought about it. I never planned it. It just happened.'

Julie gave her husband that lopsided smile of hers, and in her big hazel eyes there was that mocking look that seemed to question life itself.

'You planned it,' she said. She knew Mort well enough by now.

She looked at him pensively and suddenly her eyes were sad. She could not recall when it was that they had stopped talking to each other – really talking. When was it that he had begun to dedicate himself so completely to business that she had become just another entry in his diary? In his way, Mort was a good husband, as her friends repeatedly told her. He gave her all the material comforts she could wish for. He was kind and generous and, as far as she knew, faithful – when would he have the time to be anything else? It was simply that he no longer seemed to be aware of her as a person. He never forgot a birthday, or an anniversary; he was meticulous in his attentions, the perfect gentleman. Their marriage was an excellent one, she kept telling herself; but their perception of it was different. She needed to share her life with somebody. What Mort needed was a combination of hooker and secretary.

Perhaps if there had been kids, she thought. It was one of those things. Mort was sterile. She had come to accept it, hard as it had been at the time. If only he would agree to adopt, but it was not in his nature.

'You think I'm doing the right thing?'

'Is it important what I think?'

'Of course it is.' Mort was genuinely surprised at the question.

'Why did you leave the Oil Corporation? Not for money or position. You could have had anything you wanted.'

Mort nodded thoughtfully. 'Maybe you're right,' he admitted. 'I made an issue of those things, but they weren't the real issue. I guess I started to think about my life. It's time to be on my own.'

'You've always been that,' said Julie.

'What are you saying?'

'While you're thinking about life, maybe you should think about our marriage,' she said.

'Our marriage is fine.'

'You're sure about that?'

He was irritated by the question, though he was careful not to show it. It was quite simple: she was wrong. It could be the time of the month. You never knew with women. 'I'm quite certain it's perfectly fine. When you compare it to our friends' marriages . . .'

'Don't compare it. This is our marriage.'

'So, what's wrong with it?'

Julie shrank from the challenge. 'Times change. People change,' was all she could say.

'I haven't changed,' he said flatly.

She said nothing.

'Have I?'

When she still did not reply, he said insistently: 'No, I haven't. Nor have you. Our marriage is great. You have everything you need, don't you?'

Everything she needed. Yes. She had that. Everything except the things that mattered.

'You have a husband who's devoted to you, that's for sure.' He put his arm round her as if to prove it.

She smiled wistfully. 'In your own way you are, just like you're devoted to all your possessions. You're proud of me. I'm intelligent and decorative and I give good parties.'

'That's not fair.'

'But that's how it is. You don't share anything.'

'I share what I can,' he said.

'Not the important things.'

'What's important?'

'You are,' she said. 'I am. Children are,' she added softly.

'I'm sorry about that.'

'Don't be,' she said.

'I tried everything. We both did. You know that.'

'Except adopting.'

'That's not the answer.'

'It's what I want,' she said.

'We've been through all this. It's something I could never do. You never know what you're getting.'

'You take a chance,' said Julie. 'Like I did when I married you. How did I know what I was getting?'

'You still don't,' he said.

How true that was, she thought.

*

43

True to his principle of staying close to the source of power, Jack Greenberg was a regular at the Meyers' house on Friday evenings. The Shabbath candles were lit. Mrs Meyer was praising her own chicken matzoball soup. It was like any other Friday evening at the Meyers'.

Rachel was sitting plumply next to him with a fixed smile on her face. Her fat cheeks were pink and she was breathing a little faster than normal, because Jack's middle finger was massaging her clitoris. Somehow it was even more exciting doing it in front of the Shabbath candles. Edmund Meyer was talking about Mort. He had been talking about him for a long time now.

'When I think that yesterday he was one of us and now . . .'

Jack had heard on the grapevine that Mort intended setting up his own oil-trading company.

'He'll compete with us, E.M. Don't underestimate him. He'll be successful. The guy's dangerous. We have to break him before he breaks us.' Jack loved a touch of melodrama.

Edmund Meyer spread his heavy hands in front of the Shabbath candles. 'God will break him,' he said with the absolute assurance of an Old Testament prophet with inside information.

'No doubt about it, E.M.' said Jack. Sanctimonious asshole, he thought, smiling respectfully at his boss.

The new office was on Lexington.

'One of these days we'll move to Park Avenue,' said Mort. 'One of these days . . .'

'Lexington is good enough for me,' said Ruby. 'I'm a modest guy. Besides, I only intend to be around for a couple of years.'

'It's all I ask,' said Mort.

'Then, it's rabbinical studies for me.'

'Business will sharpen your brain, you'll see,' said Mort. 'You'll be the sharpest rabbi in New York.'

'The Upper West Side will do,' said Ruby.

'Whatever. Whatever you want, Ruby.'

'What is it you want? Money? Power?'

Mort thought about it. 'I want to be someone,' he said. 'I want to know who I am. I want everyone to know who I am.'

'That reminds me,' said Ruby. 'We're about to float a company. What are we going to call it?'

'I hadn't thought about it.' He observed Ruby, watching for his reaction. 'What would you say to "King Brothers"?'

'You've got to be kidding,' said Ruby.

'I don't kid.'

'This is not a family business.'

'So?'

'We'll have partners,' said Ruby. 'They'll never agree.'

'Who knows what they'll do?' said Mort. 'Sam is an old friend of mine. I'll talk to him.'

'Sam?'

'There are two men we have to get: Jeffrey Lewis and Sam Carlstroem.'

'Who are they?'

'The greatest oil traders in the world.'

'After you.'

'Maybe. They're good, that's for sure. I want them.'

'Knowing you,' said Ruby, 'I guess you'll get them.' Suddenly he was aware of the look on his brother's face – it was animated by a hungry, almost rapacious expression. His hands rested on the desk in front of him, apparently relaxed, but the fingers were tense, awkwardly crooked.

Just for a moment, Ruby was scared.

'Mort,' he said, a touch anxiously, 'what are we doing this for?'

'For fun,' said Mort. 'We're doing it for fun.'

He smiled reassuringly.

Jeffrey had been married for six years. Caroline had light blue eyes with flecks of green – summer sky and spring foliage. She was a psychiatrist, and a damn good one, who understood him better than he understood himself. Not, he often reflected dolefully, a difficult thing to do. He had

45

never been a great one for introspection. In addition to a wife, he also had a four-year-old son, a one-year-old daughter, a puppy of dubious breed and an ageing father whom he visited regularly. At nights and weekends Jeffrey lived in the fashionable part of Bayswater in what the estate agents called a 'bijou' townhouse – so 'bijou' and cheaply built that he could hear his neighbour peeing every morning. As the man drank eight or ten pints of beer every night, the performance was an extended one. He didn't bother to muffle the sound by directing the stream at the Royal Doulton. He peed straight into the water. At seven a.m. every day Jeffrey was racked from sleep by the thunder of Niagara Falls. It was too much. More than once, he thought of phoning the man to complain, but he never did. What was he supposed to say? . . . 'Could I ask you kindly not to pee so loudly? Why don't you pee more considerately? Please direct your willie more carefully. . . ?'

The rest of his time he passed in the threadbare office that Shell allocated him and in aircraft, airports and hotel rooms. Wherever it was he had hoped his life would be leading him by the time he was thirty-four, he did not seem to be getting there. It was like being in prison without knowing why, plagued by paranoic suspicions that someone was getting at you. There was not a single morning that he did not stand in front of the mirror and pray for his 'sentence' to be commuted. It never was. In the end, of course, inevitably, they would let him out – when he was pensionable. They would unbar the door and give him a gold watch and a leaden handshake. Shell was not the most generous of employers. Then he would go home, read the papers and watch the box. God. What a future to look forward to. What a life to look back on.

He had occupied the same office in Shell's London headquarters on the Thames embankment for the last eight years. The room contained a battered twentieth century copy of an eighteenth century mahogany partners' desk

46

and a threadbare red carpet. On one wall was a 1962 nudie calendar and a map of the Middle East on another. Jeffrey had pinned a tiny Israeli flag on Riyadh, the capital of Saudi Arabia, his only contribution to the interior decor of his office. No one ever mentioned it. Too polite – that was the British for you.

Meanwhile, what?

For Caroline, the answer was simple, as it often is for women. Jeffrey was tired of his job; he should get on or get out. He had to take the bull by the horns.

The 'bull' in this case was the Deputy Chairman of Shell, a disillusioned patrician, limpid of hand, urbane of word and expression; in looks, in fact, more like a borzoi than a bull. The man could not wait to be pensioned off. He had drifted up through the ranks by default. Never ambitious himself, he resented ambition in others.

'A failing of your people, if I may say so,' he remarked condescendingly.

'My people?' Jeffrey enquired. 'The British, you mean?'

'Actually,' the deputy chairman hesitated, looking out of the window at the reassuring neo-gothic mass of the Houses of Parliament as if for confirmation, 'actually no. What I meant was . . .'

'Ah, of course,' said Jeffrey. 'Silly of me.' He should have known. After all these years, he should have known. 'Tell me,' he said. 'Are there any Jews on Shell's board of directors?'

'Jeffrey.' The deputy chairman's hand flopped, languid, deprecating. 'The British gave the world democracy and the parliamentary system.'

'Yes, I know we did . . . er . . . I beg your pardon . . . you did.'

'We don't discriminate against anyone,' said the deputy chairman. 'That's not the way we do things in this country, nor in this company, for that matter. You should know that.'

'I see. Good,' said Jeffrey. 'Splendid.'

It was getting dark. The face of Big Ben lit up. Jeffrey

47

could no longer see the deputy chairman's features clearly. He seemed to be looking out of the window again.

'Strange,' he said. 'Very strange.'

Jeffrey waited, watching the patrician profile silhouetted against the window.

'The window,' said the deputy chairman. 'Look at it. It's filthy. Disgustingly filthy.' He was affronted. 'The window of the deputy chairman's office and no one has bothered to clean it for months. Maybe years. It shows a lack of respect, don't you think? A want of caring. A lack of commitment. Times have changed. No one gives a damn any more.'

He peered closely at the window. 'One can only see the dirt in this half light. You know I've never noticed it before. Have you noticed it?' he asked accusingly.

'No, I haven't,' said Jeffrey.

'It's quite extraordinary how one can sit in the same office, day after day, year after year, and not notice a thing like that.' The deputy chairman swivelled his chair round to face Jeffrey, who could now only see his eyes glowing in the darkening room. 'Odd, don't you think?'

'It's not something I've ever really thought about,' said Jeffrey.

'Ah,' said the deputy chairman triumphantly, as if he had trapped him into a deeply compromising confession.

Jeffrey did not know what was expected of him. The long aristocratic fingers drummed the desk impatiently.

'Details are important, you know. Some people say you have to see the broad picture, but I always emphasize the details. Details are crucial. Fatal to overlook details. Above all, a man in my position . . .'

'Quite,' said Jeffrey.

'I give you this advice in case you should ever – um – aspire to sitting where I am.' The deputy chairman touched the arms of his chair reverently as if it were a gilded throne.

'You encourage me to ask if that could ever happen,' said Jeffrey.

The deputy chairman pondered. He laid his hands on

48

the desk, palms up, and studied them. Then he turned them over and examined the carefully manicured nails. He appeared to be satisfied. 'If the board of directors saw fit . . . In the fullness of time,' he said.

'I don't have it,' said Jeffrey. 'None of us does.'

'What don't you have?'

'Time,' said Jeffrey.

The deputy chairman opened the top right-hand drawer of his desk, then closed it abruptly with a bang. 'Well, if that's all?' he said.

Jeffrey stood up to go. It was like leaving the head-master's study.

'Switch on the light as you leave,' said the deputy chairman. 'There's a good fellow.'

Jeffrey strolled down to the river in front of the Shell building. The lights of London, the capital of this all-embracing democracy, were reflected in the Thames. He leaned over the parapet and looked up to Westminster Bridge and the Houses of Parliament, downstream to Hungerford Bridge, the Festival Hall and the National Theatre and, round the bend of the river, out of sight, St Paul's and the City of London. He thought how no other place would ever be the same for him, of how much of an Englishman he really was.

As he walked along the Embankment towards the foot-bridge he stopped by one of the paving stones and looked down. It was dark now. In the dim lamplight he could barely make out the words engraved on it. No matter. He knew the poem by heart.

'Sweet Thames, run softly, till I end my Song.'

Edmund Spenser's song had ended three hundred years ago and the Thames was still running. No doubt it would be running three hundred – three thousand years – from now . . . There were things to be done.

Four generations his family had been here . . . not long enough, it seemed. Not quite long enough to be accepted. Not yet.

49

In the fullness of time, perhaps. If the board of directors saw fit.

Sam Carlstroem made neither commitments nor decisions easily. When the Swissair stewardess offered him the choice of red or white wine, he was not sure which to take. In the end she made the decision for him. Sam was chunky and fresh-faced, with a nice, complacent, bushy little moustache. The stewardess decided he was the red wine type. She poured him a full glass and gave him an intimate smile, not the airline's usual polystyrene special.

Women liked Sam, which always surprised him. A lot of things did – his marriage to Amy, a beautiful American girl, ex top model, his success in business, his two kids. When had he made all those commitments, for God's sake? He had always been a man of the sidelines by nature, one of life's spectators. Maybe it was his genes: Swedish father, Swiss mother. 'How neutral can you get?' as Amy had said more than once.

Sam walked through life self-consciously, as if he were an actor in a movie, playing a role written for him by someone else. He had the perpetual feeling that a camera was focused on him, recording everything, though who was operating it, and why, he never stopped to think. Whoever it was – this cameraman – Sam liked to feel that he approved of him, that he appreciated what he was doing. That was essential to him. The role had to be sympathetic. Who the actor was, who he was – Sam, the guy the world knew as Sam – well, that was something he would never understand. Life was some kind of dream, someone else's dream, perhaps. It was unreal. He went along with it, but it was not about him at all.

He drank a second glass of red wine. The deal had gone through flawlessly. Everything went more smoothly as the years passed. Another big one in the bag. It would make a fortune for the company and for his boss. Siegfried Gerber would be pleased with him. Sam was a good businessman – and he knew it – but, somehow, Siegfried Gerber's

50

approval gave him just that extra tingle of satisfaction, that sense of fulfilment he could never derive from his own achievements. It was not so much the icing on the cake; it was the cake itself. It convinced him that he had been successful. Without his boss's approval, there did not seem to be much point in anything.

Siegfried Gerber was a very relaxed man. He always took his time. He stood in front of the mirror admiring his handsome face and upright figure, slowly buttoning his shirt. Not bad for sixty, he thought. Amy was still in bed, stroking her long blonde hair, watching him. His assured, calm acceptance of life, his independent spirit, his absolute air of authority in everything he did and said – these were the things she most admired in a man, the qualities she had never found in Sam.

When Sam walked into the bedroom, Siegfried Gerber was zipping up his flies. Nothing was said. Gerber picked up his jacket and tie and left, head down like a small boy, as if he were ashamed of himself. Which he was – ashamed of being caught.

Sam sat on the kitchen floor, clasping his knees. He looked bewildered and uncomprehending, like a newly caged animal.

Amy tried to rouse him, to make him angry, but he would not be roused. Sam never lost his temper. He was not a man to throw tables or beat her up. So much the worse for their marriage. So much the worse for Sam.

'For Chrissake, Sam, say something. Scream at me. Hit me. Throw the furniture.'

Sam shrank further into the corner. 'What's the use?'

'What's the use of anything? You catch me in bed with another man and all you do is sulk.'

'My goddam boss, for God's sake.'

'What the fuck has that got to do with it?' she yelled.

Funny, he thought. She was the guilty party and she was the one doing the yelling.

51

'He's sixty years old.'

'Sam, in heaven's name, tell me how age comes into this.'

'He's old. You cheated on me with an old man.'

Amy shook her head hopelessly. Siegfried Gerber was young at sixty. Sam was old at thirty-seven.

'I'm a reasonable man, Amy. I believe in behaving in a reasonable way. All I want is an explanation.'

'That's the trouble. You're too goddam reasonable. That's the whole problem. I don't want a reasonable man. I want an unreasonable one. I want someone who's a little crazy, someone who gets excited about life. I want someone who isn't always in the fucking right.'

'Just tell me what it is I've done wrong,' he said.

Amy put her hands over her face.

'Oh, Jesus Christ,' she said, her voice muffled by her fingers. 'Is that what you want to do? Put it all right, everything in its place, neat and tidy, no mess, no problems, no screaming, no shouting? Don't you see, Sam, it won't work. It's not just you. It's me.'

'You're OK. What's the matter with you?'

'I don't know. Maybe I'm afraid,' she said, her voice breaking.

'Of what?'

'If I knew that, I wouldn't be afraid.' With a sudden forward jerk of the head she tossed her long hair.

'Afraid of domesticity, I guess. Afraid of life. What have I ever done with it?'

'You were only New York's top model.'

'Was. Everything's in the past tense, now. I'm married.'

'What has any of us done if it comes to that? You've still got two wonderful kids.' He raised his head and looked at her. 'You've still got me,' he said gently.

'You're a good man, Sam,' she said.

She knelt beside him on the kitchen floor, holding him tight – like a child clutching her favourite cuddly toy – the tears streaming down her face.

*

52

Sam chose to have the confrontation in Siegfried Gerber's office. It was a mistake, of course, but what else could he do? He could hardly summon his boss to his own office.

'Come in, Sam. Do sit down. I'm so glad you came. I was coming to see you, but I got tied up with phone calls.'

Sam stood in front of his boss's desk. Here he was, in Siegfried Gerber's kingdom, and the humiliating thing was that he could not find the words to tell him what he thought of him. He had prepared a speech, but it was out of place here. A close and complex affinity, layered by the years, had developed in this room; it had a life and an atmosphere as tangible as the wood panelling and the Dali prints. There was simply no way to escape it. He was the trusted employee, the faithful courtier, the King's favourite. Nothing could change all that. The atmosphere reeked of the master-servant relationship and the worst of it was that Siegfried Gerber had been a good and enlightened boss, free with his money, generous with his praise.

'What can I say, Sam? I'm deeply ashamed and most terribly sorry. Please forgive me.'

Did he really think it would be so easy? That all Sam had to do was forgive him so they could revert to the old convenient life? . . . Sam emptying his in-tray every morning, answering his mail, doing his business for him, covering for him when he played golf? Jesus. How many times a week did he play golf? How many of those times had he been with Amy?'

'It didn't mean a thing, Sam. It was just something that happened. A mutual attraction. Nothing more. I swear it. A temporary . . . aberration, I assure you. One of those things. You understand.'

So, that was OK, then. His boss had screwed his wife not because she had long slim legs, a high waist and nice little tits, not because he enjoyed her company or found her fascinating as a woman and not, God forbid, because he cared for her. Oh, no. He had fucked her ass off because of a temporary aberration. One of those things. The bastard. The sanctimonious shit.

Where did that leave Sam? Damaged, degraded, defiled. The camera was watching him. He gestured with his hand as if he were brushing away a cobweb. No one must see this. He felt exposed, ridiculous.

'One of those things,' he repeated dully.

'I swear to you, it wasn't a question of love, or anything like that. It was just . . . well, it just happened, as I said. Naturally, you have my word that it will never occur again.'

'Why my wife? There were plenty of secretaries if you needed a screw.'

Siegfried Gerber smiled confidingly, man to man.

'I . . . I did, with my secretary you know, but . . .' He raised his eyes expressively.

'Her husband found out,' said Sam. 'I remember.'

Gerber grimaced ruefully.

Sam had heard enough to forget where he was or, at least, to remember that there was a world outside Siegfried Gerber's office. For once in his life he made a commitment: he lost his temper.

'You disgusting, lecherous old man. If you ever see her again, I'll kill you.'

'I quite understand how you feel,' said Gerber coolly.

Good men were hard to find, especially traders as efficient and ingenious as Sam.

'I beg of you. Let's put this unfortunate incident in the past and forget it,' he said, congratulating himself on his self-control.

Sam laid both hands on Gerber's desk and leaned over until their faces were almost touching.

'You pig,' he said. 'You make me sick. Find someone else to make your money for you. Find another sucker to empty your tray, be your slave, shovel your shit. I'm through.'

Gerber stared right back at him. 'Please do yourself a

favour. Think about what you're doing,' he said. And then he added the final insult: 'There are not too many jobs like this around.'

Sam grabbed him by the tie and pulled. For a moment, the thought came to him that he might strangle his boss. The same thought obviously occurred to Gerber. He was choking and there was terror in his eyes.

Sam relished the terror a little longer, pulling the tie tighter and tighter. Then, abruptly, he let it go.

'Fuck you. And fuck your job,' he said.

He slammed the door of Gerber's office so hard that it seemed the building shook. It made him feel a lot better.

Until, going down in the elevator for the last time, he remembered just who it was who had been fucked.

*   *   *

The Grand Hotel Dolder, set high on a hill in the woods overlooking the Lake of Zurich, combines the baroque splendour of a French château with the remote and sinister aspect of a medieval castle.

It is sombre, complacent and dull, like most of its clientele. It is a retreat where the aspiring rich can rub shoulders with the genuine article and a bustle of expense account executives can live a quiet moment of luxury dreaming of the day when they too will be able to afford a room at the Dolder.

Whatever anyone may think of this pretentious pile with its turrets and towers, its grand reception halls and its cobbled courtyard stuffed with Rolls-Royces and Mercedes, it is, in its way, unique. There is nothing quite like it in the world.

The four new partners met in a corner suite overlooking the golf course.

Mort was in high spirits. Jeffrey Lewis and Sam Carlstroem were the best. No doubt about it. When he had phoned them, Jeffrey had said 'yes' immediately. Sam had needed time to think, like he always did. Mort, Ruby, Jeffrey, Sam. Some team.

'I chose this place,' said Mort, 'because for me it's kind of symbolic. It's on top of the world. That's where I hope we'll all end up.'

'It's perfect,' said Sam.

'Homely,' said Jeffrey ironically.

Mort gave no indication that he had heard. He had known Jeffrey a long time.

'If there's anything you guys need, just ask,' he said grandly.

'There's an emerald necklace in one of those lighted vitrines in the lobby Sarah might like,' said Ruby.

'One day,' said Mort. 'One day she'll have it. Now let's start.'

Ruby winked at the other two.

'I just want to confirm how we've agreed to divide the world,' said Mort. He opened the atlas he had brought with him; he did not forget things like that. 'OK, let's start with Europe,' he said briskly.

Sam daydreamed out of the window. The fir trees and the hillsides around the lake were dusted with snow – the first of winter.

Sam was to open an office in Wald, a little village in the east of Switzerland; Jeffrey would open up in London, and Mort and Ruby had already found their office on Lexington in Manhattan. As they allocated to themselves the responsibility for each country, the thought crossed Jeffrey's mind that here they were, dividing the world exactly as Lepidus, Mark Antony and Augustus Caesar had done two thousand years before them. The only difference was that they did not own it as those great soldiers had done.

At least, not yet.

Mort sipped a bourbon and soda, his green eyes shining, his enthusiasm tingling in the air like electricity.

This guy is serious, thought Jeffrey. He's not messing.

And, as they casually wove their grand design, talking of offices that today existed only in their minds and planning travels to the ends of the earth in pursuit of their own special dream, there came to them all a sense of high adventure, of the magnitude and stimulus of the challenge and, with all that, a hint of something else, something in each of them – awesome and intoxicating – never previously faced or acknowledged: a craving for power.

Mort slammed shut the atlas and laid it on the desk. The future of the world had been decided.

'Shouldn't we drink a toast to the new company?' suggested Sam.

He liked to do things the right way. Mort and Ruby looked at each other. What was it about these men, Jeffrey thought. They communicated without talking. Each seemed to know what the other was thinking. Theirs was a cabal of minds, the most exclusive club of all; there could only ever be two members.

'Good point,' said Jeffrey. 'What do we call it, by the way?'

Sam coughed. 'I had an idea,' he said, glancing conspiratorially at Mort. 'Just a thought,' he added.

Jeffrey caught the look and wondered what he was missing.

'Go ahead,' he said, when Sam seemed too bashful to continue.

'It has to be an entirely new name,' said Sam. 'A name never used before, or we won't be able to register it simultaneously in three countries. The name is crucial. We all know that. Once we have one, we have a handle, an identity. We're in business.'

'Agreed,' said Jeffrey. He wondered how anyone could disagree. 'So, what was your thought?'

Sam looked as though he were about to say something, but then he intercepted a glance from Mort and changed his mind.

Jeffrey did not miss that little interplay.

'How about "Nova Oil"?' suggested Ruby.

No one said a word. Then Sam spoke up. 'Could we perhaps find something a little more original?' he said delicately.

57

They all began pacing. Jeffrey had the feeling they were waiting for him to suggest a name.

'How about "Atlas International"?' he said. 'You know . . . Atlas. The guy who carries the world on his shoulders. It stresses the international scope of the company . . . and it would make a great logo,' he added, voice dropping, not even convincing himself.

'It's been done before,' said Mort.

'Maybe just a touch pretentious,' said Sam.

'Too ordinary,' said Ruby.

More pacing.

'Whatever happened to your idea, Sam?' said Jeffrey.

Again, that look between Mort and Ruby.

'I was thinking,' Sam said. 'We're agreed we have to think of a name no one has ever used before, one we can register without any delay. I guess we'd also like to give the company a name with real impact.'

No one was arguing.

'Well, then,' continued Sam a little self-consciously, 'my suggestion takes into account the fact that these two guys here were the moving spirits – the co-founders of the company.' He nodded at Mort and Ruby. 'Without their foresight and persistence we wouldn't be here. Agreed?'

Mort and Ruby bowed their heads modestly. Jeffrey stroked his chin. 'Get to the point,' he said.

'I would therefore like to propose,' went on Sam, 'that the company be called "King Brothers".'

For a long time, no one said anything. Mort examined his watch, a 1963 stainless-steel Omega, the same watch he had worn for the last ten years and would probably wear for the next ten. There was no petty vanity about the man, none of the small peacock pretensions, the little displays of wealth that other men were prone to. Not for him the gold Vacheron Constantin, the blue lacquer Dupont pen, the Dior necktie. Not for him the packaged personality, the pre-cooked image. Mort's self-esteem was solid. It needed no bolstering.

Ruby was studying his diary with great concentration.

Jeffrey felt like a man who has just seen an illusionist saw his best friend in half. Illusion or reality? Who was doing what, to whom and why?

'Remember,' said Sam, 'Mort and Ruby each have twenty-five and a half per cent of the company. In the last analysis, they have control.'

'The last analysis'. That was good. When would that be? When would the 'last analysis' come? When would the wishes of the two minority partners be ignored? Jeffrey hoped he would not be around if that ever happened. And why did this all have the smell of a setup?

'Of course, all major decisions will always be unanimous,' said Mort.

'Of course,' said Jeffrey.

'They're also putting up most of the money,' said Sam.

'Quite,' said Jeffrey.

Mort was contemplating the golf course. He spoke with his back turned to the others. 'No,' he said, 'it wouldn't be right. I'm very much against the cult of personality. After all, this is not a family business.'

'That's what I thought you'd say,' said Sam.

Another round of drinks. Sam made a few more half-hearted proposals; all of them were turned down. He persisted with his suggestion . . . 'King Brothers'. He reverted to the name three times; each time Mort shook his head firmly.

What was it that was nagging at Jeffrey's memory? And then, suddenly, it came to him: the scene in Shakespeare's *Richard III* when Buckingham persuades the indifferent and bewildered citizens to offer the crown to the Duke of Gloucester, but the Duke, with artful duplicity and sham humility, rejects it, protesting that he prefers to pray in the company of the pious friars. That had been a put-up job too. In the end, Buckingham and the citizens 'force' the 'reluctant' Duke to accept what he has schemed and murdered for, the prize he lusts after – the Crown.

Jeffrey looked at Sam . . . Buckingham, to the life. The devious bastard.

Sam returned to the battle. 'I still think "King Brothers" is far the best name.'

'No,' said Mort. 'Let's think of something else.'

Where were the friars?

'Is the King refusing to be crowned?' enquired Jeffrey pleasantly.

'I don't think I follow you,' said Mort.

'Why don't we put it to the vote?' said Jeffrey, raising his hand. 'Those in favour?'

'I don't believe . . .' Mort began.

'It's the democratic thing to do,' said Sam. 'After all.'

Jeffrey and 'Buckingham' had their hands raised. Ruby and the 'Duke of Gloucester' abstained.

'Two in favour. Two abstentions,' said Jeffrey. He raised his glass. 'The King is dead! Long live the King!' he declaimed and poured the champagne down his throat.

'I'm not sure I understand,' said Mort.

Like hell, thought Jeffrey. Like hell you don't.

'Anyway,' said Mort, 'the name isn't important. We're here to have fun.'

So that's what they were there for. Jeffrey poured himself another glass of champagne.

BOOK THREE

Make or Break

They had pushed the boat out, but it was not going any-where.

'I never gave credit a thought,' Ruby admitted.

'Well think about it now,' said Mort glumly. 'Without credit we're dead in the water. One VLCC – just one very large crude carrier – loads two, three hundred thousand tons of crude. That's ten million bucks. Where do we get that kind of money if the banks won't give us a credit line?'

'Somehow I never thought it would be a problem,' said Ruby.

'Me neither. All we need is a few banks to support us and we're in business. They take practically no risk. They hold the shipping documents till we sell the crude and get paid by our customer. Then they get their money and we collect our profit. They should be happy to have our business. Their tongues should be hanging out for their commissions. So why won't they play? What's going on?'

Ruby paced Mort's office. 'You don't think the Majors are trying to stop us before we get going?'

Ruby had a thing about huge corporations. He had a thing about anything that smelled of the Establishment.

Mort smiled. 'The Majors don't know we exist. And, if they did, they wouldn't give a nickel for us. We're not even the dust under their boots right now. No . . . it's not the Majors.'

Ruby had no doubt. 'The Oil Corporation.'

Mort shook his head. 'Not E.M. That's not his style.

He'd never try to stop me. He's too smart. He knows there's plenty of room in the oil industry for another trading organization. It might even do him some good.'

'You don't understand, do you?'

'What's to understand?'

Mort saw only what he wanted to see and did what he had to do. What he had to do, chiefly, was to succeed. It would never have occurred to him to take time out to get in someone else's way, unless, of course, they were getting in his.

'This isn't about bucks,' said Ruby. 'This isn't about the oil industry. This is about people. You made yourself enemies when you quit the Oil Corporation. You were the heir apparent, the infant protégé, groomed and approved to take over when E.M. was ready. Now, what are you? You're a rival. You're more than that. Remember what he called you? A renegade. That may sound funny to you, but to him it's serious, deadly serious. You betrayed Edmund Meyer. You committed the unpardonable sin . . . you left him. He's not going to forgive you for that, Mort. He's mad as hell – mad and powerful. He's number one – and he intends to stay that way. He's not about to sit back until you become a real threat. E.M. did not get to be where he is today by helping the competition.'

'I guess not,' said Mort.

He called Eden Morris. The guy should have an answer for him by now. Eden was once a senior vice-president of Chemical Bank, and now one of the most successful stock analysts and 'company doctors' on the East Coast.

'How are things, Eden?'

'Good, Mort. Glad you called. I can tell you what you want to know. Your problem is Jack Greenberg. He's been round the whole banking community. The Oil Corporation has a lot of muscle, and he's using it. He's threatened a whole lot of banks that he'll withdraw Oilcorp business if they give you a credit line.'

'I can't believe what I'm hearing,' said Mort. 'Collusion between banks is illegal. They could be in deep trouble.'

Eden Morris laughed. 'You know, Mort, for a smart guy you can be real naive. Who's to prove it? You think there's anything in writing? Of course not. Banks have a perfect right to grant or withhold credit. You know that.'

'What about you, Eden? Could you do something for me? Like use your influence to persuade a couple of banks to give me a small line? I'd only need, say, ten million for a start.'

Eden Morris hesitated at the other end of the line. 'I wish I could help you, Mort, but Edmund Meyer is an old sparring partner of mine and he carries a lot of weight in this town. I wouldn't want to upset him. You know how it is.'

'I know how it is,' said Mort grimly.

'If there's anything more I can do, call me.' The phone went dead.

Mort shuffled a pile of telexes, arranged them in date order, patted them into place and laid them neatly on his desk. He flipped a switch to connect him with Ruby on the intercom.

'You were right.'

'What are you going to do?'

'Call on a friend,' said Mort.

Ed Hunt was the President and Chairman of Integrated Refining. What was more important, he also owned the shop. It was a big shop. They had more than ten refineries in the USA and they processed around twenty million tons of crude a year. The company had diversified into real estate, electronics, steel and shopping malls. Ed was doing OK. He was not short of a few bucks.

'How are you, Mort? It's real good to see you. What can I do for you?'

Mort did not believe in wasting time. It was one commodity he never had enough of.

'You heard I started up a new company?'

'I heard. Sure I heard. That's great. I wish you . . . well, you know what I wish you. I wish you all the luck in the world. As much as I had. Not that you'll need it – you're a smart young fellow.'

Ed Hunt was over sixty. Anyone less than fifty was a young fellow. Below thirty-five, you were a kid.

'I'd like to buy some oil from you, Ed. I need crude to trade with, to get started. I have plenty of customers. I'll pay you the market.'

'Price is no problem, Mort. We always understood each other. After all, we've been doing business for – how long?'

'Ten years. Maybe more.'

'More,' said Hunt. 'Sure I'll sell you some crude. How much do you need?'

Mort relaxed. 'A couple of VLCCs of Arab Light. Iranian Light would do, I guess.'

Ed Hunt nodded thoughtfully. 'Five, six hundred thousand tons. That's a sizeable business. I guess we can handle that,' he said, grinning broadly. 'No problem.'

'Great,' said Mort.

'What about payment?' Hunt asked casually.

'I thought perhaps you could let me have credit for thirty days. That would give me time to sell the crude. I'll pay you one per cent over prime.'

Ed Hunt pursed his lips. 'If it's six hundred thousand tons you want, we're talking twenty, thirty million bucks. That's one hell of a lot of credit, Mort. That's a whole lot of credit to give anyone. But to give it to a new company, just starting up . . . Now, if it had been the Oil Corporation . . . You know me, Mort. We never had any problems. I trust you.'

'If you trust me, then give me credit,' said Mort.

The friendly smile froze on Ed Hunt's face. 'I'll think about it. I'll call you. That's what I'll do. I'll call you.'

Mort was weighing up the guy. Would he call him, or was he getting rid of him? He decided he was trying to get him out of his office.

'Here's what I'll do,' said Mort. 'We'll conclude the deal and I'll guarantee to transfer my customer's letter of credit to you just as soon as I sell the crude. Don't give me the crude until you have the L/C in hand. That way, you'll have no payment worries. You won't even be granting me credit.'

It was a good idea, neat and simple. He had thought of it on the way over. He was quite confident it would work. The guy had to agree. There was no reason on earth why he would not.

Ed Hunt looked embarrassed. 'Sorry, Mort. It's too risky.'

Mort could not believe it. 'Too risky? Why? There's no risk for you. None at all.'

Hunt shifted uncomfortably in his chair.

Mort let the silence pressure the man.

'I'd sure like to do this for you, Mort, but . . .'

'But what, Ed? You're the boss. You own the place. No one can tell you what to do. You know there's no risk. What's your problem?'

Hunt still looked uncomfortable, but he was also getting angry. Who was this little prick to tell him how to run his own company – needling him, trying to manipulate him, taking advantage of his good nature?

'What's the problem, Ed?'

Hunt exploded. 'Hell, Mort, if you're not the most irritating sonofabitch! Sure, we've known each other a long time, but that doesn't give you the right to order me about. I'll make my own goddam decisions. And get this. You may think you're God's gift to the oil industry, but you're not number two in the Oil Corporation any more. You're number one in some crappy little outfit no one's ever heard of. You don't carry any weight around here, now. You don't carry any weight in the oil industry. Remember what I'm telling you.'

Mort's eyes were angry, but his face remained impassive.

'I'll remember,' he said. 'You can be sure I'll remember.'

He went back to the office and drank six large bourbons straight off. After that he barely knew where his desk was. One thing he did know, though. He knew he was in deep trouble.

*

How Jeffrey had first met Henry Soames he could never quite recall. It seemed as though he had always known him. There may have been a time when Henry had observed the niceties, like making an appointment with his secretary, or even just knocking on the door before he came in. If there was, it must have been in some other life. Henry was omnipresent. He moved in and out of the lives of his adopted friends and clients with an assumption of privilege and prerogative that stemmed from his claim to be 'top drawer'.

There was no question that Henry had 'adopted' Jeffrey and Jeffrey tolerated him for his entertainment value and because, occasionally, he could be damned useful. He knew everyone and his information, especially of the scandalous variety, was invariably accurate. What Henry did for a living, no one knew. Probably he had, as they say, independent means. The word that best described his occupation was 'pedlar'. He peddled information; he peddled connections; he peddled secrets and he peddled Henry Soames. He was the quintessential flake. But, like all good flakes, once in a while he came up with the genuine article. You would be ill-advised to write him off as wholly unserious.

So, here was Henry in the office, uninvited and unannounced, as usual. Jeffrey doubted that his secretary had even seen him come in. Could it be that Henry had discovered the secret of vanishing and materializing at will? Nothing about him would surprise Jeffrey.

'Thanks for making an appointment,' he said ironically.

Irony was to Henry Soames like paper darts to a crocodile.

'You know what a good friend I am,' he said, 'and you know what good friends are worth.'

'Indeed,' said Jeffrey. 'They come very expensive.'

Having cleared up that small point, Henry was ready for business. Over the years, he and Jeffrey had developed an understanding and there was no further need to discuss

68

the sordid details of remuneration. If Henry delivered, then Jeffrey would pay and pay well.

'I hear you're having problems with Jack Greenberg.'

Jeffrey's face was a blank sheet of paper.

'That's what I thought,' said Henry Soames smugly. 'That young man is perfidious and depraved. What's more, he has absolutely no breeding.'

'He's an arsehole,' said Jeffrey.

Henry cringed. 'Must you be so anal?'

'How do you know him?'

'I had the opportunity to assist him once in a personal matter. I performed. He didn't.'

'You mean, he didn't pay up?'

'You always put things so crudely, Jeffrey,' Henry lamented.

'What can you expect from the bottom drawer? Get to the point.'

'Mr Greenberg is seeing a certain prominent, young New York lady. Very prominent. Very young.'

'Is he now?'

'He's seeing a lot of her. In fact, dear boy, he's seeing all there is to be seen.' Henry sniggered. When you heard a Henry Soames snigger, you realized that sniggering was a dying art. The release of pent-up air through the nostrils was accompanied by a leer so grotesque that it transformed his face into a loathsome gargoyle. The whole effect was rounded off by a wink which had all the subtlety of a chronic tic.

'If you take my point,' he added, just in case Jeffrey had failed to observe the convulsion. Being himself as impervious as bullet-proof glass, Henry Soames invariably assumed that everyone else was the same.

'He's screwing her,' said Jeffrey.

Henry Soames shuddered. 'Really, Jeffrey, you know how I hate that sort of language. So coarse. So . . . Transatlantic.'

'Tell me, you wicked old humbug,' said Jeffrey, 'why I should be interested in Jack Greenberg's sex life.'

'Because,' said Henry, enjoying his moment of triumph, 'his sex life involves a young lady of particular significance to you, or, should I say, to your company.'

Jeffrey looked puzzled.

'Does the name Rachel Meyer ring a tiny bell?'

Jeffrey looked reasonably impressed, but hardly overwhelmed.

'Jack's knocking off the boss's daughter. So what?'

'Do you know how old the young lady is?'

'I never examined her teeth.'

'She's fifteen,' said Henry Soames. 'My informant tells me that Jack Greenberg introduced himself – if you'll pardon the expression – when she was fourteen.'

'Ah.' Jeffrey was definitely more interested. 'She's underage.'

Henry Soames flashed his jagged piranha teeth and heaved a few top-drawer guffaws.

'What I adore about you, Jeffrey, is the subliminal speed of your intellectual reflexes.'

'Let me get this straight. You are, are you not, proposing blackmail?'

Henry covered his face with his hands and groaned. 'Would I ever suggest such a thing?' he said, outraged.

'Blackmail,' murmured Jeffrey. 'Not a bad idea.'

'I'm merely suggesting that you might feel obliged, in the interest of friendship and public duty, to have a quiet word with Jack Greenberg.'

'In fact, it's a great idea,' said Jeffrey, brightening. 'Blackmail the creep.'

A token wince from Henry Soames. 'His behaviour is reprehensible,' he said. 'It would never have happened in our day.'

'I suppose not,' said Jeffrey wistfully.

'The girl is much too young.'

'Quite so.'

'Much too young to be pregnant,' said Henry Soames, delivering the *coup de grâce*.

'You don't mean it?'

'Oh, but I do.'

'Jesus Christ!'

'No, dear boy. Jack Greenberg. No connection with the Virgin Birth, I do assure you.'

At the door, he turned. 'They tell me you're an Oil King now.'

'Just one of the little princes,' said Jeffrey modestly.

Henry bared his immaculate dentures.

'Remember the Bloody Tower,' he said.

'Shall I ever forget?' said Jeffrey.

Jack Greenberg was flattered and intrigued when Mort invited him out for a drink. It made him feel important and it confirmed that the banks were giving King Brothers a hard time. They were hurting. It could even be that Mort needed him.

'The banks are playing games with me. I need credit and they won't give it to me. It's not a matter of terms. It's something else.'

'Anything I can do to help?' enquired Jack innocently.

'Since you ask,' said Mort, 'there is. You can go right back to your account executive friends and tell them to stop hassling me.'

Jack sipped his martini and breathed deeply. Life was good. In fact, right now, life was terrific. This was the kind of conversation he fantasized about. This was that moment when the baddie plunged, screaming, into the Grand Canyon. Not only was Mort hurting, he was begging for mercy. God was in his Heaven. All was right with the world.

'I'd be real glad to do that, Mort. I don't know if they'd listen to me, but if you think it would do any good . . . Why, there's nothing I'd rather do than help an old friend.'

'That's what I figured,' said Mort.

Jack flashed his gold Rolex. 'Well, if there's nothing else . . .'

'How's Rachel?' Mort asked.

'Rachel? Rachel who?' Jack was looking round the bar

of the Pierre Hotel. His glance settled on the swelling boobs of one of the trompe l'oeil nudies decorating the walls of the Rotunda. 'Some of those dolls are really something,' he said. 'I'm getting a hard-on. Look at the ass on that one.'

'Rachel Meyer,' said Mort.

'Rachel Meyer? How should I know? Fine, I guess.'

He glanced at Mort uneasily a couple of times, considered getting up to leave and changed his mind.

'Why?' he said, with studied disinterest.

'No special reason.'

Jack shifted nervously in his chair. Mort never said anything without a reason.

'Funny you should ask,' Jack said. 'I saw her at E.M.'s place only last week.'

'How did she look?'

'OK, I think. I didn't take too much notice.'

'I heard she had a medical problem,' said Mort. 'Did you hear that? Did you hear she had a medical problem?'

'No, I didn't. Why should I?'

'These things get around,' said Mort. He put out his hand. 'Good to see you, Jack.'

'And you,' said Jack. What the hell was all this about?

'How's E.M.?'

'Same as ever.'

'You have no problems with him?'

'Problems? Come on, Mort,' said Jack. 'Why should I have problems with E.M.?'

Mort locked in on Jack with his implacable gaze. 'You mean he doesn't object to your humping his daughter?'

Jack went pale. He opened and shut his mouth like a fish. Nothing came out. Not a word.

'Why don't you ask him how he feels about abortion, Jack? I guess he might have some interesting views.' Mort waved for the check.

Jack began to splutter. 'You . . . you're out of your mind. You're fucking crazy.'

'No, Jack. Not me. That seems to be your problem.'

Mort shook his head and tutted. 'Fifteen,' he said. 'Naughty, Jack.'

'You bastard!'

'If you could call those account executives tomorrow,' said Mort, 'I'd be grateful.'

'You asshole! You blackmailing shitbag!'

Mort picked up the check and handed it to Jack. 'Thanks for the drink,' he said. 'We must do this again some time.'

The following day, Eden Morris called.

'Mort, you've been on my mind. I've been sweating my guts out for you. Would you believe, a couple of major banks are ready to offer you a credit line?'

'Fantastic, Eden,' said Mort. 'You really pulled something out of the bag.'

'Let's just say a couple of guys owed me,' said Eden Morris modestly.

'What about Edmund Meyer? I thought he was an old buddy of yours. You said you were afraid to upset him.'

'Oh, Edmund,' said Morris airily. 'He and I understand each other. You know how he is.'

'I know how he is,' said Mort.

'He'll do anything for a friend,' said Eden Morris.

'I know,' said Mort. 'I know a few friends he's done things for.'

'I'll send you round a list of a few banks. I think you'll find they're ready to help.'

'Thanks. And Eden – believe me – I know just how much I owe you.' Mort put down the phone and grinned. Within an hour, six banks called offering credit lines. The smallest was ten million, the largest, thirty.

Jack Greenberg had called off the dogs.

'All we need now is business,' said Mort.

He called Jeffrey and Sam. King Brothers was on its way. So were the partners. No one said it in so many words, but the real race was not the race for profit; it was the race to do the first deal.

*　　*　　*

73

The DC-10 dipped low over the Mediterranean. The sun was a big red ball on the rim of the world and Tel Aviv was a pink city. This was the land of the Bible, of Abraham and Isaac and Jacob. At the bottom of the steps, two soldiers were cradling Uzzi machine guns. Times had changed.

Not the most attractive city in the world, Tel Aviv stumbled into existence without foresight or planning. Most of the apartments and office buildings are reinforced concrete. They are serviceable, grey and stained with rain. The refugees who poured into Israel had neither time nor money for frills. They were not into architecture. They were into survival.

That was how it had always been and how it still was. Life was a struggle against the elements, against the British and, now, against the Arabs. Israel, besieged by hostile countries, harassed and attacked by jealous neighbours constantly threatening its borders and its access to the Persian Gulf, had, nevertheless, made itself some important friends. Mutual interests had brought them together with the most powerful country in the Middle East – Iran. The two had vital commodities to offer each other: the Israelis their know-how, their technological genius and their small but superbly efficient armed forces; the Iranians, their oil. It was a natural trade-off.

The Israeli Pipeline was one of the beneficial side effects of the Arab embargo of Israel. The forty-two-inch pipe begins in Eilat, on the northern tip of the Red Sea, the southernmost tip of Israel, and runs north across the desert sands to Ashkelon in the Mediterranean.

For many years, Iran supplied Israel with the crude oil it needed to survive. In the early sixties, the idea was conceived to construct a pipeline that would give the Iranians a Mediterranean outlet and an entirely new market for their crude oil, and the Israelis a whole new transportation system that could compete in world markets and break the stranglehold of ship owners and the Majors on crude supply, transportation and refining. It was a brilliant conception, an inspired idea. It drew the Shah and Israel closer than ever together and it changed the map of the world oil market.

To service the Pipeline and their customers, the Israelis purchased, chartered and constructed tankers of all shapes and sizes: VLCCs to ship the crude from Iran's loading terminals in the Persian Gulf to Eilat, and sixty- to a hundred-thousand-tonners to load in the deep-water port at Ashkelon and ship to customers in Europe and America, where nearly all discharge terminals had shallow draughts, unable to accommodate giant tankers.

Crude from the Pipeline was often cheaper and delivery was always speedier than shipments from the Persian Gulf. Nevertheless, not everyone would use the Pipeline. The Majors, with their huge oil concessions in Arab countries whose leaders were dedicated to the destruction of Israel, were too scared to do business with them. It made no sense to compromise their vital interests for the sake of relatively marginal commercial advantages. Equally important, the Seven Sisters – Exxon, Texaco, Standard Oil of California, Standard Oil of Indiana, Mobil, Shell and BP – the biggest cartel in history, the fat cats of the oil world, had no interest in encouraging competition. Oil was theirs to produce and sell, theirs to give, theirs to withhold. It was not, horror of horrors, a commodity to be traded by amateurs and carpetbaggers.

But there were plenty of others only too eager to trade, including the Iron Curtain countries who purchased crude on a regular basis from a country whose very existence they denied. In the oil business, profit motive speaks louder than ideology.

Bejamin Zivski, the head of the Israeli Pipeline, had known Mort and Ruby for many years: Mort, as a leading international oil trader; Ruby, as one of the very few lawyers in the world he respected and the only one he trusted. What was more, he liked them both. He also liked food, wine, classical music, conversation and pretty women

although, on the whole, he was faithful to his wife and
Wolfgang Amadeus Mozart.

Everything about Benjamin was untidy: his clothes,
the wild, white hair that sprouted from his head in all
directions, his office and his desk top – everything, that
is, but his brain. That was perfectly precise and ordered.
When you understood that, it was no surprise to learn that
his previous job had been Deputy Chief of the Mossad,
Israel's world-renowned secret service.

Ruby talked for close to thirty minutes without stopping. While he spoke, Benjamin read telexes, screamed at
his secretary and drank endless cups of coffee, none of
which disturbed Ruby in the slightest. He knew that
Benjamin was listening. Whether he was reacting favour-
ably was another question. Ruby was trying to persuade
him to support the new company; to permit King Brothers
to sell Pipeline crude, to allow them to join the big
league.

After half an hour, Ruby stopped.

Benjamin raised an eyebrow.

'I ran out of gas,' said Ruby.

'And you want to be an oil trader?'

'So, what's the answer?'

'The answer is "no".'

'Why?'

'One of my best customers is the Oil Corporation. Ask
Mort. He knows.'

'I know, too. So what?'

'Mr Edmund Meyer does not love you. He thinks Mort
is a . . . what did he call him? A renegade. A good word,
don't you think?'

'It's bullshit,' said Ruby, 'and you know it.'

Benjamin heaved his arms high and pulled a face of
mock surprise.

'Bullshit? Is that what it is?'

'The guy's afraid of our competition. He wants to stop
us before we even get started.'

'Competition from you?' said Benjamin sceptically. 'The

Oil Corporation is the biggest in the world. It's number one. What are you? Chicken soup.'

'Chicken feed,' corrected Ruby.

'That too,' agreed Benjamin.

'Just give us a chance to prove what we can do,' said Ruby.

'And lose my best customer?'

'You won't lose him. You're too important to him. You know that better than I do.'

Benjamin knew it well, but he was not going to make life easy for Ruby. He started to make one pile of all the papers on his desk. It looked like the discussion was over.

'You going somewhere?'

'Yes.'

'Where?'

Benjamin bounced up and down in his chair in irritation. 'Do I have to tell you everything?'

'No,' said Ruby calmly. 'Just tell me where you're going.'

'To Beersheba.'

'That's nice.'

'And you're not invited,' said Benjamin gruffly.

'We can talk in the car,' said Ruby.

Beersheba, the place of the seven wells, was once the home of Abraham and Isaac. Now it was a small, neatly laid-out town, with a large hospital serving the surrounding area. The descendants of the Children of Israel brought their sick to be cured and so did the Bedouins who spread their robes and sat on the hospital lawns like flowers, looking as they must have done in biblical times.

Benjamin paid his visits and they drove back to Tel Aviv. On the way, they stopped at a gasoline station and lunched in a Hungarian café. The place was little more than a prefabricated hut with four or five aluminium-framed tables and a glass counter at one end from which the food magically appeared. The wife of the owner served and the owner and his friends shouted and laughed and drank beer and played cards.

They ate sweet and sour fish, goulash and pickled cucumbers washed down with beer. Then they finished the
meal with poppy-seed cake and strong coffee.

Ruby sighed contentedly.

'You enjoyed?' said Benjamin.

'Need you ask? The place is great. Who would have
thought it?' Ruby looked around him at the bare, unpretentious room.

'Small is good,' said Benjamin.

Ruby grinned. He understood.

'I don't always eat at five-star restaurants,' said
Benjamin. 'I don't always trade with giants. Now – ' he
wiped his mouth with the back of his hand, 'let's
talk.'

'OK,' said Ruby. 'I'd like three offers: one for the UK –
Orion Oil; one for a West Coast USA refinery – Pacific
Odyssey; and one for someone very special indeed.'

Benjamin was immediately intrigued. 'Who?' he said.

'First give me the offers I need for Orion and Pacific
Odyssey.'

They haggled a little over price: not too much, just for
the hell of it. The time to negotiate was not now when
Ruby was taking the offer from Benjamin; that time would
come when they had the business in hand. That was when
the hard bargaining would be done.

'And the special one? Who is this special one?' asked
Benjamin.

Ruby paused for effect. 'The special one is Exxon.'

Bejamin bounced in his chair.

'Are you trying to bullshit me, Ruby? Exxon would never
buy Pipeline crude. They have a fat slice of Aramco. Why
should they? The Arabs would kick their ass and throw
them out of Saudi Arabia if they found out.'

'If we can keep it quiet, they're ready to buy four cargoes
of crude as a trial. Sixty thousand tonners for direct shipment to the US.'

'Who are you kidding? Are you telling me they'd risk
their necks for four cargoes? A pin in the ocean.'

'A drop,' said Ruby. 'And no one will ever find out.'

Benjamin was looking suspiciously at Ruby.

'Naturally, they would need an incentive.'

The word 'incentive' was not one calculated to put Benjamin in a good mood and Ruby well knew it, but, if his scheme were to succeed, it would have to look right. The only possible motive for Exxon to buy Pipeline crude would be if they were tempted by a price so far below the market that they simply could not resist.

'Say, fifty cents a barrel.'

Benjamin's first reaction was typical. He hit the table so hard with his fist that the coffee cups and saucers jumped several inches into the air and smashed to pieces on the stone floor. The owner and his friends stopped playing cards for a second and looked at them. No one seemed particularly disturbed. The wife came over and swept up the pieces.

Ruby was expecting a scream of anger. What came out of Benjamin's mouth was a hiss.

'Are you crazy? Do you know how much fifty cents is on a cargo of crude?'

'We're talking Exxon, Benjamin. If you break in with them, who's to say where it will end? It could open up a whole new market for you.'

'And if it ever got out, it could shut down the Pipeline.'

'That's exactly why they could never buy from you directly. They insist on King Brothers being in between. We're responsible for keeping the whole deal one hundred per cent secret.'

Benjamin was torn. The price was ridiculous, but Exxon . . . it was a dream. A dream of dreams.

'You wouldn't be playing games with me, would you, Ruby? You and that big brother of yours.'

Ruby gave Benjamin his deadpan, fish-eye look – neither innocent nor guilty. Just blank. Impenetrable.

When they said goodbye, Benjamin patted Ruby affectionately on the shoulder. 'Good luck, King Brother. Be successful. Make lots of money.'

'That's not why I joined Mort. I'll help him for a couple of years. You know what I really want to be.'

'Sure. You want to be the richest rabbi in the world.' And Benjamin thumped Ruby on the back and roared with laughter.

Mort was unconvinced. 'The only reason the guy gave you a fifty-cent discount was because you told him you were selling the crude to Exxon.'

'Right.'

'And you know as well I do that Exxon would never dream of buying crude shipped through the Israeli Pipeline. Right?'

'Right,' said Ruby.

'So, now Benjamin's all excited. What happens next?'

'I sell the crude to Houston Refining.'

Mort beat his desk in exasperation. 'You can't do it.'

'You have any idea what this means?' said Ruby. 'Four cargoes. A total of two hundred and forty thousand tons, or about one point eight million barrels. You know what we make? Nine hundred thousand bucks. Nine hundred thousand dollars is a lot of money. We need it. Or had you forgotten?'

'I know we need it. No one knows it better. Still . . . the risk.'

'Benjamin would give his right arm to sell to a Major. It would be a real breakthrough for the Israeli Pipeline,' said Ruby.

'But you're not selling to a Major, for Chrissake!'

'Benjamin will never know that. Think how happy he'll be.'

'He won't be so happy when he finds out we outsmarted him. It'll be the end for us. We'll never do business with him again.'

'I wouldn't be so sure,' said Ruby. 'If it suits him, he'll do business with us. If it doesn't suit him, he won't. He's very pragmatic.'

'It won't work,' said Mort nervously. Who else could make him nervous?

80

'OK. How's he going to find out?' Ruby was challenging him. He had become the trial lawyer, teasing his adversary, the interpreter of the Talmud debating with a student the meaning of some obscure rabbinical phrase. His astute brown eyes sparkled behind his glasses.

'A hundred ways.'

'Name one.'

'Houston Refining discharge crude at Galveston, Texas.'

'So? There's an Exxon refinery near there.'

'What if Benjamin traces the cargo from Galveston to Houston Refining?'

'Hard to imagine, but I suppose he could do it,' Ruby admitted.

'You bet. Some kind friend might tell him where the cargo really went. How would you explain that?'

'I'd tell Benjamin that Exxon exchanged his cargo with Houston Refining for Low Sulphur crude. After all, Exxon do like Nigerian. They prefer it to High Sulphur Iranian.'

'OK,' said Mort reluctantly. 'It's a plausible story. But what happens if Benjamin asks Houston Refining for confirmation?'

'If he did, they'd know nothing about it. They'd say they never did the exchange with Exxon,' said Ruby.

'Exactly,' said Mort. 'Because it only exists in your own imagination.'

'No,' said Ruby. 'Because they'd be protecting Exxon. I already told Benjamin that Exxon would never discuss the matter with anyone. The whole business is too sensitive.'

Mort was beginning to be impressed, despite his better judgement.

'What if Benjamin asks to see Exxon's buyer, or a vice-president, or the board of directors? What then?'

'The answer to that is too simple,' said Ruby condescendingly. 'Naturally, they'd deny they ever bought a barrel of Pipeline crude from us. That is, if they ever agreed to meet Benjamin, which is highly unlikely. Don't you see? That's the beauty of the whole scheme. I told Benjamin it's a condition of the sale that there can be no direct communication between him and Exxon. Not now, not tomorrow, not ever. He knows they could never admit to anyone that they bought Pipeline crude. Secrecy is essential. That's our function in the deal. If it ever got out, he'd expect Exxon to deny everything. What else could they do? Mort, I'm telling you – the scheme is foolproof. Of course, it means screwing Benjamin a little, but he does all right and he'll do plenty of deals with us in the future. Besides, if the boot were on the other foot, don't you think he'd do it to us. . . ?' There was a long pause. Ruby was watching Mort carefully.

'Am I right or am I wrong?'

'Nine hundred thousand dollars, you say?'

'Nine hundred and twenty-five,' said Ruby.

'Benjamin will suspect you never delivered those cargoes to Exxon,' said Mort.

'Maybe so. I've had to speak to him several times about his mean, suspicious nature.'

They looked at each other. The cabal was operating. Mort's lips twitched.

'So? What are you waiting for? Go ahead and do the deal,' he said.

'I already did,' said Ruby.

It was King Brothers' first major coup. The profit on that one deal alone would keep them in business for months.

They were on their way.

*　　*　　*

'The hell with Ruby.'

Caroline was cooking dinner and Jeffrey was watching her. The kitchen was his favourite place and watching Caroline his favourite occupation.

'What's he done this time?'

'He got there first,' Jeffrey said. 'He pulled off the sweetest deal.'

'Jealous?' Her eyes gleamed mockingly. They were beautiful, always greener at night.

'Out of nothing. The man's a genius. Just an idea. A great idea. Of course, he had to screw the Israelis to do the business, but then, someone always gets screwed. That's life.'

'Is that what it is,' she said. More of a statement than a question. 'It's important for you to prove you're better than the others, isn't it?'

'It's important that I show I'm just as good,' he said.

'Why?'

Jeffrey didn't answer. 'It's Friday,' he said. 'I always wind the clocks on Friday.'

He found it soothing, reassuring. Maybe because looking inside a clock was more interesting and infinitely less disturbing than looking inside himself. There was the long-case William and Mary in the hall and the mahogany *grande sonnerie* in the drawing-room that played madrigals with names like 'Fair Maid of the Village' and 'The Shepherd's Lament' and, all over the house, in various nooks and crannies, a collection of small carriage and bracket clocks with loud chimes and sturdy ticks. It took a long time to wind them all.

He went back to the kitchen. Christ, how did she do it? Up at six-thirty, Buddhist meditation till seven, pack Harry off to school, organize the baby-sitter, spend the day listening to emotionally disturbed people spewing their problems on her carpet, pick up Harry, back home to play with Charlotte, cook the dinner and deal with tired, frustrated husband when he finally showed up after all the work was done.

Did life really have to be like that?

'Smells good. Horse?'

'Pork.'

'Kosher?'

'Blooms Delicatessen!'

'Tell that to the Chief Rabbi . . . You know, I think I'm going to be a success.'

'Great,' said Caroline. 'What does that mean, by the way? A nanny? Private schools? Rolls Royce and chauffeur? Our own box at Covent Garden?'

'Something like that.'

Caroline stirred the chicken stew. 'Would that give you less time for us, or more?'

'Do I detect a hint of scepticism, a cynical inference, an atom of doubt?'

'Could be.'

'I thought so.' Jeffrey was disappointed. He tried to change the subject. 'How were the psychos today?'

'Look,' Caroline said bitterly, 'the psychos were OK. At least they know they have problems.'

'Meaning?'

'Meaning, what the hell is success anyway? If I help just one of my patients to understand what's bothering him – is that success?'

'Oh, indeed,' said Jeffrey with heavy irony. 'Now that's real success. That's the only success. The selfless kind. What I do is graft for a living. But then, who's competing?'

'You are. You're not grafting for a living. You want to be Mr Important. You want star billing. Name over the title. Well, if that's success, you can – ' She swung her arm abruptly and knocked over the chicken stew. It was all over the floor.

Jeffrey surveyed the mess. Then he knelt down and picked up two pieces – one in each hand. 'Leg or breast?' he enquired.

For a moment, Caroline was on the edge of tears. Then, she laughed instead.

'Why don't I take you out to dinner?' he said.

'That's what all the psychos say.'

'They must be crazy,' said Jeffrey.

Feet up on his desk, Jeffrey pondered the offer for Orion Oil. The crude would be shipped through the Israeli Pipeline. Orion did not care about that. They had no commitment to the Arabs, nor to anyone else for that matter. All they looked at was the landed price of the oil. Three hundred thousand tons was a lot of crude for them and they were keen buyers, tough negotiators. They were holding what amounted to a sealed auction. They would buy when they were good and ready, not one moment before. Everyone would get the same chance.

That was the problem. The offer of crude was firm for two weeks, but the cost of freight, which was tied to it, was floating. Any increase in the freight market from now until the business was confirmed would be added to Benjamin's price.

It was only natural. No one could offer firm freight these days. The freight market was going wild. Because of a strong demand for crude and an apparent shortage of tankers, freight rates were climbing at a phenomenal rate, about ten World Scale points every day, which meant on an average voyage – for example Kharg Island, Iran, to the UK – an increase of a dollar a ton a day.

Anyone can make average money in the right conditions. It takes something approaching genius to make a killing. It needs ideas; it needs inspiration, and that was what Jeffrey was searching for right now. If he waited, submitted his offer in a sealed envelope together with his competitors, he might get the business or he might lose it. He would have to take his chances. And if he was lucky, if he had the good fortune to be the cheapest, then his profit margin would be average to minuscule. Benjamin never gave anything away.

Jeffrey was friendly with Orion's chief buyer, but there was nothing doing there. The man would not help him and, anyway, he had little power. It was the board of directors who had the final say.

The board of directors. Jeffrey swung his legs off the desk and strode round the office like a tiger that just heard his keeper rattling the bars.

'That's it. What a bloody fool I am! Of course. The board of directors.'

New York was five hours behind. It was five-thirty a.m. over there. What the hell. He phoned Ruby.

'Did I wake you?'

'I've been studying the Talmud for an hour.'

'I want you to accept the offer for Orion Oil.'

'You did the deal already?'

'No, but we have to stop Benjamin's freight clock running. Phone him and confirm the business, but make the confirmation "subject board of directors' approval". Tell him it's just a formality.'

'What happens if the business falls through?'

'It's not going to fall through. But if the worst comes to the worst and something goes wrong, what can Benjamin do? He'll scream and shout, for sure. Then, he'll take the tankers away and sell the freight to another customer at a much higher price. Why should he care?'

'What happens if the freight market collapses?'

'It won't – not in the immediate future.'

'I'm with you,' said Ruby. 'I like it. Once we tell Benjamin we have the business, we lock in his price – crude and freight.'

'And we pocket any increase in the freight rate between now and the day we sell to Orion Oil,' said Jeffrey.

'I love it. I love it,' said Ruby, ecstatically. 'Just make sure you get the business.'

'You're beginning to sound like Mort already,' said Jeffrey.

Jeffrey nursed the chief buyer of Orion Oil. This was a deal he could not afford to lose. A lot of profit and a lot of pride were involved. Day after day, the freight market soared. In a week, it was eight dollars a ton higher than the day Ruby accepted Benjamin's offer.

Ruby phoned five times a day. He was getting nervous.

'Benjamin's killing me. He wants to know when shipments start. He's getting suspicious. This morning he asked what exactly "subject to the board of directors' approval" means.'

86

'Tell him we'll have a shipping schedule for him in three days.'

'Will we?'

'I doubt it,' said Jeffrey. 'In three days we'll think of something else to tell him.'

'Oyvay,' said Ruby.

The following Friday, the chief buyer of Orion had all his offers in, all except Jeffrey's. He was about ready to conclude.

'Let me have your offer on my desk by four p.m., or you'll be too late.'

'It'll be there,' said Jeffrey. What the hell was he going to do? Take his chances with all the others? No, that was much too risky.

He telexed the offer and waited till seven minutes to five. It was as long as he dared delay. He phoned the chief buyer.

'Am I the cheapest?'

'You know I can't tell you that. It's more than my job's worth.'

'I know it is. So, tell me. Am I the cheapest?'

'No, you're not. I'm sorry, Jeffrey. Better luck next time.'

Jeffrey's heart sank. Now came the tricky part of the plan.

'I imagine all the other offers are tied to a floating freight rate.'

'Of course they are. So is yours, isn't it? No one in their right mind would give us a freight offer firm over the weekend in this crazy market. They could lose their shirts.'

'So, accept my offer now.' What could he lose? Only some extra profit.

'Jeffrey,' the chief buyer said, a touch impatiently, 'you know I can't do that. I can only make a recommendation. The board makes the final decision.'

'I know that. If you confirm now, you can make your acceptance "subject to the board of directors' approval", latest Monday morning, nine a.m.'

There was a long pause on the line. 'Are you telling me that you're ready to hold your freight rate firm over the weekend?'

'If you accept my offer. Yes.'

'From this minute?'

'Absolutely. By Monday, we're sure to be the cheapest, the way the freight market is going up.'

'What happens if the board turns you down?'

'They won't, but if they do, it's my risk.'

The chief buyer was in a quandary. 'The very least I can do is give your competitors the same chance.'

Jeffrey consulted his watch. It was two minutes past five on a Friday evening. If he was right, his competitors would either be at home, or speeding along the M4 for a weekend in the country.

'Go ahead and phone them,' he said. 'I wouldn't want to have an unfair advantage.' He was almost ashamed of himself for being so devious. Almost, but not quite.

Five minutes later, the chief buyer called back. 'Wouldn't you know it?' he said. 'They've all left. Friday afternoon. Everyone disappears early on a Friday.'

'Too bad,' said Jeffrey. 'I should have phoned you earlier.' How could he be such a rotten bastard? 'If it's any consolation to you, I doubt that anyone would have agreed to leave their offer open till Monday. The freight market is boiling.'

'Don't tell me,' the chief buyer said. He sounded suspicious. 'So how can you do it?'

'Remember, we don't have to charter tankers. This is the Israeli Pipeline we're talking about. We have our own vessels. We calculate our costs in a different way.'

It sounded OK. Good enough for the chief buyer, anyway.

The poor man had a problem. If he accepted Jeffrey's offer, he was not being strictly fair to the others. If he did not accept it, he could lose Orion Oil a fortune. He could also lose his job.

'I just made a calculation. If I don't accept your offer, we could lose a million dollars over the weekend.' His ulcer was giving him a bad time.

'Actually, I calculated a million and a half. But what the hell,' said Jeffrey cruelly.

The man just could not take the risk. These days, profits were more important than the niceties of playing the game like gentlemen.

'It's a deal,' he sighed.

Monday morning at nine o'clock, the telex from Orion Oil was on Jeffrey's desk. King Brothers' offer had been approved by the board of directors. Now he really had a deal.

In ten days, the freight market had risen eleven dollars. That meant a profit of four million dollars.

'That took guts,' said Ruby.

It was the nicest thing he could have said.

Mort came on the line. 'Sounds like a good deal,' he said. 'It's just a pity you had to hold your offer firm over the weekend. The freight market went up another dollar a ton.'

Jeffrey twisted the cord in his hand, fantasizing it was Mort's neck.

'By the way,' said Mort, 'you think – uh – you think you could maybe sell them another couple of cargoes at the same terms?'

Jeffrey howled. 'Jesus, Mort! Aren't you ever satisfied?'

Mort considered the question. 'I guess not,' he said. 'Oh, by the way, congratulations!'

'Thanks a million,' said Jeffrey.

It was odd, but Jeffrey could not recall ever having a reasonable conversation with his father. Reasonable to Jeffrey meant talking about the sort of things fathers and sons were supposed to talk about, like careers, politics, marriage, even, on occasions and over a drink, sex. These trifles were not, it seemed, on the old man's agenda. He always talked to Jeffrey as if he were a well-meaning

89

distant relative. Perhaps that was the British way. Perhaps not. Certainly it was his father's way. There were even times when Jeffrey was not at all sure that his father knew who he was. Not that he was senile, far from it; he was very much all there. He was just habitually vague, tending towards the abstruse, the esoteric and, sometimes, the plain cussed. A conversation with him could be stimulating, but at the end of it, you were never entirely certain what it was you had been talking about.

It was, therefore, even odder to Jeffrey to discover that almost everything he had learnt about life had come from his father. How it ever happened, he would never know.

'What was wrong with Shell?'

'I was bored,' said Jeffrey. 'I was never going to get there.'

'Where was that?'

It was going to be one of those conversations. His father could scramble Jeffrey's brain quicker than anyone he knew.

'I wasn't moving up the ladder. They weren't promoting me. I was never going to be chairman. I wasn't earning enough money. I was overworked and underpaid. How's that for starters?'

His father surveyed him disapprovingly.

'I do hope you're not going to be disappointed with life.'

'I'll try not to be,' said Jeffrey.

'Have you seen what's happening in the Test Match?'

'No, I haven't.' Jeffrey abhorred cricket.

'It's a disgrace. A scandal.'

'Were you ever disappointed, Father?'

'I'm disappointed all the time. Look at what those idiots are doing at Lord's.'

'Disappointed by life, I mean.'

'Oh, life.' His voice dropped on the word as if he found it faintly distasteful. 'I don't think so. I was disappointed when your mother died, of course. I thought she might have waited for me. It was quite a let-down, one way and another.'

'Be serious, Father.'

'Oh, but I am. Deadly serious. It's when I'm flippant that I'm at my most serious. Only terribly earnest people like you never seem to understand that. I was never as earnest as you are about life, perhaps because I never expected much from it.'

'What about ambition?'

His father chuckled. 'I remember as a child wanting desperately to be a great composer. I liked the idea of conducting my own compositions in front of huge audiences in vast auditoriums, but – well – you know . . . that would have meant studying music and I really hated the idea of all that work.'

'No regrets?'

'Regrets? What on earth for?'

'Don't try to kid me. You were always an achiever.'

'Never.' His father was horrified.

'You were the warden of the synagogue.'

'That was your mother's idea. She enjoyed seeing her husband facing a different way to the rest of the congregation. She seemed to feel it gave her status. I think she felt it was God and the wardens against the rest. Perhaps it was. Besides, she liked me in a top hat. I hated it. It gave me a headache.'

'You were quite good at business.'

'I was quite good at a number of things. Never quite good enough, though. That's the secret of happiness, you know,' his father added contrarily.

No. Jeffrey did not know.

'But content, my boy, always content. That's not a fashionable thing to be any more, but it does for me. I have my pipe, my radio, my books, my roses. When I die, it will be no earth-shattering event. You will, no doubt, shed a few tears, but the world will not have lost one of its great sons.'

His father was performing and Jeffrey knew it. Suddenly, for no obvious reason, he felt depressed.

'Anyway, my boy, you have my blessing.'

'Your blessing?' Jeffrey was genuinely surprised.

'Thirty-four years old and you still need my blessing?'

'I need nothing of the kind,' said Jeffrey. 'I was merely keeping you informed.'

'I'm sorry,' said his father. 'I thought you were asking for my blessing. In any case, I give it freely, even without your asking for it, although,' he added mischievously, 'why you should need it, I really can't imagine.'

Jeffrey put a hand to his head. His brain was well and truly scrambled. It was time to go.

His father studied him uneasily. 'I wonder where you get your ambition from, Jeffrey. Certainly not from me.'

He looked affronted as a man might who had been unjustly accused of transmitting to his offspring some rare and incurable disease.

*   *   *

There might have been in the world a city dirtier, more polluted, more crowded than Istanbul, but if there was then Sam had never seen it. Nor, on the other hand, had he seen one more exciting or more romantic. Istanbul is a troubled confluence of seas and centuries, old and new, East and West, a hodgepodge of the ugly and the beautiful. Where else in the world can you see the slender minarets of ancient mosques fingering the sky, side by side with the smoking chimney stacks of leather factories, cement works and chemical plants?

Sam stood on the balcony of his room at the Hilton Hotel. It was a few minutes before sunset. Opposite, across the Bosphorus, was Asia; on this side was Europe. A mullah was reciting evening prayers from a nearby mosque. The mullahs used to climb to the top of the minarets five times a day. Now they stayed at the bottom and used the loudspeaker system.

Over to the left was the suspension bridge linking the two continents: to the right, the Blue Mosque and the Covered Bazaar. Irreconcilables. When you looked at a Turk, that was what you saw. What would the archeologists of the twenty-fifth century make of this place when they dug it up?

Sam decided the question was unanswerable and retired to the bar for a drink. The place was crowded, but there was no one he knew and, anyway, he did not feel sociable.

The trip had been a big fat zero. Kemal Özal, the chief buyer of Ipras, the State Refinery, was not the most flexible man in the world. When they started talking, he told Sam he was a buyer of crude at five dollars, forty cents a barrel c.i.f. Turkey. That was several cents below the market. Hard to believe he could pick up any oil at that price. An hour later, the two men had talked themselves out. Özal's price had not altered by a single cent, except that at one point in the conversation he took a call and informed Sam he could now buy at five-thirty-five, but he would still pay him five-forty if Sam made up his mind immediately.

The bastard. Sam was desperate to show the others what he could do. It was a matter of pride. He felt the challenge, the compulsion to cut a deal. The camera was focused on him.

He drank three very dry martinis straight off and looked around. Opposite him on the other side of the circular bar was a brunette with close-cropped hair and a nice smile. As she turned away from ordering her drink she caught his eye.

Her name was Jane Vogel and she was Swiss-American.

'Is this a pick-up?' she asked.

'I guess it is,' he said. 'I don't usually . . .'

'That's OK,' she said. 'I don't usually either. Will you be asking me out to dinner?'

'That's what I had in mind,' he said. Here, it seemed, was a girl with no duplicity, no humbug and definitely not a trace of shyness. He liked her immediately.

'In that case,' she said, 'I'm going upstairs to change.'

The restaurant was a houseboat moored in the Bay of Terrabia at the junction of the Bosphorus and the Black Sea. Sam had talked to her at the bar because she had great

93

legs, a cute, rather elfin face and a cool, direct glance. Now he discovered that the girl was also bright.

'OK,' she said, 'I'm twenty-eight, single, and I like men. I'm a marketing director of Sandoz which, for someone of my age, let alone a woman, is unheard of. Anything else you want to know?'

'Yes,' said Sam. 'You like raki – the Turkish national drink?'

'I adore it,' she said.

Sam warmed to her enthusiasm. It was something that had been missing in his life for a long time. In fact, if he were honest with himself, it had never been there. Maybe the Swedish father and the Swiss mother had something to do with it.

So they drank raki with *meze*, the Turkish specialities that come in numerous dishes often replacing the main course: eggplant, shrimps and lobster, stuffed vine leaves, feta cheese and black olives, a delicious dish that tasted like scrambled eggs made in paradise, and a kind of macaroni cake cut in squares that Sam always resolved not to eat because of the calories, but invariably did.

Instead of the main course, they drank red wine, then numerous cups of Turkish coffee, then more red wine. The lights of the little fishing boats twinkled on the Bosphorus and the wind blew up from the Black Sea and gently rocked the houseboat on its moorings. An old gypsy played sad Balkan melodies on his violin and talked of the good old days in Istanbul.

Through a haze of liquor, Sam gradually became aware that Jane was talking about the Turkish Central Bank. For Chrissake! What was wrong with this chick? She was obviously like those women who discussed real estate investments and the Dow Jones during the interval of *Swan Lake*.

'Did you know that?'

'Did I know what?' Disconsolately, he poured another glass of the dark red wine.

'The Turkish Central Bank fixes exchange rates between

the Turkish lira and foreign currencies and leaves them unchanged for weeks on end.'

'You don't say,' he said solemnly. 'No, I did not know that. What I do know is that I'm going to have one hell of a hangover in the morning. I did not know that the Turkish Central Bank . . . did that . . .' He was staring at her with that absurd look in his eye that people get when they have had too much to drink. He was either going to fall asleep, or off his chair – quite possibly both.

'I thought you said you were keen to do business here?'

'I am,' he said, piqued.

'Did you know that, in Turkey, the Swiss franc is under-valued by five per cent compared with the dollar?'

A sudden change came over Sam's face. He blinked a few times and then he was wide awake. It was as if someone had given him a magic energy pill.

'Say that again.'

'The Swiss franc is undervalued by over five per cent compared with the dollar,' she repeated obligingly.

Sam was trying to think, but he needed help.

'OK,' she said, 'let me explain something you might not have known. If you sell here in dollars and get paid in dollars, then, on the international currency market, you exchange every United States dollar for three Swiss francs and thirty centimes.'

'Right,' said Sam. So far, he was with her.

'But, my darling, if you sell in dollars and you ask your Turkish customer to pay you in Swiss francs, then he'll take his dollars to the Turkish Central Bank and they will give him, for every dollar, not three francs and thirty centimes, but three francs and fifty centimes. That means you make an extra five per cent, just because of some quirk in the local exchange rate. Your customer loses nothing – in fact he doesn't even know what's happen-ing – but you, Sam, you make yourself a very nice little profit.'

Sam was sober now, or at least as close to it as he was likely to get tonight.

'What happens if the Turkish Central Bank alters its rates of exchange between the time you conclude the business and the time your customer remits the money to you?'

'They do it so rarely the risk is minimal. What I do is give my customers a small price incentive for paying promptly – cash against documents. That way I get my Swiss francs in a couple of days.'

'Well, I'll be . . .' He sat and looked at her, entranced. The girl was a genius. 'How long have you been doing this?'

'About two years.'

'Do you know, I've been doing business in Turkey for five years and I never thought of this gimmick.'

'It's nothing,' she said modestly. 'Just a little trick.'

'You have any more little tricks up your sleeve?' he asked her.

'One or two,' she said.

She pushed him down on the bed and lowered herself onto him.

'Why should you do all the work?'

'You drank more than I did,' she whispered, moaning with pleasure. 'Besides, I like it this way.' She rode him slowly, feeling the length of him inside her.

The wine had deadened his senses enough to prolong the pleasure. Three times Jane cried out as she reached her climax and three times he pulled her back onto him. The fourth time he came together with her, his whole body convulsing in the final spasms of the exquisite release.

She lay beside him, her head resting in the crook of his shoulder.

'It is just sex, isn't it? I mean, we're not going to get involved, are we?'

'Why not?'

'I told you. I don't want to. You're married. I've been down that road before.'

He hated to hear her talk about her past. For God's sake, he thought to himself, how immature. How infantile. To be jealous of a woman's past.

'No,' he said, 'we're not going to get involved.'

Sam cancelled his return flight to Zurich the next morning, and flew back a day later. Jane had gone. This was strictly business.

And what business. He sold Özal seven hundred thousand tons of Iranian Light and Heavy, making apparently nothing on the deal. As they signed the contract, Kemal Özal smiled complacently. He had gotten himself a bargain and he knew it.

What he did not know was that when Sam got paid and calculated the profit, King Brothers had made one and a half million dollars – thanks to Jane Vogel.

Not to mention the Turkish Central Bank.

It was the first time Sam had cheated on Amy. He wondered whether he had done it out of spite – some macho instinct for revenge that compelled him to redress the balance. Whatever the reason, he persuaded himself that nothing had changed between them, that he still loved her. At least he thought he did. Could it really be love when you could never get close to someone, never really understand them? The moth and the candle flame. The attraction was irresistible, but inevitably moths got their wings singed, or worse. He always had the feeling that Amy was not the right woman for him, but then the right woman might have bored him to death: it was her very elusiveness, her remoteness, that attracted and tormented him at the same time.

When he thought about it, he doubted that Siegfried Gerber had been the only one. It was surely not the first time it had happened; no doubt it would not be the last. What kind of a basis for marriage was that? He would never be at peace; every day he went to the office, he would wonder what she was up to.

They had two kids. That had to be the most important

thing in their lives. How could you break up a marriage when you had young children? People did, of course, but he was the old-fashioned kind of man. Family came first and family was kids: seven-year-old Laura, sparkling, fiery, temperamental, independent; four-year-old Edward, introverted, sickly, clinging. 'Your child' Amy would often say contemptuously. Well, they were both his children and he willingly accepted the responsibility he believed that every parent had: to love them. Amy was different. She was not shackled by obligations. She took life as it came.

'If you want me to stay, I'll stay,' she said. 'If you want me to go, then say so and I'll go. You have to decide.'

'What's the point if you don't love me?' he said, half hoping she would say that she did, but knowing she would not.

'Love,' she said wistfully, as if love were a dream and an illusion. It was depressing to see her like this. She had lost her vitality, the brilliance and glitter that had once made her so exciting. She was drained and flaccid, like one of those tropical fish that lose their colour as the life force ebbs away.

'I don't know if I can love anyone,' she said.

'You said you loved me when we were first married.'

'Maybe I did. Maybe I do now. What does it matter? It's only a word.'

'Love is so complicated,' he said.

'No it's not. It's very simple. It's you who makes it complicated.' She had the knack of putting him in the wrong. Whatever he said, whatever position he took, she trapped him. He felt constantly threatened by her.

'I'm not like you,' he said. 'You want everything to be black and white. It's not so easy for me. I want you to stay, but it depends how you stay.'

'What are you trying to say?'

'It's simple. I mean you have to be faithful to me.'

'What's the big deal about being faithful? My parents were crazy about each other, but they sure as hell weren't faithful. Were yours?'

98

'I really don't know,' said Sam. 'We never talked about things like that.'

'That's your problem,' she said. 'You never talk about anything.'

'Some things are too painful to talk about.'

'Painful,' she echoed scornfully. 'The only painful thing is being honest with yourself.'

What had they decided? Nothing, as usual.

He walked the labrador in the fields at the back of the house. It was spring. He took the path that bordered a field of bright yellow colza. The cherry trees were heavy with pink blossoms. In the distance was a row of poplar trees. The young leaves were bright green. The colours of spring were uncompromising, arrogant. They disturbed him. He preferred the softer tints of late summer and the faded gold of autumn. They were about acceptance and gentleness and compromise. They were easier to live with.

In the five or so years that Karl Andermatt had worked for Sam, they had never asked each other a single personal question. It would not have been appropriate. Karl, after all, was Swiss, withdrawn, faithful and fanatically accurate in everything he did. For him, correctness was a religion. There were things you did and things you did not do. No one had to tell you; there were simply certain standards to which you were expected to conform.

Sam, for his part, had come to rely absolutely on Karl. By now, he took for granted his calm efficiency, his unfailing memory and, not least, his devotion. Somehow, in his shrouded reticent Swiss fashion, Karl conveyed the message that he would always be around as long as Sam needed him.

Indeed, when Sam decided to join King Brothers, he never even considered it necessary to inform Karl. He knew perfectly well that Karl's radar would scan the horizon with its customary precision and pick up the signals.

And so, when Sam opened King Brothers' office in Wald,

there was Karl, organizing everything with that passion-less intensity of his.

Everything important was left to Sam. Salary, for example, was too delicate a matter to be discussed. Not that Karl did not care about his salary. He cared very much. It was simply that he trusted Sam absolutely.

In their way, the two of them were both enigmas to each other and completely content that it should be so. Life was so much easier, so much more comfortable and unob-trusive like that.

Sometimes Sam wondered how it would be if they ever really communicated. He knew Karl was a complex indi-vidual; he sensed that his personality was wrapped in almost infinite layers, like an onion. The question was whether anyone would ever succeed in peeling him and what they would find if they did.

For some reason that he could not explain, it was a prospect that scared Sam.

*　　*　　*

Joe Murphy was the chief buyer of Pacific Odyssey, one of the top ten oil refiners in America and a company whose refining capacity and sales outlets for oil products far exceeded its own crude resources. Because Pacific Odyssey was the largest net buyer of crude oil in the United States, it was also the biggest and most interesting customer for any company whose business was crude oil trading. That made Joe Murphy a powerful man. A lot of people in the oil business were his friends. A lot more would like to be.

'You know I can't buy from the Israeli Pipeline,' he said.

'Why not?'

'Goddam it, Mort! I can't afford to upset the Arabs. We have too many interests out there. What I don't need is to find myself on the Arab blacklist.'

'What I need is your help, Joe. Do this favour for me. It's only a small volume.'

'It doesn't matter how small it is. Once I buy from the Pipeline, I'm contaminated.'

100

That was exactly what Mort was hoping for. The first step was always the most traumatic, like losing your virginity, but once a customer had taken it, he would keep right on walking. There was no reason to stop. The Pipeline offered a good service, and it was competitive.

'Tell me something, Joe. Is it Pacific Odyssey's policy not to buy from Israel?'

'Not that I know of. Between you and me, I'm not sure that wouldn't be illegal discrimination.'

'So, what's stopping you?'

'Let me tell you about this crap company I work for, Mort. They don't tell you what to do and they don't tell you what not to do. All they want is results. If I make the right decisions, that's great – that's what they pay me for. If I foul up, that's too bad for me. If I were to buy from the Israeli Pipeline and someone outside the company got hold of the story, I'd be dead. My management would tell the world I wasn't authorized to do it.'

'And if no one found out?'

'They'd be happy. The company gets cheap crude and the president gives me a nod and a smile from time to time. You have no idea what that does for my day.'

'I can imagine.'

'You can't,' said Joe Murphy. 'You're your own boss.'

'You know I'd never do anything to make a problem for you,' Mort said earnestly. Sometimes Mort was so convincing, he almost believed himself.

'It wouldn't be in your interest to do that,' said Joe Murphy. 'I'm your biggest potential customer.'

Mort looked hurt. 'We go back a long way, Joe,' he said. 'You're the best friend I have in the industry. There's more to business than dollars and cents,' he added sanctimoniously.

Joe grinned. 'You know, Mort, I like you. God knows why, but I do. Just do me a favour, though. Don't bullshit me.'

'Absolutely not,' said Mort. 'You know I never do that.'

'I know you never stop,' said Joe. 'I guess it's the way

101

you are. What worries me is that one of these days you might start believing yourself. Then you'd really be in trouble.'

Mort had a Perrier with his coffee; Joe Murphy, a Rémy Martin and a Monte Cristo cigar. He was in a good mood. To Mort, it seemed like as opportune a time as any to come to the point. In all the years Mort had known Joe, the man had never taken a bribe. No question, he could have made a bundle if he were ready to accept favours, but he never had done, not from Mort and not – Mort would have sworn – from anyone else. He was apparently that rare commodity in the oil business: an honest man.

But Mort believed that honest men, like unicorns, only existed in fables. Every man could be bought. There was nothing in the world that could not be traded, if the price were right.

'The word is that King Brothers is doing OK,' Joe said, lighting up.

'I'm not complaining,' said Mort. 'It's early days yet, but we're going places.'

'I believe you.'

'As you know, our business is oil, but we're doing a little commodity trading as well,' said Mort. 'Putting money into equities, precious metals, base metals. Soft commodities too – wheat, sugar, cocoa.'

'I thought you guys were the Oil Kings?'

'Sure, but we're always ready to make something extra for ourselves. And for our clients,' Mort added. He was watching Joe carefully.

'How do you mean, your clients?'

'We have a "fund",' Mort said lightly. 'Anyone who cares to can . . . invest in it. We in the company all do, naturally – the partners, our employees and, lately, quite a number of our customers.' He sipped his Perrier.

'So far, we're doing great,' he said.

'I can believe it,' said Joe. 'You guys are the experts when it comes to trading.'

'Let me think now . . . we started the fund six months

102

ago. So far, we're showing a sixty-four per cent profit on our original investment.'

Joe ordered another cognac. Usually, by this time, he would be glancing at his watch, wanting to get back to the office in case he was missing something. Today was different. He was definitely intrigued.

'Is this for real?' he asked. Joe was nobody's fool.

'Sure, it's for real. What do you think? This is a registered fund. I can show you the accounts,' said Mort.

Joe Murphy was embarrassed. 'I'm sorry. It's not that I doubted you. It's just that the whole thing sounded too good to be true.'

Mort looked him straight in the eye. Many a true word. . . .

'What the hell,' said Joe. 'I don't have any spare cash anyway.'

'That won't be necessary,' Mort said smoothly. 'The way we normally operate with our clients' money, they put up a margin – say ten per cent – and we give them a six-monthly accounting. They seem to be happy with the system.'

'I'll say,' said Joe. 'Who wouldn't be?' He finished off his cognac. 'What's in it for you guys?'

Mort flicked some crumbs off the table and smoothed down the tablecloth. He was ready for that one.

'We need all the money we can make. We're a new company. We have heavy expenses. What's in it for us? We're in it for the money. The idea to introduce clients to the fund came from one of our good customers. Now we have more outside clients than company ones.'

'Like who, for example?'

'Joe, you surely understand we have to operate on a strictly confidential basis. I can't answer that.'

Joe was thinking hard. 'Thanks for the lunch,' he said.

The car stopped outside the Pacific Odyssey building. 'The driver will take you to the airport,' he said.

'I appreciate it,' said Mort, trying not to show how despondent he felt.

'About the fund,' said Joe.

Mort maintained his poker face, green eyes watchful.

'I'll think about it. I guess I could raise five thousand bucks.'

'Ten would be better,' said Mort.

'Why ten?'

'Because ten would give you an investment of a hundred thousand dollars,' said Mort. 'That's a nice round figure.'

Joe put a finger to his lips: an unspoken request to Mort to lower his voice in case the driver heard what they were talking about. The gesture was significant. It made them conspirators of a kind, and it demonstrated as clearly as any words could have done Joe's suspicion that, if he played ball, he would be crossing a line, a line he had never crossed before.

Mort sat at a window table in the Top of the Mark, the world-famous bar on top of the Mark Hopkins Hotel in San Francisco, and contemplated his old friend, Edgar Proktor.

He was thinking that 'friend' was perhaps too simple a word to describe their relationship. But if friend was not the word, then what was?

Edgar might have been reading his thoughts. 'You son-ofabitch, it's good to see you.'

Mort sipped the same martini he had been nursing for over an hour. During that time, Edgar had drunk two double martinis and three or four singles.

'I guess you could say we're old friends,' said Mort.

Edgar grinned. 'I'll be damned if I know what we are,' he said. 'One thing I do know – you didn't fly to San Francisco just to say hi.'

Mort was ready to take his time. Not normally the most patient man in the world, he knew how to get what he wanted and if that required iron self-control and uncharacteristic forbearance, then so be it.

A few drinks later, he came to the point. 'How would you like to work for me?'

'If it's all the same to you,' said Edgar, 'I'd sooner jump off the Golden Gate Bridge.'

Mort ordered another round. This was going to take longer than he had thought. In some ways, he had even more reservations about employing Edgar than Edgar had about working for him. The two men could not have been more different: Mort, the compulsive worker, Edgar, the compulsive drinker – a lush; Mort, controlled, calculating and motivated, Edgar, irrepressible, spontaneous and lazy. But there was, despite his patent flaws, something about the man that Mort admired. Maybe it was his own alter ego that he recognized in Edgar – the relaxed amiable guy he could never allow himself to be. It was an image he could relate to, even if he could not really understand it, any more than he could understand how it was that Edgar always seemed to get results. His charming, laid-back, self-mocking, infinitely casual approach to business struck a chord in others as, indeed, it had always done in Mort.

'This is different,' said Mort.

'Anything you're involved in is different.'

'You'll never regret it.'

'I'm not nice to know.'

'I don't hire nice guys. Nice guys are losers.'

'Why the hell would you want me? You could pick up a bunch of ambitious young whiz kids – any one of them would do more work in a day than I do in a week – and, what's more, they'd do exactly what you told them. Jees, for the money you pay, you could hire the US Marines!'

'If I wanted the Marines, I wouldn't be here.'

'Why me?'

Mort shrugged. 'You get results,' he said. 'Don't ask me how, but you do.'

'You're too goddam serious for me, Mort. Life's a formal affair for you. Black tie and tuxedo. Me, I like fun. You should know me well enough by now. Don't kid yourself. I haven't changed since the last time you saw me. There are only two things in life that count for me – drink and sex – in that order. I'm a thirty-five-year-old lush going on fifty. I drink, Mort. Remember? We're talking serious alcoholism.'

'I don't give a damn what you do with your private life.'

'I don't have a private life and an office life the way other men do. It's all the same thing to me. I drink in both of them . . . I screw in both of them, too,' he added as an afterthought. 'You don't need me. I'm a professional incurable.'

'No one's incurable.'

'To you, nothing's incurable. To me, everything's incurable. It's the way I do things. I drink incurable. I screw incurable. I live incurable.'

'I don't know what you're talking about.'

'That's the trouble,' said Edgar. 'You never did.'

Mort looked out at the backdrop of San Francisco in the setting sun. It was not something he normally had time for. He did not look at views; he looked at what was in his head. Still, this was a special one, no doubt about it. The red ball of the sun was slipping behind the horizon into the Pacific Ocean and the fog was rolling in across the bridge. The city of hills pulsated with light. Who was it who said that the whole scene reminded him of a theatre? Any moment, someone would strike the set and move it into the wings. It was true. The unreality of it had a special appeal for Mort. For him, life was a little like that. He didn't trust it. The better it seemed, the less he trusted it. One day, when he was looking the other way, some creep would strike the set. And it would all be over.

Edgar poured another martini down his throat and waved at the night panorama below them. 'I love it. It's my city.'

'It's a suburb,' said Mort.

'You think so? A suburb of what?'

'Life . . . a suburb of life. I prefer to be downtown.'

'Where's that?'

'New York. Where else?'

'Who needs it?' said Edgar. 'Besides,' he added ruefully, 'my ex-wife lives in the Big Apple.'

'How is Kate?'

'She doesn't change. That's the nice thing about her.'

'Any chance of you two getting back together?'

'None at all. Why would you ask that? You never got along with her.'

'That's why I asked,' said Mort.

Edgar alone, he could handle. Edgar and Kate – that might be something different.

An hour and seven martinis later, Edgar was weakening. It was not so much the drink. Drinking didn't make him vulnerable – no more vulnerable than when he was sober. It only made life a little less unbearable.

'Give me a break, Mort, baby,' he pleaded. 'Let me die in peace. I like it here. I don't want to be the richest drunk on the block.'

'I'll make you more than rich. I'll make you a multi-millionaire.'

'How much more can I drink?'

'What you need is a challenge.'

'That's exactly what I don't need,' said Edgar. 'I already have more challenges than I can handle. Getting up in the morning is a challenge. Staying alive is a challenge. Let me go, Mort,' he begged.

But it was no good and he knew it. He had lost.

'Another martini?'

'I'll give you trouble.'

'I know that.'

Edgar shook his head despairingly. The day would come when he would find the strength to stand up to Mort.

That was what he told himself.

Three days later, the telex from Pacific Odyssey was on Mort's desk. They had purchased three hundred and fifty thousand tons of crude – Israeli Pipeline crude.

He called Joe.

'Thanks for the business.'

'Think nothing of it.'

'You know where the crude comes from.'

'I know where it comes from. I just don't want the world to know.'

'I'll take care of it.'

'You'd better.'

'I really appreciate it,' Mort said meaningfully.

'It's OK. I need the crude.'

'About the fund . . . shall I put you down for ten?'

Joe hesitated. 'I gave it some thought. If it's all the same to you, Mort – I'll pass.'

. . . Mort poured himself the first of his evening bourbons, topped it up with soda and sipped it slowly.

Unicorns . . . Could it be that they existed? Somehow, he didn't think so.

* * *

Jeffrey sounded excited and that did not happen often.

'Believe me, Mort, this could be the biggest thing yet. It's a North Sea Oil exploration consortium. BP is already in it. They're negotiating with a couple of US companies. Shell are interested, too. I hear the consortium has a great chance of being awarded three or four very promising sectors by the British government in the next round of allocations.'

'What would they want with us?'

'I have some connections here – through Henry Soames.'

'That jerk?'

'That jerk can be helpful when there's money in it for him.'

'It's too big for us, Jeffrey. Oil exploration is a risky business. You know what it takes? It can cost you hundreds of millions of bucks before you strike oil. It's for the giants. Not for us. It's out of our league.'

'Fortunes are being made,' said Jeffrey stubbornly. 'We can put aside a limited amount of risk capital. If we lose it, it'll be a blow, but not a disaster. On the other hand, we could hit the jackpot. I'm telling you, Mort, we can't afford to ignore this one. I'm not saying they'll let us in, but there's a chance they might if we handle it right.'

Mort was dubious, but Jeffrey was a level-headed sort of guy. Mort trusted his instincts. 'OK, but I need to talk to Ruby.'

'Fine. Meanwhile, do me a favour and meet my contact at BP.'

'What's his name?'

'Atherton.'

'What's he like?'

'Young, good-looking, ambitious.'

'Should I line up a girl for him?'

'I wouldn't do that,' said Jeffrey hastily.

'What's the matter? Is he gay or something?'

Jeffrey hesitated. 'Not exactly. Not too butch either.'

'Sounds like it's going to be a real fun evening,' said Mort sourly.

'It's business,' said Jeffrey. 'Who said anything about fun?'

Mort paced the foyer of the Carlyle Hotel. He was not looking forward to the evening. Atherton sounded like a real pill.

Waiting there, he admired the parade of the New York beau monde. There were certainly some beautiful women around, no doubt about it. He always marvelled how many. That was something he had never stopped noticing, thank God, even though he had not been on the market for a long time – a very long time now. Not that he had ever lost the urge; he just did not have the time. Besides, women always wanted to get involved and before you knew where you were, they had taken over. He had seen it happen too often. One thing was for sure. He had no intention of breaking up his marriage.

The elevator doors opened and two men got out. One of them looked as though he might be Atherton. It was exactly seven o'clock. Jeffrey had said Atherton was always punctual.

Mort went up to the younger of the two men. 'Mr Atherton?'

109

The man looked suprised and shook his head.

'My name's Atherton,' he heard someone say.

He turned.

'Rosemary Atherton.' She held out her hand and smiled. There was something mischievous, even cheeky, about her expression.

Mort was dumbfounded. He took her hand automatically, staring at the girl as if she had suddenly materialized from outer space. She had blue eyes that really were the colour of cornflowers.

'I was in the bar,' she said apologetically, seeing his confusion. 'You were watching the elevator.'

He was still transfixed. That devious bastard Jeffrey. Wait till he got his hands on him.

'What would you like to do?' she asked, smiling that mischievous smile again. 'Apart from staring at me, of course.'

Mort started. 'I'm sorry. I . . . where are my manners? Uh . . . you like French cooking?'

'I like any cooking,' she said.

'How about the Basque d'Or?'

'Sounds fabulous,' she said. 'What are we waiting for?'

By the time the coffee came, Mort was enchanted. He had not felt like this since he was eighteen.

'Sorry about the sex change,' Rosemary said.

Mort put down his coffee, leaned back in his chair and laughed. When was the last time he had laughed like this? When had he ever felt so relaxed? 'You knew?'

'Jeffrey said you were so convinced I had to be a man, he didn't have the heart to disillusion you.'

'Jeffrey's a creep,' said Mort.

'I adore him,' she said.

'That sounds . . . I mean, are you and he . . . uh. . . ?'

'I adore him doesn't mean I sleep with him.'

'I'm sorry.'

'Don't be,' she said.

*

When they got back to the Carlyle they sat in the bar and listened to Bobby Short making love to the piano.

'How long are you staying in New York?'

'I'm flying to Houston tomorrow,' she said. 'Then back to London.'

He looked disappointed. 'Can I see you again?'

She studied him thoughtfully with her cornflower eyes, taking her time before replying.

'If that's what you want.'

'When?'

She picked up her room key. 'In about five minutes,' she said . . .

She was already in bed.

He turned out the light and began to undress. He had taken off his shirt and was undoing his pants when she turned the light on again. For an instant he was embarrassed, like a young boy doing it for the first time.

Rosemary put out her hand and gently pulled him down on the bed beside her. She stroked his dark hair and slid her hand down his back.

'I like the light on,' she said.

'What else do you like?' said Mort.

'I'll show you,' she said. She slid her hand between his thighs and let it rest there. His penis was erect. Impatiently, he pulled off his pants. As he thrust at his underpants, she stopped him.

'Let me do it,' she whispered.

Her hand moved lightly over his tight buttocks and down his leg, taking his underpants with it. When he was naked, she looked frankly at his body for a long time without a trace of shyness, studying his thighs, his legs, his firm muscular chest and then again, his thighs. She took his penis gently in both her hands and moved her mouth close, touching the glans with the tip of her tongue.

'This is going to take a while,' she said . . .

He sighed deeply as the semen surged in her mouth. For a few minutes he held her in his arms – this girl he had

111

not even known until this evening – and caressed her firm neat little breasts and her long slim thighs.

Soon, she was breathing hard, moaning as she rolled from side to side of the bed. The blood pumped and his penis reared up again. He lowered himself into her, thrusting into the moist flesh as she spread her legs wide. She came quickly, but he continued thrusting, now deep into her body, now tantalizing her, leaving just the tip of his swollen penis at the entrance to her vagina. She began to curse him, digging her nails into his buttocks, arching her back high off the bed.

Then, suddenly, she cried out as she reached her climax and, as she did, his whole body trembled and his penis pulsated inside her. For a few long seconds they clung to each other in the exquisite tension of the shared orgasm and its delicious shuddering release.

It was a long time before they spoke.

'Stay with me,' she said.

'I'd like to,' he said. 'I can't. I'm married.'

'I heard,' she said. She was looking at him and her eyes were no longer mischievous. They were scared.

'What's the matter?'

'It sounds so damn corny. I don't want to get serious,' she said.

That suited him just fine. Nor did he.

'I never fucked a woman with cornflower eyes before,' he said lightly.

'Then you haven't lived,' she said.

'You could be right at that,' said Mort.

He sat on the edge of the bed and thought about getting dressed.

'You know something,' he said, 'we never once discussed business the whole evening.'

'I bet that doesn't happen to you too often.'

'I can't remember it ever happening,' he said. Sometimes he even surprised himself. Still, now that she had reminded him . . . 'You think I have a chance of getting into the consortium?' he asked.

'I'd say so,' she said, one hand slipping between his legs, the other gently pulling him down to her.

'I'd like to get in there,' he said. She raised her thighs to meet him as he drove into her.

'Consider yourself in,' she gasped.

*   *   *

Rebecca was a good mother – intelligent and caring. She loved her sons – son and stepson – for what they were. Moses loved them for what he hoped and believed they could become. She had married him when his first wife, Ruth, died giving birth to Mort and she had never tried to compete with the dead – she was far too smart for that. She coped with her husband's anger and his guilt, understanding them as he did not, and understanding too that the Ruth he remembered had never existed. In his gruff, grudging, undemonstrative way, he loved Rebecca, but she had always been the butt of his resentment. He resented so much. He resented Ruth for dying. He resented Mort for killing her. He resented Rebecca for supplanting her. And, above all, he resented life. Life had withheld from him what he felt was his due: money, recognition, success. Bad fortune had stalked him. Every business venture he ever embarked on had ended in disaster. Now, at sixty-five, it was too late. He would never make it. His sons would have to make it for him.

Mort and Ruby would often join their parents on a Saturday evening to celebrate at sunset the Motzeh Shabbath, the end of another day of rest. Moses would recite the brief prayers, offer his family the sweet-smelling cinnamon and extinguish the flame of the braided candle in the cup of red wine.

He placed his hands on his sons' heads, first Mort, then Ruby, and recited in Hebrew the age-old blessing:

'Y'simchah Elohim ch'Ephraim v'chiManasseh.
May the Lord bless you like Ephraim and Manasseh.
The Lord bless you and keep you.

113

The Lord make his face to shine upon you and be
    gracious unto you.
The Lord lift up his countenance upon you and give
    you peace.'

He embraced his children awkwardly, unable to express
in any other way his love for them, and they patted him
affectionately on the back, thinking of the days when they
were small and their father had scared them.

With the blessing, the spell was broken and another
week was over, but long after he had left Mort would still
feel the touch of his father's hands on his head.

This time, they had something exciting to tell him.

'We're making the world sit up,' said Ruby.

'Making it big, Pop,' added Mort. 'Guess what the
company's worth today?'

Moses loved it. His eyes were alive, shining, reacting to
their every word . . . and yet what should he say? What
could he guess? What did it mean – to make it? Something
he had never known. And to make it 'big'? . . . What could
that mean?

'Let me see,' he began.

'Go on, Pop,' Mort urged. 'Guess!'

'A million,' he ventured. 'It's worth a million bucks.'
He was watching them closely.

Mort shook his head solemnly.

For an instant, Moses seemed disappointed. Then he
recovered. 'That's too much,' he said. 'A million's too
much. How long you been in business? A year?'

'Less than a year.'

'Uhuh.' He was thinking. 'I'd say, with your brains, and
your drive, you must be worth . . . half a million.'

Mort stared at his father calmly, holding back, enjoying
the anticipation. 'Ten million, Pop,' he declared. 'We made
ten million dollars.'

Moses was stunned. 'Ten? Did you say – ten – million
– dollars. . . ?'

'That's what I said, Pop.'

114

Moses beamed, his face ten million wrinkles . . . and every one of them glowing and twinkling at his two boys.

'Hah!' he shouted. 'Ahah! You hear that, Rebecca? You hear what my son said? . . . In less than a year. You hear, Rebecca?'

He started to jump around the room, arms held high, picking up his feet as if he were dancing the hora.

'Didn't I tell you, Pop?' said Mort. 'Didn't I say one day you'd be proud of us?'

Rebecca said quietly: 'We've always been proud of you. Whatever you do, we're proud of you.'

Moses froze in mid-step. The light died in his eyes. He turned his back on Rebecca. That was for him to say. Why did the woman always try to make him feel inadequate? He was the man of the house. He was the one to give or withhold his approval.

Julie walked straight past the entrance to Leo Stendel Fine Art on Madison and stopped in front of a boutique. She had not the least idea what was in the window she appeared to be staring at so intently. Making the decision to look for a job had not been easy. And, even when made, she had lain awake for nights, wondering if it was the right thing to do. One thing at least was clear. Right or wrong, she needed a life of her own, a life independent of Mort, something that belonged to her and only her. Slowly she walked back to the gallery. It was not going to be easy to find the right career. She was married to someone special. She could not work for just anybody.

Leo Stendel, as it happened, was not just another art dealer. He was the doyen of them all. The owner of the most prestigious gallery on the East Coast, he had made his money by dealing, but he had also accumulated, with superlative taste, some of the greatest Impressionist and Post-Impressionist paintings at a time when they were little known in America. Leo did everything extravagantly, and yet with flair and style. The walls of his apartment in

Gramercy Park were hung with probably the finest private collection of nineteenth- and twentieth-century art any-where in the world. Whenever he was divorced – and, so far, he had been married and divorced four times – he settled on his latest ex a few more Picassos, Matisses, Miros, Renoirs or Kandinskys. There were plenty more where they came from to fill the gaps on the walls. Not that he cared very much. At fifty-six years old, he had reached the point in his life where a few Cézannes more or less hardly made a difference to his well-being. In some ways, he preferred the gaps.

No one was quite sure where he had emigrated from or when. It seemed as though he had always been here on the New York scene. Some said he was of Rumanian origin, some Hungarian, but, whatever he was and wherever he came from, Julie found him fascinating, charming, lively, articulate and just plain different. He reduced the Big Apple to the dimensions of a corner bistro, a bistro, however, of which he was the indisputable, unchallenged owner.

'Mr Stendel,' she said, 'I know very little about art and less about business, but I'm willing to learn and I need a job.'

'My name's Leo,' he said. 'It's what everyone calls me. Why do you need a job? Not for the money, I imagine.'

'I need something to get up in the morning for. I need something of my own. I have no children. My husband's baby is his business.'

Leo smiled. He had a beat-up face, ugly and attractive.

'You know the painter, Miro?'

'I've seen some of his paintings.'

'You like him?'

'He's the one who does all the squiggles and funny faces, isn't he?'

Leo nodded solemnly. 'He's the one who does all the squiggles and funny faces.'

'Then I love him,' she said.

'You have to understand this is a business. What I do is peddle art. I buy and sell paintings. That's how I make my money. Most of my clients don't know the difference between a Manet and a Monet and they care even less. What they want to hear about is the art market and how good an investment they're making. I tell them to buy art for pleasure, not for investment, but they don't hear me. They pretend they love art for art's sake, but what they're really doing is hanging a commodity on the wall.'

'There must be some wealthy people who enjoy art.'

'There are,' said Leo. 'About two. And I'm one of them. OK, maybe I'm exaggerating a little, but I want you to know what it is you're getting into. The art business is tough and one thing it has very little to do with is art. If you have ideals – that's great, only do me a favour: leave them on the doorstep when you come to work in the morning and pick them up on the way home. OK?'

'I'll try to remember, but I still don't think it's as bad as you make out.'

'Let me tell you something,' Leo said. 'If I showed one of my clients a pork belly and told him it was a Soutine or a Vlaminck and in five years it was going to be worth ten times what he paid for it, he'd buy it and hang it over the fireplace.'

'Wouldn't it smell after a while?'

'Sure it would,' said Leo grinning. 'But you get used to the smell of money. After a time you don't notice it any more.'

'You won't put me off,' she said.

'So when can you start?'

'How does tomorrow sound?'

'It sounds good.'

'You sure you want me?'

Leo gave a huge shrug. 'Sure?' he said. 'This is life. Who can be sure of anything? You like Miro. You're not pretentious and you have a lopsided smile. That'll do for a start.'

'I may not know much,' she said, 'but I learn fast.'

'My dear,' he said, 'please don't do that. New York is

117

full of people who know all about everything. Ignorance is a precious commodity these days.'

Julie laughed. She had not done that too often lately.

* * *

Henry Soames gave cocktail parties for the rich, the influential, the famous and the beautiful. Into which category, exactly, Jeffrey fitted, he was never quite sure, but he was a regular invitee and, in his bumbling insensitive way, Henry would introduce him around. Jeffrey's curriculum vitae – his biographical data – varied according to Henry's mood. They were rarely the same twice running and they were never accurate, but then Henry was at home in that barren no-man's-land between truth and lies, dangerously exposed yet happily uncommitted.

'Whom would you like to meet?' he asked. The question was academic. Spontaneity was not a Soames characteristic. Clearly, he had someone in mind.

The someone he had in mind turned out to be female, thirtyish and attractive – in an eccentric kind of way.

'Lady Victoria Harcourt-Smith,' announced Henry. 'Jeffrey Lewis.' And with that, he disappeared.

Victoria was front-page *Vogue*, admittedly in one of its more bizarre issues. Her face was deathly white, her false eyelashes long and upward sweeping, and she wore a cloche hat decorated with an ostrich feather. The effect of a Marcel Marceau clown was heightened by the most luminous of crimson lipsticks. She obviously felt not the slightest need to be in fashion; she most definitely needed to be different.

She took Jeffrey by the arm and guided him to a quiet corner.

'Hmm,' she murmured, surveying him. 'Interesting.'

She might have been contemplating a tasty morsel. No doubt about it though, thought Jeffrey, she was attractive – dangerous-looking, but compelling. It must, he thought, have been some similar compulsion that persuaded the

118

praying mantis to couple with its mate, knowing that his head would be bitten off for his pains.

'How do you know Henry?' he asked, for want of something intelligent to say.

'Darling, how does anyone know Henry?' she said. 'Do you mind if I take off these bloody eyelashes?'

'Go ahead,' said Jeffrey. Presumably they were her hunting gear – which meant that the hunt, for tonight, was over.

She peeled them off. The effect was startling. She looked ten years younger.

'I loathe false eyelashes,' she said petulantly. 'My husband likes me to wear them.'

Somehow, Jeffrey doubted that.

'My husband is Sir Albert Harcourt-Smith. He's in oil,' she said distastefully, as if she wished the oil were boiling and Albert were a Kentucky Fried Chicken.

The penny dropped . . . North Sea Venture . . . Sir Albert was the chairman. Henry's instincts were primitive. He had cast Jeffrey in the role of stud. All he had to do was satisfy Victoria and she would use her influence with her husband.

This was definitely not his scene. The hell with Henry Soames, the cynical, conniving shit!

And yet? This sort of thing . . . people did it every day. But what if Caroline did. . . ? He'd kill her. Of course he knew damn well that she didn't . . . the same way she knew that he didn't either . . .

'And what do you do?' she enquired. She obviously had no idea.

'I'm a trader.'

'How interesting,' she said gloomily. 'A trader. Would that be door-to-door or mail order?' She was beginning to feel that the introduction might just be one of Henry's bad jokes. The nasty little queen.

'I'm an oil trader,' said Jeffrey. 'You know, like a commodity trader – only I deal in oil.' Jeffrey never knew quite how to describe what it was he did.

119

Victoria brightened. 'They do rather well, don't they?'

'We're all multimillionaires,' said Jeffrey. 'Except for the real schmoes and they're only millionaires.'

Victoria moistened her crimson lips with the tip of her tongue. 'I can see we're going to be friends,' she said. 'You must meet Albert. He's chairman of some – consortium I think they call it. He's always drilling somewhere.'

'Did he ever find anything?' Jeffrey tried not to sound over-interested.

'No, darling. He drills away, but he's not terribly good at it.'

'That must be very frustrating,' said Jeffrey gently.

She leaned her thighs against his and traced the outline of his mouth with her forefinger.

'You have no idea,' she said.

Her apartment was just off Eaton Square. The bedroom was miniature, mostly taken up by a king-size bed. There was also a bathroom and a cute little kitchen straight out of *House & Garden* that had obviously never been used. Clearly, Victoria had her priorities right.

'This is my own secret *pied-à-terre*. I come here to do the things I like doing.'

Jeffrey could well imagine what those were.

'Are you a good oil trader?' she asked.

'The best,' he said, unzipping her dress at the back.

'How do you go about it? I'm frightfully interested in businessmen.'

'I'm glad to hear it,' said Jeffrey, pulling off her dress. She was not wearing a bra; she clearly thought them a waste of time. 'In my line,' he said, stroking her nipples with his fingertips, 'friendly relations are very important.'

The nipples were hard under his fingers. She had perfect breasts – not too big and not too small. They stood up, cheekily, asking to be caressed.

'How do you make your . . . contacts?' she asked weakly.

His hand slid into her panties and felt for the warm, wet softness between her thighs.

120

'In different ways,' said Jeffrey. 'Mostly by personal introduction.'

He tore off his clothes and stood by the bed looking down at her.

'Personal introduction is so very important,' she whispered, eyeing his penis. It was jutting out and throbbing with the pulsating blood.

'You won't be offended if I don't touch it,' she whispered coyly. 'It's such an ... intimate thing to do. And I know Albert wouldn't like it, poor dear.'

Had she really said that? He was thinking that this could not be happening.

But it was. Victoria held out her arms and enveloped him. Jeffrey thrust in to the hilt, pinning back her legs with the crook of his arms. Her feet were reaching to the ceiling, her knees hugging his face. After a few minutes, she cried out and sighed deeply.

... 'My precious,' she said, in a rush, 'you really are awfully good at it, you know. Such an asset in a man. I just know we're going to see lots more of each other. You must come round to dinner. Henry tells me you'd like to meet my husband, though why anyone should want to do that, I really can't imagine.'

Jeffrey could not get out of her apartment fast enough. He hated Victoria, he hated Henry Soames. Above all, he hated himself.

*   *   *

On the 6th of October 1973, Egypt and Syria invaded Israel. It was Yom Kippur, the Day of Atonement, the most solemn and important day in the Jewish calendar.

The timing, of course, was brilliant. Israel was caught off guard. The famous Israeli intelligence, reputedly the best in the world, had failed; it had given little or no warning of the impending invasion. When it came, few Israeli soldiers were at their posts. The first waves of Egyptian and Syrian troops destroyed the lightly manned

121

frontier positions and their tanks drove deep into Israeli territory. It seemed as though the tiny state, established only twenty-five years ago, was about to be overrun and that the Arab threat that they would one day drive the Israelis into the sea would be fulfilled in a matter of hours.

But Israel survived. In a few days the Israelis had driven back the Syrians and trapped the Egyptian army.

'We can relax,' said Ruby. The last few days they had been more than busy raising money for Israel. For once business had taken a back seat.

'Now we have time to start worrying,' said Mort.

'I don't get it.'

'Think about the freight market,' said Mort. 'The Arabs are going to be mad as a skunk. They've taken a beating and Israel has done it with American help. If Nixon hadn't organized that airlift so fast, who knows what would have happened.'

'So?'

'I'm saying there's a danger that the Arabs will turn off the tap completely, or at least place an embargo on the United States to punish them for helping Israel.'

'Meaning a shortage of oil?'

'Meaning, maybe, a shortage of oil. It could easily trigger a panic. What's worrying me right now is the freight market.'

'You're right. Of course you are,' said Ruby. 'If the flow of oil is cut back drastically, the industry won't be needing anything like the same number of tankers. The freight market will take a dive.'

'I'm worried about our position.'

'What position?' We don't have a position. We already sold the Pipeline freight. We already made our profit.'

'Let me tell you something,' said Mort. 'You don't make your profit when you sign a contract. You make it when the last tanker has discharged and, even more important, when you get paid. Until then – anything can happen.'

For a few days after the October War, the upward spiral of the freight market was checked. The industry held its breath, trying to analyse the significance of the war and then, just as Mort had forecast, the Arabs imposed an embargo on the USA.

For a brief moment, the freight market hung poised, then, slowly at first, it started to fall. The realization came to the oil industry that the market had been wildly oversold. There were too many tankers around. There always had been. The fall gathered momentum. The market was taking a nosedive and it looked like nothing could stop it. The day before the October War rates had been around World Scale three hundred. By November, the market had dropped to World Scale one hundred.

'You think we could have trouble with our customers?' said Ruby anxiously.

'I hope not.'

'After all,' said Ruby, 'a contract is still a contract.'

Mort straightened his in-tray a compulsive fraction.

It was the last week of November when the call from the chief buyer of Orion Oil came through.

Jeffrey had been expecting it.

'I wonder if you'd mind coming down to see the chairman. He'd like to meet you.'

I'll bet he would, thought Jeffrey.

Orion Oil had paid King Brothers World Scale two hundred and fifty for Pipeline freight. At the time, it had been a hell of a good deal for them. Today, things were looking different.

The chairman made his little speech.

'I thought we had an agreement,' said Jeffrey, a touch naively, perhaps.

'Indeed, Mr Lewis,' said the chairman condescendingly. 'We're the first to recognize that. All we are asking for – in the name of good business relations – is a mutually agreed voluntary reduction.'

A mutually agreed voluntary reduction. Now that was a good phrase. It had a ring to it. Jeffrey thought he might use it himself one day.

'What would be the size of this – ah – voluntary reduction?' he enquired.

'We suggest you agree to reduce the freight rate to today's market level – say around World Scale a hundred. After all, rates are still falling.' He gave Jeffrey the impression he considered it a generous offer.

'Just so I can get your proposal clear in my mind,' said Jeffrey, 'what would be the quid pro quo? For example, would you give us a first refusal on your future business for a couple of years so we could have a chance of recouping our losses?' Jeffrey thought that was a fair and reasonable suggestion. Even Benjamin might play ball with that one.

The chairman folded his lips disapprovingly.

'I regret, Mr Lewis, that I would not be able to recommend such a course of action to my board.'

'Why not?'

'I have my reasons.'

'What reasons are they?'

'We like to play fair,' said the chairman.

'Ah . . . fair,' said Jeffrey meaningfully. 'Yes, I see.'

'We don't wish to be seen favouring one supplier to the detriment of all the others. One might call that discrimination.'

'One might call it compensation,' said Jeffrey.

'Of course,' said the chairman stiffly, 'if you're going to use legal terminology . . .' He leaned back in his chair and fixed Jeffrey with what was intended to be an intimidating glare. Jeffrey, however, was not easily intimidated. 'Mr Lewis,' said the chairman, 'in my opinion, the real compensation for King Brothers would be the preservation of good relations with Orion Oil.'

'Good relations', thought Jeffrey. Now that should really impress Benjamin. He could take them straight to the Bank Leumi in Tel Aviv and cash them.

'And if we don't agree?'

'If you do not agree to a voluntary adjustment down to a level which is in line with today's market, then, Mr

Lewis, I would have no alternative but to recommend to my board a review of your contract.'

'You mean you'd cancel it.'

'Mr Lewis, I don't care to use words like that. Let's say we would suspend it, pending an equitable solution.'

'Equitable' was good too. The man had a way with words.

'You mean pending the solution you're trying to impose on us?' said Jeffrey.

'Pending a mutually agreed solution,' said the chairman. 'Yes.'

'A mutually agreed voluntary reduction?' said Jeffrey.

'Quite so,' said the chairman, pleased that he had finally got his point across.

Ruby thought of a dozen stories he could tell Benjamin, each one less believable than the last. In the end, he decided to tell him the truth. He was that desperate.

Well, almost the truth.

Benjamin shrieked and swore and threatened. When the storm died down, he became deathly quiet and syrupy – a bad sign. Ruby had learned from experience that when Benjamin capped the volcano, the next eruption would blow the whole mountain. And so it did. All Ruby could hope to do was hang in there and dodge the lava. One thing he could not afford was to lose the Pipeline as a supplier. It had become a key factor in their business.

'How did it go?' said Jeffrey. He was worried.

Ruby was noncommittal. 'Could have been worse, could have been better. We lost our profit on the deal, but that was unavoidable.'

'Is that all?'

'Isn't it enough?'

'Don't tell me he agreed to reduce his freight rate to World Scale a hundred?'

'Sure, he did.'

'Why on earth would he do that?'

'It took a little while, I have to admit,' said Ruby modestly.

'How the hell did you get him to come down?'

'I told him Orion Oil had given us first refusal on their business for the next five years. He thought that was fair compensation.'

'Ruby, for God's sake. I already tried that. I asked for first refusal for only two years and they turned me down flat. I told you.'

'I must have forgotten,' said Ruby, who never forgot anything.

Jeffrey could have throttled him. 'You mind telling me what we're going to do when Orion put out their next tender?'

'There won't be a next tender.'

'What are you talking about?'

'Read the papers,' said Ruby.

Jeffrey leafed through the *Financial Times*. Suddenly, there it was: 'British Petroleum buys controlling interest in Orion Oil.'

Orion had been taken over by BP. His brain was buzzing. That meant no more business with the Pipeline. The takeover still had to be ratified by the Orion Oil board. By the time they had done that, the four Pipeline cargoes would have been delivered. After that, zilch for the Pipeline. BP simply did not do business with Israel. End of story.

So that was why the chairman would not give him first refusal on future business. He couldn't. He knew he was going to be taken over by BP.

Jeffrey called Ruby back.

'What's Benjamin going to say when he sees this?'

'Plenty,' said Ruby. 'But what can he do? It's *force majeure*, isn't it?' Innocently.

'That's not what I'd call it,' said Jeffrey grinning.

Some guys had it and some guys didn't. Ruby had it in trumps. They call it 'chutzpah'.

*

126

They were not so fortunate on the sale of freight to Pacific Odyssey. Joe Murphy told Mort that management insisted on a reduction of a hundred World Scale points. If they did not get it, they would cancel. Simple as that.

'How can they do it to us?' said Ruby.

'Easily,' said Mort.

'We have a contract,' said Ruby.

'You know,' said Mort, 'sometimes, even lawyers can be naive. Contracts aren't what they used to be.'

'First Orion. Now Pacific. How can we survive if even the top companies renege on agreements?'

'We'll play the game by their rules,' said Mort. 'One day the market will change, then we'll be the ones to dictate what happens. Meanwhile, we have to try and stay in business.'

'What do I do with Benjamin?'

'Tell him the truth. What else can you do?'

'I don't like it. We need him.'

'You think I don't know that?' said Mort. 'If we didn't need him, we could tell him to get lost.'

Ruby was trying to adjust, but it wasn't easy. 'No one said it was going to be like this.'

'This is a tough business,' said Mort. 'You'll learn.'

Benjamin was kind. He gave them back twenty-five points. They lost ten million dollars on the deal.

They were back where they started.

*　　*　　*

In December '73, the partners met at the Dolder. Their second annual meeting.

They had planned a celebration. That was before the Yom Kippur War.

'We're about covering overheads,' Mort announced. 'I had hoped to be doing better by this time. We were doing just great, but . . .'

'It's only a year,' said Sam. 'Our name is already well known. We're trading. That's something.'

'We're not setting the world on fire,' said Jeffrey. 'But I think we're doing OK . . . considering . . .'

Mort turned away to the window and looked down at the golf course. This morning he had hoped to play, but everything was fully booked. It must be nice to own a golf course. Some guys did. A nine-holer would do. That way, the course would never be booked. No one could shut him out. He could always get a round . . . if he ever had the time to play, that is.

'Doing OK is for the birds,' he said. 'It's for all the others. That's not what we're here for.'

'We're making a living,' said Ruby.

Mort shuddered. 'For Chrissake, I can make a living selling brushes. We wanted to set the world on its ear. We can still do it.'

'You have something in mind?' said Jeffrey.

Mort always had something in mind. The guy never stopped. The other three were watching him. That was the way he was. He did not have to say too much for people to take notice.

'We put King Brothers on the map. No one questions that. What we need to do now is make some money – some real money.'

They were all listening.

'The industry is running down stocks. The Arabs have embargoed the USA. People are getting nervous. OK, they're not falling over themselves to buy, but they're asking what's available.'

The other three nodded.

'Not much business, but a hell of a lot more enquiries than usual at this time of year,' said Sam.

Mort continued. 'If we wait until every buyer in the industry panics, it'll be too late. The crude won't be there to buy.'

'What are you suggesting?' said Ruby.

'I'm suggesting we go to a couple of producers and buy some crude – a few million tons of crude.' Mort spoke as casually as he could.

'For crying out loud,' said Jeffrey.

'You want us to go long millions of tons?' Sam sounded anxious, incredulous.

'Why do we have to take risky positions when we can make money trading spot cargoes?' said Ruby.

Mort poured himself a bourbon. 'Taking risks is the way to make real money. It's the way to make it big.'

'It's the way to lose your shirt,' said Sam.

'Not if you know what you're doing. Not if the risks are reasonable. Which one of you guys thinks the market's on a downturn?'

No one did.

'Who thinks we're in for a boom?'

Only Mort raised his hand and then, hesitantly, Ruby.

Mort faced Jeffrey and Sam. 'So you two think nothing much will change over the next two or three months?'

'Who the hell knows what will happen?' said Jeffrey. 'Why don't we trade from day to day until things are clear?'

When would things ever be clear, Mort wondered. 'OK,' he said. 'Taking into account your reservations, I propose we buy the crude and then lay it off. Right away. If you like, we can keep a few hundred thousand tons to play around with on the spot market.'

No one said anything.

'Lay it off to whom?' asked Jeffrey.

'Pacific Odyssey, for one. They'll buy. They need crude.'

'The Italians are talking of buying and it sounds like it might be a large volume,' said Sam.

'Who else?' said Ruby.

'There'll be others,' said Mort. 'You'll see.'

Jeffrey was not so sure. 'It's a gamble.'

'A gamble is when you risk all your stake,' said Mort. 'This isn't a gamble. It's a calculated risk. If we can't sell all the crude within a few weeks, then we'll certainly be able to move eighty or ninety per cent of it.' Mort's absolute assurance, his confidence in his own judgement, was compelling, hard to resist. Few people know what they

129

want. Even fewer are ready to back their judgement – to go out and do it.

'Well?' Challenging them to decide.

Ruby nodded. 'I agree.'

Jeffrey hesitated, then he, too, nodded. 'OK,' he said. 'If we lay off the crude quickly.'

Sam was undecided.

'Sam?' Mort wanted the decision to be unanimous. You could see that.

The words came into Jeffrey's head: 'Of course, all major decisions will always be unanimous.' The first Dolder meeting.

'I'm not sure,' Sam said. 'But if you guys are for it, then I'll go along with it.'

That was Sam. He went along with a lot of things.

The British Caledonian night flight from London arrived around five-thirty in the morning – not the high point of anyone's day. After the cosseted pampering of the B. Cal. First Class cabin, Lagos Airport was a shock to the system. What was needed was patience, humility and about twenty pounds in loose change. Experience saves you a lot of time and hassle in Nigeria. Fortunately, Jeffrey knew the ropes.

It can take up to six hours, sometimes longer, to run the gauntlet of the arrival lounge. This time, Jeffrey was lucky; he was out in one hour flat, and flat was just about how he felt. As he emerged from the baggage area carrying his suitcase, it was grabbed by a young boy in rags who ran whooping, chased by ten more, to look for a taxi. Jeffrey let him go. Occasionally it happened that you saw neither boy nor bag again, but on the whole these kids performed a service. They found you a cab and put your bag in it. They were the embryo middlemen, the budding entrepreneurs, the young hustlers of the big city.

Jeffrey gave the boy a pound and climbed into the cab. It was still dark as they drove off. The sides of the road were lined with clusters of Nigerians crouched around fires, cooking breakfast. As the cab passed each bloom of black faces, they looked up hopefully, willing it to stop, as if they expected someone to leap out and offer them a contract on the spot. Any contract would do. The Nigerian lives in hope and on hope. However often life kicks him in the teeth, he'll come back for more.

About a mile or two down the road, Jeffrey noticed a huge crate by the roadside. It was one of those crates that automobile manufacturers use to export cars. There were people inside, a whole bunch of them.

'What are those people doing?' he asked the driver.

'They live there,' the man said offhandedly, as if it were the most natural thing in the world.

No wonder everyone you met was on the make. From the age of four or five, every Nigerian was trading. He was trying to get out of that crate.

Between the outer corridor and James Timba's office was an anteroom. It was tiny and invariably crammed with visitors, all of them wanting to buy crude oil. Some waited hours, some days. The electric fans whirred away. There was no air-conditioning. Each time the door opened, every piece of paper on the secretary's desk was blown all over the room – letters and contracts, bulletins and projections, statistics and production figures. The visitors crawled on their hands and knees to pick up the litter. They did it partly out of boredom, partly out of politeness, partly hoping to read something secret and interesting, but mostly hoping that the grateful secretary would use her influence to speed up their appointment. That was where they made their big mistake. Gratitude was not part of her make-up, and her influence was nil. She was bored with her job, she hated James Timba, she loathed visitors and she scowled her way through every day of her life at the offices of the National Nigerian Oil Corporation.

Whenever James Timba, Marketing Manager of the NNOC, opened the door of his office, every face in the anteroom looked up, pleading for an audience like dogs begging for tidbits. The expression on their sweaty faces

131

was pathetic. Most times, he appeared only to ask his secretary for a letter or a contract. Now and again, he levelled the finger of fate at the lucky man whose time had come. The first appearance this morning was to say 'hi' to Jeffrey. They were old friends from Jeffrey's days with Shell.

'Two minutes,' James Timba whispered loudly. 'I'll be with you in two minutes.'

Three hours and five visitors later, he showed Jeffrey into his office.

'Sorry to keep you,' he said.

'Think nothing of it.'

'What can I do for you?'

'You know I'm with King Brothers, now.'

'I heard.'

'I sent you all the references you need. I'd like to sign a crude contract.'

'You and the rest of the world.'

'James, I know the situation. It's not easy, but you could do it for me if you really wanted to.'

Timba rubbed his stubbly chin and grinned. He had a great smile – the smile of a man who loved life.

'You have an agent?'

'No.'

'You know the rules,' said Timba.

In theory, the rules – such as they were – expressly forbade the use of 'agents'. The practice was different. It was a way of involving the Nigerian business community in the biggest business of all. It was also an opportunity for politicians to repay favours and for businessmen to channel money to their friends in high places. Not that anyone would admit it.

'Anyone you can suggest?' asked Jeffrey.

The request was somewhat unusual. Normally, you had to find your own channel and hope that it would prove effective, although that was easier said than done. All Nigerians claimed to have influence. Few had. Like the boy who carried your bag at the airport, they operated in

132

a thin market against heavy competition and they only got paid by results.

'I'll think about it,' said Timba. 'Where are you staying?'

'The Federal Palace.'

'I'll get back to you.'

For the next two days, Jeffrey tried to relax in the decayed splendour of the old, colonial-style hotel, drinking numerous cups of bitter coffee and fighting off the tarts in the air-conditioned bar, the lobby and the corridors. His room was OK, if you did not mind having no electricity and no running water. In these conditions, the only thing to do was open the windows, day and night, and let the mosquitoes do their worst.

The third night, there was a huge storm. Jeffrey sat on the terrace and watched the display. The lightning split the sky from end to end and the thunderclaps left his ears singing. After a few moments' calm, the wind came up and the awnings struggled and flapped on their frames. Then the rain started: a solid sheet of water that beat the earth and rebounded six inches in the air. It was a tropical storm, as wanton and irresistible as Africa itself. Jeffrey breathed easy again; he could smell the rain and the heavy scent of the tropical garden.

Harry Dosumo appeared between a flash of lightning and a thunderclap. One moment there was no one there; the next he was sitting beside Jeffrey.

He had huge, pale, almost colourless eyes and very dark brown skin. The contrast was dramatic. He introduced himself monosyllabically and then stared at Jeffrey with his big pale eyes saying nothing. He held himself upright, very still, not relaxed, but tense and watchful, like a lizard waiting to flick out its tongue and trap some incautious insect. A lizard, thought Jeffrey. That was what the man reminded him of, with his unblinking, heavy-lidded eyes and his impassive, expressionless features.

Jeffrey's glance moved from Dosumo's face to his wrist. Strapped to it was a gold Rolex set in a wide, finely woven gold bracelet. As he moved his arm a fraction, the gold flashed a warm, expensive glow and, for an instant, his brown wrist was encircled with a bracelet of light like a magic charm.

Jeffrey did most of the talking, which was not difficult.

' . . . So you see, what I need is to get King Brothers registered with NNOC.'

'No problem.'

'And then a contract for, say, fifty thousand barrels a day.'

'No problem.'

'I want at least ninety per cent Bonny Light. The rest could be Medium.'

'No problem.'

Nothing appeared to be a problem for Harry Dosumo. Jeffrey allowed himself a more probing question than he had so far thought it prudent to ask.

'You have certain – ah – contacts, I understand?'

The inflection of his voice made it clear that it was a question. Dosumo chose to take it as a statement. He fixed his huge eyes on Jeffrey and said nothing.

So that was how it was going to be. The man was giving nothing away. Why should he? He had been introduced by a good enough source – no less than the Marketing Manager of NNOC. Why compromise his contacts? All he had to do was perform. It was just that Jeffrey would have liked to be convinced that Dosumo's connections, whoever they were, had real clout.

Dosumo was human enough, at any rate, to feel that some response would be in order. He considered Jeffrey and delivered his final pronouncement.

'No problem,' he said.

For a moment, the bizarre thought occurred to Jeffrey that perhaps those were the only two English words the man knew.

Harry Dosumo stretched the tight skin of his face in a grimace. Apparently, it was intended to be a reassuring smile. His tongue darted between his lips.

Jeffrey was glad he was not a fly.

*

134

Two days after that first meeting, there was a knock on Jeffrey's bedroom door at three o'clock in the morning. It was Harry Dosumo.

'I hope I'm not disturbing you,' he said.

Anywhere else in the world, the comment would have been absurd. In Nigeria, it was normal. There were many businessmen – and Dosumo was undoubtedly one of them – whose most active time was between midnight and four or five in the morning. Doing business in Nigeria depended on whom you knew. The more influential your contact, the less likely it was that he wanted to be observed talking to an agent or con man. The important meetings were held in the small hours, in the dim light of guest houses and private homes. It was then that the deals were struck or the takings calculated and distributed.

'Not at all,' said Jeffrey sleepily. 'Come on in and sit down.'

'You have an appointment with James Timba tomorrow morning at ten. Meanwhile, we have one or two matters to discuss,' said Dosumo, moistening his lips with that reptilian tongue of his.

So, that was it. He wanted to agree the commission before tomorrow's meeting.

'I suppose it couldn't wait, could it?' Jeffrey suggested hopefully.

Harry Dosumo sat on the bed. He seemed not to have heard the comment. 'This won't take long,' he said.

At five-fifteen in the morning, they shook hands on twenty-five cents a barrel. The amount was outrageously high, but Dosumo could not be budged. As far as Jeffrey knew – and as far as he wanted to know – it was all for Dosumo. But that was not the way the system worked. Or at least, Jeffrey hoped it was not. It would be comforting to know that someone up there on Olympus had blessed the union.

On forty thousand barrels a day – that was to be the size of the contract, according to Dosumo – someone would make five million dollars in commissions. Who would pocket the 'take' in the small hours, Jeffrey wondered.

Nigeria had a lot of pockets.

James Timba was as friendly as ever. Maybe a touch formal. 'I'm glad to inform you that the General Manager has approved your application. You're registered with NNOC and you've been awarded a contract of forty thousand barrels a day – twenty thousand Bonny Light and twenty thousand Bonny Medium.'

'I thought . . .' Jeffrey hesitated. It was not the deal – not the deal Dosumo had promised to deliver.

'Yes?' asked Timba. 'What did you think?'

Jeffrey began again. 'I would have liked . . . I understood the contract would be ninety per cent Bonny Light.'

'Who gave you to understand that?' Timba enquired gravely.

Jeffrey considered the question. 'No one,' he said firmly. 'It was just something I was hoping for.'

'Why don't we see how it goes?' said Timba. 'Perhaps I could use my influence with the operations staff.'

So Harry Dosumo had screwed him. Or was it James Timba? Most likely he too wanted a piece of the action. He knew as well as Jeffrey that the Americans liked Bonny Light. It was tough to sell the Medium. Timba would 'use his influence'. His influence was considerable. And expensive.

'If you could,' said Jeffrey, 'I'd certainly appreciate it.'

'I'm sure you would,' said Timba grinning.

The contract price was nineteen dollars a barrel for the Light: the highest price ever paid for crude oil. The market had to be taking off. It just had to be.

As he opened the door of the anteroom, a dozen sweaty faces looked up hopefully. A moment later, the draught struck and they were all down on the floor scrabbling for papers. Jeffrey stepped over the bodies and made for the outer door.

On the way out, he waved goodbye to the secretary and

136

she scowled at him malevolently, like she always did. It gave him a reassuring sense of continuity.

When Edgar Proktor checked into the Inter-Continental Hotel in Tehran, the reservations manager looked at him shrewdly, shrugged, consulted his guest list, shrugged again, closed the book and disappeared into his office without a word.

Edgar was irritated. He smacked the bell angrily with the palm of his hand and, as the guy re-emerged, pulled out of his pocket the indisputable evidence of his booking and laid it on the desk: the letter from King Brothers confirming the phone booking, the reply from the hotel acknowledging the letter, the telex from King Brothers reconfirming both the booking and the arrival time and, finally, the telex from the hotel signed 'Reservations Manager' acknowledging receipt of the telex and wishing Mr Proktor 'bon voyage'.

It seemed to Edgar that he had a reasonably strong case.

'I'd like my room,' he said.

'Unfortunately, Mr Proktor, we have no reservation for you.' Another Iranian shrug, the shoulders almost touching the ears.

Edgar tapped the row of letters and telexes in front of him.

The manager read them. 'This is not a confirmation,' he said.

'This is not a confirmation?' enquired Edgar, sarcastically. 'What is it, then? The American Constitution? The Treaty of Versailles? Let me read it again ... It couldn't be my mother's recipe for pumpkin pie, could it?'

He read aloud the exchange of letters and telexes.

'Doesn't it kind of give you the impression that it's some sort of confirmation?' he asked, with heavy irony.

'Bon voyage,' said the reservation manager positively, 'is not a confirmation.'

'What is it then?' said Edgar. 'I mean, allowing for ethnic and language differences, would you not say that the words "bon voyage", following a clear acknowledgement of a reservation, indicate that you are holding a room for me? So, please, I'm tired and I'm hungry. I just got off the plane. I need a shower. Give – me – my – fucking room.'

'We don't have a fucking room for you,' the reservations manager said apologetically. 'We wished you a good trip, that's all. If you like to come to Iran, this is your business. I hope you had a good trip,' he said, remembering his manners.

Edgar bit his lip so savagely that he drew blood. There were several possibilities – a number of choices. He could grab the reservations manager by the tie and choke him to death; he could take hold of that little bitsy quiff of hair flopping over his forehead, twist it real tight and pull it out by the roots, or he could pick up the ballpoint used for signing in and stab the guy in the neck. Each option had its attractions.

The downside of all three courses of action was that none of them was likely to result in his getting a room; not, at least, in the Inter-Continental Hotel. He had heard about Iranian jails. There were better ways to spend his time.

'Could I talk to you in the bar?' he said.

'I'm too much busy right now,' said the manager. 'Perhaps tomorrow?'

'On a matter of considerable mutual interest,' said Edgar. 'Considerable,' he repeated.

The reservations manager looked at him reflectively. 'Mutual interest' was something he could perhaps relate to. 'Considerable' was impossible to resist.

'What's the story?'

'The story, sir?'

'Who did you give my room to?'

The reservations manager hesitated. 'There was another

138

gentleman . . . a gentleman with a great deal of . . . influence.' The manager patted his left breast, indicating the spot where, by happy coincidence, his heart and his wallet lay.

'How much . . . influence?'

'A hundred dollars,' said the reservations manager, smiling ingratiatingly.

'That's a lot of influence.'

'Indeed.'

'Where is Mr Influence right now?'

'In the dining room.'

'And his key?'

'In his pocket, I believe. Our guests do not like to part with their keys.'

'I can imagine,' said Edgar drily. 'OK. Here's what we're going to do. You will send someone up to Mr Influence's room and clear out his gear. You will also give me a duplicate key. I'm going to move in and bolt the door. Here's two hundred bucks for you.'

The eyes of the reservations manager grew round and greedy.

'Certainly, Mr Proktor. It will be too much pleasure.' Then he had an unpleasant thought. 'What shall I tell the other gentleman?'

'Tell him His Imperial Majesty needed the room for a friend of his.'

He had only just fallen asleep when the knocking on the door started. First it was knocking, then thumping, then kicking. Fortunately, it was a good solid door.

Edgar smiled, patted his pillow and went back to sleep.

The next morning, the reservations manager was indisposed. Apparently a maniac had stabbed him in the neck with a ballpoint pen.

Ali Nagaar was grey-haired and sickly-looking. His dark brown eyes peered anxiously at the world through outsize tortoise-shell spectacles. He was a soft-spoken, meek-looking man of about forty-five who had a habit of inspecting the ceiling while he was talking to you as if he lived in constant fear that something heavy might fall on his head.

Considering that this was Iran and that he was the Commercial Manager of the National Iranian Oil Corporation, the expectation was not entirely unreasonable. Behind him on the wall hung a portrait of His Imperial Majesty, Shah Mohammed Reza Pahlavi, attired in military uniform, surveying the room sternly, appearing to warn visitors not to take advantage of the miserable representative of the Peacock Throne who sat so timorously beneath him. No one messed with Iran. No one, goddam it, messed with the Shah. That was the message. Ali Nagaar worshipped HIM. After all, was he not the fount of all goodness, all virtue, all power, the vindication of the past and the hope for the future? Was he not, also, the guy who paid his salary?

On Nagaar's desk was a contract for fifteen thousand barrels a day of Light and the same volume of Heavy crude. The prices were, respectively, sixteen-fifty and seventeen-fifty dollars, the highest prices ever asked, let alone paid, for Persian Gulf crude. Edgar was shattered. 'Gee, I'm sorry, Ali, but I just can't pay these prices without consulting my head office. I'll have to get back to you.'

'Mr Proktor, how many visitors did you see in the waiting room?'

'Thirty, I guess. Maybe more.'

'Did you ever see so many visitors before?'

'Not that I recall. But I'll tell you something, Ali, even if the whole world is queueing up to buy your crude, your price is still screwy.'

'Tomorrow it will be still higher,' said Nagaar, 'and there will be fifty visitors in my waiting room. The market is booming.'

'What goes up must come down,' said Edgar. Not, he was thinking, one of his more original observations.

Ali Nagaar glanced up at the ceiling, apparently fearing

140

that Edgar's prophecy might come true sooner than expected.

'Mr Proktor,' he said, 'take my advice. Sign. You won't get the opportunity again. We have only a limited volume of crude to sell.'

'Can we discuss the price?' said Edgar.

At the best of times, Ali Nagaar was given only minimal authority to negotiate. Right now it was clear he had none. What he did have was a great line in reactions. His eyes, his nose, his mouth, all of them managed to look disgusted. Even his tortoise-shell spectacles, by some freak of osmosis, reflected his distaste. Words were unnecessary.

'OK,' said Edgar. 'You win.'

As he signed the contract, he looked up at the portrait of His Imperial Majesty. He could have sworn that the eyes were gleaming triumphantly.

On the flight home, the stewardess took a shine to him. Women usually did.

'Why are you looking so depressed?' she asked.

'No one likes getting screwed.'

The tip of her tongue showed for an instant between her teeth.

'Well now, honey,' she said. 'That depends on who does the screwing.'

Her name was Sandra. As a name, not the greatest turn-on, but who worries about advertising when the product is so succulent? Sandra had some very unusual tastes. Edgar was a meat and potato man himself, but Sandra liked it exotic and spicy. He found it exhilarating but exhausting.

She was insatiable. He gave it to her forwards, backwards and sideways. She presented him with every known orifice and a few he had forgotten even existed. She also screamed the place down most of the time.

'You're the biggest ever!' she kept shrieking, which was nice to hear, but exaggerated, he thought, and it played hell with his concentration. He liked a little relaxation

141

with his sex. When she wasn't screaming she was talking, mostly about her sexual exploits.

'Honey, have you ever done it in a Jumbo la-va-to-ry?' She dwelt salaciously on all four syllables of the word. 'I tell you it's the greatest turn-on, especially when they start hammering on the door. I tried it on Concorde once, but the lavatory's minuscule and the poor guy had a disc problem. They carried him out on a stretcher when the plane landed.'

There was only so much of this a man could take. It was at times like these that Edgar wondered why he could never leave it alone. It did not make for self-respect. He was not even sure he liked sex. The only woman he had ever really enjoyed it with was Kate.

When it was over, she limped across to the phone and called Mom.

They all seemed to have a mother. Edgar had some experience of mothers and, not a little, of fathers – none of them pleasant. But this was not one of your average run-of-the-mill mothers, or so it appeared from the phone conversation.

'Mom,' she said, 'this one is something special. You have to meet him. Come on over.'

Edgar leapt out of bed, grabbed Sandra's clothes and threw them at her.

'Out!' he said. 'I have a business engagement.'

Sandra pouted. 'But my mom wants to meet you. I'm telling you, she's a real classy lady and, boy, can she fuck!'

Fuad was a prince of the Royal House of Saudi Arabia – he and about seven thousand others. He had a round, olive-complexioned, untroubled face into which he stuffed, at frequent intervals, the good things of life.

The menu of the dining room of the Hotel de Paris in Monte Carlo featured a great many of them and Fuad had eaten his way through most of it without once pausing for breath, let alone speech.

142

Mort ate like he always ate: lightly. Fuad ate with rapacious greed and fierce concentration.

When the third plate of petits fours had been washed down by the final cup of espresso, Fuad took his napkin, wiped his shiny red lips, his pencil-thin moustache, his little pointed beard, his forehead and the back of his neck. Lifting his hands in a gesture of appreciation far more eloquent than words, he raised his black eyes and looked at Mort for the first time since they had sat down to lunch.

He was ready for business.

'You understand, Mr King, that few Arabs are willing to do business with a Jew.'

Mort inclined his head, showing neither surprise nor resentment.

'There is, of course, nothing personal in this. It is a political matter, a question of principle.'

Mort knew all about Fuad's principles.

'It is just that the intransigence of Israel and her fascist friends in the Zionist world conspiracy make it difficult for a man in my exposed position to have any business relationship with a Jewish company. Not that I personally have anything against Jews.'

'Quite so,' said Mort. 'Some of your best friends . . .'

'You have Jewish colleagues?' said Fuad.

'Yes. I have Catholic and Protestant colleagues, too. I also have Muslim colleagues. You see, we are not anti-Semites,' said Mort gravely.

Fuad permitted himself a half smile acknowledging the jest.

'It is simply,' he said, eyeing a passing nubile French girl, her neat bottom snug in a skin-tight mini-jupe, 'a question of priorities.'

'I think I understand your priorities very well,' said Mort. 'After all, we have known each other a long time.'

'Does your company trade with Israel?'

'Never,' said Mort, looking Fuad straight in the eye as he lied.

143

'Do you support the Arab embargo of Israel and South Africa?'

'Absolutely,' said Mort. Sure he did. Why not? Without embargoes, how would traders make a living? Mort wondered what the next question would be.

Fuad's expressive eyes were darting around. He scratched his little beard. 'Do you think,' he said, 'do you think you could get me one of those?' He nodded in the direction of a second French *derrière* quivering by in a mini.

'Dozens,' said Mort.

Fuad sighed resignedly. Was not the whole of life a compromise?

Principles were principles. And ass was ass.

Fuad went through a lot of girls. How exactly he managed, Mort was not sure. He must have been, as they say, a man of parts. Mort sent round six a day to his apartment. Some were turned away at the door; some were tried and found wanting and a favoured few made the trip every day for a week. Satisfaction all round.

By the end of the week, Mort was getting nervous. He was not a man who enjoyed hanging about, but Fuad had his own timetable and his own needs. More important, he also had his own personal princely allocation of Saudi crude. The government took care of him and if the Saudi government took care of Fuad, then Mort was ready to do the same.

Approximately nine days, thirty-eight girls and five gargantuan meals later, Mort signed a year's contract with Fuad to buy fifty thousand barrels a day of Arab Light at fifteen dollars a barrel. The price was the official price and both of them expected the sales price to be far higher. The profit was to be shared – sixty per cent to Fuad, forty per cent to King Brothers.

It promised to be a profitable deal for both of them.

When they said goodbye, Fuad embraced Mort and kissed him on both cheeks. It was a singular honour. 'I think we can work together,' he said. 'We both know what we want.' One of his eyelids quivered. It could have been a wink, or maybe, thought Mort, he was just plain exhausted.

On his way back to New York, he had an hour or two to kill at Heathrow. He thought of phoning Rosemary, but he changed his mind. Instead, he had a large bourbon in the First Class Lounge, and then another one. The New York flight was called. He picked up his bag and headed for gate twenty-four.

On the way, he decided to call Rosemary. What the hell.

'Mort, this is fantastic. You're here. When did you get in?'

'I just arrived,' he said.

'Why didn't you let me know you were coming? When am I going to see you? How long are you staying?'

'Hold it. Hold it. Slow down.'

'OK, I'll slow down. Just tell me when I'm going to see you.'

'Honey, I'm sorry. I've been away from New York a few days. I'm on my way back home from Monaco. My flight leaves in a few minutes. I just wanted to say hi.'

'That was thoughtful of you.' Her voice was drained of expression. Clearly, she was disappointed.

'It really would be great to stop over and see you, but things are piling up in the office. You know how it is.'

'Do I? Yes, I suppose I do. I should be grateful a one-night stand even merits a phone call.'

'It wasn't like that. You know it wasn't.' It was a mistake to have phoned, only he had wanted to hear her voice.

'I'm sorry,' she said, 'I'm being silly. Forget I said that. It was good of you to call and I'd love to see you next time you're in town.'

She had set him free. So that was OK. There was no guilt attached. He picked up his bag and headed for gate twenty-four.

*

When Rosemary arrived back at her flat in Kensington, he was waiting for her outside the front door. He watched her park the car and walk towards him. She was not expecting him to be there, which made two of them. What was it about the way she moved? There was a lilt to it, as if she were doing it to music, an unselfconscious grace and a nonchalance that was somehow typical of her whole attitude to life.

She raised her head and, as she saw him, she cried out: 'Oh, my God!' And with that, she ran into his arms.

The moment they were in the flat, they tore off their clothes, leaving a trail that led directly to the bedroom.

Later, she opened her eyes and looked at him as if surprised to see that he was still there.

'What about you?' she asked.

'I was trying so hard to please you, it never happened. It was great, though,' he said.

'Oh, baby,' she whispered.

She worked her way down his body, unhurriedly, with little kisses and caresses . . . his chest . . . his stomach and thighs . . .

They slept in each other's arms. When they woke, it was dark. She cooked him spaghetti bolognese and they drank two bottles of Beaujolais Nouveau.

He was less outgoing than he had been that first night in New York, a little tense and withdrawn. She sensed that their relationship was moving too fast for him and wondered if she would ever see him again.

'What is it?'

But he only shook his head. 'It's nothing,' he said. 'It's just me.'

Rosemary smiled a little sadly.

'Before I built a wall I'd ask to know
What I was walling in, or walling out . . .

'Robert Frost,' she said. 'One of your poets.'

'I'm not building any wall.'

146

'You don't even know it's there,' said Rosemary. 'Look, I don't want to own you. You're married and you live in New York. I live in London and I have my own life. Believe me, it's a good one. I like it. I wouldn't give it up for anything. Or anyone.'

'I know that,' he said.

'Let's just enjoy this while it lasts,' she said.

He nodded. The shadow had passed. He grinned at her. The grave cat eyes lit up for a second or two.

'You should smile more often,' she said.

'So I've been told.'

'You still interested to get into the consortium?'

'What brought that on?'

'Are you?'

'Maybe.'

'I'm working on it.'

Mort stood there, holding his dark blue raincoat. 'Look, I never . . .'

She put a finger to his lips. 'I know,' she said. 'Anyway, you thought I was a guy.'

'Some guy you turned out to be.'

He walked down the Old Brompton Road at four in the morning until a stray taxi came along. He had not wanted to stay the night and she had understood.

*   *   *

They were set for the kill, ready to ride the wave when it came.

'So what have we got?' said Ruby.

'Here's how we stand,' Mort said. 'We bought forty thousand barrels a day Nigerian, thirty thousand Iranian and fifty Arab Light. That's a total of a hundred and twenty thousand barrels a day, or about six million tons of crude.'

'At the highest prices ever paid,' said Ruby nervously.

Mort grinned. 'Relax. Now, all we have to do is sell. There are plenty of customers around. Sure, the prices are high, but we'll make good profits. You'll see.'

147

Ruby hoped his brother was right. He was not accustomed to playing around with these kind of figures. This was a lot different from any game he had ever known. It was the oil game, the biggest game of all, played for the highest stakes in the world.

'Let's get moving,' he urged.

'What's the hurry?' said Mort. 'Let's wait for the panic to spread a little. It's already started. Look at the statistics; they show that crude and product stocks are at an all-time low. Now that the Arabs have embargoed the US for supporting Israel in the October War, I'm beginning to hear more and more anxious noises in the industry. Everyone's asking what OPEC's going to do next. This is the first time they really flexed their political muscles. Maybe they only just realized they had any. Well, they have. That's for sure.'

'You think the Arabs would turn off the tap completely?'

'I guess they're too scared, or too smart to do that. A world embargo could lead to military intervention by the West and that would be a disaster for everyone. Besides, they need the money. They'll keep the oil industry guessing. It's good for business and it'll make the world sit up and take notice.'

'They could overplay their hand,' said Ruby shrewdly.

'One day, they probably will. Meanwhile, the West depends on them for oil. It's the world's key strategic product, the one commodity no one can survive without.'

'With all that crude in our position, let's hope you're right,' said Ruby.

What Mort was counting on was a panic based on the illusion of a shortage. It was not that there had been any dramatic increase in demand. Far from it. It was the sudden awareness of what could happen if there really were a shortage that would bring the panic to the boil. OPEC had become a force to be reckoned with. The puppet master was making the world dance.

Pacific Odyssey were desperate for crude. At the best

of times, they were crude short and these were not the best of times. The squeeze was on. It was a seller's market and the pressure on Joe Murphy was unrelenting – from management, from his refinery managers and from every executive in the company who considered himself in any way involved in maintaining an adequate supply.

The peak of the pressure came when Joe received a call from the president himself.

'Joe, I hear you're doing a fine job. I'm counting on you to maintain the supply of crude. We need to keep the pipelines full. As you very well know, this company is one of the biggest refiners in North America and there's a lot of money in refining these days. We sure as hell need crude and we need it at the right price, Joe.'

'Yes, sir.'

'Remember, there's no panic. If we panic we're in trouble. Don't panic, whatever you do.'

'No, sir.'

'And don't relax, either.'

'No, sir.'

'Just be sure we don't run short of crude.'

'Right on, sir.'

'Whatever you do, Joe, don't overpay. We can never afford to overpay.'

'No, sir.'

'I hope you found our little chat helpful.'

'I can't tell you how helpful, sir.'

'Keep up the good work, Joe.'

'Thank you, sir.'

The guy made over a million bucks a year. Joe made fifty thousand. Something was wrong somewhere. It seemed like in this business you were paid according to the size of your genitals: the bigger the prick, the bigger the salary.

An hour later, even his sense of humour failed him. Joe was red in the face, shouting down the phone at Mort.

'You must be out of your goddam mind. You expect me

149

to pay twenty-two dollars a barrel for crude? Why, that's ten dollars more than I was paying a month ago.'

'I'm paying twenty-one fifty for the crude myself, Joe. I can't sell it any cheaper than twenty-two.'

'I heard you paid nineteen dollars in Nigeria.' Joe was nobody's fool and he was invariably very well informed.

Mort hesitated. He could not afford to be caught out in a lie. Joe trusted him.

'Absolutely right. But you heard about agents' commissions?'

'I never heard of anyone paying two bucks fifty a barrel. How many agents you got in that place, Mort? You employing the goddam Nigerian army?'

'Look, Joe, we got extra crude allocations. For that, we had to pay over the odds.'

'So, go find somebody else to pay your fancy prices. I just had the president of the company on the phone telling me not to overpay. No deal, Mort.'

'You need the crude, Joe. It's hard to come by these days.'

Joe did not appreciate other guys trying to run his business for him.

'You're a pain in the ass, Mort. Don't tell me what I need and what I don't need. I'm Pacific's chief buyer, not you.'

Mort was beginning to realize that he would never do a deal on the phone. Not at these prices.

'Let me come and see you. We'll talk.'

'You do what you like,' said Joe huffily. 'It's your time.'

The next day, Mort was in Bakersfield. Joe was edgy, showing the strain of being pressurized from both sides: his management and Mort. Since his last phone conversation with Mort, he had spoken to every possible seller in the market. One thing was clear; there was very little crude around. Mort was right. Joe could buy cheaper, a lot

150

cheaper, but not the volumes he needed. What was it that sleazebag had said? 'Don't panic.' What a jerk. Joe's instinct was to hold out until the market fell, but that would be a risk. It would mean running down refinery stocks to danger level; they were already too low. He could just imagine the calls he would get from his refinery managers all over the USA. For a while he could take the heat, but what would happen if he misjudged the market and it kept moving right on up? Whose head would be on the block? Joe Murphy's. No one else's.

They argued and quarrelled for two hours or more, Joe always on the verge of losing his temper, Mort endlessly patient, probing, pushing Joe into a corner, never tiring, never weakening, never giving up.

At the end of it, Joe was exhausted. He was about ready to throw Mort out of his office.

'It's no good, you sonofabitch. I can't do it. The price is over the moon. The president would crucify me.'

'I guess it's no deal, then,' said Mort.

Joe would never understand Mort. The guy didn't negotiate like normal people. After two hours, he had not even offered a one cent reduction.

'I'll pay you twenty-one dollars.'

Mort made a face. 'The price is twenty-two dollars,' was all he said. He walked across the room and stood at the window for a moment, looking down over the polluted haze of Bakersfield. He had lied about his cost. Twenty-one dollars was a hell of a good price. As Joe had said, the crude cost them nineteen dollars, plus, say, fifty cents a barrel commission. Joe's offer would leave King Brothers a dollar fifty a barrel. On forty thousand barrels a day, that was about twenty-three million dollars' profit. But for Mort, it was not enough. Nothing was ever enough – not if you could get more.

'You're making a mistake, Joe.'

'So? I made mistakes before. I'll make them again.'

'In a few months, your management will bless you for your foresight.'

151

'I don't get paid for foresight. It's hindsight that counts here.'

'That's tough.'

'It's a tough life,' said Joe. He glanced at the photograph on his desk.

'How's Mary?' said Mort, following his glance.

'She's been sick.'

'I'm sorry.'

Joe picked up the photograph. 'Those heart surgeons know their business.'

'You never told me,' said Mort. 'An operation?'

'Open heart surgery. She's doing fine though. But she needs a break. I thought of taking her to Hawaii, but . . .'

But he could not afford to. Mort could have finished the sentence for him.

'If you would only let me, I could . . .'

'You could what?' said Joe quietly. 'Bribe me?'

'I didn't say that, Joe. I have too much respect for you.'

'I don't take bribes. I never have. I never will.'

'You think I don't know that? Helping a friend isn't bribery. I could help you.' Mort looked concerned.

'You could pay for the vacation. Is that what you mean?'

'A loan. That's all it would be.'

Joe's face flushed with anger and resentment. He was a man who lost his temper quickly.

'Go screw yourself, Mort! You have a way of putting things that makes them sound so innocent, don't you? You talk quiet, but by God, do you use a big stick. You think you can buy the whole goddam world? Well, you can't buy me.'

'I know it,' said Mort patiently. 'I'm not trying to.' He hoped he had not pushed too hard, too fast.

Joe paced his office for a few moments until he calmed down. 'I'm sorry. I shouldn't have said those things. There's a lot of pressure right now.'

'I understand,' said Mort. He always seemed to understand. 'Listen, Joe, I have an idea. The fund is booming.

We're re-investing all the time. Why not take an advance against anticipated profits? It really wouldn't be a problem to let you have, say, fifty – if you could use the money, of course.'

'Fifty thousand bucks?'

'Sure. Why not? If you invested, it would be your money. Not ours.'

Joe was finding the idea a bit tough to take in.

'All the fund needs is a ten per cent margin, like I told you. Send me a cheque for ten thousand – whenever you have the money – no sweat. The fund will credit you with ten times that. You can draw any amount, any time . . . like I said, fifty thousand – more if you want.'

'Ten times.'

'Sure.'

'For an investment of ten thousand dollars, I get an immediate return of a hundred thousand?'

'That's what I said.'

'It's incredible! You guys must be wizards.'

'We know our business,' said Mort smoothly. 'Well? How about it?'

Joe was thinking about his wife and that vacation. 'It's generous of you. Real generous.'

'Think nothing of it. It's the way the fund operates.'

For a long moment Joe played with the steel paperknife on his desk.

'I can't,' he said. 'I can't take it.'

'Why not?'

'I can't explain. God knows, I could use the money. I just can't take it, that's all.'

Mort tried to hide his disappointment. It was the end . . . no sale. He was in trouble. No one else would buy that quantity of crude.

'About the Nigerian . . .' said Joe.

Mort was wondering how he could climb down on the price without losing all his credibility.

'You swear to me you paid twenty-one fifty? You swear it, Mort?'

Mort looked him straight in the eye. Who could check? How could Joe ever find out?

'I swear,' he said. 'You have my word. Trust me.'

Joe nodded. 'I'll recommend the purchase at twenty-two,' he said. 'I'll talk to the president. It'll be my job on the line ... but just as long as I have your word, that's good enough for me.'

The next day, there was a long telex from Pacific Odyssey on Mort's desk.

He buzzed Ruby on the intercom and he came rushing into the office.

'You made how much?'

Mort had a problem sounding casual. Even Mort. 'Two dollars, fifty cents a barrel.'

Ruby's eyes were round. He took out his pocket calculator.

'Don't trouble yourself,' said Mort. 'The profit is forty million dollars.'

'My God!' Ruby collapsed into a chair. 'How the hell do you do it?' he asked, a touch of envy in his voice.

'Let's not count our chickens,' said Mort cautiously. 'You know the old saying.'

'What the hell!' said Ruby ecstatically. 'Let's count them. Let's start a chicken farm.'

Sam called the next day. Suppressing his excitement. Or trying to.

'What did you sell?' Mort was never one to waste time.

'The Iranian.'

'What volume?'

'The lot. The Italians bought the lot. Thirty thousand barrels. The Light and the Heavy. I could have sold sixty. Their tongues were hanging out.'

'The price?'

'Man, you should see the women here. When they look at you, it's a mortal sin.'

'Sam,' said Mort patiently. 'The price?'

154

'Eighteen dollars for the Heavy. Nineteen for the Light.'

Mort whistled. A margin of a dollar fifty a barrel. He buzzed Ruby.

'Chickens!' he said.

'Eh?'

'More chickens for you to count.'

'How many?' said Ruby eagerly.

Mort told him.

'That's sixteen million bucks.'

'I know,' said Mort. He sounded pleased but not really surprised – as if he always knew it would happen.

Ruby put down the phone, reached into the right-hand drawer of his desk and pulled out a bag of chocolate eclairs.

Mort, too, was in the mood to celebrate, but, when he looked at his watch and saw it was only five p.m., he hesitated. A man who needed to organize his day strictly, his obsessions stood guard between him and chaos, keeping him this side of anarchy.

Just the same, there were times when rules were meant to be broken. Today was one of them. He poured himself a bourbon, carried it to the window and looked down at Lexington. If they only knew, those guys down there . . . if they only knew.

Martin Field was the chief buyer of Atlantic and Orient – number seven or eight in the United States – a company with enormous business and political influence. A. and O. was big and tough and Martin Field had the manner and the ego to match it.

It was not easy for a man of his importance to demean himself by personally receiving this flabby flake who looked like he had just escaped from a spin dryer. In God's name, what was the oil industry coming to? This was not at all the kind of man Martin Field was accustomed to dealing with, not the calibre of executive he should be compelled to meet just because the jerk claimed to have crude to sell. As far as Martin Field was concerned, there was a certain natural order of things and Reuben King did

155

not belong in the same solar system as he did, let alone in the same room.

He began the way he intended to continue.

'Personally, I never heard of your company before, Mr King. There's a whole lot of mushroom companies springing up in the oil industry these days, thriving on the miserable conditions we find ourselves in, but, just as soon as things get back to normal, you and I are going to see a high mortality rate in mushrooms.' He fixed Ruby with a hostile glare, making it clear where he thought the mushroom blight would start.

Ruby was unperturbed. He had done his homework. He knew exactly how much crude A. and O. consumed a year. He knew what their refining capacity was, where their oil fields were and how much they produced. Finally, and most important, he knew where they bought their crude, what they paid for it and how much they still needed to buy. Martin Field deluded himself. He was entirely convinced that this crumpled little fat guy sitting opposite him would have a problem finding his way back to the elevator. But then he was not the first one – and, no doubt, would not be the last – to underestimate Ruby.

'Meanwhile,' he continued grimly, 'I understand you claim to have some crude to sell.'

'Claim' was snide, thought Ruby. 'Claim' really put him in his place. Without actually saying so, the man was telling him he thought he was either a liar or a flake or, more than likely, both.

Ruby smiled benignly. 'We have some Saudi crude,' he said. 'Arab Light.'

'Where does it come from?'

Now, one thing a trader never does is to name names, reveal his sources. Why should he? That kind of information could lose him a valuable supplier if his customer went direct and cut him out of the deal. It was none of Field's business and he knew it.

'It comes from Saudi Arabia,' Ruby said and grinned cheekily.

People did not mock Martin Field. Apparently, this cocky little shitbag had not got the message.

'Mr King,' he said acidly, 'I know Arab Light comes from Saudi Arabia. Every idiot knows that. I'm asking you to reveal the name of your supplier so I can assess the seriousness, or otherwise, of your source. I don't buy from anyone unless I know who my supplier is.'

Ruby nodded his head vigorously, indicating that he understood exactly what it was Martin Field was asking for. 'No problem,' he said. 'Your supplier is King Brothers.'

Either the guy was an insolent bastard, or he was obtuse. Martin Field inclined to the latter view. He considered himself to be a good judge of men; this one was plain dumb.

He could see that he was not going to get too much out of the idiot, but he had already made the decision to do a deal if the price was right. What could he lose? The worst that could happen was that the jerk would not perform; that would be inconvenient, but not disastrous. In times of shortage, as he knew from experience, it was always wise to buy more than you needed. The odds were that you never got everything you bought, especially when backstreet traders and middlemen were involved. And if, against expectations, all his suppliers performed, well, Martin Field had a trick or two up his sleeve. It was his boast that at the end of the year, his crude oil inventory was always exactly what it should be – not too big, not too small. Atlantic and Orient had more than enough muscle to rewrite contracts when it suited them. If they decided they needed to renegotiate, then the suppliers had better jump, or they would never do business with them again. True, years ago, a small trading company had been foolish enough to sue them for breach of contract, but after five years of litigation they were now in Chapter Eleven – bankrupt. The lawyers were richer and A. and O.'s inventory was still exactly the right size: not too big, not too small.

'What volume of Arab Light do you need to sell?' asked Martin Field.

'Need' was another jibe. Still, Ruby was not about to get irritated for no reason. He was here to do business.

'I'd be glad to sell you fifty thousand barrels a day for a year,' he said.

Even Martin Field looked impressed. That was a lot of crude. Of course, he would never see it, but even if he got half of it . . .

'Your price?'

'Nineteen dollars a barrel.'

'That's a hell of a price.'

'It's the market,' said Ruby simply.

He was right and Field knew it.

'Send me a telex. I'll confirm the deal,' he said imperiously.

Ruby held out his hand. Martin Field did not take it. He looked at it as if it were a toad.

'I'll see you to the elevator,' he said abruptly.

'I can find my own way out,' said Ruby.

Which was something Martin Field very much doubted.

It was a bonanza.

'It's the greatest deal,' said Mort. 'It's out of this world.'

They were paying Fuad fifteen dollars a barrel. The profit was four dollars a barrel. Since King Brothers' share was forty per cent, they stood to make a dollar sixty a barrel on nineteen million barrels. That made thirty million dollars.

'The only problem,' said Ruby, 'is Martin Field. I don't trust the bastard. He has a lousy reputation in the industry for breaking contracts.'

'Why worry?' said Mort. 'The market's booming.'

There was no denying that. 'We're doing OK, eh, Mort?' said Ruby.

'Didn't I say we would?'

'You said it, but this is something else.'

'It beats working for E.M.'

158

Ruby nodded thoughtfully. 'Less than a year,' he said. 'I wonder where we'll be five years from now.'

'At the top,' said Mort. 'Where else?'

*   *   *

Edgar always said the only woman a man could really love was his ex-wife.

'Why did we ever get divorced?' he asked Kate.

'Why did we ever get married?'

'Touché.' He grinned ruefully. 'Why you ever had me, I'll never know.'

'Anyone can have you,' said Kate. 'It's being married to you that's the problem.'

That goddam sharp tongue of hers.

'I never wanted to come back to New York,' he said.

'Why did you?'

'To be near you.'

She looked incredulous. 'Liar. You came back because Mort asked you to.'

'Hell, Kate, how can a man still be in love with his ex? It's freaky.'

'You still a great screw?'

'Try me.'

'Still drinking?'

'Am I still breathing? Am I still living? Do I still love you? Sure, I'm still drinking. What's wrong with that?'

'You're like Peter Pan,' she said, fondly, sadly.

Edgar rushed round the room flapping his arms, Then – throwing the window wide open – 'Watch me fly,' he shouted, leaning way out.

She rushed over and grabbed him. 'You're crazy.' For a moment she was terrified he was going to jump.

'I can fly!' he shouted. 'Watch me.'

'Are you nuts? You want to kill yourself?'

He was still hanging out. 'Naw. I haven't got the guts.'

'Shut the window, Edgar,' she said, still holding him. 'You scare me.'

He shut it. 'Sometimes I scare myself,' he said quietly.

159

'I don't see you for months, years. Then, suddenly, you show up. You never change, you know that, Edgar? Never. I do, though. I'm getting older.' She said it with resignation, but a touch forlornly.

'How can you say that? You've never looked better.'

'It's not just age. Me, I learned a few things along the road. You never did. You're Peter Pan, the boy who never grew up. You never will, either. The funny thing is, you don't even notice that I've changed.'

'For Chrissake, Kate, what's eating you? You should be happy to see me.'

'There's no place for you here.'

'Are you serious?'

'Sure, I'm serious. I've built a life without you. I'd rather you didn't come round.'

'The season of goodwill,' he said wryly. 'I love you.' He kissed her.

She kissed him back. 'I love you too.'

'Don't say things like that,' said Edgar. 'It plays hell with my blood pressure.'

'Go home,' she said.

He finished his martini. 'Home? . . . Where's that?'

'Don't, Edgar,' she said reproachfully.

'Sorry.'

'I'm sorry, too,' she said. 'For everything.'

'If I gave up drinking, would you marry me again?'

'You never would. What's the point of asking?'

'You think I couldn't?'

'I didn't say you couldn't. I said you wouldn't. I don't think you want to.'

'If I did?'

'If you could fly . . .' she said.

'I can,' he said. 'Watch me, Kate. Just you watch me.'

He went back to the apartment and drank a bottle of gin. Then he called Sandra. She was out.

But her mother was in. 'I've been expecting your call,' she said huskily.

'Is this Wendy?'

'Wendy? Who's Wendy? My name's Gloria.'

'Gloria in Excelsis?'

'No,' she said. 'Gloria Weintraub – Sandra's mother.'

'Sorry,' he said, 'I was trying to reach Wendy.'

'What's so special about Wendy?'

'I was teaching her to fly,' he said.

The walls of Gloria's apartment were stippled cream, the mirrors pink, the carpet shag white and every armchair stuffed with cuddly toys.

'I can't believe you're Sandra's mother,' Edgar said, just to be friendly. As far as he was concerned, she could have been Whistler's mother. She looked old enough.

Gloria simpered. 'That's what all my men friends say. Of course, I had Sandra when I was seventeen and she's only twenty now . . .'

Sandra was thirty if she was a day. Gloria looked about fifty-five in a good light. The pink mirrors helped. Not that Edgar was too sensitive about age. Young or old, it was much the same to him; they all had the same basic equipment.

'You like to talk?' Gloria asked. 'I like to talk. I mean, screwing is great, but I'm an intellectual girl. I like a man who talks.'

She slipped off her pink angora sweater and unhooked her bra. The enormous blue-veined breasts hung down to her waist. She was looking at Edgar as if she expected him to make some contribution. 'What do you think?'

Her nipples were the size and colour of horse chestnuts.

'Never seen anything like them,' he said bravely, but ambiguously.

She wriggled her monstrous thighs out of the tight skirt and stood there, coyly, in her panties. She was oddly appealing, in a grotesque sort of way.

'I like a man who knows how to talk to a girl,' she said.

'I was in my college debating team,' said Edgar.

He had his clothes off in record time. His penis was jumping; it was not too fussy. Thank God. It seemed to lead a life of its own.

161

'You think I'm intelligent?' Gloria asked.

'Do I ever,' he said, clearing his throat.

Gloria knelt at his feet. Edgar winced as she dug her nails into his buttocks. 'Because I think that's real important,' she said. She began to joggle his alter ego with the tip of her tongue. 'I always say there's more to a relationship than sex,' she said.

'How right you are,' said Edgar, weakly.

'Sandra's good, isn't she?' Gloria murmured, suspending operations for a moment.

'She's OK,' said Edgar. 'For a kid. I like mature women myself.'

Gloria really appreciated that.

When she was through, Edgar lay back, gave a deep sigh of pleasure and thought wistfully about sleep. His eyes started to close, but Gloria was having none of that.

'Now, it's my turn,' she said.

... Sometimes, just sometimes, Edgar wondered whether it was all worth it. He could see himself in the pink mirror spanning the wall beside the bed and he certainly did not, objectively speaking, look like a guy who controlled his own destiny. His face had that half-puzzled, half-bewildered expression of a man who's been lured into a trap and doesn't know how to get out of it. Trap was the word for it. Gloria's fat thighs had his neck in a scissors grip.

All good things come to an end – even Gloria's orgasms, which were numerous, interminable and deafening.

'You're the greatest!' she screamed, over and over again. 'Oh God, you are so great! Where did you learn to make love like that?'

Before he could answer, she was asleep, sprawled on the bed surrounded by her soft toys, the limp folds of her plump white body reflected in the pink mirror. There was something sad about her, sad and pathetic. She was curled up in the foetal position, her knees touching her breasts. The pendulous flesh round her chin lay on her collarbone, her mascara was streaked, her lipstick smeared. He pitied her and he pitied himself.

162

What was the matter with him, for Chrissake? What was he doing with his life? He needed a drink. As he stood up, he felt a twinge of pain in his neck and winced. Jesus, what a grip she had. Never again.

How many times had he said that before? He closed the door quietly behind him, not wanting to wake Gloria. She was lying on her back now, her mouth gaping, snoring like a rhinoceros.

Sam thought about Jane all the time. One thing he had discovered – and it had been a revelation – was that it was actually possible to enjoy making love to someone. He could never have admitted it to himself before, but, over the years, bed with Amy had been a yawn. Now that he had found someone to compare her with – he had never played around before – he realized that Amy was simply not interested in sex. In fact, she seemed to find it vaguely distasteful. She rarely had an orgasm and, when she did, he suspected her of faking it.

He tormented himself wondering if it had been different with Siegfried Gerber, but what was the use? That was past. She would never discuss it. The subject was taboo.

Ten days before Christmas, he came home to find the place empty . . . an austere note on the mantelpiece explaining everything. And nothing. Amy needed a break. She had taken the kids and flown to the States to stay with her parents in Connecticut. She must have planned it carefully, booking the flights, packing after he had left for the office. How come the kids had said nothing? She must have sprung it on them that very morning.

He waited a couple of hours and called Connecticut. The kids were excited. It had been a great surprise. When was he coming over?

But Amy made it clear that she was not expecting him. He pleaded with her, but she was adamant. He tried losing his temper, shouting at her, but it was no use; that was something he had never been too good at. Anyway, she sounded low and depressed, reluctant to fight.

Something was wrong, but then something was always wrong with Amy.

He made up his mind to spend Christmas alone, catch up on his reading, watch TV. He would contact a few friends. Someone would surely invite him round. It would not be so bad.

He began to read *War and Peace*. He started it once a year. This time he would finish it.

After a day or two, he began to feel lonely. He picked up the phone and called Jane. 'I guess your Christmas plans are all set?'

'They are,' she said, 'and they include you.'

She was so open and spontaneous, so generous-spirited. She could not have been more different from Amy. And she liked him. Right now, it would feel good to be around someone who liked him.

He packed in record time – just a few necessities. As an afterthought, he tossed in *War and Peace*. Then he thought some more and tossed it out again. When would he ever get round to finishing it?

So, there was Jeffrey at Christmas and Chanukah in the bosom of his family . . . a Buddhist wife, an agnostic father, two confused kids and a dog of uncertain sex, let alone breed. In the corner of the room was a huge Christmas tree and, on the table, a Chanukah menorah. There were candles everywhere, reflections in gold and silver balls, a twinkle in the menorah, the spirit of Christmas, the spirit of Chanukah: tiny lights in a dark universe. Small comforts. Might as well enjoy everything while it lasted. It was all a gleam in a kid's eye. It was all, in the end, the same and, such as it was, Jeffrey loved it.

Soon, they would be moving to Kensington, to a street where chestnut trees grew and the walls of the five-storey house were monastically thick. And yes, they would have a nanny and a new car. Not a Rolls – when would he ever want one of those? – but a British racing-green Jaguar Saloon.

Things were looking good, Jeffrey reflected contentedly,

and they were going to get better. He watched Caroline laying the presents at the bottom of the tree: ties from the kids, a book from his father – probably Dickens. He had given him *The Pickwick Papers* five times. Caroline's present was different every year, unpredictable, like her.

He wondered what the New Year would bring. Whatever it might be, someone had knocked on the door and let him out. And for that he would always be grateful.

What the hell was Edgar going to do over Christmas?

What about Arlene? Arlene was his secretary. He had had Arlene over a couple of years. Regularly. At home and in the office. Never over Christmas though. Why not? It would be a first. He could gift-wrap it for her.

'Arlene?'

'Is that you, Edgar?'

'No, it's President Nixon. I'll be celebrating Christmas at the White House with a few buddies and I thought that, being a religious holiday and all, you might like to come over and screw in the Oval Office.'

'Sorry, Edgar. I'm spending Christmas with my mother.'

'I hope she's a good fuck.'

'You're naughty,' said Arlene. 'OK, so it's my boyfriend. I need to spend Christmas with him, Edgar. It's kind of a family time, isn't it?'

'I guess so, Arlene. Make sure he gives you a big helping of pudding.'

Arlene giggled.

Edgar drank another couple of martinis and called Sandra. No reply. Gloria was in, though. Gloria was always in.

'You doing anything special over Christmas?'

'Come on over, honey. I'm sure we can think of something.'

He rubbed the back of his neck. It still hurt. It still hurt quite a lot.

But then, so did being alone.

*

The twenty-fourth of December. The day before Christmas. Mort and Ruby were in the office going over the figures. Things were looking good. The company had made eight million dollars. Only about a third of that amount was so far liquidated. The balance was estimated profit based on spot purchases and sales already concluded.

'Not counting the 1974 long-term contracts,' said Ruby.

'The Nigerian,' said Mort.

'The Arab Light.'

'The Iranian.'

They niggled at their mini-calculators for the hundredth time. Then they leaned back in their chairs and looked at each other in wonder.

'I can't believe it,' said Mort.

'It's wild,' said Ruby.

'You make it what I make it?'

'What do you make it?'

'Eighty-five million dollars' profit. And that's being conservative.'

Ruby frowned. 'Strange. I only make it eighty-four million five hundred thousand.'

They eyed their calculators critically. Mort caught the puzzled expression on Ruby's face and exploded with laughter. Then Ruby was chuckling. They laughed until the tears ran down their cheeks and they had to hold their sides to stop the muscles from cramping. They were on the verge of hysteria.

'This is serious,' Ruby gasped.

'A – major – discrepancy,' said Mort weakly, between eruptions.

As their laughter subsided, they sat there, shaking their heads incredulously.

Less than a year . . . That's what they were both thinking. It was less than a year since the first Dolder meeting.

'Still,' said Ruby, 'we can't have discrepancies.'

'Absolutely not,' said Mort.

'Why don't we go over the figures again?' said Ruby.

'Sounds like a great idea,' said Mort.

166

For a few minutes longer they played with their calculators, both men totally absorbed, as though in some kind of trance, hypnotized by the hieroglyphics that wriggled on the tiny grey screens they cradled in the palms of their hands.

Mort finished checking his figures and sat back, watching his brother, waiting patiently for him to finish. Ruby's eyes were shining. As the numbers bloomed on the screen of his pocket calculator he muttered to himself excitedly and, suddenly, Mort understood that this was still a game for Ruby, the best game of all, a child's game played by men. It was not real; it did not relate to the world he lived in. Not at all. There, men were accountable for their actions. In Ruby's world of fantasy, no one could be called to account. Each time a number appeared, as if by magic, at the tip of his fingers, it represented another triumph, another victory of the intellect, another confirmation that, in this mediocre world of commonplace people and average achievement, there was still a place for excellence, still a chance to show that you were better and smarter than anyone else. That was all that truly mattered. He was like a child, peering through a kaleidoscope, exulting in his own skill at producing a different but still captivating image every time he shook it, astonished and delighted at the ease with which the coloured shapes rearranged themselves.

'I make it eighty-six million,' said Ruby, at last. 'What do you make it?' He was beaming with happiness.

'I make it the same,' said Mort, lying. Who cared? A million more or less. What the hell did it matter? Mort was tired of playing with toys. It was time to put away childish thoughts. He slipped the calculator into his pocket.

Last week, one of their tankers had sunk. Ruby had scampered off to be sure that the insurance was in order. It was. He had not thought to ask if the crew were safe. Two men had drowned, but Ruby was not interested. Mort had been surprised, but now he understood. These were not real tankers Ruby was chartering, nor real men who

167

crewed them. His fantasy world was not inhabited by real people. They were counters in a game, pieces on a board, coloured lights winking on a screen, numbers on a pocket calculator.

'Eighty-six million dollars,' said Ruby wonderingly. 'It's unreal.'

'No,' said Mort. 'It's real.'

'Who can believe it?' It was too much for Ruby to absorb. But not for Mort. 'Believe it,' he said.

BOOK FOUR

The Facts of Life

Mort and Ruby breakfasted two or three times a week at the Brasserie in the Seagram Building on Fifty-Third Street. Ruby's favourite food was anything fattening: croissants and strawberry jam, cheese Danish, blueberry muffins and honey, pancakes and syrup. Mort ate, like he did everything, with fastidious self-control: a slice of melon, a cup of coffee and, once in a while, as a special indulgence, a boiled egg. Such indulgences had to be controlled, otherwise there was a danger of their becoming chronic weaknesses and, of all things, Mort despised weakness.

He watched his brother with distaste as he stuffed yet another blueberry muffin into his mouth.

'Who would have dreamed?' Ruby was saying with his mouth full. 'Less than a year's trading and we're multi-millionaires. You were so right, Mort. Everything you forecast has come true.'

Mort did not answer. He seemed preoccupied this morning. He was leafing through the *New York Times* in a purposeless, desultory kind of way.

'We're shipping out the first cargoes in a couple of days,' continued Ruby. 'Isn't that something?' It was the fifth of January. The shipments were scheduled to run through the end of 1974.

Mort sheltered behind his paper as Ruby packed in a succulent cheese Danish.

'You want one?' Ruby held the plate under his nose. There was only one left. 'The best in New York. Go ahead.'

Mort moved the plate away impatiently. 'Do me a

171

favour, Ruby. Take the goddam thing away. All you think about is food.'

Ruby looked offended. 'Why so irritable?'

'It's warm,' said Mort. He shook his head. 'It's January and it's warm. It should be snowing. It should be freezing.'

'Is that bad?'

Mort handed him the *New York Times*.

For a moment, Ruby was bewildered. 'What am I supposed to be looking at?' He could see nothing of any great interest.

'The weather. Temperatures around the world. Look at the goddam weather. It's a freak winter.'

Ruby glanced at the weather page and handed back the paper.

'You're right,' he confirmed. 'It's warm. So?'

He sipped his coffee while Mort looked at him. For a few moments, they stared at each other. Suddenly, Ruby knew what Mort was telling him. The cabal was operating. 'Oh, my God!' he exclaimed. 'What a dumb idiot I am.'

'Look at these reports from the European ski resorts. It's the warmest winter for years. No snow. It's a disaster.'

'Heating oil,' said Ruby. 'That's it, isn't it? No one will buy any heating oil.'

Mort folded the paper and waved his hand for the check. 'If only it were just heating oil,' he said. 'But if we don't get a normal winter damn quickly, the whole product market will be shot to hell and when product prices start falling . . .'

'Crude prices follow,' said Ruby.

'You got it,' said Mort. 'Finally, you got it.'

'We made the right decision to sell all the crude,' said Ruby. 'If we hadn't, we might be stuck with it in a falling market.'

Edmund Meyer read the oil journals and the financial press, the investment analysts and the bank forecasts. He read them exhaustively and he read them every day. He noted carefully the experts' recommendations and then he

172

consulted the palm of his hand, stroked it with the tip of his third finger and did what he wanted to do; usually, it was the opposite of what the experts advised and, invariably, it was right.

Since the end of 1973 he had been telling Jack Greenberg: 'Sell short. Don't buy. Don't take long positions.'

And Jack had protested: 'But E.M., the market's booming. Everyone in the industry is going the other way.'

'Then everyone in the industry is wrong,' said E.M.

'How do you know?' said Jack. There was nothing more exasperating than E.M.'s arrogance. You could never argue with the guy. He and the Pope; they were both infallible.

All E.M. did was look at the palm of his hand. How could he explain? The gesture was an unconscious one. That was how it was. He did not know himself how he read markets. There was, in truth, no rational process. It was like the very high notes; some people heard them, some didn't. He did.

Of course, Jack did as he was told, but he resented being overruled. He resented it all the more when it started to become clear that E.M., as usual, was right. Nothing is more irritating than a guy who is always right.

Well, he knew a couple of things that E.M. didn't.

'You hear about King Brothers?'

Edmund Meyer tensed. 'What about them?'

'They did all right the first year. Nothing spectacular . . . pretty mediocre, I'd say . . . but they're paying their way.'

E.M. pondered. He'd rather Mort was in Chapter Eleven. Still . . . 'paying your way' didn't get you into the Forbes One Hundred.

'But now I hear something very interesting . . .'

He paused, enjoying E.M.'s obvious curiosity.

'Mort has had a rush of blood to the head. You know how he is. He never could tolerate being Mr Average.'

'Get to the point.'

'He's bought his goddam head off, E.M. More than five million tons of crude. Five – million – tons.'

173

Five million tons was a sizeable position even for the Oil Corporation. For a small company like King Brothers it sounded foolhardy. E.M.'s shrewd eyes glittered.

'They lay it off?'

'I'm told they sold every barrel.'

E.M. nodded. Mort was a renegade and a sonofabitch, but he was no one's fool. And he had learned on the slopes of Olympus.

'Listen to me, E.M. We're short of crude. We read the market right.'

'What you mean is – I read the market right,' interrupted E.M. 'You did what you were told, like you always do.'

Jack looked dazed for a moment, like a football player who has picked up a pass only to run into a block tackle. But just for a moment. He carried on as though his boss had not spoken. Pride was not one of his weaknesses.

'This is the moment we've been waiting for. The guy bought and sold more than a hundred thousand barrels at the highest prices in history. And now what? The market is dead. It's the warmest winter anyone can remember.'

'So?'

Jack put his hands on his boss's desk, his face only a few inches from E.M.'s. 'They're vulnerable. If you want to hit them – do it now.'

'How?'

'What would happen to King Brothers if all their customers cancelled on them?'

E.M. stood up abruptly, partly because he needed to think, partly to distance himself from Jack's unctuous features.

'Why would they do that?'

'Because we go to them and offer to replace their contracts at a huge discount, say a dollar a barrel.' He glanced sideways at E.M. to see how he was reacting to the suggestion. With E.M., you never knew.

'Good thinking,' said E.M., grudgingly.

174

The patronizing shitbag. Still, a compliment from Edmund Meyer was rare; it was like rain in the desert. Jack's smile blossomed. His face was shinier than ever. 'We could offer an even bigger discount.' He was watching E.M. closely. What was he thinking? 'Two dollars. Three maybe.'

E.M. said nothing.

'Face it, E.M. You and I both feel the same way about the bastard.'

'You and I?' E.M.'s heavy face was impassive, but there was a hint of something ominous, intimidating, in the way he echoed the words.

Still Jack ploughed on. Envy was a great spur. He envied Mort a lot of things, his business acumen, his strength, his dedication, his success, his independence. He envied his independence most of all. He hated him for being free of E.M. and he hated him for not taking him with him. That was the unforgivable slur.

E.M. was looking at the chair in the corner of his office that Mort used to sit in.

Loyalty. Not in fashion any more, it seemed. People were too greedy. Still, he missed Mortimer King. He would never admit it to anyone, but he missed him.

'We'll sell the crude today,' Jack was saying, 'and cover in a falling market. The market is going to keep on falling, isn't it, E.M.?' he asked, almost anxiously. E.M. always knew.

E.M. nodded absently.

'These are huge corporations,' said Jack persuasively, 'respectable companies quoted on the New York Stock Exchange. They're not going to walk away from a contract for peanuts.' That was Jack's philosophy. Respectability, like reputation, was a tradable commodity indispensable to business success – unless, of course, someone made it worth your while ... He held out his hands to E.M., appealing to him. 'Three bucks a barrel! Who can refuse that kind of money? After all, they have an obligation to their shareholders and there's nothing like a satisfied

175

shareholder to ease a man's conscience. Mort will take a bath. He'll drown.'

E.M. tucked his thumbs in his blood-red suspenders and looked down at Jack.

Jack grinned and nudged him, an insinuating gesture, an affirmation of intimacy.

Edmund Meyer drew back, frowning. He detested familiarity in anyone, whoever they were, especially in his employees, most especially in Jack Greenberg.

'No,' he muttered, 'I won't start a vendetta. I won't stoop to that.'

'But E.M.,' protested Jack. 'This is trading. It's for the Oil Corporation. It's for you.'

E.M. turned his back on Jack. 'No,' he said. 'I want no part of it.'

The Titan had spoken.

*   *   *

Leo Stendel handled it to perfection – so neatly, in fact, that Julie was not sure what had happened until it was all over.

How long had she been working at the Gallery? A week? Two weeks? It was, in fact, just about six months, but the time had passed so pleasantly and Leo was such a honey to work for that she had not exactly counted the days. She was so contented that she rarely knew what day of the week it was or what time of day. She stayed late every evening because she enjoyed being around the Gallery and, if anyone asked her whether it was Wednesday or Thursday, she looked blank. Only the weekend dragged. The best part of it was Sunday evening; she could look forward to being at the Gallery the next morning.

She could also look forward to seeing Leo, but that was not something she dared to admit to herself.

Right now, the Gallery was busy. Leo was planning his quarterly exhibition. He had a few paintings that none of his customers had seen, but not enough for a show, and he and his staff were chasing round the dealers and contacting

176

private clients to beg, borrow or buy some more. Good quality paintings, however, were scarce and getting scarcer. There was too much money around. A rich man rarely sells a painting; he holds on to it. If you have the cash, why not hang it on the wall and enjoy it?

Julie was on the phone in the tiny cubicle he had given her that everyone in the Gallery except her called an office. She called it 'my closet' and she loved it. He had offered her a larger space, but she had refused it. The 'closet' contained a chair, a miniature desk, a trash can and a filing cabinet. The walls were covered with reproductions of Miro, Bonnard and Matisse, her three favourite painters. There was one exception – a tiny Toulouse-Lautrec – a man and a woman at the opera. That was an original. She had arrived one morning and there it was. Leo's idea, of course. When she protested that it was too valuable to hang in her closet, he looked apologetic and said he had nowhere else to put it.

Leo appeared in the doorway and waited there, quietly, until she saw him. She put her hand over the mouthpiece of the phone. 'I think I've found you a Chagall,' she whispered.

He wrinkled his nose. There were a lot of Chagalls around: most of them third rate.

'A good one,' she mouthed.

He pointed to his mouth and mimed food. Then he tapped his watch and said something quietly. She nodded. They often had lunch together, sometimes alone, mostly with a client.

She looked forward to it. Leo was fun. She waited for him to appear around twelve-thirty, but he did not come. At one o'clock, he was still not there.

No reply from his office. Tina, his assistant, said she thought he had gone out with a client. Obviously he had forgotten, or something had come up unexpectedly.

She picked up a diet soda and an apple at the deli round the corner and 'lunched' in the office.

She saw Leo in the afternoon and he said nothing, which

177

she thought a little strange. He was not the kind to forget things.

Around four p.m., the Chagall arrived. It was a forties painting of a huge vase of flowers. In the background was the Russian village of Vitebsk where he was born. The painting was a beauty. She wanted to buy it for the Gallery. The owner wanted six hundred thousand dollars – a high price – but she thought they could still make money on it.

An hour or so later, Leo popped his head round the door and saw the Chagall. He could hardly miss it. The canvas was three and a half feet by two and the colours were vibrant.

'What do you think?' she asked timidly. What Leo thought was important. He was the boss, sure, but, more than that, he knew about paintings. He loved them and he had a shrewd eye, not simply for what would sell – he always knew that – but for what was good.

He studied the Chagall from a few inches away, picked it up, looked at the back, put it down again, stepped back to the doorway and contemplated it with his head on one side.

Finally he smiled. 'It's magnificent! The best Chagall I've seen around for years.'

Julie flushed with pleasure, hazel eyes wide, excited. 'She wants six hundred thousand. It's a lot of money.'

He popped his eyes and puffed out his cheeks as he always did when he wanted to tell a client, without actually saying anything, that their asking price was unrealistic.

'Too expensive?' she asked tentatively.

'What do you think?'

She had no doubts. 'I think we should buy it.'

'So buy it.'

'You mean you agree?'

'Sure, I agree. We may have to sit on it for a while, but when are we ever going to find another Chagall like this?'

That was exactly how she saw it.

'Congratulations,' he said.

'Thanks,' said Julie. It was her first coup for the Gallery. Leo was pleased. She felt great.

'What time shall I pick you up?' he asked.

She looked blank.

'I thought we were having dinner together,' he said.

'But I thought . . .'

'It's not convenient? You want to make it some other time?'

'Oh no,' she said. 'It's fine, perfectly fine.'

'I'll stop by at seven-thirty, then. We'll eat in the Village.'

Mort was on a trip to Washington. Not that it mattered, of course. It didn't matter at all. He knew all about her work.

It was funny, though. She could have sworn Leo had said lunch.

La Tulipe was a restaurant on the fringes of Greenwich Village. Julie had never been there before. It was noisy enough to make you feel you were one of the crowd, but not so noisy that you had to raise your voice. She loved it.

'If you like seafood, they have the best crayfish in town.'

'You choose for me,' said Julie. When had she last said that to a man?

She had dressed carefully, trying on and discarding a dozen dresses before settling for an elegant but simple Galanos. Her hair was piled high on her head and she wore little make-up.

'You look amazing,' Leo said. He was appraising her with those dealer's eyes of his. Then he smiled lazily, and he was plain Leo Stendel again. He liked women; that was obvious. He liked her; that was obvious too.

He was surprisingly serious. She had expected smart chat. He could be very amusing in the Gallery. Here he was just relaxed, as though he saw no need to impress her. She might have been offended, but she was not. She wondered, all the same, why he had asked her out. He saw

179

her every day at the Gallery and they lunched together
often enough.

'Why are we here?' she asked.

'I've been meaning to do this for a long time, but I didn't
know how.'

'Are you telling me you're shy?'

'Not so much shy,' he confessed, 'as devious.' He grinned
sheepishly. 'It's been on my conscience all day.'

'What has?' she said.

'When I was mouthing my invitation at you, what I was
really talking about was dinner, but I was trying to make
it sound like lunch.' He looked like a small boy caught
stealing candies.

Julie laughed. 'That's exactly what I thought. You said
lunch. Then, when you confirmed dinner, I guess I was
too chicken to refuse.'

'Would you have turned me down if I'd come straight
out and asked you to have dinner with me?'

She thought about it. 'I guess not,' she said.

'I feel silly.'

'Don't. Just tell me why you asked me out to dinner.'

'I asked you out because you're a beautiful woman and
I'm a lonely old bachelor.'

'If you're lonely, that must be your choice.'

'You have a point. It's not easy to find what I'm looking
for.'

'What are you looking for?' she asked gently.

He considered the question. 'Someone like you,' he said.
'My apartment's round the corner, I left my car there. I'll
drive you home. Unless . . .'

'I'd like to see your place,' she said.

'I could offer to show you my etchings,' he said, 'but I
don't have any.'

He had a lot more than etchings.

Never in her life could Julie have imagined that one
man owned such an incredible collection of paintings. For
variety and quality, few museums could have equalled
it.

There were seven interconnecting rooms, each dedicated to a different period, from Old Masters, through the eighteenth century, on to the Impressionists and Post-Impressionists and up to the present day. Leo Stendel had not attemped to cover every period; his collection was not representative. It was eclectic, rather, but one unifying element held it together and made it uniquely great: the taste of the collector. Every painting was a masterpiece. There were the great Picassos and Cézannes and Monets, but there were also the great works of lesser painters – a middle life landscape by Vlaminck, an exquisite painting of a yacht harbour by Derain and a warm, atmospheric interior by Vuillard.

Leo gave her a running commentary. He talked fascinatingly about the paintings, the painters, and the story of every purchase. Sometimes, he would talk about the empty spaces on the walls. 'Now that's a Claudette: French, talented, sexy, not too bright – fun though. We had fun.' Claudette had been his number three wife.

'What used to hang there?'

'A cubist Picasso.'

'She liked Picasso?'

'Loathed him.'

'Then why did she take it?'

Leo gave her an old-fashioned look. 'It was the most valuable painting I had at the time,' he said.

'Why don't you fill the spaces? You're always buying paintings.'

'There's something about the spaces,' said Leo. 'They're kind of nostalgic. Each one has its own personality; it reminds me of one of my ex-wives. How else would I remember them?' he said and smiled a rather forlorn smile.

'Why so cynical?'

He pulled a wry face. 'My wives gave me very little. Except Claudette. She gave me a son. David's a fine boy. I wish I'd spent more time with him. The others – they took – but, what the hell. I had too many paintings anyway.'

181

'You're very self-centred aren't you, Leo? Life hasn't really touched you.'

'Not until now.'

They stared at each other.

'Are you going to stay?' he asked.

'Yes,' she said, 'I'll stay.'

He was a gentle lover, as she had expected him to be. His body was strong and hard, like that of a much younger man. He made love, not just with his male organ, as so many men do, but with his whole body. For the first time ever, she felt that the act of love was not just sex, but a communion of bodies, a shared, almost spiritual experience. She had always admired those words in the Christian marriage service 'With my body I thee worship'.

Leo worshipped her with his body, with passion and hunger and desire, but also with a kind of reverence for her smooth, rounded limbs and for the beauty of the act itself.

He drove her back to her apartment and they kissed goodbye at the entrance – not prudent, but who cared?

For some reason, she was embarrassed. God knows why, but she felt like a teenager.

'I could get used to this,' he said.

'Me too.'

'Julie,' he said, 'I need to tell you – '

She kissed him gently on the mouth. 'It's been fun,' she said.

Mort was not home. He must still be in Washington. Or wherever. It didn't seem to matter too much these days.

*   *   *

It was eight-thirty p.m. Ruby had already left. Mort was still in the office, on his third or fourth bourbon, or was it his fifth or sixth? He had lost count. He sat in the circle of yellow light around his desk and contemplated the New York skyline. They said it was the most spectacular view in the world. Not that he ever had the time to appreciate

182

it. When Mort stayed late in the office it was not to enjoy the view.

Right now he was not working. He was thinking about Sam's phone call.

'They're wriggling,' Sam had said.

'Who are?'

'The Italians. They want out.'

'Hold their feet to the fire, the bastards.'

'The fire? What fire, Mort?'

Sam was right, of course. They were not exactly in a position of strength. Still, why couldn't the little creep have sounded angrier? Nothing ever seemed to bother Sam, damn him!

'Sue the shitheads!'

'You want to sue the Italian government?'

'I'd like to,' Mort had said furiously. And so he would. But for what? Years of litigation. And what then?

It was bad news. Bad, bad news. The market was slipping. If the Italians walked away, what would their other customers do?

He thought about how much it cost to open the doors of the New York office every day, not to mention London and Wald. They had been talking of opening others. Now what? They had only just begun to get their act together. Jack Greenberg had nearly destroyed them before they even got off the ground. Now the nightmare was starting all over again.

'They were, well, decent about it. I think they have a conscience.'

So. The Italians had a conscience. Wasn't that something?

'What do we do, Mort?'

Now, there was a good question. What do we do? What you did was have another drink. That's what you did.

He bullied his pocket calculator as he had done for the last two hours, trying to make the numbers on the Italian contract look better, glaring angrily at the tiny black figures on the miniature screen. No matter how he calcu-

183

lated, the numbers always came out the same. The loss was huge. Unthinkable. He had told Sam to negotiate, compromise, agree to reduce the volume – if necessary by half – to spread out the shipping schedule so they wouldn't have to take all the losses in one year. Compromise. Compromise. Compromise. And all Sam could say was: 'I think they have a conscience'. Jesus, what a wimp! What did he know about trying? Trying was never giving up. Trying was making people do what you wanted, not lying down so they could walk all over you. What did Sam know? . . . You had to try everything . . . clutch at straws . . . clutch at the barrels floating away before they disappeared . . . all those barrels floating away from the sinking ship . . . MS King Brothers . . .

Just after ten, Sam phoned back. 'I'm sorry, Mort. I tried again. Believe me, I tried. It was hopeless. They cancelled. All they would say was they had an offer three dollars a barrel cheaper than ours. They're lying, of course. It's just an excuse. I'm really sorry.'

Well, that was OK, then. Sam was sorry. That made everything OK.

So all they had to do now was cancel with the supplier. Who the hell was the supplier? Oh, yes, the Iranians. Edgar would take care of them. It would be a piece of cake, wouldn't it?

Mort smiled, laid his head on the desk next to the calculator and fell asleep.

At around eleven p.m., the phone rang. It was Julie wondering why he had not come home yet. He was always late, but this late was a record. It rang eight or nine times until it disturbed him in his sleep and he shifted his arm and knocked off the receiver.

Edgar was not a contentious man. For him the best way out was the easy way out. The prospect of travelling to Tehran to try to cancel a contract he had only just concluded was not his idea of a good time. It worried and disturbed him. Business – and life, for that matter – should be straightforward. Of course, they never were. Which was why he drank. Breakfast in his room at the Inter-Continental was designed to give him courage; he lined up half a dozen dry martinis and tossed them back in a few seconds. Then, thinking of his health, he ate the six little slices of lemon rind.

As he passed the desk, the reservations manager saluted him jovially. Edgar had brought him the latest *Playboy* magazine and stuck a hundred-dollar bill on the centre-fold's pubic hairs. He thought his friend would find the combination irresistible.

Ali Nagaar looked as apprehensive as ever. He fussed his papers and kept an anxious eye on the ceiling, while His Imperial Majesty covered the rest of the room.

Edgar explained the problem.

'Our customers have cancelled,' he said. 'It's very unfor-tunate. Morals are not what they used to be in the oil business.'

Ali Nagaar was nodding his head, it seemed, sympatheti-cally, but you never knew with this guy whether he was agreeing, or just twitching. He heard Edgar out. From the way Edgar presented it, the future of the Western Alliance would depend on whether NIOC were cooperative or not.

'My company anticipates a long and mutually beneficial relationship with NIOC.' Edgar wished he could remember the speech he had prepared, but the gin had frayed his concentration round the edges. He was hoping that a few appropriate clichés and an engaging grin or two would do the trick. 'There has to be some give and take in a . . . in contractual . . . uh . . . relationships,' he droned on. Was he repeating himself? He didn't feel so hot. Must be the lemon rind.

Ali Nagaar waited for him to finish. He took off his worried-looking tortoise-shell spectacles, rubbed them with a tissue and put them back on. Then he held his wrists together and laid them on the table.

'My hands are tied,' he said dramatically.

Edgar did not have the stamina to hard-nose this dis-

185

cussion out for hours, even if Ali would make the time available, which was doubtful. Edgar was not, by nature, a negotiator; he had neither the endurance nor the guile needed to play that game. Salami tactics – the laborious and infinitely patient surrendering of bits of one's position, slice by tempting slice, hoping with each sliver of concession that your opponent might be tempted to settle – no, that was not for Edgar. He liked to talk some and grin some and then – with a grandiose gesture – slam the whole goddam salami on the table. That was what he did now.

'How would it be,' he volunteered, 'if we agreed to maintain the price and cut the volume by fifty per cent. You yourself said you only have a limited volume of crude to sell.'

'That would be an excellent solution . . .'

'Ah,' said Edgar hopefully.

' . . . For you,' continued Ali Nagaar mournfully. He swivelled in his chair and gazed up at HIM. 'But not, alas, for His Imperial Majesty the Shahanshah.'

Edgar looked like a man who has just laid down four aces and lost to a royal flush.

'We might, however, agree to reduce the contract volume by ten per cent,' said Nagaar.

'But we already have that right,' said Edgar. 'It's in your standard contract.'

'The ten per cent tolerance, Mr Proktor, applies to each individual shipment. It does not apply to the whole contract. I am, nevertheless, prepared to make you this major concession, even at the risk of His Imperial Majesty's displeasure. I make it for the sake of our old friendship.'

'Ten per cent,' said Edgar dejectedly.

'Ten. Not eleven. Ten.'

Edgar was looking thoughtful.

'Tell me, Ali,' he said, 'speaking hypothetically, of course, what would happen if some company – not King Brothers, naturally, but some unscrupulous, flaky company – what would happen if they told NIOC to . . . uh . . . well, to . . .'

186

'Go screw themselves?' said Ali Nagaar, blinking anxiously.

'I guess that would be the gist of the example I had in mind, although I wouldn't have phrased it exactly that way.' Fuck the Shah! That was how he would have phrased it.

Ali Nagaar, for the first time in the whole of their acquaintance, actually looked cheerful. The effect was grotesque and sinister.

'Mr Proktor,' he said, with the gentlest of smiles, 'the answer to your hypothetical question is that such an unscrupulous and – how did you put it? – flaky company, would be blacklisted, first by Iran, then by every oil producer in the world. I personally would arrange it, on behalf of His Imperial Majesty. It would be difficult for this hypothetical company to trade in oil if you – I beg your pardon – if they – had no oil to sell. Now wouldn't it?'

'I can see that,' said Edgar. 'Yes, you have a point.'

'That's the scoop,' he said. 'I'm sorry, guys.'

'Don't be,' said Ruby. 'What else could you have done?'

'Walk away from the contract.'

'If we walk away from the Iranians, we might as well shut up shop and go home.'

Mort said nothing. He was thinking they might have to do that anyway.

'That's what Ali said. He threatened to have us blacklisted worldwide if we didn't perform.'

'He could do it,' said Ruby. 'No question.'

'How much do we stand to lose?' Edgar had made his own calculations; he just hoped they were wrong.

'We're still working on the Italians to take part of the volume at the contract price, but it's tough going,' said Mort. 'We're dealing with government officials and they're not the most flexible guys in the world.'

'We have a contract. Why don't we insist they lift the crude at the contract price?' said Edgar indignantly.

'We did,' said Mort.

'They weren't impressed,' said Ruby.

'Those Italian bastards – they're all the same. You can't trust them,' said Edgar.

'Not like the good old Americans,' said Ruby.

'Right,' said Edgar. 'In this country, at least, a contract is still a contract.'

Mort and Ruby stared at him impassively.

'So, tell me,' said Edgar, 'how much do we lose?'

'Twenty million dollars,' said Mort.

'That's what I was afraid of.' Edgar was astonished how calmly they seemed to be taking it. 'I guess we'll make so much on the Nigerian and Saudi contracts, we'll come out OK. I mean, we are going to make a killing on them, aren't we?'

'Sure we are,' said Mort.

But Edgar could not escape the feeling that he had let the team down. He should have done better. He should have come back with some concession.

He needed someone around to tell him what a great guy he was.

The closest to a steady girlfriend he had was Arlene – how much closer could she get than sitting outside his office door all day? She was twenty-two, with short, curly blonde hair, big blue eyes and a neat little butt. Everything about Arlene was neat – her desk, her work, the way she walked. She was a good secretary; she rarely made mistakes; she knew how to cover for Edgar when he was shooting the breeze at the bar of the Bistro Français and she was as pliant and uncomplicated as it was possible for a woman to be.

She just walked into the office one morning and asked Edgar for a trial. So he took her back to his apartment the same evening and gave her one. She passed with flying colours.

The next day she started full time. The amazing thing was she could type as well. It really surprised Edgar how efficient she was. Her curriculum vitae had not done her justice. She was fast and untiring; she could screw all night and take dictation at eight the following morning.

When he left Mort's office, he wandered disconsolately back to his own. He didn't have the stomach to get on the phone and trade. He sat at his desk and stared at the wall. His brain was paralysed. He buzzed Arlene. She walked in with her precise little steps, sat down, smoothed her skirt and held her pen at the ready.

'You love me, Arlene?' he asked.

Arlene was never surprised by anything – certainly not by anything Edgar said. That was one of the nice things about her. She took life as it came; she was never fazed.

'Would you believe me if I said yes?'

Edgar grinned bashfully.

Arlene said nothing. Once, she had kidded herself that maybe she and Edgar . . .

'But you're crazy about me.'

'I like you a lot,' she said.

Edgar thought some more. 'You wouldn't leave me, would you?'

'No.'

'Not even if you got married?'

'No.'

'How can you be so sure?'

'I got married three months ago,' she said calmly.

Edgar snapped forward in his chair. 'Jesus Christ! You never told me.'

'I didn't think you'd be interested,' said Arlene.

'Is he . . .? I mean . . . you like the guy?'

'He's OK. He has a good job, a nice apartment and a car.'

Arlene had her priorities right.

'What kind of car?'

'A 1968 Lincoln.'

Edgar nodded solemnly. 'That was a good year . . . for Lincolns . . . Well, that's great. Congratulations.'

'Thanks.'

Arlene locked the door, pulled up her skirt, slipped off her panties and came round the desk. By the time she got there, Edgar was nude from the waist down. He was a fast operator.

'What can I give you for a wedding present?'

'This'll do fine,' she said, clasping the rock in her cool hand.

'I'm not kidding,' he said. 'Something you really need.'

'There's nothing I need more than this,' said Arlene, deadpan. Then, seeing his disappointment, 'OK,' she said, 'how about a TV?'

'What kind of TV?'

Arlene laid her hands on his shoulders and eased her shapely bottom up and over.

'Full size,' she said.

'Any particular make?'

She thrust down on him, hard. Arlene was very small and Edgar had the member of the year.

'Oh God!' she gasped, 'I love it. Jesus, you're big!'

Edgar lay back in his chair, his eyes closed. Iran and the NIOC were far from his thoughts. The phone rang. He picked it up with one hand, supporting Arlene's hard little ass with the other.

'I'm in conference,' he gasped.

'Enjoy,' said the switchboard girl, who knew Edgar well.

'How about a Sony?' he suggested.

'Oh . . . Fuck!' she moaned. 'A Sony would be . . . aah . . . great.'

She rammed her thighs down on his penis a few more times, taking as much of it as she could inside her, squeezing it adroitly with her sinewy vaginal muscles. Then she gave a moan of contentment, shuddered and laid her head gratefully on his chest.

'You're the greatest, Edgar,' she whispered. 'There'll never be another one like you.'

And that was exactly what he needed to hear.

Arlene repaired her make-up, stuffed her panties in her

pocket, smoothed her skirt and sat down again, ready for dictation.

'I'd like one of those twenty-five-inch models,' she said.

Edgar sighed. 'Some girls are never satisfied,' he said.

Ten days later, Ruby was summoned to Atlantic and Orient. He said nothing about it to Mort; no sense to get everyone excited until he knew whether there was anything to get excited about.

A lot of people can't stand the sight of blood. Martin Field was definitely not one of them. When he wielded a knife, he did so with pleasure. He plunged it in with relish and then twisted it round a few times, just for the hell of it. The sadistic delight he took in administering the *coup de grâce* was something Ruby would never forget.

'We're both businessmen, Mr King,' he said. 'You know how these things are.'

'I know exactly how these things are,' said Ruby coldly. 'I know that you signed a contract to lift two and a half million tons of crude. So far, you've lifted only five hundred thousand. You have a contractual obligation to lift the balance.'

Martin Field bared his teeth in a grimace that was apparently intended to be a grin.

'Let's be realistic. There's no way you can force me to lift.'

'Who says? You have no excuse not to. We performed to the letter.'

'Sure, you did. Because you were making a killing. It suited you to perform.'

'We would have performed whatever the market. Even if the price had gone against us, we would have performed.' Ruby wanted to believe what he was saying.

'Don't be so damned naive, Mr King, and don't take me for a fool. Your kind of people stick to contracts as long as it suits you and, if it doesn't, you're like the Bedouins. You pack your tent and steal away in the night.' He emphasized the word 'steal' with snide sarcasm.

'My kind of people?' said Ruby, raising an eyebrow.

'Mushroom companies. Remember? It just stopped raining. The sun came out.'

'Spare me the meteorological lecture,' said Ruby. 'You have a contract. We expect you to perform.'

'Is that so?' said Martin Field. 'I'm a busy man, Mr King. If you have nothing more to say . . .'

Ruby had handled tough guys before. Business was no different from the law. You took an extreme position in order to weaken your opponent's resolve. This was a negotiating tactic. It had to be. Everyone knew American companies honoured their contracts . . . Didn't they?

He breathed deeply, controlling his anger. 'Perhaps we could discuss some kind of compromise,' he said. 'I have an absolute commitment to my suppliers. There's no way I can cancel the contract. If I did, King Brothers would be in deep trouble.'

That was exactly what Martin Field was hoping, but he didn't say so.

'I understand your predicament,' he said, feigning concern. 'I really wish I could help you, but I'm up to my ears in crude. As you may know, my company is one of the biggest users of the Caribbean terminals and, I can tell you, every darn tank is full. I won't be buying any more crude for the rest of this year – not at the price I've been paying you, anyway.'

'But you might if the price were cheaper?'

Martin Field grinned unpleasantly.

'Cheaper? How about three dollars a barrel cheaper?'

'Three dollars a barrel?' Ruby sounded sceptical. 'That's hard to believe.'

'I don't give a goddam what you believe, Mr King,' Field snapped angrily. 'I can show you Mr Greenberg's telex.' He blurted out the name and then, catching the look on Ruby's face, he bit his lip, annoyed with himself for giving too much away.

So, that was it. The Oil Corporation had offered them crude at way below the market. It was a smart move. They would cover – buy in a falling market – and they would probably make money. Of course, the real incentive for them was to give King Brothers a hard time.

'I'm willing to discuss price,' said Ruby. What else could he say? It was either negotiate or lose everything. Sure, he could sue for breach of contract, but he knew it would take years and a small fortune to get a judgement against A. and O.

'I really wish you'd told me that before. The Oil Corporation offered me a price that I – my board that is – could not refuse. Not with all those greedy shareholders.' He waved vaguely at the window as if suggesting that the shareholders were out there with binoculars, watching his every move.

'How could I?' Ruby protested. 'You never gave me a chance. You summon me here to tell me our contract is cancelled and expect me to salute smartly, turn on my heel and leave. You've acted in bad faith.'

Martin Field smiled sourly. 'Mr King, we're not talking good faith or bad faith. We're talking business. This is the oil industry. I can't justify paying you three dollars a barrel more than your competitors are asking.'

'You know goddam well the market has dropped since we made our deal with you.'

'You're so right. And I intend to take full advantage of that fact. You sold me crude when the market was at its peak. That's your bad luck and your bad judgement. Your competitors are smarter than you are.'

'I'm ready to talk a substantial price reduction. I could help you by delaying shipments, or even reducing the contract volume. There has to be a way to reach a reasonable compromise.'

'Don't try to nickel and dime me, Mr King. We're past compromise.'

Ruby folded his arms. 'I'm not leaving this room until we've made a fair settlement.'

Martin Field stood up. 'In that case, Mr King, I'll say goodbye. My office is yours as long as you want it. I'm going out to lunch.'

'You won't talk?' said Ruby.

'I already did,' said Martin Field. 'I said all I had to say.'

'He cancelled on me,' said Ruby. 'The bastard cancelled on me.'

'You shouldn't have let him,' said Mort. 'You shouldn't let people dump on you.'

Ruby loved his brother, but sometimes he was hard to take. 'That's easy to say. You weren't there. The guy refused to talk. He wasn't interested in making compromises. He wanted a cancellation, not a settlement. It was Jack Greenberg – '

Mort did not let him finish. The very mention of Jack's name enraged him. It was rare for him to lose his cool, but the cancellation of a second major contract in a few days had shaken him.

'The hell with that little creep! He's nobody, you hear. Nobody. He can't touch us.'

'Maybe so,' said Ruby quietly. 'And maybe I'm never going to be the businessman you hoped I'd be.'

'You can be whatever you want. Anyone can, if they work at it.'

'You think it's so easy?'

'No one said it was easy.'

'I can always go back to being a lawyer,' said Ruby.

'You're staying where you are. You're not going anywhere. How do you expect to get to the top if you throw in the sponge when the going gets tough?'

'It's my life,' Ruby said. 'I make my own decisions.'

'Sure you do.' Mort walked over to the window and looked down at Lexington. 'You pay a price, Ruby,' he said. 'You pay a price for being successful. It's a high price. Not everyone thinks it's worth it. I happen to think it is. Don't try to be the nice guy. The world is full of nice guys and they're all failures.'

'That depends what you call a failure,' said Ruby.

Mort rounded on him, furiously. 'For Chrissake, Ruby, who needs philosophy? This is not some kind of game.

This is for real. This is life. This is it. You only get one crack at it and then it's dust and ashes.' He grabbed Ruby by the arm and pulled him over to the window. 'You want to be one of them? You want to be one of the crowd down there? Go ahead. Join them. It's easy enough. It's safe, too. You're anonymous. No one knows who you are. No one cares. Up here, it's different. Everyone knows you, but one thing, Ruby – you have to be able to defend yourself. You have to know how to fight back.'

'I'm not sure I can do that,' Ruby said quietly.

'Then learn, goddam you! Learn!'

For a long time neither of them said a word. At last, Ruby spoke. He sounded weary.

'I never thought it would be like this.'

'No? What did you expect? Overnight success?'

'I expected fun,' said Ruby. 'I guess I never really thought it through. You did tell me it was going to be fun, didn't you?'

'Is that what I said?' Mort grinned wryly. 'Well, isn't it?'

'It's a riot,' said Ruby. He paused, searching for the right words. Then, abruptly abandoning the search, he asked: 'How bad is it?'

'Bad enough.'

'Do we file for Chapter Eleven?'

'It's a possibility. We'll have to ask the other two.'

'Didn't I hear you say something about fighting back?'

'I can't do it on my own.'

That was some admission, thought Ruby, coming from Mort.

'I made myself a promise,' he said. 'One day – whatever it takes – I'll get even with Martin Field.'

Mort nodded. Ruby believed what he was saying. But talking about it was one thing – doing it was something else. You had to fight steel with steel.

'You still think Jack Greenberg can't touch us?'

'I'll tell you,' said Mort. 'I'd be surprised if he had the guts, but if I find out he did this to us . . .'

'What will you do?' said Ruby.

'Let's say, I'll make him see the error of his ways,' said Mort, slowly.

His face relaxed in a smile, but his green eyes were cold and unforgiving.

Fuad was the supplier of the Arab Light. Mort thought of a dozen ways to break the news to him and rejected all of them. In the end, he decided to give it to him straight.

'We made two mistakes. We thought the market would take off and it didn't. Worse, we sold the whole volume to one customer and he cancelled on us.'

Fuad paddled his podgy fingers in the jacuzzi in the pool room of the Four Seasons restaurant. He had eaten well and he appreciated the care Mort had taken in entertaining him. The meal had been superlative and a table by the Four Seasons' pool was a singular privilege reserved only for the favoured ones. Fuad, however, was not a man to permit such marginal considerations to cloud his judgement. Business and pleasure, like oil and water, did not mix.

'This is not an auspicious start to my relationship with King Brothers,' he said. Fuad was drawn to plump, pompous words like 'auspicious'.

'What can I say?' Mort said. 'You're right. I just hope we can reach some kind of amicable settlement.'

Fuad examined his immaculate manicure. 'Let me tell you something, Mr King. I've been in the oil business many years and, in my experience, there is no such thing as an amicable settlement. There are good settlements and bad settlements. There are no amicable settlements.'

'I don't agree,' said Mort glibly. 'I believe that personal relationships count for a great deal in this industry. It doesn't pay to be too tough. I was telling my brother only a couple of days ago how much people respect a nice guy. At least, that's how I see it. Maybe I have too much faith in human nature.'

Fuad smiled cynically. 'You?' he said. 'Too much faith in human nature.' He chuckled. 'You're a strange man, Mr King, difficult to fathom, a man who hides his true nature in the shadows. You don't reveal yourself to anyone, not even to yourself, I would venture to say. Otherwise, how could you say such things and believe them? Or, maybe you don't? Maybe you pretend to be the nice guy in order to get your way?'

Mort looked offended. 'If you think that, then you really don't understand me.'

'Perhaps I don't,' said Fuad. 'Or, perhaps I understand you very well. We have a contract. If I force you to observe it, you will do so. The alternative would be too unpleasant to contemplate. If I raised a finger, you would be out of the oil business.'

It was no exaggeration. Fuad had the power to make life very uncomfortable for Mort. They both knew that.

'All I ask is that you are as cooperative as our other suppliers have been,' said Mort. His green eyes were unwavering. Lying was an indispensable tool in business. Morality had no relevance in the jungle. You did what you had to do to survive.

Fuad explored his gums with the sharp nail of his little finger, all the time considering Mort, weighing him up. For a few moments, the two adversaries assessed each other, then Fuad lowered his eyes. Mort noticed, for the first time, that his eyelashes curled upwards, like a woman's.

'How is Mr Nagaar?' Fuad asked casually.

'He's OK.'

'You sent one of your men to reach an "amicable settlement" with him, I believe?'

Mort did not answer. Fuad contemplated the pool. He was in no hurry.

'Tell me,' he continued. 'How amicable was the settlement?'

'Very,' said Mort, looking Fuad straight in the eye.

'That's not what I heard.'

197

'Then you were misinformed.'

It was a stand-off. The two men stared at each other, their eyes expressionless.

'We have a deal, Mr King. I sold you fifty thousand barrels a day at fifteen dollars a barrel. You confirmed to me that you sold everything at nineteen dollars a barrel. My share is sixty per cent of the profit. You owe me two dollars, forty cents a barrel. That makes a total of forty-five million dollars – unless my calculation is at fault?' Fuad slipped a large champagne truffle into his mouth, looked around for his napkin and, not finding it, dunked his fingers in the pool.

'Your calculation is accurate,' Mort said grimly. 'Your problem is you won't accept the truth.'

'What is the truth?'

'The truth is I can't pay you.'

Fuad gazed into the pool, fascinated by the turbulent blue water. 'The truth . . . You know how I perceive truth, Mr King?' He waited politely for a reply, without really expecting one. He waved at the pool. 'I perceive truth like I see these reflections. Pretty, are they not? From where I'm sitting I can see colours – over there, the red of some-one's glass of wine, and there, the gold of a woman's hair and, in that corner, some flowers . . . yes, I see the reflection of some flowers . . . violet and pink and yellow. Do you not see them?'

'I see only blue water and white bubbles.'

Fuad retrieved his napkin and wiped his red mouth. 'Truth is like reflections, is it not? It depends on where you're sitting.'

'From where I'm sitting, I see Chapter Eleven,' said Mort.

'Bankruptcy is the resort of cowards. Whatever you are, Mr King, you are not a coward.'

'Thanks,' said Mort ruefully. 'Thanks for the compli-ment.'

'It's not a compliment. It's a statement of fact. And I'll give you another fact, Mr King.'

198

Mort waited, saying nothing. There was not too much he could say.

'One day, you'll need me again. You would do well to keep me as a friend.'

'How do I do that?'

'Pay your debts, Mr King.'

'In full?'

'In full.'

'You refuse to help me?'

Fuad looked pained. 'You have my sympathy.'

'Sympathy doesn't pay the rent. It doesn't keep the banks off my shoulders.'

Fuad stroked his worry beads. 'You have broad shoulders, Mr King – broad enough to carry the world.'

Two down, Mort was thinking. One to go. Pacific Odyssey. If they pulled the plug – it was the end.

Every day without news was a bonus and a reason for hope. They pretended to each other that one of their contracts had to stick, that one company at least would honour its commitments, that King Brothers would still be saved. If Pacific continued to lift, they would hopefully break even – live to fight another day.

By the sixth day following his meeting with Fuad, Mort was beginning to feel confident.

On the seventh, the blow fell. He was summoned by no less than the President of Pacific Odyssey. On the flight west, he was thinking that his shoulders might just not be broad enough.

Joe Murphy was there, but apparently only to show solidarity with management. Never once did he look at Mort. Most of the time, he stared straight ahead, avoiding eye contact. From time to time, he nodded slowly when the president was speaking, like a robot programmed only to agree.

The heavyweights of Pacific Odyssey sat in a semicircle, opposite Mort – the president in the middle, next to him, Joe. Present, also, were the executive vice-president in charge of oil acquisitions, the area vice-president for the Middle East and Africa and a group of vice-presidents with unspecified functions. To round off the numbers, there were also the finance director and four lawyers.

'Mr King,' the president began, ponderously, with a happy smile on his puffy face, 'we're going to be very frank with you.' He looked at Mort, frankly. Then he looked at Joe Murphy who studied his feet and nodded in agreement.

From years of experience, Mort knew that when a businessman claimed he was going to be 'frank' with him, it was a clear signal that he was about to tell a gigantic lie. Moreover, the rules of the game precluded the expression of scepticism or outright incredulity.

The president rambled on. He had a harsh, rasping voice that irritated Mort only slightly less than the ingratiating hypocrisy of his manner.

'We've invited you here to sit down with us to share our thoughts and yes, our problems. You should feel free to be as frank and open with us as we shall be with you.'

He was obviously sublimely unaware that he was being nauseatingly sanctimonious and patronizing.

He paused dramatically. 'Sometimes, in commerce, a contractual relationship can turn sour due to the profound inequity of the basic agreement. The agreement might be inherently legal. It might be capable of standing up to the most minute and critical scrutiny in any court of law, but, in the arena where we businessmen act out our days, it would receive the thumbs down – if you get my meaning.'

In case Mort did not, the president demonstrated the concept with his own thumb. Mort observed that it was large and crooked.

The president beamed at Mort benevolently, like a missionary hoping to convert a savage to Christianity. Mort stared right back, hard-eyed and unsmiling. He was trying to imagine how the man would look with a neat round bullet hole in the centre of his forehead.

The president was disconcerted. He had expected some

reaction – if not a sympathetic one, at least something. What he got was zero, so he switched off the winning smile and turned, as if for support, to the cluster of lawyers. They bent their heads to him in unison, like sunflowers to the sun. They eyed each other doubtfully for a moment or two. Then one of them spoke.

'Mr King,' said the lawyer, 'if I might amplify . . . this company has a legal obligation to protect its shareholders and – '

Mort cut in. 'Shareholders, bullshit!' he snapped. 'What your company has is a legal obligation to honour its contract with King Brothers.' He tapped his briefcase. The implication was strong that he had not only brought the contract along with him, but a legal opinion as well. The lawyer looked hurt. The president acknowledged the futility of his contribution with a dismissive wave of his hand.

'Mr King,' he said flatly, 'we have received, from a highly reputable competitor of yours, an offer of identical Nigerian crude at a price three dollars a barrel lower than yours.'

Now, this was talk that Mort could understand.

'That, sir,' said Mort, 'is entirely possible. Our contract with you was concluded several months ago when the market was much higher. It cost us three dollars a barrel more then, and you were happy to pay the price. If the market had risen three dollars, you would not be bellyaching now.'

'The market has not risen, Mr King. The market will not rise.'

True. The market was not going to improve in the foreseeable future. It was the president's strongest card.

'You can take us to court or you can be smart. I hope you see it my way. There's a lot of business in this building for you in the future. There's a lot of business out there, too. The industry does not look too sympathetically on uncooperative middlemen, especially in these hard times.'

And with that parting jibe and that crudely blatant threat, the president walked out of the room.

'What can I say, Mort?' Joe was mortally embarrassed. 'I'm real sorry. Believe me, I never dreamed this would happen. For me, a contract is a contract. I guess I'm old-fashioned.'

'I expected more help from you,' said Mort bitterly.

'They wouldn't listen to me. I was the one who pushed the deal through in the first place. They blamed me for it. Matter of fact . . .'

'What is it, Joe?'

'The president said something . . . something I didn't like. He said they'd be watching me more carefully in future . . . that I was getting too close to some of my customers.'

'Why should you care, Joe? Your conscience is clear.'

'That's right,' said Joe. 'My conscience is clear.'

'I need your help, Joe. If they cancel, I'm finished. Don't let them cancel, whatever you do.'

'I'll do what I can, Mort.'

Mort put his arm round Joe's shoulders. 'You know you can count on me, don't you, Joe? If you're ever in trouble, real trouble. If you should ever need help.'

'Thanks, pal.'

Mort hesitated at the door of Joe's office. 'Oh, by the way . . . funny thing . . . I know you never invested in the fund . . . not yet. But, if you had, your ten thousand would be worth two hundred thousand today. If you ever change your mind, I'm keeping a place warm for you.'

'Thanks, Mort, but Pacific take good care of me. I owe them.'

'Sure, Joe. You owe me too. We've been friends a long time. If I go under, everyone loses. Don't let them do this to me. We shook hands on the deal, Joe. I even told you my cost price. I gave you my word. Remember?'

'Like I said, Mort – I'll give it my best shot.'

But Joe's best shot was not good enough. Next morning, Pacific Odyssey's telex cancelling the deal was on Mort's desk.

The same day, Jeffrey was on the British Caledonian flight to Lagos. It was a forlorn hope. No one really expected the Nigerians to play ball. The Saudis hadn't, the Iranians hadn't, so why should the NNOC agree to cancel a valid contract? It didn't make sense. But then, in this business, nothing did. It wasn't about sense or logic; it was about meeting impenetrable barriers and penetrating them; it was about making the dreams come true, achieving the impossible. It was about believing in yourself.

Harry Dosumo's guest house in Lagos was famous. Visitors from all over the world, as well as Nigerians in their multi-coloured robes, filled the salon from ten in the morning every day of the week. Some stayed an hour, some a few hours, some until midnight, and it was not unusual to find a few hollow-eyed remnants still lounging around semiconscious at three or four o'clock in the morning. They talked business and drank Harry's booze. Running a guest house was expensive, but it was a symbol of success, and success attracted the prosperous, the powerful and the influential.

Jeffrey relaxed in one of the huge armchairs that lined both sides of the long sitting room and gloomily sipped a Scotch. He was exhausted. He was also freezing. The air-conditioning in the guest house was super-efficient, so cold you had to drink or risk frostbite. Over in the far corner of the room, a group of robed Nigerians and a few foreigners sat around in a half-circle. It might have been a prayer meeting, but it wasn't. They were watching a hard porn movie on a huge TV screen. In the kitchen there were ten enormous fridges stacked with champagne and beer, mostly champagne. Upstairs, round the gallery, were twelve bedrooms – every one with palatial en suite bathrooms, air-conditioning, TVs, and the choicest girls, black, white, and shades in between. Harry catered for all tastes, most of them depraved.

Jeffrey had been asleep for a while; he had no idea for how long. He woke, suddenly, to find Harry sitting next to him. He looked at his watch; it was five a.m. The salon was empty except for one Nigerian still watching the TV screen in the far corner. It looked like the same porno movie. But then, didn't they all?

The lizard eyes blinked. 'You seen the movie?'

'No, I haven't seen the movie.'

'You should see the movie,' said Dosumo. 'It's very artistic.'

'I'll try and catch it,' said Jeffrey. 'Look, Harry, I know this is an embarrassment for you, but it's a crisis. You have to help us get our NNOC contract cancelled. There'll be more contracts and more commissions, you can be sure.'

'You been upstairs?' Dosumo enquired.

Jeffrey did not seem to be getting through to him. 'No, I haven't been upstairs. I've been down here waiting for you since eleven o'clock yesterday morning. I drank two bottles of your Scotch. I've had nothing to eat. I'm hungry, my blood is congealing from the cold and I'm tired.'

'You should go upstairs and get some sleep.'

'I hear you don't get much of that upstairs,' said Jeffrey.

'You get whatever you want,' said Dosumo.

'I need your help, Harry.'

'You want to watch the movie or go upstairs?'

'Harry. If you can't help me do this right, I'm going to cancel anyway.'

'No one cancels on NNOC. No one.'

'I wouldn't count on it.'

'You'd be blacklisted if you cancelled.'

'We'd be finished if we didn't. Our customers walked away. We're dead, Harry. If you don't help us, King Brothers is through. You can't blacklist a company that doesn't exist.'

Harry sat there immobile. Then, suddenly, he began to

sway angrily from side to side. 'I was the one who persuaded the government to award you the contract. What's this going to do to my reputation?'

'What's it going to do to your reputation when we cancel?'

Again Harry was still. For a second or two a paroxysm – a violent spasm – disturbed his leathery features. It looked as though the strain of controlling his aggression was tearing at his nerve ends.

'Are you trying to blackmail me?' he said.

Jeffrey turned on Harry a deeply reproachful look and said not a word.

'What about my commission?'

'We'll pay you every cent – on the whole contract – every barrel we signed for.'

'Even if you don't lift?'

'Even if we don't lift.'

'Twenty-five cents?'

'Twenty-five cents.'

'Hmm.'

Jeffrey took another swig of whisky and waited.

'I don't know . . . I'm still concerned about my reputation.'

'Five cents for your reputation,' said Jeffrey.

With massive dignity, Harry Dosumo raised himself upright in his chair and froze Jeffrey with a contemptuous look.

'You insult me, Mr Lewis. You think Harry Dosumo trades his reputation for money?'

'I apologize,' said Jeffrey. 'Seven cents.'

'Fifteen.'

'Eight.'

'Ten.'

'Very well,' said Jeffrey. 'Ten it is.'

'Say that again,' said Jeffrey.

James Timba folded his hands on his desk and lifted his shoulders apologetically.

205

'I regret to inform you that I have instructions to cancel your contract.'

'On what grounds?'

'On the grounds that you've been shipping Nigerian crude to South Africa.'

'What?' Jeffrey was stupefied. 'Whose idea? I mean . . . who told you that?'

Timba shifted around in his seat. 'I'm not at liberty . . .'

'Come on, James. Who told you?'

'Harry Dosumo.'

Jeffrey nodded. The less he said, the better. Harry was a genius. Worth his weight in gold – or, at any rate, thirty-five cents a barrel.

'Naturally, we believe him. He would hardly tell us a lie. Besides, he stands to lose a fortune in commissions. We consider his sacrifice to be highly patriotic and public-spirited.'

'What happens to King Brothers?'

'You, my dear Jeffrey, will lose your crude entitlement under your current contract. We do not propose to make an example of you by blacklisting you, although of course you realize that we could easily do so. We consider the cancellation of your contract to be punishment enough.'

'Oh indeed,' said Jeffrey. 'It's a blow, a bitter blow.'

'You should have thought of that before diverting our crude to a prohibited destination,' Timba pointed out.

'I can assure you that it will never happen again,' said Jeffrey. He was reflecting that, despite everything, James Timba was looking remarkably cheerful. Maybe he had come into an inheritance . . . or something of that kind.

Timba inclined his head. 'I imagine not,' he said. Did the upper lid of his right eye quiver just a fraction?

There were no visitors in the anteroom. No one wanted to sign contracts these days. The secretary had to gather up the fan-blown papers herself. She scowled at Jeffrey ferociously as he left and he scowled right back.

Could this be love, he wondered.

*   *   *

206

The sixth of December 1974. The partners were holding their third annual meeting at the Grand Hotel Dolder.

It was a gloomy one.

Mort gave them the facts of life.

'Three customers – the Italians, Atlantic and Orient and Pacific Odyssey reneged – cancelled on us. We went to the suppliers to see what help we could get – either to cancel, or at least to get some relief. From Fuad we got zilch. From the Iranians we got nothing either. They made some noises about giving us a ten per cent volume reduction, but that's something we can always arrange by adjusting the size and number of shipments, so it doesn't mean a damn thing.

'From the Nigerians – well, thanks to Jeffrey, they agreed to cancel. It cost us thirty-five cents a barrel in commissions, or about five million dollars, but it saved us a whole lot more. Jeffrey – you're a goddam genius.'

Sam and Ruby patted Jeffrey on the back and he did his best to look modest.

'That's the good news,' Mort went on. 'The bad news is that we stand to make huge losses on the other two contracts. Now, we can play around ... we can delay shipments even longer, we can spread the red into next year's balance sheet. But whichever way you cut it, the position is bad. We're in trouble, deep trouble. We're long nearly eighty thousand barrels of crude a day. That's four million tons, or thirty million barrels. Right now, at this moment, we're losing a dollar fifty a barrel.'

Sam whistled.

'Forty-five million dollars,' said Jeffrey. 'It's a disaster.'

'And the market's still falling,' added Mort.

'What's the bottom line?' asked Ruby.

'Hard to say.' Mort crossed to the bar, calmly poured himself a bourbon, topped it up with soda and sat down. 'We're trading spot cargoes. The market is not exactly booming, but there's business out there. We're scratching around, looking for counter-business, barters, whatever ... we'll need to be more adventurous and more active.'

He made it sound like they had been asleep until now.

207

'Tell us the worst,' said Jeffrey.

Mort studied his glass. 'OK. Here it is. With luck and a superhuman effort, I calculate this year's balance sheet will show a loss of twenty-five million bucks. Next year's . . . who knows? Maybe less, maybe more.'

Sam collapsed in an armchair. 'We're finished.'

Ruby's face was a mask, as usual. 'It's not too great,' he said.

'It's the end,' said Jeffrey. 'Whichever way you look at it . . . it's the end of the line.'

They all looked at Mort. He sipped his drink, nodded, satisfied that the mixture was right, and set the glass down on the table beside him.

'Who says so?'

'For God's sake, man.' Jeffrey had a sudden urge to grab Mort round the neck and shake him. He found his steely control, his damned supercilious arrogant manner, irritating as hell. 'We say so. We're finished . . . bankrupt.'

Sam glanced at Mort from under his brows, shamefaced. 'I'm sorry . . . I . . . no one wants to, but I have to agree with Jeffrey.'

Ruby looked at the floor. He too agreed with Jeffrey, but he wasn't ready to say so. Not yet.

Mort revolved his glass on the table. Then he moved it a fraction to the right.

'Bankruptcy's a voluntary act. We're bankrupt when we choose to be. Not before.'

'Bullshit!' Jeffrey strode across the room and towered over Mort. 'Don't give us that crap. When the banks see our year-end figures they'll jump on our backs like hungry tigers. They'll call our loans and that will be that. Finito. You don't have to file under Chapter Eleven to be bankrupt, you just have to be broke.' He turned away, his voice dropping. 'Mort . . .' He shook his head helplessly. Just for a moment he felt the prick of tears at the back of his eyes, then he was in control again. 'It's a tough business . . . we had a dream . . . now it's time to face reality.'

For a long time no one said a word. Mort sat with his head bowed.

When he raised it, they were looking at him again.

'I won't let them win,' he muttered.

'Who are you talking about?' said Jeffrey.

'Edmund Meyer . . . Jack Greenberg . . . they did this to me.'

Jeffrey's face was hard. 'That's the trouble with you, Mort. This isn't business for you. This is some damned private war between you and the Oil Corporation. Let me tell you – no one else in this room gives a fuck about those guys. What we care about is the company, and right now the company is down the drain. I say we file for a reorganization under Chapter Eleven.'

Mort stood up slowly, moved across to the window, and looked down, way down to the Lake of Zurich. What was it he had said at the first meeting? . . . 'It's on top of the world . . . that's where I hope we'll all end up . . .'

He turned to face them.

'Jeffrey's right. We're dead. The only question is, do we want to lie down? We've taken a hard knock. It's a setback – more than a setback – it's a goddam catastrophe. But don't you see? There's only one way to go now, and that's up. Any of you have anything better to do? . . . OK, let's put it to the vote. On this one we have to be unanimous. Either we file under Chapter Eleven, or we keep right on going. Whatever you decide, you should know that the last couple of years have been the most exciting, the happiest of my life. You're the greatest partners any man could have.'

You had to hand it to Mort, Jeffrey was thinking. He was at his best when the odds were against him. What a speech! The sneaky bastard!

'If Mort has that much confidence in us, I don't think we should let him down,' said Sam.

They were looking at Ruby.

'There's this deli on Sixty-Eighth, round the corner from the office . . . they sell the best chocolate eclairs. Good eclairs are tough to find. I'd like to stick around.'

209

'Up to you, Jeffrey,' said Mort.

Jeffrey was shaking his head as though he could not believe what he was hearing.

He picked up a bottle of champagne and examined the label. 'Who needs this shit?' he said. 'I suggest we order Cristal next year.'

'Next year?'

'Cristal,' said Jeffrey firmly. 'That's my proposal. Of course, all major decisions have to be unanimous.'

'So let's vote on it,' said Sam. 'Those in favour of Cristal?'

Four hands were raised.

Mort turned away to the window. 'Thanks,' he said. His voice sounded a little strange.

'It's not going to be a piece of cake,' said Sam.

'Tell me about it,' said Ruby.

Mort was grinning. He felt good. He felt terrific. For some reason, he was more confident than he had ever been.

Now he knew they were going to make it.

*   *   *

'You think we'll survive?' said Ruby.

Mort did not answer the question directly. 'We need to do something about Jack Greenberg.'

'And Edmund Meyer?'

'Jack's his dog. Let's deal with him first. He was the one who destroyed our contracts.'

'He damn near destroyed us, too.'

'If we don't stop him now, he'll finish the job.' Mort tapped the telexes on his desk into a neat pile, perfect, symmetrical.

'What are you going to do?'

'I'll do something. I'll put out a contract on him.'

Ruby was startled – until he saw the grin on Mort's face. 'You're joking.'

'Sure I am,' said Mort. 'What else?'

*

210

Jack's face was shinier than ever. His dark grey worsted suit was close-fitting and immaculately pressed. His light brown hair fell just the permissible inch over his unruffled forehead and not a wisp of grey blemished the young, dynamic, upwardly mobile image Jack so assiduously cultivated. His barber saw to that.

He was pleased with life – even more pleased with himself. And he cared not a damn who knew it. He allowed himself a scornful glance at Mort's ill-cut, sombre suit, nondescript tie and plain white polyester shirt. The man did not know the meaning of the phrase 'custom-made' – so much was clear. There was something primitive about Mort. He simply did not belong in the circles he so clearly aspired to.

Mort, for his part, did not even notice how Jack was dressed. The custom-made suit, the Yves Saint Laurent tie, the Rolex chronometer, the Tiffany gold cuff-links – none of them impressed him. He saw only Jack – smiling, devious Jack – saw him still playing games. Dangerous games. Jack was no longer a joke. Jack was life-threatening. Not that Mort's thought processes were complicated by base emotions like fear or resentment; they were a waste of time. Jack Greenberg was in the way. Something had to be done about him.

'I thought we agreed to call a truce?'

Jack smiled his friendliest smile. 'No idea what you're talking about, Mort. If anyone's fighting, it sure isn't me.'

'First the banks. Now, you're stealing our customers.'

'Aw, come on, Mort. It's not like you to squeal when you're hurt. This is a tough business. You know that. You've been in it long enough. If your customers prefer to trade with a well-established company with a proven track record, why then, that's their privilege. Don't come whining to me.'

'You can't stop me,' said Mort.

'I can have a ball trying,' said Jack, grinning.

For a few seconds the two men challenged each other with their eyes.

'Why?'

Jack lay back in his chair and stretched his legs. He was enjoying himself.

'They call it competition, Mort. That's all it is. Healthy competition.' He raised his glass. 'May the best man win.'

It was obvious to Mort that he was not getting any-where. Jack was not the kind to appreciate subtlety. The only thing he respected was the sword in the hand.

'I gave you a break, once,' said Mort. 'If I had turned your file over to E.M., you'd have been out of a job in five minutes. You'd have been in jail.'

'Bullshit!'

'Stealing? Stealing from the Oil Corporation? You call that bullshit? I call it theft. So would a grand jury.'

'You can't prove a thing. You gave me the file,' said Jack sullenly.

'That's right, Jack. I gave you the file. But what I never told you was I kept a copy. I have it all, every phoney invoice, every fake charter party.'

'So what?'

'I'll accept fair competition, but if you keep on playing dirty, I'll turn the file over to E.M.'

'That's not your style, Mort,' Jack said. 'You don't like to soil your hands. You lurk in the shadows and let others step in the shit for you. I know you. I know every mean little trick you ever played, so don't pretend you're a fucking saint. Who do you think you are, telling me how to run my business?' Jack's mouth twisted. He enjoyed tormenting Mort.

Mort looked at him with contempt. 'Do what you like – just as long as you don't tread on my toes.'

'You have big feet, Mort.'

'I'm warning you – do your own thing and stay away from me.'

'Tell that to E.M. He's the one who hates your guts.'

'Let him play the Godfather if that's what he wants,' said

Mort, 'but don't you get involved. It could be dangerous.'

Jack wagged his finger in mock rebuke. 'Threats, Mort? Naughty. A nice Jewish boy like you.'

* * *

'Your wife on line three.'

Mort was uncertain what to do. He and Julie had a dinner date with Leo Stendel. And yet right now he had more important things to do with his time.

He flipped the button. 'Julie, I'm sorry. I can't make it. I have problems.'

'Let the problems wait. They'll still be there tomorrow. We already cancelled on him once.'

'You go,' said Mort. 'I'll try to catch up with you later.'

'How long is it going to be like this?'

'Like what?'

'Like sixteen hours a day. Like we don't have a life together any more.'

'I told you the first year or two would be tough.'

'Sure, you did. The first year or two. What about the last ten? Whatever happened to them?'

'I'll make it up to you, honey.'

She wondered how he was going to do that.

'Mort isn't coming,' she said. 'Maybe we should call it off.'

Leo looked disappointed. 'Must we?'

'I feel badly, Leo. It's getting to be a habit.'

'Not all habits are bad ones,' he said.

'This one is.'

'Not for me, it's not. It's the best thing that ever happened.'

'I bet you say that to all your mistresses.' She laboured the word. It was troubling her.

'I don't have any mistresses. You're not my mistress.'

'Let's postpone it,' she said. 'Please.'

'What will you do?'

'What I always do. Go home, grab a bite, watch the tube, go to bed. Alone.'

'Maybe Mort's the guy with a mistress.'

'He is. Name of King Brothers.'

'Look, I know a quiet place in the Village. They specialize in cheese soufflés and the wine is superb. How about it?'

Julie was torn, but she couldn't face the prospect of yet another lonely evening.

'It sure beats Johnny Carson,' she said.

The 'quiet place' was Leo's apartment. The mixture for the cheese soufflé was in the icebox. It seemed it was Leo's speciality.

'You're very sure of yourself, aren't you?'

'I was hoping,' he said.

She shook her head. 'You knew I'd come.' She resented it. She resented being taken for granted. On top of feeling guilty about the relationship, it made her feel cheap.

'Look,' said Leo, 'let's spell it out. We're having an affair. You're married, I'm divorced. If that's something you can't live with, then we can stop having sex. That's OK. I would hate it, but it's OK. I could handle it. But if we stop having sex, it doesn't mean I stop loving you. I want you to know that. It also doesn't mean you stop working in the Gallery, because you do a superb job there. Most important of all, it doesn't mean that we stop being lovers, because we can still be lovers without screwing. Do I make myself clear?'

'Very clear,' she said.

'So you let me know what you want to do,' he said. 'I'm going to put the soufflé in the oven.'

'That gives us fifteen minutes,' said Julie.

The corners of his mouth rose, just a little.

'Twenty,' he said, 'if you like it to rise real high.'

'That's the way I like it,' she said.

They twisted and turned on the bed, biting and clawing, digging their hands into each other's bodies, frantic with the torment of their craving. Julie moaned and clasped him tight as he plunged into her . . . tighter and tighter . . . until they were like one body. She wanted to be part

214

of him, always . . . but he broke away from her, turned her over roughly and held her face down, digging between her buttocks, as his fingers – his whole hand – beat the warm, wet cavern of her thighs. They hung poised, at the peak of ecstasy for a few brief seconds . . . pulsated . . . and slowly, dreamily, drifted down, down, back to the consciousness of who they were, the awareness of time and place.

Surely it could never be as good as this with anyone else, they were both thinking, but neither of them dared say it for fear of breaking the spell.

He woke her gently. 'How do you feel?'

'I can't tell you how I feel. I feel, that's all.'

He understood what she meant. He always seemed to understand.

'What are we going to do?' he said, hopelessly.

Julie put her arms round his neck. 'We're going to do the same thing all over again,' she said.

*　　*　　*

He should have been more accepting, less jealous of Amy now that he had Jane, Sam reflected, but, of course, things never worked out like that. The fact was, he was more jealous than ever.

He took to phoning her at irregular intervals – from the office, from restaurants, from airport lounges. When she was not at home – and that was very often – he suffered for the whole day, tormenting himself with the suspicion that she was with some man. When she answered, he was embarrassed, not knowing what to say to her. She knew exactly what he was up to. Naturally, she knew. Whenever he convinced himself that he was being most subtle, she saw right through him. In the evening, she would challenge him to cross-examine her. She said nothing, only daring him with her eyes, but he would look away, afraid to meet the challenge, afraid, he supposed, to lose her. There were some things too painful to talk about, some problems best left unresolved.

215

One day, he left the office on an impulse and drove to their apartment. He parked down the road, where he could see the street entrance, turned off the engine and waited.

What in God's name was he doing? He didn't even know if she was in or out. He had not planned anything; he was acting on impulse, something completely out of character for him. An hour later, he was suddenly overcome with shame. He drove back to the office and phoned her.

She had been in all morning, she said. Edward had a cough, so she had kept him home.

For the rest of the day, he felt good.

The next day, he was twitchy again. There was too much to do and he really shouldn't leave the office, but he felt compelled to. He was like a junkie needing a fix.

He buzzed Karl and told him he had to go out. Karl would hold the fort. Karl was born to hold the fort. It was what he most enjoyed doing. What would he ever do without him?

He drove to the apartment, parked thirty yards away and waited. He had no idea how long he was going to stay there; he only knew that this was where he had to be.

Thirty minutes later, a taxi pulled up outside. Amy ran out and jumped in. He followed it – with some difficulty, at first. He had never done such a thing before. Who did, except in movies?

The taxi appeared to be heading for Zurich. Why had she not taken her own car? Was there a parking problem where she was going? Perhaps she thought she would reach her destination quicker that way. Maybe – and this had been his first thought – she suspected that she might be followed by someone who knew her car. Someone like Sam.

The taxi stopped outside, of all places, the Kantonsspital on Rämistrasse. Amy ran into the hospital.

He sat in the car and waited. The traffic police kept moving him on, but each time he would circle the block and return. After an hour or so, he began to wonder if he had missed her. When she had still not appeared after two hours, he started the engine and left it running for a few minutes, undecided what to do. Then he turned it off again. To hell with the police. He jumped out, locked the car door and walked quickly into the hospital.

To the left of the entrance was the reception counter. Until he approached the glass partition, he had not the slightest idea what he was going to say.

'Ist . . . Ist Herr Siegfried Gerber einer ihrer patienten?'

The girl was writing something on a yellow admissions card. She didn't bother to look up.

'Darf ich sie fragen wer sie sind?'

'Ich bin sein bruder.' His brother . . . all men are brothers.

She consulted the index. 'Herr Gerber ist im Zimmer 328. Dritten stock.'

'Danke.' He walked across to the elevator. The girl was not looking. She had gone back to her writing.

He hesitated, turned abruptly, hurried out of the entrance hall and drove off.

On the way back to Wald, he kept thinking how lucky he was not to have got a parking ticket.

'What's the use of lying? You're still screwing around with him. I know it.'

'It's over.' Amy was calm, in a flat disinterested way that infuriated him.

'That's what you said last time.'

'It's over,' she said. 'This time it's different.'

'Why different?'

'Because he's dead. Siegfried's dead.' Her mouth was set in a firm line and her eyes were dull and lifeless.

Sam was shocked. He did not know what to say.

'It was quick,' she said. 'Cancer. He refused treatment.'

She was, suddenly, infinitely pitiable, like that tropical fish, dead now, drained of colour, floating on the surface of the tank. He wanted to put his arms around her, to say it was all right, that he forgave her.

217

'They wouldn't let me see him at the end. I wasn't family . . . only the woman he loved. His wife was there. She meant nothing to him.'

The woman he loved. So Gerber had lied to him. And Amy? Had she lied too? He wanted desperately to know if she had loved Gerber, but he dared not ask. Not now. Anyway, what was the point? What did it matter any more?

What a dumb question. It mattered.

What was it she had seen in the man? What was so special about him? Sam recalled his own attachment to Siegfried Gerber; how he had admired his strength, his self-assurance and, above all, his drily humorous, wry acceptance of life and whatever problems it brought.

He tried to take Amy's hand, but she pulled it away abruptly. She wanted nothing from him, neither compassion nor love. She was cocooned in her grief. He desired and hated her at the same time. That man, that old man had reached out to her, had touched her, made her love him in a way that Sam had never been able to.

He went into the kitchen and made himself some coffee. The touch of the warm cup and the cold metal spoon, the hum of the icebox, the ticking of the clock on the wall – all these were reassuring. He needed to feel and hear such ordinary, commonplace things, things that had always been there in his life and always would be.

If Gerber had lived, Sam might have been able to win Amy back. Now that he was dead, he knew for certain that he had lost her.

*   *   *

In a side street, downtown Manhattan, just off Park Avenue, was the Bistro Français, Edgar Proktor's favourite restaurant. It was a cosy corner of Paris, American-style; a few tables with the mandatory red and white check tablecloths, hanging lamps covered in the same, murals of the Côte d'Azur and an intimate softly lit bar where the rich and the overdrawn of Manhattan could rub shoulders

218

with the impoverished and the disillusioned, the famous and the infamous. They could also, as they say, touch base with some of the choicest female bases New York had to offer.

Some said Edgar owned the place. If he did not, he ought to have done. He spent most of his spare time there and a great deal of his money. The bar must have paid its way on the liquor he alone consumed.

He had his reservations about Jack Greenberg, but Jack could be very convincing and the tale he had to tell was a fascinating one.

'The guy's a wheeler-dealer. Known him for years. He's Dutch – name of Van Gelden.'

'I've heard of him,' said Edgar. 'Isn't he an arms dealer?'

'He dabbles,' said Jack laconically.

'His reputation isn't so hot.'

'There's a whole bunch of guys in our industry whose reputations aren't so hot. If we cut them all from the pack there wouldn't be anyone left to do business with.'

He was not so wrong at that.

'So, what's he offering?'

'Crude. Iranian. Light and Heavy. It's cheap and there's only one explanation. It has to come out of an arms barter. The guy knows nothing about crude. I can tell you for a fact that he burnt his fingers badly on an oil deal six months ago. He's happy to take his profit on the arms and offload the crude to someone he can trust – someone who'll keep the whole thing stum.'

'What's wrong with the Oil Corporation?'

'E.M. won't touch it. He won't have anything to do with the arms business. He says it's dealing in death and misery. The usual crap.'

'Why us? I hear Mort and you are not exactly buddy buddies.'

'If I tell you something, will you swear to keep quiet about it?'

'OK,' said Edgar.

'Van Gelden has promised me a fat commission if I can

219

find a reliable buyer – someone who can be trusted to keep his name out of it.'

Edgar had heard a few stories about Jack . . . taking personal commissions on company business was one of them.

He would check it out, of course. As it happened, Edgar badly needed a success, something to salvage his pride after the NIOC fiasco. That had cost the company plenty. Success . . . the one thing Mort respected. Mort was a little cool towards him these days, or was he imagining things? That guy was the one person in the world who could get under his skin. Edgar loved the bastard – almost as much as he hated him. What he craved more than anything else was Mort's approval. This could be his chance to earn it.

The story was true. Van Gelden had two hundred and thirty thousand tons of crude on a VLCC – the *Golden Fleece*. Edgar checked out the tanker carefully. It was genuine. It had already loaded and was heading out of the Persian Gulf. The owners confirmed that they had signed a charter party with Van Gelden. That meant it was his crude.

He phoned Van Gelden who was expecting his call. They agreed a price without too much haggling: ten dollars and fifty cents a barrel. Edgar calculated conservatively that he should make a couple of dollars a barrel. Three and a half million dollars. That should please Mort.

But he was not taking any chances. He contacted the man's bank. They too confirmed that they knew about the deal. He opened the letter of credit in favour of Van Gelden. It would give him the ultimate protection he needed. If the original shipping documents were not presented, Van Gelden could not draw his money.

A week later, Edgar sold the cargo to an East Coast refinery for thirteen dollars ninety – a profit of nearly three and a half dollars a barrel. Six million bucks! It was a killing. The largest profit the company had ever made on a spot transaction.

He called Jack to thank him.

'Think nothing of it. Van Gelden paid me my commission. It's me who should thank you. Just don't tell Mort I made him a millionaire. He might not appreciate it.'

Edgar laughed. He decided to tell Mort – not the whole story, or that Jack Greenberg was involved – just the basic facts.

Mort was ecstatic. He called in Ruby.

'This is a great day, Edgar,' Ruby said. 'I'm happy for you and I'm happy for the company.'

Mort smiled benignly. Edgar was over the moon. He went back to his office and called in Arlene.

'I just realized something,' he said. 'Those guys get their orgasms doing deals.'

Arlene locked the door. 'Sounds like fun,' she said. 'Want to try it?'

Henry Soames minced into Jeffrey's office. 'And how is dear Victoria?'

'Victoria who?' asked Jeffrey innocently.

'Please, dear boy, do not be coy with me. It doesn't suit you and it's an insult to my intelligence. Victoria Harcourt-Smith, wife of Sir Albert, chairman of North Sea Venture, is the lady in question.'

'As far as I know, Lady Harcourt-Smith is fine,' said Jeffrey.

'So is Sir Albert. I'm told he has an excellent chance of striking oil.'

'Are you serious?'

'While you've been drilling away in Eaton Square, Sir Albert has been sinking bore holes all over the place. The latest area looks promising.'

'What are you up to, Henry?'

'I'm trying to do all of us some good. That's what I'm up to. North Sea Venture is a consortium of BP, a UK bank and a few wealthy businessmen. Rosemary Atherton, whom you know – and whom our friend Mort knows even better – has the ear of the BP board. Victoria has the ear

221

of Sir Albert and he's not only the consortium chairman, he's also the representative of the independent investors. Thanks to you, he's well aware of King Brothers' interest in a possible participation in North Sea Venture.'

'I only hope he's not aware that . . . I mean . . . that we're . . .'

'Shafting in Belgravia? He probably is, but he's so besotted with Victoria he'll do anything she wants as long as she stays with him.'

'We talked about taking a participation,' Jeffrey said. 'Mort is against it. He thinks too much money is lost in oil exploration. I must say I tend to agree with him.'

'High risk it may be, but the potential is enormous. If they strike oil – and they will – it'll be too late. They'll never let you in.'

'You think they'd let us in now?'

'Some of the independent punters are getting cold feet. Costs are increasing and, so far, they've seen nothing for their money. Most businessmen look for quick returns.'

'Who can blame them?'

'Twenty-five million dollars will buy you five per cent,' said Henry.

'A snip.'

'You may jeer, dear boy, but I tell you it's a bargain. What's more, it may be the only chance you ever get to join an oil consortium.'

'How about five million dollars for twenty-five per cent?'

'Don't make bad jokes so early in the morning,' said Henry, flinching. 'Especially about money.'

'It won't fly,' said Jeffrey.

'It won't fly,' echoed Henry mockingly. 'What a hip, new-world expression. Beware the insidious influence of your transatlantic partners, Jeffrey. What will it do then? Run? Walk? Hop? Crawl, perhaps?'

'Henry,' said Jeffrey patiently, 'I'm a busy man.'

'Another sparklingly original observation. For shame, Jeffrey. I thought you were an original – a font of creativity, not a dripping fawcet.'

222

'Dear God!' said Jeffrey, head in hands. 'How have I deserved this?'

'You've committed the unpardonable sin, my son. You have wandered from the paths of sound business judgement. Say three Hail Marys and make me a reasonable counter-offer.'

Jeffrey's patience had expired. 'I took by the throat the uncircumcised dog and smote him – thus!' he said, threatening Henry.

Henry backed away. 'I'm Catholic,' he said. 'They don't circumcise Catholics.'

Jeffrey grabbed a paperknife from his desk. 'There's always a first time,' he said, advancing menacingly.

Henry ran.

The partners talked about it and decided to submit an offer. It would be a new development for King Brothers: risky but tempting. One thing was for sure: if the consortium struck oil it would put King Brothers in a new category. To have long-term supply contracts was the dream of every trader; to have your own oil – that was something else. It put you up there with the real oil companies. It meant you could go anywhere in the world and talk to producers as one of them. The possibilities were exciting, unlimited.

They left the negotiating details to Henry Soames. Jeffrey phoned Sir Albert a couple of times. He sounded pompous, but pleasant enough. Henry was right. Victoria had done her stuff. So, apparently, had Rosemary. It paid to have the right kind of influence.

Jeffrey sat in the bar of Brown's Hotel in Albermarle Street waiting for Henry. The offer was on the consortium's desk. It expired at close of business: twenty million dollars for ten per cent participation. According to Henry, the initial reaction to the offer had been 'caustic, dear boy'. And yet it had not been thrown out. They were getting to the end of a long process of negotiation. Either the consortium accepted, or the deal was dead.

223

At five o'clock, Victoria appeared, ordered a bottle of Dom Perignon and drank three glasses straight off.

Jeffrey had been drinking steadily since lunchtime; he gazed in fascination at Victoria's swelling right breast, two-thirds of which was spilling over the snug embrace of her black lace bra, attracting the light of day and a great deal of attention. The hell with it, the damned consortium could wait. He swept up his coat, grabbed Victoria by the arm and rushed out of the hotel.

The first session was a battle. They sprang out of their respective corners and attacked each other like boxers fighting for a million-dollar purse. At this rate, their lovemaking could not last long. After a few minutes, they lay back on the bed, panting. Jeffrey was drained – literally and emotionally. He was also conscience stricken.

Victoria had other ideas. She turned her back on him and nestled her buttocks against his thighs, tempting him to take her from behind. Her buttocks were firm and full. One of them had a tiny dimple on it, Jeffrey noticed. He was guiding the tip of his stone-hard lust between the cheeks when the phone rang.

'Let it ring,' he groaned.

'It might be Henry.'

He twisted round and grabbed the receiver.

'I trust I'm not interrupting anything,' said Henry.

'Fuck off!' said Jeffrey.

'That's no way for an oil producer to talk.'

'Henry, why don't you – ' Jeffrey suddenly focused on what Henry had said. 'An oil producer!'

'They accepted your offer.'

'I don't believe it.'

'They need the money. I told you. Congratulations! This is the biggest deal you ever made – or ever will.'

'You're a genius, Henry. I love you. See you later. Right now I'm in conference.'

'Fancy,' said Henry. 'Is that what you're in?'

*

Two weeks after Edgar concluded his famous transaction with Van Gelden, the arms dealer, Karl Andermatt was on the line from Wald.

'You remember your arms dealer friend? The one you bought the Iranian from?'

'Don't I ever,' said Edgar. 'Van Gelden. My hero.'

'The cargo you bought – was it afloat?'

'Sure.'

'What was the tanker's name?'

'The *Golden Fleece*. Why?'

'Van Gelden sold another cargo of Iranian to a Lebanese friend of mine.'

'So? He had more than one cargo to sell. No sweat.'

'That's what I thought,' said Karl, 'until I checked the name of the other tanker.'

Edgar went cold.

'What was it?'

'The *Golden Fleece*,' said Karl.

'That's impossible. There's some misunderstanding.'

'There's no misunderstanding.'

'It's a later voyage,' said Edgar. 'It has to be.'

'I checked. The dates are identical.'

Edgar's hands started to shake. He was sweating. 'What are you saying?'

'I'm sorry, Edgar. I'm saying Van Gelden sold the same cargo twice – to two different buyers. It's a sting. You've been conned.' Karl waited. At first he thought he'd been cut off. 'Edgar?'

Edgar couldn't speak.

'My friend already paid him. Van Gelden drew under the letter of credit. Edgar, did you open the L/C?'

'Yes.'

'Did he draw the money yet?'

'Not yet.' Edgar slammed the phone down. He needed help. He needed help badly, but he could not go to Mort. He could not do that to save his life.

*

Edgar and Ruby sat opposite the Vice-President of the Bank of Geneva. Edgar was still shaking. He craved a drink and there wasn't any around.

Ruby was icy calm.

'We opened the letter of credit through your bank,' he said. 'The seller has to present the shipping documents under the L/C, thirty days from bill of lading date – that's today.'

'He already presented them,' said the vice-president of the Bank of Geneva.

'They're forgeries,' said Ruby.

'Wrong, Mr King. The documents are perfectly genuine. I already asked my Letter of Credit Department. They're checking them right now. If there are no discrepancies, then the documents are in order and we have to pay the supplier. We have no option. We have an obligation to do so.'

'You also have an obligation to protect your client,' said Ruby.

'The supplier is our client, too,' said the vice-president.

'We're talking twenty million dollars,' said Ruby. 'The man's a crook – a con merchant. He sold the same cargo twice to two different companies.'

'Where's your proof?'

'I don't have any proof. Not yet. We only just found out. I need time.'

'Our bank's responsibility is only to check the documents,' said the VP. 'You know about documentary letters of credit. We have no reason not to pay.'

'Goddam it! I just gave you a reason.'

'I regret. It's not good enough.'

'I can't believe what I'm hearing.' Ruby banged his fist on the table so hard the ashtray jumped. 'You're going to hand over twenty million dollars to a crook, just like that?'

One of the phones on the banker's desk rang. He picked it up, listened briefly. Put it down again.

'The documents are in order. They're absolutely genuine and there are no discrepancies.'

'I need a drink,' said Edgar. No one was listening to him.

Ruby stared, unblinking, at the vice-president. 'What do you intend to do?'

'I'd like to help, Mr King,' said the VP, 'but there's nothing I can do.'

'Give me one hour.'

'What for?'

'To check the documents.'

'We already checked them. They're in order.'

Ruby's eyes were cold, his expression stony. Edgar had never seen him like this before.

'Mister, you'd better be sure, because if you pay out and this guy really is a crook – and if I find one single discrepancy, just the tiniest little discrepancy between the documents we listed in the L/C and the documents he presented, then I'm going to sue you – not for twenty million dollars, but for five hundred million. The damages for negligence will be a record, I promise you,' said Ruby.

There was a long silence while the banker fingered a glass paperweight on his desk. Judging from the expression on his face, he would gladly have thrown it at Ruby.

'I'll give you an hour,' he said.

Ruby and Edgar sat at a small table in one of the bank's claustrophobic waiting rooms. They sat opposite each other, checking every document meticulously, word for word, letter for letter, against the L/C, searching vainly for a discrepancy. As Ruby read the documents he handed them over to Edgar to re-check: weight certificates, quality certificates, certificates of origin and bills of lading. There was nothing wrong with them. They were all in order.

'The hell of it is,' said Ruby, 'they're not forgeries, either. Somehow, the guy was able to get his hands on two sets of genuine documents. He must have bribed a lot of people.'

'What now?' The sweat ran down Edgar's neck. He felt nauseous.

'We check them again,' said Ruby. 'What else?'

Edgar looked at his watch. Five minutes to go. His eyes

were swimming. He could no longer focus on the words . . . it was hopeless. He could feel the panic crawling up from his stomach to his throat, like some loathsome parasitic monster growing inside him. It was the end – the end of his career and the end of King Brothers. And who was responsible? Edgar Proktor, drunk, womanizer, lay-about and smart ass. The sweat was welling up in his armpits, the saliva oozing from the back of his mouth. He was about to throw up.

Opposite him, Ruby was not even aware that Edgar had stopped checking the documents. His concentration was absolute. Edgar watched him, fascinated. Who would have thought this baby-faced, plump little Jewish guy with the bland expression and the clever brown eyes – who would have thought he had steel in him? He looked about as macho as Mickey Mouse. Not, it seemed, a man's man, not the sort of regular guy someone like Edgar could respect – not, that is, until this moment. Now, he realized that the power was in that nondescript, dumpy figure. Where it came from, God alone knew. But it was there, no question about it. Ruby sat in the tiny room, totally absorbed, moving only to turn a page or brush the cigarette ash off his shirt, his pot-belly resting comfortably on the table, his attitude relaxed, like a scholar studying a passage in a law tome of great theoretical but little practical interest. Maybe that was Ruby's secret. He had the knack of switching off his emotions, of standing back from the problem and illuminating it with the cold blinding beam of his intellect. Edgar remembered what Ruby had once said to him about success. 'It's a game you play. I want to play it better than anyone else.'

One minute to go. Ruby sat back and looked at his watch. He had small hands, Edgar noticed. The phone on the desk rang. Edgar jumped. Ruby picked it up, grim-faced.

'I know,' he said. 'Time's up.'

And how it is, thought Edgar. For all of us.

'We found a discrepancy,' said Ruby.

Of course, it had to be a lie. The guy was playing for

time. There was no way he could have found a discrepancy.

'I suggest you move your ass over here,' said Ruby, and slammed down the phone.

Edgar had never heard him talk to anyone like that. The guy was really something. You had to admire him. He was going down, but he was going down fighting.

Ruby jabbed the letter of credit with his finger.

'There it is,' he told the banker. 'The L/C calls for bills of lading to ship "Iranian Light Crude Oil".'

'Exactly so.'

'Look at these bills of lading. They describe the oil as "Iranian Light Crude". The word "Oil" is missing.'

The banker smiled condescendingly. 'It's quite obviously the same thing,' he said. 'Iranian Light is Iranian Light.'

'It's a discrepancy,' said Ruby.

'It's an insignificant difference in phraseology,' said the VP.

'It's not your function to decide what is significant and what is insignificant,' said Ruby. 'A difference in phraseology is a discrepancy. I'm a lawyer.'

'If that's a discrepancy, then half the documents we process in this bank have discrepancies,' said the banker.

'Tell that to the court when we sue you. That should impress them. They'll be interested to hear it,' said Ruby. He sat back, arms folded. 'It's a discrepancy,' he repeated.

The banker winced. 'It has no practical significance,' he insisted.

'It's a discrepancy.'

The man was clenching and unclenching his fists, fighting to control his temper.

'A – minor – discrepancy. That's all it is.'

'Major. Minor. Who cares? The documents are not in order. You agree?'

The banker looked at Ruby with venom in his eyes. For a long moment he was silent. 'The documents . . . are not . . . in order,' he muttered.

Ruby leaned back in his chair and grinned cheekily.

'I knew we could count on your cooperation,' he said.

*   *   *

Sam never questioned whether it was right that he and Amy should stay together – right for him, right for her, or right for the children. He knew only that he wanted her around, that, somehow, they should try to work things out.

He began, consciously, to court her again. They had intimate dinners in candlelit bistros, lunches at lakeside hotels. More attention was what she needed, he felt certain. That would solve everything. He had neglected her. The subject of Siegfried Gerber was never mentioned again. As far as he was concerned, it never would be. She seemed happier now, more like her old self and, seeing her happy, he too was content.

They stood outside the grey, concrete, box-like building in Wald where Sam had his office. It was raining – a light, steady, autumn drizzle. The only touch of colour that relieved the misty Swiss October day was the red of the geraniums, still gallantly blooming in the windowboxes.

And then, of course, there was Amy herself. She would have brightened the gloomiest day. She was wearing a tailored suit of canary yellow and her long silky blonde hair had no adornment and no cover. Amy scorned such things. She derived a sensual pleasure from the soft touch of the breeze in her hair and the brush of rain on her cheek. Sam was forever trying to protect her with coats and scarves and umbrellas, but she laughed and evaded him. She wanted to be open to the wind and the rain, to see the clouds chasing across the sky, to be, in a word, free.

She kissed him lightly on the cheek and squeezed his arm. 'It was fun,' she said. From her, that was the best compliment of all.

'Me too,' he said. 'Remember, you promised to say hi to Karl.'

Amy wrinkled her nose. 'Must I, honey? He's so dull.'

'I wish you would. The man's been such a treasure over the years. Just give him a few minutes. He's a good guy. He's very Swiss and reserved. That's his style.'

'Just my type,' she said.

'Besides, he's the hero of the hour. He'd really appreciate it if you took some notice of him.'

'If it's important,' she said.

'It is.'

She tossed her hair. 'Lead me to him.'

Sam left the two of them alone together. For Karl, the embarrassment was manifestly acute. He grinned and squirmed and was tongue-tied. How lost he was around women. Being with the boss's wife was purgatory. Shifting and shuffling in the centre of his office, he clasped his hands in front of him apologetically, almost protectively, like a small boy. She noticed how pale they were – his hands – the backs covered with a down of black hair. Pale hands, pale face – a colourless man. She wondered if he ever saw the sun, or felt the wind on his face.

She sat on the sofa in the corner and was amused to see that he took the chair furthest from her, so threatening did he appear to find her.

'You've been with Sam a long time,' she said. 'Longer than I have, I guess.'

'Ten years,' said Karl, studying his shoes.

'You must be very attached to him.'

Karl said nothing.

'I know how fond he is of you.'

'Sam's a good man.'

'Yes,' she said. 'Sam's a good man.' She had to think hard what to say next. Obviously, Karl was not going to be much help. 'When did we last meet? It was quite some time ago, wasn't it?'

'It was at one of Mr Gerber's parties,' he said. He was rushing his words. 'I . . .' He looked embarrassed again. 'It was years ago.'

He knew about them, of course. Not that she gave a damn. He was trying desperately not to make her feel

231

uncomfortable and that was kind. It seemed that the world was full of kind men, like Sam and Karl.

'Are you married?' she asked, after another pause.

He blushed and stammered. 'No, I'm a . . . what I think you call a . . . confirmed bachelor.'

'Don't you like women?'

Scarlet again, an even darker hue. 'I . . . I . . . If what you're asking me is . . .'

'I'm not,' she said, although, of course, she was.

'I'm not a homosexual. I like women . . . perhaps I'm a little shy.'

'Just a little,' she said and smiled.

Suddenly, he was not embarrassed any more. He smiled back at her spontaneously, for the first time, responding to her casual, natural warmth. Women were so rarely interested in Karl. He was flattered and pleased.

'I like computers,' he said suddenly. 'You want to see?'

It was the last thing she had expected. He was like a kid desperate to show her his favourite toy.

'Why not?' she said.

Sitting at the computer, he was a different person: amusing, self-assured, stimulating. He was in command. He explained what he was doing, how he was achieving the extraordinary effects she saw on the screen. To her astonishment, she was having fun. For nearly an hour she sat there beside him while he performed his magic – conjuring words, numbers and intricate green pictures on the blank grey face in front of them. Some of the time she watched the screen. More and more she watched Karl, fascinated by his dedication, stirred by his excitement. Now his face was no longer pale – it was pink and animated. It was a transformation. She had breathed life into a robot.

When he turned to her, as he did from time to time, to explain some especially complex spell he had cast on the screen, something about him, some electrical charge perhaps, generated by his almost fanatical intensity, made her shiver. She felt the hairs rise on the nape of her neck.

*   *   *

It was clear. Either Jack Greenberg had been involved in the Van Gelden con, or he had known what the man was up to. One way or the other, he had contemptuously dismissed Mort's warning. He was proving, somewhat to Mort's surprise, to be an unrelenting and dangerous enemy. He had become a threat to the existence of King Brothers. Mort could not be sure when or where he would strike next. It was a situation he could tolerate no longer.

'It's the third time he's tried. Next time he might succeed,' said Ruby.

Mort was not in a good mood. He was jumpy.

'What do you want me to do?'

'You once said you'd make him see the error of his ways. Talk to him.'

Mort made a face. 'Sometimes you're so goddam naive. I already did. Jack's not a man you can reason with. He understands only one thing.'

'What's that?'

One day, Ruby would have to face the facts of life, the kind you never found in books, nor, apparently, on the Upper West Side or in Midtown Manhattan.

'I'll tell you, Ruby. What Jack understands is punishment.'

'Punishment? How do you mean?'

'It's very simple. He knows how to hand it out, but he's not too good at taking it. When he hits you, you have to hit him back.'

'An eye for an eye?'

'Something like that.'

'So, let's hit him.'

'This isn't like the movies, Ruby. If it were, it would be easy. We could have him dressed in a cement overcoat and dumped in the river.'

'Don't make jokes like that, Mort. I know you don't mean it, but it makes me nervous.' He blinked. 'It is a joke, isn't it?'

The catlike eyes were unwavering. 'Sure, it is. But I told

233

you before, this isn't a game. This is the real thing. If someone tries to destroy me, then I do what I have to do to defend myself.'

Ruby eyed his brother uncertainly. For a moment, it occurred to him that, perhaps, he did not know him quite as well as he had always assumed he did.

'You wouldn't do anything without talking to me first, would you?'

'Why would I do that?' said Mort. 'You're my brother. We're partners.'

Ruby nodded, satisfied.

On Mort's desk was a bunch of files. 'You read them?'

'Yes.'

'What do you think?'

'They're dynamite. The evidence is incontestable.'

'I put these together over a period of two years. Then I told Jack what I had. After that, he behaved himself. I promised him I wouldn't use them if he stopped stealing from the Oil Corporation.'

'And did he?'

'I think so.'

'You're going to send them to E.M.?'

'Yes.'

'I don't like it.'

'Why not?'

'I don't know. It's not right. It doesn't feel right.'

Mort smiled. 'It's not in the rule book – is that it? Well, how about Jack? Does he play by the rules? Was he playing fair when he fixed the banks? Or when he stole our customers? Or when he conned us? Grow up, Ruby. It's sink or swim. We're not talking morality here. We're talking survival.'

Ruby looked unhappy. 'I still don't think it's right.'

Mort picked up the files. 'I'm sending these to E.M. today.'

'What do you think he'll do?'

'Fire Jack Greenberg.'

'He won't,' said Ruby.

'Sure he will.'

'And hand you an easy victory? Never.'

'You don't understand E.M. like I do. He doesn't care about me any more. It's over and done with. The guy's a realist. If I saw him today, he'd probably wish me good luck.'

'And you say I'm naive.'

'Wait and see. He'll fire Jack and that will be the end of it. Jack will have lost his power base. End of story.'

'He'll keep him on the payroll and watch him. You deserted E.M. Remember? You broke faith. You're still a renegade.'

Edmund Meyer leafed through the files with distaste. They made painful reading. There was something deeply depressing about treachery.

It had all happened a long time ago, but it still hurt. He had been too generous to the man, foolishly generous. One thing was clear to him now. You could not buy loyalty. If you could, Jack Greenberg would have been the most loyal employee in the world, instead of which he was an ungrateful treacherous little thief.

Why had Mort sent him all this . . . this filth? To get even with Jack? Or to humiliate his former boss? Whichever it was, he was damned if he was going to give the bastard what he wanted. What a triumph it would be for Mort. How he would crow over the Oil Corporation. Think of the scandal. How could that be good for the company?

On the other hand, how could it be good to keep Jack on the payroll? A man so obviously devious and corrupt? There was something wrong with him – something about him – there always had been. He had the big wheel complex without the brains and the guts to go with it. Still, the man was a brilliant trader – with the right guidance, of course. He could no longer be trusted, but then, as E.M. had learned a long time ago, the guy you don't trust can't harm you.

235

He determined to watch Jack carefully. He would set something up, keep careful check on his activities. If Jack were still passing phoney invoices through the books, falsifying contracts and charter parties, then E.M. would hear about it. What was more, this time he would be sure to keep a record of it.

He looked again at the topmost file on his desk. The last entry was in 1965. That meant that, in a year or two, Jack Greenberg could no longer be prosecuted. The Statute of Limitations took care of that. E.M.'s sharp lively eyes were thoughtful. Not that he would ever want to have the guy put away. Or would he?

He sat there, fingering Mort's visiting card. It was typical of the man – small, modest, unpretentious. There was someone he had trusted. Not any more though. Now he was the renegade, the enemy, the man dedicated to destroying him and his life's work. So be it. There had been enemies before. He had known how to deal with them. When the time came, he would know how to deal with Mortimer King.

He locked the files in the wall safe and walked back to his desk, rubbing his hands as though trying to clean off something dirty.

Then he wrote on Mort's visiting card: 'What's new?' and had his secretary post it.

Ruby read the message from Edmund Meyer and smiled. 'What did I tell you?'

Mort's face was grim.

'There has to be a way to fix Jack Greenberg.'

'You tried. It didn't work,' said Ruby.

Mort nodded. 'There'll be a way. One day I'll find it,' he said. 'Losing those contracts set us back two years, maybe more. And that bastard did it.'

'No,' said Ruby. 'We did it. We made the decision to buy when the market had peaked. It was our mistake.'

'You think those guys would have walked out of the contracts if Jack hadn't shown them the way? Goddam him!' Ruby had seen Mort angry before, but rarely as angry as this. 'We were going to be such a success. What a dream I had. Look at us now.'

* * *

Mort flew over for the signing ceremony with North Sea Venture. Jeffrey was surprised. It was not like Mort to waste time over formalities. He was happy to have him around, but he had a sneaking feeling that Mort had another reason for his trip to London.

And of course Jeffrey was right. The truth was that Mort was missing Rosemary. For the first time in his life, he was actually missing the company of a woman. The thought of it made him apprehensive; he was not a man who cared to be 'involved'; it meant sacrificing time and it could lead to loss of control – control of his life and of the people around him. A woman could be a perilous distraction for a man so single-minded.

It was not simply loving someone that he shied away from. In his way he loved Julie, but a wife was necessary, functional; she fulfilled a useful purpose; there was a place for her in a man's life. It could even be argued that she was necessary to his success, his well-being. But what, he asked himself, was a lover? A lover was certainly not necessary. What purpose did she fulfil? What did she, in the end, con- tribute? Sexual urges could be satisfied at home. Infidelity was not only risky – it was superfluous. He had in Julie everything he truly needed. She was beautiful, efficient, a popular hostess, vivacious, intelligent and, on the whole, obedient, as a woman should be. She was also good in bed – sufficiently interested in sex to retain his interest, but not so obsessed as to disrupt his timetable. What more could a man ask? Marriage was a definable, controllable state. An affair was not. It was an acknowledgement of weakness.

A long time ago, Mort had calculated the cost of success and achievement. It was an equation that he had com- pletely accepted. Rosemary was not part of that equation.

And yet, despite all his misgivings, here he was together again with the girl in her apartment – a girl he scarcely

237

knew. He had even made a special trip to see her. He was honest enough with himself to admit that.

And what, for Chrissake, was he doing drinking cheap Chianti and eating spaghetti?

'I had two helpings,' he said. 'It's incredible.'

'No, it's not,' she said. 'It was damn good spaghetti. It was me who cooked it.'

'All those calories.'

'You watch your weight?' She was surprised. His body, as she well knew, was hard and muscular.

'I watch everything,' he said wryly, mocking himself with a candour unusual for him. He was relaxed, and that rarely happened.

What was it with this girl? There was something about her that he envied, something perhaps that he hungered for in his own life. He looked round the simple apartment, at the travel posters taped to the wall, at the huge double bed and the colour TV in the corner. It was all so eloquent of a simple, casual kind of existence, an uncluttered life, a life that he himself had long since sacrificed – if sacrifice were the right word.

The whole of this would fit into the study of his Fifth Avenue apartment. But that was not what impressed him most. What struck him was the casual disorder of the room. Nothing was in its place and yet, in a way, everything was. As a tidy man he could not have lived in this mess, but in Rosemary he found it acceptable, enchanting even. There was in her surroundings – as there was about her, too – a sense of freedom. She was carefree, untrammelled by material things, not trapped by things at all, as he was constantly. Things had taken over his whole existence.

This young girl was still dreaming dreams, still clinging to illusions he had long since abandoned. He was drawn to her and to her vulnerability – a quality he pitied and, at the same time, envied. Her uncomplicated trust in life, in people, in him, saddened Mort. It was, after all, a precious gift – one that a fortunate few treasure all their

238

lives, and many lose with the years – a gift he had never even possessed.

'You ever think of living in a better apartment?' he asked. Why had he said that? It was such a banal observation. Why was he trying to change what he so admired? He envied her freedom and yet he wanted to deprive her of it.

Rosemary laughed. 'Are you suggesting I become a kept woman? Isn't the Big Apple a little far from London for that? You'd hardly get your money's worth.'

'That's not what I meant,' he said. But he had.

'I like you, Mort,' she said. 'I really do. I don't normally jump into bed on the first date and I never had a married boyfriend before. You can believe me or not. There's something about you. You have this tremendous conviction, this strength. You walk the world as if you owned it.'

'Not yet,' he said laughing.

'Well, you don't own me and you never will. I don't want another apartment. I like this one. I love it, in fact. I don't want furs and I hate jewellery. Those things are for wives and mistresses.'

'You have to be one or the other.'

'No, I don't,' she said. 'I'm my own mistress. As long as you're around, I'll be here, but don't try to take me over and don't look over your shoulder when you're gone. You know what I mean?'

Mort sat on the bed and poured another glass of wine. 'I haven't drunk Chianti since I was twenty,' he said softly.

'When were you ever twenty?' she mocked.

He thought about that. 'You're right,' he said. 'I never was. I missed a lot.'

She began to unbutton his shirt. 'You have some catching up to do.'

*   *   *

Every week, the private investigator reported to Mort. He was the archetype of the commonplace, the quintessence

239

of the undistinguished. He walked bowed, as though crushed by life's burdens, and he dressed crumpled, like an underpaid bank teller. His hair was thin – the colour of stained cement – and his eyes watery. His face was devoid of character, empty of expression. He was a wisp, a cipher, a scuttler in cracks and corners. You would scarcely notice him in an empty room, let alone a crowded one.

He consulted his notes. 'Mr Jack Greenberg is still screwing Miss Rachel Meyer,' he said tonelessly.

Mort was no prude, but he found the choice of words inappropriate, coming, as they did, from a hired man. He would have preferred a more respectful, serious presentation. 'Screwing her?' he repeated tartly, giving the man the opportunity to adjust the description.

'Right on, sir,' the PI confirmed. 'That exactly describes it.'

Clearly, the guy was thick-skinned. But then, if he were anything else . . .

'Are you telling me you have actually seen them . . . in the . . . act of sex?'

The PI guffawed. 'The act of sex. That's good,' he said approvingly.

The man was a prize a-hole. Mort's lip curled. 'I told you I need tangible evidence,' he said. 'You're only confirming what I know already.'

The PI pulled out a bundle of photographs from a brief-case that looked like a piece of flotsam washed up from the Flood. 'These tangible enough for you?'

Mort picked up the first one, glanced at it and then quickly thumbed through the rest.

'How about the one in the shower,' said the PI. 'Thirty years in the business and I never got a better shot. And I thought I knew all about positions. Long focus lens, of course – two hundred ASA Kodacolor – a hundredth at F. one-point-eight.'

'Spare me the technical details.'

'Personally, I go for the one in the kitchen,' the private

investigator said. 'Now we know how to keep the little woman happy while she's slaving over a hot stove, eh?' He winked.

Mort flinched. He could not wait to show the slimebag the door.

The PI sensed that the meeting was at an end.

'You have the negatives there, Mr King. The whole shooting match. I guess you have everything you need.' He licked his lips. 'He's been servicing the young lady since she was fourteen.'

'Stick to the facts,' said Mort. 'I didn't ask for your comments.'

'It's all there in my report.'

Mort opened the door of his office. He despised the man. He despised himself for associating with him. But then, what else was he supposed to do? He nodded 'goodbye'. In all the time he had known the PI, he had never shaken his hand. He could not bring himself to touch him.

'It's a dirty job,' he said.

'It's a dirty life,' said the private investigator.

'I guess it pays well.'

'All of us, Mr King,' the man said. 'It pays all of us.'

Mort shut the door in his face. He slipped the photographs into a large manila envelope, sealed it and pressed the intercom.

'I have a letter for you to post to Edmund Meyer,' he told his secretary. 'Mark it "Private and Confidential".'

The spices that Moses held up to Mort were full and pungent in his nostrils. It was the Jewish custom, the symbol of a pleasant start to the week. As he inhaled the exotic scent, it brought back the innocent world of his childhood. It was the bitter-sweet smell of nostalgia and it made him feel, just for a moment, like a child – vulnerable and uneasy. It was not an experience he enjoyed. Mort lived for today and tomorrow. Yesterday, he could do nothing about and, for that reason, he rarely gave it a thought.

Right now, he was feeling happy, even exuberant. So was Moses.

'Soon, my boys will be the richest men in the world.'

'Don't be ridiculous,' said Rebecca crossly.

'What's ridiculous? Why shouldn't they be?'

'What for?' asked Rebecca.

Moses was angry. His face flushed with irritation. 'What for? What for?' he echoed. 'To be the best. That's what it's for. Why can't they be what they want to be?'

Rebecca reflected sadly that it was hardly the point. Why did they have to be what Moses wanted them to be?

'More corned beef?' she offered, keeping her thoughts to herself.

'I had enough,' said Ruby.

'Me too,' said Mort.

'I never have enough,' said Moses, holding out his plate. 'Not corned beef. Not anything.' He glared defiantly at Rebecca.

'Am I missing something?' said Ruby. 'There's an atmosphere.'

'No one says what they think any more.' Moses addressed the remark to his second helping of corned beef.

'How's my Julie?' asked Rebecca.

'The world is changing. I don't like it,' said Moses.

'Julie's OK,' said Mort.

'You should spend more time with her,' said Rebecca. 'She's a good girl,'

'I try,' said Mort. 'The business takes a lot of my time.'

'They tell me Edmund Meyer is the sixth richest man in America,' said Moses.

Was that really all his father cared about, thought Mort. There were times when he wanted to grab the old man's face . . . squeeze it and pummel it with his fists . . . make it smile and be gentle, make it show approval, affection even. But what was the use? It would be pointless and frustrating – like beating and savaging one of those trick rubber faces until, for a few seconds, it assumes a benign

242

expression in your hands, only to return slowly, inexorably, to its original malignant shape.

It seemed that the private investigator had something to say, but he was taking his time. For some reason, Mort had the impression that the man was enjoying himself. Why had he come back so soon?

'Anything more on Jack Greenberg?'

The PI shook his head. 'Just more of the same.'

Mort picked up a telex. 'If that's all?'

The man hesitated. Again, Mort had the feeling that he was playing cat and mouse.

'You have something on your mind? Go ahead and say it.'

'It's about your wife, sir.' The PI avoided Mort's eyes.

It was the last thing he had expected. 'My wife?'

'It was kind of a coincidence. Mr Jack Greenberg and Miss Rachel Meyer were having dinner in Greenwich Village. I was following them after they left the restaurant. That's when I saw your wife.'

'You had no right to follow my wife. You had no goddam right to do that.'

'No, sir. I thought you might say that.'

'You exceeded your authority.'

'Yes, sir. I'm with you. I'm sorry.'

Mort was trying to read the telex. His brain was spinning like wheels in mud. It was not going anywhere.

'I guess you don't want to hear any more.'

'No.' He struggled with the telex for a full minute. Then he gave up. 'Go on,' he said.

The PI looked out of the window. 'She seems to know the gentleman quite well,' he said. 'Quite well.' His face was expressionless. For all the animation he showed, he might have been a garden gnome. 'I made some notes,' he added. 'Nothing too detailed, you understand, she being your wife and all.'

'Notes?' said Mort, trying not to hear what the man was saying, but hearing only too well.

243

'Times, places . . . that kind of thing. I'll destroy them . . . if that's what you want.'

Mort's eyes flicked back and forth. He was looking for a way out, but there wasn't any. He was trapped.

'What the hell are you suggesting? I don't care for your snide insinuations.'

'I'm not suggesting anything, Mr King. It's not my job to do that. I deal in facts.'

'What facts?'

'You want to hear them?'

'Damn you,' said Mort. What choice did he have?

'It could all be a misunderstanding.' The man was breathing a shade faster than usual.

He's getting off on this, thought Mort. He set his mouth resolutely and controlled his anger. 'I'll be the judge of that.'

'You're the boss. The facts are that your wife has been seeing a lot of a Mr Leo Stendel. Of course, it might all be perfectly innocent.'

Mort breathed a sigh of relief. 'I see,' he said. 'You can stop right there. I know all about it. She works for him. He owns an art gallery on Madison.'

'That's the guy,' said the private investigator. He grinned. 'Well, that's OK, then,' he said. 'I guess . . . if you're satisfied, I'm satisfied.'

'Do me a favour,' said Mort. 'In future, do what I tell you to do. No more. No less. You understand me?'

'Sure, Mr King. I understand you. Boy, am I relieved.'

Mort looked at the man contemptuously. 'It's not your business to be relieved,' he said coldly. He would like to have picked up the insolent little bastard and thrown him out of the window.

'Absolutely not, sir.' He clasped his worn briefcase to his chest and stood up. 'She sure works long hours,' he murmured, as he walked to the door.

'What are you talking about?'

He turned. 'Your wife, sir. She works long hours.'

Mort shrugged indifferently. 'I guess she does. Sometimes. So do a lot of people.'

244

'Into the small hours?' said the PI very softly.

Mort said nothing. Jesus Christ, what was the disgusting piece of filth still doing here? Why hadn't he disappeared?

'At Mr Leo Stendel's apartment, too,' the man continued relentlessly. 'Sometimes till three or four in the morning . . . All night once in a while.'

Mort's shoulders slumped. He did not want to hear any more.

'She must like her work,' the private investigator said.

'Get the hell out of here,' said Mort savagely. 'Get out!'

'You want me to put a tail on her, Mr King?'

'Get the fuck out of here, you little creep!'

'If you need photographs . . .'

Mort leaped up, his features contorted with pain and rage, but the private investigator was out of the door before he could get to him.

He fell back in his chair. 'Oh, God,' he whispered, 'not Julie. Not her.'

*　　*　　*

It was a director of Crédit Suisse, an old friend of Sam's, who introduced him to Ricardo dos Santos.

Dos Santos was the President of Luandol, the Portuguese oil company that had owned concessions in Angola for many years.

A few days later, Sam flew to Lisbon to meet him.

Ricardo dos Santos was short, dapper, soft-spoken and polite. He was a gentleman of the old school. He wore a double-breasted waistcoat from which dangled a thick gold chain attached to a fob watch which he consulted regularly and a little anxiously, like the white rabbit in *Alice in Wonderland*. The gorgeous red handkerchief in his top pocket perfectly matched his tie. Every article of his clothing blended in discreet harmony, each complementing the other, in a quiet unostentatious display of good taste.

'I'm delighted to meet you,' said dos Santos and actually looked as though he meant it. 'Let me explain why our

245

mutual friend introduced us. My company has been in Angola for many years. We own oil concessions. We export crude and we also refine it in our Luanda refinery. For how much longer, we don't know. Our days there are certainly numbered. The time will surely come when the new government will take us over. Which government that will be, no one knows. The country is still torn apart by a terrible civil war. Whoever it is, the story will be the same. We shall be out and the compensation we receive will be ludicrous.'

'Who do you think will win the war?'

Dos Santos adjusted his pocket handkerchief. 'Hard to say. Since 1975, when Portugal gave Angola independence, the MPLA, in the centre of Angola, backed by the Cubans and the Russians, have been fighting the FNLA in the north, backed by the Americans and some Portuguese extreme right-wing political groups. Then there is UNITA, backed by South Africa.' He brushed a speck of dust from his sleeve. 'My hope is that the FNLA will win, but who can say? Meanwhile, Luandol's situation has changed. Our refinery in Portugal does not like our crude and they can no longer afford to pay us the international price. We think we can do better on the world market. Since we have no experience of selling our crude overseas, we thought, perhaps, that King Brothers might be interested to buy it and give us a fair price.'

'We can handle it,' said Sam.

'Good. We don't have enormous volumes of crude to sell. We load a hundred thousand tons every month in the estuary of the Soyo River in the north.'

'That should be OK. What about Cabinda crude?'

'That's still owned by Gulf. There's talk that the government may nationalize fifty per cent of the production, but I doubt if they'll be so kind to us when our time comes. They'll take everything.'

'Can we make a long-term contract for Soyo?'

'The situation is too uncertain, as I explained. I'll sell you one cargo now, and, if you give me a good price

246

and if it works out OK, we'll be friends. I never desert my friends.'

Sam liked the way dos Santos did business. They agreed terms very quickly. Maybe this would be a flash in the pan. Maybe, it would lead to something big. In the oil business, you never knew.

For a few weeks now, Laura's health had been poor – not that she seemed ill, just a little tired. She was very pale and she started to have prolonged nosebleeds.

The doctors gave her exhaustive tests and assured Sam and Amy that there was nothing seriously wrong. Still, they worried. Laura just did not have the energy and the spirit that a ten-year-old should have.

Edward, the child Amy had always derided as the sickly one – Sam's child – was now a healthy, energetic, seven-year-old, devoted to Amy and suspicious of his father. It was ironic.

Until Laura recovered, Sam tried to cut down on business trips. As a result, his relationship with the kids and with Amy, too, improved.

Soon Laura was her old self again and Sam's peace of mind returned. For the first time in years, he felt like a family man. He was confident he and Amy could make their marriage work.

The Angolan business was proving to be highly profitable and trouble-free. In a way, he was surprised how smoothly it was going, considering that Angola was constantly in a state of civil war.

And then, one morning when he arrived at the office, there was a telex on his desk that changed all that. The message was signed by Count Luis Corte Real, a gentleman who described himself as President Designate of the Provisional Revolutionary Council of the FNLA. Sam had never heard of the man. The gist of the telex was simple; King Brothers' tanker had been hijacked. The *Roman Eagle*, the second tanker chartered to load a hundred-thousand-ton cargo of Soyo crude, had completed loading and was about to

247

sail when the Count and thirty heavily armed FNLA troops boarded, took over the ship and seized the loading documents, including the original bills of lading. The Count demanded payment for the full value of the cargo – about ten million dollars – and the money was to be remitted to him immediately. As soon as it was received, the telex stated, the tanker and the crew would be free to sail and the documents of title would be mailed to King Brothers.

Sam and Karl Andermatt stayed in the office for two days and nights, exchanging telexes with the Count. His messages were tough and uncompromising. He would make no deals. All he would do was exchange the documents of title for the value of the cargo. Sam feared what would happen if he did not accept the Count's terms.

On the second night time ran out for Sam.

He read the telex while the machine was still chattering its message: 'Full value of cargo to be remitted immediately and confirmed directly to me by first-class Swiss bank or charges will be set and tanker and crew blown up. You have twenty-four hours. Corte Real.'

That was clear enough.

Who could help them on this one? Whose police? Whose army? No one's. It was strictly a problem for King Brothers. They were on their own.

Ricardo dos Santos was adamant. 'You must not pay the man. He's a crook, a pirate.' He consulted his fob watch anxiously.

Easy for him to say. It was not his tanker. He was not on board. It was, however, his crude – at least until he was paid for it. Sam had to remember that.

'If you pay him, I shall be forced to sue you for the money,' said dos Santos. 'At the same time, I must also warn you that if the MPLA win the struggle for Angola, they too will undoubtedly take action against you and you will never do business in the country again.'

Sam was between a rock and a hard place. He could see no way out. Except to play for time. Time was what he needed – and time was the one thing he did not have.

248

He dictated a carefully worded telex to the Count. Two hours later, the answer came. The Count would receive him in two days in his Paris apartment.

Sam breathed a sigh of relief. He had no idea what was going to happen, but he had won a minor skirmish in the war. The man was at least ready to talk.

The Count's driver met them at Charles de Gaulle. He drove at speed to the Eighth Arrondissement. Then, slowing down, he picked up the car phone.

'Nous arrivons dans deux minutes.'

As the black Mercedes limousine approached the eighteenth century château, the huge oak metal-studded doors glided open, operated by remote control. The car swung round the cobbled courtyard and drew up at the steps of the main entrance. Two servants in dark blue gold-braided uniforms, with gold buttons, opened the rear doors on either side and bowed out Sam and Karl.

The salon was vast, stuffed with Louis XV and Louis XVI furniture. There was, Sam could have sworn, not a reproduction in the place. Clearly, the Count was a wealthy man.

On either side of the doorway, opposite the large bay windows, hung two paintings, presumably of the Count and his wife – she seated in an arbour with two poodles in her lap – he attired in what appeared to be a hussar's uniform, affecting an aristocratic pose, one knee slightly bent, right hand arrogantly on hip.

Suddenly, the salon doors were opened by two uniformed servants, revealing the original of the portrait.

Count Luis Corte Real hardly looked your typical hijacker. He was tall, slim, elegantly dressed in a rather tight-fitting suit in the French manner. He sported a brocade waistcoat with obvious pride and frequently fussed the bunched curls at the back of his neck with his long, exquisitely manicured fingers. He looked as though he would have been more at home at the court of Louis XV than on the deck of a VLCC.

He offered them the back of his hand in such a way that Sam almost felt constrained to bow and kiss it.

'Champagne, messieurs,' he said. It was a declaration, not a question. As he spoke, the doors swung open again and in walked yet another uniformed servant. Sam noted with approval the silver tray and the bottle of Dom Perignon and accepted the bubbling glass from a white-gloved hand.

The Count was in an excellent mood. Why not? He had every reason to be.

'*Santé*!' He raised his glass and pointed to a desk smothered in ormolu. 'There, gentlemen, are the shipping documents of the *Roman Eagle*,' he said. 'You are welcome to study them.' For a moment, Sam considered grabbing them and making a run for it.

'They are copies,' said the Count slyly. 'Naturally.'

'Naturally,' said Sam.

'The originals will be handed over to you against a banker's cheque, drawn on a first-class Swiss bank for ten million, three hundred thousand dollars. The matter is very straightforward.'

'Not entirely,' said Sam. 'My company has certain obligations to Luandol and the MPLA.' He examined the documents. They were genuine, no doubt about it.

The Count frowned. He was seriously displeased. He posed by the fireplace, looking very much like his portrait.

'Within four weeks – less, probably – the FNLA will have liberated the whole of Angola. The criminal leaders of the MPLA will be tried and executed and the country will be reunited. I myself am the President Designate of the FNLA as you know. The money will therefore be in safekeeping until that time.' He smiled benevolently. 'I can guarantee you the gratitude of the legitimate government of Angola.'

It was then that Sam had a flash of inspiration.

'May I suggest that, pending settlement of this matter, as you propose, you send a telex to your men allowing the *Roman Eagle* to leave Angola. As long as she remains there, she's incurring demurrage of over forty thousand dollars a day and those costs will have to be borne by someone. Without the shipping documents which are in your possession we cannot discharge the tanker, as of course you know.'

'If I allow the tanker to leave, do I have your word that you will instruct your bank to pay me the value of the cargo?'

Sam hesitated. 'Very well,' he said.

The Count was triumphant. 'Then I agree to release the tanker. There is no reason to endanger further the lives of innocent men,' he added unctuously.

And that was Count Luis Corte Real's first mistake.

He left the room to dispatch the telex. When he returned, Karl addressed him with great respect.

'If I might just bring one small point to your attention,' he said, tentatively.

'Please do,' said the Count. He could afford to be gracious. The battle was won.

'There is a letter of credit which my company opened. According to the very strict banking code – which a man of your experience is obviously familiar with – you are obliged to present the original shipping documents under the L/C. Against those documents, the bank will release the cash to you.'

The Count pondered. 'Which bank would that be?'

'The head office of the Banque Internationale de Genève,' said Karl.

The Count inclined his head. 'In that case, gentlemen, we shall meet in Geneva at ten tomorrow morning. I advise you to set matters up in advance.'

'You may rely on us to do that,' said Sam.

'I regret,' said the Vice-President of the BIG, 'but I cannot release the money to you.' He consulted the visiting card. 'Monsieur le Comte. I regret . . . infinitely.' He shrugged a big, Gallic shrug.

Count Luis Corte Real's aristocratic features turned white with rage, almost as white as his lace cuffs.

251

'Are these not the original shipping documents?' he demanded.

'Indeed, they are,' said the vice-president. He looked at them again. 'Indeed,' he confirmed.

'And are they not fully in accordance with the letter of credit?'

'Fully,' said the banker. 'Fully,' he repeated.

'Then, pay me immediately,' said the Count curtly. 'You are wasting my time.'

Sam nodded in agreement and confronted the banker with a most aggressive frown.

The banker looked uncomfortable. 'I regret, monsieur . . . infinitely. I regret.'

'What, in God's name, do you regret, you idiot?' said the Count rudely.

'Monsieur le Comte, there is legally a dispute as to title between the FNLA and Luandol,' said the banker with dignity.

'My business is with this gentleman,' said the Count, waving at Sam.

'This gentleman, Monsieur le Comte, is not in dispute with you,' said the banker.

Sam looked relieved.

'Who, then, is disputing the title?' the Count asked. He looked for support at Sam, who nodded furiously and glared at the banker, challenging him to answer the unanswerable. When it came to the crunch, Sam was a frustrated actor.

'Monsieur Ricardo dos Santos,' said the banker.

'Ricardo dos Santos!' the Count snapped. 'That little worm is a common criminal!'

Sam nodded his head in agreement. He was enjoying himself.

'Perhaps, monsieur, but until the rightful owner of the crude is established, the BIG has no option but to freeze the money. Otherwise, we could ourselves be involved in a most serious legal dispute.' The banker looked at Sam. Sam looked out of the window.

'Freeze?' The Count raised his voice in outrage.

'Yes, Monsieur le Comte,' the banker confirmed. 'Freeze.'

'And how long will it take to establish that the FNLA are the legal owners?'

'That depends, monsieur.'

'On what?'

'On developments in Angola,' said the banker reasonably. 'On whether the FNLA or the MPLA or UNITA win the war. Whoever wins will be the legitimate government of Angola and the legitimate owner of the cargo. We shall have to wait and see.' He spoke calmly, rationally, as if the matter were self-evident.

The Count's face distorted with impotent fury. 'I have been tricked,' he said, rounding on Sam.

The banker intervened. 'No one has tricked you, monsieur. Monsieur Carlstroem has instructed the BIG to pay you. But this bank cannot, by law, do so until a Swiss court gives us that authority.'

The message was clear enough. The banker had played his part well. After all, King Brothers was amongst his best clients.

The Count paced the room.

'Very well,' he said. 'If that's the way it is, I shall not pursue the matter of payment. You have the money. You can keep it. I have the shipping documents and the crude. You will never see it. I shall discharge it in the Caribbean and sell it.'

He had a point. Sam and Karl exchanged glances.

'What is the discharge port?' the Count demanded.

'Curaçao,' said Sam reluctantly.

'And how long is the sailing time from Angola to Curaçao?'

'Twenty-five days,' said Sam. 'Approximately.'

Karl was about to intervene, but, catching the look on Sam's face, he coughed instead.

'My representatives and I will be there,' said the Count. 'You can be sure of that.'

And that was Count Luis Corte Real's second mistake.

*

253

'For Chrissake,' said Karl. 'Twenty-five days. If it took fifteen it would be a slow voyage.'

'I must have made a mistake,' said Sam mildly.

'That was no mistake. What are you up to?'

'I'm planning a little reception committee for the *Roman Eagle*.'

'The Count will check the voyage time with the owners.'

'I'm sure he will,' said Sam. 'I already spoke to them and explained the situation. They'll confirm twenty-five days.'

A smile began to disturb the corners of Karl's mouth. 'So, when the Count gets to Curaçao . . .'

'The tanker will have discharged, the crude will have been shipped to the US and refined, and the products will be burning up in Cadillacs and Jumbo jets.'

The smile spread slowly across Karl's face. 'There are times,' he said, 'when you are reasonably intelligent.'

'Thanks.'

'Are you certain you can discharge the tanker?'

'Sure I can. That's what most people don't know. I could do it with an indemnity if I wanted to.'

'You don't think the Count might fly to Curaçao a week or two early to sit and wait for the tanker?'

'He might.'

'What then?'

'It won't do him any good.'

'How come?'

'Because I gave the owners secret instructions to radio the captain just two hours before he reaches Curaçao.'

'What instructions?'

'To divert the tanker to Bonaire.'

'Bonaire?'

'Bonaire,' said Sam.

Karl thumped his fist on the desk. 'I can just see the Count standing on the quayside at Curaçao, looking out to sea,' he said, chuckling with delight.

'With his hand on his hip.' For the first time, Sam allowed himself a smile.

'You know something?' said Karl. 'You really are a devious sonofabitch.'

Sam took that as a real compliment.

Amy stopped by the office unexpectedly.

'I thought I'd do my duty and congratulate Karl,' she told Sam.

He was pleased. 'That's a nice thought. He'll appreciate it.'

Karl looked up as she opened the door of his office. This time he was not embarrassed at all. On the contrary, he was obviously happy to see her.

'It wasn't me. It was Sam,' he said modestly.

'I hear you helped,' she said smiling, 'just a little.'

'Maybe just a little.'

She smiled again. She was smiling a lot these days.

'It's not over yet,' said Karl. 'We discharged the tanker three weeks ago, but the Count is still sending us letters from Angola claiming the ten million dollars.'

She nodded. She was not really listening. She was reminding herself how intense Karl could be.

'The problem for our friend the Count is that the FNLA are losing the war. They're being driven further and further north by the MPLA. Every time we get a letter, the last town he occupied is crossed out and the next one typed in. He's retreating so fast, he doesn't even have time to get a new letterhead printed. If this goes on, he'll be writing to us from Zaire.'

Amy laughed. She did not really understand about business, but she was sure that Karl was smart. Otherwise, he would not have been around Sam for so long.

'I have to go.'

'Thanks for stopping by.'

'No big deal. I had to drop by the office anyway.'

'How have you been?' He asked as if he really wanted to know. It was such a routine question – a cliché. Coming from Karl, though, it was more than a little unusual. It meant something.

'I've been OK,' she said. 'Great.' And again she was smiling.

*　　*　　*

'You remember the first cheese soufflé?'

'The first and all the others,' said Julie. Leo poured her a glass of St Emilion.

How was she going to tell him goodbye? And then she realized that she didn't have to. He knew. Leo always knew.

'I have to try and be there for Mort,' she said.

'Is he there for you?'

She didn't know what to say.

'I'm sorry,' he said. 'That wasn't fair.'

She took his hand in hers. 'You remember what you said about being lovers, even if we never made love?'

'I remember saying that. We were about to screw at the time.'

'That doesn't sound like you.'

'It's true, though. It's easy to be philosophical about life when everything's going your way.'

'How old are you, Leo?'

'Strange you never asked me that before. No complaints, I hope. My soufflés always rose to perfection?'

'No complaints. Your soufflés will be a hard act to follow.'

Leo grinned. 'Thanks for the compliment. I'm sixty.'

'Sixty!' It was hard to believe. 'You never told me.'

'I never told myself, either.'

'Do you mind? Being sixty, I mean.'

Leo contemplated his glass of red wine. He held it up to the candlelight.

'I try not to. I mind, though. Yes, I mind.'

'In a lot of ways, you're younger than Mort,' said Julie.

'Not in years.'

'What do years matter?'

'They matter when you're sixty. Take it from me,' said Leo. 'They matter when you're about to lose the only thing that gives your life meaning.'

256

'Don't, Leo. That's not fair.'

'Did I say it was meant to be?'

'Don't be bitter. It's not like you.'

'It's an extraordinary thing you did for me, Julie. For the first time in my life, you made me feel. I realize now that all these years I've been playing a part. Good old Leo Stendel, the guy who's always fun to be with, the guy who never takes life too seriously. Mr Charm. That was always my secret weapon, you know – charm. All that stuff that gets to most people – broken marriages, business problems, the son I never got to know – I held it all at arm's length like it wasn't happening to me. Well, I'm beginning to realize that charm has its limits. It hides a lot of heartache, but it doesn't solve a darn thing. You see, I learned a couple of things.'

'We both did,' said Julie. 'I want you to know that I thought of leaving Mort. But I can't. I believe there's still something worth saving.'

'I hope you're right.'

'I wish things were different.'

'We don't always want what's good for us,' he said. 'If we did, life would be a whole lot less complicated.'

'I'm sorry I complicated yours.'

'There are some complications you can't live without.'

'What about the Gallery? You really want me to stay?'

'It's your job. You made it. You didn't get it for screwing the boss. I'm damned if you're going to lose it for not screwing him.'

'Thanks, Leo. You know how much I love it.'

He looked round the room and grinned. 'You want a Matisse or a Renoir?'

'Thanks a million,' she said, 'but I just don't see myself as a gap on your wall.'

The next day, she told Mort there had been someone else. He fixed her with his cat green eyes, saying nothing, showing neither surprise nor pain. What was he thinking?

What was he feeling? She had no idea. She could not believe that he was indifferent. If he was, then she was wasting her time.

'Who?' he said.

'Leo Stendel.'

There was no change in his expression, but she noticed that line across his forehead, the one that only appeared when he was disturbed.

'Why?' was all he said.

For Chrissake. Why? What was that supposed to mean? Why Leo, or why anyone? She tried to explain. 'He was there. I guess that's the reason. He was just there. Oh, God, that makes me sound like a whore. It's not only that he was physically present – though God knows he was, every day – I mean he was there for me when I needed someone to talk to, someone to listen to me, someone to hear what I was saying. Can you understand that, Mort?'

'Wasn't I there?'

Suddenly she was smiling that lopsided smile of hers and crying at the same time. She spoke quietly, intensely, moving her head to emphasize her words, the tears trickling down her face. 'You, Mort? You're never here. Don't you know that? Never.'

'I've been trying to get home earlier from the office these days. Hadn't you noticed?'

She wiped two tears from the corners of her hazel eyes with the back of her hand, an innocent, strangely touching gesture. 'Yes,' she said. 'I noticed. What has that to do with anything? We don't communicate any more. It makes no difference whether you're home or not.'

'Do you love him?'

'Love,' she said scornfully. 'What's love? I don't know. I care for him. He's important to me.'

'When did all this happen?'

'What does it matter when it happened? Jesus, you ask the goddam dumbest questions. It's not the when or the where that matters. It's the thing itself. I've been having an

258

affair with another man. That means we have a problem, doesn't it?'

'How long?'

'Oh, Jesus Christ!' She started beating him on the chest with her fists. He stood there, taking the blows without flinching. He did not try to stop her, to grab her hands. He just let her hit him while the line across his forehead deepened. Then, abruptly, she gave up. What was the use? She sat down and wept. He had never seen her cry like that before. She sobbed violently, rocking from side to side, nursing the pain and the frustration. He watched her. When she stopped, he handed her a box of Kleenex.

'Good old Mort,' she said. 'For once he's there when he's needed.' She blew her nose and wiped her face, but it was obvious that she had no interest in how she looked. She did not so much as glance at a mirror. 'It's the details that are important to you. Isn't that so? The facts and the figures, the whys and wherefores. The whole schmear. The bullshit. Well, if you want the dirt, you can have it. I'll tell you when and where and how often.'

'You don't need to,' he said quietly.

It dawned on her what he meant. 'You knew! You knew all along.'

He nodded.

'And you said nothing.'

'What could I say that would do any good?'

'For God's sake, weren't you jealous? Weren't you angry? Didn't you want to strangle me?'

'That's not my style,' said Mort calmly.

'Your style. What is your style, then? Don't you ever just get mad? Even if it doesn't do any good? Your style. Don't you ever say what needs to be said and to hell with the consequences? Don't you ever . . .' She was searching for the right words. 'Don't you ever just – *feel*?' Oh, God, what was it Leo had said? She had made him feel – the one thing she had never done for Mort in all these years.

'You think I don't care if you screw around?' he said stiffly.

259

'I never screwed around. I had a relationship with one guy – a relationship, Mort. You know what that is? It's where you share things. It's where two people actually care for each other. You wouldn't understand, would you? The only person you care about is Mortimer King.'

'That's not how it is,' he said. 'You don't know me if you say that.'

'When did I ever get the chance to know you? When did anyone? Here I am, going through all kinds of hell, telling you something most wives would lie in their teeth about. I'm doing it because the other hell was worse. The other hell was a cheat and a lie – every day, every hour. And what happens? You tell me you knew about it already. And you kept quiet. And you say you care. How can you care? Why didn't you say anything, for Chrissake?'

'I didn't want to lose you,' he said simply.

He meant it. She could see that. He had been afraid to face the truth, hoping, somehow, to save their marriage. She, on the other hand, had felt compelled to face it for the same reason. It was ironic.

'We have to be honest with each other,' she said more calmly. 'I'm not sorry for what I've done, but extra-marital affairs are not my scene. I can't handle them.'

'Are you saying you want a divorce?'

'Don't you understand a goddam thing?' The question infuriated her. 'Can't you see I'm trying to save our marriage?'

'What about Leo Stendel?'

'It's over with him.'

'You don't love him any more?'

'I told you. He's important to me. That's not something that's going to change in a couple of days. But you're the man I married.'

'Only you've forgotten why,' he said bitterly.

'I don't know who you are any more.'

'You used to know. They call guys like me over-achievers. We're tough to live with.'

260

'I understand what you want. I don't have any problem with that. It's who you are that's the problem. I don't know what goes on in your head. I don't know what you're thinking and I sure as hell don't know what you're feeling. Sometimes I wonder if you feel anything.'

'Most of the time,' said Mort, 'I'm too busy doing things to know what I'm feeling.'

'What a confession,' she said.

She stood at the window and looked down on Central Park. A girl knelt on the grass, and a toddler – about two or three – was running into her arms. Julie wondered if she knew how lucky she was. No, of course not. No one ever did, did they?

'It's going to be OK,' he said. 'It was good we talked. We communicated, didn't we?'

There was something endearing about his eagerness to please her.

She tried to smile.

'Maybe we should talk about adopting again.' It was hard for him to say.

'Not now,' she said. 'Not like this.'

And that was how they left it. Something had happened. For a moment, it seemed, they had almost reached each other, but, in the end, what had it meant? What had they achieved? It was as if she had seen, or imagined she saw, someone she used to know – an old friend – on the other side of the street, and crossed over to greet him. But when she came close, she realized that she had made a mistake.

The man was a stranger.

*   *   *

It was almost a year to the day since Laura had first complained of feeling tired.

Sam and Amy sat at the doctor's desk. He was wearing a white coat and he had a pleasant, untroubled face.

'Laura has acute monocytic leukemia,' he said.

Sam knew, of course, that it was ridiculous. Obviously there had been a mistake. There could be no question of

261

that. Some mix-up. Laura was perfectly all right. It was a young girl's problem – hormones or glands – something of the kind. The man was an incompetent fool. How could they employ people like that in hospital? An idiot. He let the doctor drone on.

'Other forms of leukemia . . . acute monocytic very rare . . . nosebleeds gave us the clue . . . should have known sooner . . . exceptionally high leucocyte count . . . white cells . . . anaemia . . . various forms of treatment . . . chemotherapy, blood transfusions . . .'

The man had a mole high on his left cheek with a few black hairs sprouting from it.

Amy sat stony-faced. Never once did she take her eyes off the doctor.

'Can you cure her?'

The doctor hesitated. 'We can treat her,' he said carefully.

'How long?' She was perfectly calm.

The doctor showed her the palms of his hands, as if to dissuade her from thinking like that. Then he placed them deliberately on the desktop. 'We can't predict these things. With good response to the treatment . . .'

'How long?' she insisted.

'Six months,' said the doctor. 'A year at the most.'

Sam lost his temper. 'This is bullshit! The man's a screwball. We'll find another doctor.'

Amy stood up. 'Thank you,' she said quietly.

The doctor walked them to the door. 'I'd like to keep Laura here under observation. With your permission, we'll start the treatment right away.'

Sam blustered: 'You'll do no such thing. I won't listen to this nonsense. We're getting a second opinion.'

They got a second opinion, and a third and a fourth. Finally, Sam had to accept what in his heart he had accepted that first day. For a time, he and Amy played a game; Laura was sick, but she was going to get better like other sick children got better, like Laura had always got better before.

A few weeks later, they were on their way to visit Laura in the hospital and Amy said: 'We have to stop it, Sam.'

'Stop what?'

'Playing this game of hope. There isn't any. She's going to die. We both know it.'

'There has to be hope,' Sam whispered. 'If there wasn't . . .'

'First you tried to convince yourself she didn't have leukemia. Now you accept it, but you still want to believe she'll get better. It's just another pretence.'

'What's wrong with pretending, if it keeps me sane?' said Sam. 'You can face the reality. I can't.'

'You have to, Sam. We both have to. We need to prepare ourselves. And Laura.'

'You tell me . . . How do you prepare an eleven-year-old kid for death?'

'I don't know,' said Amy. 'I only know we have to try.'

But it was not necessary. Laura knew. She had known for a long time. She read it in her body and in their faces. She understood about death in the uncomplicated way that children do.

When Sam realized that she knew, he began to talk to her about God and the afterlife and how they would all meet again in heaven. And Laura held his hand tightly and listened with round eyes, like she used to listen to the fairy tales he told her before she went to sleep. She knew they were stories and yet, in her way, she believed them, just as she had once believed the fairy tales.

She showed him a pencil drawing she had made of a man and a little girl. They were floating in the sky, holding hands. The two figures looked familiar.

'Don't I know him?'

Laura was delighted. 'It's you,' she said. 'But the nose isn't right.'

'No,' he said. 'The nose isn't right.'

She knelt on the bed for a long time, chin cupped in hands, studying his face, as if she needed to remember

263

every detail. Then she hugged him so tight he could scarcely breathe. 'Don't be afraid, Dad,' she said.

'Dear God, how does she know so much? How can she be so brave?'

'She's your daughter, Sam,' said Amy quietly.

'You used to say that Edward was my son because –'

She cut him off. 'I know what I said. I said a lot of things. I was wrong.'

As they had done so many times since they first learned about Laura's illness, they clung to each other for the comfort it gave them, sharing their sadness, mourning those lost days when love, not grief, was the bond that held them together.

Edgar was drinking heavily these days. He was on a bottle of gin a day, plus a few dry martinis here and there to vary the presentation, if not the content. He took to phoning Kate in the middle of the night, two or three times a week. She never once complained or suggested he might call her back the next day. If he called, he needed her and Kate, in her way, loved Edgar. She couldn't live with him, but that was something else.

He would talk to her about nothing – nothing, that is, of any significance. All he needed was someone to listen to him, and the knowledge that the person at the other end was a friend – someone who knew him and maybe even understood him a little. There were not too many of those around.

But as he drank more and more, it became clear to her that she could never help him. What he needed was professional help. He had to be convinced that he was an alcoholic.

'Whatever it is you say I am,' he told her, 'I guess it's true. I trust you.'

'Jesus, Edgar, don't do that. The morgue is full of guys who trusted women. Trust yourself.'

'I'm too far gone, Kate. No one can help me any more.'

'Try helping yourself.'

'If I thought it would do any good – if I thought you'd have me back, I might make the effort. As it is, I'm OK. Life's a gas, Kate. Most guys would envy me the eighteen-year-old dolls, the divorcees. My butt is getting sore sitting on bar stools, but what the hell!'

'I wouldn't want you to give up anything for me. I don't want to spoil your fun.'

'Fun?' said Edgar. 'Yeah, I guess you could call it fun,' he said doubtfully.

'Why don't you leave King Brothers?'

'And do what?'

'What did you do before?'

'I screwed around.'

'And now?'

'I still screw around, but at least I can kid myself that I'm doing something useful.'

'Mort will destroy you, like he does everything he touches.'

'Why do you hate him so much?'

'I don't hate him. I understand him. He's for himself, not for you, not for anyone. If you think any differently, you're fooling yourself.'

'I need you, Kate.'

'Think about leaving Mort. Then, maybe we can talk.'

Ricardo dos Santos was reading the morning paper and sipping coffee in his Lisbon apartment when the bomb exploded. Later, the police told him that the device had been planted in the waste disposal unit in the kitchen. His wife had been standing next to it, making his breakfast. It blew away her left breast, and her intestines were hanging out. After two days in intensive care she gave up the struggle and died.

'They say they have no proof,' dos Santos told Sam, 'but I don't need proof. I know.'

'The Count?' said Sam.

'Who else?'

'I'm deeply sorry, Ricardo. What can I say? If only I'd

known. No amount of money is worth a human life and to think it had to be your wife –'

'You didn't know. How could you? You have nothing to blame yourself for. You did what you had to do. Like I must do now.'

Sam put his hand on his friend's shoulder. 'Don't, Ricardo. The man is ruthless. That's clear. He's an animal. Let the police take care of him.'

'What gave you any other idea?' said dos Santos. 'Naturally the police must take care of him.'

Sam told Jane that he had been thinking a lot about divorce.

'Are you sure you're not still in love with Amy?'

'How can you love someone who walks all over you?'

'You have a lot to learn, Sam.'

'One day, you and I will get married.'

'What about Laura?'

'Laura's illness has brought Amy and me closer together, but I think we both know that our marriage can never work.'

'Have you discussed it with Amy?'

'You can't discuss important things with Amy. Only trivialities.'

Jane studied Sam's face – not a strong face, but kind and caring. He was a decent man. The lines around his eyes and forehead seemed to express perplexity, as if the world were too much for him. He was defenceless and he showed it.

She found it an attractive quality. She was strong enough for both of them.

A week later, Laura came home. The treatment had been more successful than the doctors had predicted – far more than Sam and Amy had dared to hope. They kept her indoors over the weekend and played riotous games of Ludo and Snakes and Ladders.

On Monday, she went back to school.

'Isn't it too soon?' said Sam nervously.

'Let her go,' said Amy. 'She can't wait to feel like a normal kid again. She's so much better.'

And, indeed, she was. Her cheeks, that had been white

for so long, were pink and glowing, and her eyes bright and lively again.

Their lives returned to normal.

The doctors were cautious. It was too early to be certain. It could be a temporary remission, but, as time went by, they became more optimistic. Laura's response to the treatment had been dramatic.

'Is she really cured?' Sam asked the doctor, willing him to say 'yes.'.

'It's too soon to be certain, but the indications are good – very good.'

Sam had no doubts; he had heard what he wanted to hear.

He put out of his mind all thoughts of divorce. They were a family again. They needed each other. What had been broken was mended.

In Angola, the hammer and sickle had struck. The MPLA, the new government, descended on Luandol: the Portuguese directors were replaced and the company was nationalized and renamed Natoilco. Sam was summoned to Angola to discuss 'future cooperation'.

'In Angola, there are three main players in the oil business right now,' Ricardo told Sam. 'The first is the President – he makes the decisions and they are ratified by the cabinet. The second is Eduardo Cabrillo, the managing director of Natoilco. He is intelligent, suspicious of foreigners and difficult. He is also a dedicated Marxist. I doubt if he would ever be your friend, but watch out. He could be a dangerous enemy. The third is the Minister, José Rocha, an ex-soldier, a friend of the President and an easy-going, pleasant man who likes the good things of life . . . You follow me?'

Sam followed him.

'These two men are close to the President and they are bitter enemies. Somehow, you'll have to find a way to work with both of them if you want to succeed. It will not be easy.'

267

'And you?' asked Sam. 'What will you do?'

'I shall remain a director of Luandol in Portugal. In Angola I'm finished and that makes me sad. It was my home for many years and I love the country. My life has changed. I have lost my wife and my country, but not, I hope, my friends.'

'I don't forget my friends,' said Sam. He could not resist asking about the Count. 'What news?'

Ricardo opened wide ingenuous eyes. 'How should I know? For me, the man does not exist. He is as good as dead.'

In the New Year of 1977, Sam received a registered envelope from Portugal. There was no letter inside, nothing to indicate who had sent it. It contained only a press cutting – a photograph of Count Luis Corte Real and, underneath, an obituary notice. It seemed that the Count had died ten days ago, blown up in his car in the courtyard of his Paris château. There were no clues to his assassin, but the motive was thought to have been political. The obituary mentioned his support for the now defunct FNLA, his distinguished service to Portugal in war and peace and his unique collection of French antique furniture.

Sam phoned Ricardo. 'You saw the news about the Count?'

'Certainly I did,' said Ricardo. 'It came as a great shock.'

'I'll bet it did,' said Sam.

*   *   *

Jack Greenberg reclined on one elbow and looked down at the slim body lying beside him on the bed. Rachel was nearly twenty now. The silly, feckless girl was no more and in her place was a woman, a robust individual with her own strong views and attitudes, someone who could no longer be manipulated.

For Jack, it was disconcerting and, at the same time, compelling. Not being himself a man of any great strength of character, he had long indulged a taste for dominating

268

other people; a taste which, in large part, had been frustrated, but it had once been easy enough to dominate Rachel. These days, he sensed when he talked to her that she no longer regarded him as a hero – a demi-god, whose every word and action was to be accepted without question – but as a fallible, an all too fallible, human being. She had not pushed him off his pedestal overnight. She had eased him down from it gently, almost without his noticing. Now she was beginning, by slow degrees, imperceptibly, to play the leading role in their relationship. She was learning how to manage, if not to control, him, and Jack, for his part, was learning how to enjoy it.

If he had been honest – and Jack could never be entirely that – he would have acknowledged to himself long ago that Rachel's allure was in no way diminished by her financial expectations. When they were wrestling in the act of love, Jack's fantasies took on many shapes. Sometimes he imagined that he was making out with the fourteen-year-old she had been when he first seduced her. At others, he saw himself sitting at the head of the long boardroom table in the panelled conference room of the Oil Corporation, dispensing wisdom and – the greatest turn-on of all – orders to his employees.

As time passed, he found himself increasingly preoccupied with Rachel. At the morning meetings when the talk was dull, he would daydream about her and he would often catch E.M. looking at him with an odd expression on his face. It could be his imagination – after all, E.M. did not readily tolerate inattention in his minions – or it could be something else. But no, it was absurd. Jack had covered his tracks too well. The old man could not possibly suspect a thing.

He lightly fingered Rachel's nipples. She had large and very firm breasts. Why did so many women's breasts flatten like fried eggs when they lay down? There was that Matisse drawing of a reclining nude in the boardroom: she was asleep, flat on her back, her nipples erect and firm as

269

berries. Perhaps they were Matisse's fantasy, or maybe he had a supply of exceptionally endowed models. Lucky Matisse! Lucky Jack, for that matter! That was one thing he had no need to fantasize about. Rachel's breasts jutted out aggressively, inviting – no, demanding – attention. They were, somehow, symbolic of the new Rachel.

'It's time we thought about getting married,' she said lazily.

Jack's heart fluttered nervously. He could feel the disturbance in his chest. 'Honey, why spoil everything? You know I love you. I look after you, don't I? One day, perhaps, but not yet. What's the hurry? Besides, I have some things that need doing.'

'Business? Who cares?'

'Other things.'

'Mort?'

Jack did not answer.

'Be careful, Jack. Leave him alone. He's dangerous.'

'Honey, I'm not a child. I can take care of myself.'

'No, you can't. You need someone to look after you,' she said affectionately.

Look after him. That was a new angle. He had been doing OK for the last thirty-eight years, without help from anyone.

'Somehow I don't think your father would welcome me as a son-in-law.'

'Leave him to me,' said Rachel firmly.

Now, there was a woman talking. A woman who was very sure of herself.

'I just don't see that we would be any better off – not right now. We spend more time together than most married couples.'

'And look how we spend it. Screwing!'

'What's wrong with that? Don't you like it?'

'Sure, I like it. I'd like to eat out in a restaurant once in while, too.'

'I never had any complaints before.'

'Grow up, Jack. There's more to a relationship than

270

fucking. We've been going together a long time now and we hardly know each other.'

'You're out of your mind. What do you mean, we don't know each other?'

'Oh, sure, in bed we do. But that's all,' she said. 'You're so scared of E.M., you won't even take me to a movie in case someone he knows sees us together. What kind of a relationship is that? Are you ashamed of me or something?'

Jack protested. 'Of course I'm not. It's just that your father's such a goddam reactionary. He disapproves of sex before marriage. He told me so. Why he told me, God alone knows, but he did. I guess he thinks you're still a virgin. He probably thinks I am.'

Rachel began to kiss the inside of Jack's thigh. 'I think he knows about us.'

Jack could feel that ominous tightening in his chest. 'Don't say things like that. I get a pain.'

'It's psychosomatic,' she said, caressing him with her lips. He was breathing heavily. 'Maybe I'll tell him,' she said.

'For Chrissake,' Jack gasped, 'you want me to have a heart attack?'

'Isn't this just the greatest?' she whispered.

The image of the Titan – E.M.'s big face and knowing brown eyes – slowly faded.

'Say something dirty,' he said, pushing open her legs.

She smiled. Her eyes were closing.

'Marriage!' she whispered in his ear.

Jack plunged into her vengefully. 'Honey,' he protested, 'there's a time and a place for everything.'

The Lake of Zurich was calm under a blue sky. The hillsides were already touched with autumn tints. It was a day of perfect tranquillity; the ideal time for a lakeside lunch and the ideal setting.

Sam and Jane powered across the lake in his speed boat and found a tiny restaurant with a miniature harbour and a garden with red and purple geraniums and, at the

271

water's edge, a willow tree whose leaves were turning yellow.

They ate trout, drank a bottle of Swiss Dôle. Then another. There were things to be said and yet they hardly spoke a word. They were both depressed and Jane knew, without Sam saying anything, that something important between them had changed.

They sat on the lawn until the sun sank behind the top of the hills. She shivered. The air was getting cold.

'Let's go.'

'We should talk,' he said.

'Better not,' she said. 'What's the point?'

'I wanted to,' he said, 'but I can't. There's too much guilt involved. Things are different, now. Who knows? Amy and I might even have a chance.'

'I understand,' she said. 'I hate her guts, but I understand.' She smiled and rested her hand lightly on his shoulder, possessing him for a moment.

Sam stared out across the lake. It was a national holiday. The water was dotted with small boats. A man in a yellow oilskin was reeling in a wriggling fish. The setting sun flashed red on its scales.

The boats were making for the shore now. It was time to go home.

*　　*　　*

December '77. Another year gone.

The Dolder was the same. When did the Dolder ever change?

Or we? thought Jeffrey. Well, maybe just a little. The lines around Sam's eyes . . . weren't they just a touch deeper? And Ruby . . . ? Ruby had the same baby face and his smooth hair was still brown, but there was a circle of white, not grey, pure white, and perfectly round, about two inches in diameter, just over his left ear. Mort . . . well, Mort was like Cassius. He still had that lean and hungry look, still waiting, still hoping. When would he ever be satisfied?

272

'It's been a long time – three years, to be exact – since we voted to keep the company going.' Mort always made the speeches. 'It's been a struggle, but now I have something to tell you, something we can all be proud of. This year, for the first time since that meeting, King Brothers has broken even. We're in the black, guys. In fact we're more than in the black. In 1977, we made a million dollars.'

They all cheered.

Ruby had eyes only for Mort. Over the years, his admiration had turned to idolatry. As far as he was concerned, his brother could do no wrong.

Jeffrey, too, admired Mort, but in a very different fashion. He had learned from experience that what Mort said was not always an accurate indication of what he was thinking. He held him in the same esteem that the master of hounds has for the fox.

'There's only one thing that troubles me,' said Sam.

'What's that?' Mort scorned negative thinking.

'The Oil Corporation. Last time we were getting to be successful, they moved in on us. It's taken us three years to recover. I hear Jack Greenberg's bad-mouthing us again.'

'Forget Jack Greenberg,' said Mort harshly. 'No one's going to stop us. Not this time. No one. You all concentrate on business. Leave him to me.'

Ruby wondered exactly what he meant.

'We have more important things to talk about,' Mort continued. 'I'd like to hear what you guys think is going to happen to the market in 1978.'

'I left my little crystal ball behind,' said Jeffrey.

Sam shifted from foot to foot. 'Hard to say,' he came out with finally.

'I have a hunch,' Ruby said. 'I have a hunch that this is the year when we're going to see the price of crude take off.' He stroked his palm with the tip of his third finger: an unconscious gesture that did not escape Mort. He had only seen one other man do that.

'Remember 1973,' said Jeffrey. 'Let's not forget what happened.'

273

'Conditions are very different now,' said Ruby. 'OPEC has become a major power in the world.'

'There's a surplus of oil,' cautioned Sam. 'The Middle East . . . Alaska . . . the North Sea.'

'True,' said Mort. 'But the US still imports thirty per cent of its requirements and Germany, France, Italy and Japan depend a hundred per cent on imports. If there's a crisis in the Middle East, they'll all panic. That's when the market will move.'

'I guess you're right,' said Sam. 'But let's be careful.'

Mort grinned. 'Sure, Sam. Why not?' 'Careful' didn't get you to the top of the heap. He didn't have to say it. Everyone knew what he was thinking. 'One thing, though. We waited a long time. If our chance comes, let's make the most of it.'

By mid-1978, industry stocks were at their lowest level ever. The disturbances in Iran were beginning to look less like isolated protests against the regime of the Shah and more like the start of a planned, concerted revolution.

Still, everyone was convinced that there was no real danger to the Peacock Throne.

'Our generals are on first-name terms with the military in Iran,' said President Carter. Presumably that was intended to mean that the Shah was secure. It meant, too, that there was still time to buy crude. No one was panicking. Yet.

In July 1978, President Carter announced a number of new measures limiting imports of foreign crude to protect US domestic production.

It was generally assumed that the oil market was desperately weak. The protective measures were widely welcomed.

*   *   *

On a Monday morning in the first week of September, Mort strolled into Ruby's office.

'It's time,' he said casually.

274

'I'm not sure,' said Ruby doubtfully.

'It's time, Ruby.'

The two men stared at each other, saying nothing. The cabal was operating. They were reading each other's thoughts.

Ruby picked up the phone. Jeffrey came on the speaker. 'Mort thinks it's time. What do you think?'

'He said that once before. He was wrong.'

'This time I'm right,' said Mort.

'Well?' Ruby puffed at his cigarette, dabbing the ash on his shirt-front.

'I'm not sure,' said Jeffrey.

'Nor am I,' said Ruby glumly.

'The signs are there, but if we buy and the market doesn't take off we could be in deep trouble again. Maybe we should wait a few weeks.'

'We have more experience now,' Mort said. 'We would handle the producers better.'

'Maybe. What does Sam think?'

'Jeffrey, Sam's good – we all know that. He's a great negotiator and he's sharp as a whip, but when it comes to decisions – forget it.'

'OK, I'm with you. I hope you know what you're doing.'

'When will I ever know that?' said Mort.

'Sam, we think it's time. What do you think?' said Mort.

'Well . . .' said Sam uncertainly.

'Ruby, Jeffrey and I – we all agree – but of course we need your agreement too.'

'I see,' said Sam. 'Well, I'll go along with you guys.' It was Sam's signature tune.

Mort slammed down the phone and turned to Ruby. 'Let's go!' His eyes were shining.

The contingency plans had been worked out months ago. They knew what they had to do – buy up the world. They would buy crude anywhere they could find it – in Nigeria and Iran, in Saudi Arabia and Angola, in Algeria and Tunisia, in Dubai and Kuwait, Iraq and Syria, Israel,

Venezuela, the North Sea . . . They would move aggressively and they would move fast.

Ruby had long promised himself his own special treat.
For some months he had been registering dozens of new
companies, each sufficiently capitalized to operate inde-
pendently. No one could trace a connection between any
of the companies and King Brothers.

His plan was daring and ingenious. He intended to corner
all the storage space he could lay his hands on in the
Caribbean. The idea had come to him years ago, when he
learned that every drop of crude imported by Atlantic
and Orient – Martin Field's company – was transhipped
through the Caribbean terminals in Bonaire and Curaçao.
Like many American oil companies, A. and O. was wholly
dependent on the terminals, because it shipped its
crude from the Middle East in huge VLCCs, reducing
dramatically the freight cost of each ton of crude
shipped. The crude was then stored in the Caribbean
and transhipped in small tankers to refineries in America.
A. and O. had not one single discharge facility in the
US that could accommodate a VLCC. The Caribbean
terminals were their lifeline. Without them, they were
dead.

Ruby was still mad. He had a long memory. Martin Field
had it coming to him. The man had been hard-nosed and
remorseless. He had offered no way out, no compromise,
no hope.

In the name of King Brothers, but also in the names of
the dozens of other companies he had registered, Ruby
began to buy up options on Caribbean storage space. That
meant he could use the space or not, as he chose. If he
used it, he had to pay the rent. If he did not, he would have
to turn it back or sell it. The options were expensive, but
he was not concerned. He calculated that if the market
took off he would be able to sell the space easily and
probably turn over a nice profit.

It was clear to him that the terminal owners would
never agree to rent so much storage space to one company.

They would have been deeply suspicious of its motives. Hence the need for the 'dummy' companies.

In a few weeks, 'Operation Terminal' was successfully completed. For the first time in the history of the oil business, one company effectively controlled over sixty per cent of the storage space in the Caribbean.

Ruby sat at his desk, day after day, like a chubby cheerful spider patiently waiting for its prey. It was one particular fly he was lying in wait for – one phone call he was expecting with voracious anticipation.

When Jeffrey told Harry Dosumo how much crude he wanted to buy, Harry stretched the skin of his face so convincingly that it looked – just for a moment – like a smile.

'You sure about this?' he asked warily.

'Sure.'

'What happened to the market?'

'Nothing.'

Harry knew that was true. Otherwise the place would be swarming with buyers. Unable to resist the temptation, he took out his pocket calculator and, with feverishly clumsy fingers, worked out his fee.

He sat back, stunned.

'James Timba will kiss your backside,' he said.

'I assure you,' said Jeffrey hastily, 'that won't be necessary.'

What the NNPC – as it was now called – what the Nigerian National Petroleum Corporation needed was a big fat stick to beat the oil companies with. As long as they depended on Shell and BP to lift the bulk of the country's production, they would never run their own show. If NNPC could only develop some substantial customers of their own, they could talk to the companies from a position of strength. The Majors had to be convinced that, whatever they did, the Nigerians could do it better. The more crude NNPC sold, the more the Majors would have to lift. And the more they lifted, the more revenues

277

would increase and the more commercially independent Nigeria would become.

The Minister would be delighted. The President, General Obasanjo, would be delighted and James Timba would be a hero – a wealthy hero, too, he was thinking. He regarded Jeffrey almost as a messenger from God. He was carrying in his hand the big fat stick NNPC had been looking for all these years.

'Fifty thousand barrels a day!' He could scarcely believe his ears.

'Fifty,' said Jeffrey.

James Timba's head was shaking doubtfully. It was an automatic reflex. Never make things too easy for your customer. Anyway, he was naturally suspicious.

'The market's dead. No one is buying and you stroll in here calmly wanting to buy fifty thousand barrels. How come?' It was a fair question.

'We have a special deal,' said Jeffrey smoothly. 'Oil products against fertilizers. A barter. We're making enough on the fertilizers to subsidize the loss on the crude.'

Timba was eyeing Jeffrey shrewdly, but he learned nothing from the expression on his face. Was it the truth? You could never tell with these Englishmen. They were always so damned plausible – never more than when they were lying their bloody heads off.

So be it. So King Brothers knew something about the market that he didn't. So what? He needed a big sale. He needed it desperately. He was not a man to look a gift horse in the mouth, but, being Nigerian, he could also not resist the temptation to turn one gift horse into two.

'Why not buy a hundred thousand barrels?'

'I don't need a hundred thousand barrels.'

'Management will not sign contracts with traders right now,' said Timba.

'Management would sign a contract with the devil if he was in the market,' said Jeffrey drily.

James Timba sighed. Negotiating from weakness was no fun. The only weapon you had was bluff. 'I might be able to sell the Minister the idea of a hundred-thousand-barrel contract.' As if it were a new thought.

'No deal,' said Jeffrey.

'Even if you only had to lift fifty?'

Jeffrey was puzzled. 'I don't get it.'

'Let's say, for example, we do a deal for fifty thousand barrels and make it look like it was a hundred.'

'What for?'

'I have my reasons.'

'Whatever they are, I don't like it. It won't work.'

'Then,' said James Timba, 'I suggest you buy from someone else. I don't know who would have all that Low Sulphur crude to sell, but you're an ingenious chap. I'm sure you'll find another source of supply.'

He wouldn't. Not for fifty thousand barrels. They both knew that.

'Just give me that again,' said Jeffrey reluctantly.

Timba beamed. 'Let's say we have an agreement for fifty thousand barrels a day – and a side letter to confirm it – but we sign a contract for a hundred thousand barrels. That's five million tons of crude. I can tell you, in confidence, that I need a contract for a really big volume to show the Majors. With that in my hand, I can force them to increase their liftings. It's what the Minister wants. It's what the President wants. They're on my back every day. I can assure you, you'd only have to lift fifty thousand barrels. You'd be helping Nigeria,' he said, coaxing Jeffrey. 'We need help.'

Jeffrey thought about it. The stuffing was oozing out of the arm of the filthy brown plastic chair he sat in.

'You need new furniture,' he said. 'It's a deal.'

James Timba flashed the ivories. 'I need a lot of things,' he said. 'I won't forget it.' He was a happy man.

Which was more than anyone could say for his secretary. This time again, there was no one in the waiting room to pick up the fan-blown debris for her. For a moment Jeffrey was tempted to help. Just for a moment. She crawled on the floor, grabbing papers, and scowling at him even more venomously than usual. It was sad, he thought, closing the door gently behind him, how quickly love faded.

By late 1978, there was a noticeable change in the streets of Tehran. The demonstrators were more aggressive, the police more panicky and much more violent. Most of the time, the city was calm, but the calm had about it a tense, menacing quality. The Iranians, at the best of times a suspicious people, trusted no one – neither brother nor friend. The secret police were everywhere. A careless word could lead to arrest, torture and death. Behind the scenes, in the bazaars, the mosques and market places, the mullahs did their work, spreading the word of the saviour to come – the Ayatollah who sat patiently in Paris, waiting to be called.

The moment Edgar walked into Ali Nagaar's office, he sensed that there was something different about it. What it was exactly he could not, at first, make out. Ali was his old self, a little more anxious perhaps, a shade twitchier, but still, nevertheless, the commercial manager of the NIOC, still in the same office, still at the same desk.

He even seemed pleased to see Edgar. There was no one in the waiting room. The market was dead. These days, Ali Nagaar spent most of his time shuffling papers.

'I'm here to buy crude, Ali.'

Ali sucked in air noisily, shook his head in a reaction intended to convey the enormity of the problem Edgar was causing him, and peered anxiously at the ceiling.

Edgar was accustomed to Ali's performances. He passed the time looking at the huge photograph hanging behind Ali Nagaar's desk – a magnificent view of the Holy City of Isfahan . . . Isfahan! That was it. The Shah had taken a walk. Where was he? And then Edgar noticed His Imperial Majesty hanging on a side wall. It was the same portrait, the same proud bearing and arrogant expression, the same god-like pose, but not the same wall.

The Shah was still there, but he had been subtly de-

moted. Edgar knew his Iranians. Ali Nagaar was keeping
his options open. If, as he always seemed to fear, the ceiling
should ever fall on that worried little man, he had his alibi
ready. Loyalty was a fine and noble thing, as long as the
object of your loyalty was in a position to protect you.
Edgar was sure that Ali had a portrait of a certain well-
known Ayatollah stashed away – just in case.

'Very difficult,' said Ali. 'We have so little crude to sell.'

'I heard differently.'

'Rumours spread by our enemies.'

'The market's dead. I'm willing to buy fifty thousand
barrels.'

He knew, of course, that if Iran erupted, if the revolution
ever came, then all bets would be off. King Brothers would
never get their crude. The whole Persian Gulf could be
closed, contracts with the West cancelled and there was
not a damn thing anyone could do about it. The Iranians
would simply stamp 'force majeure' across all their commitments.

Edgar got his contract and Ali Nagaar had fun making
him sweat for it. When they signed, Edgar asked: 'What's
going to happen, Ali?'

Ali Nagaar took off his spectacles and laid them on the
desk in front of him. 'It is Allah who will decide.'

'Not His Imperial Majesty?'

Ali lowered his voice and cast a nervous glance at the
portrait of his lord and benefactor. 'There are those,' he
whispered, 'who say the peacock is an unlucky bird.'

The Natoilco car sped from the airport through the wide,
empty boulevards of Luanda.

The sidewalks were deserted, the shops and restaurants
boarded up, the banks closed, their Grecian facades decay-
ing, their marble halls silent and abandoned.

Sam checked into the Panorama, a hotel built on a finger
of land no wider than a hundred metres dividing the Bay
of Luanda from the Atlantic Ocean.

He opened the windows of his room and pushed back

the shutters. Russians and East German ships lay at anchor in the bay, line astern, all the way to the horizon, waiting to discharge their cargoes. A few – not many – carried foodstuffs . . . fish and meat, fruit and vegetables, flour, powdered milk, sugar, beer and canned foods. Most of them brought tanks and guns, bombs and ammunition. Angola's 'friends' had their priorities right.

He looked down at the Panorama's swimming pool that no one ever bothered to fill. The carcass of a dead cat lay rotting in the deep end. The garden on the edge of the bay was untended, choked with weeds, but still a fairyland of tropical trees and bushes: scarlet poinciana, orange bougainvillea, cream and pink frangipani, bird of paradise, giant flowering cactus.

On the rocks bordering the bay, a sea bird wandered on spindly legs looking for crabs.

Sam was hot and sweaty after the long flight and the drive from the airport. The air was heavy and humid. He stripped off and stepped into the bath to take a shower. He turned on the tap, but there was no water, nor, when he checked, was there any electricity. No power meant no lights, no air-conditioning and, probably, no sleep.

So, what else was new?

Eduardo Cabrillo, the Managing Director of Natoilco, had the look of a bird of prey. His glance was sharp, his eyes cold and keen, the curl of his mouth predatory. Whatever he believed, he believed passionately. He was a dedicated Marxist, a patriot and a fanatic. A dangerous combination. Dangerous for him and even more so for his enemies.

He loathed the Minister, José Rocha, with a concentrated, passionate loathing that only he was capable of, and Rocha responded with a characteristically bemused, casual hostility. Since Rocha was Sam's special friend, it followed that Cabrillo needed careful handling. Unfortunately for Sam, Cabrillo was convinced that Angola needed no one's help in selling its crude and that, far from calling on additional outside assistance, they should throw out

Gulf and all the other capitalist exploiters who, he insisted, had robbed the country blind over the years.

'We have studied your draft agency agreement, Mr Carlstroem. It is admirably presented and cleverly argued. It is not, regrettably, for us.'

'I'm sorry to hear that, Mr Cabrillo,' said Sam. 'If there's anything you would care to change – we are naturally very flexible.'

'Naturally,' said Cabrillo drily. 'It is not, however, a question of changing the small print. I am fundamentally opposed to any such agreement.'

'We can help you find new markets for your crude,' said Sam. 'In a few years, you will have built up an oil corporation to match those of Iran, Algeria and Nigeria, for example. At that time, we shall gladly bow out.'

'And meanwhile, King Brothers would have the exclusive right to sell half of our production of Cabinda crude. Half the nation's biggest natural resource would be in your hands, half in Gulf's – none in ours.'

'It seems to us to be an ideal compromise for you. After all, you have no national oil corporation yet and hardly any qualified staff – except, of course,' he added slyly, 'one or two experts like yourself.'

'I'm aware of your proposals,' said Cabrillo acidly. 'I have read the contract. I am opposed to it in principle, not only because you would make far too much money but also, and more important, because, frankly, a privately owned Western trading organization should not represent a Marxist state. It makes no sense, either commercially or politically.'

And that was that.

José Rocha was another story. 'The man is a fool,' he said. 'He has no judgement. Except,' he added wistfully, 'where women are concerned. His wife is ... she is very ... efficient. In fact, I'm thinking of asking her to be my secretary.'

Sam had heard about Cabrillo's English wife. She was,

apparently, dynamite. Cabrillo would be mortified if she came to work for the Minister. Rocha had a certain reputation where women were concerned. No one had actually seen any of his secretaries type a letter. Their work seemed to be done for them in the typing pool where accuracy was valued above other more personal attributes.

'He's opposed to the agency agreement in principle,' said Sam. 'Naturally, that doesn't concern me in the least, since I know you favour it.' He hoped he sounded convincing, but he was far from confident. He imagined Rocha must be a baby compared to Cabrillo when it came to political in-fighting.

'The agreement will be signed in the next few days. I have the President's promise,' said Rocha.

Sam brightened. That was good news. Rocha had never before sounded so confident. There was only Cabrillo to worry about. Rocha the soldier against Cabrillo the politician. Well, he had no choice. There was little more he could do now. He could only sit back and wait.

'How long do you think . . . ?'

'As soon as possible,' said Rocha and smiled.

'I'll be at the Panorama.'

'Leave everything to me.'

'What will you do if Cabrillo convinces the President not to sign?'

'I'll cut out his heart,' said José Rocha, throwing back his head and laughing heartily. As he did so, either consciously or unconsciously, he straightened his gun belt. Sam could imagine him zapping a few FNLA troops in the bush and consuming a pack of South African Lion Lager before lunch.

Such is war. Such is business.

To Sam's surprise, the call came through the following morning at about nine o'clock, just as he was finishing breakfast. The President must have made a quick decision. His heart was beating fast as he rushed to reception.

But it was not José Rocha. It was Amy. A sharp pang of fear sliced his stomach.

'It's Laura. You'd better come home quickly.'

He landed in Zurich the next morning and took a taxi directly from Kloten to the hospital.

He was too late. Laura had died the night before.

Amy was sitting in the kitchen. He tried to put his arms round her, but she pushed him away.

'I caught the evening flight,' he said. 'She must have . . . it must have happened while I was on the plane.'

Amy said nothing.

'She seemed so well. I had no idea. I would never have gone if I'd thought . . . never. If only I'd stayed home.'

Amy just sat there, stiff and upright, staring out of the window. 'You had your business to do,' she said. There was no anger in her words, no reproach, but he felt the distance between them. This was something too terrible for their marriage to bear. It would never survive it. There was nothing left to share – not even their grief.

He went upstairs to Laura's bedroom and closed the door carefully behind him. There was a photo of James Dean in the frame of the mirror by the bed and a poster of the Rolling Stones taped to the wall. On the desk was an untidy pile of pop magazines and a faded Polaroid of Laura skiing in Zermatt. She must have been four or five. She was speeding down the nursery slopes, hair flying in the wind, arms and legs wide apart. Sam was waiting for her at the bottom with his camera and she was calling out to him. He could hear her now.

On her bedside table was a pencil drawing of a man and a little girl floating in the sky, holding hands. He picked it up. Now that he looked at it again, it really was very like him. Only the nose was not quite right . . . she would have to do something about the nose.

He looked round for her school uniform, but he couldn't see it. She had not come home yet.

He sat on the bed and waited for her.

*

During the funeral service, Sam cried and Amy stared ahead with dead eyes. Once, as he watched her, she seemed to brush away a tear, or perhaps she was making the sign of the cross. He was not sure which. Maybe she wasn't either.

The next day, she flew to New York with Edward.

There was nothing for him to do in the morning but go to the office. Karl did not say much. What was there to say? Thank God for Karl. At least Sam still had him. His wife and his family had gone, but Karl would never desert him – honest, dull, faithful Karl. What would he ever do without him?

The telex from Luanda arrived in the afternoon. The President had given his OK. José Rocha had signed the agreement. Five minutes later, Mort was on the phone. He had already seen a copy of the telex in New York.

'Congratulations, Sam. What a coup!'

'Not right now, Mort. Can we talk later?'

'I'm sorry. It's a bad moment. I heard about – your daughter.'

He can't remember her name, thought Sam. 'It's OK,' he said. 'I need a little time, that's all.'

'Sure you do. Take a few days off. Unless, of course, you feel you have to get back to Luanda. I leave that to you. Maybe it would do you good – take your mind off things.'

Even now, Mort was pushing him. The guy never stopped. But then he had no kids. No, that wasn't it. He had no fucking heart.

'I'll be OK,' said Sam.

'I wrote you a letter of condolence. You should get it tomorrow. I sent it by courier.'

That was important, thought Sam. He would get the letter tomorrow.

'I'm sorry, Sam. Deeply sorry. I know how you must feel.'

How would he know that?

The line was quiet for a few moments. At first, Sam thought Mort had put down the phone, but, in fact, Mort was wondering whether or not he should give Sam another nudge. He decided in favour.

'Perhaps you should jump on a plane after all,' he said, 'just to make sure there are no foul-ups with the agreement. This is the biggest yet. Of course, you must do what you think is right,' he added quickly. 'You know I trust your judgement.'

Sam tried to think about tomorrow. All the other tomorrows. Maybe Mort was right. He should jump on a plane. The truth was that he had nothing better to do.

It was a coup all right, no doubt about it. Never before in history had a trading company – a six-year-old one, at that – been appointed the exclusive sales agent of an oil producing country. He picked up the telex from Angola. This was what he had been working for, wasn't it? This was his, no one else's – not Mort's, not Jeffrey's, not Ruby's and not fucking Siegfried Gerber's. They had taken his daughter from him, but this was one thing they could never take away.

It was his. For the first time in his whole life he had done something he could really feel proud of.

Mort was in bed reading the yellow copies – the telexes he never had time to read in the office.

Julie sat in front of the mirror, brushing her long black hair, stroking it with the bristles, turning her head this way and that, studying her reflection in the glass, eyeing critically the skin on her neck and the line of her chin.

'How's it going?'

'It's going great. Matter of fact, this is a real important time for us. We've bought every barrel of crude we could lay our hands on – half the goddam world. I'm guessing the market's about to take off.'

'I'm sure you're right. You always are.'

At thirty-three her complexion was still perfect – well, nearly perfect. Perhaps, she was thinking, there were one or two wrinkles here and there . . . not wrinkles exactly, but faint, very faint lines . . . the sort only another woman would notice in a side light. She acknowledged to herself that she was still a beautiful woman, but it gave her no great pleasure. In a few years she'd be forty and Mort would still be in bed reading the yellow copies.

'What about Jack Greenberg?'

'What about him?' Mort paused, holding a half-read telex.

'Wasn't he giving you a hard time?'

Mort went back to the telex. 'He won't bother us any more.'

He seemed to be making an effort. He was taking more notice of her. But his attentions were so studied, so unspontaneous, that they had the opposite effect on her to the one he obviously intended. Sometimes she wondered if he had his secretary remind him about birthdays and wedding anniversaries. Otherwise how would he ever remember? Maybe she misjudged him, but she would not be surprised if his marital sexual obligations were not carefully noted in his diary together with all his other appointments.

Tonight, it seemed, was one of those nights. She knew the signs all too well. He had finished the telexes, but he was sitting up in bed waiting for her. Usually he turned out his bedside light and went straight to sleep. He never took sleeping pills; he did not need them. It was unusual for him to be in bed later than midnight and he rose at four-thirty every day, including weekends. He seemed not to need more than four hours' sleep and he did more while other men slept than most of them did in their whole working day. There was a certain tension in the air; she could feel the vibrations. He was waiting for her to come to bed and she, reluctant to go to him, went on brushing her hair with long unhurried strokes and examining herself in the mirror with her big hazel eyes.

Every day brought Mort closer to his dream of heading up the most successful oil company in the world. Once, that would have been enough – more than enough for him – but not any more. For one thing, he missed Rosemary.

There were times, like now, when he hungered for her easy sexuality, her uncritical approval. It was what Julie had once given him. Now he had the feeling she despised him. It was tough to live with, especially when the rest of the world put you on a pedestal.

'Are you coming to bed?' he asked impatiently. She put down the brush, took a last look at her reflection in the mirror and went to him.

He turned out the light and moved over to her in the bed. She lay there in the dark, hoping that this time it would be different. He kissed her on the mouth gently and caressed her breasts. As a lover, he had always been unselfish but predictable. She remembered when he had been passionate. Now he was cool, clinical and skilful. He gave her physical pleasure, but that was all.

Sometimes, copulation became a mental struggle between them and they wrestled passionately, but without affection, each willing the other to reach their climax first, though it was always she who surrendered in the end. In some extraordinary fashion, when the orgasm overwhelmed her, she would feel defeated, as if she had lost a battle.

Tonight, she had no heart for a prolonged struggle. She reached her climax quickly and, as she did, she was thinking of Leo.

Mort turned on the light and drank some water. 'How was it?'

'Need you ask?'

'I like to hear.'

'You're very good at it,' she said. 'You know that.'

'You make it sound like a fault.'

Julie sat up and looked at him. 'Oh no, it's not a fault to be good at sex. I just wish it felt more like making love.'

'You mean you don't feel anything?' His pride was hurt.

'Of course I do.' Suddenly, she was angry. 'You're a great screw, I told you.'

He turned out the light. Why did it seem like an insult? 'I'm trying to make things better for us,' he said.

289

Julie did not answer. He reached out his hand and felt the tears on her face. 'What is it?'

'I don't know,' she said. 'I guess I always thought I'd have a real family life . . . kids . . . a loving husband – you know, like a normal marriage.'

'If you wanted a normal marriage, you should have married a normal man.'

Maybe so. Maybe he was right and that had been her mistake. She wondered if she would have been happy with a 'normal' man.

'How is Sam taking it . . . Laura, I mean?'

'You knew,' he said, surprised.

'Yes,' she said. 'I knew. Why didn't you mention it?'

'I didn't want to upset you.'

Even that he had not known how to share.

Jack Greenberg drove back to his apartment with the radio turned up full blast. He was in high spirits. Rachel and he were engaged to be married. The future looked rosy. Not that he was in love with her exactly, but he had to admit that he was fond of her. And she loved him – that was for sure. E.M. would be treating him differently from now on. He might not like it too much but, like it or not, he was getting Jack Greenberg for a son-in-law. And Jack? Well, he was getting the sixth richest man in America for a father-in-law and that couldn't be bad.

He glanced at his gold Rolex. It was nearly midnight. He thought of grabbing a couple of drinks at his favourite disco and maybe picking up a piece of ass, but he was tired. It was Sunday night. It was late. Tomorrow was another day.

As he got out of the Cadillac, the two men in stocking masks jumped him. The streets were deserted, but who asked questions anyway? They dragged him down an alley and flung him against a wall. One of them grabbed him by the hair, forcing his head back until it felt like his neck would break. The other placed an enormous hand round his throat and laid a thumb on his Adam's apple.

290

Jack was terrified, but not so terrified that he was unable to think. If they were going to beat him up, they would be doing it right now. If they were going to kill him, then surely they would be waving a knife or a gun in his face and there were no weapons in sight.

'My money's in my back pocket,' he managed to say. It was tough to talk when all you could see was the stars and a thumb was massaging your Adam's apple.

'That's where your head'll be if you don't shut your fucking mouth!' The thumb jabbed savagely on the cricoid cartilage and Jack was choking. The thumb eased back, just a little. 'A friend of mine says you've been a bad boy. He wants you to stop being a bad boy. You think you could do that for him?' The thumb increased the pressure again. Jack was fighting for breath. Again, the thumb relaxed.

Jack gulped in air. He was feeling better now. This was not the way he would have chosen to spend his evening, but he was no longer terrified.

'Who is this friend of yours?' he asked boldly.

The rubbery lips moved behind the stocking mask. The face was a sea creature, slimy, deadly.

'Don't get cute. You know who he is. And if you don't, then play it smart. Make a resolution – be nice to everyone. Otherwise my friend will be angry. Can I tell my friend you'll show him and his family respect? Can I tell him that?'

'Tell your friend to go screw himself! You too while he's about it! I'm sure you'd love it, you bastard!' Where the words came from, Jack would never know. But then no one ever knew how they would react in a situation like this.

The thumb dug deep into the cricoid cartilage again. 'You hear that? The fat guy's calling me a fruit. You calling me a fruit, little fat guy?'

Jack twisted free for a moment and tried to run, but the man grabbed him by the neck and threw him against the wall. The sea creature writhed venomously in its cave. The man drew back his arm slowly, so that Jack could see what was coming, and drove a fist into his face again and again with great hammer blows, taking his time, working carefully, systematically, first on the mouth until his teeth were shattered and the lips blown up like red balloons, then on the eyes, until the eyeballs were obscured behind obscene red-veined swellings that grew and grew until finally they burst, spewing blood across Jack's forehead and down his face.

For the first time, the other man spoke: 'This ain't right. We was only to scare him.'

'So what? You heard what he said. He insulted me. This is between me and him. The guy called me a fruit.'

His hand was still round Jack's throat, but now it was holding him up against the wall.

'Or did I hear wrong?'

The rubber lips widened in a smile. The sea creature loomed through the mist.

The words grated painfully in the back of his throat, oozing through the swollen mouth.

'Fucking fruit!'

His lips bubbling blood, he spat in his tormentor's face. It was a defiant, brave, crazy gesture and he paid for it.

The great fist slammed into his nose. That first blow broke it. The next five sliced it from top to bottom, spattering bloody slivers of bone down Jack's shirt-front.

Moaning quietly, only partly conscious, he slid down the wall until his haunches touched the ground. For a moment he sat there. Then he toppled over onto his side.

'You shouldn't have done that. We broke our contract. No violence, he said. He said strictly no violence.'

The laugh was more like a giggle, ending with a gurgling and a scratching on the roof of the mouth, as though the man were about to spit. He bent down and carefully separated Jack's legs. Then he kicked him seven times in the genitals with the steel-capped toes of his boots. A professional job.

'You call this violence?' he said.

*

On Christmas Eve, the whole of New York was home. Every businessman in town was with his family – every businessman except Mortimer King.

He was sitting at his desk drinking bourbon. Being alone, planning the next day, had become his favourite occupation. The end of the year was special – this year, above all. He could look back on the last six years and feel satisfied. Despite everything – despite all the problems and setbacks – he was coming out on top, as he had always known that one day he would. It was where he belonged.

The office was nearly in darkness. Only the desk-top lamp threw a dim circle of light on the yellow telexes spread out in front of him. He had read them all before, of course, several times. He knew them practically by heart. But he found them relaxing, soothing – therapeutic. Besides, what was there to go home for? Julie was cool and distant these days and he was almost too caught up in business to care.

It was like a dream come true. They had the oil to sell and the whole industry was lining up to buy, desperate for crude – any volume, any quality. It hardly seemed to matter any more. It was a seller's market to end all seller's markets. And he was a seller – a seller, moreover, of almost unlimited quantities. He was the guy who could call the shots. Finally. He was sitting on a fortune, millions and millions of barrels, selling them slowly, grudgingly, as if each barrel were a gold bar. Every hour the price rose. Every single hour. And he should know. He was the one pushing it up.

This Christmas, while the other guys were eating their turkey and Christmas pudding, giving themselves a pain in the belly, he would still be here in the office.

And when they returned from their Christmas vacation, he would be waiting for them.

The phone rang. It was Ruby.

'You heard about Jack Greenberg?'

'Yes.'

'He's badly beat up. They're not sure he'll recover.'

'So I heard.'

'Who would do a crazy thing like that?'

'I can think of a few guys who might have liked to.'

'For Chrissake, Mort!'

'You think it was me?'

'No.' Ruby faltered. 'How can you say that? It's just that we talked about Jack so many times . . . what we should do about him . . .' His voice trailed off.

'It wasn't me,' said Mort. 'Someone did it for me.'

'You're working late.'

'Just winding up a couple of things. I'm leaving soon.'

Mort put down the phone and poured himself another bourbon.

He was on his way. No one could stop him now. No one. Not Jack Greenberg. Not anyone.

BOOK FIVE

Gusher!

When the revolution in Iran erupted it blew with all the power of a giant volcano. Overnight the supply of Iranian crude was cut off and the fear of even greater disasters in the Middle East created the biggest panic the oil industry had ever known.

Cosseted and pampered by years of security, reassured by the power of the Majors, deceived by the docility of the producing countries, the industry was caught with its pants down. It reacted as people do when the earth shakes and their idols tumble. Buyers did not know which way to run to escape disaster. The industry was in turmoil. Everyone joined the mad mindless rush to buy. But where was the crude? It was tough to find – at any price.

The tired gaunt face of the Shah of Iran as he stood for the last time on his country's soil was a symbol of a change much more fundamental than the overthrow of the Peacock Throne.

The telephones in the offices of King Brothers never stopped ringing. The word soon got around that they had crude to sell. There were not enough hours in the day to take all the calls. Messages from panic-stricken buyers piled up on traders' desks. The industry had run down its stocks almost to zero. This was a crisis for the whole world and a bitter experience for the oil companies.

Already, they were calling it the Crunch of '79. The lights were out in Washington. The speed limit in the US was down to fifty miles an hour. Gasoline queues circled every gas station and senators and congressmen all wanted the answer to the same questions. Why hadn't they been warned? Why hadn't the industry done its homework? Where were the strategic stockpiles? Who was responsible? Someone had to be.

The Arabs had the West by the throat. It was beginning to look like the end of the world.

But not for the oil traders. For them it was the dawn of a new golden age.

It was a long time – five years, eight months and twenty-three days to be exact – since Mort had last spoken to Ed Hunt, President, Chairman and owner of Integrated Refining. From the way Hunt talked, it might have been yesterday.

'Mort, how are ya? Ed here.'

'Hi, Ed.'

'I'm in the market for some crude, Mort, baby, so naturally I thought of my old buddy. How are things?'

'Just great, Ed.'

'We weren't able to do much last time we spoke, but things were different then, eh?' Hunt laughed, a little too heartily

'They were,' said Mort.

'I could use some Arab Light. You have any?'

'Plenty.'

'Gee, that's just fantastic. How much can you sell me?'

'Not a barrel,' said Mort.

'Could you let me have that again?' said Ed Hunt. 'The line isn't too great.'

'None,' said Mort distinctly. 'I said none, Ed.'

Ed Hunt laughed. 'I'm a buyer, Mort. You don't seem to understand.'

'I'm not selling.'

'I thought you said you had plenty of Arab Light, Mort, baby. How come you're not a seller?'

'I am a seller, but I'm not selling to you, Ed . . . baby.'

'Why not, for crying out loud?' Hunt's urbane manner was beginning to fray at the edges.

'Well, I'll tell you, Ed. Last time we spoke you refused me credit, even though there was no risk to you.'

'You were just starting up,' Hunt protested. 'You were nobody. How was I supposed to know you'd become one of the biggest oil traders in the world in six years?'

'You weren't.'

'Right you are. I need crude, Mort. This is a major crisis for my company. I need your help.'

'I needed yours,' said Mort. 'Remember?'

'I don't recall the details exactly,' Hunt stammered.

'You want me to remind you?'

'For Chrissake! I'll pay you over the market. I'll be generous.'

'I make the market,' said Mort icily. 'Buyers pay my price. I'm the one who decides what's generous.'

'OK. Name your price. I'll pay it.'

Mort hesitated. What the hell, this was business. He was in the game to make money, after all.

'How much crude do you need?'

'Now you're talking. I need a million tons. More, if you got it.' Hunt sounded relieved.

'You can have two hundred thousand.'

'I'll take it,' said Hunt quickly.

'The base price is nineteen dollars a barrel.'

'Nineteen? But . . . but . . .' Ed Hunt was torn. The price was way over the market, but there was no other place he could go to buy crude. He knew. He had tried everyone else. 'It's a deal.' He had not fully absorbed what Mort had said. 'Wait a minute. Base price?' he said nervously. 'What do you mean by base price?'

'The base price is nineteen dollars. I'm adding a premium of two dollars a barrel to it.'

'Jesus Christ, Mort, that's usury! What in God's name for?'

'You called King Brothers a crappy little outfit. That was very insulting. I never forgot that. That's what the premium's for – Ed, baby.'

'You've got to be kidding. You're charging me a premium for something I don't even remember saying six years ago.'

'Five years, eight months and twenty-three days,' said Mort. 'And you said it.'

Hunt gasped. 'I got to tell you, Mort . . . I got to tell you . . . you are . . .' He broke off. He could see the crude disappearing down the tube if he said any more.

'Yes, Ed? What am I?'

Ed Hunt was holding the phone so tightly his knuckles were white. The blood had stopped circulating in his arm.

'If you could just see your way to . . .' he muttered . . . 'Reducing the price a touch, I'd be real . . . I'm sorry if I said . . .'

Mort cut in. 'Twenty-one dollars is the price. Take it or leave it. I don't give a damn.'

'I'll take it. But I'll remember, Mort. You can count on it. I'll remember.'

'Glad to hear it,' said Mort. 'That's exactly what I want you to do.'

The telex from the NNPC, Lagos, was signed, 'Timba, Marketing Manager'. It was brusque and distinctly un-friendly. It contained phrases like 'flagrant abuse of agree-ment' and 'failure to comply with clear contractual obligations'. Altogether, it was a lulu and, like most un-pleasant surprises, it came without warning. Jeffrey booked the British Caledonian night flight and phoned Mort.

'It's a shot across our bows,' said Mort.

'It looks like a direct hit to me. Cancellation is in the air.'

'Cancellation? You're out of your mind. What have we done? They have no legal grounds for cancelling the con-tract.'

'Legal grounds?' Jeffrey scoffed cynically.

'Yes, legal grounds.' Jeffrey could be so damned obtuse and irritating. 'You don't think they need legal justifi-cation?'

'No, I don't. But if they needed it, they'd get it.'

'Maybe you know something I don't. We're lifting all the oil we're entitled to. Why shouldn't we? We're making a killing on every barrel.'

'Quite so,' said Jeffrey. 'I'll be in touch. And remember one thing: we're not dealing with fools. They know the contract price is way below the market now and they haven't forgotten how we wriggled when we were hurting back in 1974. Would it be so surprising if they cut us back, or even if they tried to cancel on us?'

'They can't do that!' Mort was as close to being agitated as he ever got. 'We have a contract.'

'We do?' said Jeffrey innocently.

Why was it, thought Mort, that even his own partners did their best to frustrate him? If only people would just do what he told them, the world would be a simpler place.

This time the anteroom was crowded. Nigerian crude was top of the hit parade again and James Timba's miserable secretary had more than enough helpers to pick up her papers.

The turnover of appointments was rapid: a bad sign. If any confirmation were needed, you only had to take a look at the misery on the faces of the would-be buyers as they left the marketing manager's office to know that none of them had got what they wanted. James Timba was having a ball. At regular intervals he stood there, framed in the doorway and – like the proud black emperor of some ancient tribal kingdom – surveyed his petitioners, humble representatives of his client states and, face blank of expression, raised his hand, forefinger extended. The chosen one leapt swiftly to his feet, before the Emperor changed his mind. The rest sank gloomily back into their chairs to resume their patient vigil.

A buyer's life in a seller's market is not an enviable one.

Jeffrey's 'reprieve' came after a couple of hours, to the great irritation and envy of those many unfortunates who had been waiting for days.

'So what can I do for you, Jeffrey?' said Timba breezily.

'Don't tell me you want to sign a contract with NNPC like all the other chaps out there.'

An ominous start. Jeffrey had his secret doubts that pestered and buzzed him, like mosquitoes in the night – sharp fears that stabbed him in the small gloomy hours before dawn. It was hard to have to accept in the glaring light of day that these fears might, after all, be justified. 'Why would I want to sign a contract,' he said, 'when I already have one?'

'Had,' corrected James Timba.

'Had?'

'Had,' repeated the marketing manager firmly.

'What happened to it?'

'The Minister cancelled it.'

'On what grounds?'

'Breach of contract,' said Timba.

'We lifted fifty thousand barrels a day,' said Jeffrey. 'We never missed a lifting. Not once. We never sent in a tanker outside its laydays.'

'Correct.'

'So where's the breach of contract?'

'Look at the contract.' Timba offered him a copy.

Jeffrey waved it away. 'I've read it – many times.'

'I imagine you know what you signed?'

'Certainly I know what I signed.'

'You will recall, then, that you signed a contract for a hundred thousand barrels a day,' said Timba. 'You only lifted fifty. You're in breach of contract.'

James Timba's eyes never wavered. Jeffrey's mouth fell open.

'Do I need to jog your memory, James?' he said when he had recovered. 'We had a side agreement. It was your idea, remember? You wanted to show Shell and BP that you'd concluded a huge contract with an independent buyer. And you did show them, didn't you? I recall your telling me how they agreed to increase their liftings by ten per cent. You even thanked me for the help I gave you.'

'I did?' Timba said innocently.

'Look at your records, James. You must have the original side agreement on file. It confirms that the contract was really only for fifty thousand barrels.'

'Well, now you see . . . the thing is . . . I don't have any side agreement in the dossier,' said James Timba. 'Here, look for yourself.' He handed the dossier to Jeffrey. This time Jeffrey did not wave it away. He examined it carefully. No side agreement.

'I could have my secretary look through her files,' said James Timba helpfully.

Jeffrey raised a hand. 'Spare me that.'

Timba shuffled the papers in the dossier and shook his head. 'No,' he said, 'I don't see any side agreement. You wouldn't have a copy on you by any chance?'

'As it happens,' said Jeffrey, 'I do.' If the devious bastard thought he was going to get away with this . . . He produced it. 'There are plenty more where that came from,' he said. He sat back, studying James Timba's reaction. He had to hand it to the guy. He was a cool customer. His smooth black face betrayed not a ripple of agitation; his features were relaxed and composed. The man was a pro, no doubt about it.

James Timba nodded and handed back the agreement. 'I don't see a signature,' he said.

'Of course there's a signature. Look. Here it is. Here's mine and here's . . .' Jeffrey was about to point to the Permanent Secretary's signature when he suddenly realized that it was not there. And then he remembered . . . James Timba had been rushed or, at least, that was the excuse; his secretary had only typed one copy; they had signed it here in the office and Timba had run off to get the Permanent Secretary's signature, promising to mail the copies to London. He had done so. Only they were not signed. Jeffrey had signed a couple of copies and sent them back to Timba, but Timba had not returned them. Jeffrey had forgotten to follow up.

It was hard to believe that even James Timba could be so devious.

'I imagine it's no use protesting that you are completely misrepresenting the true agreement between us?'

'If you put your protest in writing, I'll see it reaches the right destination.'

So much for protests. It would take years to get an answer and there was no doubt what the answer would be: 'Your letter is being looked into, etc . . .' Meanwhile, they could kiss goodbye to doing business with NNPC.

Jesus, what a mess. What a bastard. He had to think. Maybe Dosumo could do something.

But Harry Dosumo was on a trip up north. How long for . . . ? Indefinitely.

Catching flies no doubt.

Jack Greenberg lay on his back in the hospital bed and stared at the ceiling. His brain was functioning all right, but it was the only part of his body that was. They injected him with painkillers every few hours, but even so the pain was acute, almost unbearable. A few days after they brought him in, they took the dressing off his eyes. They were swollen and pulpy, like over-ripe melons, and they hurt like hell, but he was beginning to see again. A week later and he had come to know the ceiling intimately, every lump, bump, crack, peel and stain. He would close his eyes and memorize them. There wasn't much else to do. Pain was something he could live with, but boredom could not be deadened with pills and injections.

Rachel sat at his bedside every day. He liked that. He was surprised how much he liked it. It could have been a disaster for their relationship, especially since Rachel had to do all the talking. There wasn't too much talking you could do with a splintered jaw. During this difficult time, Rachel revealed qualities he never knew she possessed: tenderness, understanding and a great deal of tact. She seemed to know instinctively when to talk and when to be silent, and she never smothered him with either the phoney cheerfulness or the syrupy sympathy he endured from most of his visitors.

304

It was a long time before he could speak – even longer before anyone could understand what he was saying. Not once did Rachel mention the vicious beating he had taken; she never asked him a single question about it, afraid that he was too ill to be upset. Jack, on the other hand, thought about little else. Finally, he came out with it. 'I'll get him,' he muttered, his face twisting with pain. 'I'll get him.'

'Who?' said Rachel. 'Who did it?'

'He did.'

'Who? Tell me,' she begged. 'And why? We have to tell the police.'

But slowly, painfully, he turned his face away from her and stared at the wall. The subject was closed.

In time, they said, his jaw would heal – and his nose. The kidneys, too, though at first the doctors had feared permanent damage. But the prognosis for Jack ever having children was poor. It was something he had never even considered. If anyone had asked him if he wanted kids, he would probably have said no, but when Rachel told him what the doctors said, he cried.

'It's not for sure,' she said. 'You need rest. In a few weeks, they'll give you more tests.'

'Tests,' he grumbled. 'Who needs tests?'

Rachel started to unbutton her blouse.

'For Chrissake, what do you think you're doing?'

'Let's do some tests right now,' she said softly, uncupping her bra.

'Honey, I'm not sure I can handle it.'

'I'll handle it,' said Rachel.

'How was it?' she said afterwards.

'It was beautiful.' He grinned. 'Painful, but beautiful.' He tried to grab her again.

'Slow down,' said Rachel. 'Remember what the doctors said.'

'Doctors,' said Jack scornfully. 'Who needs doctors? What I need is more tests.'

*

305

When in London, James Timba invariably took a corner suite on the third floor of Claridge's, overlooking Davies Street and Brook's Mews. The ambiance pleased him. It was dignified, Art Deco and very English.

The room service waiter, immaculate in black trousers and white jacket, wheeled in a trolley of Earl Grey tea and a large plate of McVities digestive biscuits – James's favourite – and left the sitting room murmuring respectful thanks for the fiver tip.

'Nice of you to call,' said Timba.

'You asked me to,' said Jeffrey. 'We have an appointment.'

'We do?' said Timba. He eyed the digestives. 'I'm sorry. I'd forgotten. My memory is not what it was.'

'I noticed,' said Jeffrey drily.

Timba poured the tea. 'This matter of the side –whatever you call it. It may be hard for you to believe, but I have absolutely no recollection of anything like it. Sugar?'

'No sugar.'

'Naturally, if you tell me that there was such an agreement – and I know you're an honest man – then I ask myself how such a misunderstanding could have arisen? How could such a thing have happened?'

'It happened,' said Jeffrey. He was enjoying the performance. James Timba excelled in the histrionic art.

'You know me,' continued the Nigerian Laurence Olivier, 'and you know that when I give my word, you can rely on it – absolutely. That's what hurts me – the thought that you might have even a sneaking suspicion that I deliberately deceived you.'

'Now where would I get such an idea from?' said Jeffrey.

'You know what a contract means to me,' said James Timba.

'Indeed I do,' said Jeffrey solemnly. 'Indeed I do.'

The one dollar fifty cents a barrel to be deposited in the numbered Swiss bank account was not all for James Timba – not, at least, according to James. And Jeffrey believed him. Twenty-five million dollars. Some 'misunderstanding'! Some 'commission'! Too large for Timba to handle. He was acting as the bagman, fronting for someone far more powerful and exalted than he. Once the commission was agreed, it was astonishing how quickly his memory recovered. The original of the side agreement was found and, this time, Jeffrey made certain that plenty of copies were signed. It seemed that King Brothers was, after all, not in breach of contract.

'I'm absolutely mystified how I could so completely have forgotten about this side . . . what do you call it?'

'Agreement,' said Jeffrey. 'I call it an agreement.'

'It just flew away. The memory flew away, like a bird – like a migrating bird,' James Timba added poetically.

'They say that birds always return home in the spring,' said Jeffrey. 'To feather their nests.'

'They say that, do they?' said Timba.

In July '79, Mort was summoned to the West Coast by the Chairman of Pacific Odyssey. It seemed he was displeased with King Brothers. Early in the year, when the oil market began to take off, Joe Murphy had bought a million tons of Nigerian from King Brothers at the Official NNPC export price, plus a premium of three dollars fifty cents a barrel. Deducting King Brothers' 'expenses', it had left them with a profit of two dollars a barrel, or fifteen million dollars on the contract. At the time it had looked like a nice profit. At the time. But as the market tested new highs almost daily, the profit margin began to look less and less attractive to Mort. Today, King Brothers was selling spot cargoes at a premium of six dollars a barrel over the market. And tomorrow?

'Why don't we just cancel the contract?' said Ruby. 'They did it to us, the bastards.'

'Let's not do anything in a hurry,' said Mort characteristically. 'We might regret it if the market turns against us.'

'What do you suggest?'

'Why don't we just cut them back? We'll give the

reduction an impressive name like "OPEC interim market cutback" and reduce shipments by twenty per cent. Then we can cut them back another ten per cent for "operational tolerance". That'll give us plenty to sell in the spot market. We'll make at least four bucks extra on every barrel we take away from them. Nothing wrong with that.'

'They won't accept it,' said Ruby.

'They have no choice,' said Mort.

The president of Pacific Odyssey thought otherwise.

'Mr King, you have a commitment to ship us a million tons of crude – a million, not seven hundred thousand.'

Joe Murphy nodded dispiritedly. The lawyers tried to look triumphant and belligerent at the same time, as if the president had just won game, set and match and they were daring Mortimer King to dispute it.

'As I explained to you,' said Mort patiently, 'we are being cut back by the Nigerians.'

'I would want to be satisfied on that point,' said the president aggressively.

'Satisfied?' said Mort innocently.

'Personally satisfied,' the president said, folding his arms to emphasize the point.

Mort stood up. 'Could I have a word with you in private?'

The president hesitated, then he nodded. He showed Mort into a small anteroom adjacent to the boardroom.

Mort closed the door and turned to the president. 'Look, wise guy,' he said, 'let me tell you something. You have a big mouth, but all that comes out of it is mashed potatoes. You cancelled on me once – outright, no warning. I don't forget things like that. I'll give you a choice. Accept the cutback or I'll suspend shipments. You can sue me. Then we can both waste our time and money in the courts. Meanwhile, not one drop of oil will you get from me.'

The president set his lips in a hard line. He was a proud man, but an astute one, too. There was a time to swallow your pride. That time was now, and he knew it. He could be as flexible as the next man. That was why he was president of Pacific Odyssey. He held out his hand and

Mort took it. 'I sure do appreciate your straight talking, Mr King,' he said. Somehow he succeeded in sounding as though he meant it.

'You can expect more of it,' said Mort.

They returned to the boardroom and the president addressed his minions succinctly. 'Mr King has clarified the position for me,' he said. 'I'm satisfied. Personally satisfied.'

Not nearly as satisfied as Mort. He had picked up three hundred thousand tons of crude that he could sell on the open market at an extra profit of ten million dollars.

Before leaving for the airport, he had a drink with Joe at the Oil Club, two blocks away from the Pacific Odyssey building. For some reason, Joe was ill at ease.

Mort was triumphant. He had waited a long time for this day. 'What's the problem, Joe? You hate the jerk as much as I do.'

'No problem. It's just that he has a way of sticking the tail on the donkey.'

'You being the donkey?'

'Who else? I signed the contract with you. It has to be my responsibility if it goes sour.'

'Why should you care? What could he do to you?'

'Plenty. I might be asking you for a job one of these days.'

That was the last thing Mort wanted. Joe Murphy was much more useful to him where he was than he could ever be in King Brothers. 'Any time,' he said lightly. 'By the way, the fund is still doing great. It's a real shame, Joe. If only you'd invested – you'd have been worth a million dollars today.'

Joe just stood there, looking at Mort.

'A million bucks! Jesus!'

'It wouldn't matter a goddam who they stuck the tail on, would it, Joe? Not if you had a million bucks in the bank.'

'You can say that again.'

'How's Mary?'

'She's OK. Not great. Just OK.'

309

'You could still invest, Joe. I could maybe give you a special price for your shares. At today's valuation, well, the price is way too high for you.'

'It always was, Mort.'

'How do you mean?'

'The price was always too high.'

'Just trying to help.'

Joe wanted to be sure about the fund. Mort was so damned convincing. Could it be genuine? 'I'm wondering,' he said. 'Since the fund seems to be such a great investment . . . would you have any objection if I mentioned it to one or two guys in the office? Very discreetly, of course. I'll bet they wouldn't mind putting some cash into it.'

Mort was caught off-guard. This was something he had not expected. For a moment, he was thrown, but he soon recovered.

'Sorry, Joe. We're limiting membership right now,' he said. 'When things get to be too big, you lose control of them. We would like to keep it in the family. Know what I mean?'

Joe knew exactly. Now.

'Sure you won't change your mind?'

'I'm sure, Mort. Like I said. The price is too high.'

It was more than five years since A. and Orient had cancelled their contract with King Brothers. When Ruby had nothing better to do, he ran past his mind's eye the film of that last encounter with Martin Field. He could still hear every word, every syllable that self-important, condescending shitbag had uttered. He could still see every sly look, every mirthless, patronizing smile.

As the market soared, more and more crude poured into the USA. The Caribbean terminals were booming, operating to peak capacity. Ninety per cent of the oil discharged on the US East Coast was transhipped in the Caribbean. It was only a matter of time before Martin Field would be compelled to contact Ruby. The trap was sprung.

*

310

The call came on a Tuesday morning in September. It was a day Ruby would never forget.

'Ruby! How are you? This is Martin Field. How's it going?'

Ruby was amused at Field's glib assumption of intimacy, as if they had been friends for years. 'Never better, Martin,' he said, stressing the man's first name. 'How are things with you?'

'Great, Ruby. Just fine.'

'What can I do for you? You need some crude?'

'Hell, no, I'm up to my eyes in crude, Ruby. But I don't have to tell you that you're right up there on top of my list the moment I'm in the market. You can count on me,' Field assured him.

'Gee, thanks,' said Ruby. He knew just how much he could count on Martin Field. 'Are you phoning to shoot the breeze or is there something I can do for you?'

'Could be,' said Field, trying to sound casual. 'It's really nothing. I sure hate to waste your time over such a trivial matter.'

'Think nothing of it,' said Ruby. 'How can I help?'

'I have a couple of VLCCs berthing at Bonaire tomorrow. Would you believe the goddam terminals are full. I tell you, Ruby, if you and I ran our business the way those guys do we'd both be bankrupt.'

'I can imagine,' said Ruby.

'Hell, I know it's a real dumb question, but would you happen to have some spare storage capacity I could trade with you? You know – like you lend it to me now and I give it back to you in a few weeks?'

Ruby leaned back in his chair and sighed a sigh of the deepest contentment. This was better – better by far – than the first cigarette of the day. 'Gee, I'm sorry, Martin, but right now I don't have a thing to offer,' he said. 'I'll be glad to call you just as soon as I have anything for you. Meanwhile, you're right up there on top of my list the moment I'm in the market. You can count on it.' Ruby liked that speech. He liked it a lot.

'How about if I bought some space from you? I'd be glad to cover your costs and, if it's important to you, I'd even throw in a few bucks. I know how you guys love to make a profit,' Field said snidely.

Ruby loved that. How to win friends and influence people. 'That's more than generous of you, Martin, but, as I say, right now, I have nothing available.'

'That's not what I hear,' said Martin Field. His voice was a touch strained.

Ruby said nothing. Field waited for an answer. He could have waited till doomsday.

'That's not what I hear,' he repeated.

'I heard what you said,' Ruby confirmed jovially.

'Ruby, I need to buy storage from you. I'll give you a twenty per cent profit. How about it?' It must have hurt the guy to be so magnanimous.

'I really couldn't accept that.'

'That's real friendly of you,' said Martin Field, breathing easier.

'I wasn't referring to the profit,' said Ruby. 'I couldn't accept to sell you any storage space. That's what I'm saying.'

There was a hiss at the other end of the line. It sounded like steam escaping under high pressure. 'Look,' said Martin Field slowly, as though to an idiot, 'let me explain. I – need – storage – space – in the Caribbean. I always need it. Everyone knows that. If I don't have storage capacity, I can't discharge my tankers. If I can't discharge my tankers, then I can't tranship the crude. If I can't tranship the crude, then I have nothing to refine in the United States. That means A. and Orient have no products to sell and if A. and Orient have no products to sell, then the company goes down the tubes, the gasoline lines will get even longer and . . . Jesus, man, you need any more?'

'No thanks,' said Ruby. 'It's all quite clear.'

'For some reason,' continued Martin Field, 'which no one in the oil industry seems to understand, your company has cornered all the available space in the Caribbean –

your company and a few ghost outfits no one's ever heard of. Do you realize this is the first time in thirty years in the business that I can't rent the storage space I need?'

'That must be frustrating for you.'

'You see my predicament.'

'Absolutely.'

'If I gave you the impression before that it's not serious, then I – apologize.' 'Apologize' was not a word that came easily to Martin Field's lips. 'This is real serious – not just for my company, but for the USA. Not to mention that my president is giving me all kinds of hell.'

'I can imagine,' said Ruby sympathetically.

'Now I know, and you know, that you couldn't possibly, by any stretch of the imagination, need all the storage space you're sitting on. All I'm asking you to do is sell me your excess space,' said Field reasonably.

'I understand what you're asking,' said Ruby. 'It's very clear.'

'Would you please sell me some space then?'

'No.'

'What the fuck do you need all that storage space for?' he screamed.

'To store crude,' said Ruby.

There was a long silence on the line. And some heavy breathing. 'OK,' said Martin Field, deadly calm, 'I'll tell you what. Sell me some crude in storage. I'll ship it out right away. Then I can discharge my tankers into the empty storage tanks. I don't need crude. I don't want to buy crude, but if it helps, I'll do it, just to please you. You can make an extra buck or two.'

'Smart idea,' said Ruby.

'Great! So sell me a million tons of crude.'

'I don't have any crude to sell you.'

Martin Field made one last superhuman effort to control his rage and frustration.

'Mr King,' he said. It was disappointing to Ruby that their friendship had been so short-lived. Where had his first name gone to? 'Mr King – you're making life real

313

difficult for me. I'm trying to keep my cool, but believe me, it's tough.' His voice was trapped deep in the back of his throat.

This was the moment where Ruby always felt, in retrospect, that he had excelled himself.

'Now, Martin,' he cautioned him, 'that's where you're making your big mistake. You shouldn't try to bottle up all that anger. It's not good for you. You'll make yourself sick. Talk to any shrink. He'll tell you. You have to learn to externalize your emotions. You may not believe this,' he added, 'but, in spite of all the effort you're making to be polite to me, I can still sense your anger. If that's how you feel – if you're really angry – go ahead and express it – share it with me.'

There was a howl at the other end of the line, followed by a stream of abuse. It sounded like Martin Field was externalizing all over his office. 'What's the matter with you, you slimebag?' he screamed. 'I have a major problem here and you're giving me a telephone course in psychotherapy! Stop screwing around! If you don't sell me some goddam storage space, my whole company will be in jeopardy. Not to mention my career. That bastard will fire me!'

'I understand,' said Ruby.

'What do you mean, you understand, bonehead! How does that help me?' Martin Field was choking into the phone.

'It always helps to talk to someone who understands you,' Ruby explained.

Martin Field was calm again, calm and desperate. 'What do you suggest I do?'

'Try Curaçao,' said Ruby.

That did it. The effect was like throwing a lighted match into a crate of fireworks. 'I already tried Curaçao!' Field shrieked. 'You got that tied up, too, mother fucker!'

Ruby was shocked. 'Please try to control your language, Martin. Some young person could be listening in on this conversation.'

314

Martin Field could not take any more. 'If you don't release me some space, by God I'll ... I'll ...' He was panting into the phone now. He could have committed murder.

'You'll what?' Ruby asked gently.

The line went quiet. Martin Field could see that threats and bluster would not pay. His options were limited. 'Ruby,' he said quietly, 'could we meet and discuss this like two civilized people?'

'Sure. Why not? Always happy to see you.'

'Why don't you fly over to the West Coast tomorrow,' Martin Field suggested. 'We can have lunch and a few drinks.'

'I'll see you in my office at eight o'clock tomorrow morning,' said Ruby curtly, and put down the phone.

Martin Field arrived, punctual and subdued. He had taken the overnight flight from the West Coast – the Red Eye Special – drunk too much bourbon on the plane and slept not a wink. By the time he showed up at King Brothers' office, he was physically fragile and mentally distraught. Being in control of every situation was what he was accustomed to; being totally out of control angered him. It also scared him.

Ruby was his usual friendly, phlegmatic self, even a touch playful – like a cat with a mouse. Tooth and claw, however, were discreetly hidden.

'Coffee, Martin?'

'Thanks, no.' Martin Field was impatient. He could not wait to solve his problem.

'Fruit juice?'

'Really, no. Could we start, please?'

'How about a chocolate eclair?' Ruby continued relentlessly, opening the top right-hand drawer of his desk. Martin Field turned pale. The thought of a chocolate eclair at eight o'clock in the morning made him feel nauseous. The saliva jetted at the back of his throat: a bad sign. His stomach was definitely queasy.

315

'You don't mind if I . . . ?' Ruby held up a fat chocolate eclair oozing cream right under Martin Field's nose. The man shuddered, tried unsuccessfully to speak and waved his hand desperately in the air in mute and helpless resignation.

Ruby beamed vaguely and munched his way steadily through the eclair. When he had finished, he licked the cream noisily off his fingers, one by one. Martin Field's complexion turned a whiter shade of pale. Ruby appeared completely oblivious to the fact that anything was wrong. He devoured two more eclairs, grinning engagingly at the man on the other side of his desk and, when he was done, wiped his mouth on his shirtsleeve and heaved a satisfied sigh. 'Breakfast,' he said, 'is important. You're quite sure you won't . . . ?'

'Quite,' Martin Field managed to mouth. He sat there, looking wretched.

Ruby appeared concerned – like a Jewish mother trying to tempt an anorexic daughter to eat. He dug in his drawer and held up another eclair. Field flapped his hand again, opening and closing his mouth like a goldfish, and began searching frantically in his pocket for a tissue. His complexion had that shiny, translucent look of tombstone marble.

Ruby opened the drawer to replace the eclair, thought better of it, shrugged and sank his teeth into the voluptuous concoction. The cream spurted from the sides of his mouth. A large pat fell on the desk between the two men. As Martin Field looked at it, transfixed, his stomach began to spasm.

Ruby looked distantly interested, obliquely sympathetic. First, he finished the eclair, sucking his fingers diligently, then he focused his full attention on the sickly face sweating on the other side of his desk.

'You don't look well,' he said solicitously. 'Is there anything I can do?'

If Martin Field had had the courage to say so, what Ruby could do was jump out of the window – and that would only be a start.

'The problem with a lot of guys these days,' said Ruby, 'is that they just don't eat right. I'm always telling Mort – eat a good breakfast. The rest of the day will take care of itself.'

'Ruby,' said Martin Field weakly, 'we have some things to talk about.'

'Health comes first,' Ruby drove on. 'What's the point of our shaking hands on a deal if, tomorrow morning, God forbid, they put you in a box?' He shook his head like a man saddened by the foibles and failings of humanity, but philosophical enough to tolerate them.

Martin Field could not believe what was happening to him. 'Ruby,' he began again, 'could we . . . storage space . . . ?' He leaned back in his chair, exhausted.

'Absolutely,' said Ruby. 'Exactly what I was about to suggest.'

'Couldn't we settle this thing amicably?' It sounded a lot like a plea.

'No question.'

Martin Field waited for Ruby to speak, like a dog waiting for its master's command.

Ruby nodded vigorously. 'Absolutely,' he repeated, taking another eclair from the top right-hand drawer of his desk. Martin Field cradled his head in his hands. It was too much.

'Martin,' said Ruby, his mouth gushing cream, 'I've discussed the situation with my partners and we'd really like to help you out.'

Martin Field raised his head. There was, in his eyes, a pathetic gleam of hope.

'I have a proposition.'

Finally! It seemed like the bastard was getting down to business. Martin Field perked up.

'We agree to sell you as much storage space as you need,' said Ruby. 'A million tons if you want.' He waved a hand expansively.

'I need two million over the next six months,' said Field sullenly.

317

'No problem. On one condition . . .' Ruby finished the last mouthful of chocolate eclair, held his fingers up to his mouth, noticed that Martin Field was looking at him again in horror, changed his mind and wiped his hands on a telex instead. Field shuddered.

'The condition is,' Ruby continued, 'that you sell us crude oil – a ton of storage space for a ton of crude.'

'I don't have that much crude to sell,' Field protested. 'I need all the crude I can get for refining.'

'Then use your contacts with producers. You're a big corporation. Buy a couple of million tons of crude surplus to your requirements.'

Field nodded. It was really not such a bad idea. True, his company had never traded in crude oil. They were refiners. They bought crude from producers, refined it and sold the products. But why not? Why not use their buying power and their connections to trade crude and make some extra bucks? If he put himself out, he might just squeeze an extra couple of million tons of crude over six months out of two or three of his regular suppliers. Naturally, it would cost him. The commissions would have to be fat ones, but he would make a killing, buying at the producer price and selling to King Brothers at the market price. He was beginning to feel better already.

'OK,' he said. 'It's a deal. You sell me two million tons of storage space in the Caribbean over the next six months and I'll sell you two million tons of crude.'

'Fifty per cent Iranian Light or Arab Light from the PG and fifty per cent Bonny Light,' said Ruby casually.

Martin Field grimaced. That would make life a lot harder. The cunning bastard wanted only the best: Light crude and Low Sulphur crude. That meant A. and Orient would be stuck with Heavy crude – always difficult to sell. It was not going to be easy, but he guessed he could just about handle it. He would have to. 'Agreed,' he said. 'Half PG Light, half Nigerian Light.'

Ruby nodded, satisfied. Martin Field relaxed. His blood pressure dropped thirty points. 'There's the matter of price, of course,' he said. 'Naturally, it'll have to be in line with the market. I suggest four dollars a barrel over the official producer selling price. I guess that's reasonable today – if anything, it's below the market. We'll review it on the first day of every month and adjust it in line with market conditions.' The market was boiling, he was thinking to himself. Even if the producer price kept on going up, the market price was always going to be way above it. Depending on the commissions they had to pay, A. and Orient should wind up making two or three dollars a barrel – a profit he had never dreamed of. It would be a killing. He would get a fat bonus. An unexpected windfall . . . 'I think that's a fair proposal,' he concluded.

Ruby polished his glasses and blinked a couple of times. 'We'll pay you the official producer price – not one cent more,' he said coolly.

Martin Field's blood pressure began to take off again. 'That's below our cost,' he protested. 'That's outrageous! You know goddam well we'll have to pay fat commissions to get the crude.'

'That's your problem,' said Ruby. 'I understood you to say you wanted some storage space.'

Martin Field's face turned bright red. He looked as though his head was about to explode, hurling small bloody fragments to the far corners of Ruby's office. 'You asshole!' he yelled. 'This is price gouging. This is blackmail.'

'No, Martin,' Ruby said quietly. 'It's not blackmail. It's business. Blackmail is what you did to me when I was helpless. You could have negotiated with me, but you decided I was too small to fight you, so you never gave me a chance. That's why I never forgave you. You had me over a barrel, didn't you? A barrel of crude. It didn't matter a goddam to you if you destroyed me and King Brothers. My guess is that's exactly what you had in mind.'

'So, that's it. All these years you've had it in for me.'

'What did you think it was, Martin? Bad breath?'

'You set me up. You planned this whole scam, you scumbag!'

319

'Go ahead, Martin,' said Ruby. 'Externalize. It's good for you.'

'You devious, fucking sonofabitch! You lousy douche-bag!'

'Does this mean we have a deal?' said Ruby cheerfully. He had good reason to be cheerful. He calculated that King Brothers would make eighty million dollars on this one.

Martin Field slumped in his chair, unnerved. He nodded despairingly. It had to be a nightmare. Things like this just could not happen to guys like him.

*   *   *

The Iranian revolution was a major blow to the state of Israel. The Israelis had lost their only friend in the Middle East. Economically and politically it was a setback. The country was forced to look elsewhere for its oil and the days of the highly successful and lucrative Pipeline were numbered. There was simply no oil to pump through it any more. Israel was out of the oil business.

'What will you do, Ben?' asked Ruby. He was in Tel Aviv to wind up their Pipeline business.

Benjamin scratched his unshaven face. 'I'll read the papers in the morning, walk the dog, cook dinner for my wife – maybe I'll read a book once in a while. Who knows? I might even take a job. Groceries cost money.'

Ruby grinned. Benjamin knew very well that numerous oil companies – Israeli and foreign – would compete for his services.

'If I'm really in the bread basket, as they say . . .'

'On the bread line,' corrected Ruby automatically.

'I could always go into politics,' said Benjamin unheeding. 'God forbid,' he added fervently. 'That would be the rock's bottom.'

Ruby kept a straight face. 'Why don't you come and work for King Brothers? We'll make you a partner. You'll be a rich man.'

Benjamin gazed into the middle distance. 'A rich man,' he reflected. 'That would be a new experience.' He said it without enthusiasm. 'I'm not sure I was born to be a rich man. What would I do with the money?' he asked Ruby.

'Who cares?' said Ruby. 'Spend it. Give it away. The money's not important.'

'Not when you're rich, it's not.'

Ruby shook his head. 'You don't understand, do you?'

'No,' said Benjamin, 'I don't. But one thing I do understand. I understand we've known each other a long time. We did business together. We had some laughs. Sometimes we screwed each other a little – I think sometimes you screwed me a lot. But it was fun.' He beamed at Ruby. 'Was it not?'

'It was fun,' agreed Ruby. 'I'm going to miss you. I have a hunch next time I see you, you'll be Prime Minister of Israel.'

'I'm not that desperate for a job,' Benjamin growled.

*　*　*

It had finally happened. Edgar had given up drinking.

'Thirty days, ten hours, twenty-eight minutes,' he told Kate proudly. It was the first time for years – the first time ever for such a long period.

Kate was impressed. 'That's fantastic! If you can give it up for a month, you can do it for good.'

'I intend to. There's a lot riding on this one.'

Kate pretended not to understand. 'Like what?'

'Like our marriage.'

'I never said I'd marry you again, Edgar.'

'It's what keeps me going.'

'That's not fair. It's emotional blackmail.'

Edgar grinned. 'What's wrong with that?'

'I told you before. First, you have to learn to depend on yourself. Not on me – just on yourself.'

'Kate, let's cut the small talk. If I don't touch a drop for a year, will you marry me?'

'How will I know you're telling me the truth?'

'You'll know,' he said. He was right. Of course she would. He would be on her doorstep the next morning,

321

drunk and apologetic. Edgar was not the devious kind.

Kate thought about it. How could she do such a dumb thing? They had tried it once and it had been a disaster. On the other hand, how could she turn him down? She was his lifeline, his only hope. Already, he had lost that drawn look. His face had some colour in it, his whole appearance had changed. He was like the old Edgar, perkier, smarter, more alert than he had been for years. It would be good to have him back. She still loved him; that was the dumbest thing of all. But she was afraid that if she took him on and he started drinking again, she would not be able to handle it. Next time, he would drag her down with him too. If only she could get him away from Mort. The guy was bad news.

'Let me think about it,' she said.

He kissed her on the cheek diffidently and stood there, not wanting to press her any more, but unable to leave.

'What is it?' she said.

'I just wanted you to know that I need you,' he said.

She knew. That was the hell of it.

Edgar was offhand, so offhand that the warning bells rang for Mort immediately.

'By the way,' he said, oh, so casually, 'I'm thinking of getting married again.' He tried to say it like he would say he was going out to lunch.

'You are?' said Mort, equally casually, pretending to read a telex.

'I just thought I'd let you know.'

'Great! Congratulations!'

'Thanks.'

'Anyone I know?' said Mort, picking up another telex.

'I said I was thinking of getting married – again.'

'I heard you.' Mort straightened his in-tray very precisely so that it was absolutely parallel with the side of his desk. 'Ah,' he said, 'you mean . . . again.'

'Right on,' said Edgar.

'Again . . . as in again . . . or again, as in again to . . . ?'

'The same woman,' said Edgar. 'You got it. See what you can do when you try?'

'I don't believe this. Are you telling me you're marrying Kate again?'

'That was the name,' said Edgar. 'I'm sure it was.'

'They call it remarrying.'

'Is that what they call it?'

'That's what they call it.'

'Well, I'll be . . . what will they think of next?'

'It usually doesn't work,' said Mort.

'It's usually no one's fucking business.'

'Then why tell me?'

'Because, goddam you, Mort, I thought you'd be pleased. You know . . . pleased like being happy for your old friend . . . like thinking of another human being for a change, instead of the crap oil business.'

Mort pushed aside the telexes. He was angry with himself. This one he was handling badly. No one was going to take Edgar away. He was too valuable to the company, but if he wasn't careful, he would lose him through his own stupidity. 'Sit down, Edgar,' he said gently. He came round the desk and sat next to him. 'I'm sorry for what I said. I didn't mean it to sound that way.'

Edgar fidgeted in his chair. When Mort talked to him like that, it made him feel uncomfortable.

'You're my friend, Edgar,' Mort said ingratiatingly. 'My friend – my colleague. I care. I care what happens to you. If you decide to get married to Kate again, that's your decision and no one in this world – no one – has the right to say a thing. It's your life, after all. I'll be happy for you and I'll wish you everything you wish yourself.'

Edgar was feeling ashamed of his outburst. 'Hell, Mort, I know that. You and Kate – well, it's never been exactly a love match. I know that, too. But she's good for me. I need her.'

Like hell you do, Mort thought. No one needs that bitch. If anyone was going to take over Edgar, it was not going to be her. It would be ironic and tragic if she were to force

323

him to leave the company just when they were hitting the jackpot.

'It won't change a thing, Mort. I promise you. I'm here for you – as long as you need me.'

'I'm happy to hear it,' said Mort. 'You're a pro, Edgar. I like to have professionals round me.'

'You can count on me,' Edgar assured him. 'Oh and when the time comes, I sure would appreciate it if you'd be my best man.'

Mort's expression never changed. 'I'd be glad to. Thanks for the compliment. When will the great day be?'

'We haven't fixed a date yet. In a few months, I guess. She needs to be convinced I'm a reformed character.'

'How do you mean?'

'I've given up, Mort. I don't drink any more. I'm clean. I promised her I'd never touch another drop. If I do, the wedding's off. That's the deal.'

'You don't say?' said Mort, his eyes widening.

Ruby decided when he was a small boy on the Upper West Side that he was the smartest kid on the block – on any number of blocks for that matter. Since that time, nothing had happened to make him change his mind. Not only was he endowed with a fine brain, he had the guts and the motivation to use it. While most men were still in bed clutching their pillow, Ruby was sitting at his office desk, meditating, analysing, planning. Every day he rose between four-thirty and five and said his prayers. Then he would think. He thought a lot. He thought like a chess grand master, pondering an almost infinite variety of possibilities, the expected and the unexpected reactions to every move he might make in the next few days. Ruby prided himself on being ready for anything. Aside from his formidable intellect, he possessed a sixth sense which, like a radar dish, scanned the horizon, enabling him to see what few other men ever glimpsed. He had, too, a capacity for flexible response to any situation and a determination never to take no for an answer. Nothing was impossible.

There was no obstacle that could not be overcome. If you couldn't remove it, you could always get round it. Secretly, he scorned and despised authority and bureaucracy, as many Jews before him had done in the shtetels of Poland and Russia. For Ruby, the real enemy was the Establishment. If you were smart – and Ruby was smart – you got them before they got you.

As a lawyer, his skills had been employed on his clients' behalf – often in an effort to beat the legal system over the head with its own laws. Now, as an oil man, he had come to realize that here, too, was a system he could manipulate, and he was not about to allow anyone to play the game better than him. If that meant bending the rules, then, by God, he would bend them.

One day, sitting at his desk at seven in the morning, he had an idea. By the time Mort arrived, half an hour later, he had developed it, checked and crosschecked it and satisfied himself that his scheme was foolproof.

'Sit down,' he commanded Mort.

Mort, who was not accustomed to taking orders – even from Ruby – looked a little surprised, but he did as he was told: an indication of his respect for his brother.

'OK, now. Listen.' He was smoking his fifth cigarette of the day and, even this early, his shirt was already hanging out of his trousers. His expression was intense, almost enraptured.

'What day is it today?'

'The twenty-eighth of March.'

'OK . . . It's the twenty-eighth of March. And what's today's official price of Arab Light?'

'Twenty-six dollars,' said Mort.

'Twenty-six dollars a barrel. Right,' said Ruby.

Mort leaned back in his chair, relaxed but a little bemused. Ruby was rushing all over the room, puffing his cigarette and abstractedly brushing the ash off his shirt-front.

'OK, tell me. What's going to happen to the official price on the first of April?'

'You know as well as I do. The Saudis are increasing it to twenty-eight dollars a barrel. They already announced it.'

'They already announced it.' Ruby repeated the words as if he were an automaton. 'So we already know that the official price will be hiked two dollars a barrel on the first of April.'

Mort nodded. He was following Ruby's wanderings with his eyes.

'Even if we didn't know, it wouldn't matter. These days, the price only moves one way – up!' He pointed up with his forefinger.

'Right.'

Ruby continued. 'All our contracts are subject to official price hikes, aren't they?'

'Sure they are. If the tanker sails on the first of April, or later, we pay the Saudis the increased price and our customers have to pay us the new price, too.'

'How do we know the tanker's sailing date?' Mort was beginning to look impatient. 'Bear with me,' said Ruby.

'By the date on the bill of lading,' said Mort.

'By the date on the bill of lading. Exactly. So . . . If we had – just as an example – if we had two sets of bills of lading for every cargo – one dated the twenty-ninth of March and the other dated the first of April? . . . What then?'

Mort sat up sharply. Suddenly, he understood what Ruby was getting at. 'We would pay the Saudis this quarter's price and collect an extra two bucks from our customers.'

Ruby grabbed a sheaf of typed lists from his desk. 'Here's a list of every cargo we sold this quarter. Ten are scheduled to be shipped yesterday, today or tomorrow – the twenty-eighth, twenty-ninth and thirtieth of March – a total of nearly three million tons. You realize what this means? If we present ten bills of lading to our customers dated the first of April or later, we could make an extra forty-five million dollars. Extra! Over and above our normal trading profit.'

'We can't do it.'

'We can't not do it, you mean,' said Ruby.

Mort was thinking and shaking his head at the same time. 'What about the set of documents on the tanker? The copies of the genuine bills of lading will have the correct shipping date.'

'No problem. I can have someone meet the tanker and take the documents from the captain. We've done it a hundred times when the loading documents weren't in our hands before the tanker's arrival at the discharge port.'

Mort was trying hard to find a flaw in Ruby's reasoning. He couldn't. He couldn't, because there wasn't one.

'What's it all for, Ruby?' he asked. 'I don't like it.'

'I tell you,' said Ruby. 'I'm sick of getting screwed. The world screws us and we say thank you.'

'We're doing OK, Ruby. We don't need it.'

'Who said anything about need? This is the greatest game in the world. There's only one way to play it, Mort.'

'Yeah, I know. To win. Whatever happened to Ruby, the Midtown lawyer? The old soft touch?'

'I haven't changed. I'm still the same old Ruby. Just a bit smarter. A little more streetwise, maybe.'

'We'd be crossing a line. We've looked at it before. We've come close to it a few times, but we never crossed it,' said Mort.

'Then we're just about the only ones who haven't.'

That was true enough, but still. What would this make them? Best not to analyse it too much. What the hell. 'I'm just glad you're on my side,' he said.

'We do it?'

Mort hesitated. It was a turning point. 'We do it,' he said finally.

When Mort had left, Ruby stared down at Lexington Avenue where the first commuters were racing each other to work. He had beaten the rest of Manhattan by a couple of hours – just like he did every day.

*   *   *

327

It was nearly a month since Jack Greenberg's release from hospital. He was still only able to walk with a stick – painfully and laboriously – but he would never allow Rachel to help him. When she tried, he would push her away, panting and grey in the face.

'I'll do it myself.'

'We'll see about that,' Rachel would say briskly.

All that time she stayed at his apartment, tactfully and inconspicuously supportive – always there when he needed her. As the weeks passed, he became stronger; he could take care of himself. Soon he would be back at work. But the longer she stayed, the more Jack depended on her and the more he depended on her the more he resented her presence. One afternoon, without warning, he exploded.

'Do me a favour. Stop doing a Florence Nightingale. I really don't care to have you around any more. If you get your jollies playing nursemaid to invalids, then go work for the geriatrics. I don't need a nurse. You hear me?'

Rachel was no longer silly, fat and fifteen. She was a mature twenty-two-year-old, poised and self-assured, with a stubborn streak and a strength of character that she had inherited from her father.

'I hear you,' she said coolly and without resentment. She packed her bag and looked in to say goodbye.

'I'm real sorry if I offended you,' said Jack, with heavy irony. 'Me and my foul mouth. They should put me away with all the other maladjusted psychopathic social misfits. Maybe I'd learn better manners.'

'I don't give a goddam about your manners,' said Rachel. 'It's your self-pity I find hard to take.'

'Then take a walk,' said Jack wearily.

Three days later, he called her. 'Nurse, I can't find my bedpan. It's embarrassing. You don't happen to remember where you put it?'

'In the freezer with the TV dinners, where I always put it,' she said.

'I should have known,' said Jack.

She was back at the apartment in fifteen minutes. He opened the door and took her in his arms.

'What do you really think of me?' he asked.

'You want to know?'

'Sure I do.'

'I think you're boring, trivial, shallow and self-opinionated.'

'You're right,' he said. 'You want to screw?'

'Now you're talking,' she said.

'We never discussed it,' said Rachel. 'I mean, who did it. I think we should talk about it.'

'I know who did it,' said Jack.

'Mort?'

'Who else?'

'Why would he hate you so much?'

'I'm the competition. I've been hassling him.' He grinned.

'I never liked Mort, but still it doesn't seem to be in character.'

'What do you know about his character? What does anyone know? He's from the dark side. He's out of a black hole. Those weird eyes. That goddam poker face. You ever seen him smile?'

'Sure.'

'Really smile?'

'Sort of,' she said doubtfully.

'Sort of,' he repeated. 'Sometimes – sometimes he smiles with his face. But with his eyes – never. He never says what he thinks. No one knows what goes on behind that mask. I say he paid those guys to do it.'

'You have proof?'

'Who needs proof? Forget it, honey.' He didn't want to talk about it any more, but she couldn't let it rest there.

'If you're so sure it was Mort, the least you could do is tell the police.'

'Why ever would I do that?'

'I don't understand you, Jack. Isn't it the normal thing to do?'

329

For a moment, Jack looked uncomfortable. 'I don't want to involve the police.'

'Why not?'

'I have my reasons.'

Rachel wondered what they could be.

Edgar had made his deal with Kate, and Mort was part of the bargain. For weeks he worried how he was going to break the news to Mort. Finally, he plucked up the courage to tell him.

'Hell, it's not that I want to leave. I love this business. I love the company. These last seven years have been a blast.'

'So why leave?'

'I promised Kate.'

'You seem to have promised Kate a lot of things. You sure she's worth it?'

Edgar avoided Mort's hypnotic eyes. Yes, he was sure, but the obligations of married life were already beginning to get to him and he was not even married yet. 'It's been months, man. I couldn't have done it without her. I could never have given up drinking.'

'You did it,' said Mort, 'not her.'

'It was both of us.'

'Why leave now? What's the hurry?'

'Kate thinks the pressure's getting to me. You know how the oil business is. It's the whole lifestyle, the jet setting, the high rolling. It's hard for me to stay away from liquor, harder than if I were leading a normal life.'

'Who leads a normal life?'

'You know what I mean.'

'I don't. What's normal? Get up at ten, drink a coffee, read the *New York Times*, work out, go for a jog maybe, call your stockbroker a couple of times, fall asleep in front of the tube every night? Is that normal?'

'What's wrong with it?' said Edgar defensively.

'Nothing. It's just not for you and me, that's all. We're different.'

330

'You're different, Mort. I'm not. I'm just a regular guy.'

Mort shook his head. 'What you call a "normal life" isn't living, Edgar. It's existing. You'd be bored in six months.'

'No, I wouldn't. I'd be married to Kate.'

'Is that all you want out of life? To be married to Kate? Don't you see? You'll be doing what she wants for the rest of your life – not what you want. Hell, Edgar, you have a mind of your own, don't you?'

'Not when I'm boozing, I don't. Kate says you control me when I'm drinking.'

'That's bullshit, man. And you know it.'

But of course it wasn't. Mort remembered the Top of the Mark. He could never have persuaded Edgar to join him without the help of a bottle of gin. The disturbing truth was that Edgar was now beginning to show the first real signs of independence.

'It was killing me. The doctors gave me a couple of years.'

Mort pulled a face. 'Doctors.'

'I was a wreck. I was screwing around.'

'So what? You always screwed around. You always will. You do your job well. That's how you get your real kicks.'

'I made my choice. I'm sorry, old buddy,' Edgar said quietly.

Mort hesitated, nodded and patted him on the shoulder. 'I understand. When do you have in mind to leave?'

'As soon as we're married.'

'When's that?'

'Next week.'

'Wow! I thought it was months away still.'

'That was months ago.'

Mort put out his hand. 'You know what I wish for you.'

'I know,' said Edgar. 'You still my best man?'

'You can count on it,' said Mort. He smiled, but his cat-green unfathomable eyes were cold.

*

Whenever Jeffrey saw his father it comforted him that someone, somewhere, was devoting himself to the daily, commonplace round of life – of real life; that the world was still turning. Whatever the latest crisis, whatever his current obsession with his own crazy, volatile existence, he could always be sure that the unremarkable routine of his father's day remained unchanged. There was too, about the old man's calm acceptance of the passage of time, about his daily involvement with the minutiae of existence, something infinitely touching. Trivial as it might seem to some, a day dedicated to such things as cooking stews, brewing beer, pruning roses, reading the papers – mostly the sections devoted to books, theatre, the arts and cricket – and, in the evening, a selective viewing of the 'goggle box' – such a day had about it an unvarying rhythm and a calm melody that was to Jeffrey deeply reassuring. In some way that he still did not fully understand, his father seemed to him to be closer to life's realities than he would ever be. The old man trod the earth with measured, confident and wholly independent steps. Jeffrey buzzed here and there like a demented bumblebee.

'Yesterday, I sold a cargo of Arab Light and made ten million dollars. Today, I cut back a customer ten per cent, took back one of his cargoes, resold it and made another ten million. And they say money doesn't grow on trees.'

'What did you do with it?'

'What did I do with what?'

'The ten million dollars.'

'Nothing. It appears in the balance sheet at the end of the year.'

'Ah, the balance sheet.'

Jeffrey had the impression that his father was making a point: a philosophical reflection on the futility of wealth, perhaps. But then his needs were different from Jeffrey's, so how could you argue with him? It was not so much that he was a moving target. He was no target at all. It was all very unfair.

'I have a Jaguar and a bigger house and Caroline has a

nanny. That's the only real difference in our lives. Suddenly, we have all this money and we don't know what to do with it.'

'Very nice, too.'

'I wondered if there was anything I could do for you?'

His father considered. 'As a matter of fact, there is. I need a new pair of gardening gloves.'

'Gardening gloves,' repeated Jeffrey gravely.

'To prune the roses with. The ones I have are eleven years old. No, I lie. Twelve. They're getting a bit worn. Mrs Jenkins can't darn the holes any more.'

'You wouldn't like a safari holiday in Kenya, or maybe a cruise in the Norwegian fjords?'

His father did not appear to have heard him. He was contemplating his gardening gloves. 'I could still use them as a second pair, of course, in case I mislaid the new ones. You know how forgetful I am.'

Jeffrey tried again. 'Caroline and I were thinking that maybe there was something you needed to improve the quality of your life. After all, we have all this money now, as I said, and what the hell is it but a blip on a screen, statements in a bank, a computer print-out. We'd like you to have some benefit from it. We want to buy you something you need. You're still fit and active. How about a new house? This one isn't what you'd call . . . well . . . Camden Town isn't exactly Belgravia. Hell, Father, tell me. What do you really need?'

The old man looked at him, surprised. 'I told you what I need, Jeffrey. I need a pair of gardening gloves. Nothing fancy, mind you. The canvas sort will do.'

Jeffrey turned away to hide his disappointment. When would the old man give him the satisfaction of accepting a helping hand? How the hell could you reach someone whose world had shrunk to the dimensions of a pair of gardening gloves? 'Canvas ones, mind you. Nothing fancy.'

His father had given up the struggle, damn him . . . And then, as his anger cooled, he began to wonder whether, after all, he was not misjudging the old man. Had he really

333

lost the will to struggle or was he, perhaps, telling Jeffrey something he needed to hear? At his age, what could a man do with new houses and world cruises? His lifestyle fitted him comfortably, like a pair of old slippers . . . or old gardening gloves. He was not rejecting Jeffrey; he was reaffirming his own identity.

As he looked at his father, what did he see but a tranquil man? And suddenly he knew. He knew that buying him a house – buying him any damn thing he had no need of – would merely be a gesture designed to please the giver, not the receiver. He turned to the old man, put his arms round him and hugged him. He had not done that since he was a small boy. It was like returning home after a long voyage, like rediscovering where he belonged.

Jeffrey's father patted his son gently on the shoulder. 'My cup runneth over,' he said quietly.

And with that, he returned to the Sports Section of *The Times*, savaging the page furiously as he read about England's disastrous collapse in the Test Match.

Two days before Edgar's wedding, Mort took over the Bistro Français for the night. It was to be a 'surprise' party – the best food, the best booze and the best music in town.

'It starts at seven. It's in your honour – you and Kate.'

Edgar dug the toe of his shoe into the carpet. 'Mort, you know how Kate feels. She won't come. She doesn't . . . well, she doesn't care much for the whole business scene.'

'She doesn't care much for me, you mean.'

'I didn't say that.'

'So, come alone.'

'I can't come. I daren't. All that booze. The temptation would be too much.'

'Edgar, trust me. I'll take care of you. The goddam party's in your honour. The whole office will be there.'

'Leave me out,' pleaded Edgar. 'I'm scared.'

'Look, just put your head in and say hi to the guys and gals. That's all I ask. It wouldn't be fair to disappoint them.'

Edgar hesitated.

'For me, Edgar. For old times' sake.' Mort spread his arms, smiling ingenuously. 'Where's the harm?'

Edgar capitulated. 'You got it, you bastard. But I'm not coming in.'

'You can stay right out there on the sidewalk and shout "hi",' said Mort. He put his arm round Edgar's shoulder. 'I knew you wouldn't let me down,' he said.

When Rachel needed to talk to her father, she made an appointment to see him in his office. As a child, he had never had too much time for her. She remembered talking to him through the door when he was in the john and, sometimes, as a special favour on Friday evenings after dinner, he would call her over to sit on his knee while he talked to his friends. E.M.'s friends were invariably either employees or business contacts – oil men, lawyers, accountants, real estate developers – anyone who might be useful to him.

'This is my baby girl,' he would say, patting her on the knee, and then he would expound on how a man should invest his capital these days. Rachel learned a great deal about investment, but not too much about love.

Later on she learned that the only reasonable place to talk to her father was in his office. There were distractions, of course, and the interview could always be terminated by a visitor or a crisis. But at least as long as the two of them were alone, she had his full attention.

E.M. had noticed and wondered at the change in his daughter. It was a mystery to him what had happened to the wilful, self-indulgent teenager, but here, suddenly, miraculously, butterfly from chrysalis, was a young woman he could relate to. He waved her to the corner of his office where the armchairs were and, after a moment's hesitation, left his desk and joined her.

They rarely talked and never about anything personal. He had not, for example, ever mentioned those filthy photographs. Not once. It was a part of her life he simply could not face; it disgusted him. She had been soiled by that shyster. It was not his girl's fault. He stood looking down at her for a moment without speaking.

'Now then, Rachel. I'm a busy man. Come straight to the point,' he said gruffly.

'Pop, I want your blessing.'

'My blessing? For what?' E.M. was not accustomed to giving anything away for free – certainly not without good reason.

'I want to get married.'

Edmund Meyer was amazed. 'Married? How old are you?'

'Twenty-two.'

'I remember when you were born. You were bald. Did I ever tell you that?'

'No, you didn't,' she said. She smiled a little sadly. No one had ever mentioned that to her before.

'So, I'm to have grandchildren after all. That's good. I'm going to tell you something, Rachel. I worked hard all my life. Sometimes I think maybe I worked too hard. There was never enough time for you. It didn't seem to be all that important when you were young. It's a woman's job, isn't it, looking after babies? And then, suddenly, you were a teenager and I had lost touch with you. I'd like to give my grandchildren what I never gave you.'

'Don't blame yourself,' she said. 'It's not your fault.'

E.M. shook his head gloomily. 'I don't know whose fault it is, if it isn't mine.' His eyes were sombre as he reflected. 'Children,' he whispered. 'How many kids are you going to have?' he asked her suddenly.

'Pop, I . . .'

'Because I hope your husband-to-be wants kids. I want lots of grandchildren to play with.'

Rachel bowed her head. 'There won't be any grandchildren, Pop. I'm sorry.'

Edmund Meyer was stunned. 'What are you telling me? No grandchildren. What are you getting married for? Sex? Forget it. It's OK for the first couple of years. Now, I'd

336

rather read Platts Oilgram. Don't tell your mother I said that. What do you mean, no children?'

'My fiancé had . . . an accident.'

'What kind of accident?' E.M. snapped.

'He was beaten up by thugs.'

Edmund Meyer pushed himself up from the chair. 'Who is this man?' His voice was trembling.

'It's Jack,' she said. 'Jack Greenberg.'

'Jack Greenberg!' He was swaying on his feet. Rachel jumped up and took his arm.

'What is it, Pop? What's the matter?'

'I won't let you!' he shouted angrily. 'You can't marry that . . . that . . . he's not the man for you.'

'He's the only man for me,' said Rachel firmly. 'I love him.'

Edmund Meyer walked slowly across the room to his desk and sat down. Somehow, he felt safer there. 'I won't give you my blessing.' He was close to tears.

'Yes, you will, Pop.' Rachel stood behind her father and slipped her arms round his neck. 'It's the only thing I ever asked you for.'

He patted her hand. 'I wish you'd asked me for something else,' he said. 'Does it have to be . . . him?' He could not say the name.

'Yes, Pop,' she said.

He threw up his hands in despair. 'What can I do?' he said. 'Take my blessing and go. I'm a busy man.'

Rachel kissed him.

'No children, you say?'

'No.'

'You see, Rachel . . . what I want to ask is . . . is he . . . ?'

'No, Father, he's not impotent. The beating-up left him sterile. He can't have kids, that's all.'

When Rachel had gone, Edmund Meyer picked up the silver-framed photograph of his wife and daughter taken nearly twenty years ago. Life had been so much less complicated then. He had still been dreaming dreams, still had everything in life to look forward to. Most of the things

337

he wanted, he had gotten. But, now that he had them, they did not seem to be all that important any more.

Not even the Oil Corporation.

At three in the morning, Kate was woken by a loud banging on the door. She unlocked it. Edgar was standing there, swaying.

'Hi! Ish me!' he said. 'Party . . . shurprise party . . . !' He pitched forward on his face and passed out.

In the morning, she made him black coffee. He was feeling bad. He had a bruised forehead where he had fallen the night before and a migraine which felt like it was slicing his head in half. His tongue was so swollen he could hardly speak. 'God,' he moaned, 'what have I done to deserve this?'

'What happened?' Kate asked.

He poured himself a tumbler of bourbon. 'Do I need this,' he mumbled and drank it, not lowering the glass until he had finished.

Kate watched him, her face stony.

'Say something,' he groaned. 'I know what you're thinking. Talk to me. Tell me what a bastard I am. Throw a plate at me. Whatever you do, I deserve it. Just say you forgive me.'

'What's to forgive?' she said. 'I want to know what happened, that's all.'

'They threw a party for us – for you and me – for the wedding, you know.'

'No, I didn't know.'

'Honey, it was for the both of us.'

'Why wasn't I invited?'

'You were. Of course you were. I knew you wouldn't come, that's all. Believe me, I didn't want to go either. The guy twisted my arm.'

'What guy?'

'Mort,' he said.

'Mort,' she echoed flatly.

'He just wanted me to say "hi" to everyone. "Just say

338

hi and go," he said. I wasn't going to stay, Kate. I swear I wasn't.'

She was looking at him in a strange way. 'And you fell for it?'

'I didn't fall for anything,' he protested. 'He took over the Bistro for the whole goddam office. It was a party. Just a harmless party. What's the big deal?'

'The big deal is you hadn't touched a drop of liquor for months and now you're back on it again.'

'Who says I'm back on it? For crying out loud! One lousy toast. One lousy toast – that's what started it. And you know who I was drinking to? To us. I was drinking to you and me. You surely can't blame me for that?'

'No,' she said quietly. 'I can't blame you for that.'

'Well then,' he said, as if that finished the discussion.

'Who gave you the drink?'

'What is this? A Senate investigation? How the hell do I know who gave me the drink? What does it goddam matter who gave me the drink? Some guy gave me the drink.'

'Some guy.'

Edgar hung his head. 'It was Mort,' he mumbled.

'You fool!' she said disdainfully. 'You big, soft, gullible fool.'

'OK, smart ass! What was I supposed to do? Stand there and refuse the glass when Mort is proposing a toast to us? The guy's like a brother to me. Who else would have taken the trouble? I had to take a sip. Just a little sip. Hell, you understand that. I felt awkward.'

'That's how he meant you to feel,' said Kate. 'That's exactly how he planned it.'

Edgar stared at her, uncomprehending.

'What are you talking about? Honey, I just can't believe you're making this big a deal over a couple of drinks. This was a once in a lifetime. How often do I get married, for Chrissake? I told you I was through with drinking and I meant it.'

'What are you doing now?' she said.

339

Edgar stared at the tumbler of bourbon in his hand. He had refilled it without even noticing. He slammed it down on the table, wiping his hands on his trousers as if, with that one gesture, he was wiping away his addiction. 'There,' he said. 'I'm through. Finished.'

'You're not through, Edgar. You'll never be through. It's not just the drink. It's Mort. I don't know what it is about the guy, but he has the power to manipulate people. He's got you, Edgar, and he's never going to let you go.'

'Jesus, this is some kind of nightmare. Please God, tell me it's a nightmare. Any minute now I'm going to wake up.'

'It's no nightmare,' she said dully. 'It's real.'

He put his head in his hands. 'I'm nothing without you.'

'I'm sorry,' she said. 'It won't work.'

For a week, Edgar disappeared. No one knew where he was, but the word got around that he was drinking. Eight days after the party, Ruby rushed into Mort's office.

'He's back.'

Mort nodded, showing no surprise.

'You knew he'd be back, didn't you?'

'I hoped,' said Mort laconically.

'You knew.'

Edgar walked into Mort's office after lunch and stood there in the middle of the room, lurching from side to side.

'Hi, Edgar,' said Mort. He was studying a contract.

'Bastard!'

Mort looked up. 'I see you've been drinking again,' he said.

Edgar staggered back two melodramatic steps, rolled his eyes and affected amazement. 'Shit, Mort! God, you're sharp, man! Those little green marbles of yours, they don't miss a thing, do they?'

'Why the sarcasm?'

'Because you piss me off. Because you're an asshole!'

'Pacific are looking for some Algerian. Tunisian would do,' Mort said calmly.

340

Edgar belched and leaned against the wall.

'Last quarter delivery. I suggest you get to work on it. Tell Jeffrey, will you?'

'Sure I'll tell him. I'll tell him you're a fucking asshole!'

Mort picked up a telex.

'She wasn't right for you,' he said quietly. 'If she had been, she wouldn't have called off the wedding for a minor thing like that.'

Edgar's face twisted in rage and torment. 'None of your goddam business!' he shouted, thrusting out his neck, veins bulging. For a moment he stayed in that position, still swaying, and then, without warning, the tears began to stream down his face. He tried to wipe them away with his sleeve, but they kept on coming. 'How could you do it to me?' he sobbed. His face was all screwed up, the way a child's is when it cries. He was making blubbering noises and his lips were trembling. 'I loved you and you fucked me, you rotten, heartless bastard.'

Mort came round the desk, took Edgar in his arms, and held him close until the sobbing quietened down. Then he led him down the corridor, back to his own office. 'It's for the best,' he said.

Edgar wiped his face with the palms of his hands and collapsed into his chair.

'It's good to have you back. Call Jeffrey,' said Mort and closed the door gently behind him.

Edgar swivelled in his chair to face the Manhattan skyline. Then, with dead eyes, he picked up the phone and dialled London.

As the months passed and the physical pain eased, Jack began to think more and more about revenging himself on whoever it was who had been responsible for the savage beating he had received. He suspected Mort, of course, but he could not be sure. He had no hard evidence; he needed to convince himself that Mort was capable of that kind of calculated savagery. Maybe he had hurt him more than he had thought. He had always seen him as a superior, almost invulnerable being, supremely confident in his own ability. Why would he strike out so viciously? After all, what had he done but rattle his cage a few times? Somehow it didn't seem to be in Mort's nature to react so impulsively, so primitively. He was too controlled, too careful for that.

Jack had hated Mort for a long time. Now, there was another dimension to his hate. He had to go see him. He had to know. He had to be sure. It was only when you looked in a man's eyes that you knew the truth.

'You're looking good, Jack. Glad to see it. You made an amazing recovery.' Mort seemed genuinely concerned.

'It took a year,' said Jack, 'but I'm OK now.'

'I heard you took quite a beating.'

'They messed up my face pretty good. I had to have a nose job. Several, in fact. You like it?' He turned side on to Mort, displaying his profile.

Mort grinned. 'Better than the old one.'

'I should hope so,' said Jack. 'It cost enough.'

'You're a lucky guy,' said Mort. 'They might have killed you. All for a lousy Rolex and a few dollars. Doesn't it make you sick?'

'Hard to believe what some guys will do for money,' said Jack.

'Isn't it just? Anyway, be thankful you're OK. No permanent damage?'

'Nothing you'd notice.'

'How do you mean?' The question came too pat – a little too quickly, it seemed to Jack.

'When they finished working on my face, they went to town on my balls. It was a real good job they did, I tell you. Maybe they had their instructions. Maybe they kicked me once too often. Who knows?'

'What are you saying?' Mort seemed nervous.

'What I'm saying is the doctors are talking sterility. I

342

can't produce the goods any more. No kids, Mort. No bambinos. Funny, isn't it? You and me, both. The one thing I could do that you couldn't and now I can't even do that. It's as if someone wanted it that way.'

'I don't get it.' Mort's cat eyes were levelled at him unwavering.

'Someone had me worked over. I think those guys had their orders. They sure did a thorough job.'

'I thought they were muggers,' said Mort. He looked genuinely bewildered. But then he would, wouldn't he? 'Didn't they steal your watch and take your money?'

'Muggers don't do what they did.'

'It happens. Muggers kill.' Why was he so anxious to convince Jack it was only a mugging?

'Sure they kill,' said Jack. 'Sometimes. They shoot people. They knife them. I never heard of anyone who was systematically beaten up from head to foot like I was. Not by muggers, anyway. Did you, Mort?'

Mort looked uncomfortable. 'No, I didn't,' he said, 'now you mention it.'

Jack nodded. Then he grinned suddenly. 'I guess it could have been worse. I can still get it up. If I couldn't do that, I don't know what I'd do.'

'I'm sorry, Jack.' There was no question about it, thought Jack. Mort had the look of a guilty man.

Suddenly Jack's eyes filled with tears. 'I always thought I'd have kids. They make a difference to your life. You can't take a thing for granted these days, can you?'

'What can I say? I never knew.'

'How would you?' Jack stroked the bridge of his new nose. It felt numb. 'I need to ask you something.'

'Go ahead.'

Jack looked into Mort's eyes. 'Was it you?'

Mort's facial muscles tensed, but his eyes were calm. 'Was what me?' he asked coldly.

'Come on. You know what I mean. Did you do it? Was it you who had me beaten up?'

First Mort looked astonished, then angry. He spoke

343

quietly, intensely, emphasizing every word. 'No, it was not. I don't do things like that.'

'No, you sonofabitch, you don't, do you? The only question is, would you have someone else do it for you?'

'No, I wouldn't.'

'You threatened me more than a couple of times.'

'You tried to destroy my company.'

'I intend to keep right on trying.'

'You do and next time I might do something we'll both regret,' said Mort furiously. He bit his lip. It had come out wrong.

'Next time!' Jack seized on the words triumphantly.

'Hell, Jack, that's not what I meant. You provoked me. Don't be an asshole. You can't believe I would do that to you.'

Jack was satisfied. He had what he came for. No sense to show his hand any further. He had looked into Mort's eyes and found the truth.

*   *   *

Mario's in Greenwich Village was crowded and noisy. After a couple of drinks Leo made a face and pointed at the door. Julie nodded.

For a few moments they walked in silence. 'I'm sorry,' said Leo. 'I needed to talk. I'm not in the mood for the in crowd tonight.'

'We said we wouldn't meet again outside the office.'

'I know what we said.'

They walked some more. He stopped in front of the lighted window of an art gallery, one of those places that discover young talent. There wasn't too much evidence of it in this particular window.

Leo looked up at the night sky. 'It's a full moon.'

'They say it makes people crazy,' said Julie.

'You need a full moon for that?' He sounded bitter. Not like Leo.

'What is it?' She was concerned.

'Seeing you every day in the Gallery is tough.'

'You want me to quit?'

'That would be even tougher.'

They moved on.

'I saw the watercolour you did,' he said. 'It's good.'

She laughed. 'You don't need to flatter me.'

'I'm not. I mean it. It's good. Keep at it. You have real talent.'

She slipped her arm through his as they walked. 'Talk to me.'

'It's a crap life,' he said. 'What else can I tell you?'

She squeezed his arm. 'What's the problem?'

He stopped dead on the sidewalk. He did that sometimes when he wanted to talk. People turned and stared. Who stopped on a New York sidewalk? If you weren't rushing somewhere, you had to be crazy.

'They arrested my son. They picked up David.'

She was shocked. 'It's a mistake isn't it, Leo? It has to be.'

'Yes,' he said. 'It's a mistake. My mistake.'

'Why did they arrest him?'

'Drugs.'

'Oh, my God, I'm sorry. When did it happen?'

What did it matter when it happened? Why had she asked a damn fool question like that, she wondered. The facts and the figures . . . the whys and the wherefores . . . she remembered what she had once said to Mort.

'Yesterday.'

He started walking again. They went back to his apartment.

' . . . No,' he said. 'It couldn't have been yesterday. Yesterday he was a kid – just a little kid. He used to hug me when I put him to bed. Sometimes he wouldn't let go. The goddam little tyke just wouldn't let me go. He would hold on so tight, I had to drag myself away. Then he would shout "Goodnight, Dad! Don't let the bed bugs bite! Goodnight! Goodnight! Goodnight!" over and over again – long after I'd shut the door and gone downstairs. It was like an

345

obsession, some kind of ritual he had to perform so he wouldn't feel he'd lost me. It was the only way he could fall asleep. Funny thing, I'd be in the Gallery or walking down Madison and I'd hear him calling me. Imagination, of course. Long after he'd grown up and left home . . . I still hear him sometimes.'

'You love him very much,' she said. 'I'm sure he knows that.'

'I'll be sitting in a bar or on some aircraft and I'll hear him trying to reach me from somewhere, far away, with that little love prayer: "Goodnight, Dad! Don't let the bed bugs bite!" '

Julie was crying.

'Trouble is – he never did reach me. I never reached him, either. In the end I threw him out of the house. What happens to people, Julie? They say he's a heroin addict now. How do you get to be a heroin addict?'

She held Leo in her arms until he went to sleep. He sat up once and said sternly, 'I don't want to see you ever again – you hear me, boy?' Then he went back to sleep again.

In the morning, he didn't want to talk. He was embarrassed. 'You stayed here all night?'

'Sure.'

'What are you going to tell Mort?'

'No problem. I have a bunch of friends in New York.'

'That must be nice.'

'Don't, Leo,' she said. 'Don't be sorry for yourself. It's not like you.'

'What have I done with my life?'

Julie was silent.

'I'll tell you what I've done with it. When I'm gone he'll have the finest collection of Impressionists in private hands,' said Leo. 'Thanks to me. And he's a junkie . . . that's thanks to me, too.'

'You did your best.' What else could she say?

*   *   *

346

The English girl, Eduardo Cabrillo's wife, Anne, was now José Rocha's secretary. She was something special. She was maybe twenty-three or twenty-four. She wore her long' silky, blonde hair in two pigtails down to her waist. The hem of her black leather skirt was three inches above her shapely knees. God knows the tropical heat all that leather must have generated around her thighs and buttocks – well, God and José Rocha. When she was around, air-conditioning was no luxury; it was one of life's necessities.

'Poor girl,' said Rocha, comforting her hard little butt with his hand as he spoke. 'She is unhappy. Look at her. You can see it. She has such a hard life. Her husband does not appreciate her.'

Anne tried to look miserable as she wriggled out of the room, pouting sexily.

Rocha was something of a local hero. A veteran of the civil war, a bush fighter, he wore a fawn-coloured safari suit with a .38 revolver strapped to his waist. He was also, in theory, the most important man in Angola after the President when it came to making decisions affecting the country's oil production and export. In theory. His rival Cabrillo, the fervent Marxist, not only had many influential friends in the Party, he had made himself an expert on all matters relating to oil. He was as hard-working, fanatical and suspicious as Rocha was lazy, pragmatic and trusting. Cabrillo was a thorn in the Minister's flesh.

The telex from Rocha had said there was a problem – no details.

'Cabrillo is making trouble. He is violently opposed to the agency agreement. He is trying to have it cancelled.'

So that was it. 'Why?'

Rocha shrugged. 'Who knows? No one ever knows with that man. He's so cunning, so devious. Maybe, because he hates the Americans.'

'I'm Swedish. The company's international.'

'This man is not rational, like you and me,' said Rocha.

347

'Everything that isn't Russian or Cuban is shit. Marxism is the only creed. Oh, we are all supposed to be Marxist in theory, but you know very well that we are not. Marxism and Africans don't mix. We are tribal. That is our politics. If we have to do business with the devil, we will.'

'Thanks,' said Sam.

Rocha grinned. 'Don't take it personally.'

Anne swayed into the office and deposited some mail on Rocha's desk. Rocha nodded, hypnotized by her leather-encased bottom. 'The man hates me. I can't think why. He is – how you say – a paranoic. He sees slights and insults in everything. He is so jealous of me. Can you explain that?'

Sam looked at Anne and shook his head solemnly. 'Inexplicable,' he said. He could see little beads of sweat forming on her thighs just above the knees. You could have grown an orchid in there. The climatic conditions were perfect.

'Cabrillo and his friends in the cabinet spread vile rumours about me,' said Rocha indignantly.

'Rumours?

'Rumours of corruption and such things. Can you believe he has told the President that your company is paying me a commission. Imagine that.'

'Imagine,' said Sam.

'He has slandered me. He has said that I am a wealthy man, that I have bank accounts in Switzerland and other countries. I am deeply hurt.' Rocha looked deeply hurt. 'I shall take you to see the President. We shall convince him that the agency agreement is in the best interests of Angola.'

'When?'

'Tomorrow at ten.'

Rocha was worried. Clearly there was no time to be lost.

The heat and the mosquitoes kept Sam awake, as they so often did. About three in the morning, the power came on and, with it, the air-conditioning. He closed the windows and soon the room cooled down and he was able to get some sleep.

It seemed only a few minutes later that he was awake again. He looked at his watch. It was four a.m. What had woken him? . . . And then he heard it – the crackling on the other side of the bay, the unmistakable sound of automatic gunfire. There were four or five huge explosions. He could see the flames lighting up the sky from the direction of the radio station and from another building about a mile away – the Presidential Palace, perhaps.

He opened the window and watched the display. From where he stood, it was like watching *son et lumière*, but there was no doubt what was happening. This was not show business. This was a coup. Bad news. If the coup were successful, it would mean the end of the agency agreement. Even if it were not, it could still mean disaster. What if Cabrillo were involved? His own life could well be in danger.

He kept the room in darkness. Outside, he could see the first faint wash of light on the horizon. The gunfire was more intense now and there were figures – soldiers presumably – running in the garden. He hoped they were here to defend the hotel and not to attack it. Whichever way, there was not a damn thing he could do except stay in his room and keep his head down.

After an hour or so, he began to doze intermittently, but his twilight sleep was interrupted by nightmares. He was being tortured in a cellar by two men. They were holding up a huge, crumpled sheet of paper with the words 'Capitalist pig' on it. Then Cabrillo appeared and ordered him to sign a confession. It seemed to be an admission of his adultery with Anne, but then she swayed into the room, unbuckled her black leather skirt, slid down her panties, sat astride his chest and tried to strangle him with her pigtails. All the time José Rocha was ringing a bell in his ear and screaming: 'Slander! Slander!'

Suddenly, he was awake. The phone by his bed was ringing.

'Telex for you, sir.'

'What?' He shook his head to clear it. 'What time is it?'

'Eight-thirty, sir.'

'What's going on?'

'Telex for you, sir,' the man repeated. The line went dead.

Downstairs at reception there were, in fact, two telexes: one from the Minister: 'Meeting with President cancelled. Rocha.' Short and to the point. Not exactly informative. The other was from Cabrillo: 'Please stay in hotel. Will meet you as soon as possible. Natoilco, Managing Director.' Not too friendly, but a damn sight more helpful than Rocha's. The guy was telling him to stay out of trouble. Not that he needed telling.

It looked like every guest in the hotel was standing there, all of them talking at the same time. They were being 'protected' by a nervous-looking kid in battle fatigues who shifted uneasily from foot to foot, with his finger on the trigger of an AK 47 assault rifle and the safety catch off. It was the first time Sam had felt really anxious. He was more likely to be killed by this kid than by the revolutionaries.

Everyone in the place had his own theory, of course; the President and the whole cabinet had been murdered by the Cubans who had replaced them with their own puppet government; the Cubans had saved the President from a suicide squad of UNITA guerillas; a regiment of East German paratroopers had gone berserk and wiped out two barracks of Cuban troops. Sam liked that one. It showed imagination. There were plenty more – the whole thing was a propaganda exercise to strengthen the President's position and drum up popular support; the Vice-President had murdered the President and taken over the government; the South Africans had landed marines from fast gunboats, slaughtered the cabinet, destroyed the port installations, the refinery, the radio station and the Presidential Palace and sunk three Russian cargo ships.

The only indisputable fact was that the airport was closed and all flights cancelled until further notice.

Around three in the afternoon of the third day, Cabrillo

350

phoned. 'I'm sending you the Natoilco car and driver. He'll be with you in ten minutes. Everything's back to normal now. We have to talk. The President is not satisfied with the agency agreement. Nor am I.'

Sam wanted to say something, but the phone went dead.

A few minutes later, the car arrived. Since the uprising, no one had been allowed to leave the hotel, but it was now clear that the attempted coup had failed.

The driver drove him directly to the Natoilco building. Sam took the elevator to the third floor where Cabrillo had his office. The whole place was deserted – no receptionist, no secretaries, no telex operator – no one. Sam knocked politely on the door of Cabrillo's office. There was no reply, so he opened the door and walked in.

Cabrillo was sitting at his desk. He would not be signing any more contracts – or cancelling them either. He had been shot, obviously with a heavy-calibre gun at close range. One side of his face had been blown away. A wash of blood was congealing on the wall behind him and there were fragments of scalp or brain embedded in it. What was left of the neck was a pulpy oozing mess. Cabrillo's shirt was bright red, swamped with the blood that had pumped from his carotid artery in the seconds following the shooting.

Sam had never seen anything like this before. He rushed out of the room and retched in the corridor until his stomach muscles ached. The Natoilco driver clattered screaming down the stairs. He must have seen Cabrillo. Sam chased after him. When he ran out onto the street the car was there, but the driver had disappeared.

It was another three days before he could see Rocha again.

'For God's sake, what happened?' It might not have been the best way to open a discussion with a minister, but he couldn't help himself.

José Rocha was as cool and immaculate as ever. He was dressed in a white safari suit. Sam noticed that he had discarded the gun.

351

He spoke calmly. 'As you know, there was an attempted coup. Two ministers were taken hostage by the criminals and murdered. Their bodies were found this morning in a baker's oven on the outskirts of the city. The criminals have been captured and executed – after a fair trial, of course.'

'What happened to Cabrillo?'

'Shot by the criminals,' said Rocha.

'But why?'

'We think they may have tried to hide in the Natoilco building and found him there. He was in their way.'

'But why would they kill him?'

'Who knows? Perhaps he tried to resist them.'

Sam was still puzzled. 'When did this happen?'

'The morning of the coup. About ten o'clock.'

'The morning of the coup?' Sam had spoken to Cabrillo two days after the coup!

'Correct.'

'It couldn't have happened later than that?'

'Impossible. The criminals were captured at eleven o'clock the morning of the coup and executed at noon.' Rocha looked at Sam shrewdly. 'Cabrillo could be a very obstinate man, you know.'

'I know,' said Sam.

'He is a grievous loss to the country. I, personally, shall miss him.'

'My condolences.'

Rocha inclined his head in acknowledgement. 'Anne is devastated, of course. I do my best to comfort her, but . . .' He raised his arms helplessly, indicating the limitations even of a minister's power to console the bereaved.

'When shall we see the President?'

'What for?'

'We had an appointment. You remember?'

'Circumstances have changed,' said Rocha. 'The President is satisfied with the agreement. There is no opposition to it. The cabinet has ratified it. It was always a formality, as I told you.'

352

'You did? I thought . . .'

'Tonight the airport will be open,' said Rocha gently. 'You can go home.'

'That's nice,' said Sam.

Rocha held out his hand. 'I believe,' he said, with a sly look on his face, 'there is an English expression – something about an ill wind?'

'Indeed there is,' said Sam.

'The driver will take you to the airport,' said Rocha.

'The Natoilco driver?'

'Ah no,' said Rocha. 'The ministry driver. The Natoilco driver met with an accident. It seems his eyes deceived him. He had hallucinations. He was seeing things.'

'That could be dangerous for a driver,' said Sam.

'Fatal,' agreed the Minister sadly.

*   *   *

'By North Sea standards, it's a mini-strike,' said Henry Soames casually. 'Fifteen to twenty thousand barrels a day – at most. Of course, one never knows. It could turn out to be a little more, but nothing spectacular, you understand. At least it's not a dry hole.' He meandered on. Jeffrey was confused, but the essence of what Henry was saying seemed to be clear.

'Hold it, Henry. Let me understand this. Are you telling me we struck oil?'

'The consortium did. Yes,' said Henry.

Jeffrey let out a yell of delight and grabbed the phone. 'I have to tell the others.'

'Don't get excited, dear boy. It's bad for the arteries. You have a ten per cent share of a tiny production. Nothing to get your knickers in a twist about.'

'Tiny production be damned!' said Jeffrey exultantly. 'We struck oil. We're not just traders any more. We're producers. Don't you see what this means? It's going to open all sorts of doors that were closed to us before – quite apart from the profits we'll make on the crude.'

Henry flapped a deprecating hand at Jeffrey – a gesture

353

intended to express mild displeasure. 'Calm down, Jeffrey. Listen to me. Sir Albert wants to see you. He has a proposal – a very generous proposal, I may say – to buy you out. If I were you . . .'

'You're not,' Jeffrey cut in rudely. 'And don't forget, you represent King Brothers at a highly inflated fee.'

'I'm only trying to advise you in your own best interest,' said Henry stiffly.

'Henry,' said Jeffrey drily, 'the only interest that counts with you is self-interest.'

'Brutal,' said Henry. 'Brutal and slanderous.' He looked beaten and betrayed – a latter-day Julius Caesar expiring on the steps of the Capitol.

The bland features of Sir Albert Harcourt-Smith, Chairman of North Sea Venture, were plump, pasty and a little sweaty – rather, thought Jeffrey, like a large mozzarella cheese.

Behind his ostentatiously grand partners' desk he sat playing with calculators, leather-bound diaries and gold pens. He opened and shut drawers as if they contained documents germane to their discussions, but far too secret to be revealed.

Jeffrey amused himself by fantasizing that the drawers concealed the very latest state-of-the-art microchips whose function was to trigger the phantasmagoria of expressions that flowed smoothly over Sir Albert's porcine features: gratification, displeasure, brotherly love, venom, condescension, outrage, candour – an ever changing, apparently infinitely diverse display that never once disturbed the unvarying, balefully antagonistic glare of his protruding eyes.

'You will of course understand, Mr Lewis, being an intelligent man,' he droned on, 'that our offer to buy you out is motivated not simply by considerations of profit, but by matters which are, I may say, not unrelated to the security of this country and to vital government energy policy.' Click! Portentous solemnity. Click! Engaging candour. Click! Ingratiating smile. Sir Albert leaned back in his chair, placed the tips of his fingers together and waited for a response.

He consulted his diary, unscrewed his gold pen and wrote something on a desk pad. Then he closed the diary, screwed the top on his gold pen and opened and shut a couple of drawers noisily. After a time, he realized that his tactics were not working. He was waiting in vain.

'We intend,' he continued, 'to spend, and – more import-ant to be seen to be spending – some very substantial sums in the North Sea and, in particular, in the area of this first strike. The amounts involved could well run into hundreds of millions of dollars.' He paused for effect and contem-plated Jeffrey. Jeffrey appeared to be looking out of the window, studying the City skyline with great interest. It seemed clear to Sir Albert that he was casting pearls before swine. He was obliged to continue. 'The more money we invest in exploration, the better Her Majesty's Govern-ment will like it, and the better HMG likes it, the more inclined it will be to award us concessions in the future.'

Click! Conspiratorial cunning. Click! Transparent sin-cerity.

He leaned back once more and, with a grandiose gesture, swept a glass ashtray from one side of his desk to the other. He stared at Jeffrey expectantly and Jeffrey stared right back.

Henry Soames shifted in his seat. The interview was not proceeding according to plan. Time, it seemed to him, for intervention. 'It appears to me,' he said, 'as an entirely impartial observer, that Sir Albert's proposal is eminently fair and reasonable – if I may say so,' he added, with phoney patrician diffidence. 'Twenty-two million dollars for King Brothers' ten per cent holding. Cash on the table. A profit of a hundred and twenty per cent on your original invest-ment.' He shook his head in wonder, implying that Sir Albert's generosity left him speechless. 'I am, of course,

355

as everyone well knows, a neutral party in this affair but I would have thought ... well ... grab it before the consortium changes its mind. Eh, Sir Albert?'

Sir Albert inclined his head. It was not he who had spoken. That would not have been proper. He had merely concurred in another's opinion.

'After all,' said Sir Albert, 'you are only traders.' Click! Distaste. 'Not producers.' Click! Smiling condescension. 'You would be, would you not, somewhat out of your league?'

The moment had come, Jeffrey sensed, to enter the arena. 'That didn't seem to worry you when you needed our exploration money,' he said.

Sir Albert flushed. He glanced at Henry Soames, a look of serious displeasure on his heavy features. 'The stakes, Mr Lewis, are higher now – a great deal higher. We cannot afford to have passengers who are unable to pay their way. Do you have any conception how much it costs to operate and develop an oil field in the North Sea – quite apart from the enormous investment in further exploration to which I already referred? One needs oil rigs, pipelines, pumping stations, tankers, onshore landing and distribution facilities and so on and so forth.'

'Does one?' said Jeffrey.

'Not only the costs, but the risks – the risks, Mr Lewis – are astronomical.'

'For a small operation of fifteen to twenty thousand barrels a day? Surely "astronomical" is an exaggeration,' said Jeffrey innocently.

Sir Albert and Henry Soames exchanged glances. Sir Albert carefully considered his next pronouncement.

'It is normal business prudence to make provisions.'

'Provisions for what?' Jeffrey enquired.

'In the event – the unlikely event – that the field turns out to be, well . . .' Click! Captivating beam.

'A bonanza?' said Jeffrey helpfully.

'Somewhat larger than initially indicated,' said Sir Albert. The sweat was dripping off the mozzarella cheese.

How had the conversation taken this regrettable turn?

'Good,' said Jeffrey, jumping to his feet. 'I think that's clear.'

'If I could have your answer tomorrow,' said Sir Albert sweetly, 'I would greatly appreciate it. There are many things to be done. If there's any way we can assist you, if there's anything at all we can do to help you arrive at the right decision, please do not hesitate to call on us.' He smiled a fat complacent smile that seemed to Jeffrey to grow and grow like the smile of the Cheshire Cat in *Alice in Wonderland*. It grew so large that Sir Albert's dumpy body appeared to shrink behind it.

'You can have my answer now,' said Jeffrey. 'We're not selling.'

'Are you seriously suggesting that your company would wish to be involved in such a costly and risky venture?' said Sir Albert, still managing somehow to smile while he was talking. The effect was grotesque.

'We ain't selling,' said Jeffrey. 'Thanks all the same.'

Sir Albert's smile began to fade gradually, like the Cheshire Cat's, leaving behind only a pair of very cold eyes focused malevolently on Jeffrey.

The silence after Jeffrey's departure was long and sinister.

'Correct me if I'm wrong,' said Sir Albert at last, icily, 'but did you not say he would be a pushover?'

'I did,' said Henry. 'I was wrong, wasn't I?'

The next day the news hit the headlines. It was, said *The Times*, the biggest North Sea oil strike for years. After two dry holes, the consortium – North Sea Venture – had struck oil, not too far from BP's Forties field. The exact size was not known, but the estimates were between seventy and eighty thousand barrels a day. Two tabloids ran the same headline: 'Britain Strikes It Big!' Another contented itself with the more eye-catching and dramatic one-word headline: 'Gusher!'

'Effective, don't you think?' said Jeffrey to Henry Soames, showing him the tabloids. He was enjoying himself. 'Strange how the press seems to have access to information not available to you and Sir Albert, isn't it?'

'Rumours, dear boy,' said Henry, 'nothing but rumours. The usual superficial coverage by the uninformed gutter press. Half truths, distortions and outright inventions.'

'Time will tell,' said Jeffrey.

'You don't have time.' Henry was agitated. 'Sir Albert's offer expires today.'

'Let it expire,' said Jeffrey.

He phoned Mort and asked him to fly over. This was a biggie – perhaps the biggest yet. Major decisions would have to be taken. He could do with some support. The transatlantic phone was fine to discuss most deals, but this was not most deals.

He picked Mort up at Heathrow. They talked in the car, heading into town on the M4, and continued their discussion in Mort's suite at the Dorchester.

'Where do you want to eat?'

Mort hesitated. 'Why don't we meet at seven-thirty tomorrow morning and have breakfast together. I feel bad keeping you away from your family. You go home. I'm sure Caroline will be happy to see you. I'm going to roll into bed. The jet lag got to me.'

If Jeffrey was surprised, he did not show it. It was not often that Mort was so solicitous of his partners' families.

Rosemary was excited to hear his voice. 'Mort, what a nice surprise. It's been so long.'

'I thought I'd give you a call,' he said casually, 'just to see how things were.'

'I'm flattered,' she said. 'Not just a call, but a long-distance call. The line's great. It sounds like you're next door.'

'I'm not next door,' he said. 'I'm in the phone booth across the road from you.'

Rosemary let out a shriek. 'You bastard!' she said. 'Come on up before I rush down there and rape you in the phone booth.'

'Sounds good,' said Mort. 'I think I'll stay here.'

At the door, she threw her arms round him. 'Why didn't you warn me?' she protested. 'I could have been entertaining a lover.'

Mort had been half afraid of that. He knew she might be out – or worse, in bed with a boyfriend. He had considered the possibility, but if that was how it was, he would prefer to know about it. It would, indeed, have been the perfect excuse to break off the relationship – not that he was looking for one. What he was looking for was a reason not to fall in love with her. So far, he had not found one.

The passion was greater than ever. To Mort, it was almost frightening. He made love to her hungrily, clumsily, as if for the first time and, in her way, she understood and loved him more for it. But that scared him too. The second time they made love slowly and gently, like two people in love. After she reached her climax, she held him tight, her face next to his, and he could feel the tears on her cheek.

They woke two or three hours later. It was nearly midnight. 'I'm hungry,' he said.

'You mind spaghetti?'

'I love it.'

'Just as well,' said Rosemary. 'It's about all I have in the flat.'

It reminded them both of last time. The wine was Chianti – red, strong and heady. It reminded him, too, of his student days when spaghetti was pretty much the staple diet and girls entertained him in their apartments with candles and wine and Nat King Cole and sex.

While they were waiting for the spaghetti, they took a quick shower together. Neither of them wanted sex. They soaped each other gently and kissed under the hot water until they were gasping for air.

Then they sat in white bathrobes and listened to her favourite late-night music – Nat King Cole.

'I don't believe it,' he said.

'What's wrong with Nat King Cole?' Defiantly.

'Nothing,' he said. 'I just didn't think people listened to him any more.'

'Well, here's one who does.'

'I'm glad.'

Naturally, she knew about the oil strike. It was only that they had a tacit understanding to try to avoid talking business when they were alone together. She couldn't resist it though. It seemed to excite her.

'You think the strike's a big one?'

'Hard to tell. You know more than I do.' Not that he didn't trust her. It was his habit not to give anything away unless it was absolutely necessary.

'You know how rare that is?' she said. 'To strike oil? And on your first time around?' Her eyes were shining. 'You have the touch, don't you? What will you do when you own half the North Sea?'

'Buy the other half,' he said.

'I really think you will,' she said. Something strange was happening to her. Her breathing was coming faster and her face was flushed. She sat on his knee and, kissing him hungrily, slipped her hand into his bathrobe between his legs. He was still holding his glass of wine. A few drops spilled on her nipples and he started to lick them. She took the glass from him and slowly poured the red wine on his chest, licking it as it trickled down to his stomach. The last dregs she poured, very deliberately, on the tip of his cock and tasted it with her tongue, lapping the glans the way a cat licks its paw.

He tried to stand up to carry her to the bedroom, but she wouldn't let him. She sat astride him on the chair – eyes closed – hands on his shoulders – thrusting herself up and down slowly and rhythmically until they cried out together.

'My God!' he gasped. 'Wasn't that the greatest!'

Rosemary threw back her head and sighed a deep sigh.

'Gusher!' she breathed.

That night, for the first time, he stayed with her. In the

morning he dressed while she took a shower. 'I'd like to buy you some clothes, but I don't know what to get you,' he called out. She didn't hear him. They never had time to go shopping – besides, it would not be good to be seen together. He decided to take a look in her closet to give himself some ideas.

It was surprising how few clothes she owned. He could not help thinking of Julie's collection of designer dresses. The contrast in the lifestyles of the two women could not have been greater.

She came out of the shower and wrapped herself in a towel. He was sitting on the bed, shoulders hunched. Something was wrong.

'What is it?'

'Nothing.'

She sat beside him on the bed and tried to touch him, but he shrank from her.

'Are you going to tell me what's wrong?'

He stood up and put on his raincoat.

'There's a suit of clothes in there,' he said. 'A couple of shirts ... ties ... nothing much. I was looking at your dresses to see what I could buy you. I had no business poking around. I'm sorry. It was a shock after last night, that's all. I had no right to expect anything else. You warned me once.'

'Yes, I warned you,' she said quietly. She tried to put her arms round him, but again he pushed her away.

'We're both free agents. That's what we agreed, isn't it?' he said.

'Something like that,' she said.

He nodded. 'I remember.' It seemed like a long time ago.

After he left, she wandered around, looking in the cupboards, the drawers, the bathroom – even under the bed. She had no idea what she was looking for – anything at all, she supposed – anything that belonged to Mort, something of his to hold, to keep, to remind her of him. But there was nothing, not even a damn toothbrush.

*

'Ok, what have we got if we stay in?' said Mort.

'Hard to say. Sir Albert now claims that the strike is twenty-five thousand barrels a day – say about one and a quarter million tons of crude a year. Our ten per cent would only represent about a million barrels – not too much, but at today's prices we'd make a gross profit of thirty to thirty-five million dollars a year.'

'Less development costs and overheads.'

'Which initially will be very high. After a year or so, they should drop dramatically – once the pipeline and onshore facilities are in place, that is.'

'You believe Sir Albert's estimate?' said Mort.

'No, I don't. I think he wants us out. We don't belong there, not in his book. My guess is he's deliberately underestimating the size of the field. The press is probably nearer the mark. They say it's a biggie and I tend to believe them. I've talked around the market and the experts are estimating eighty to a hundred thousand barrels a day.'

Mort whistled. 'Four times what Sir Albert told you. The lying bastard!'

'It's only their guess.'

'Let's assume their guess is right. What would you do?'

'No doubt in my mind. I'd sell our share – if they give us our price, of course. If we stay in, we'll be involved initially in very heavy outlay. And if they hit exploration snags, the costs could double or treble.'

'On the other hand,' said Mort, 'we could visit producing countries and talk like producers. That would open up new sources of oil that are closed to us right now. We could buy a couple of refineries in Europe and the States and go downstream. Think of the profits.'

'Think of the risks,' said Jeffrey. 'We'll do fine as long as the boom lasts, but one day it'll be over. I prefer today's profits to tomorrow's dreams.'

Mort's eyes had a faraway look in them. 'Think of it, Jeffrey. We'd be an oil company in our own right. The world would really have to sit up and take notice of us.'

'They do that already. We're making money. Big money. We're doing what we know and we're doing great. The risks we take are the risks we understand. Let's leave it that way, Mort. Let the others stick their feet in cement. We should stay flexible. We're traders.'

'One day,' said Mort, 'I'd like to be something better.'

The final meeting with Sir Albert was brief and to the point.

'We're prepared to offer our shares to the consortium,' said Jeffrey.

Sir Albert's mozzarella cheeks beamed damply. His chins wobbled with pleasure.

'If you accept our terms,' Jeffrey continued, 'we shall require a banker's cheque one week from today for the full amount. If you don't, we shall remain in the consortium and exercise our rights as a shareholder and partner.'

It sounded like an ultimatum. It was intended to.

'Your terms?' asked Sir Albert, looking slightly less cheerful.

'Two hundred and fifty million dollars,' said Jeffrey and sat back in his chair to enjoy the reaction.

Henry Soames choked on his coffee and broke into a paroxysm of coughing. Sir Albert's mouth fell open – the entrance to a dark cave. His face was as pale as any face could be. The skin was translucent, beaded with little droplets of sweat. He removed his handkerchief from the sleeve of his jacket and wiped his face with it. Jeffrey wondered idly how it stayed up there. He also wondered who did Sir Albert's laundry.

'Since you will no doubt wish to consult the other consortium members, you may let us have your reply by ten a.m. tomorrow,' said Jeffrey. 'If we do not receive your acceptance by then, we shall assume our proposal is rejected.'

Sir Albert made a brave effort at a smile – brave but desperate. He was floundering, a stately galleon holed below the waterline. Henry Soames was still recovering from his choking fit.

They both looked sick.

At nine forty-five the following morning, Henry Soames crept into Jeffrey's office and slumped in a chair.

'Ah, Henry,' Jeffrey greeted him jovially. 'What brings you here?'

'You know damn well what brings me here,' said Henry. He threw an envelope at Jeffrey.

Jeffrey ignored the paperknife on his desk. He tore open the envelope and read the brief message. His expression betrayed nothing.

Mort could not endure the suspense.

'What do they say, man? What do they say?'

Jeffrey looked up. 'They accept,' he said calmly. He threw the letter up in the air, leaned back in his chair and gave a whoop of joy. 'Two hundred and fifty million bucks!'

'For Chrissake,' said Mort, 'how about that!'

'It was always in the bag,' said Jeffrey immodestly.

'It was a very close-run thing,' said Henry Soames indignantly.

'Indeed?' said Jeffrey.

'I had to do some pretty ruthless arm twisting, I can tell you.'

'Did you?' said Mort. He sounded unimpressed.

'Tell me, Henry,' asked Jeffrey, 'how do you explain all those low production estimates you kept feeding us?'

'I never – fed you anything, as you so crudely put it. Those estimates were what Sir Albert gave me. I had no reason to doubt them.'

'You had every reason to check them,' said Jeffrey.

'Why should I?' Henry blustered. 'I acted as I thought best.'

'Ah,' said Jeffrey, 'I thought you were acting for me.'

'Of course I was,' Henry stammered, 'only . . . the matter was highly complex . . . the whole thing was . . .' He seemed to lose his way.

364

'How much were they paying you?' asked Jeffrey.

One of Henry Soames's more engaging qualities was his ability to recognize when he was beaten.

'More than you,' he said apologetically. 'A great deal more.'

'You conniving bastard!' said Jeffrey. 'You took money from me to get me the true production estimates and you took a bribe from the consortium to tell me a pack of lies.'

Henry demurred. 'Not a bribe. A retainer, dear boy. A retainer. There are civilized words for everything.'

'What's the civilized word for a shit?' said Jeffrey.

'Please.' Henry dabbed a pained hand to his brow. 'Have some consideration. That bastard refuses to pay me my commission because of the enormous settlement you extracted from him. You won't credit it, but they had the impudence to accuse me of betraying them – of being some kind of double agent. They said I was working for you all the time.'

'Which, of course, you were,' said Jeffrey.

'Quite so,' said Henry. He seemed confused.

'On an ex gratia basis.'

'Ex gratia?' stuttered Henry. 'What – what do you mean by that?'

'By ex gratia? – Oh, I'm sorry, Henry, I thought with your classical education you would understand. I mean free – for nothing – without remuneration – gratis,' said Jeffrey. 'That's what the word means.'

'I know what the word means,' said Henry. 'I simply don't consider it fair to apply it in this case.'

'I do.'

'Not a bean?'

'Not a bean. And next time you make an agreement with me,' said Jeffrey, 'I suggest you stick to it.'

Henry was horrified. The look on his face was telling Jeffrey that he was asking far too much of him.

* * *

It was nearly two years now since Laura's death. The day after the funeral Amy had flown to New York with Edward. There was nothing else to do. She had needed to start all over again. After fifteen years of marriage she was compelled, for the first time, to acknowledge that, at thirty-three, she was no longer a girl, and that the passing of youth was not something to be mourned, but to be celebrated.

Now she began to see herself as she really was. She was able to be what she wanted to be – not obliged to play a role chosen for her by someone else. She could stop looking back and start making plans and dreaming dreams.

She enrolled Edward in a prestigious East Coast school as a boarder and returned to her former career of fashion modelling. At first, it was tough; the business had changed, the models were younger than ever – kids. She had to live on promises and the money Sam sent her every month. And then, after a few months, a door opened. She was hired to model five dresses by a top New York fashion house. She got the job through influence – a friend of a friend. Then another door opened and another and another. Within six months she was, once again, one of New York's top models; the world of fashion re-adopted her. She had it made. Her fragile beautiful face was on the front cover of every fashion magazine. She was seen at the best restaurants and discos. Society hostesses competed for her favours. She was more popular than she had ever been in her youth. Now, to her American flair and panache, she had added a dash of European sophistication and mystery.

She was courted by bankers and senators, pop stars and painters; she was adopted by the wealthy and sought after by fashionable intellectuals. She had that poise, that tantalizingly remote quality that Sam had found so fascinating and, at the same time, so frustrating. She was the planet and her dependent satellites swam around her, thriving on her approval, marvelling at her beauty, drawing their strength from her controlling power. In less than a year she had totally discarded her old life and created for herself a new one. It was, after all, she discovered, her life and she could do with it as she pleased.

Sam constantly tried to tempt her back to Switzerland. For the first few months, he phoned her two or three times a week. 'I need you. I want you back,' he pleaded.

But she was merciless. 'What you need, Sam, is a large pair of tits to suck. I can't be your mother and your wife. It's time to be honest with each other.'

'We have a son. We have all those years of marriage behind us. How can you just throw that away?'

'I don't care any more,' she said. 'I don't care about the past. I don't care about what we've been to each other – or what we might have been. It's finished. I'm living for the present.'

'You don't want to be alone for the rest of your life,' warned Sam.

'Why not?' she said. 'We're all alone. The only difference between us is that I have the guts to accept it. You don't.'

Finally, they stopped talking about themselves and began to confine their conversation to the weather, to Edward's education and to money transfers. Once, only once, Sam tried to talk about Laura, but Amy interrupted and changed the subject. Whatever her reasons, Sam was hurt. It seemed that she wanted to behave as if Laura had never existed. He, on the other hand, needed to talk about her, and Amy's apparent indifference when he mentioned her name only confirmed what he could not bear to admit to himself: their marriage was over. Why he still needed to cling to Amy, he was not able to understand. Sometimes, he thought he must be a masochist. He was not even sure that he loved her any more. One day he was convinced that he did, the next he was quite certain that he hated her. Whatever it was that he missed – her allure, her strength perhaps – he hankered after her.

Then, one night, the phone rang. It was three in the morning. Amy never knew about time differences, never cared. She always acted on impulse, anyway. He struggled to clear his head of sleep.

367

'I want a divorce,' she said. And that was all. He tried to call back, but she had left the phone off the hook.

The next thing he knew, she had filed for divorce. It was something he had to accept. What choice did he have? Fighting would only prolong the agony and the result, in the end, would be the same.

He had not seen Jane for three years – not since that day by the lake when they had said goodbye. Things had changed now.

He called her. 'I must see you.'

'What for?'

'I want you to move in with me,' he said. Why the hell had he said that? Why in God's name was he so afraid of being alone? Did he really want to share his life with Jane when he had not yet accepted the break with Amy? He was totally unable to analyse his own emotions.

'I'll think about it,' she said.

'Please do,' he pleaded.

'What about Amy?'

'We're getting a divorce,' he said lamely.

'So, now you come running back to mother.'

Jesus! Women! One was as bad as the other. 'I don't think that's fair, Jane. Do you?'

'Oh yes,' she said. 'It's fair all right.'

'Shit!' he said and slammed down the phone. He was through with women – finished.

If only it were true. But it wasn't. It was a pose. Who was he kidding? Who was he living his life for? That goddam camera? The fat shiny lens was still focused on him.

It was a quiet wedding – family and a few close friends – not the kind Edmund Meyer had planned for his only daughter, but then Jack Greenberg was not the kind of son-in-law he would have chosen either.

It was far from being a happy day for E.M. There were times when he longed to wipe the complacent smile off that chubby, shiny face – most of all, when Jack was

368

standing with Rachel under the chupah, looking exactly like the cat who had got the cream.

Still, if Rachel was happy with the bastard, what could he do?

Life was full of compromises. That was one thing E.M. had learned.

*　　*　　*

Winter came early in 1980. By December, the cars needed chains to drive up the hill to the Dolder. The trees were weighed down with clumps of snow clinging to the branches like plump white lobsters. When the first thaw came, they would lose their hold and tumble to the ground.

Mort was exultant. 'We made it. We're up there,' he said. 'We finally made it.'

From their mini-Olympus, they looked down on the snow-covered world. It was theirs. All they had to do was reach out and grasp it. They had dreamed and their dream had come true.

Six years ago, they had been on the edge of bankruptcy. Two years ago, when the price of crude was twelve dollars a barrel, they had made the decision to buy. Now the price was over thirty-five dollars a barrel. They were the second largest oil-trading corporation in the world.

'Our assets today are over five hundred million dollars,' Mort announced proudly. 'We have thirty-three offices in twenty-nine countries.'

'It's incredible,' said Sam.

Mort nodded agreement. 'We can all be very proud of what we've achieved. There isn't one of you who hasn't made a major contribution to the growth of this company.'

'Think about it,' said Ruby, in awe. 'Just think what we're all worth.'

'The champagne tastes the same,' said Jeffrey wryly.

'Now that's a typical Jeffrey Lewis put-down. Enjoy, man. You did it.' Mort patted Jeffrey on the shoulder affectionately.

'I enjoy,' said Jeffrey. 'I'm just trying to keep a sense of perspective. So we made it. Does anyone know what that means?'

'Money isn't important,' said Mort, 'I'm with you there. It's what you do with it that counts.'

'And just what are we going to do with it?' said Jeffrey.

'That's what power is all about,' said Ruby.

'Is this Rabbi King talking?' said Jeffrey, grinning.

'I'll tell you something,' said Ruby. 'When I first stayed in this joint, I couldn't afford the price of a room. Now, I could buy the place.'

'You don't suppose you're getting to be too big for your boots?' said Jeffrey.

'You don't suppose you're getting to be a sanctimonious prick?' Ruby retorted angrily.

There was an awkward silence. Sam gazed out of the window. He usually did when the going got rough.

Jeffrey persisted. 'So we're worth half a million dollars. What are we going to do with it?'

As Ruby considered the question his face drained of expression — as though the essential being, the life force that normally animated it, had temporarily vacated. Then he smiled, but in his smile there was little humour.

'Take over the world,' he said.

Mort's green eyes were glittering. Then he too smiled. 'Lighten up, Jeffrey. Let's make the next half billion. A billion is a nice round number.'

Jeffrey nodded slowly. 'And then?'

'It's snowing,' Sam said.

'Terrific,' said Jeffrey.

These guys are not kidding, he thought. 'Let's not take ourselves too seriously,' he said. 'We're in this for the fun, aren't we?'

'You said it,' said Mort. 'Not me.'

'No,' said Jeffrey. 'You said it. At the first Dolder meeting. Remember?'

'That was a while back. We've come a long way since then.'

'Haven't we just?'

'Why don't we concentrate on putting King Brothers on top of the world?' said Ruby.

'It's what we all want, isn't it?' said Mort.

'The American dream,' said Jeffrey caustically. 'If you're not number one, you're nothing.'

Sam was looking down on the golf course. On top of the world. The sun had broken through the clouds. One of the snow lobsters slipped off a branch at the top of a towering pine tree and the spray shimmered in the sunlight as it fell.

*　　*　　*

Melvin Craig was short, chunky and Texan. He wore blue crocodile shoes with gold buckles, a vivid scarlet silk shirt puffed with frills at collar and cuffs, a figure-hugging cream linen suit and a bootlace tie. He was soft-spoken, smiling and friendly. He wanted only one thing out of life – to be rich.

Edmund Meyer and Jack Greenberg watched him with a blend of fascination and incredulity, as if he were a visitor from outer space. Neither of them had seen anything quite like him before. Their gaze followed his busy, neat little hands nestling in their bed of frills as they gestured the accompaniment to the grandiose schemes he was outlining. E.M.'s nose wrinkled distastefully at the disagreeable odour of his cheap cigar.

Exactly why his son-in-law had granted the man an appointment, he was not quite sure. If ever he had seen a flake, this was one. After five minutes, he was less certain. After ten, he was beginning to take the little man seriously. The scheme he was proposing was brilliant.

It also made E.M.'s nose wrinkle – like the cheap cigar.

'You ever handled Domestic crude?' Craig began by asking them.

'Here and there,' said Jack. 'Not on a regular basis.'

'Then you know there are three tiers.'

'I know,' said Jack. 'Maybe you should explain to Mr Meyer. He's not in day-to-day trading.'

371

'Sure,' said Craig. 'Here's how it works.' He puffed on his cigar. 'The Department of Energy, or DOE as we all lovingly call it, has designated three categories of Domestic oil: Old Oil or Lower Tier, New Oil often called Upper Tier, and Stripper. Forgive me if I'm teaching you to suck eggs, but Old Oil is produced from a well at or below the production level fixed in 1972. Crude discovered after 1973, or any crude obtained from existing wells in excess of the 1973 level of production, is termed New Oil. Stripper is any crude produced from a well whose average daily production is less than ten barrels.'

Edmund Meyer nodded thoughtfully.

'Bureaucracy, eh?' Craig laughed scornfully. 'The Carter administration thought their idea was the greatest discovery since chocolate. What they were trying to do, of course, was to stimulate new production. DOE regulates the price levels of each category of crude. So, for example, you're allowed to sell a barrel of Old Oil for ten dollars, a barrel of New Oil for twenty-five dollars and a barrel of Stripper for thirty dollars.'

Melvin Craig put his blue crocodile shoes on E.M.'s desk and leaned back in his chair.

'You with me so far?' he said, his voice a touch patronizing. E.M. glared and looked at Jack.

'Mr Meyer does not like anyone to put their feet on his desk,' said Jack.

Melvin Craig was thrown for just a moment, but he soon recovered. He was a man who could adapt rapidly to any situation. He removed his feet hastily, pretending not to notice the look of disgust on E.M.'s face.

'I don't get it,' said Jack. 'You haven't told me anything I don't know already.'

'Let him go on,' said E.M.

'The scheme is kind of confidential,' said Melvin Craig. 'I'll give you an outline, but I wouldn't want it to get around.'

'You have my word,' said Jack.

Craig pulled out a packet of wooden gum massagers and started in on his teeth. He was considering what Jack

Greenberg's word was worth. Not much, he decided. He also decided that he had no choice.

'Well now, you all see that these three categories of crude are way different from each other. They have different names, different descriptions and they sure as hell have different prices. But you know the funny thing? They all look alike. One goddam barrel of crude looks the same as any other. You can call it what you like. It don't change what it is. Know what I mean?'

Jack was beginning to realize that the man in front of him was no one's fool.

'It's what you might call a paper distinction – and who tells us what to put on all those little pieces of paper? Our old friend, DOE.'

Jack was getting the idea. He was looking at E.M. to see how he ought to react, but E.M.'s face was impassive. He was listening carefully.

'But now, if you think about it,' Craig went on, 'what's to stop some enterprising businessman with a little more imagination than your average jerk putting his own designations on those pieces of paper? What's to stop him buying a barrel of Old Oil and changing the category to New Oil? All he needs is to type out an invoice describing the Old Oil as New Oil and he's made himself fifteen bucks a barrel. If the next guy in the chain feels like it, he can turn the New Oil into Stripper and that's another five bucks.' He took a drag on his cigar. 'And all they've done is type a couple of invoices.'

He had the two men's complete attention now.

'Clear?' asked Craig.

Jack nodded. E.M.'s face was like a plank of wood.

'Let me tell you. No one's really organized this the way it needs to be organized. Me, I have a few buddies who are just waiting to go. They're ready to form a daisy chain of small companies to buy and re-sell crude, so every time the crude is passed on in the chain, it changes a piece here and a piece there, bit by bit, volume by volume. It's a great little machine. Magic! You put in the Old Oil at one end

373

– now you see it, now you don't – and hey presto! What comes out at the other end? New Oil and Stripper! And the beauty is, the whole goddam scheme is so simple. It's not even done with mirrors. It's all done with paper.'

'I don't know,' said Jack doubtfully.

'You all have any idea how much money there is in this?' said Melvin Craig eagerly. 'I figure you could make a few hundred million bucks a year. Maybe more. No sweat. I'll do the shit work with the daisy chains. All you need to do is sell me the Old Oil and, at the end of the chain, I'll sell it back to you as New Oil and Stripper. I don't have the financial strength to buy the crude I need. That's where you come in. You'll make a fortune – and at no risk. What more can you ask?'

Nobody said anything.

Melvin Craig fidgeted in his chair. 'Well? You interested?'

Jack was more than interested. He was slavering. He could see himself retiring on this one. 'Interested?' He glanced across at E.M. The greedy grin died on his face. 'I guess not,' he said hurriedly.

'Mind if I ask you why?' Craig asked, disappointed.

E.M. said: 'No one questions the way I made my money. No one ever will.'

'You're making a big mistake,' said Melvin Craig.

E.M. looked down at him from Olympus. 'I like to do things big,' he said drily.

At the entrance lobby Jack laid a hand on Melvin Craig's shoulder. Friendly Jack. Smiling, friendly Jack. 'Ever heard of a company called King Brothers?'

'Who hasn't?'

Jack didn't like that, but he made no comment. 'They're more – how shall I say – entrepreneurial than we are. E.M.'s the old school. You know what I mean? This scheme of yours could be right up their street. Why don't you go see them?'

'Can I mention your name?'

'I wouldn't do that,' said Jack hastily. 'Uh – E.M.

374

wouldn't like it. In fact, in return for this favour I'm going to ask you to keep my name out of any discussion you have with King Brothers, or anyone else.'

'No problem. You have my word. Let me just ask you: why King Brothers?'

'I tell you,' said Jack smoothly, 'Mort King may be a competitor, but he's a former colleague and still a very dear friend. I try to help my friends. There's more than enough to go round. That's my motto, Melvin. More than enough for everyone.'

As Jack walked back down the corridor to his office on the thirty-fifth floor – seat of power without the mace of authority – he was thinking to himself how good it felt to throw an old friend a rope. He might just hang himself with it.

It took Melvin Craig less than fifteen minutes to explain the Domestic scam to Mort and Ruby.

'Is that it?' asked Mort.

Melvin Craig grinned appreciatively. 'You guys don't take long to grasp things, do you? Are you in?'

'Give us a little time. We'll get back to you.'

The two brothers sat in Mort's office. For a while, the only sound was the hiss of the air-conditioning and the muted hum of traffic. They were thinking.

'So?' Mort said.

'I don't like it.'

'I just made a calculation. You think we could buy, say, a hundred thousand barrels of Domestic a day?'

Ruby considered the question. 'A hundred thousand? I guess it should be possible. Yes.'

'OK, let's make that assumption. I estimate we should wind up with an average profit of ten to fifteen dollars a barrel. Agree?'

Ruby lit another cigarette and spread the ash over the front of his shirt.

'I'd say closer to fifteen.'

'So . . .' Mort's fingers dabbed at his pocket calculator . . . 'we'd make a million and a half dollars a day. A day, Ruby. Think of it. In addition to our normal profits. We're talking – half – a billion – dollars a year. Conservatively.'

' "Conservatively" I like,' said Ruby. He stubbed out his cigarette and set off round the office. He needed to prowl when he was thinking.

'It's scary,' he said.

'It's one hell of a lot of money.'

'That's why it's scary.'

'If it were peanuts, we wouldn't even be considering it,' Mort said. 'Do you realize what this could do for the company? No one could stop us. We'd be number one in the world. Less than a year from now.'

'We never did anything like this before,' said Ruby.

'Pay-offs?'

'Commissions,' said Ruby, 'not pay-offs. That's the name of the game.'

'Bills of lading, Ruby?'

'This is different.'

'How different?'

'We'd be going out there and taking on DOE for one thing. For another, the amounts are staggering. We could never keep them secret. Sooner or later, someone is sure to sit up and take notice.'

'So what? If we do it right – and I think we can – who cares who notices?'

'Let's talk morality, Mort.'

'Oh. Morality.' Mort sounded bored.

'Yes,' said Ruby. 'Morality.'

'Does it bother you?'

'It's not the way we were raised,' said Ruby. 'It's not what Pop taught us.'

'Pop was a failure,' Mort said. 'You said it once. Now all he wants is for his sons to be a success. You don't get to the top by being a saint.'

'Why does it have to be the top?'

'Where else is there?'

376

Ruby didn't answer. He lit another cigarette and puffed at it nervously. 'I need to think.'

'We are thinking.'

'I need more time.'

'If you don't want to do it, say so now. We'll forget the whole idea.'

'I'm no saint,' said Ruby. 'I bend the rules. I don't like to break them.'

'The rules are crap,' said Mort contemptuously. 'As a lawyer, you know that. Lawyers spend their lives finding loopholes.'

'Is it legal?' said Ruby. 'That's the one thing that bugs me.'

'What's your problem?'

'The daisy chains.'

'What if we could do it without being involved in the daisy chains?'

'How?'

'We buy the Domestic. We sell it. Then, later on, we buy another category of Domestic from another supplier. What happens in between is not our business. We're not involved. We don't touch the daisy chains.'

'How do we collect the profits?'

'I'll think of something,' Mort said. His eyes were emerald green. Ruby could read the excitement in them. Contagious. Frightening.

He began to laugh. 'I guess you will,' he said. He had no idea why he was laughing. It was not amusement. It felt closer to hysteria.

Midtown Manhattan was a long way away.

The phone rang in Amy's East Side apartment. It was Karl Andermatt. Of all people.

'I'm in New York for a couple of days,' he said. 'Sam gave me presents for you and Edward. I'd like to send them to your apartment.'

'Come on over,' said Amy. 'Don't be so formal, Karl. Edward would love to see you.' She sounded different, more relaxed, more self-assured. 'Me too,' she added gently. 'How about this evening?'

'Well,' said Karl uncertainly, 'I'd love to, but . . .'

'Great,' she said. 'See you around seven.' The phone went dead. Karl put down the receiver slowly. It was not exactly how he had planned it.

He had not planned to take her to Regine's, either.

The 'Beautiful People' came to their table to greet Amy – movie and TV actors and actresses, a couple of pop stars, a senator, a gossip columnist.

'I never knew you were such a celebrity.'

'I'm sorry, Karl, but it's like this wherever I go, now. I suggested Regine's because the food's good and it's not as frenetic as some of the other night spots. I thought you'd like it here.' She seemed anxious to please him. He wondered why. It never occurred to him that she liked him. He thought she was being polite, for Sam's sake.

'How's Sam?' she said, over coffee. So that was it, he thought. She really wants to know about Sam – if he misses her, if he has any girlfriends.

'Sam's OK.' He sipped his coffee and watched her light a cigarette. She was a beautiful woman – poised and graceful in all her movements. 'He misses you. I think he misses you a lot.'

Amy drew deeply on her cigarette. 'How well do you know Sam?'

'Pretty well. After all, I've worked for him for fifteen years.'

'I lived with him longer than that,' said Amy, 'and I don't know him at all. I don't know what he wants out of life. I don't know who he is.' For a second there was a glimmer of moisture in her eyes. Karl felt uncomfortable and, to his surprise, a little protective.

'He loves you,' he said quietly. 'That much I know.'

'Then you know more than I do,' said Amy. 'Let's have some champagne.'

They finished another bottle. She touched the back of his hand with the tip of her forefinger. She did it pointedly, deliberately. 'You know, in all these years, you've never really spoken to me. Except once – that time you told me how computers work. Remember?'

'I remember.' Every day. He'd remembered it every day since.

'I think you like me,' she said, stubbing out her cigarette and looking at him from under her long eyelashes. 'Just a little. Huh, Karl?'

'You're the boss's wife. I work for Sam,' he said uncomfortably.

'Our marriage hasn't worked for a long time,' said Amy. 'We're getting a divorce.'

'I'm sorry,' he said. He had suspected as much, but hearing it from her made him feel awkward.

'So, what's the problem?' said Amy.

'What are you saying?'

'You know what I'm saying,' she said. 'I'm saying I like you.'

'Thank you,' said Karl. 'I like you, too.' He was looking down – embarrassed – earnestly brushing the breadcrumbs off the tablecloth.

'I mean, I really like you,' she said.

Karl didn't know where to look. Amy laughed, enjoying his discomfort.

'You're so goddam constipated,' she said. 'But you're cute.'

And with that, she dragged him off to Club 54.

She called him at seven-thirty the next morning. 'How would you like to take a celebrity to lunch?'

Karl considered, like he considered everything.

'Be spontaneous,' she said, teasing him. 'Tell me you'd love to.'

'I'd love to,' he said.

'That's cool,' she said. 'You see, you can do it if you try. Just keep practising.'

They lunched at Le Relais on Sixty-Third and Madison: fashionable, French, unpretentious and noisy. Karl could not remember enjoying himself as much – not ever – except maybe the evening before.

379

'You actually talked about yourself,' said Amy as he paid the check. 'I still have a lot to learn about you, though. Let's find a quiet place tonight where no one knows me and we can really talk.' Her eyes were shining, her cheeks flushed.

Karl put down the ballpoint and looked at her. She was so beautiful it was difficult to say what he had to say.

'I can't.'

'You have a dinner date?' she said lightly.

'If that were the reason, I'd break it,' he said. 'I can't – because of Sam. It's been too long, Amy, too many years, too much trust.'

'I told you. We're separated. Practically divorced. Why should he care?'

'He would,' said Karl. 'He'd care. Even if you were divorced, he'd care. Sam always says you and I are the only two people in the world he can depend on.'

'He thinks differently about me now.'

'Maybe he does,' said Karl. 'All the more reason why I can't let him down.'

'It's none of his goddam business,' said Amy. 'Besides, he'd never find out.'

'That's not the point,' said Karl.

Amy flushed. She had a quick temper. She scooped up her cigarettes and lighter. 'What *is* the point then?' she asked. 'Poor Karl. Poor timid Karl. Afraid to cross the street in case he gets hit by a truck.' She grabbed her purse and jumped up. 'You don't give a shit, do you? You're programmed, just like one of your lousy computers. You're someone else's invention. There's no such thing as Karl Andermatt.'

And she ran out into Madison Avenue.

Karl sat there for a few moments, stunned and miserable. How could she misunderstand him so? Or did she? he wondered. Maybe she was right. Maybe he did pay too much attention to the old-fashioned bourgeois virtues: respect, devotion, loyalty. They were not too highly rated these days, it seemed. He longed to be someone else, to be

380

free of Karl Andermatt, to be out of control, not to give a damn what anyone else thought of him. How did you get to be like that? How exhilarating it must be to live like Amy – to be a free spirit.

He was a fool to let her go. She took him seriously. No woman had ever done that before. He caught sight of his reflection in one of the gilt mirrors on the other side of the room. It was true what she said. There was no such thing as Karl Andermatt or, if there were, he didn't know who he was. He couldn't recognize himself. Just for one wild moment, he had a crazy urge to pick up the empty Chablis bottle and throw it at the glass, to hear the crash, see the mirror fragment and enjoy the outraged reaction of all these people dining so complacently in their smug little enclave . . . Fantasy . . . that's all it was. He knew he would never have the guts to do it. He would never know what it felt like to break the mirror, or the rules.

He straightened his tie, patted his hair self-consciously and walked out of the restaurant, certain that everyone must be looking at him.

Tex was a tax lawyer, acknowledged by those who knew to possess the most ingenious and flexible mind in the game. His speciality was representing businessmen who sailed close – often too close – to the wind. He was the best known, if not the most popular, lawyer in town, but then he was not in the business to be loved. What counted with Tex, above all, were the astronomical fees he invariably extracted from his grateful clients. Once in a while, of course, even Tex couldn't keep them out of jail, but then that was their problem, not his.

For some reason best known to himself, Tex affected his version of the English look. No doubt he thought it was good for business. He wore tweeds, two-tone striped shirts and club ties that he bought in Jermyn Street when he visited London. He thought himself one hell of a guy.

At lunchtime, Mort's secretary brought in bagels, cream

381

cheese, lox and cold beer. This was one meeting everyone preferred to hold in the privacy of an office rather than in a restaurant. Ruby was there, of course – and Edgar. they had also invited Melvin Craig.

'Look, Tex,' said Mort wearily, 'you've told us the law and Melvin has told us how the scheme works. What we need to hear from you, now, is what happens if we get found out? Is it legal?'

'You won't be,' said Tex. 'DOE is finished. The next administration will kill it. The goddam Energy Regulations are a joke. Everyone screws around with them.'

'Everyone?' said Ruby.

'You'd be surprised,' said Tex. 'There's at least a dozen companies in Houston stringing the daisy chains. I happen to know that some of the biggest goddam oil corporations in the USA are involved up to their neck.'

'How?' Mort asked.

'Selling Domestic at a big premium over the market price to companies who operate the daisy chains. Why are they getting premiums? The market doesn't warrant it. They know damn well what's happening to their crude.'

Mort nodded. 'That's what I thought. It's not the same as being involved.'

'It's goddam close,' said Tex. 'Technically, though, you're right. What you have to do is sell into the daisy chains and buy out of them. The way I'm telling you to go it's someone else's ass on the line, not yours. Melvin here – now that's another story, but he's willing to operate the daisy chains and he's a smart fellow.'

'What happens if we're found out?' Mort repeated.

'You won't be,' said Tex confidently.'

'If we are?'

'It's my opinion you're in the clear. If I'm wrong – and that doesn't happen too often – remember one thing. There's nothing that can't be negotiated. The US Attorney has neither the time nor the inclination to go through all that grand jury shit – you'd be fined and rapped over the knuckles. Believe me, that would be the worst. And even that won't happen.'

'I hope you're right,' said Mort.

'Trust me,' said Tex.

That was Mort's line. 'I want a written opinion,' he said.

'You'll have it on your desk in the morning.'

Mort glanced across at Ruby. Ruby stared back at him. Not a muscle moved in his face. His brown eyes were bland. The mask was on.

Mort nodded at Melvin. 'If we go for this, we'll need your help. Are you in?'

'That's what I'm here for,' said Melvin Craig, fingering his bootlace tie. 'Does this mean we're in business?'

Again, Mort glanced at Ruby and Ruby stared right back at him. It seemed to the other three men that, somehow, they were communicating without talking. After a moment or two, Ruby nodded so slightly that only Mort spotted it.

'That's what it means,' said Mort.

Melvin Craig beamed. 'We're going to remember this day,' he said.

*　　*　　*

The stroke was a major one. Leo Stendel had been in the Mount Sinai Hospital for a week. Every day, Julie sat by his bed. He was still in a deep coma. When she spoke to him, he neither stirred nor gave any sign of recognition. Sometimes, he would yawn deeply and moan, so that she thought he was on the point of waking up; but he never did. The nurses told her it was normal – a symptom of the condition.

On the eighth day, he opened his eyes and seemed to be looking at her, but they were unfocused, blank. The light of intelligence was not in them.

After two weeks, they moved him out of intensive care into a private room and he lay there with his eyes shut for another two days.

Then, one morning, quite suddenly, he opened his eyes

again and, this time, they focused on her. They were tired, very tired, but she could see that he knew her. He was asking what had happened. She told him gently and he closed his eyes again and slept.

Each day, now, he made a little progress, but his recovery was painfully slow. He had no interest at all in what was happening around him, little even in Julie. Often, when she came to see him, he turned his face to the wall, refusing to look at her. Perhaps he was ashamed to be seen like this. The right side of his body was paralysed. His speech was fragmented, unintelligible. The only sound he could make that resembled words was the one sound – 'da-da-da'. He would repeat it for minutes on end. It was agonizing to listen to him. He lay on his back, not moving, staring at the ceiling and stammering 'da-da-da'. She had no idea what it signified, but the nurses told her not to worry and, above all, to avoid showing any concern in front of him. They said it was a comforting noise for him to make. He was reverting to his babyhood. It was a happy release. They pampered and coddled him as if he were, indeed, a baby.

Julie was wretched – certain that the stroke had damaged his brain. The only hint to the contrary, the only thing that gave her hope, was the fact that he seemed to stop making the noise whenever nurses were around. He stammered it out only when she was there. He seemed to be asking her for something and she was acutely frustrated that she could not understand what he was apparently trying so laboriously to convey.

The doctors could not help. They gave her the technical jargon, the medical words that they erected, like a barrier, between her and the truth. They told her to wait, to be patient, to persevere.

Then, one morning, as she was sitting by his bedside, it came to her. She knew what it was that he had been trying to say. What a fool she had been. Of course! He was trying to speak the name of his son. He wanted news of David.

The news was that the young man was getting help. He was on a farm in Southern California that specialized in the treatment of drug addicts. So far, all was going well. The jail sentence had been a suspended one. She told Leo what she had learned: David was making a real effort to kick the habit. She had spoken to him and told him that his father was sick, but recovering, and David had said that when he had completed his cure he wanted to see him. Leo never again stammered his insistent question. Instead, he told her, without speaking, something else. She saw in his eyes what she had never seen there before: the poignant and frank expression of his feelings for her, neither gratitude nor devotion, but clear and strong, like a bright shining light – love. She was, for the moment, his only link with the outside world, his only link with his son, his only link with sanity. She was the one person who knew what he was enduring.

It was the first time in her life that anyone had truly needed her, had depended on her so completely and, in a way that she did not fully comprehend, the knowledge of it restored to her some of the self-respect she had lost living with Mort all these years. It was important – not everything – but it was important to be needed.

It was also, for Julie, infinitely ironic and inexpressibly sad, that, from the prison of his paralysis, lacking even the power of speech, Leo Stendel was communicating to her immeasurably more than her husband had ever done.

*   *   *

'I can remember exactly the day I stopped believing,' said Jeffrey. 'I was ten years old and it was Yom Kippur. The priests were praying up there on the Bimah in front of the congregation and you told me not to look. You said the Angel of God was hovering over them. Even the priests had to cover their heads with their talesim.' His father smiled and nodded.

'Remember how you used to cover me with your prayer shawl? You held it over my head so I couldn't see. It was like being in a little tent.'

The old man chuckled. 'Do I remember!'

385

'Once I took a peek,' said Jeffrey. 'You know what I saw?'

'What did you see?'

'I saw nothing.'

'That's because you didn't believe.'

'You mean if I'd believed I would have seen the Angel of God?'

'If you'd believed, you wouldn't have looked,' said his father shrewdly.

'Perhaps. Anyway, I was disillusioned,' said Jeffrey. 'I suppose I thought I'd see God – or a spaceship at the very least.'

'The trouble with you, my boy, is that you only believe what you see.'

'They say seeing is believing, Father.'

'It's no such thing. Seeing is very misleading. Sight is the most primitive of all our senses.'

'What do you believe in?'

His father smiled. 'After all these years suddenly you ask me that?'

'After all these years maybe you know something I don't.'

His father pondered. 'I'm an old man. I've seen bad things, but I still haven't lost hope.'

'What do you believe?' Jeffrey insisted. The child and the adult in him both wanted to know the answer.

Jeffrey's father gave a little shrug and his eyes were dreamy. Was he looking into the past or the future? 'I believe in shaving every day. I believe in eating right and sleeping when I'm tired. I believe in life and I believe in death. One of these days I won't wake up and my wicked old spirit will hover over you while you're praying for me.' He patted his son's head and grinned mischievously.

'I'll try not to peek,' said Jeffrey.

The kids were in bed and Caroline was in the kitchen cooking.

'I'll take you out to dinner,' he said fondly.

386

'No, you won't. We're eating in. Chicken stew.'

'Leg or breast?'

Caroline laughed. 'We were poor then . . . Say goodnight to the kids.'

He went upstairs and sat on Charlotte's bed. The dog was curled up, head on her shoulder.

'What's he doing?' said Jeffrey.

'He's armpitting of course,' she said. 'He's very good at it. I taught him,' she added proudly. She looked down at the dog as he lay there with his nose in her armpit, eyes closed. 'What is he?' she asked.

'Nothing special,' said Jeffrey. 'Just a mongrel.'

'What's a mongrel?'

'It's a dog whose parents are of different breeds – like a Pekinese and a poodle. They call that a Peekapoo.'

'No, they don't,' said Charlotte firmly.

'They do,' said Jeffrey.

'Am I a mongrel?'

'I suppose you are.'

'Then I'm glad,' she said. She hugged Jeffrey with all her strength, lay down and gazed at him solemnly for a long time. Suddenly, she closed her eyes and was asleep. Life was so uncomplicated at ten years old.

His son was happy to see him, but less demonstrative. He would be thirteen soon – a Bar Mitzvah boy, a young man. Jeffrey selected a book from the shelf over the bed and prepared to read Harry a story.

Harry lay down and pulled the sheet up to his chin. 'Goodnight, Dad,' he said.

'What do you mean – goodnight?' Jeffrey looked astonished. 'Don't you want a story?'

'No thanks.'

Jeffrey was hurt. 'But I always read you a story before you go to sleep.'

'That's kids' stuff,' said Harry dismissively.

Jeffrey looked down at his son. 'When did this happen?'

'Not long ago,' said Harry. 'I just decided one night I was too old for bedtime stories.'

'And why wasn't I consulted about this major decision?'

'I don't know, Dad. I don't remember. I expect you were working late at the office.'

'Seen the latest figures?' said Mort.

'Not for a month or so.'

'Up to the end of last week we made two hundred million dollars on Domestic crude alone.'

'You've got to be kidding!'

The profit margins had taken even Mort by surprise. As Melvin Craig had forecast, they were handling over a hundred thousand barrels a day, selling Old Oil into the daisy chains, buying it at the other end as New Oil and Stripper and selling the redesignated crude at huge profits.

When the company began trading in 1973, a profit margin of five cents a barrel was considered acceptable. Ten cents was a windfall. Now they were making ten, fifteen, twenty dollars a barrel. Mort was beginning to worry that New York was making too much money. How could they explain it? One day the IRS might start asking some awkward questions. Then, in September, the axe fell. The Department of Energy passed a regulation limiting a reseller's permissible profit or mark-up on Domestic crude to twenty cents a barrel. The implications were dramatic.

What were they to do with the stellar profits?

'You know what this means?' said Mort.

Ruby said nothing. He knew.

'It's the end of our Domestic business,' said Mort. 'If we make more than twenty cents a barrel we'll be in breach of the DOE regulations.'

'Right,' Ruby said thoughtfully.

'I'd hate to give up the Domestic business.'

'Who said anything about giving it up?' Ruby said.

Mort looked puzzled.

They met together with Edgar, Tex and Melvin Craig in Mort's office. The atmosphere was intense. Ruby was covered in ash – not just his shirt-front but his pants as well.

Mort was looking down on Lexington as he often did when he had a problem. 'We found the pot of gold at the end of the rainbow and now they won't let us keep it.'

Ruby was mumbling to himself.

'What are you saying?' said Edgar.

'The pot of gold,' said Ruby. 'That's it. Don't you see?'

'No, I don't,' said Mort, puzzled.

'Nor do I,' said Tex.

'How do you hide a pot of gold?' It was not a question that needed an answer – at least not an answer from the others. He was asking himself. It was Talmudic, rhetorical. He was figuring something out.

He lit a cigarette and carefully paced the length of the room as if he were measuring it, pressing his feet down into the thick pile carpet with slow, deliberate, bouncy steps. 'You hide a pot of gold . . .' He turned sharply, drew deeply again on his cigarette and walked slowly back towards them, bouncing even more at the knees as his mood changed from gloomy to playful. 'In a bigger pot!' he said dramatically.

Tex raised his eyes to the ceiling. 'For Chrissake, Ruby, stop prowling. You're like some goddam polar bear in the zoo.'

'It helps me to think,' said Ruby. He paced about for a few more moments, then he stopped, crossed over to Mort's desk and began feverishly drawing boxes and diagrams on a pad. No one else could think. He had destroyed their concentration and captured their attention. When he fell back into an armchair, four pairs of eyes were focused on him.

'It might work,' he said to himself. 'It – might – just – damn well work.'

Mort was beginning to lose patience. 'What might?'

'It's only an idea,' said Ruby, 'but I guess it could fly.' He nodded. 'It will,' he said.

'Do me a favour, Ruby,' said Tex, 'cut the crap and let us into the secret before we all die of curiosity.'

'OK,' said Ruby. 'Here's what we do. We create a "pot"

389

and into that "pot" we put all the profits we make from Domestic crude.'

He stubbed out his cigarette and immediately lit a new one. He still had their attention. No doubt of that. Tex's cigar had gone out. Mort was leaning forward in his chair.

'And how,' intoned Ruby, 'you are thinking, do we create this "pot"? Simple. Melvin will make the profits for us.'

'Are you saying that he's going to make the mega bucks?'

'That's exactly what I'm saying,' said Ruby. He was enjoying himself just like he did when he held his Talmudic tutorials every Shabbath. 'He puts the big bucks into a "pot" and keeps them warm for us.'

Mort's shoulders were hunched. His chin almost touched the desk top.

'How does he transfer the profits from his books back to ours?' he asked. 'New York can't handle them, or we're back in trouble.'

Ruby spread the ash around his shirt-front. 'We transfer the profits to Sam in Wald.'

'How do we do that?' said Edgar.

'Simple,' said Ruby. 'Melvin is going to be selling a lot of crude to Sam in Wald and Sam will be making some profits that even he might get excited about.'

Mort was not convinced. 'But aren't the IRS going to claim that we're transferring profits to Switzerland when we should be paying US taxes on them?'

Tex nodded, but not too hard. He did not want to scare anybody.

'What the hell has this got to do with the IRS?' said Ruby. 'All we need to do is set the thing up in such a way that the source of the money is offshore and the profits are not subject to US tax. In fact we would have an obligation to transfer the profits to Switzerland. If we didn't, the Swiss could go after us. The IRS can't claim what doesn't belong to them.'

They were looking at Tex. Slowly, a big grin lit up his

face. 'Where does this guy come from? He's a goddam genius!'

Melvin was grinning too. A little uncertainly. But he was grinning.

Ruby waited for his brother to react. The green eyes were clouded. Then they too lit up.

'I love it,' he said.

So did they all. Mort opened a bottle of champagne – something he rarely did in office hours.

'Gentlemen,' he said, raising his glass in tribute to Ruby, 'they tried to take it away from us, but Ruby wouldn't let them. I give you Ruby and the pot. The pot of gold.'

'The pot!' they echoed.

Ruby patted his shirt-front and blushed modestly.

*   *   *

Six weeks after the stroke, Leo was back at the Gallery. It was the fall of '81 and the weather was chilly. The last yellow leaves tugged at the trees in Central Park and the north wind blew down Madison.

Leo wore a heavy dark blue cashmere overcoat and a scarf. His eyes were rimmed with shadows and he walked, hesitantly, with a stick. His summer days were over.

'David left the rehabilitation centre last week,' he said.

'That's wonderful news,' said Julie.

'What's more, we're communicating now. He's flying across to stay with me for a while. There's a girl he wants me to meet.'

Leo was happy. He had a son again. 'It took me a lifetime to learn how to be a father.'

'Many fathers never learn,' she said. 'I'm happy for you.'

'I'm happy too,' he said, 'except for losing you. How is it with Mort?'

'Sometimes it's better, sometimes it's worse, but at least we're both making an effort.'

'I'm glad,' he said, pulling a sly face to show it really was not at all how he felt.

391

Julie laughed. So did he. Then, quickly, he was serious. 'Thank you for allowing me to love you,' he said.

She wanted to tell him that it was not like that, that she had needed him more than he needed her, but talking about it still hurt and she didn't trust herself to be as strong as she had to be.

The flame hissed as Moses dowsed the Shabbath candle in the goblet of wine. He blessed his two sons, his hands trembling more than usual as he placed them on their heads. The heart attack of three months ago had been a mild one, so the doctors said, but it had pushed him over the threshold of old age. He forgot things – Moses who had never forgotten anything. His mind often wandered these days and sometimes he talked strangely. Oddly enough, he was less cantankerous than he had ever been before. His fiery spirit was subdued, almost at times benign. But there were flashes of the old Moses to remind his family that the unbending authoritarian was still there, brooding and unpredictable. The ageing lion, brittle of tooth and claw though he might be, was still dangerous.

'So it's going well,' said Moses, nodding to show that he always knew it would, but eager to hear it all again.

'We're multimillionaires, Pop. It's our dream come true,' Ruby said.

'Sure it is,' said Moses sternly. 'Wasn't it me who gave you the dreams to dream?'

'Aren't you proud of us, Pop?' said Mort.

'Ruth was proud of you,' said Moses, 'but she died.'

Ruby put his arm round his mother's shoulders, comforting her.

'I saw her, you know,' Moses said in a savage whisper. 'Outside the deli. She was carrying the bags herself – cream cheese, bagels, lox. You'd think they'd deliver.'

'We're famous, Pop,' said Mort. 'Number two in the world. Isn't that great?'

'My wunderkinder,' said Moses ironically but proudly, his eyes shining. He patted his sons. They were still kids

392

and he was giving them candy for getting good grades.

Mort and Ruby grinned, pleased with the old man's praise, despite themselves. Suddenly, Moses frowned.

'Number two? You have to be number one. Didn't I always tell you?' He was challenging them, thrusting his lips forward belligerently.

'The day will come when you're satisfied,' said Rebecca bitterly.

'When I'm dead,' said Moses. 'That's what you mean, isn't it? A nice thing to say to your husband.'

'We're doing great, Pop,' said Ruby hastily. 'Soon we'll be the richest men in America.'

'Will that buy me a new heart?'

'I'd buy you one if I could,' said Mort.

'If you did,' said Rebecca, 'he'd say the old one worked better.'

Moses concentrated on a stain on his jacket lapel. He scratched and scratched at it, as if nothing else in the world mattered, except removing it. Rebecca looked sadly at her sons.

'It's no use. He doesn't understand any more.'

'When did he ever?' said Mort.

'Bagels aren't as good as they used to be,' Moses complained.

'Nothing's as good as it used to be,' said Rebecca.

'I want a bagel,' said Moses. 'Why doesn't Ruth come back with the bagels?' He sounded weak, querulous and scared, like a kid abandoned by his parents. 'You'd think at her age someone would help with the schlepping.'

Mort turned away from his father, a look of disgust on his face. In his whole life he had never known such misery.

Edmund Meyer felt about doctors the same way he felt about lawyers. You got a second opinion and a third. Then you ignored what they all said. He had a theory that all doctors were, to a greater or lesser degree, on power trips. The more serious your illness, the more they enjoyed it.

The first one gave him pills for angina; the second told

him he needed surgery to correct a faulty valve and the third was adamant that only a triple bypass would ease the pain from his blocked arteries and prolong his life.

'The heart is a pump, Mr Meyer,' he told him. 'It needs a regular supply of blood.'

'Don't tell me what the heart is,' said E.M. acidly. 'I've had mine a long time. I know what it is. Give me some pills and leave me alone with operations. No one is going to cut me open. Especially not you.'

The surgeon tapped the X-ray. 'These three arteries are partially blocked – this one ninety per cent, this one seventy per cent, this one fifty per cent.'

Edmund Meyer was familiar with the percentage game. He played it every day, calculating the odds, the chances of making a profit or a loss, the upside and the downside. This time it was a little different. The upside was life. The downside . . . well, there were no second chances.

'If I don't have the operation, how long have I got?'

'A year,' said the doctor. 'Two at the most, but I recommend you, I strongly recommend you to have it. The prognosis would be excellent. You could live to be a hundred.'

E.M. doubted it. He looked at the backs of his big hands . . . the blue, bulbous veins . . . the crinkled skin. He remembered, all those years ago, how he had looked at his father's hands . . . his cruelly direct child's eyes had noticed everything. Now he looked at his own and saw what he had seen then. He saw death.

'Young man, I know the meaning of the word "prognosis". It has to do with assessments, analyses, opinions. Am I right?'

The surgeon nodded.

'I don't want a prognosis. I want a guarantee.'

'No one can give you that. All I can give you is my opinion.'

'Then do me a favour,' said E.M. brusquely, 'and keep your opinion to yourself.'

*

E.M. and Mort shook hands, awkwardly. Neither of them was at ease. There was too much distance, too much distrust between them. They were rivals now. Mort had made it. He was treading on the heels of the master, crowding him, and E.M. was looking over his shoulder knowing that the man who had deserted him could soon overtake him.

It was several years since Mort had seen his former boss. He was still the same giant of a man, still the Titan dwarfing the world. Brobdingnagian in Lilliput. Perhaps the brown eyes had lost some of their sparkle, and the crop of white hair was receding just a little. But that was all. How old would he be now? Sixty-six? Sixty-seven maybe. Not bad. Not bad at all. Still a man to be respected, yes, and feared by his competitors. But the Titan had aged. He had changed. Their relationship had changed even more. He could no longer feel friendship for him. Those days had gone. In a way he was sorry for him. He could see the hurt in his eyes when he looked at him. E.M. had been damaged and somehow diminished – not as a businessman, but as a person. And why? Because Mort had left him. Mortimer King, renegade. What was it Ruby had said? No one left Edmund Meyer. You stayed with him, or you were fired. To leave was a crime. To leave and be successful was the ultimate sin.

As they sat opposite each other in the corner of Mort's office, E.M. looked around him, approving despite himself the look of the room. It was not ostentatious; it was elegant, workmanlike and well-appointed. E.M. shunned indulgence in his own life. In others he despised it.

'You've done well.' It was as if E.M. were speaking to the son he never had.

Mort inclined his head in acknowledgement. He knew how he had done. He needed no one to tell him – not even Edmund Meyer.

'Number two in the world,' said E.M. softly. 'Who would have thought it?'

Mort permitted himself an intimation of a smile. 'Not for long,' he said. His meaning was clear. E.M. drew in his brows. His face flushed with anger, but he controlled himself. He was not here to lose his temper. That would not achieve what he wanted.

'You had a reason for coming here?' Mort asked pointedly.

Edmund Meyer nodded. 'First, I want to pay you a compliment,' he said. 'I always knew you were a first-class businessman, but what you have achieved in nine years . . . incredible.'

'Thanks,' said Mort. More compliments. What was E.M. trying to soften him up for?

'Things will get tough from here on in,' said E.M. 'Take my word for it.' He leaned back, patting the blood-red suspenders that Mort remembered so well.

'Things were always tough,' said Mort. 'You saw to that.'

'You get nothing without a struggle,' E.M. said curtly.

Mort made no comment.

'I hear you're under-capitalized and over-staffed. That's not healthy, Mort.'

'It's not what my balance sheet says.'

'Balance sheet!' All E.M.'s contempt for the whole breed of accountants and lawyers was in those two words. 'I came here to make you an offer.'

Edmund Meyer smiled, flashing his perfect crowns for an instant. When he smiled his brown eyes flashed and twinkled. And there, genie from bottle, there he was, the E.M. Mort had once known, sardonic, disenchanted, world weary but still, at the same time, paternal, caring.

'It's an offer you can't refuse.'

Mort surveyed him coolly. 'You said that once before, if you remember.'

'I remember,' said E.M. He kept Mort waiting.

'What's the offer?'

'A merger of our two companies,' said E.M. and, having thrown the thunderbolt, he sat back to enjoy the effect. He was not disappointed. Mort's mouth gaped. For once in his life, his reaction was spontaneous.

His gaze fell on the chrome cigarette lighter lying on the glass-topped table between them. He moved it two inches to the right, a small, unconscious action, a hint of obsession, a mini-eruption from a capped volcano.

'Well?'

Mort was shaking his head, subconsciously rejecting the proposal before he had even given it serious consideration. His life's ambition – the one that had tormented him for as long as he could remember – was the passionate desire to be number one. Not number two to E.M., not to live in his shadow any more. Was that not, after all, why he had left him?

E.M. showed him the palms of his great hands. 'Before you say "no", listen to the terms I'm proposing. I'm ready to exchange – at par – one share of the Oil Corporation for one share of King Brothers. Naturally, we'd arrange it so we both had an equal number of shares. The assets of the Oil Corporation are worth at least thirty per cent more than King Brothers'. Well?'

The offer was extraordinary, incredibly generous. But why? E.M. saw the suspicious look on Mort's face and chuckled. 'Like they say,' said E.M., 'if you can't beat them, join them.'

'Why really?' said Mort.

'Why really?' E.M. pondered. He decided, on the spur of the moment, to tell Mort the truth. He tapped his chest. 'They tell me I need a triple bypass. The schlemiels say I only have a year or two to live.' For a second, Mort wondered, ungraciously, if this was another of E.M.'s tricks, but when he looked at him again he knew he was telling the truth. Something about his eyes. Besides, the story could easily be checked.

'I'm sorry,' he said.

'Don't be,' said E.M. indifferently. 'I've had a good life. It's just that before I go I'd like to head up the biggest oil-trading corporation the world has ever seen – or is ever likely to.'

'What more can a man want, E.M.? You're already number one.'

'Number one is not what it's cracked up to be.'

'You want an empire?'

'Not much of an empire if you compare it to the Greeks and the Romans.'

'But still, you'd be emperor,' said Mort slyly.

'For a year or two. Surely you wouldn't grudge me that?'

'Haven't we been through this before?'

'When I die, you can buy my shares. You'll have first option on them.'

'What about your son-in-law? What about Jack? Isn't blood thicker than water?'

Edmund Meyer snorted angrily. 'Blood! That man is not my blood. Rachel, my daughter – she's taken care of. So is my wife. I have no son to take over when I'm gone.' His voice shook. 'I'll tell you what blood is. Blood is your life's work. It's what you do with the precious time God gives you. The Oil Corporation – that's my blood. It'll be my only memorial when they put me in the box.'

Hard to imagine the box that would hold the Titan.

'What more can I offer you?' E.M. pleaded. 'Think of it, Mort. The whole company will be yours. You've earned it. It's time to come back,' he said softly. 'It's time to come back where you belong.'

The prodigal son, thought Mort. The fatted calf. 'It's a generous offer,' he said. 'Tough to turn down.'

'Then don't.'

'I have to. Naturally, I can only speak for myself. My partners would have to be consulted.'

'I'm not interested in your partners,' said E.M. impatiently. 'If you're fool enough to turn down the offer of a lifetime . . . I don't understand you, Mort. I never did. I never will.'

Mort moved the lighter back two inches. 'Second-hand goods,' he said gently.

'You're crazy!' Edmund Meyer clutched his chest. He looked ill. 'How can you turn me down?' he gasped. 'You're going to regret this.'

'I don't think so. I'll get to be number one and I'll do it without your help.'

E.M. shuffled across the room to the door. Sick giant lumbering home. It was sad to see him like this. 'Let me tell you something,' he said savagely, 'you'll never be number one. Not without me. And I'll tell you something else. This is your second mistake.'

'And my first?' Mort waited for him to continue, but E.M. waved his hand in disgust and opened the door. With his back to Mort, he said: 'Give my regards to Melvin Craig.'

Mort nagged at that remark long after the old man had left. Clearly, he was intended to. It sounded like a warning. He wondered how sick E.M. really was. It was hard to imagine a world without him.

Jack was not surprised to receive a summons to E.M.'s office. What did surprise him, however, was the reception he got. E. M. opened his arms and embraced him. But Jack could not read E.M.'s thoughts. The old man was thinking that he could so easily have slipped a knife under his son-in-law's ribs at that moment. That was how the Mafia did it, was it not? They smiled and killed you while they smiled. Was that not what Jack deserved?

He led him to the corner of the room, the one Mort used to sit in. What a contrast in the two men. Why had a smart young woman like Rachel chosen such a nebbisch? She could have had anyone. This little creep had no class, no style, no balls. What was it she saw in him? Many times, E.M. had been on the point of telling her that the man was a thief, but what was the use? She would never have believed him and he would most likely have lost her love. Maybe, one day, someone else would deal with Jack. But not him. Life was too short. A platitude: but for him the platitude had become a cruel reality.

There had been a time, before he discovered what a creep Jack was, that he had been quite fond of him. Not any more. He loathed him. Now that he was part of the family, he loathed him all the more. He was all too obviously waiting for him to die so that he could reach out and grasp the prize – his father-in-law's creation – the Oil Corporation. It was too much to bear.

Outside, the sky was overcast, tinged with yellow. Snow was falling in big flakes. Whatever happened to summer? Time passed so quickly.

Time . . . not much left. That was the problem. There were no choices any more. If only there were something else he could do, but there was not. He had tortured his brain, over and over again. Now that Mort had turned him down, what alternative was there? The succession had to be secured. If it were not, if he did not pass the reigns to experienced hands, the company would die with him. But God in heaven, what hands he was forced to pass it to!

Jack grinned at E.M., trying to be friendly, but hell, it wasn't easy. E.M. could be very intimidating. He noticed that his eyes were tired and a little watery, the way old men's eyes were.

'I hoped I would live to see my grandchildren,' E.M. said softly. Who was he talking to, himself or Jack?

Jack shifted uncomfortably in his chair. 'The doctors say we can't,' he said, 'since the . . . accident. I thought Rachel told you.'

It was as if E.M. had not heard him. 'I would like to have had grandchildren to spoil,' he said.

Jack glowered sullenly and held his tongue.

E.M. leaned forward, crooking his broad shoulders. 'I have something to tell you – something that for the moment has to stay in this room. No one must know about it. No one. You understand?' His cheeks quivered. It was intended to be a smile, but it was no more than a spasm of the face. The man must be in some kind of trouble, Jack thought. For the first time he noticed how perfectly white

400

and even his teeth were. Why hadn't he noticed that before? But then, why should he? How often did E.M. smile at him?

'I understand,' he said.

Edmund Meyer looked out of the window at the falling snow.

'I'm dying,' he said.

Jack's eyes widened. Then he shook his head violently, like a boxer trying to clear his brain after a heavy blow. He was genuinely shocked. 'I don't get it,' he said.

Edmund Meyer spread his hands. 'What's to get?' he asked. 'It's simple. I have a heart condition. They say I need surgery, but no butcher is going to cut me up. I don't have too much time. A year. Two years at the most. Who knows? It's not important.'

'What can I say?' Jack was still shell-shocked.

'What can you say? You can say nothing. Nothing. Not to me, not to anyone. Just keep your mouth shut.'

'You should live forever,' said Jack piously.

'Do me a favour,' said E.M. 'Try not to be two-faced. Your tongue is telling me to live forever and your eyes are looking at my desk like you owned it already.'

It was true. Jack's face turned crimson. E.M.'s sharp eyes had caught him out. The old man walked slowly to his desk and sat down, clutching the padded arms of the black leather chair. Something stirred in his memory. Once, a long time ago, Mortimer King had wanted all this. What had he told him? 'No one's ever going to take it away from me.' How wrong he had been. Now that little shit, that devious, slimy little wimp over there in the corner . . . that was exactly what he was going to do. 'Fifty years,' he reflected bitterly. 'Fifty years it took me to build up this corporation. A life's work. A life's dream. And now those bastards tell me I'm dying.'

Jack was not always too smart, but right now he was smart enough to keep quiet.

'My wife will be well taken care of. Naturally. So will Rachel. God bless her, she's a good girl.'

Jack nodded his head in solemn agreement. It seemed like a safe thing to do.

'My big problem,' continued the old man, 'is the company. Who's to run the company when I'm gone? Three thousand people on the books. Three thousand people who draw their salaries from the Oil Corporation. Three thousand people who depend on me.' He sat tall in his chair, proud and upright. He was silent for a long time. Then he cleared his throat. Whatever it was he had to say, he seemed reluctant to say it.

'I intend to leave half my shares in the company to Rachel.'

Jack murmured gratitude.

'The other half, I shall be leaving to you.'

Jack's eyes grew big. This was more, far more, than he had hoped for.

'Such a shareholding will be appropriate to the office of Chairman and Chief Executive.' Edmund Meyer sat back again in his chair. There. The goddam thing was done.

Jack's face flushed with pleasure.

'I can't tell you how much I appreciate it, E.M.,' he said. 'To show your confidence in me like this.'

Edmund Meyer thrust the palms of his big hands down on the desk. For a moment, it looked as though he were about to stand up, but, in reality, he was strengthening his resolve, preparing himself to say what he had wanted to tell his son-in-law for a long time.'

'Get this straight,' he hissed. 'I'm not doing it to show my confidence in you. I don't have any. What I do have is no choice. You're my daughter's husband. I'd like to keep the business in the family. When the time comes, you can tell your wife what you like. You can tell the world what you like. But do me a favour – don't kid yourself. Don't pretend you've earned this inheritance. You haven't.' He leaned back, glaring malevolently at his son-in-law.

Jack swallowed his saliva and his pride. 'I hope to make you change your mind about me,' he said ingratiatingly.

He was going to inherit the Oil Corporation, after all.

He would not have to put up with this kind of crap much longer. He would get what he had always wanted. True, he would not get it out of merit, or respect for his qualities, but out of family obligation. He would get it because an old man was sick and cornered. Well, what the hell, that was fine with him.

Just as long as the apple fell in his lap, he was not too fussy how it got there.

*   *   *

Jack Greenberg checked into the Waldorf Astoria at fifteen minutes to three in the afternoon.

'How many nights, Mr Andrews?' the receptionist asked.

'Just one.'

'How will you be paying, sir?'

'Cash,' said Jack.

'We shall need an advance payment.'

'No problem.'

He collected the key, walked back through the crowded lobby and took the elevator to the sixth floor. Room 606 was a long walk. The corridors were deserted.

He sat on the bed and waited. At three o'clock, exactly, the phone rang. He grabbed the receiver.

'Mr Andrews?'

'Speaking.'

'This is Mr Jones. I understand you're interested in finalizing the contract.'

'Right.'

'I have the biographical details and the photographs you mailed me. Please remit a hundred thousand dollars by telegraphic transfer to the head office of the Commercial Bank Corporation in Geneva, account number 21403/86, reference "Porcelain".'

'I'll take care of it tomorrow.'

'In case of extreme emergency, call the number you were given, but only, you understand, in case of a crisis – like a change in your instructions.'

'There won't be any change,' said Jack.

The man ignored him. 'Leave a message on the machine. No names. Just the code word – "Porcelain". Understand?'

'I understand. When will you . . . ?'

'I don't know. I don't care to be pressured. It might be next week. It might be in three months.'

'There has to be a time limit.'

'Maximum six months from today. Is that acceptable?'

Jack hesitated. It was a long time to wait. 'OK,' he said. 'But the sooner the – '

'Goodbye, Mr Andrews.' The phone clicked.

He put down the receiver. His heart was pounding against his ribs and his hands were sweaty. He needed a drink badly.

He went down to the desk and checked out, then he sat at the Peacock Alley bar and gulped down four large dry martinis. After that, nothing mattered too much. He eased himself carefully off the bar stool and walked unsteadily across the lobby, out into the anonymity of Park Avenue.

*   *   *

Suddenly, without warning, Amy was in Zurich. Sam had not seen her since Laura's death. He tried to pretend to himself that he was indifferent, that he didn't care where she went or what she did, that it was all over; but it wasn't and he knew it. It would never be over between them.

She came round to the apartment with Edward. The boy was twelve now and tall for his age. When Sam tried to hug him, he pushed him away. 'You'll muss up my hair, Dad,' he said and went upstairs to potter about in his room and make contact again with his childhood.

'How have you been?'

She bobbed her head in that odd way she had, talking and nodding jerkily like a puppet on a string, as if she were not real, as if the words she spoke had been written for her.

'It's been good,' she said. 'It really has. Great.' There was something disjointed about her reactions. He had the impression she was thinking of other things, afraid, perhaps, that he might ask her to come back.

'Are you happy?'

'I am,' she said, nodding again, puppet-like. 'I'm real happy.' He sensed that she needed to convince herself of the truth of what she was saying. He wanted to reach out to her, but it was as if she had drawn a line on the floor between them. She was so polite, so considerately distant that he felt constrained to talk and act in the same guarded way. Both of them knew that if they crossed the line, it would be like abandoning safely charted territory and straying into a minefield.

'I'm still modelling.'

'I know,' he said. 'I often see your photograph. You must be doing well.'

'Doing great.'

To think they had once been married, that they had two kids together. It was strange – sad and painful, even now. They had done all the things married couples are supposed to do, except understand each other the way people need to do when they live together.

'What happened?' he said. He was quite deliberately putting his foot over that line. But there it was again: the strained look on her face. She was not going to enter the minefield.

'You should try to spend some time with Edward while we're over here,' was all she said.

'Of course. How long . . . ?'

'A few days.'

'Any special reason for the trip?'

She shook her head, but she was hiding something. He could see that.

'Could we meet . . . maybe have dinner . . . ?'

'I need to do my own thing, Sam. You understand.'

'Sure I do.'

Did he? What did he understand? Had he ever really understood Amy?

As she said goodbye, he must have looked unhappy,

405

because, quickly, in a spontaneous gesture, she touched his face. 'You should have beaten me,' she said. 'Every day.'

'Next time,' said Sam lightly.

But there would never be a next time. They both knew that.

On Friday morning, Sam drove down to Lake Como with Edward for a long weekend. Amy was staying at the Baur au Lac in Zurich. Karl waited for her call. He found it impossible to concentrate on work. A dozen times he started to dial the hotel's number. A dozen times he changed his mind and put down the phone. He was not going to scare her off. If she wanted to see him, she would surely call. Besides, even though Sam was away and the divorce had come through, he still had a conscience about phoning her.

At six-thirty in the evening, he snapped shut his brief-case and was about to switch off the lights when the private line on his desk rang. He let it ring four times, enjoying the anticipation. He picked it up. It was a man's voice. His heart sank.

'*Hier ist der Concierge vom Hotel Baur au Lac. Ist Herr Andermatt am Telefon?*'

Joy! Karl was already smiling as he answered: '*Ja. Am Telefon.*'

'*Ich habe eine Nachricht von Frau Carlstroem.*'

'*Ja?*' He tried to sound calm.

'She asked me to inform you that the software is waiting for you.'

'The software?'

'She said you would understand.'

'Where?'

'At the Baur au Lac. *Danke*, Herr Andermatt.' The phone clicked.

He rehearsed his lines on the drive into Zurich. He intended to be casual and light-hearted. He would try to sound spontaneous. As he handed the car keys to the doorman outside the hotel, he decided that what he proposed to say was shallow and glib. Crossing the lobby, he changed the whole thing. He was still rehearsing the new speech as the elevator doors opened on the second floor. To his surprise, she was standing there waiting for him. He forgot everything. All he could think of was how beautiful she looked.

Amy led him by the hand to her room and shut the door. As he tried to speak, she put her arms round his neck and kissed him. 'I missed you,' she said.

He wanted to return the kiss, but she pushed him gently away.

'I decided the only way to interface with a computer was to programme it myself,' she said, smiling mischievously.

'I wanted to say sorry for New York.' He was trying to remember the speech.

She put a finger to his lips. 'You like the software?'

Karl grinned. 'I think it's prima.'

'You think it's compatible with the computer?' she asked coquettishly.

'I think,' said Karl, 'that the only way to find out is to try.'

She came over, stood close for a moment, not touching him, and kissed him on the mouth gently, almost tentatively, as if she were sampling a new dish. He held her tight, thinking to arouse in her the intensity of feeling that was already beginning to overwhelm him. Never in his life had he experienced anything like this. The faculty of rational thought drained from him when he touched her, to be replaced by something he had always shied away from – dreaded even – the compelling power of passion.

She lay on the bed scarcely moving, while he made love to her. The first time, he reached his climax quickly. There was nothing he could do to control himself. He wanted her too much. For a few minutes they lay there, side by side, not speaking.

'I'm sorry,' he said. 'Next time it'll be better.'

She smiled her distant smile and patted his cheek almost consolingly.

Soon he was inside her again, relentlessly determined to satisfy her, moving in and out with perfect control, touching her breasts, stroking her inner thighs gently to give her the maximum pleasure. He had to hold back two or three times. After fifteen or twenty minutes, he lost control. He lay on her for a few moments, his whole body quivering. He was mortified. Her head was turned away from him.

'It was no good for you,' he said, rolling onto his back.

'Give me a cigarette.'

'You like to smoke?'

'Once in a while.'

'After making love?'

'After sex,' she said, correcting him.

'You didn't . . . ? I mean it never happened for you?'

Amy inhaled deeply and blew a long stream of smoke. He watched it swirl around the ceiling.

'It doesn't matter.'

'Did I do something wrong? Tell me how I can make it better next time.'

She giggled. 'You want to improve the service? You sound like a headwaiter trying to please a dissatisfied customer.'

'Isn't that what you are?' If only she wouldn't ridicule him. He couldn't bear it. Anything but that.

She stubbed out her cigarette and kissed him lightly on the cheek. 'Don't take it so seriously.'

'Does it happen like that with other men?' He despised himself for asking the question.

'You're sweet, Karl,' she said.

'Does it?' he insisted.

She shrugged. 'Sometimes. I'm not frigid, if that's what you mean. I do have orgasms. It depends.'

'Why not with me?'

She started to roll on her stockings. Her legs were perfect – long and shimmering. She was altogether perfect – maybe too perfect – serene, remote and distant. Like a goddess, he thought.

'Next time,' he said, 'I promise you it'll be perfect.'

She was hooking on her bra, thrusting out her small breasts as she arched her back. 'Sure,' she said. 'Next time I'll have the orgasm of the year and fall madly in love with you and we'll live happily ever after.'

The pulse in Karl's throat began to throb. 'Don't mock me,' he pleaded. 'Please don't mock me.'

'I'm not mocking you,' she said. 'Or if I am, I'm mocking myself, too.'

'I love you,' he said.

She pulled on her sweater and tossed her long, blonde hair. 'Let's go eat,' she said. 'I'm starving.'

*   *   *

December 1981 . . . The Dolder.

Mort spoke calmly, soberly, but you could tell he was floating. He was way up there where he had always wanted to be.

'We now have fifty offices,' he said. 'After the Oil Corporation, we're the biggest – the biggest trading company on earth.'

'On earth' was good, thought Jeffrey. 'On earth' was very good. Why did it sound so much more impressive than 'in the world', for example? He didn't know. Mort had a way of putting things that stemmed, no doubt, from his own vision of himself.

Mort went on: 'I thought you'd also be happy to know that our auditors confirm, as of the fifteenth of September 1981, that King Brothers' net worth exceeded one billion dollars.'

For a moment, there was no reaction. Then everyone clapped and cheered.

Sam popped another bottle of Cristal. As they sipped, Jeffrey said quietly: 'There's been a quantum leap in the last few months, hasn't there, even though the market has levelled off? How come?'

409

One of those looks passed between Mort and Ruby.

'We're still selling off old stocks of low-cost crude,' said Mort. 'Some of it we've had in our position for over a year now.'

Jeffrey was not satisfied. 'I've been keeping a running estimate of profits, transaction by transaction,' he said. 'My estimate is about seven hundred million dollars – that's three hundred million lower than yours.'

'What's three hundred million dollars between friends?' said Ruby.

'How come?' Jeffrey repeated.

'I don't have the detailed breakdown with me,' said Mort lightly. 'I guess we've done some outstanding deals in Domestic.'

'What exactly are we doing in Domestic?' Jeffrey asked.

Mort turned on him quickly, resentfully. 'You know damn well what we're doing.'

'I know in general terms. I haven't seen the document-ation and I certainly don't know what the repercussions might be.'

Mort's face was stony. 'Repercussions? What are you saying, Jeffrey? What the hell are you saying?'

'I should have thought it was abundantly clear.'

'Oh, you would, would you, you patronizing English shithead!'

Sam was bewildered. 'What's this all about?'

'What are you up to, Mort?' said Jeffrey.

'Just remember one thing,' said Mort heatedly. 'We're all benefiting. You can't turn your back on it. You're involved, just like Ruby and me.'

'OK, so I'm involved. What exactly am I involved in?'

'Will someone please explain what the hell's going on,' said Sam plaintively.

Mort explained.

'I outlined the scheme to Jeffrey at the time. I never mentioned it to you, Sam. I'm sorry.'

'He thought you might prefer not to know,' said Jeffrey.

Sam was offended. 'You involve a partner in fraud and you think he'd prefer not to know?'

'Who said anything about fraud?' said Mort.

'We've been told by the lawyers,' Jeffrey explained, 'that what we're doing is not illegal. I'm not so sure, especially now I hear these profits.'

'You want to stop?' said Mort.

'Yes, I want to stop. Now! We don't need it.'

'Before we do anything we're all going to regret, remember one thing – tax evasion is negotiable,' said Ruby. 'Besides, why worry? The set-up is perfect. We'll never be caught.'

'And if we are?' said Jeffrey. He was remembering . . . In the last analysis . . . they have control.

'You worry too much,' said Ruby.

' "Major decisions will, of course, be unanimous," ' said Jeffrey. 'Now who said that?' Twenty-five and a half per cent each. In the last analysis.

Mort and Ruby looked at each other. 'OK, we'll stop,' said Mort.

'When?'

'Soon as we can,' said Mort.

'The sooner the better,' said Sam.

'I'm beginning to worry about where we're going,' said Jeffrey.

'Who gives a damn where we're going?' Mort said. 'Just as long as the world knows we've been here.'

The Lord had always been good to Edmund Meyer and that seemed only right to him. Had he not attended the Temple regularly? Beat his breast on Yom Kippur? Kept a strictly Kosher house, as his parents and grandparents had done before him? Had he not tried to be a good husband and father? And had he not, despite all his manifold virtues, accepted, without complaint, the Lord's punishment? The Lord had decided to test him, as Job had been tested in his time. It was his fate, part of the mysterious order of things. What else was there to do but accept it? He was not

411

resentful. On the contrary, he was grateful for the many gifts that God had showered on him.

The one he had always taken for granted, of all gifts the most precious – the gift of life – God, in his unfathomable wisdom, had decided to take back. For what purpose he had never questioned, any more than he questioned why the Lord had now apparently decided to return it to him. The Lord giveth, the Lord taketh away. And rarely, very rarely, the Lord changeth his mind.

'I can't give you a clean bill of health, you understand,' the cardiologist said. 'Your heart isn't perfect. At your age I wouldn't expect it to be, but these latest tests . . .' He shrugged, whether expressing puzzlement or disappointment was unclear.

'What about my arteries?' said Edmund Meyer.

'The first scan was inaccurate. The second scan showed a greatly improved blood flow.'

'So you're giving me back my life?' E.M. said.

'I hoped you'd be happy to hear the news,' the cardiologist said defensively.

'You expect me to congratulate you on a wrong diagnosis?'

'Mr Meyer, I can only say I'm sorry. These things happen. I don't know how they happen, but they do. I don't understand it.'

'Why should you understand?' said E.M. 'One thing only you understand – so send it to me and I'll pay it.'

The office was dark except for the circle of light around Mort's desk. He was reading the day's telexes and sipping his first bourbon of the evening.

The phone rang . . . Edmund Meyer. Mort had not expected to hear from him so soon. He sounded cheerful, ebullient even.

'You sound good.'

'Never better,' said E.M.

'How's your medical problem?'

'I told you all doctors were schlemiels. They're also

incompetent assholes. Now they tell me I'm superman.'

'I'm delighted to hear it, E.M.'

'I owe you,' said E.M. 'If you'd accepted my offer, I would have been committed by now. I would have been stuck with you as a partner for the next twenty years. Two years would have been bad enough. But twenty . . .'

Mort chuckled. 'Waiting to fill dead men's shoes is not for me. Besides, I never believed you were dying.'

'I did,' said E.M.

'What are you going to do with the Oil Corporation now?'

'None of your goddam business,' said E.M. 'One thing I can tell you, it won't be moving in Jack Greenberg's direction.'

'How is Jack?'

'As slimy as ever.'

'You really don't like your son-in-law, do you?'

'An understatement.'

'Well, do me a favour and keep him off my back.'

'I'm not in business to do you favours,' said E.M.

'I did you a favour, once. I sent you that dossier on Jack.'

'It was useless,' said E.M. 'you forgot the Statute of Limitations.'

Mort beat the desk with his fist. Of course! E.M. was right, as usual. That was the one thing he had forgotten. So Jack could never be punished now. He was in the clear.

'Hell,' he said. 'That's too bad. He was getting to be a nuisance – to both of us.'

'Let me give you a piece of advice,' said E.M. 'Don't try and divide my camp, Mort. I know all about Jack, but he's still my son-in-law. I know all about you, too. There's only one thing in your life that counts and that's Mortimer King.'

Mort restrained himself. What was the point of arguing with the old man?

'People don't change,' said E.M.

Well, that was true enough, thought Mort.

'You're still a renegade and Jack is still a thief,' said E.M. and cut the line.

Mort put the phone down slowly. Why had the old man

phoned? E.M. garnered his words. He was not a man to shoot his mouth off for nothing. What was that he had said about Jack? . . . Jack was still a thief. Hard to believe. Jack up to his old tricks? Jack, married to the boss's daughter, wheeling home an enormous salary, loaded with stock options? Was Jack Greenberg biting the hand that fed him? Would he really be so dumb? Why would he do it? Mort could not imagine. Of course, there was one thing about Jack. He had always craved recognition. He was a proud man, a small man, and E.M. had never given him respect. Naturally, he would despise him, knowing he was a thief. If he showed Jack his feelings – and most likely he did – then Jack would be sore . . . revengeful maybe. Supposing he was still milking the Oil Corporation? Taking what he considered to be his due? What then?

E.M. would find out about it – that was for sure. He had been blind once, but he was not a man you could cheat twice. Besides, Mort had put him on his guard. The question was – why had E.M. dropped the hint? Why had he phoned?

Mort poured himself another drink. If Jack was still stealing and E.M. knew about it, then he must be keeping records. But what was the use of the records to him? Surely he would not put his own son-in-law in jail? What would the world say? More to the point, what would his daughter say? No. E.M. was too big a man. He would never do that. But what if someone out there had a reason to step on Jack's toes? Someone else . . . like Mortimer King.

Was that it? Surely it must be. E.M. was not a man to leave anything to chance. He did not say 'good morning' without weighing the consequences.

The private eye was even more nondescript, puny and pallid than the last time Mort saw him. He looked as though he had just made a substantial contribution to a blood bank.

'Files, you say?'

'I guess quite a lot of them. Enough to fill a canvas bag or a small suitcase.'

'Where are they?'

'If they exist, they're on the thirty-fifth floor of the Oil Corporation building – in the president's office.'

'The president?'

'Edmund Meyer.'

The private eye was taking notes. Mort noticed he was writing with a disposable ballpoint and his fingers were stained with ink. For just a second, he felt sorry for the guy. Such a nebbisch, such a piece of flotsam. The world had flung him overboard and he was trying hard to exact his revenge.

'In a safe?'

Mort nodded.

'Know anything about it?'

'I know everything except the combination. Here's a diagram showing the location. Here's a note of the make and the model.'

'That's good. That's very good.' The private eye seemed satisfied. 'What do I do with the files?'

'You photocopy every sheet of paper in every file. Then you return the originals to the safe and bring me the copies.'

The private eye sighed. 'Mr King, you're asking me to break the law. That's something I don't normally do – especially since Watergate. Maybe you heard about Watergate?' he said, with heavy irony.

'I heard,' said Mort laconically. 'This is different. That was the president stealing. This is stealing from the president.'

'That's very funny, sir,' the private eye said, gloomily.

'I'm kidding,' said Mort. 'I'm not asking you to steal.'

'So tell me,' the private eye said. 'How am I going to do it?'

'I don't know. Use your imagination. There might be a girl in the office – you know, someone you can get close to. Real close.'

'I don't do things like that,' the man said sadly.

Mort surveyed him. 'No,' he said, 'I guess you don't. It

415

was hard to imagine the private eye seducing a girl. There were not too many short-sighted nymphomaniacs around.

'What if I get caught?'

'If you do, I'll take care of you.'

'Just as long as I don't talk, you mean.'

'Either way,' said Mort softly.

The private eye pondered, then held out his hand. Mort eyed the ink stains fastidiously and, after a moment's hesitation, took it. 'When will you do it?'

'Can't say exactly. This is going to need some preparation. I like to do things right. Over a weekend, I guess – this one or the next.'

'Phone me,' said Mort, 'to confirm you have the package. Nothing else.'

Two weeks later, Mort took a call on his private line.

'I have the package. No problems. It's in a suitcase. I'll send it to you as agreed.'

When Mort studied the contents of the files, he was well satisfied. His hunch had been right. Jack Greenberg was still stealing from the Oil Corporation and E.M. had kept a complete record of his activities. The records could not have been more up to date.

They could prove useful, one day.

'Sit down, Jack,' said E.M. 'I have something important to tell you.'

'Not bad news, I hope?'

E.M. looked at him with a sardonic smile. He was enjoying himself. 'No,' he said. 'Not bad news. At least, not for me. For me, it's good news. Very good.'

'Then I'm happy,' said Jack. 'What's good for you is good for me.'

'Wait till you hear it,' said E.M. drily.

Jack waited. There was on his face the strained look of a man who had every right to expect the best and yet, despite everything, feared the worst.

'It's about my health,' said E.M. and paused. He was not

trying to spare his protégé's feelings by breaking the news gently. Far from it. He was relishing the situation, anticipating with mischievous delight the effect of what he was about to say.

'I've taken your advice,' he said.

'I don't understand,' said Jack.

'I intend to live forever,' said Edmund Meyer. 'The doctors tell me I'm cured – or maybe there was never anything wrong with me. Who knows with those schlemiels?'

'That's wonderful,' said Jack dully. 'That's the best news I've ever heard.' He jumped up and wrung E.M.'s hand in both of his. 'Mazeltov!' he said. 'Long life!'

E.M. nodded. Jack had taken it well, disappointingly well. So far. But there was more to come. Having plunged in the knife, E.M. began to turn it.

'I have something else to tell you,' he continued. 'I've changed my will.'

Jack looked hunted. 'Changed? How changed?'

'For one thing, I'm thinking of going public – selling my shares on the open market,' said E.M. calmly.

'For Chrissake, E.M.! Why would you do that? We'd wind up with a thousand shareholders and no company. The Oil Corporation would be swallowed up by some flaky predator who knows nothing about trading or the oil business. It would be the end.'

'On the contrary. The value of the shares would rocket and my family would make a fortune.'

'But they would lose control of the company,' Jack protested.

E.M.'s voice cracked like a whip. 'You mean you would!'

Jack winced at the venom in the old man's voice.

'Be fair, E.M.! You promised me the company. I always kept faith with you. You gave me your word.'

'What would you know about keeping faith?' said E.M. contemptuously. 'I promised you the company when I thought I was dying. Well, I'm not dying. I don't owe you a thing. Thank God for that. You think I enjoyed the

417

thought of leaving my company – my life's work – to a thief who robbed me all these years?'

'What are you talking about?' Suddenly, Jack was sweating with fear.

'I'm saying you're a goddam cheap little crook. The worst kind. The kind who steals from his own. I've been keeping a file on you for years. It's in that safe over there. I know exactly what you've been up to and I have all the proof I need.'

'Mort told you that. It's all lies. He hates me!' Jack screamed.

'It wasn't Mort. It was me. Mort kept a file on you, but it's out of date now. Nobody can touch you with that evidence. Time ran out under the Statute of Limitations. But you made a big mistake screwing the company after Mort left. You thought I was a fool, didn't you, Jack? No fool like an old fool, eh? You never knew I was keeping an eye on you. You couldn't resist, could you? You started milking the company again seven years ago and you've never stopped. My God, what a son-in-law I have. What a husband for my daughter.'

'If you'd ever paid me a decent salary. If you'd ever shown me respect.' Jack was distraught, his eyes red with tears of self-pity.

Edmund Meyer shrank from him in disgust. 'Respect! For you? You make me vomit. Get out of here and thank your father-in-law for not turning you over to the Feds.'

'You'd never do that,' Jack sneered. 'What would Rachel think of her beloved father then?'

'You're a slimebag!' said E.M. savagely, the disgust distorting his face. 'To think that my beloved Rachel married such a piece of shit. Every day I live I thank God that I'm not leaving the company to the man who seduced my daughter.'

A sharp pang of terror – almost a physical pain – sliced Jack's guts.

'What are you saying?' He was wiping the sweat from his face with the back of his hand.

'Did you think I never noticed? Did you think I was blind?' The old man was trembling with hate and fury. The saliva dribbled from the corners of his mouth. He was remembering things that he had seen and had not wanted to see, unspeakable things that he had thrust deep down into his subconscious. Now they had reassumed their loathsome shapes and crawled out to torment him.

'Even in my own house, on the Shabbath . . . You think I don't know the vile things you did to her? You defiled my Rachel with filth. Perversion and filth. She was an innocent young girl and you – you raped her.'

Jack shrank from the huge, avenging Titan.

'It's not true!' Jack was gasping for breath, backing away from E.M., dreading what he might say or do next.

'Those filthy obscene photographs.'

'What photographs? What are you talking about?'

'Paddling your fat lecherous fingers in her thighs. Squeezing her breasts.' E.M. ranted on, pouring out his venom, vomiting the bile of his sexual revulsion and his long-repressed hatred.

'Rapist! Murderer!'

'What are you talking about, you crazy old man?'

'You made my daughter have an abortion. You murdered my grandchild!'

The giant figure advanced, eyes streaming tears, face twisted with loathing.

'Stop it!' Jack screamed. 'Stop it!' He slapped E.M. across the face, trying to shock him out of his hysteria. But it only made matters worse.

E.M. began to hit him with all his strength. He beat him about the face and head with his hands clenched together in a single fist. Jack retreated in terror, trying vainly to protect his head, his eyes bulging with fright, unable to associate this raging incoherent madman with the controlled, caring father figure he had served for so many years.

And then, as suddenly as the fury had seized E.M., it left him. He stood there, bewildered, in the middle of his office, pale and shaking, scarcely understanding how he came to be there, still less what was happening to him. He staggered to his desk and fell back into the haven of his chair, clutching the arms for support and comfort.

Jack made, uncertainly, for the door, conscious only that he had to escape from this lunatic. He felt as though he were going to faint.

Edmund Meyer sat up straight and tall. He was himself again. 'What's done is done,' he said in a tired voice. 'For better or worse, it's over. You're my son – my daughter's husband. If you weren't, you wouldn't be here. And for what you did to her, you've already been punished.'

For a moment, Jack stared at him, blankly, and then, suddenly, he understood. 'Oh my God! Jesus Christ! It was you!'

E.M. stared back at him coldly.

'You crazy old man. It was you who had me beaten up. It was you!'

The phone was answered by a girl. It was a brief recording instructing the caller to leave a message after the beep. Jack was trembling. The sweat ran down his face, drenched his clothes.

'This is "Porcelain". Cancel. For God's sake, cancel! Do not – I repeat – do not carry out operation.' He racked his brain in desperation. What else could he say? Nothing. There was nothing more he could do. He replaced the receiver and leaned his head against the side of the phone booth. Someone was knocking on the glass.

'Oh, God,' he moaned. 'Let him get the message.'

The knocking was louder, insistent.

'You OK, buddy?' The man was looking at him curiously. Jack's eyes were scared, confused.

'Hey, buddy. You OK?' He put his hand on Jack's shoulder. Jack started, terrified, pushed past the man onto the crowded sidewalk and rushed blindly down Park Avenue, not knowing or caring where he was going.

It was dusk. Soon there would be two stars in the night sky and another Shabbath, another day of rest, would be over.

Mort cleared the papers from his desk top and shuffled them into his bulky briefcase. Time to go to his parents' house. As he reached the door of his office, the phone rang. It was Tex.

'Hi, Tex. I'm in a hurry. Can I call you back later?'

'This won't keep.'

Mort put his briefcase on the desk. 'Trouble?'

'With a capital "T".'

'What's up?'

'I just heard Melvin Craig is appearing before a grand jury next week.'

'Melvin? How come? It's not possible. He would have warned me.'

'I don't think so. You remember our last meeting with him?'

'Sure I do. We discussed the "pot". We agreed the whole thing.'

'The Feds were already on to him. I figure he made a deal with them. He may have been wired.'

Mort sat down heavily. 'Are you saying that whole meeting . . . everything we said . . . it was all taped?'

'Could be.'

It was hard to grasp. Most men could not have handled it. They would have been unable to think, overwhelmed by the enormity of the disaster. Not Mort. Nothing ever stopped Mort from thinking. He was calculating the odds, weighing the consequences, much as he always did.

'What about Edgar?' He had never been sure about Edgar.

'I don't know, but I wouldn't rely on him too much if I were you,' said Tex. 'One more thing,' he added. 'This is the last time we discuss anything on the phone.'

Tex was warning him that his phone might be bugged. That meant the Feds were using Melvin Craig as bait. They were after bigger fish.

'I'm sorry about this, Mort, but I did ring the alarm bells.'

'You did? I thought you gave me the green light.'

'You weren't listening good,' said Tex.

'I was listening OK.'

'You hear what you want to hear.'

'Let's not argue,' said Mort. 'What do we do now?'

'Talk,' said Tex. 'Try and make a deal. It may never come to trial, but I wouldn't count on it.'

'White man speaks with forked tongue,' said Mort derisively.

'Look,' said Tex, 'if you prefer to, go get yourself another lawyer. Maybe it's better for you if I don't represent you. Remember – I know what you've been up to. I know how the scam works.'

It sounded like Tex was talking for the record, in case someone was listening in. Were the phones already bugged? Maybe so. Well if they were, he sure as hell wasn't going to let him get away with that one.

'I'll say you know how it works,' he said. 'You're the one who suggested it in the first place. You helped us set it up.'

'I don't know what the fuck you're talking about,' said Tex coldly. 'I warned you all along you were going too far, but you wouldn't listen to me.'

'You're a goddam liar,' said Mort and hung up.

He picked up his briefcase and stood there for a moment in the darkening room. Outside, the skyscrapers of Manhattan were alive with light and there were two stars in the sky.

Mort and Ruby were subdued. They had a lot to think about. Moses was in one of his rare happy moods.

'Why is everyone so quiet? Is this a funeral or something?'

'We're OK, Pop,' said Ruby. 'We were talking business, that's all.'

'My boys,' said Moses fondly. 'My two fine sons. You should be proud of them, Rebecca.'

Rebecca sighed. When the old man was in a good mood, he was even harder to take.

'Who needs number one?' said Moses abruptly. 'In this house my boys will always be number one.'

Mort looked at his father oddly. He was thinking it was a little late for him to say that.

The candle flame died in the red wine. Moses turned away to get his pipe.

'The berachah,' Rebecca reminded him. 'You forgot the blessing.'

'Who forgot?' Moses said angrily. He laid trembling hands on his sons' heads, first Mort, then Ruby, in the Shabbath evening ritual.

'Y'Simchah Elohim ch'Ephraim v'ChiManasseh . . .

The Lord bless you like Ephraim and Manasseh.
The Lord bless you and keep you.
The Lord make his face to shine upon you and be
    gracious unto you.
The Lord lift up his countenance upon you and give
    you peace.'

He embraced them in his rough awkward way, patting them on the shoulder. Mort noticed that his father's head only came up to his chest now. The old man was shrinking physically, as if a hand were pushing him slowly, but inexorably, into the grave.

They lay back in the company limousine and looked through the tinted glass at the streets of Manhattan. The driver's partition was closed. The querulous taxi horns, a howling police siren leaping at them, frenzied, fading, all the street noises of New York at night were muted, drifting in to them distantly, as though from another world. The loudest sound was the rain beating on the car roof. Clouds of steam, silhouetted in the street lights, billowed from the air-conditioning system of the subway.

'It's like hell,' said Mort.

'Just a small branch office,' said Ruby drily.

For a few moments, each was occupied with his own thoughts.

'You think Ephraim and Manasseh were ever in trouble with the Feds?' said Ruby.

423

They looked at each other and smiled. Then they chuckled. Then they began to laugh hysterically. They laughed so much, the tears ran down their faces and they had to hold their stomach muscles to prevent them cramping. The driver looked back to see if anything was wrong. Mort waved and grinned.

They were silent again.

'All those people out there,' said Ruby. 'You ever wonder what they do? How they live? Who they are?'

'They're just people – like us,' said Mort, shrugging.

Ruby shook his head. 'They're not like us.' He lit a cigarette, drawing the smoke deep into his lungs. 'Whoever thought it would end like this?'

'Don't worry,' said Mort. 'You worry too much. We'll handle it. In six months this will all be forgotten.'

Silence.

'Mort?'

'Yeah?'

'You ever afraid?'

'Never. What's the point? If you're afraid, you don't win, you don't lose. You're nothing.'

It was quiet. The rain had stopped. It was as if, here, inside the limo, in this encapsulated luxury, this air-conditioned bubble, they were beings apart, unaccountable, untouchable.

The car stopped outside Mort's apartment. He turned to Ruby. 'Everything's going to be OK,' he said. 'You'll see.'

'Sure it is,' said Ruby.

As the limo moved off, the man standing in the shadow of the apartment building shot Mort in the stomach. For a moment he stood upright, shocked by the heavy blow. Then, slowly, he bent over, covering the wound with his hands in a reflex reaction. He felt no pain, only a slight burning sensation and a rush of blood in his ears like the wind in the trees. As he fell, the street lamps spun across the night sky.

And then the lights went out.

BOOK SIX

The Untouchables

The surgeon clipped four X-rays onto the X-ray machine and switched on the light. 'That's what you looked like when they brought you in, Mr King,' he said, tapping the first one. 'Really something, eh?' He was talking to the X-ray as if Mort's persona were in there somewhere.

The only thing that interested Mort was how he felt right now, and that was good. In four weeks he had made a complete and impressive recovery. He had no time for sickness, no time for being a patient. Mortimer King was a doer, not a sufferer. What was past was past. If he endured even this brief, clinical, post-factum chat, it was because he was grateful to the man in the white jacket, not because he was at all involved in what he was saying.

The surgeon tapped the second X-ray with a large finger. 'There's the entry point. It was a two-two-calibre bullet from a Ruger suppressed – so the police say. Did you know that?'

'No, I didn't know that,' said Mort.

'You were lucky it wasn't the explosive variety.' The man paused for a moment, lost in a daydream of shredded arteries and mangled guts. 'Thank God,' he added, not very convincingly.

Mort sensed the regret in the man's voice, the nostalgia for technical challenges that might have been.

'Here's where it passed clean through the left dia-phragm,' the surgeon continued enthusiastically, 'missing the heart by this much – ' There was about half an inch between his thumb and forefinger as he demonstrated. Mort noted with surprise the large, apparently clumsy hands, like a carpenter's or a butcher's, but then, he thought, that was really what he was.

'This is neat!' The surgeon emphasized the point by tapping the third X-ray with one of his cucumber fingers. 'You can see quite clearly where the bullet ripped through the colon. Did I have a ball in there!' he enthused.

In a weak moment, Mort tried to imagine those huge hands having a ball in his guts.

'And this – ' another tap – 'this is the bullet's exit point. It missed your kidneys by a whisker. God knows how.' Again, just a hint of regret. He turned out the X-ray light looking like a small boy whose favourite toy has been confiscated. 'You're one lucky guy, Mr King,' he said.

'Not lucky,' said Mort, 'I had a great surgeon – a maestro.'

'Thank you.' The surgeon did not disclaim the extravagant compliment. He acknowledged it as appropriate. 'You're a courageous man,' he volunteered, after a moment's thought and, for the first time, he looked at Mort. It was as if he had never seen his face before. Perhaps he hadn't.

Mort nodded curtly. He had been called a lot of things, complimentary and otherwise. What people thought about him was really irrelevant in his life.

'They ever get the guy?' The surgeon held out his hand. The consultation was over.

'They're working on it.'

'I hope they do. I'd sure hate to see you back here.'

Unless of course, Mort thought, as he strolled down the corridor, it was something exciting that brought him in – like an explosive bullet.

He grinned to himself as the elevator sped down to street level. Life was good. Never better than when you had so nearly lost it.

Rosemary had called him at least a dozen times at the hospital and, later, at the office. He had refused to take the calls. Why was it? Hurt pride? The fear of getting

428

involved? He could not explain it to himself. Was it, perhaps, the sense that she was the first woman he had known since Julie with the strength and spirit to measure up to him, the first, without exception, to love him and ask nothing in return? What was it that he really wanted from her? At first, she had been little more than a sexual convenience, all the more desirable because she seemed not at all vulnerable. He had too many problems, too many commitments already in his business career to contend with more in his private life. So, why did he now feel betrayed, resentful? There was a perverse streak in him, an intractable obstinacy, a refusal to face up to his own demons that made it impossible for him to answer such questions. It was always his way. First he convinced himself that the problems need not be faced, then, that they did not exist.

A few days after he had received the green light from the surgeon, Rosemary called again. He was working late in the office. The phone was switched through to him. When he picked it up, she was on the line.

'I was worried about you.' No rebukes, no protests, no mention of all the fruitless calls he knew she had made.

'I'm OK,' he assured her. 'Never better.'

'Do they know. . . ? I mean . . . who. . . ?'

'No, they don't,' he said. 'Not yet.'

'I heard you were doing great.'

'I'm OK,' he repeated. 'I'm fine.'

'You have any travel plans?'

'Not to London. Not right now.'

'If you do . . .'

'I'll let you know.'

' "Something there is that doesn't love a wall . . ." ' she said.

'More Robert Frost?'

'More Mortimer King.' And then, her voice softening, 'I cleared out the wardrobe. Sorry, closet.'

'You didn't have to do that for me.'

'I didn't,' she said. 'I did it for me.'

429

He said nothing.

'I miss you, Mort,' she said.

He could not bring himself to say so, but he missed her too.

Mort signed the check and he and Ruby strolled out of the Seagram Building onto Fifty-Third. It was around eight-thirty in the morning. The street was crowded.

He steered Ruby across to Park Avenue. It was the usual scene of mass neurosis in action: a million New Yorkers stampeding to work like mindless lemmings rushing to the sea.

Except, of course, for Mort and Ruby. They had taken their breakfast break at seven-thirty, an hour or so after arriving at the office, and now, coolly, unhurriedly, telexes memorized and day planned, they moved up Park Avenue on their way back to Lexington.

'Why are we going this way?' said Ruby.

'We can cut back to Lexington,' said Mort. 'I want to show you something. A building. It's on the corner of Park and Fifty-Second.' He stopped. 'Well?'

'Well, what?' said Ruby.

'You like it?' Mort was looking up at the latest, the tallest, the most beautiful and spectacular of all Manhattan skyscrapers – the fifty-five-floor Glass Tower, a giant multi-faceted crystal that shimmered and glowed perpetually – sun, rain or snow, day or night. The Glass Tower was 'it', the zenith, the architectural talk of New York – or any other city, for that matter. By day the sun lived and died in its glass walls; at night, its fifty-five floors vibrant with light, it rode above the city like a great ship sailing in the sky, dimming the stars, a symbol of every New Yorker's aspirations and achievements.

Especially Mort's.

'Who wouldn't?' said Ruby. 'It's the greatest building in New York. It's number one.'

'That's where our new office is going to be,' said Mort.

Ruby's face was a comic caricature of astonishment.

430

'You're kidding.'

'No, I'm not. They're looking for tenants. They have five empty floors.'

'Five floors?' said Ruby. 'All that space.' He considered the building. 'Why move? What do we need it for? It's too much for us.'

'Nothing's too much for us,' said Mort. 'Nothing.'

He asked his in-house lawyer, Jim Sullivan, to take care of it. Three days later, Sullivan came back to Mort.

'They won't deal,' he said.

'I don't follow,' said Mort. 'You mean the space is taken?'

'The space is free,' said Sullivan. 'It's for rent. They just don't want to give it to us.'

'Why?'

'I have no idea.'

'Then find out,' said Mort tersely.

'I already tried, Mort. All thy would tell me is that they weren't interested.'

Mort decided to do the job himself. He had no patience with sloppiness. To get the right answer, you had to ask the right questions. You also had to put the questions to the right people.

It did not take him long to discover that the Glass Tower was owned by Milton Luce, one-time scrap metal merchant, now the most successful real estate developer in New York, entrepreneur, philanthropist, one of the world's leading art collectors and, not least, a billionaire several times over.

Tracking the man down was one thing. Getting to talk to him was something else.

But when Mort wanted something, he did not give up; persistence was second nature to him. Milton Luce was never there to take his call, but he would not be discouraged. He had his secretary phone twice a day to leave the same polite message: Please tell Mr Luce that Mortimer King would like to talk to him and would be grateful if Mr Luce would return his call whenever it's convenient.

After more than a dozen attempts, Luce finally called back or, rather, his secretary did.

'Mr King?'

'Speaking.'

'I have Milton Luce for you. Please hold.'

Mort was not accustomed to holding – not for anyone. Invariably, it was the other way around. He didn't like it, but he could be patient as well as persistent. He held for two or three minutes.

'Milton Luce here.' The voice was rasping, the manner abrupt. He was telling you without actually saying so that he had no time to waste.

'This is Mortimer King.'

'What can I do for you?' No acknowledgement, no indication that he knew who Mortimer King was. He knew all right. Mort was sure of that.

'I understand there are several empty floors in the Glass Tower. You're looking for a tenant, I hear.'

'We don't look for tenants, Mr King. They look for us.'

Insolent. Self-important. Provocative. Mort did not bite.

'I'm not surprised,' he said jovially. 'The Glass Tower has to be the most beautiful building in New York.'

'People seem to think so,' said Milton Luce, just a shade less brusquely.

'I've been thinking of relocating for some time, so naturally I was interested when I heard there was office space in the Glass Tower,' Mort said.

'Rentals are normally discussed with my agents.'

'We tried. They seem reluctant to talk to us. I heard five floors were empty. I'd be willing to rent them all. I believe you may have heard of me, Mr Luce. If not, I can give you all the necessary bank references.'

'I've heard of you,' said Luce laconically.

'Fine. Can I take it you'll instruct your agents to talk to us?'

There was a pause. 'Mr King, what you say is correct. There's space available in the Glass Tower. I won't deny it. But it's not available to your company.'

432

'I don't follow.'

'Then let me give it to you straight. The Glass Tower is a prestige building. We only rent to prestige clients.'

'And we're not?'

'Your company has had astonishing, almost overnight, success. But our tenants are banks, airlines, mining houses. Every one of them is a household name, companies with established reputations. That's how I'd like to keep it.'

It was hard for Mort to believe that anyone still talked that way. The man was a top-flight bigot. Someone should teach him a lesson. Obviously, the Glass Tower was for him the supreme symbol of his success and, more than that, of his acceptance in the New York business and social worlds. But whatever else it had done for him, it had not helped him to come to terms with his complexes. He clearly regarded Mort as one of his own kind, or the kind he used to be and no longer wanted to associate with.

'I think you're being unreasonable,' said Mort.

'And I think you're being presumptuous,' said Milton Luce.

At Mort's request, the lieutenant was not in uniform. The last thing Mort wanted to do was upset the office staff. The attempt on his life had not, of course, been forgotten, but at least it was no longer the subject of gossip and speculation. That kind of talk was destructive, bad for morale, bad for business. He himself had put the episode where it belonged: right out of his mind. Almost.

'We don't have any leads, Mr King. You sure you told me everything you know?'

Mort looked and felt irritated. 'There's nothing to tell you, lieutenant. The man was a loony, a nutter. What's to know?'

The lieutenant nodded, unconvinced. 'He knew your movements. That much is for sure. He was waiting for you.'

'So was the guy who murdered John Lennon.'

'John Lennon was a public figure. The whole world knew

him. You're a prominent businessman, sure, but not many people know about you outside of the oil industry. You're not exactly the flavour of the month. Your name doesn't appear in the *New York Times* every day.'

'So?'

'It points to someone who had a motive, a grudge, a reason to hate you. Someone in your business. The oil business.'

'I already told you,' said Mort. 'There's no one who hates me that much. Sure, there may be guys jealous of my success, but that's not a reason to kill, for God's sake.'

'People kill for much less,' said the lieutenant.

'It could have been mistaken identity,' said Mort thoughtfully.

'Maybe.' It was clear that the lieutenant did not buy that one. He was convinced Mortimer King was hiding something.

'I want to warn you, Mr King, that if I'm right, there's a good chance this guy will try again.'

Mort held out his hand. 'I thought of that. It's a possibility. I appreciate your concern, Lieutenant, but what can I do? I can't ride around for the rest of my life in a bullet-proof plastic bubble, now can I?'

'The strange thing is,' said the lieutenant, 'we can't trace the guy who saved your life – the one your brother saw apparently trying to scare away the gunman. That was a pretty unusual thing to do, Mr King, wouldn't you say? Why would he run off? If he was just passing by, coincidentally, then the guy's a hero. I'd sure like to find him.'

'Keep trying,' said Mort. 'I'd like to thank him.'

The lieutenant stopped at the door. 'We figure it was a professional job. A hit. That makes it even harder to understand. A mystery stranger – if he was a stranger – saves your life by frightening off the gunman. If he'd taken a second shot at you, you'd be dead. Why would that guy risk his life for you? And why, for Chrissake, doesn't he come forward?'

*

434

'Why me?'

Leo Stendel was puzzled. If Mort needed an art adviser, there were plenty of them around. No need to consult his wife's lover, or ex-lover. Of course, Mort might not know about Julie and him, but somehow Leo felt instinctively that he did. There was something in Mort's eyes when he looked at him, an uncharacteristic evasiveness, a hint of unease.

'Because you're the best,' said Mort.

That was typical of the man, Leo thought.

'So you want to start collecting?'

'Paintings, yes.'

'What kind of paintings?' He was surprised – not just that Mort would choose him as an art adviser, but that he would suddenly want to get into collecting paintings. His perception of Mort was that he did not have time for such things, that, in fact, he rather despised people who did.

'Impressionist, Post-Impressionist,' said Mort.

'You know anything about the art market?'

'I know a bit about the oil market. Is there any difference?'

Leo laughed. 'A little. Just a little. If you want me to help you, I'll do it gladly. How do you see it working? Our cooperation, I mean.'

'If I see a painting I like, I'll let you know. Then you tell me if I should buy it and how much I should pay for it. You take five per cent commission.'

Leo nodded. 'OK, it's a deal. Let me give you some advice, though. Before you buy anything, get to know the market. Visit a few galleries. See what painters and paintings you like and how much the galleries ask for them. Get the feel of the auction houses and how they operate. The more paintings you see, the better, even if you don't see any you like. Whatever you do – don't be in a hurry to buy.'

It was good advice and Mort took it.

Over the next couple of months, he learned a great deal about the art market. He seemed especially interested in auctions and, whilst his time was limited, he found opportunities to dash out of the office and view sales of Impressionist and Modern paintings at Christie's and Sotheby's . At one of these – a Sotheby's auction – the star lot was a magnificent Degas pastel of two ballet dancers stretching at the barre. The estimate was three to four hundred thousand dollars. At six hundred thousand, there were still two bidders, one on the phone, the other sitting in the front row.

'The guy in the front row?'

'Stephan Milani. He's an art dealer,' said Leo.

The bidding had reached eight hundred thousand dollars. Almost everyone in the auction room was on his feet, craning to get a view of the one man in the room still bidding.

'Is he bidding for himself?'

'No. He's bidding for the man sitting at the end of the front row.'

'Then how does he know when to stop?'

'Depends on the arrangement. Often the client gives the dealer a sign. He scratches his nose, or takes off his glasses, or holds up the catalogue.'

'I don't see anything.'

'This is exceptional. Look at the dealer,' said Leo. 'He's staring straight ahead. He's not looking out for any sign.'

'Why not?'

Leo gave a wry smile. 'You know who his client is?'

'No.'

'Milton Luce,' said Leo.

Mort felt the tingle on the nape of his neck. 'So that's Milton Luce.'

'He only goes for the best. Collecting art is his passion in life and he never yet lost anything he bid for.'

'So I heard,' said Mort.

The Degas was finally knocked down to Stephan Milani for one million two hundred thousand dollars: the highest price ever paid for a Degas pastel.

*

A few weeks later, Leo was on the line to Mort. 'You saw the catalogue for the next Christie's auction?'

'On the twenty-first?'

'Yes.'

'I saw it. They're auctioning the last Van Gogh sunflower painting still in private hands. The press is full of it.'

Leo laughed. 'I know,' he said. 'They're calling it "The Auction of the Century". Have a look at lot thirteen. It's a little early Vuillard, a Nabi, a real gem. The estimate is reasonable and it's just a beautiful painting. Time to get your feet wet? What do you think?'

'You could be right,' said Mort . . . 'I see they're estimating the Van Gogh at eight to ten million dollars.'

'Wild, isn't it? Even so, it'll go for more than that,' said Leo confidently. 'There are some real big punters in the market – including our friend Milton Luce. Remember him?'

'Indeed I do,' said Mort. 'So you think he'll bid for the Van Gogh?'

'He already said as much. What's more, he'll get it. That guy hates to lose. He has collector's fever and the money to indulge it.'

'I'll take a look at the Vuillard,' said Mort. 'But there's another painting I'm interested in.'

'Great!' said Leo. 'I guess it's time you bought something. Which one is it?'

'The Van Gogh,' said Mort calmly.

'Jesus Christ! You're not serious?'

'Sure I'm serious,' said Mort. 'I like sunflowers.'

On the twenty-first of September 1982, at eight o'clock in the evening, the most widely advertised event in the history of fine art auctions was scheduled to begin. In all, only fifteen paintings were to be auctioned, each of them beautifully reproduced in Christie's magnificent hardback catalogue. There was a crystal vase of flowers by Manet, two late Picassos and a marvellous early one – a portrait of Dora Mar – a landscape by Monet, a portrait of a girl in

437

a hat by Renoir, A Cézanne landscape, two interiors by Matisse, a Pissarro, a Vuillard, an Odilon Redon, a Derain, a Rouault and, last to be auctioned, the most famous painting in the sale, one of the most famous in the world – the *Sunflowers* by Van Gogh. It was undoubtedly the finest sale of Impressionist and Post-Impressionist paintings ever.

By six o'clock, crowds of sightseers filled the pavement outside 502 Park Avenue, eager to catch sight of the millionaires who could afford to participate in such a spectacle, much like the Roman crowds must once have waited for the gladiators as they entered the Colosseum. The lucky, flustered and sweating ticket holders fought their way through the throng of people, to be searched in the entrance hall for concealed weapons before making their way up the grand staircase to the first floor where the auction was to be held.

The auction room itself was vibrant and noisy. Every seat was taken and the aisles and the back of the room were crammed. It was standing room only. Most had come to look and wonder, to enjoy the vicarious thrill of rubbing shoulders with the mega-rich, to see the show, to goggle at power and money and acquisitiveness in action.

By seven-thirty, there was not an inch of space left. The crowds spilled into the outer rooms where the mass of people heaved and swayed in an effort to get a better view of one of the TV monitors that would relay the dramatic events from the main auction room.

There, the auctioneer had already positioned himself on the podium, high above the audience and, flanked by his assistants, was studying the lists of reserves – the minimum price limits set by the owners of every painting. Not that he expected any of the reserves to be tested. In a normal auction, he might be compelled to indulge in one of the traditional tricks of the trade – pulling bids out of the air from phantom bidders, a piece of fairground chicanery intended to convey the impression that there was someone in the auction room bidding when in fact no one was. The purpose was always to push the bidding up to and beyond the reserve and to try to tempt a genuine bidder in the room to take a plunge.

But this was not a normal auction. There was not one single painting in the sale which was not a masterpiece, and the advance press publicity, the promotional hype and the extraordinary interest that the auction had generated amongst collectors and would-be collectors more than guaranteed its success.

There were probably more multimillionaires gathered in this one room than had ever been seen at an auction before. They were the kind of men who hated to waste time – workaholics all. For sure, then, none of them was here for the fun of it. These were the actors, not the spectators. They had come to bid. They had caught the most contagious and deadly disease around town – collector's fever.

But it was not only from the room that the bids would come. Every one of the auctioneer's six assistants was holding bids from anonymous clients unable or unwilling to attend the auction – clients in London, Tokyo, Singapore, Geneva and Zurich, Paris, Amsterdam and Hong Kong – clients who had left their secret upper limit above which they would not go, and up to which one of Christie's staff would bid on their behalf.

There were, too, the mystery bidders, the big punters, their names known only to Christie's, who bid directly to the auction room by telephone, from the USA itself and from all over the world. On the right-hand side of the room, against the wall, sat ten girls, each with a red telephone in front of her. It was their responsibility to phone each client on their list a few minutes before their chosen lot came up, and to relay to them the bids in the room and pass on their bids to the auctioneer.

Mort sat in the third row, next to Leo. From his seat on the centre aisle he could see the whole auction room. Leo had already told him who was there and, in some cases, which lot they were likely to bid for.

Milton Luce was in his usual place – the aisle seat on the left of the front row. Next to him, on this occasion, was his art dealer.

At precisely eight o'clock, the auctioneer raised his hand, and the room, in an instant, was silent. On a table below and to the right of the podium, a porter was supporting the first painting to be auctioned – the Derain still life. The estimate was a hundred to a hundred and twenty thousand dollars.

'We'll start at seventy thousand,' said the auctioneer.

The bids came fast from the room. At least ten people raised their hands.

'Eighty!'

'A hundred!'

'And twenty!'

At two hundred thousand dollars, the bid was in the room. Then one of the telephone girls raised her hand and, talking all the time into the red phone, she kept on raising it until the bidding reached three hundred and fifty thousand. The electronic screen flashed the last bid in dollars and, simultaneously, its equivalent in pounds sterling, Swiss francs, German marks, French francs and yen.

The bid was in the auction room and every eye in the room was on her. For a few more moments she talked earnestly to her client and then, clearly disappointed, shook her head. The auctioneer brought down his gavel with a bang. The first painting in the auction had trebled its estimate.

And so it continued . . . every lot achieved a record price. The two late Picassos fetched five hundred and six hundred and twenty-five thousand dollars respectively. The portrait of Dora Mar, seven hundred thousand. The Monet landscape, nine hundred thousand. The little Vuillard that Leo had so wanted Mort to buy fetched two hundred thousand, and the Manet – a staggering one million, three hundred thousand dollars.

The auctioneer was taking it nice and slow. After all,

what was the hurry? He believed in giving the customers plenty of time to think. That way, he could, perhaps, tempt them into making that vital extra bid. By eight-thirty, he had reached Lot Number Fourteen, the Cézanne landscape, a view of Mont Sainte-Victoire, one of a series of almost cubist paintings in which, according to many experts, Cézanne broke new ground and reached the height of his powers.

The bidding started at a million dollars. At first, it was a battle between three or four collectors and a dealer, all of them in the auction room. When the first frenetic flurry was over, only the dealer and one of the collectors were still bidding. The last bid was with the dealer at a million eight hundred thousand. The collector shook his head. He was out of the race.

The auctioneer looked round the room and raised his gavel, but, in the second before he was about to bring it down, Milton Luce nodded his head and made a sign. The auctioneer came close to betraying surprise.

'Three million dollars!' he announced and, with a token glance at the deflated dealer, brought down his gavel with a dramatic thump.

Leo whispered in Mort's ear: 'That's a typical Milton Luce tactic. He waits until the very last second, when the only guy left is about to walk out with the painting, then he steps in and stuns the opposition with a massive jump in the bidding. It works every time.'

'I thought he didn't bid for himself?' said Mort.

'He does when he's after something really important. He loves an audience. Milton Luce is not a man to hide his light under a bushel.'

The porter held up the *Sunflowers*.

'Lot Number Fifteen,' the auctioneer said, casually, as if he were offering the room an afterthought that the porter had just found lying in the cellar.

The bidding started at five million dollars – three million below the lowest estimate. It moved up rather slowly, a hundred thousand dollars a bid, until it reached nine million five hundred thousand and there, for a few moments, it stuck. The room was quiet as people twisted and turned their heads to see who would be the next to bid. If anyone.

'What's going on?' said Mort.

'No one wants to lead the bidding . . . we're not done yet.'

But it seemed as if, for once, Leo might be wrong. The pause – if pause it was – was so prolonged that the auctioneer was compelled to raise his gavel.

And then one of the telephone girls raised her hand. The bidding took off again, this time at a faster pace. Soon the auctioneer was only accepting increases of two hundred thousand dollars a bid. In less than two minutes, the bidding reached nineteen million dollars. The last bid was on the phone. Another pause.

Mort's pulse was beating fast and the palms of his hands were sweating.

Leo could feel the electricity. 'Take it easy,' he said. 'This is dangerous. Don't lose your head. It's only a painting.'

The auctioneer raised his gavel, held it high for a second or two, lifted it an inch higher and was already lowering it when Milton Luce nodded.

The auctioneer's arm stopped on its way down.

'Twenty million dollars!' he announced and, this time, he was unable to keep the excitement out of his voice.

The girl spoke again into the red phone. She nodded.

'Twenty-one million dollars!' The auctioneer raised one finger. From now on, any bidder would have to increase the last bid by a million dollars. Or drop out.

Milton Luce nodded again and made a sign.

'Twenty-five million dollars!' There were beads of sweat on the auctioneer's forehead. 'In the room, with Mr Luce,' he added.

A moment of silence. No one made a sound. Then those who were still seated jumped up and the whole room applauded.

The telephone girl grimaced and shook her head.

The auctioneer signalled for silence, looked round the room and raised his gavel to bring it down on the most memorable auction ever held.

And, at that precise moment, Mort raised his hand.

The auctioneer peered at him. He knew who he was looking at. It was his business to know such things.

'Are you raising the bidding another million dollars, Mr King?'

Mort showed five fingers.

'Thirty million dollars!' The auctioneer grabbed a bunch of tissues and wiped his forehead and neck.

Again, the applause. Everyone in the room was talking at once. At a signal from the auctioneer, there was silence. The atmosphere was rapt, intense, devotional, as if the auctioneer were the priest and the audience his congregation. They were looking at Milton Luce who seemed completely oblivious to the interest he was arousing. He mouthed his next bid to the auctioneer who, by this time, was so disoriented that he had to clasp the podium to steady himself.

'Thirty-five million dollars!'

The reaction in the room was immediate – a spontaneous cheer. This was the stuff of drama. This was what they had come to see.

Mort waited for the noise to die down. He knew very well that the whole room was watching him, waiting for his next move, and, knowing it, revelling in the sensation, he took his time, inhaling and exhaling deeply to try to steady his nerves. His heart pounded and the blood raced in his veins. It was the biggest high he had ever experienced. Leo put a hand on his arm, not so much to restrain him or calm him down, as to keep him in touch with reality, to remind him that he was sitting next to someone he could talk to.

Seeing no reaction from Mort, the auctioneer lifted his gavel and prepared to bring it down for the last time.

Mort nodded again and made a sign. The auctioneer was

too proud – or maybe too concussed – to ask a question, so he merely looked astounded. Mort repeated the sign. Again, the room was hushed. The auctioneer swallowed hard.

'Fifty million dollars!'

The spectators were too mentally exhausted, too shell-shocked, or too afraid to do or say anything in case they missed the next act in the drama. The room was deathly quiet.

'The bid is against you, sir,' the auctioneer said softly to Milton Luce.

For nearly thirty seconds, Luce sat there in the front row, unmoving, staring ahead impassively, showing not a trace of emotion. Then he stood up, looked at Mort as if about to say something to him, and then, changing his mind, turned away abruptly and, as the crowds fell back to let him pass, strode out of the auction room.

The gavel descended with a bang. The auctioneer jabbed his finger in Mort's direction and declaimed at the top of his voice, above the cheers and applause: 'Lot Fifteen – sold to Mortimer King!'

It was a name no one was ever likely to forget.

'If I take you on, Mr King, I want you to know there are no short cuts. It's a long hard road. An expensive one, too. And there are no guarantees – not for you, not for me, not for anyone.'

Maxwell Parkes was the unlikely name of the most celebrated public relations man in the USA. Known sometimes as the king-maker, sometimes as the rain-maker – neither very original, but both accurate – he had spawned, sponsored, guided and damn near created at least one president and more than a few congressmen and senators. Some of them he cared to remember; some he did not. But all of them were well aware to whom they owed their political careers. There is nothing as generous as a grateful politician. Maxwell Parkes was a wealthy man.

444

'I never charge fees, Mr King. I make my money from grateful clients.'

'I think I know what you mean,' said Mort.

'I guess you do,' said Maxwell Parkes drily. 'OK,' he continued, tired of the preliminaries, 'what do we have? A young, phenomenally successful business tycoon. Incidentally,' he asked, 'how old are you?'

'Forty-eight.'

'A child. A mere child.'

'John Kennedy was President at forty-three,' said Mort seriously.

Maxwell Parkes observed Mort's strong, saturnine face. He noted the determined features, the intense steady gaze of the green eyes. They glowed with a fire he had only rarely seen. He sensed the inner reserves of energy, the absolute self-assurance. A man not easy to come close to – this; a man of mystery, an enigma, a careful man who did not readily reveal himself to others; not subtle, not an intellectual, but then neither quality was especially desirable in a politician – quite the reverse, in fact. He guessed that Mortimer King could be devious. He was certain he could be ruthless. This was an exceptional man, one that others leaned on, a man with that special gift that attracted others to him and made them give of their best. He had charisma, not the obvious, flashy kind, but a strong, powerful magnetism. He understood power. Maxwell Parkes could see that. He sought it and he knew how to wield it.

He would need burnishing; he was introverted and uneasy. He would have to be taught how to smile, how to sparkle. Well, nothing was impossible. It was a question of the right packaging. It was not a major operation that was needed, only cosmetic surgery. The raw material was there, no doubt of that. Mortimer King had the strength, the power to move mountains. The man was formidable.

He surveyed him and approved of what he saw.

'You'll do, Mr King. There's something about you . . . One thing, though, one thing I need to know.'

'Shoot.'

'Why? I need to know why. You're a rich man – a tycoon. You've made it. What more do you want? You have all the money you need. Money is power.'

'No . . .' As Mort brooded, measuring his reply, Maxwell Parkes could feel the tension, sense the coiled spring under that calm, relaxed exterior.

'No,' Mort repeated firmly. 'Money isn't power. Money can buy power . . . but you have to know how to use it.'

'And that's where I come in.'

Mort acknowledged the accuracy of the comment by his silence.

The other man was looking at him reflectively. 'There's one other thing . . . that little cloud on the horizon . . . no bigger than a man's hand, as they say.'

Mort's eyes were unblinking.

'It is going to disappear? It's not going to get bigger, is it? I mean, no one's going to give it a face and a body, are they?'

'It's going to disappear.'

Maxwell Parkes looked shrewdly at his client. 'You're quite sure of that?'

'Absolutely,' said Mort. Unfazed. Confident.

Maxwell Parkes grunted. 'Good,' he said. 'I just wanted to get that out of the way. Now, here's what we have to do. . . .'

An hour or so later, Maxwell Parkes was about through. 'So that's the scoop. I'll arrange for you to be a member of the Empire Club – that's a good way to meet the right kind of politician.'

'What kind is he?' asked Mort.

Parkes laughed. 'The kind that can help you. The only kind that matters. Like I told you, it's a two-way street. You scratch their backs and – sooner or later they might – they just might scratch yours. Help them when they're campaigning for public office, help them raise funds and, one day, they may do you a favour in return. It takes time, though. There are no short cuts – no microwave miracles in politics. It's a long wait on the back burner. In a year or two, you'll be rubbing shoulders with candidates and fund raisers and, more importantly, with the rain-makers. They're the guys who make things happen in politics. Guys like me. You get enough of them together, make yourself a team and you could have the start of a political career.'

'I'm not sure I can be that patient.'

Maxwell Parkes shrugged. 'Then forget it,' he said indifferently. 'If you think you can hustle, make things happen tomorrow, if you so much as look as though you might be a candidate, then you're wasting your time – not to mention mine.' He folded his arms and squared his shoulders self-importantly.

Mort kept his cool. He was accustomed to handling people with inflated ideas of their own importance. He was not accustomed to being told what to do, but what the hell, this guy seemed to know what he was talking about.

'One final question, Mr King. What's your ambition? Where are you going?'

Mort pondered the question. 'How about governor of New York . . . maybe a cabinet post?' he said tentatively.

'You don't sound very convinced.'

Mort grinned. 'Maybe I'm not.'

'Then get convinced.'

The PR man walked across to the window and looked down at Lexington. Manhattan was lighting up in the grey mist-shrouded autumn day. 'You didn't get to sit up here by playing Hamlet,' he said. 'You're not the kind to lie around and brood. You knew what you wanted in business and you went out and got it. Let me tell you something. It's no different in politics. If you don't know – and I mean really know – what you want, then how am I going to? And, if I don't know, then no one does.' He looked at Mort challengingly.

Mort leaned back in the armchair and carefully adjusted

447

the cigarette lighter's position on the table. How to explain a pathological hunger, an insatiable thirst? 'I know,' he said, quietly.

'Well, that's OK then,' said Maxwell Parkes.

'I never asked you about your politics,' said Mort. 'You know I'm a Republican. What are you?'

Maxwell Parkes considered the question. 'Me?' he said. 'I'm a professional.' He made it sound like he was a mercenary, which, in a way, thought Mort, was exactly what he was.

Van Gogh's *Sunflowers* was on the floor, leaning against the bar in Mort's office – all fifty million dollars of it. Most people would have it enshrined by now, spotlit, hanging proud in a place of honour. Not Mort.

'It looks neat,' he said nonchalantly. 'Like it belongs there – don't you think?'

Milton Luce coveted the Van Gogh with greedy eyes. 'It's magnificent,' he murmured, licking his lips.

Mort nodded agreement. 'It kind of goes with the decor,' he said.

Milton Luce blanched.

'So what brings you here?' Mort asked casually.

'You don't know?'

'Should I?' Innocently.

Luce nodded at the Van Gogh. 'That's what I came for.'

'I get it. You came to see the *Sunflowers* in its new home. Or should I say – their new home?' He was toying with Luce, and loving it.

Milton Luce tried hard to conceal his contempt. 'I came to buy the painting.'

Mort did not react. No change of expression. No comment. He gestured at a chair, sat behind his desk and turned his serious gaze on the man sitting opposite him.

'You heard what I said?'

'It's not for sale,' said Mort shortly.

Luce carried on as if he hadn't heard him. 'You paid fifty,

448

plus ten per cent buyer's premium – that's fifty-five. I'll give you sixty million dollars for it.'

Mort picked up a bunch of telexes from his in-tray and leafed through them idly.

'Seventy,' said Luce, a shade desperately.

Mort studied one of the telexes intently. Then he looked up. 'That's more than generous, Mr Luce . . . around five million bucks a flower. But I guess you didn't hear me right. The painting's not for sale.'

Milton Luce threw up his arms in mock surrender. 'OK. I think I know what all this is about. You're sore at me for not renting you those five floors in the Glass Tower. Admit it. It's not the painting you want. Hell, you're no collector. You bought the *Sunflowers* from under my nose just so you could cut a deal with me. Why the hell I didn't go on bidding I'll never know. I could have kicked myself. I guess you had me psyched. I was so shocked by the price I lost my cool. But you were right. No question. The Van Gogh is priceless. You're a smart man, Mr King. I underestimated you and now I have to pay the penalty. Tell you what I'll do – I'll give you seventy-five million. And I'll throw in a ten-year lease on the five floors you want in the Glass Tower.'

Mort smiled. Was there the merest hint of triumph on his face? 'You can keep your lousy five floors,' he said rudely.

For a moment, even Milton Luce was speechless.

'Anyway, why should I part with a priceless Van Gogh? It's the greatest investment I ever made.'

'There has to be a price, Mr King,' said Milton Luce. 'Everything has a price.'

Mort flipped through some more telexes. 'Could be,' he said.

Luce beamed. Hope! 'Name it,' he said.

Mort reclined in his high-backed chair and let out a small sigh. 'OK, Mr Luce. Here's my price. I want you out of the Glass Tower in seven days,' he said calmly. 'For good!'

449

Milton Luce's face turned beetroot red. 'You're fucking crazy!' His voice rose. 'What's more, you're the most impudent sonofabitch I ever met! Out of the Glass Tower? I own the goddam property!'

Mort inclined his head. 'Sure you do, Mr Luce,' he said. 'And I own the *Sunflowers*.'

It was nearly four weeks since the Christie's auction. Mort and Ruby strolled out of the Brasserie, took a right turn out of the Seagram Building and right again into Park Avenue. They made their way downtown in the direction of Fiftieth.

'So, when's the unveiling?'

'What unveiling?'

'What unveiling?' Ruby echoed. 'What unveiling do you think? The Statue of Liberty? The Van Gogh, of course.'

'Oh that,' said Mort.

'Yeah, that. What is it with you, Mort? You act as though it was nothing. The whole world is talking about you. You've arrived.'

Mort looked up at the Glass Tower as if he had not heard his brother. 'How about that for a great building?'

Ruby was confused. 'What? Oh. The Glass Tower. It sure is.'

'You said the rent was too high, didn't you? You said five floors was more than we could handle.'

'I thought about it some more,' said Ruby. 'Funny thing. When you know for sure you can't have something, you want it all the more. I guess that's human nature.'

'That's what Milton Luce said.'

'What's Milton Luce got to do with it?'

'He came back to me,' said Mort. 'I knew he would. He hates to lose. So do I.'

Ruby was puzzled. 'Came back?'

'About the Van Gogh.' Mort was still looking skywards, contemplating the Glass Tower. 'I got to thinking about it and how much money it cost and then I thought – what

450

do I know about art anyway? And here's this guy who understands things like that – a genuine collector. He really hankered after the damn painting.'

'I don't get it,' said Ruby. 'Why would you want to do that bastard a favour? Especially after he refused to rent to us.'

'You know how it is,' said Mort. 'He wanted the Van Gogh. His tongue was hanging out for it. He told me he could have kicked himself for walking out of that auction room. Wanted to make me an offer there and then – in Christie's. It was the first time in his life he had ever denied himself something he wanted. Imagine.'

'Big deal.'

'So, I got to thinking.'

'What are you trying to say, Mort?'

'I sold him the Van Gogh,' said Mort casually.

'You what?' Ruby stopped dead on the sidewalk. 'Are you out of your mind? That's the most incredible thing I ever heard. What made you do a dumb thing like that?'

Mort smiled gently.

'Wait a minute,' said Ruby, understanding dawning. 'Now I get it. You made a fat profit on the deal. That's my boy.'

'Not a cent.'

'Then why, for Chrissake, did you do it?'

'I made another kind of deal. I gave him a cheque for a hundred million dollars.'

'You what!' Ruby took a step back and Mort held him by the arm to stop him stumbling off the sidewalk.

'And I threw in the Van Gogh.'

Ruby's mouth fell open. He shook his head, bewildered. 'What in God's name for?'

Mort pointed at the Glass Tower. 'For that,' he said.

Ruby followed Mort's eyes. 'You . . . bought . . . the Glass . . . Tower!'

'It seemed like a good idea,' Mort said.

'You paid a hundred and fifty million bucks for a goddam

451

skyscraper! And you're the guy who won't even buy himself a new watch!'

'I already have a watch,' said Mort.

Ruby was more than angry. He was hurt – bitterly hurt. 'Whose money did you use?'

'I bought it in the company's name. If you think it's a mistake, I'll be happy to buy it back from the company. I'll borrow the money against my shares.'

'That's not the point. Sonofabitch! You know that's not the fucking point. Why didn't you tell me? Why didn't you say what you were up to? You set the whole thing up, didn't you? All that shit about the Van Gogh . . . It was the Glass Tower you wanted all along. What if he told you to take a walk? What then?'

Mort gave a little shrug. 'So what? I'd still own one of the finest paintings in the world. As it is, we own the greatest building in New York – in the United States. In the world.'

'You could have told me, Mort. I'm your brother. Your partner. You could have told me.'

'I'm sorry. OK? I'm sorry.'

'You shouldn't have done it.'

'Come on. It'll be worth double in a few years. Meanwhile, we have the greatest offices money can buy – at a knock-down price. What did I do wrong?'

'You don't know, do you? You really don't know.' Ruby shook his head. All his life he had admired Mort. Now. . . ? 'All my life, Mort . . . All my life I looked up to you. Whatever you did was OK with me. I never criticized you . . . not once . . . all these years I never criticized you.'

'What is it, Ruby? Why are you so upset?'

Ruby spread his arms wide. 'We have everything we need . . . more than we could possibly need . . . more than we ever dreamed of. What do we need with . . . that?' He pointed accusingly at the Glass Tower.

'I want more than we've got, Ruby. Much more.'

'Then you want more than I do.'

Was this the parting of the ways?

'We want the same things. You know we do. In your heart you know it's true.'

'We've always been modest, private, unostentatious. Why change now?'

'The meek don't inherit the earth, Ruby. All they get is dust and ashes.'

Ruby started walking back to Lexington, repeating over and over: 'You scare me, Mort, you know that? You scare me. You really scare me.'

*   *   *

Every name in the oil business was there – and not only in the oil business. Mort had invited three senators, two congressmen, a former Secretary of State and two highly influential members of the White House administration, including one with a cabinet post. No one turned down an invitation from Mortimer King. They were flattered to be asked and eager to come. It was the sort of party you simply had to be seen at.

The meteoric rise of King Brothers, the ultimate success story, the quintessence of the American dream, had been a talking point around town for a long time. Money attracts all kinds of men – those with power and those who feed on it – the jungle cats and the parasites. The progress of the company was being tracked by people of all sorts and conditions, fascinated by this rapidly burgeoning phenomenon, much as astronomers are by an approaching comet.

With this, their first major acquisition – the Glass Tower – the King Brothers had truly arrived. Mort promptly renamed it 'Kings' Tower'.

His speech of welcome was serious and brief. An articulate speaker, never lost for words, he referred only rarely to the minuscule notes he concealed in the palm of his hand. But, though his delivery was smooth and fluent, his manner was maladroit. There was about him an air of unease. He moved uncomfortably from one foot to another, avoiding eye contact with anyone in the room. It was a speech he was giving, not an informal chat; he was addressing an audience not as individuals but collectively, and his discomfort and gaucheness infected them all. They looked at the ground and shifted restlessly, like a flock of sheep in the presence of a predator.

'We are grateful for your help, for the help of all our friends . . . and our competitors, too. We make no distinction between the two of them. We are all one family in the oil industry.'

'Does he really believe this bullshit?' said Edgar, sotto voce to Jeffrey.

'He does when he's saying it.'

'Why doesn't he say something funny?'

Jeffrey grinned. 'You don't think this is funny?'

Mort was into his peroration. 'We accept, with pride and gratitude, our responsibility, indeed our solemn duty, to maintain our position as the indispensable and trusted suppliers of the American oil industry.'

Mort turned away to polite and sporadic applause.

'What did you think?' Sam asked.

'It was OK,' said Jeffrey. 'You know – not exactly Roosevelt or Churchill, but OK.'

'He's a great bullshit artist,' said Sam, 'but who does he think he's kidding?'

'Maybe you're asking too much of him. What did you expect? Profundity?'

'How about the truth?' said Sam.

'In that case,' said Jeffrey, 'you're definitely asking too much of him. Or any of us, for that matter.'

'Who are all these politicians?' Sam asked Edgar.

'Search me.'

'What are they doing here?'

'Haven't you heard?' said Edgar. 'Mort is running for President.'

Sam looked thoughtful. 'Many a true word . . .' he said.

Corks popped incessantly. The vintage champagne gushed orgiastically. 'It's a strike. We hit champagne!' cried Edgar, gulping down a glassful and pouring another.

454

The conversation in the room was so loud now, you had to shout to make yourself heard.

Ruby was pumping Mort's hand, congratulating him on his speech.

'You think he's trying to make oil come out of his mouth?' said Jeffrey.

Edgar chuckled.

'Great speech,' said Ruby. 'I found it very moving.'

'You really think so?' said Mort, doubtfully. As a public speaker, he had a problem finding the right words. People seemed to doubt his sincerity. He couldn't imagine why.

'Yes, I do,' said Ruby. 'It was a fine speech.'

'I agree, sir,' said the senator from the South. 'You have a natural flair for oratory and the appropriate word. You should be in politics.'

Mort raised his hands in mock horror. 'Me? In politics? I could never do what you guys do. I'm just a simple businessman.'

The senator's reaction was unexpected – at least to Mort. He backed off. 'I guess you're right,' he said. 'We all should stick to what we know best.' He moved away to refill his glass.

Ruby could see that his brother was disappointed. He understood, for the first time, where his real ambition lay.

'If you want to go into politics,' said Ruby, 'never ask a politician to help. It only makes you a potential competitor.'

Mort nodded. 'The guy didn't believe what I was saying. He was looking at my face and he could see I was interested. It wasn't smart.'

'No, it wasn't,' said Ruby. 'First, let them find out they need you.'

'Who needs an oil trader?'

'The meek don't inherit the earth,' said Ruby. 'Isn't that what you said?'

Jeffrey grew more sardonically mellow with each glass of champagne.

455

'How long,' he asked Karl Andermatt, 'does it take Mort to get to work in the morning?'

'I have no idea,' said Karl uneasily. 'Why don't you ask him?'

'This is a joke,' explained Jeffrey patiently. 'I just made it up.'

'Oh, I see. A joke,' said Karl and smiled to show he knew about jokes. 'Well then, how long does it take him?'

'Fifteen minutes from his apartment to the door of his office, then another ten to the desk,' said Jeffrey, poker-faced.

'He's lucky,' said Karl. 'It takes me an hour.'

'Does it really?' said Jeffrey despairingly. 'That long?'

Sam asked Jeffrey: 'Have you noticed this is vintage Dom Perignon?'

'Vaguely. I can never tell the difference. Why?'

'Take a look at the label,' said Sam, holding up a bottle. Jeffrey read it: 'Vintage 1973'. 'Was that a good year?'

'It was for us,' said Sam meaningfully. 'The best.'

The penny dropped. 'Oh, my God,' said Jeffrey. 'The year we launched the company. You mean this is deliberate?'

'Are you kidding?'

'What a throwaway.'

'Impressive, no?'

'If you're impressed by that sort of thing,' said Jeffrey.

'How do you like the new office?' said Edgar, politely, to Julie.

'Neat,' said Julie. 'Real . . . neat.' She had drunk more than a little too much.

'Out of sight,' said Edgar. 'Remote-controlled bars, carpets a foot deep. And how about the padded walls?'

'I think they're quite appropriate,' said Julie.

Edgar nodded automatically. Then he realized what she had said and started laughing. So did Julie. She had always liked Edgar.

'Ruby's like a teddy bear,' said Caroline. 'He looks so crumpled and cuddly.'

456

'Ruby's about as cuddly as an MX missile,' said Jeffrey tartly.

'Something tells me you don't love your partners any more,' said Caroline.

'I love them to bits,' said Jeffrey. 'It's just that I don't always like them too much.'

'If it hadn't been for them . . .'

'Oh sure,' said Jeffrey. 'If it hadn't been for them, I'd still be peeling the paint off the walls of my office in Shell.'

'So, what's the problem?'

'I have the feeling we're losing our way – getting involved in a lot of crap we don't need, throwing money around to impress people. Who's impressing whom, I wonder?'

'The company can afford it,' said Caroline reasonably.

'The company can afford to paste Picassos on the wall and throw darts at them. That doesn't make it a good idea.'

Caroline laughed. 'Maybe you're disillusioned with the business world,' she said.

'Me disillusioned? When did I ever have any illusions? All I wanted to do was make some money and I'm making it. There's nothing wrong with that. It's the direction we're taking I don't like. You think we need offices in the Glass Tower – sorry, Kings' Tower? You know why we're here? We're here because it's bigger and swankier than the Oil Corporation building. We're here because Mort's office is twenty floors higher than Edmund Meyer's. We're not traders any more – at least not in oil. You know what we're trading? Power and influence. That's heady stuff. You know why he invited all these politicians?'

'No. Why?' Caroline had been dying to ask. In spite of herself, she was impressed. Some of the faces she recognized.

'Mortimer King for President,' said Jeffrey.

'You don't mean it? The first Jewish President!'

Jeffrey chuckled. 'If anyone can do it, he can. Can you

457

imagine? Bagels and cream cheese in the Oval Office? Chicken soup and matzoballs on the front lawn?'

Caroline giggled.

'It's no joke,' said Jeffrey. 'Mort is using the company to achieve his personal ambitions. He and Ruby think it belongs to them.'

'But it does, doesn't it?' said Caroline.

Jeffrey stared at her. He was shocked and resentful. He hated to hear it, but it was true. He and Sam had forty-nine per cent between them . . . minority shareholders.

In the last analysis. It seemed that the 'last analysis' was getting closer.

'Why such big offices, Mr King?' the reporter asked Mort.

Mort smiled. 'I like space,' he said. He loathed reporters and he hated the press. The truth was, he was scared of them. Being by nature a secretive man, he had schooled himself in the art of poker playing, bluffing the competition, never showing his hand, never saying exactly what he meant, always weighing his words, delicately placing one after the other on the scales, as if he were weighing diamonds – here a flawed stone, there an outright imitation, but, intermingled with everything, a kind of truth – the only kind that counted – Mortimer King's kind.

The press – now they were different. You could never control what they said about you. They wrote what they wanted to write. Not what you wanted. Still, it was important to seem at ease, to appear open and friendly with this guy.

'Space is essential to me,' he said. 'Walking about my office is the only exercise I get.' He grinned engagingly . . . the light-hearted touch.

'I can vouch for that,' said Julie loudly, slurring her words.

Suddenly, the room was quiet. A woman giggled. Everyone was listening.

The reporter sensed that there was more here than the averagely dull story he had expected. He 'pointed' like a hunting dog at the scent of his prey. 'Why would anyone hate you enough to want to kill you, Mr King?' Not an appropriate question for such an occasion. Not friendly.

Julie moved closer . . . attention focused on her.

'No one hates me,' said Mort coldly. 'It was obviously a mentally deranged individual.'

The reporter did not pursue the question. He knew his time was limited. 'Are you surprised at the phenomenally rapid success of your company?' A loaded question. Seemingly innocent.

'Gratified, not surprised. And it's not my company,' Mort added quickly. 'It's a partnership – a team.'

There was a murmur of approval in the room.

'Then why call it King Brothers?' The question cracked like a whiplash. And immediately – not giving him time to reply: 'And why did you rename this building "Kings' Tower"?' Pressure on pressure.

Mort hesitated. He was talking himself into a corner.

'Thash unfair,' said Julie. 'Unfair queshtion,' she shouted. 'Shtrike that queshtion out.'

'Honey,' protested Mort, trying vainly to shut her up. 'Let me answer the guy.'

'Unfair queshtion,' she shouted again. 'Ish not King Brothers. Ish the King and I.'

'Julie, please!' Mort was warning her, not pleading.

'God shave the King,' said Julie. 'The King needs a shave,' she added. 'Didn't I shay before we went out thish evening, "King", I shaid, "you need a shave." ' She started to sing, ' "Getting to know you, getting to know all about you . . ." ' She hiccuped loudly.

Edgar put his arm round her shoulder.

'You're nishe, Edgar,' she said affectionately. Edgar was warm and flawed and vulnerable. He was all the things Mort was not. He took her arm and began to move her towards the door.

'Time to go home, honey,' he said gently and bent his head protectively to hers. She was crying soundlessly, the tears rolling down her face, streaking the mascara.

'Where was I?' said Mort calmly to the reporter, but he saluted Mort and ran. He already had his story. Several, in fact.

Julie wiped her face with the back of her hand. 'We're rich as Croesh . . . as Croesh . . .' She couldn't get the name out. 'I'm rich,' she shouted.

Edgar was trying to steer her through the door, but as they reached it, she pulled away from him. She had stopped crying. 'Didn't mean to be a bitch,' she said loudly. 'A rich bitch . . . Mort.' She giggled. 'It was jush – I shaw you acrosh the room – acrosh a crowded room.' She pondered a moment. 'Shome enchanted evening,' she added. 'And you looked sho kind, I thought you must be . . . Leo. No, what I thought was . . . I thought you looked sho . . . shin . . . shincere . . . you had to be lying your fucking head off. So I came back to shay goodbye.' She put one arm on Edgar's shoulder to steady herself. 'Goodbye!' she declaimed, the other arm outstretched histrionically.

Mort turned away, humiliated and disgusted. Edgar, gently but firmly, manoeuvred her out of the office.

The huge room was deathly quiet for a moment and then, as the embarrassed guests turned away from the door, everyone started talking at once.

'A smash hit,' said Jeffrey.

'The night of the year,' said Sam.

'I'm sorry for Mort,' said Caroline.

'Have some 1973 Dom Perignon,' said Jeffrey, 'and don't waste your pity.'

The last guest had left and there was no trace of the party – no empty bottles, no glasses, no post-reception debris. The caterers had done their job, the cleaners had descended with their machines and Mort's vast office was neat and tidy, the tabletops polished, the thick-piled carpet pristine.

He sat at his desk, but, for once, he was not thinking of business. In some way that he preferred not to try to analyse, his marriage was a mess. He wished it were as easy to put in order as his office had been. But there was

460

no one to call, no marriage cleaners, no one you could pay to come in with plastic bags and vacuum cleaners, to sweep and shampoo and polish and leave things as they had been before – just as they ought to be. No, he would have to do it himself. But how? Where to start?

It was tough enough to claw your way to the top of the heap, tough but rewarding. It was a simple game with simple rules. But marriage? Now that was different. What were the rewards for staying together? He could remember loving Julie. He could remember being excited by her presence – how, when she walked into a room unexpectedly, it had been the highlight of his day. But now, when the fireworks had burned themselves out, when the display was over and nothing was surprising any more – what should he do now? Strangely, it seemed that the less demanding he became, the more she wanted. He must pay more attention to her, give her more of his time. Business was going well. The company was on top of the world. Soon, the Domestic oil problem would be forgotten, behind him. He could fix it. Of course he could. Anything could be fixed if you were smart, if you knew the right people, if you had enough money – anything, that is, except a marriage that was in trouble, or a wife who didn't love you any more.

*   *   *

By reputation, Matthew Rowland was the greatest trial lawyer in the New York district, possibly in the USA. A neat, well-manicured, exquisitely barbered and altogether immaculately groomed little man, not a hair of his silver grey coiffure, nor a word in his trial memorandum was ever out of place. His custom-made suit streamlined what might otherwise have been a somewhat dumpy body. Cut, stitched and fitted in Savile Row, London, it told his clients what Matthew Rowland wanted them to know – that he had good taste and that his services did not come cheap. He had a way of patting his stomach and hips, a mannerism that unconsciously expressed how extraordi-

461

narily satisfied he was with his shape, his professional expertise, his life and . . . himself. In the opinion of many – not least Matthew Rowland – he was a superstar.

But Matthew Rowland was not altogether what he seemed. In appearance and speech, he was a typical product of an Ivy League campus. In thought and action, he was an alley cat.

As he stood there in Mort's office, composed and elegant, wafting Aramis, his light tan camel's-hair coat draped casually over his shoulders, no one could have guessed that, until the age of sixteen, he had spent most of his days and a good part of his nights on the backstreets of New York, educating himself in the power struggles and intrigues of the teenage gangs who roam the Bronx. He learned lessons there that he applied with equal success in the more affluent downtown neighbourhoods he frequented in his later life, and he never forgot the most important one, the only one that mattered: survival. Privileged or underprivileged, rich or poor, people, he believed, were fundamentally the same the world over. They were weak, fallible, devious and dangerous. The risk might vary, but the risk was always there. 'You can get mugged in Disneyland' was his favourite aphorism.

'I sure am glad Tex jumped overboard,' he said. 'Not that he's a rat. He's just not a very good lawyer and not,' he added smoothly, 'that your ship is sinking. No, sir. It may be drifting a bit, but we'll soon have it back on course.' He patted his hips complacently.

Ruby's lips curled. In his book, anyone who talked like that had to be a wimp or a schmuck – probably both. Mort was not too impressed either.

'Mr Rowland,' he began.

'Call me Matthew.'

'Matthew. Ruby and I are plain speakers. We heard you were sharp – a smart lawyer – not a walking filibuster. You hear what I'm saying?'

Clients did not talk to Matthew Rowland that way. He didn't like it. It showed lack of respect.

'You have to take me the way I am,' he said.

'I don't have to take you the way you are,' said Mort brutally. 'I don't have to take you any way at all. I'm the client. I pay you for advice. When it comes to action, you do what my brother and I tell you. Right now, we have a problem. If you help us solve it, you'll make a small fortune. More important, you'll make powerful friends. You want it or you don't? There's your chair. There's the door.'

For a second or two, it looked as though Matthew Rowland would walk. He was miffed. But at the same time he was intrigued, and not a little impressed. Tooth and claw was not his overt style, but it was the only thing he truly understood. He admired a man who had the guts to say what he thought.

'The chair looks pretty comfortable,' he said.

Mort glanced at Ruby. Ruby shrugged resignedly. Mort smiled at Rowland. 'Sit down, Matthew. Tell us what you think. You studied the documents we sent you?'

'I did.'

They leaned forward, concentrating on his words.

Matthew Rowland was at his best when he had his audience's attention. 'Let's be frank with each other. The Domestic crude stunt you pulled was a scam. Others have done the same thing – many others – and a lot are still doing it. Not only little guys, either, not just the mushroom companies springing up overnight in Houston and Dallas and Fort Worth, no, the big guys are at it too. Big oil companies.'

'We know that,' said Mort.

'But there's a difference. To be precise, there are two vital distinctions between you and all the other guys on the block.'

They were listening carefully.

'The first is, you've been successful – too darn successful – the most successful oil-trading corporation anyone has seen in a long time.'

'That's a crime?' asked Ruby.

463

'It is to some people,' said Rowland. 'There's a whole lot of envy out there.'

Mort nodded. To him, that made perfect sense. 'And the second distinction?'

'You put your name on the door: "King Brothers". You made yourself a target. What the heck made you do that?'

'We're majority shareholders,' said Ruby. 'Why shouldn't we have our name on the door?'

'You guys like to play humble,' said Rowland, 'but that's not your true nature at all, is it? You don't want to get suntanned, but you just can't stay out of the sun.'

'You read us wrong,' said Ruby. 'We're not the ostentatious kind. We're modest guys. Anyone will tell you that.'

'Modest? . . . Is that what you are?' He walked across to the plate glass that spanned the side of Mort's huge office. 'There aren't too many views like this in the world. You're up here with God. You see what I see? I'm looking down on clouds. The clouds are between us and Park Avenue. Don't you ever get the feeling you're above it all? Above the struggle? Above the rat race? Above the ordinary schmoes?' He turned back to face them. 'Above the law?'

'No, we don't,' said Mort.

'Then why did you buy this building? And why, for Chrissake, did you call it Kings' Tower? You couldn't resist, could you? Modest!' he said scornfully. 'Huh.'

'This is all hindsight,' said Ruby. 'What's the point of it?'

'The point is,' said Matthew Rowland, 'that the Feds might come after you two personally and, if they do, they're going to want their pound of flesh. It seems to me,' he said, looking around, 'that you have more than enough flesh for them to get their knives into.'

'We're not the only successful company in town. You said it yourself,' said Mort.

'Yeah, but with you two they can attach names to the crimes. Suppose – just suppose – that Exxon had been

464

naughty boys like you. I guess it's possible the Feds might target them. But who would they hit? Who would they indict? It's no fun hounding a major oil company and it sure as hell isn't easy to get a conviction.'

'What are you saying?'

'What I'm saying is that if the worse comes to the worst – and in my experience it usually does – we're going to have to negotiate a settlement with the US Attorney's Office.'

'Surely it hasn't come to that?' said Ruby. 'What do they know? What can they find out?'

'What do they know? Very little,' said Matthew Rowland. 'What can they find out? Plenty.'

'How?' asked Mort.

'You heard Melvin Craig was indicted?'

'We heard,' said Ruby.

'He'll be sentenced in a couple of weeks. Now, I happen to know that, so far, he's refused to cooperate with the US Attorney's Office. They offered him a reduced sentence in exchange for the names of any companies he knew that were involved in the Domestic scam. He told them to get lost. He's a cussed sonofabitch.'

'Tex told me he thought Melvin was wired during one of our discussions,' said Mort.

Matthew Rowland chuckled. 'I heard that too. The truth is, they talked him into it, but he never turned the tape on. He changed his mind at the last minute. That's Melvin Craig for you. He hates the Establishment and he loathes the Feds.'

'Thank God for that,' said Mort. Things were sounding better every minute.

'OK,' said Matthew Rowland. 'Here's what I suggest. The threat of jail is kind of depressing. It burrows into the mind like a little parasite. It doesn't exactly bring out the best in a man. Go see Melvin Craig before he's sentenced. He's still out on bail, of course. Try and talk to him. Make a deal – if you know what I mean.'

'I know what you mean,' said Mort.

'His lawyer is still trying to persuade him to do a deal with the Feds. You have to convince him to do one with you instead.'

'How do you rate our chances?' said Ruby. 'I mean, how do you rate our chances of. . . ?' He couldn't bring himself to finish.

'Staying out of the pen?' Matthew Rowland was back on top, where he liked to be. It reassured him to see a little healthy fear in his clients' eyes. Fear engendered respect. But whatever happened to these two guys, he would still be walking the streets at the end of it all. Of course, he cared what happened to his clients. Failure was bad for business. But, one way or another, this case would ring the till and, God knows, he needed cash badly enough. His lifestyle was extravagant.

'Ninety-nine per cent. That's my opinion.'

'Only one chance in a hundred of going to jail,' said Ruby. 'Pretty good odds.'

'Not if you're the one per cent,' said Mort wryly.

*   *   *

Reassured by their talk with Matthew Rowland, Mort and Ruby returned with their usual zest and dedication to the oil business. They had taken full advantage of the boom years, but now, the boom was over. The slowdown was accompanied by the most prolonged and devastating recession since the early thirties. Soaring interest rates destroyed many small and medium-sized businesses and left even some of the biggest corporations vulnerable. Third World countries were burdened with huge debts on which they could not even pay the interest, let alone repay the capital. Many a Western bank that could not open its doors wide enough to borrowers only a few short years previously, now came perilously close to closing them for good.

Corporations that had grown fat and lazy during the boom years were now vulnerable to predators. The quarry was sluggish, disheartened and defenceless. The hunting

466

had never been so good. It was the perfect opportunity for Mort. His attention was diverted from oil trading, at which he had been so brilliantly successful. Now he saw a new opportunity. The economic situation was tailor-made for him. It perfectly suited his expansionist ambitions. Money was no problem. King Brothers had more than enough.

'With bank loans and plenty of leverage, we can take over the world,' he said grandly.

'What do we do with it when we've got it?' said Ruby.

But Ruby too was beginning to catch the fever.

Their entrepreneurial activities had already attracted the attention of the press. Mort and Ruby were written up in *Newsweek* and *Time*. Almost weekly, their names appeared in articles and interviews in the *New York Times* and the *Wall Street Journal*. Finally, to their delight, they were accorded the accolade of a four-page article in *Fortune* magazine and named in the Forbes One Hundred list of the richest men in the United States.

Publicity had spurred their ambition. They swallowed a mining house producing copper, lead and zinc, a medium-sized US oil corporation, eight super-tankers, two large real estate corporations – one in California, one in Texas – an investment bank, a transport conglomerate, a meat-packing plant, a brokerage house, and, finally and most glamorous, a hotel casino in Atlantic City.

Jeffrey read about the hotel casino in the London *Times* – not the best way to find out what your partners were up to. Certainly, neither he nor Sam was being consulted these days.

He phoned Mort. 'Tell me. I'm getting confused,' he said. 'What am I? An oil trader, a meat packer, or a crap shooter?'

Mort chuckled. 'I love your sense of humour, Jeffrey.'

'It might surprise you to know I'm not being funny. When you buy a hotel casino and don't even tell your partners about it – something's wrong.'

Mort had a way of sounding innocent when he was at

467

his most devious. 'You're absolutely right, Jeffrey. It's just that you and Sam were busy trading.'

'True enough. We're making money. You and Ruby are spending it.'

'That's not fair,' protested Mort.

'No, it's not,' said Jeffrey perversely. 'So why do it? I've just been talking to Sam. He tells me the company is leveraged ten times over with all these takeovers. Now that's not sound business. It's downright dangerous. We're paying the bankers more interest on our loans than we're making in a year. How can that make sense?'

'We're sitting on companies worth many times what we paid for them,' said Mort. 'One day, when we choose to sell them, we'll make more money than we ever made out of oil trading. Trust me.'

'Whatever happened to King Brothers, the oil traders?' said Jeffrey. 'I remember when we made fortunes trading, and that was good enough for us. What's happening, Mort?'

'Times change. We're moving with them. You'll see. It's going to be great.'

'And if it isn't?'

'I tell you what. Then you can say: I told you so.'

'So help me, Mort, if this were a public company, I'd have you and Ruby voted off the board.'

'It's not,' said Mort bluntly. 'Save your threats for your enemies. I'm your friend. Remember?'

Mort's secretary buzzed him. 'Edmund Meyer on line one. Shall I say you're in conference?'

'No. Put him through.'

'You well, Mort?' E.M. was in a good mood.

'My health is good, thanks,' said Mort carefully.

'Recovered from the shooting?'

'A hundred per cent.'

'They ever get the guy who did it?'

'They will.'

'I doubt it.' E.M. sounded pretty sure of himself. For a moment there, Mort wondered if E.M. had been behind it.

Then he dismissed the idea as too fantastic. Not the old Titan. It was just not his way of doing things.

'What can I do for you, E.M.?'

'You remember our last discussion?'

'Sure. I thought you'd given up on the merger idea.'

'I have. I'm giving you one last chance to come back to the Oil Corporation.'

The old man was crazy. His brain must be softening. 'Forget it,' said Mort curtly.

He could imagine the expression on E.M.'s face. What he wanted, he had to have. He never gave up.

'I hear you're having a few problems,' said E.M.

'Nothing we can't handle.'

E.M. said: 'These things have a way of getting out of hand. You don't know who your friends are.'

Mort wondered what he meant by that.

'You can name your terms. One day you'll be President – own the company. I'm ready to talk. You and I should be working together, not fighting.'

'I'm not fighting you. I'm not fighting anyone,' said Mort. 'You're the one with the grudge. Let go, E.M. I'm not coming back. Not now. Not ever.'

'I'm asking you again, Mort. For the last time. I'll be honest with you, it's the only way I know to secure the Oil Corporation's future.'

'That's your problem, E.M., not mine. The future of King Brothers – that's all I have to think about – and that'll be a great one.'

'It may not be as great as you think,' said Edmund Meyer.

Again that warning. What was E.M. trying to tell him?

Bob Rosenfeld, an Assistant United States Attorney, climbed, grunting, into the Cadillac. He was a veteran of the Korean War with a replacement hip to remind him of it. Jack had borrowed the company stretch limo. He told the driver to cruise around Manhattan, then he flipped the button that closed the glass partition separating the front from the rear of the limo. They were in a sound-proof bubble.

'Now we can talk.' He turned to the man sitting next to him. He knew he must be pushing fifty-five, but he looked much younger. He also looked intelligent. His suit was badly fitting and crumpled, the knot of his tie pulled frenetically tight, the wide end hanging much too low. The top shirt button was undone. His face had that sallow shadowed look of a man who was always short on sleep and a day behind in his shaving, but his gaze was steady and his eyes sharp and shrewd behind his glasses.

'Sorry about the limo,' said Jack. 'This is not where I usually meet people.'

Bob Rosenfeld made no comment. He had met people in stranger places. They were heading downtown on Park Avenue. They passed Kings' Tower. Jack gestured towards it. 'You know the building?'

'Kings' Tower. Formerly the Glass Tower.'

'Used to be a colleague of mine – Mortimer King. That was a long time ago.'

'I know that too,' said Rosenfeld.

The flat As, the slightly affected accent. A Bostonian.

They turned west, then north up Madison. For a couple of minutes, neither of them spoke. To Bob Rosenfeld, silence was good news. It was often the forerunner of an interesting disclosure.

'What I have for you is not really information,' said Jack. 'It's nothing concrete – just a feeling I have.'

'Feelings can be useful,' said Rosenfeld encouragingly. He was accustomed to reluctant informers. In his experience, most informers were reluctant. Conscience was something he had learned to contend with, but it still got in the way. It was in the nature of things that informers most frequently ratted on their friends and colleagues.

'I don't want to get involved,' said Jack, looking out of the window on his side of the limo.

Rosenfeld wished he had a dollar for every time he had heard those words. No one ever wanted to get involved.

470

'If you're not breaking the law yourself, there's no reason why you should,' he said.

Another long silence. They were crossing Central Park now.

'It's about Melvin Craig,' said Jack.

Bob Rosenfeld kept quiet. He was a good listener.

'Or, to be more accurate, it's about one of Melvin Craig's business associates – former business associates I should say.'

Rosenfeld's keen eyes gleamed.

'I hear Craig was offered a deal if he talked about his connections.'

'Could be,' said Rosenfeld.

'I also heard he refused to cooperate?' said Jack. It was a question.

No reply.

'I guess you already know from Craig's files who had dealings with him.'

Rosenfeld shook his head. 'We have enough evidence to convict Craig, but nothing to speak of on anyone else. His records were very incomplete.'

Jack told the driver on the intercom to head back to the office. Rosenfeld waited for more, but they drove on in silence. When they stopped outside the Oil Corporation building, Jack turned to Rosenfeld. 'Glad to have met you,' he said. 'The driver will take you back to your office.'

'Thanks.'

Jack started to get out of the limo, as the driver held the door open for him.

'By the way,' he said, casually, 'you should take a good look at Kings' Tower. It's quite a building, isn't it? Incredible how quickly that guy made it.'

As the limo pulled away from the sidewalk, Rosenfeld relaxed in the cushioned seat, stretching the stiff leg. 'Isn't it just?' he said softly to himself.

In not one of Rosenfeld's discussions with Melvin Craig had the name King Brothers come up. It was hard to

471

imagine why a man like Mortimer King would involve himself in daisy chains and all the crooked paraphernalia of the Domestic crude scam. But then success could do strange things to people.

He saw Melvin Craig the next day. At ten the following morning, he was due to appear at the Southern District Federal Court for sentencing.

'It's not too late.'

'Too late for what, Rosenfeld? A Presidential pardon?'

'It's not too late to make a deal.'

'You know what you can do with your deals,' said Craig belligerently.

In a way Rosenfeld admired Craig, but his business was justice, not morality, and anything he could do to persuade a man to stick a knife in his friends or partners, or his family for that matter, was fine by him. It was legitimate. It was lawful. It might be distasteful, but the end justified the means.

'Look, Melvin, being noble is fine. It might even do something for you up there when your time comes. But it's not going to shorten your stretch in the pen.'

'You guys will never understand, will you? I don't like you. I don't like your methods. I don't like the whole goddam system. Do me a favour. Go screw yourself!'

'How well do you know Mortimer King?' asked Rosenfeld patiently.

'I've heard of him.'

Bob Rosenfeld smiled with only one side of his face. It was a habit of his.

'You heard of him?' he said, inviting Craig to elaborate.

'Sure, why not? Who hasn't? He's a nice successful Jewish boy. Like you,' he added mischievously.

'I need your help to get him,' said Rosenfeld.

'Too bad.'

'You could save yourself, Melvin. Know what I'm saying?'

'I know what you're saying,' said Melvin Craig. 'You

want me to tell you that Mortimer King was involved in the Domestic scam.'

Rosenfeld nodded. His sharp eyes glittered. It sounded promising.

'Well, he wasn't,' said Craig and grinned cheekily.

Rosenfeld scowled. 'You're a fool,' he said angrily.

'Fools sleep nights,' said Melvin Craig.

Two days later, he appeared in the Southern District Federal Court and was sentenced to three years on each count of fraud, tax evasion, mail fraud and wire fraud, the sentences to be served concurrently. It was a heavy punishment. Mort decided to waste no more time. Soon, Craig would begin his sentence – probably in thirty days. It was time to talk to him. Matthew Rowland was right. Once he was inside, it would be difficult to talk, unwise even to visit him.

'What can I say, Melvin?' said Mort. 'What can I say except I'm sorry?'

Melvin Craig was thinner than the last time they met. His eyes were tired, sunken and shadowed. The blue crocodile shoes had not been near a brush in months, the cream linen suit was grimy and crumpled and the shirt unbuttoned to the waist. The frills had gone with the jaunty smile. He was a mess.

'Sure you are,' he said. 'You'd be a whole lot sorrier if it was you going to the pen instead of me.'

Mort said nothing. What was there to say? It was true. He watched Craig gulp his second neat vodka in five minutes. It was not yet noon.

'I used to envy you, Mort. You know that? Your success, your money, your cool. You always acted like you belonged on top of the heap. That's where I wanted to be. Funny isn't it, how the whole goddam ball game changes overnight? I still envy you, but it's not your success I envy now, you sonofabitch. It's your freedom. You'll be up there on top of Kings' Tower giving orders, cutting deals, drinking bourbon – eh, Mort? And I'll be in the pen.'

473

'It'll pass,' said Mort. 'Time passes. You won't serve more than half the sentence.'

'Don't tell me what I'll serve, you bastard. I know what I'll serve. Don't patronize me.' Melvin Craig swallowed another vodka and stared sullenly at Mort.

'I didn't mean to.'

Craig gazed into his empty glass. 'Power,' he mused . . . 'It's all about power with you, isn't it? Now, with me it's different. Big bucks. That's all I ever wanted. A nice house, a weekend place on Long Island, maybe a small yacht, money in the bank. But you, Mort, you want more than that, don't you?'

'I don't know what I want.'

'I believe you. That's why you'll never stop. But me?' said Craig. 'If I had enough, I'd retire.'

'Enough? What's enough?'

'If you need to ask you'll never find out. Believe me, most of us know what enough is. Enough is when you don't need any more.'

'Then you're right,' said Mort. 'I'll never stop.'

'You can buy a lot of things, but you can't buy power. Who needs it, anyway? Power's a whore. You pay her for her favours and she fucks you around. Isn't that right, Mort?' His speech was slow, affected by the vodka, but he was still thinking clearly enough.

'I don't understand you.'

'So? You don't understand me. Ain't that a pity.' Melvin Craig poured himself another vodka, tossed it back and refilled his glass. 'You don't comprehend me? Well, try comprehending this. I won't be serving three years. I won't be serving eighteen months.' He downed the vodka and banged the glass on the table. 'I changed my mind,' he said. He looked around him. 'I like it here. I like my apartment. I like my house in Connecticut. It's neat. You should see it. You never came round, did you, Mort? You never met my wife?'

Mort shook his head.

'No. We were business . . . associates. Isn't that what

they call it? We weren't on social terms, were we? We were never buddy buddies, eh, Mort?'

'I thought we were.'

Melvin Craig's face twisted briefly in a convulsive spasm that was as close to a smile as he could get.

'Bob Rosenfeld – now he's a buddy of yours. But of course you know that, Mort. He was asking after you. Seems to be quite an admirer, would you believe? Wanted to know all about you – how you made your money – where I met you. All that stuff. He seemed to think we might have done some deals together. How about that? Where would he get an idea like that from?' Craig frowned suddenly. 'I don't dig Rosenfeld. He's a hard bastard. Like you, Mort. You're a hard bastard too, aren't you?'

'I try not to be,' said Mort quietly.

'Do you? I wonder. I really wonder. You have any friends, Mort? How about family? Oh yes, you have a wife, don't you? I have a wife too . . . I'm not going to enjoy being away from home . . . I'll miss the kids. I'll miss my wife. I like my wife. You like your wife, Mort? You have a dog, Mort? You ever go to the movies? You ever go fishing? I guess not. What's with you, Mort? What makes you tick?'

'I'm just a regular guy like anyone else.'

Melvin Craig chuckled. 'Oh, no. That you're not. That's one thing you ain't . . . Those bastard lawyers. They told me I'd get six months, a year at the most. Never trust a lawyer, you hear? The Feds offered me a deal, you know. I was too goddam proud. I spat in their eye.'

'I'm grateful,' said Mort.

'Grateful? Well, thank you,' said Melvin Craig sarcastically. He reached again for the bottle. 'The man's grateful. Now isn't that nice.' He raised his glass in a mock toast to Mort and tossed back the vodka. His expression changed in an instant from taunting to belligerent. 'Let me tell you something, Mort. Grateful is cool, but grateful doesn't pay the bills, grateful doesn't give me back my reputation and grateful doesn't get me out of the pen.' His voice broke and his eyes filled with tears. He put his head in his hands.

'Jees,' he muttered. 'If there's one thing I hate, it's self-pity.'

'Tell me what I can do,' said Mort after a while.

Melvin Craig looked up and grinned. 'I know why you came to see me, Mort. Like I said – power's a whore. Right? One day she's in the sack with you, the next, little Melvin Craig is screwing her. My lawyer says I'll do two years. Of course, if I were to help the Feds catch a few little fish . . . or maybe just one big one . . . just one Biggie. Now that would be another story. I might only do a year. Not bad, eh? A year of freedom for a little information. That's all they're asking. It's not much they want, is it?'

'They want your self-respect, too,' said Mort.

'Aw, now, just listen to the guy,' Melvin Craig mocked. 'Listen to who's talking self-respect. Mortimer King, tycoon, top of the shit heap. Tell me how you got up there, Mort? Did you float up on your cute little cherub wings?' He chuckled drily. 'You really are something, aren't you?' he said contemptuously. 'Watch out. One of these days you'll start believing all that garbage you give people. That'll really be the end of you.'

'I never did you any harm,' said Mort. 'I never harmed anyone that I know of. I can understand your bitterness, but why turn on me? All I want to do is help, if I can. I'm offering you my friendship.'

'Friendship? Is that what you're offering? Well, that's fine with me. Let's not use unpleasant words like suborning a witness or perjury or bribery or any of those goddam things. Who cares about them, anyway? You and I – what we care about is people, loyalty and friendship. We like to do good by our neighbours. Right, Mort?'

'Right,' said Mort, ignoring the sarcasm.

'Who are you kidding?' said Craig disdainfully. 'You don't give a goddam about anyone except Mortimer King. You're afraid to call a spade a spade. That was always your problem. Your scruples begin and end with terminology. If you were to offer me a bribe in the name of friendship, it would still be a bribe, Mort. Face it. That's your game – controlling everyone. You'll do it till the day you die. And

476

after. I can just see you trying to sweet-talk St Peter – no, I forgot, it'll be Moses or some character like that, won't it? "What's the going price for a ticket to paradise?" you'll ask him. "Whatever it is, I'll double it." ' Melvin Craig giggled and poured himself another vodka.

'This is all crap,' said Mort. 'I care about my friends. I care about you, Melvin. You know I do.'

Craig looked at Mort intently. 'How much?'

'What?' Mort was startled.

'How much do you care?' This was not the way Mort had planned the discussion.

'I care a lot,' he said, evasively.

'How much, asshole? How much is a year of my life worth?'

What would it take? Ten million dollars probably. Fifteen would do it for sure. And twenty? Twenty would bury the body, nail it down and bind the coffin with brass.

'It's not worth a goddam,' said Mort.

Craig looked at him, blinking his eyes. 'What? What did you say?'

'I can't compensate you for a year of your life, Melvin. Besides, I could offer you the moon and you wouldn't take it. I know you. You're a proud man.'

Melvin Craig put down his drink and stared at the floor. His body was swaying from side to side, reflecting his confusion.

'Sonofabitch,' he muttered. He was trying to decide if this was an insult or the greatest compliment anyone had ever paid him. He sat up, suddenly, straight and still, folding his mouth in a determined line. 'It was going to cost you plenty,' he said. 'I was going to ask you for ten million dollars.'

'I don't believe you,' said Mort.

Craig chuckled – a wry humourless sound. 'Just a gag,' he said. He finished off his drink and picked up the bottle. It was empty.

'If anything happened to me, you would take care of my family.'

477

'Nothing's going to happen to you.'

'Nah, I'll be OK,' said Craig. 'But just in case.'

Mort nodded. 'You know I would.'

Melvin Craig raised his glass. 'Here's looking at you, old buddy buddy. You discovered something about Melvin Craig today.'

'I discovered something about myself,' said Mort.

Mort finished his third bourbon of the evening. Time to leave. He was putting the telexes in his bag when a thought occurred to him. He picked up the phone, hesitated, changed his mind, replaced the receiver and poured another bourbon. What the hell was he doing? Why was he acting so indecisively, changeable as a teenage girl?

It was a couple of months since he had last spoken to Rosemary: a long time. What was she doing? What was she thinking? He only had to lift the phone to find out, but that simple act, one that he performed a hundred times a day, would signify a degree of involvement alien to his nature; it disturbed him even to contemplate it. He picked up the phone again. It was late to call, but she never seemed to care if he woke her up. She slept easily and peacefully and she woke the same way. He recalled, when he had slept overnight with her, the way she had woken in the morning. The moment she opened her eyes, she was alert – not a trace of sleep in her face or her manner.

'What time is it?' she said.

'It's seven-thirty here. Half an hour after midnight with you. Did I wake you?'

'No. I was thinking about you. Strange you should call.'

It was not just her voice that was close; it was her. He could sense her presence in the room, see her, smell her, touch her almost. There was a curious intimacy in the habit she had of taking up the conversation as if it had never been interrupted. Her artless acceptance of his midnight call, without protest, without question, told him how close they had drawn to each other. The thought was

478

engaging and, at the same time, disturbing. How and when had it all happened?

'What were you thinking?'

'I was wondering if you'd like to have a wardrobe – sorry closet – or maybe a couple of drawers?'

He laughed. 'Is that what you buy the man who has everything?'

'Funny,' she said. 'I mean in my flat.'

'What for?' He knew what for, of course.

'You could keep a few suits here . . . pyjamas . . . that sort of thing.'

'You don't have to do that for me.'

'You always say things like that. It's such a rebuff. I know I don't have to. The question is, do you want me to?'

Did he? Hard to say. She was telling him that she was willing to make him the only man in her life. Is that what he really wanted?

'Sure I do.'

'Then that's settled,' she said, almost primly, as if she were a child and they had just agreed a name for her new doll.

What, he wondered, had they settled?

'When will I see you?'

'I'm trying to find a reason to come over.'

'Does there always have to be a reason?'

She was pressurizing him. He did not like that and she sensed it. 'I'm sorry,' she added quickly. 'That was silly. Of course there has to be.'

'I'll see you soon,' he said, sounding more confident than he felt.

'We can have a grand opening.'

'Grand opening?'

'Your new closet.'

He laughed. 'Wardrobe will do.'

'I love you,' she said wistfully, as if she wished she didn't.

'Thanks.'

'You're embarrassed,' said Rosemary. 'Women shouldn't say things like that to you, should they?'

She was right, of course. It was tough to handle. He sat at his desk and thought about her. Why did he feel so depressed? Was it because Rosemary had said she loved him? It was the first time she had said it – the first, maybe the last. It could be the start of something important in his life, but somehow it felt more like an ending than a beginning.

Since the celebration party for the opening of Kings' Tower, Mort and Julie had barely spoken to each other. When they did, he had been, as ever, distant and courteous. Never once had he referred to her behaviour at the party or the stories in the gossip columns. The only time, in fact, that he had mentioned the party was to say what a success he thought it had been.

As the weeks passed, Julie grew desperate. She had to talk to her husband, but she knew it wasn't going to be easy.

He was in the library sipping a bourbon and soda and reading the inevitable yellow copies. It seemed as good an opportunity as any.

'I'll be right with you, honey. Just give me a moment to finish reading these.'

For a few minutes he read on, totally absorbed. Then he set aside the last telex, carefully placed the two bundles in his briefcase – one for filing, one for follow-up the next day – and turned to her. 'Drink?'

'A martini.'

As he poured it, she asked him: 'Do you ever not do anything?'

'How do you mean?'

'Do you ever do nothing? Sit in a chair and do nothing?'

'Not that I can recall.'

'Every second accounted for. Not a moment wasted.'

'It's a short life. I try not to waste time.'

'How long did our wedding take?'

'I don't remember,' he said, puzzled.

'Wasn't that a waste of time?' she said harshly. She drank the martini and held out her glass. 'I'll have another one.'

He poured the drink, handed it to her and sat down heavily in his chair. 'Kings' Tower . . . the Grand Opening. Is this going to be a repeat performance?'

'No,' she said. 'That was a performance. This is a conversation.'

'Not the kind I care for.'

'You'll get used to it,' said Julie. 'It's called communication and I'll have another martini.'

'You pour it,' said Mort curtly, looking at his watch.

'No problem,' said Julie. 'How long have I got?'

'I don't know what you mean,' he said irritably.

'You looked at your watch. I want to know how much time I've been allocated. You do allocate time for your interviews, don't you? I mean, it's a short life. You try not to waste time. Isn't that what you said? You see, my problem is I don't know how long things should take. What do you give a crude oil deal, for example? Or a business lunch? Or a heart-to-heart talk with one of your employees? Or a chat with your tax lawyer? Or a fuck, Mort? How long do you give a fuck these days?'

Mort said nothing. He looked at the carpet uncomfortably.

'You mean you don't know?' she said. 'I'm real disappointed . . . How about saving a marriage? Is that worth a couple of extra minutes? Come on, Mort. Tell me. How long have I got?'

Mort helped himself to another bourbon. 'You did your goddam best to ruin the greatest day of my life.'

'Good!' she cried. 'I like it! A touch of feeling – real feeling. What do you know? For once in your life, you actually said what you meant.'

'I won't stoop to brawling. It's degrading and undignified.' He turned his back on her.

'Bullshit!' she scoffed. 'Go ahead – stoop. Be undignified.

481

Let's have a brawl. You have to lose your dignity sometimes. That's when you really know you're living. Come
on, Mort. Let's fight.' She put up her fists and started
dancing round the room, shadow boxing, breathing noisily
through her nostrils.

'You're being ridiculous,' he said distastefully. 'It's impossible to have a meaningful conversation with you.'

The effect of his words on Julie was dramatic. She stood
there in the middle of the room, frozen, a figure of comedy,
still holding up her fists, staring at Mort, incredulously.
'What did you say?'

'I said it's impossible to have a meaningful conversation
with you.'

Suddenly, she was laughing. She laughed until the tears
ran down her face and then the laughter turned to a dry
rasping sound and she was fighting for breath. Mort slapped
her across the face. The blow was calculated, controlled,
without anger. For a second or two, her eyes were full of
venom, her face distorted with hate. She wanted to hit
him back. Instead, she hid her face in her hands and began
to cry. Mort stood there, not knowing what to do, holding
her to him roughly, wanting to show tenderness, but not
knowing how.

'I'm sorry,' he said. 'I love you.'

She shook her head. 'No you don't. I've tried to reach
you all our married life and you block me every time. Now
you say it's impossible to have a meaningful conversation
with me. You don't know what a meaningful conversation is. You never did. That's what's so tragic.'

'Of course I do,' said Mort. 'It's just that my life . . . I'm
so busy all the time.'

'Doing what?' she said. 'Being a success. Buying approval, buying admiration. And when you're number one
– what then? You won't be satisfied. I just about learned
how to handle being a tycoon's wife, now I have to adjust
to being First Lady. You're like a child whose teddy bear
was taken away from him. Your father should have
spanked you less and hugged you more.'

482

'Those are just psychological clichés,' said Mort.

'Sure they are,' she agreed. 'So are you. You're forty-eight years old and you're still not ready for a mature relationship.'

He shook his head helplessly. What could he say? 'I could try. Maybe you can help me understand these things better.'

'These things,' she said, 'are the only things that count. Don't knock them.' She picked a piece of white cotton from the shoulder of his jacket. It was a touching, possessive gesture, a shy confession, despite everything, of her love for him.

*   *   *

The office of the Assistant United States Attorney in charge of the case was about a third of the size of Edgar's. The sludge-brown walls looked as though they had not been painted since the Depression. They were bare, except for a faded black and white photograph of President Reagan, and a graph tracing the rise in the rate of teenage pregnancies in the State of Arkansas from 1960 to 1970. The floor tiles were lavatory grey and the tangled warp and weft of what might once have been a rug lay brittle and decomposing on the floor.

Bob Rosenfeld was hyperactive, fast-talking and sharp. Everything about him was sharp – his nose, his expression, his mind. Everything except his Bostonian As. They were flat. Clearly, he did not care much what he looked like. It seemed as though he was not too fond of shaving and his shirt and trousers would not have been out of place on a wino in Central Park. His keen eyes peered at Edgar through rimless glasses. He conveyed the impression of a man who had plotted his course at an early age and thrown away the chart. He was dedicated, uncompromising and ruthless.

Beside his desk, in the corner of the room, perched on a tiny chair, sat a large, sleepy-looking man with melancholy eyes. He, too, was in shirtsleeves.

'Ed Goldwyn,' said Rosenfeld indicating him.

Goldwyn inclined his head without disturbing the mass of his frame. Edgar grinned nervously. 'No relation of Sam?' he said and instantly regretted the fatuous remark.

Ed Goldwyn did not reply. He just inflated one plump cheek in dour acknowledgement. Somehow, his weary disillusioned manner conveyed that he had heard the dumb crack before, more than once – that, in fact, he had heard most things before.

'Ed was transferred to this department from the FBI on temporary assignment. He's a specialist in tax evasion and fraud,' said Rosenfeld casually. His sharp eyes noted Edgar's uneasy glance move from Ed Goldwyn's impassive face to the gun he carried in a holster under his left arm. It was a 'three-five-seven'. Edgar knew a little about guns. You didn't see too many three-five-sevens in the oil business.

He felt shocked, disoriented, as if the grab of a crane had descended on him without warning, lifting him out of his own safe familiar territory and dumping him in hell. Surely this brown, featureless, sinister room was some place in hell.

He shifted on his chair and tried to look unconcerned.

'This is a private discussion, as I explained,' said Rosenfeld. 'There's nothing official about it and it's not for the record.'

'Sure,' said Edgar. Just a cosy fireside chat between friends. He could have thought of better places – better company, too.

Bob Rosenfeld turned up the sleeves of his white shirt, one by one, slowly and carefully, to just below the elbows. Like an old soldier would. He did not roll them; he folded them and, when he had finished, he lined them up and patted them. Considering the wrinkled mess his shirt was in, the compulsive care with which he fussed it was ludicrous. Then he removed his glasses and rubbed his eyes. For a moment, he looked almost vulnerable.

Edgar was disturbed by the brooding presence in the

corner. He kept glancing across at Ed Goldwyn, trying to catch him out. He had the impression that the man was studying him, analysing his reactions, but Goldwyn always seemed to be looking straight ahead at the wall behind Edgar. The heavy face was grubby, not exactly unshaven, but messy. From time to time, he moved his bulk on the chair, crossing or uncrossing his short legs. He had remarkably neat little ankles, Edgar noticed.

'The company you work for, King Brothers. It's under investigation. That's no secret. You probably knew already.'

'What for?' said Edgar. A Bostonian. Like the Brits, Bostonians made him feel inferior.

Rosenfeld hesitated. 'We have a way to go before we frame charges, but I guess you could say fraud and tax evasion – for starters.' He was watching Edgar carefully. The absence of any surprise was, he thought, significant. 'I guess you know that when this office is involved, it's no bullshit. We may not have all the evidence we need right now, but we'll get it. We'll get a conviction, too. That you can be sure of.'

Ed Goldwyn's chair creaked as he heaved one leg over the other. He looked as though his mother had just died.

'We're talking to a few guys. Some in King Brothers, some in other companies. We're questioning just about everyone who ever did business with you people. We're getting good cooperation,' said Rosenfeld, stressing the word. He paused to give Edgar time to think.

Cooperation. So that was what they wanted. They needed him to put Mort and Ruby in the pen. Well, that suited him just fine. It meant, of course, that Rosenfeld was lying. He had no evidence and no hope of getting it – not enough for a conviction, anyway. Melvin Craig was a hard-nosed sonofabitch and if he had decided not to cooperate, then the Feds had no case.

'We're getting so much information, we're having a real hard time processing it all. Strictly between you and I . . .'

Edgar winced. He considered himself Phi Beta Kappa in grammar, if nothing else. Rosenfeld caught the look and stumbled. For a moment, he lost his cool.

'Strictly between you and I,' he went on, 'you're about to see some action in the next few days. There's going to be a Federal grand jury appointed and the subpoenas will be flying around like autumn leaves. They'll be queueing up outside this office like it was Noah's Ark and the flood was coming.' He liked that. Edgar could tell. He enjoyed talking, did Rosenfeld.

Even Ed Goldwyn seemed to have appreciated Rosenfeld's turn of phrase. The pall over his head appeared to lift for a second or two.

'Meanwhile,' said Rosenfeld, 'it would be helpful to know where you stand.'

Where he stood . . . how delicately put, thought Edgar. They were offering him a deal. What kind of deal? As far as Mort was concerned, Edgar knew exactly where he stood. The guy had screwed his life up. He was responsible for everything bad that had happened to him in the last few years. In the guise of friendship, he had trapped him into joining King Brothers and then destroyed his only chance of happiness. No, Edgar was neither burdened by guilt nor tormented by doubts. If they were offering him a deal, he was ready to listen.

'Where I stand? What does that mean?'

'It means, Mr Proktor, that you're a friend of Mortimer King's. We know that.'

Then they knew more than he did.

'You've been friends for years. He's made you a millionaire many times over, hasn't he?'

Edgar did not reply. What did money have to do with anything?

'So, what we're asking you to do might not be so easy for you. We recognize that.' Rosenfeld took off his glasses again and polished them on his sleeve. He looked younger without his glasses.

'What is it exactly that you're asking me to do?' He was

being led by the nose. So what? It wasn't that big a deal. They were leading him the way he wanted to go.

'If you cooperate with us, we'll offer you immunity.'

'What's that?'

'I suggest you check it out with your lawyer. Basically what it means is that you tell us everything you know. If you do, and as long as you tell us the truth, you can't be indicted. Whatever you got up to in King Brothers, you'd be clean.'

Clean. This Bostonian lawyer with the grubby shirt and the steamy glasses could wash him clean. 'And if I don't cooperate?'

The chair in the corner creaked. Edgar flashed a glance in that direction. Ed Goldwyn was looking at the wall behind his head.

'We'll cross-examine you and, when the time comes, you'll take your chances. If you don't cooperate you run the risk of being indicted. My guess is that you'll serve a lengthy jail sentence.' Rosenfeld sat back and waited.

'I'll think about it,' said Edgar, after a while.

Rosenfeld sighed and blinked a couple of times. Then he grinned broadly. 'I appreciate it,' he said. 'You'd be doing the right thing.'

The right thing. For whom? Edgar wondered.

Rosenfeld walked Edgar to the elevator. 'I'll be in touch, Edgar,' he said. He used the first name naturally, as if there were already a bond between them. In a way, there was.

'If I accept your proposal,' said Edgar, 'would my co-operation . . . would it be kept secret? I mean, I wouldn't want it to get out that I . . .'

Rosenfeld tried to conceal his contempt. 'That's something I can't guarantee,' he said. 'You'll have to assume that the grand jury will want to question you.'

Edgar nodded uneasily. 'I'll have to think it over.'

'Don't think too long,' said Rosenfeld. 'We need to know soon.'

'I'll get back to you.'

As he rode down in the elevator, past the long, bare,

forbidding corridors of the US Attorney's Office building, he shivered.

This was hell all right.

'He's shaky,' said Rosenfeld. 'He wants to save his skin and be a goddam hero, too.'

'Why do we need Edgar?' said Goldwyn.

'We may have to lean on him. Hard. He's all we've got.'

'As far as we know, he's innocent.'

'Everyone's innocent,' said Rosenfeld, wincing. His hip was hurting.

'He seems like a nice guy.'

'Real cute.'

'I'm not kidding.'

'You going soft or something?'

'This is not the Mafia we're dealing with.'

'Ed, O'Reilly was lashing me this morning.' O'Reilly was Rosenfeld's boss. 'The Attorney General has been on to him. He wants a prosecution. He wants an example made. And quick. Someone's been playing hell with the DOE regulations.'

'Yeah! Half the oil companies in the US. The regulations are shit. They should dump them.'

'The Attorney General wants a Biggie. He doesn't care who. King Brothers would do fine.'

'Uhuh. Worth a few votes.'

'Not for us to say, Ed. Our job is to get a conviction.'

'I thought our job was to catch criminals,' said Ed Goldwyn drily.

'Once we start subpoenaing records we'll have all the evidence we need.'

'I wouldn't be so sure,' said Goldwyn. 'Those guys are smart. If they do have anything to hide, they'll clean up their records.'

'They have plenty to hide.'

'You know that do you, Bob?'

'Sure I know it. And I'll prove it.'

Ed Goldwyn shook his head gloomily. He was not so

sure. Not so ambitious either. Not so single-minded. Not so hungry. He sighed.

'Let's just say, for the moment, that you're right. You think that their records in the US will help us?'

'No.'

'Well, I'll tell you. If we go after their Swiss records, the Swiss government will block us.'

Bob Rosenfeld grinned. 'That's right, Ed. That's why we're going to need Edgar.'

*   *   *

Sarah gazed dreamily at the Shabbath candles. Friday evening was for her the highlight of the week, the time she most enjoyed being a wife and a mother. It was a total vindication of her humdrum life.

She beamed at her family, poured out her love with the chicken matzoball soup and heaped her approval on their plates with ample portions of roast chicken, corned beef, potato latkes, sweet carrots and hemischer cucumbers.

Ruby was looking, in his vague way, at Ruth.

'I'm seventeen, Pop. My name's Ruth,' she reminded him.

'I know,' said Ruby patiently.

'It's a joke,' said Ruth.

'I know it's a joke,' said Ruby.

Sarah beamed at the candles for a while and they beamed back at her. She had heard it all before. 'When I think,' she told Ruby adoringly, 'what you used to be and what you are now.'

'None of us is getting any younger,' said Saul. 'He can't help it.'

'Shut your face,' said Ruby.

'How old were you when you met Dad?' asked Ruth.

'Seventeen,' said Sarah. 'I was just seventeen.'

'When I'm eighteen,' said Ruth, 'I'll be married.'

'With three kids,' said Saul.

'You were on the shelf,' said Ruby.

489

'How can a girl be on the shelf at seventeen?' said Sarah sharply.

Ruby smiled. 'I remember in Anatolia, in the south of Turkey, I saw these empty bottles on the roof of a house in a small village. They were sitting up there, next to the chimney stack. You know why?'

'Why?'

'Every bottle signified that a girl in the house had reached marriageable age. The parents were advertising – looking for husbands.'

'That's disgusting,' said Ruth, horrified.

'So primitive,' Sarah said.

'Sure it's primitive,' said Ruby. 'That's how it is in Anatolia. And you know what? That's how it is in most places – how it was with you. I remember it clearly. Your father put a bottle on the roof.'

'What are you talking about?' said Sarah. 'I would have died!'

'Your parents invited the approved suitors round for tea on Sunday and they all took a good long look.'

'Forget it,' said Ruth. 'You're not going to do that to me. Besides, I hate tea.'

'For you we'll serve gin,' said Saul.

'That was different,' said Sarah.

'I got more than a look. You let me touch your knee under the table.'

'Ruby!' Sarah was outraged. 'I did not!'

'You remember we used to sit out in the yard and talk?' said Ruby.

'What did you talk about?' said Ruth.

'Sex,' said Saul. 'What else would they talk about?' He recognized a familiar look in Ruby's eye. 'Just joking,' he said hastily.

Sarah was embarrassed. 'We never talked about ... things like that in those days. Your father was always a perfect gentleman.'

'How dull,' said Ruth. 'So, what did you talk about?'

'He would tell me things he was studying in the Talmud.

490

Sometimes we talked politics and life and, oh, I don't know what else. He wasn't like the other boys. He was different.'

'Sounds like it,' said Saul.

'Do you remember what you said when you asked me to marry you?' Sarah was dreaming into the candles again.

Ruby shook his head. It was another world, another life. It might have been his. It might have been someone else's. He remembered only bits here and there, like snatches of an old song.

'I remember, if you don't,' said Sarah. 'You said you loved me and you would try to make me a good husband, but you couldn't offer me any great material comfort. You said material things weren't important to you, and if what I wanted was a rich husband I should marry someone else because you would never make any money. That's what you said.'

'That was very romantic, Pop,' said Ruth.

'Did I say that?' said Ruby.

Sarah nodded. 'That's what you said.'

Ruby rubbed his eyes. It was hard to remember – not just the words – but the young man who had spoken them.

*　　*　　*

On Maxwell Parkes's recommendation, Mort planned to host regular cocktail parties at the Fifth Avenue apartment, with Julie playing the role he most valued: the elegant, beautiful, and always charming hostess and devoted wife.

'I'm sorry to have to ask you,' said Mort when he first mentioned the idea.

'I'll do it,' said Julie, without enthusiasm. 'If you want me to, I'll do it.'

'I want you to.'

'But why? What's it all for?'

'It was Maxwell's idea. He wants me to join the right clubs. He says it will help.'

'Help launch your political career, you mean,' she said.

'Business, political, whatever.'

'You're not being honest with me.'

'I didn't know how you felt about my ... political aspirations.'

'What should I feel? I thought you were a businessman. Don't you get enough kicks being the most successful tycoon around? What did *Fortune* magazine say? "Today, the tenth richest man in the United States ... tomorrow the richest".'

'It's the most natural thing in the world,' he said. 'I've taken a lot out. Now I'd like to put some of it back.'

Julie laughed. 'You're putting me on. This is me – Julie. You're not barnstorming me. Tell me what's really going on in that brilliant brain of yours – apart from flashing dollar signs.'

'I don't know,' he said. 'Being a billionaire is great, but I guess I want something more out of life than money.'

'Like what?'

'Call it respect,' he said.

Julie looked astonished. 'You don't have respect? Who doesn't respect you?'

'It doesn't matter,' he said lightly. 'I want to be something more than an oil trader. I want to go into politics. I won't lie to you. It's going to take time – maybe years – before I'm even accepted as a prospective candidate and it's going to be hard work, especially for you.'

'You quitting King Brothers?'

'Not in the foreseeable future,' he said. 'I need the company. I need its power. I need its image.' The green eyes glowed with excitement.

So that was it. For him the company was a means to an end. How to understand the man she had married? She tried to push her mind to its utmost limits in an effort to get inside his head but, despite her clear intelligence, despite all those years they had spent together, she was still bewildered. His motives were shadowed, subterranean, mysterious to her.

'Where does it end?'

'When they put me in a box,' said Mort.

'I hear there's trouble.'

'It's nothing. Believe me,' he assured her. His face was calm and confident. She felt relieved.

'We need to try and remember why we got married,' she said.

He was touched. He remembered how vibrant and carefree she was when they first met. He had envied her. She had lost all that, but, in his eyes, she had become infinitely more fascinating: a free spirit, if no longer a carefree one.

'I never forgot,' he said and touched her face gently with his hand.

'I'll do what you want,' she said. 'I'm not crazy about it, but I'll do it. Just be honest with me.'

'I will,' he promised, conscious that he had lied to her yet again. The company could be in big trouble.

'Tell me,' she said, 'what are these clubs it's so important to join?'

'There's the Century on Forty-Third. They don't take women members, though.'

'Great,' said Julie. 'I love it.'

'Then there's the University on Fifty-Fourth and Fifth – a whole bunch of important people are members there. They take a very limited number of Jews.'

'Sounds terrific,' said Julie. 'And this is the road to the White House. I'm learning something.'

'On the other hand, I'm also applying to the Harmonie on Sixtieth. That's very German-Jewish – the best people – our sort of crowd.'

'Do they take Wasps?'

Mort laughed. 'I doubt Wasps would want to join.'

'Maybe the Jews should learn a lesson from that,' she said.

'I guess you're right,' said Mort. It felt good to be communicating again. He had forgotten how intelligent his wife was.

'So, this bunch of racists are going to help you win votes.'

'I wouldn't say they were racists. They're just picky.'
'So was Hitler,' said Julie.

*   *   *

The appointment with Bob Rosenfeld was at two thirty. Edgar had hardly slept. He had waited a long time to settle his score with Mort, but now that it came right down to it, now that he had the opportunity to hit him where it would hurt most, he was having second thoughts.

He was not sure he could go through with it. Maybe he could live with his own conscience, but if the whole world knew that Edgar Proktor had taken immunity and betrayed his friends . . . what then? Rosenfeld had said if he didn't cooperate, would be indicted. Edgar doubted that. The planning and execution of the Domestic scam had been Mort's and Ruby's. Edgar had been an employee of the company, acting on instructions. He could probably convince a grand jury that he had not understood the implications of the scheme.

A grand jury he could convince – but not himself. Not Edgar Proktor. He had known what was going on. He had always known. So had a lot of guys in the office. How could he send someone to the pen for doing what he himself had done? He had to talk to Mort. They hadn't talked in a long time, not like they used to. Mort would know what to do. He always did.

He walked south through Central Park. He would be late at the office, but he needed to clear his head. It was a chilly November morning. A few tangled clouds rushed across the sky, chased by a brisk north wind. The sunlight was pale, almost white. The effect was strange, eerie, like the end of the world, like a day out of time.

The breeze tumbled the autumn leaves around him as he walked. He had the feeling they were jostling him, chuckling drily as if they knew something he didn't. The debris of yet another year, he thought . . . just millions of dead leaves.

494

He wandered out of the park and up the steps of the Plaza Hotel.

'What is it, Edgar? Where are you?'

'The Plaza.'

'What the hell for?' Mort snapped. He was busy. He was always busy – under most pressure first thing in the morning.

'I need to talk to you, Mort.'

'Hang on . . .' The line went dead as he took another call. Edgar waited, twisting the cord round his finger.

'Yeah?' Mort was back on the line. 'Oh, it's you, Edgar.'

'I need to talk to you.'

'Talk. I'm listening.'

'I can't talk on the phone – I want to see you.'

'When?'

'Right now.'

'Is it important?' He could hear Mort dictating a telex to his secretary.

'It's personal,' said Edgar.

'Oh.' More dictation. 'What did you say it was?'

'Personal,' Edgar said desperately.

'Hang on . . .' Mort was talking on another phone with his hand only half over the mouthpiece . . . Something about 'too many "heavy ends"' in the crude . . . he couldn't 'pay the price'. It would have to be 'a dollar less'.

'Sorry, Edgar, it's like a madhouse here. What was it you wanted? Personal, you said?'

The way he said 'personal' made it sound like it was an intrusion. 'Personal' didn't pay the overheads. 'Personal' was like sinking a dry bore hole. 'Personal' was a goddam waste of his time.

'Edgar?'

Edgar didn't reply. After all these years, what the hell could he say anyway? Why had Mort driven Kate away? Why had he screwed up his life?

'Edgar? You there? Can this wait? I have to take a call.' Mort sounded harassed.

495

'I just phoned you to say have a nice day,' said Edgar. It had waited too long already. It could wait some more.

'Edgar, is something wrong? You OK?'

'I'm just fine.'

'You sure it can wait?'

'Take your call,' said Edgar. 'First things first.'

He hung up and stood there a moment or two, twisting the cord. He walked away, stopped, and came back again. He picked up the phone and felt in his pocket for a quarter. He was out of change. That did it. It was how all the biggest decisions were made, he reflected ironically. He would have phoned Mort back, but he was out of change.

The Plaza bar was one of his favourites. The guy behind the bar knew him well. What barman in town didn't?

Thirty minutes later, he paid the check and walked out. He had an appointment to keep.

Bob Rosenfeld was alone. That was the way he had planned it. Ed Goldwyn would only appear this time around if they had to lean on Edgar.

Nevertheless, for Edgar, the empty chair in the corner was a presence almost as oppressive as Ed Goldwyn's.

'I see the Giants won again,' said Rosenfeld.

'Wouldn't you know,' said Edgar.

Rosenfeld shuffled papers.

'The Jets are coming up.'

Edgar nodded. 'Seems like it.'

Rosenfeld crossed his arms on the desk and examined his sleeves. They were folded again, exactly parallel, each two inches below the elbow. It was the only neat thing about him.

'They've been playing like a new team this season,' he said.

'They sure have,' said Edgar. 'Like a new team.'

'Of course, the coach deserves a lot of the credit,' said Bob Rosenfeld.

'I decided to take immunity,' said Edgar.

Rosenfeld eased his hip and sat back in his chair. 'That's a courageous thing to do,' he said.

Such a facile judgement to make. What was courageous about it? Edgar wondered. 'You think so?' He really wanted to know.

Rosenfeld's glasses glowed. 'Never doubt it,' he said. 'It couldn't have been an easy choice for you to make. Believe me, I know that. I respect you for it.'

Well, that was great. That was something he could always console himself with; the thought that, however much he despised himself, whatever kind of a treacherous creep his friends would judge him to be, he would still have earned the respect of an Assistant United States Attorney. That should help him sleep nights.

'It's the right thing – it's the public-spirited thing to do,' said Rosenfeld.

The right thing. He never knew that. Would you believe? Public spirited. Saving your own skin was public-spirited. Stabbing your partner in the back was public-spirited. He wondered how many public-spirited things Bob Rosenfeld had done to get to be a US Assistant Attorney – and how many times he would have to do 'the right thing' to get wherever it was he wanted to go from here.

'There's one condition,' said Edgar.

Bob Rosenfeld stiffened. He didn't like conditions. In his experience, that one little condition was usually the impossible one, the rock that the deal foundered on.

'What's that?'

'You have to keep it quiet. I'll tell you everything I know, but no grand jury. I won't testify. I won't sign anything unless you promise me that.'

It was the rock all right. Rosenfeld did not have the power to make a deal like that. No one did. If Edgar were subpoenaed, he'd have to testify, not just to the grand jury, but to the court at any trial.

He picked up the phone. In a minute, Ed Goldwyn appeared. He went straight to the corner chair, sat down and crossed his legs.

'Edgar's ready to sign an immunity agreement,' said Rosenfeld.

Ed Goldwyn stared at the wall.

'He has one condition. We have to keep him away from the grand jury. He doesn't want anyone to know he's cooperating with us.'

Ed Goldwyn folded his lips. Then his legs. He was giving nothing away.

'In view of the exceptional importance of Edgar's testimony,' said Rosenfeld carefully, 'I'd like to help him.'

Ed Goldwyn said nothing.

'I'd like to help him,' Rosenfeld repeated.

Goldwyn was still staring at the wall behind Edgar's head.

Rosenfeld sat up straight. Old soldier. Edgar and Ed Goldwyn looked at him.

'Of course,' he said, 'I'd need to talk to my boss. But I happen to know he feels strongly about this case. He wants those guys inside.'

'I'd like it in writing,' said Edgar.

'I'm afraid that's not possible,' Rosenfeld said. 'This will have to be unofficial. But you could trust my boss.'

Edgar looked at Goldwyn. 'You agree?'

Ed Goldwyn turned his face towards him. It was weird. It was the first time the two men had ever made eye contact.

'I agree you could trust his boss,' he said carefully.

Edgar nodded. It was as much as he could get. He knew that. If he did not have to appear before the grand jury, then Mort would never find out.

And that was all that mattered.

He moved his eyes over the document Rosenfeld handed him; but his brain was not absorbing it.

'Read it carefully,' said Rosenfeld.

'I read it.'

'You want your lawyer to read it?'

'I don't need a lawyer.'

'It's important you understand what you're doing.'

498

So that's what lawyers were for. Edgar was learning a whole lot today. It was not psychiatrists or priests who helped you understand. It was lawyers.

He signed the agreement and handed it back to Rosenfeld.

He rode down in the elevator wondering where he could find him – this lawyer who could help him understand why the hell he was destroying his life.

Bob Rosenfeld was reflecting on what the successful prosecution of the case would do for him and his career. Star status might be a mixed blessing, but he thought he could handle it.

He straightened the files on his desk.

'You must want those guys real bad,' said Ed Goldwyn.

'Mort and Ruby. Yes, I do.' They might have been his friends the way he talked about them. There was a special intimacy, a unique bond between the hunter and his prey.

'Don't let it get too personal.'

'I won't,' said Rosenfeld. He was still moving files around his desk. He looked as though he had something to say. Goldwyn waited, but Rosenfeld said nothing.

At the door, Goldwyn turned. 'You think he has the impression that we made him a promise? That we have some kind of a deal?'

'I don't deal in impressions,' said Rosenfeld. 'All I know is that without that guy we have no case.'

'He doesn't think. . . ?'

'How could he? I never made any promises. I told him I'd talk to my boss.'

Ed Goldwyn inflated his cheek rapidly a few times. 'I'll look forward to that,' he said drily.

Matthew Rowland's plump, unctuous tones boomed through the speaker on Mort's desk.

'I see you took my advice. Congratulations.'

'What are you talking about?' said Mort, not too gently.

499

'Rosenfeld made a big play with Melvin Craig. I think he offered him a huge reduction of his sentence – to less than a year. Craig told him to stick it.'

'Melvin's a pigheaded guy. He likes to buck the system. Nothing he likes better.'

'Except maybe money,' said Rowland, malicious, insinuating.

'What is that supposed to mean?'

'Aw, come on, Mort. You're talking to your lawyer. This is privileged. Still, the phone could be bugged, so maybe you're right. The less said the better.'

The furrow appeared in Mort's forehead. He was angry. 'I don't give a damn if the whole of the Justice Department is listening in. I don't bribe and I don't appreciate your snide comments.'

'I guess I jumped to conclusions,' Rowland said humbly.

'I guess you did,' said Mort and slammed the phone in its cradle.

There were questions Ruby wanted to ask, but this was not the time.

'He's the only man who could cause us a real problem with the Feds.'

'Right.'

'I hear this Rosenfeld is taking an interest in us.'

'Let him.'

'Funny thing. He's a member of my congregation.'

'Those who pray together stay together,' said Mort.

Ruby chuckled. 'Seems like a nice kind of guy.'

'I'll bet he's a dreamboat,' said Mort.

'You ever think of morality?' Ruby said.

'Morality?'

'Some of the things we've done. Heavy stuff.'

'Sometimes. Mostly I think about staying out of jail. What do you think about?'

'I try not to,' said Ruby.

★　　★　　★

'I'll be honest with you, Mr King. We haven't made too much progress. We're still sure it was a professional hit. Aside from that, we have no real leads.'

There was something about a cop in plain clothes, thought Mort. He wore them as if they were rented for the occasion. He looked uncomfortable. Maybe it was Mort's huge office that unnerved him. What was it Edgar called it? Megaspace. It amused Mort to see the lieutenant shifting uneasily in the padded shoulders of his badly fitting jacket, but he wished the man would go away and be uncomfortable somewhere else.

'Except maybe one.' The lieutenant stopped fidgeting for a moment and considered Mort, sitting there on the other side of his gigantic glass-topped desk. Even in the lieutenant's considerable experience, he had never seen a desk like it.

'Is that glass, Mr King?' he enquired with almost child-like naivety.

Mort started. The question was so unexpected. He followed the lieutenant's glance. 'The desk top? Sure it's glass.'

'Must be fragile.'

Mort smiled. 'Not at all. It's tough.' He thumped the desk top with his clenched fist to demonstrate. 'Indestructible,' he boasted.

'Indestructible,' said the lieutenant. 'You don't say!' He looked impressed. 'Still,' he said dubiously, 'it is glass.'

Mort was irritated. 'No one's going to beat it with a hammer.'

The lieutenant considered the remark. 'You never know,' he said and grinned.

'You mentioned that you might have a lead,' said Mort impatiently.

'The man who shielded you. Remember? The one who left without giving his name.'

'I remember,' said Mort. 'What about him?'

'We think we know who he is,' said the lieutenant. He was watching Mort carefully. 'We think his name is Jack Greenberg.'

Mort sat there, staring at the desk top as if, indeed, the lieutenant had hit it with a hammer and it had shattered into a thousand pieces. 'That's impossible.'

'I'd be interested to know why you say that, Mr King,' said the lieutenant. He wasn't looking uncomfortable any more. Or naive.

Mort shrugged. 'It's just impossible, that's all.'

'Wasn't he an associate of yours at the Oil Corporation? A friend?'

'An associate,' said Mort. 'Why would Jack Greenberg risk his life to save mine?'

'You tell me,' said the lieutenant.

'I came to see Jack,' said Mort.

'What for?' Rachel stood at the front door of her apartment, barring his entrance. This was not the plump, silly teenager he had once known, but a slim, attractive young woman, erect, assured – formidable even – a lioness protecting her cub.

'He doesn't want to see you. Leave us alone.'

'Rachel,' said Mort quietly, 'I want to talk. Just talk, that's all.'

'What is there to talk about?'

'Why don't you ask Jack that?'

She stared at him coolly for a few moments, trying to read the expression in his eyes. He returned her gaze without hostility. She must have found his manner reassuring, because she stepped aside without a word, not inviting, but allowing him on sufferance to enter. 'Wait in the library. I'll tell Jack you're here.'

As he opened the library door, he could hear voices: Jack's loud, high-pitched and angry, Rachel's relaxed but insistent. Mort closed the door behind him, shutting out the sound of the argument. It was a man's room or, perhaps, an interior decorator's conception of a man's room: clubby, wood-panelled walls, shelves crammed tight with books, mostly leather-bound – more for show than use, thought Mort – heavy Regency-style chairs upholstered in bottle-green leather, concealed ceiling lights and, in one corner of the room, a large mahogany partners' desk with the obligatory French bouillotte lamp. Everything more decorative than functional.

Mort guessed that this was all Rachel's doing – creating the right image for Jack, who had neither the taste to choose nor the judgement to know what he wanted.

Jack entered the room almost sheepishly. Without acknowledging Mort, he moved across to the bar and stood there a moment or two in silence with his back to the other man.

'Bourbon?'

'Right.'

'You got it.'

Jack handed him the drink.

'You remember,' said Mort.

'A lot of things,' said Jack. 'I remember a lot of things.'

They sipped their drinks in silence. Jack was looking everywhere but at Mort. His eyes flicked uneasily from side to side. He had nothing to say and yet, as so often in Mort's company, he felt impelled to speak, being acutely aware that silence often betrayed a man's guilty thoughts more eloquently than words. He hoped Mort had not noticed his hands shaking as he held his glass.

'What brings you here?'

Mort crossed the room to the bar. It was a small thing in itself, but it aggravated Jack. It was not just that Mort was making himself at home in another man's house; it was as if he really were at home. There was something about the assurance, the complete unselfconsciousness of the gesture, that placed it beyond criticism, beyond comment.

Why don't I say something, thought Jack petulantly. It's my goddam bar. My bar, my library, my house.

But it was Mort's world. That was the impression the bastard always succeeded in conveying.

'I think you know,' said Mort.

Jack had to put down his drink and clasp his hands

503

together to control them, so violently were they shaking. 'How should I know?'

Mort studied him gravely. 'What's bugging you, Jack?'

'I don't know what you're talking about.'

'Look at you. You're twitching. Is it me?'

'It's not you,' said Jack. 'I have a fever.' It was a pathetically obvious lie.

'I always thought you hated me. I never understood why.' Mort sounded dispassionate, but curious.

No. Mort would never understand and he could never explain. You didn't hate people for what they did to you. You hated them for what you did to them.

Jack's hands were shaking a little less now. The alcohol was taking effect.

'I came here to thank you.'

'What the hell for?'

'Jesus, man, you know what for,' said Mort patiently. 'For saving my life.'

Jack's face was a comic caricature of astonishment.

'I don't know how you happened to be there, but you stood between me and that guy with the gun. If you hadn't, I wouldn't be around now.' Mort was embarrassed. 'I guess you saved my life,' he repeated lamely.

Jack sat down heavily in the nearest armchair and cradled his drink in his two hands. What a goddam crazy world it was. To be thanked for saving his life by the man you had tried to kill. Oh, it was true enough. In the end, he had wanted to stop the killing, but he had not stood between Mort and the killer. He wasn't crazy. The hit man had seen him after the first shot and taken fright. Maybe he had recognized him. How, he had no idea since they had never met, but these guys had a way of knowing who they were working for.

'Why did you just disappear? Why didn't you ever say anything?'

'How did you know I was there?'

'The police. They found out somehow. I don't know how. They call you?'

504

'They called,' said Jack nervously. 'Asked me some questions. I wondered why.'

'I guess they hoped you might be able to identify the hit man,' said Mort.

'Hit man? How do they know it was a hit man?' His voice was edged with hysteria.

'They don't – they're guessing. I have the impression they know nothing.'

For a moment, the thought flashed through Mort's mind that Jack looked relieved, but he dismissed it as imagination.

'It was dark,' said Jack. 'I saw a man with a gun – that's all.'

'I was wrong about you,' said Mort. 'I came to apologize.'

Jack poured himself another drink. Strange. It was easier to take Mort's contempt than his gratitude. Approval was difficult to stomach – from him or from Edmund Meyer. The two men were very alike. They both patronized the world.

Mort held out his hand and Jack took it, awkwardly.

'If there's anything I can do,' said Mort, 'let me know.'

Jack tried to smile.

'Lucky for me you happened to be around,' said Mort.

It didn't sound like he wanted an answer, but it was the second time he had dropped the hint. It was a way Mort had of asking questions and Jack recognized it as such. 'I had a row with E.M. the week before,' he explained. 'I was coming to see you about a job. But then I got to thinking how you'd react if I asked you for one.'

Mort left a pointed silence.

'That's what I thought you'd say,' said Jack.

Rachel had never felt comfortable with Mort, partly because she sensed his uneasiness in the presence of women, partly because she knew only too well that he had little respect for Jack.

But, in spite of her misgivings, her deep distrust of Mort, she could not help but admire him. To her surprise, she

505

was even beginning to recognize in herself some of those same qualities that set him apart from the norm: tenacity, self-confidence and, above all, a kind of inner strength that drew other men to him.

There was, nevertheless, a profound difference in their natures. Mort despised weakness, afraid perhaps of some real or imagined weakness in himself, whereas she not only accepted it but found it compellingly attractive. If she had not, she would never have been drawn to Jack. He depended on her resoluteness, she on his vulnerability.

'What did he want?'

Jack lied. 'He wants me to join him, to leave the Oil Corporation.'

'Mortimer King wants you to work for him?'

'Not to work for him. To join him,' said Jack, 'be his partner.' He mixed another martini.

'You've had enough.'

'My last,' he said.

'What did you say?'

'Turned him down, of course. Flat. You think I'd ever leave the old man?'

'It might not be such a bad idea,' said Rachel. She could imagine how it must feel to work for your father-in-law.

'The old man's OK. We understand each other. He thinks he's God Almighty. I think he's a sleazebag.'

'Jack!' Rachel was first shocked, then angry.

'Sorry, honey. I'm a little drunk.' He often was, these days.

'How can you talk like that when he's so good to you?'

'Sure he is,' said Jack. 'He's all heart.'

Jack hated E.M. only marginally less than Mort. E.M. played this role – and everyone thought it was genuine, everyone except Jack – the benevolent boss of the Oil Corporation, all probity and sanctity, the archetypal father figure, the scrupulous, warm-hearted gentleman, beloved by his employees, respected by the industry. What was it he was always saying to the press? 'I tell my young people not to do anything in business that I wouldn't do.' Well, that left them plenty of goddam scope. What was the other piece of vomit? 'Anyone who works for me is family. There are no employees in my office – only sons and daughters.' Jesus! Hard to understand how people could read that shit and believe it. They actually believed that E.M. was the patriarch of the oil business, and not the condescending, slave-driving scumbag Jack had worked for since he was a kid fresh out of college. God, he had been so innocent in those days.

'I love him,' he said lightly. 'And you know what I really dig most about him? He's never wrong. Isn't that something? Can you imagine how it feels, never to be wrong? Me, I'm wrong now and then, but E.M., never.'

'That's not funny, Jack.' She went to the bar and locked it, taking the key.

'It's not meant to be,' he said. 'It's tragic.'

'So why don't you join Mort?'

'Why don't I join Mort? . . . I'll tell you why I don't join Mort.' Jack finished off the dregs of his martini. 'Because he's a bigger shit than your dear father, if that's possible. Because the next time somebody tries to kill him, they'll probably make a better job of it. And because, my darling wife, he wouldn't have me if I worked for free.'

'You said he offered you a job.'

Jack grinned boyishly and a touch shame-faced. 'Not in this life,' he said.

'You still think it was Mort who had you beaten up, don't you?'

'An eye for an eye,' Jack intoned. 'A mouth full of teeth for a tooth.'

Rachel had no idea what he was talking about, but then, nor did he. It was the drink talking, wasn't it?

Ruby sat on the Bimah of the synagogue. He was feeling pleased with life. Very pleased. It was his first morning in this place of honour and already he felt at home; he had that reassuring sense that this was where he belonged. Up here – Ruby on one side of the Ark of the Covenant, the rabbi on the other – looking down on the congregation, almost all of them relatives, friends or acquaintances, it was difficult not to feel special and apart. Of course, he told himself, he was still the same old Ruby. Nothing could, nothing would ever change that. So they had elected him to the Board of Trustees. That didn't make him any different from all those people down there . . . not really . . . well, perhaps, just a little. Was there ever a man so ruthlessly single-minded in business and, at the same time, so compassionately involved in the community? So orthodox in his religious views and so liberal in his outlook? Talmudic scholar and student of the world? Why not admit it to himself? Why not enjoy it? He was special. All these years he had sold himself short, working backstage, cowering in the wings, leaving it to others – less talented and infinitely less qualified – to take all the credit. Now, finally, he was tired of all that skulking, that false modesty; he was ready to step into the spotlight, to be recognized, to be acknowledged for what he truly was, someone exceptional – tycoon, scholar, philanthropist. Sure it felt good. And why not? He had worked hard enough for it. He shifted around. The chair – more like a throne than a chair – was uncomfortably hard. Mort had once said that you paid a price for success. He had not warned him it would hurt his ass.

After the service, there was a reception for Ruby and Sarah in the communal hall adjoining the shul. They shook hands with two or three hundred people while Ruby chuckled and cracked jokes incessantly. Suddenly, in front of him, was a familiar face – Bob Rosenfeld, Assistant United States Attorney.

Rosenfeld introduced his son Daniel. 'My wife you already met. We have to go. I just wanted to wish you mazeltov.'

'Stay,' Ruby urged. 'Have a drink. It's a cold day.'

Rosenfeld hesitated and then nodded. 'Thanks, I will.' He disappeared into the crowd with his wife.

Daniel was tall, taller than his father. His features were

intelligent, lively and sharp like his father's, but softened by an abundance of wavy black hair. He wore heavy black-rimmed glasses intended to make him look older than his twenty-one years.

'Quite a crowd,' he said to Ruth.

'Yes.'

'Yes,' said Daniel. He pushed his glasses down on his face a little and back up again on the bridge of his nose. He dug his hands into his trouser pockets and nodded, first with his head, then with his neck and shoulders as well. He couldn't stop. Ruth started to giggle.

'I'm sorry,' she said. 'I didn't mean to laugh.'

'That's OK,' he said. 'You can laugh. You laugh real nice,' he added shyly.

'I have to go,' she said, not moving.

'Could I see you again?' he said quickly, wondering, as he said it, where the courage had come from.

'Sure,' she said. 'I'm here every Shabbath.'

'I mean . . .'

'You mean like a date?' she said.

'Yes.'

She made a face. 'I don't think my father would approve.' She looked down at her shoes. 'He's kind of old-fashioned about things like that.'

'How do you meet boys then?'

'I don't,' said Ruth.

'But then . . . what I mean is . . . how will you ever. . . ?'

Ruth looked embarrassed. 'My father – I guess he'll introduce me to someone.'

Daniel was outraged. 'You've got to be kidding! What if you don't like the guy?'

'I'm sure I will,' she said. 'Of course, if I really hate him . . .'

'What then?' Daniel looked concerned.

'Then I'll give you a call,' said Ruth and rushed away.

'See you next week,' he shouted after her.

But he couldn't wait that long. He was an enterprising young man and he soon found out that Ruth spent two or

509

three afternoons a week in the New York Public Library on Forty-Second and Fifth, studying for her first-year college exams.

He sneaked into the library and sat down opposite her, pretending to read. After a while, she looked up and saw him.

'What are you doing here?' she whispered fiercely.

'I'm reading,' he said.

'Then go read somewhere else,' she said crossly.

'I like it here,' said Daniel and returned to his book.

A lady with a pince-nez shushed them.

Ruth found his presence disturbing. It was impossible to study while he was sitting there.

'This is ridiculous,' she whispered.

'I agree,' said Daniel.

'Shush!' hissed the bespectacled lady.

'Then go away,' whispered Ruth, a little louder.

'Only if you agree to go out with me,' said Daniel.

'I can't. I told you,' she said.

'Just for a coffee?'

'I don't drink coffee.'

'Tea then?'

'No.'

'How about Coke?'

'Definitely not,' she said firmly.

'Water?' he said despairingly.

They looked at each other and started to laugh. The lady waved her pince-nez and hissed like a whole colony of snakes. Daniel nodded towards the exit. Ruth hesitated, but only for a moment.

The coffee shop was neither the best nor the cleanest, but it was warm.

'It's not exactly the Four Seasons,' said Daniel.

'I don't care,' she said.

'I do.'

'Why?'

'It's our first date.'

'It's not a date.'

'Sure it is.'

'I would say you're behaving very immaturely,' said Ruth.

'I know,' said Daniel, 'but I'm cute, aren't I?'

Ruth set her face in a frown of disapproval and looked down at her Coke, but she couldn't keep it up for long. Despite herself, her lips started to twitch. In a moment, she was smiling.

'Yes,' she admitted. 'You're cute.'

'So are you,' said Daniel generously. 'And what's more, you're real pretty.'

Ruth blushed. 'What do you do?' she asked, to change the subject.

'I'm studying to be a lawyer. I'm in my fourth year. My dad's a lawyer. He's an Assistant US Attorney,' he said proudly.

'That sounds important.'

'It is, but there's no money in it. When he's made his name, I guess he'll quit and start up his own law practice, or maybe go into politics.'

'My dad's in business.'

'I know,' said Daniel. 'Everyone knows that. He's a senior partner of King Brothers. He's famous. I think that's cool.'

'He used to be a lawyer, too,' she said.

'That's what I'm going to do. When I have my law degree I'm going to get me some legal experience and then it's business for me.'

'It doesn't sound like much fun,' she said. 'No deviations, no surprises?'

'Sure there are. I wasn't expecting you,' said Daniel.

Ruth blushed. 'Look,' she said. 'We're having a Coke together. That doesn't mean we're made for each other.'

For the first time since his early teens, Daniel became a regular visitor to shul on Saturday morning. As in all

511

Orthodox Jewish communities, the men and women were separated, the men sitting downstairs where the real 'action' was and the women sitting upstairs in the gallery, where they chatted and watched with pride as their husbands and sons carried out the honoured rituals of their ancient religion.

Daniel sat next to his father, a regular attender, trying, without success, to catch Ruth's eye. He was totally convinced that no one but he and, hopefully, Ruth could possibly be aware of his clandestine glances. Unfortunately, a pillar partly obstructed his view of that part of the gallery where Ruth was sitting and the contortions of his body, the noddings of his head and the convulsions of his neck could scarcely have been missed by a single member of the congregation.

His father, a keen observer of men both by nature and profession, found his son's eruptions and upheavals amusing.

'You have a problem with your neck, Danny?' he asked solicitously.

'My neck?' said Daniel. An uncomprehending, distracted, almost demented look froze on his face for a second. He was trying to look innocent.

'Why do we have to sit so far back?' he asked his father abruptly.

'Where would you like to sit?'

'Anywhere. Anywhere we can see – see better that is.'

'See what better?' said Bob Rosenfeld.

Again the look of panic.

'See what? Uh . . . whatever there is to see.'

'You mean the Bimah?'

'Right. The Bimah,' said Daniel, thankfully grasping the solution to his problem.

'I'll see what I can do,' said Bob Rosenfeld. 'It sure would be nice to get a better view of the – uh – Bimah.'

'Thanks, Dad,' said Daniel gratefully. It was a real mystery to him how his father could call himself an Assistant US Attorney and still be so gullible.

At the end of the service, Daniel thrust a note at Ruth with a convulsive spasm of his hand, giving the gesture the appearance of a major espionage operation. He might have been handing over the comprehensive technical data of the United States Strategic Defence Initiative for the next ten years. A dozen pairs of eyes were irresistibly drawn to the clumsy 'drop' and a dozen faces turned away, smiling. Daniel assumed his demented expression and walked away, convinced of his own cleverness. Sarah, who had naturally seen everything, thought he was cute and said so.

'He's a nurd,' said Ruth, acutely embarrassed. 'Totally immature.'

'Yes, dear,' said Sarah who had not realized until then that her daughter was interested. She made a mental note to discuss the boy with Ruby.

'What's so important that you had to see me urgently?'

Daniel hesitated. 'It's kind of tough to say.'

She wondered what was coming. It seemed too early in their relationship for anything serious and, anyway, she would not know how to handle a 'declaration'. She was not ready for it.

'It's about your dad,' he said – the last thing she had expected him to say.

'My dad?'

'I don't know how to say this,' said Daniel, 'but I hear he's in some kind of trouble. I don't know what exactly, but it's something to do with King Brothers. They have problems.' Afraid to look at her, he stared earnestly at his coffee.

'I can't believe what I'm hearing. My dad is a very successful and respected businessman. How can he have problems? He's on top of the world.'

'He's being investigated,' said Daniel in a rush of words.

Ruth's face was suddenly pale and strained. Her blue eyes appeared huge in her face. 'You're out of your mind. Who's investigating him?'

513

'My father.' Daniel looked up for the first time. He took off his glasses and laid them on the table beside his coffee. She thought again how ridiculously young he looked without them, like a teenager. But his eyes, as he looked at her now, were not the eyes of an adolescent. They were the eyes of a man.

'Why are you telling me all this bullshit?' she asked angrily.

'I'm sorry if I'm upsetting you, Ruth, but I had to say something. I don't give a damn about any screwball investigation, but it's my dad and yours and I don't want it to affect us. I mean if anything should happen . . . oh hell, you know what I mean . . .' he ended lamely.

'I don't give a damn either,' said Ruth. 'It's none of your business what my dad is, or what he does.' She stood up. 'I tried to be kind to you, Daniel. You seemed like a nice guy, but you're really not. You're a pompous asshole.'

'Thanks,' said Daniel wearily and watched with hurt eyes as she ran out of the coffee shop.

*   *   *

The bickering at the Dolder meeting of December '82 started early on.

'Did they ever find out who tried to kill you?' said Jeffrey.

'What's the big deal?' said Mort. 'It's a private matter. How does it affect you?'

Jeffrey bridled. 'Someone tries to kill the president of the company and it's a private matter,' he said with heavy irony.

'The chairman,' Ruby corrected him.

'Who gives a shit?' said Jeffrey.

'I do,' said Ruby. 'I'm the president.'

'Ruby, old pal,' said Jeffrey, 'some things aren't funny. The crucifixion wasn't. The holocaust wasn't. And, whatever you might think, the attempted murder of one of our partners isn't either.'

514

'Why bring it up now, Jeffrey?' Mort asked. 'What's the problem?'

'The problem,' said Jeffrey, 'is communication. You know, like talking, like telling your partners what the hell's going on. I mean what are we doing here? We meet every year in this bloody baroque monstrosity to pat each other on the back, and no one ever says anything.'

'How can you talk like that?' protested Mort.

'Because it's true,' said Jeffrey. 'Our senior partners aren't talking. Look what's happening to King Brothers. We used to be a trading organization. That's the only business I understand. Now what? We're into shipping, real estate, beer, engineering, casinos, mining, petrochemicals and God knows what else. Tell me – what have you bought since yesterday? We've borrowed from every major bank in the Western world. We're leveraged up to the hilt and what the hell is it all for? So we can take over the world? Well, it's one thing to own it and it's quite another to control it. Who's going to run all this shit?'

There was a long silence.

'Is that it?' said Mort.

'For the moment,' said Jeffrey.

'OK,' said Mort. 'I can understand how you feel, but . . .'

Jeffrey cut in. 'Look, don't give me your usual phoney rubbish about how you understand what I'm saying and the important thing is that we all love each other. I want to know what's happening.'

'What's happening,' said Mort patiently, 'is that we're expanding. We're getting into new and even more profitable areas . . . projecting the company into the eighties . . . taking the next logical step forward.'

'One small step for the company, one giant leap for Mortimer King.'

'Fuck you, Jeffrey! You sarcastic shit!'

'What's with the clubs? What's with Maxwell Parkes?'

'None of your goddam business!'

'Isn't it? When the company's under siege and you're playing ostrich?'

515

'What are you talking about?'

'We're under investigation. That's what I'm talking about.'

'For what?' said Mort softly.

'Fraud and tax evasion. Are we or aren't we?'

Mort looked at Ruby.

'Don't look at him,' Jeffrey said angrily. 'Look at me. I'm the one who's asking.'

Mort fixed him with his green eyes. 'We're innocent.'

'Who says so?'

'Matthew Rowland. He should know.'

'It's not your skin,' said Ruby. 'It's mine and Mort's. You and Sam are not US citizens. You're not involved.'

That was too much, even for Sam. 'How not involved? We're partners. If the Feds go after the company, the consequences will surely be serious for all of us. Cut out the bullshit, Ruby.'

'What happens if they find you guilty?' said Jeffrey.

'They won't,' said Mort. 'Never.'

'What would the sentence be?' Jeffrey insisted.

Mort was compelled to answer. 'Three years,' he said. 'Maybe five.'

'Jesus!' Jeffrey was shocked. Sam went pale.

'How much more is there?' Jeffrey asked. 'How much more that we don't know?'

'Relax, man,' said Mort. 'If we have a problem – and I don't think we do – it's a minor one. After all, what are we? What have we done? We're not thieves. We're not murderers. We're not drug dealers. What in heaven's name have we done that's so terrible? Besides, we're innocent.'

'You and Sam knew we were playing around with Domestic,' said Ruby.

Sam looked out of the window.

'I knew,' said Jeffrey. 'I just hadn't thought it through. I never knew what was at the end of the road.'

'Who ever knows that?' said Mort.

*

516

Downstairs in the lobby the sleek, well-groomed men wandered around smoking cigars. Their wives and girl-friends paraded in their couturier dresses. Was this where he was going? Jeffrey wondered. Was this the end of the road?

Damn Mort! Damn him! What the hell was he up to? Jeffrey didn't understand him any more. Where was he going? Did he know? Did he care? Or was he just pushing on – to the limit and beyond? If only he'd look around, if only he'd slow down, he might see the dangers. Who knows, maybe he did. Maybe he simply didn't care. He was not, and never would be, one of those frightened, timid souls that the world abounded in. He dared. He would take on anyone or anything, win or lose. In a way it was to be admired, but it was frightening to be around.

There had to be more to life than this. Jeffrey, too, craved the excitement. His pulse raced to the challenge and the triumph as fast as Mort's. But what if the challenges and the triumphs became an end in themselves? What happened when the body craved them like a junkie craved drugs? There had to be more. What was it they said? Money gives you freedom. That's what the smart ones wanted. All the rest wasn't worth a damn. Freedom. That's what you worked for. Freedom to go where and when you wanted, freedom to live life your way, freedom from the daily round that imprisoned all the others. Freedom. That was the prize.

So how come he was beginning to feel trapped?

BOOK SEVEN

Know Your Friends

Temp O'Reilly sat in his office in One St Andrew's Plaza and stared out of the window at the grim outline of the Municipal Building where all the city officials sat. He was not happy. For one thing, it was Monday morning. For another, it was raining, and the mist swirled around outside the window as if he were in swampland. Which, in a way, he was. One wrong step . . . He thought about the lousy press he was getting and shuddered.

'What a fucking day,' he said.

Bob Rosenfeld kept a discreet silence. For his boss to be miserable was nothing new. That was what they paid him for.

'What's with the King Brothers' case?'

Rosenfeld removed his glasses and wiped them carefully. It wasn't necessary, but it gave him time to think.

'There's no case yet,' he said.

'Bob . . .' O'Reilly tapped one of the phones on his desk. 'I just had the President of Channel Two on the line. He wants to do a programme on white-collar crime. Wanted to know if I could give them a scoop. Bob, he dared to insinuate that this office was soft on Wall Street and big business. He made a point of mentioning the oil industry. Now why would he do that?' He sat back and looked at Rosenfeld.

'I don't know.'

'He knows something we don't. The President of Channel Two. The President of Channel Two, Bob. He knows something we don't. Now, what do you think of that?'

Bob Rosenfeld replaced his glasses. What he thought was that his job didn't look too secure. It was a lousy job, but it was a means to an end and he wasn't ready to leave. He sure as hell wasn't ready to be fired.

'We're working day and night on the case, Temp. I have a hunch it's big, but I can't be sure. These guys are smart. We have to walk on tippy-toes.'

Temp O'Reilly opened his mouth wide and yelled. When he yelled, the stenographers could have written it down five floors away. He thumped his desk in time to the words.

'What's – with – the tippy-toes? You ain't fucking Baryshnikov! I – want – results. You hear me?'

'I hear you,' said Bob Rosenfeld.

No one was sure how Temp got his name. One rumour was that his first wife divorced him because of the number of secretarial 'temps' he had been through. Another, equally scurrilous, was that he had beaten a drunk driving charge by pleading temporary insanity. The truth, if that's what you believed in, was that, for twenty years, he had been a member of the Milwaukee Temperance Society – that is, until they discovered that Temp O'Reilly liked his martinis straight up, ice cold and often.

'I was in Le Cirque, Friday.' Temp O'Reilly would kill for an invitation to Le Cirque. He liked the food. He liked the social scene. And he liked people to know who he was. 'Some goddam reporter at the next table. He knew who I was all right, the schmuck. He wanted me to hear. You know what he said? You know what he said, Bob?'

Rosenfeld waited politely.

'He said, "The Feds aren't interested in white-collar crime. It's a hot potato. And they like to stay cool".'

'He said that?' Even Bob Rosenfeld was shocked.

'That's verbatim.'

'We should sue.'

'Terrific idea, Bob. Then we'd really look great. We'd be laughed out of town.'

'Maybe you're right.'

'Bob . . .' Feline. Dangerous. 'Bob, I want those two guys inside. Mortimer and Reuben King. You follow me? I mean you really follow me?'

Rosenfeld nodded.

'Nobody tells me I'm soft on crime. I don't care who the criminal is. I don't care how big he is. In fact, Bob, the bigger the better. You understand me? What this office needs is to get its hands on a few less hoodlums and a few more nice, big, fat successful "respectable" citizens.'

'I understand, Temp.'

'Good. And remember, Bob. A nice big, fat conviction won't do either of us any harm with the media. You know what I mean? You're a smart fellow.'

'It's just that it's going to be tough to get the evidence.'

Temp O'Reilly leaned menacingly across his desk. 'Tough is what life is,' he said. 'Get it!'

Three days later, the Office of the United States Attorney subpoenaed the New York records of King Brothers for the years 1978 – 1982: letters, telexes, files – the whole shooting match. Temp O'Reilly announced at a press conference that over thirty companies which had business contacts with King Brothers had agreed to hand over large numbers of unspecified documents without any court order being issued.

The following week, the Federal grand jury served subpoenas on nearly forty employees of the New York office.

When Mort read the list he noticed a strange omission.

Edgar Proktor's name was not on it.

'We got a bunch of subpoenas,' said Mort.

Edgar nodded.

'Pretty much the whole office was served.'

'I noticed.'

'We haven't talked too much these last few months.'

'Time passes. You've been busy tycooning.'

'I always felt badly about Kate and you. I want you to know that.'

It was a little late for that – a few years too late.

'It's not that big a deal. I guess it wouldn't have worked out.'

'What was it you wanted to talk to me about when you phoned me from the Plaza that day? I've been meaning to ask you.'

'Nothing.'

'Nothing?'

'Nothing important,' said Edgar.

Mort moved across to the window and stood there looking down at the crowds in Park Avenue. Even this high up he could see the people clearly. They walked in a funny way, with splayed legs. It was the perspective. The tops of the bodies were flattened and the legs elongated. That's how it was. Fuad was right. Everything looked different, depending on where you stood when you looked at it.

'Where do you stand, Edgar?'

'What's that supposed to mean?' Where did he stand? Rosenfeld had asked him the same question.

Mort faced him. 'Why didn't they subpoena you, Edgar?'

Edgar flushed and stammered. 'What the hell? What is this? An interrogation? I come in here to talk – try and make some contact with the guy who used to be my friend, and he gives me the third degree. What is this crap? I'm with you, man. You know that.'

Mort came over and put his arm round Edgar's shoulder. 'Do I, Edgar?'

'Why do you keep calling me "Edgar" like that?'

'It's your name isn't it . . . Edgar?'

'I told you, I'm with you, man.' He was nervous.

'I hope you are,' said Mort. 'If you're not with me, you're against me. There are no half measures.'

'Like Jesus Christ?' said Edgar. He couldn't resist it.

'Where do you stand?'

'What are you talking about?'

524

'I'm talking about loyalty, Edgar. Don't I deserve loyalty?'

'Who knows, Mort? Who knows what any of us deserves?' He took the envelope out of his pocket and threw it on the desk.

Mort opened it and read the subpoena.

'So you did get one.'

You could never be sure with Mort. Was he convinced? It was dumb of Rosenfeld not to subpoena Edgar the same day as the others. He had overlooked it. Edgar had balled him out.

'I'm sorry I doubted you,' said Mort. 'My old buddy.'

'Think nothing of it.'

'They'll offer you immunity. That'll be the next step.'

'They already did.'

'What did you say?'

'What do you think I said? I sent them away with a flea in their ear.'

Mort patted Edgar on the back of the neck. 'You won't lose out,' he said. 'I promise you. Loyalty pays.'

'Is there any way we can stop them grabbing our records?'

'We can delay them for a time,' said Matthew Rowland.

'And then?'

'Then they'll grab the records.'

'Hold them off as long as you can.'

'They just subpoenaed the Swiss records. Anything incriminating in them?'

Mort and Ruby exchanged one of their cabal looks.

'I asked you a question,' said Rowland.

After a while Ruby said: 'We don't like the word "incriminating". There's an assumption of guilt in there somewhere.'

'I beg your pardon,' said Matthew Rowland with heavy irony. 'Let me put it differently. Is there anything in the Swiss records about the Domestic scheme or the distribution of profits?'

'Could be,' said Mort.

'It would be better if there weren't. Know what I mean?'

'Matthew,' said Ruby, 'you're as subtle as green hair. We know what you mean before you say it.'

'We don't do things like that,' said Mort.

'Sure you don't,' said Rowland coolly. 'Any other records?'

'Not that we know of,' Ruby said. 'What about the guys they've subpoenaed?'

'They'll offer them immunity,' said Rowland. 'At least the ones they think can be helpful.'

'Let's see how many of them talk,' Ruby said.

'They'll talk,' said Mort. 'All of them.'

'In that case, they'll give us a hard time,' said Ruby.

'The hell they will. They'll get bits and pieces of hearsay and circumstantial evidence,' Mort said. 'This is a complicated case. They're going to need hard facts, and that means records.'

'As far as I can see, you have nothing to worry about,' said Matthew Rowland. He patted his Savile Row suit, as if he were complimenting it for concealing his paunch.

'As far as you can see?' Ruby made it sound like Matthew Rowland couldn't see beyond his nostrils.

'I wish you'd try and remember I'm on your side,' said Rowland acidly.

'I'm working on it,' said Ruby.

'We're OK,' said Mort. 'Everything's going to be OK.'

'What about Edgar?' said Ruby. He had a way of putting his finger on the sensitive spots.

'He won't talk,' said Mort.

'You sure?' said Ruby.

'Sure as I can be.'

'He have any records?' said Rowland.

Mort hesitated. 'None that I know of. I have a hunch he may have kept his own private notes.'

'Get hold of them,' said Matthew Rowland.

'What's the point?' said Mort. 'He could always keep a copy and I'd have no way of knowing. Forget Edgar. I can handle him.'

Matthew Rowland draped the camel's-hair coat round his shoulders.

'There's going to be a lot of heat, a lot of pressure, a lot of bluff. Just let everyone keep his cool and we've got it made.' He sounded as if he were trying to convince himself.

*   *   *

It was the anniversary of Laura's death. Sam left the office early. He wanted to be with Jane, but she wasn't home yet. He started drinking – beer at first – but then, when that had no effect, he changed to dry martinis. He fell asleep in an armchair, his arms folded tightly across his chest, cradling the memory and the pain.

Jane woke him gently, smiling down at him. She was so obviously happy that, involuntarily, he shrank from her touch.

'What is it?' she said startled. 'What's wrong?'

Sam kept his arms folded. A strange look came into his eyes, part cunning, part resentful. 'Nothing,' he said. 'Nothing. I was lonely, that's all. I had a few drinks.'

Jane knew when Sam was lying.

'You're late,' he said casually, getting up and pouring himself another gin. He looked at her for a moment, gulped it down and poured a refill.

Jane was puzzled. Clearly, Sam was not drinking for pleasure.

He indicated the gin. 'You want one?'

'I don't drink gin,' she said.

'Of course not,' he said, pouring himself yet another. 'I forgot. You don't drink gin.' He made it sound like something contemptible – a weakness. He stood there, holding the bottle in one hand and the empty glass in the other.

'It's Laura, isn't it?' she said.

He was still holding the bottle and the glass, his back turned to her. 'I had a daughter once. I keep telling myself I used to have two kids. Now I only have one.' He shook his head disbelievingly.

527

'You have to let go.'

'I can't.'

'You could if you wanted to. You don't want to – not Laura, not Amy.'

'You don't understand,' he said. 'How could you?'

'Oh, I understand,' said Jane. 'You want to believe I don't, but you know I do. It's your exclusive and private pain and you don't want to share it. You want to keep it all to yourself. You won't let anyone in. Not even me. Above all, not me.'

'That's not true,' said Sam. 'It's just that today – another anniversary – I can't handle it.'

'I'll make dinner,' she said.

'Why are you late?'

'I went to the doctor.'

'Anything wrong?' He faced her, suddenly anxious.

'Nothing,' she said. 'I'm fine, just fine.'

He waited, but she didn't add anything.

'How can you just say "nothing", like that? Tell me what's wrong.'

'Nothing's wrong,' she said. 'I'm pregnant, that's all.'

For a while, he stood there stunned, unable to think, mesmerized by the gin bottle and the empty glass.

She was standing in the kitchen looking wretched. He took her in his arms and held her, not knowing what to say.

'I wasn't going to tell you,' she said. 'It didn't seem right and then I thought – no – it has to be right. Life comes first. Life goes on.'

'It's a sign,' said Sam, making an effort. 'It must be.' He was not sure he could handle this one.

'Bullshit,' said Jane happily. 'It's just a baby.'

She clattered around the kitchen, aimlessly, for a while, waiting for Sam to suggest they go out to dinner, open a bottle of champagne – anything to show that he was happy, that tonight was special.

But he never did.

*

Maxwell Parkes looked a little fleshier than the last time they had met and – or was it Mort's imagination? – his hair seemed a couple of shades darker. He slowly unbuttoned the neat-fitting dark blue cashmere coat with the mink collar and laid it carefully on a chair. Then he lit a slim, gold-banded cheroot, leaned back his head and blew a perfect smoke ring.

'How's it going?' He was watching the smoke ring disperse.

'It's going great,' said Mort, guardedly. 'How are things with you?'

'Can't complain.'

'Julie and I are looking forward to seeing you at the cocktail party next week. It should be fun.'

Maxwell Parkes studied the gold band on his cheroot. 'I wanted to talk to you about that,' he said. He sat in a chair by Mort's desk.

'I thought we'd sit over there in the corner,' said Mort. 'It's less formal.'

'Formal's OK,' said Parkes.

Mort tensed. It sounded ominous. Parkes leaned forward. 'We have a problem,' he said. He stubbed out the cheroot viciously as if he hated it. Long after the ash was dead he kept moving the stub around in the ashtray. 'We have a problem,' he repeated.

Mort stared at him stolidly.

'What kind of problem?'

'That cloud on the horizon – no bigger than a man's hand,' he said. 'You remember?'

'I remember,' said Mort. The supercilious bastard was about to tell him to put his house in order. Who the hell did he think he was?

'You said it was going to disappear.'

'That's right. So I did.'

'It got bigger. It's developing a body and a face. People are talking.'

'It's not true,' said Mort. 'Not a word of it.'

Maxwell Parkes ignored him. 'More press coverage,

more publicity, more talk. It's not good, Mort. My people are uncomfortable.'

His people. The self-important jerk.

'They don't like it. And I'll be frank with you – I don't like it either. It's my name and my reputation on the line. We're not just talking money here. You can't buy reputation you know.'

Mort kept his cool. What he wanted to do was punch the patronizing shithead on the nose. He would have felt a whole lot better for doing it, but he didn't, because any chance he had of getting into politics would have walked out the door with Maxwell Parkes.

'You know how people talk. It means nothing,' was all he said.

'It means a hell of a lot. You hope to be a political frontrunner. Today you're up for membership of the best clubs, tomorrow you want to be a candidate for political office.' He shook his head. 'You got to be clean, Mort.'

'I'm being investigated for an alleged technical infringement of a meaningless law.'

Maxwell Parkes raised his hand as if he were St Peter barring entrance to the Kingdom of Heaven. 'Spare me the details,' he said. 'You're being investigated. You said it. That's all that counts – not what you're being investigated for, not whether the law makes sense or not, not even whether you're innocent or guilty. Who gives a damn? We're not talking guilt or innocence here. We're talking suspicion. We're talking taint. You're tainted, Mort. You're tainted.'

'So I've been tried by your anonymous friends and found guilty. Is that it?' said Mort furiously. 'Some fucking jury!'

'Jesus, Mort! Don't be so goddam melodramatic. You know how it is in this business. We're in the public eye and, believe me, the public is merciless. You want to be a public figure. Learn to play by the rules.'

'The hell with the rules! There are more crooks in politics than there are in business, so don't lecture me.' Mort's self-control was cracking.

'Maybe so, but in politics there's only one rule that counts. It's the eleventh commandment. "Thou shalt not be found out". And you broke it, Mort. No one wants to be around a loser. No one's going to help a loser up the ladder. I tell you that for nothing. No one. It's a long way up there, Mort, and by Christ, it's a short way down.'

Mort was feeling the strain of controlling his temper. Hiding his aggression had become a way of life to him, but at what cost. 'If anyone says I've broken the law, I'll sue him. And don't you ever tell me again that I'm a loser. You hear me?' The jibe had hurt.

Maxwell Parkes looked unimpressed. 'I'll do what I can, Mort, but I have to tell you there are no second chances in this business.' He stood up. 'For the time being, I suggest you cancel the cocktail party.'

'What happens when the US Attorney drops the investigation?'

'From what I hear that's not likely. If he does, we can talk again.'

Mort pressed him. 'We'd pick up where we left off?'

Parkes pulled a face. 'Mort, do me a favour. Let's talk about it when it happens.' He held out his hand. For a moment Mort hesitated. Then he took it, gingerly, as if the guy had psoriasis, but he took it. He was going to need him again one day. Meanwhile, he felt betrayed.

'I thought even in politics there was such a thing as friendship,' he said sourly. 'Whatever happened to friendship, Maxwell?'

Maxwell Parkes patted the mink collar of his cashmere overcoat. 'I don't know,' he said. 'I'll ask around.'

Mort was sitting at his desk in the darkening room when his private line rang. He poured himself a large bourbon and sipped it slowly. Normally, he could never wait to answer the phone; now it seemed like an intrusion. He waited until it stopped ringing.

A police siren yowled in the distance. The sound died.

It was quiet, as quiet as it ever was in New York. Even fifty-five floors up he could hear the traffic down there moaning like some doomed monster trapped in the canyons. We're never going to escape, he thought. None of us.

The phone rang again. It was ten minutes past eight, late for a business call. He poured himself another bourbon. If the phone was still ringing by the time he took his first sip, he would pick it up. It was.

'Hi!' Rosemary. He could picture the eager face, the cornflower-blue eyes.

'Hi.' Suddenly he felt more cheerful. 'What time do you have?'

'It's past one here.'

'You should be asleep. But I'm glad you phoned. It's been an age since I heard from you. What have you been doing with yourself? Getting into mischief?'

'You could say that,' she said. Her voice sounded strange.

'I thought of coming over,' he said. 'Do I still have the closet – or is it wardrobe?'

The line was quiet.

'Rosemary?'

'I heard you. Look, Mort, I phoned to give you some news. I've been meaning to phone you for weeks, but you know how it is.'

'News?' He tried not to sound apprehensive. 'What news?'

'I'm getting married.'

'Oh,' he said. He was stunned. 'When?' What the hell did it matter when?

'Tomorrow.' She made a brave effort to be light-hearted. 'Isn't it ridiculous? God, I must get some sleep or I'll never make it up the aisle.'

'I'm happy for you.'

'Thank you, Mort. That's sweet. I knew you wouldn't exactly be devastated, but you might at least sound just a teeny bit upset, or disappointed . . . or something. I mean, you did like me a little, didn't you? It wasn't just sex?'

532

'No,' he said.

'Don't you want to know who he is?' She prattled on without waiting for a reply. 'His name's Giorgio. He's American, well, half Italian really, and he's loaded. He buys and sells companies which sounds frightfully boring, but he seems to do it awfully well. And he has green eyes, just like you. And he's dynamite in bed. Just like you,' she added.

He couldn't believe what she was telling him. This wasn't Rosemary. It couldn't be.

'Do I sound frantic?' she gasped. 'Well, I am. I'm getting married tomorrow, I can't sleep and I'm shit scared.'

'Then why do it?' said Mort. 'What's so different about this guy?'

'He asked me, darling,' she said wistfully. 'I'll miss you, Mort.'

'Sure you will,' he said. He wished her good luck and tried to sound as if he meant it. 'I hope everything works out fine.'

'I hope so too,' she said.

Whatever it was that Rosemary had meant to him, he had never allowed himself to acknowledge that he loved her. What was love anyway? One thing, though, he had to admit: somehow she had got to him. She was not just another shapely ass; there was plenty of that around. That wouldn't have tempted him to risk his reputation, maybe his marriage. Strangely enough, when he thought about her it was not her looks he remembered. It was her free spirit. Now his heart went out to her. She had been vulnerable after all.

And he? Was he vulnerable too? Surely his life would never be quite the same. Just for a moment – for one moment in time – he had been touched by the predicament of another human being and, now that he had lost her, it occurred to him that it might be the nearest he would ever come to loving someone.

*

533

Mort read through the transcripts of Edgar's last three sessions with Bob Rosenfeld.

'You did well,' he said. 'You talked a lot and you said nothing. There's not a damn thing here that need give us any concern. I love it.' He was pleased with Edgar.

Which was exactly how Bob Rosenfeld wanted him to feel. It was essential to his plan that Mort should trust Edgar.

'What happened about the immunity they offered you?'

It seemed to Edgar that Mort had asked him that question before. Maybe he needed reassuring. Or was he testing him out?

'I told them where to put it,' said Edgar. 'If I took immunity, I might get careless. This way, I'm still in the same boat as you are. I have to watch every word I say, or I'm in trouble.'

'You never took immunity?'

'I told you. No.'

Mort looked at Edgar approvingly. 'You're doing a great job,' he said. 'Ruby and I – we talked about it. We'd like to express our appreciation.'

'You don't have to do that,' said Edgar uncomfortably.

'I know we don't. It's something we want to do. We want you to accept an allocation of five hundred shares in the company. All you have to do is pay us the face value – a hundred dollars a share. You can keep them, or you can sell them back to us at today's book value. Whatever you want.'

'What's today's book value?'

'Ten thousand dollars a share.' Mort flashed a glance at him, relishing the look of astonishment on Edgar's face.

'Jesus, ten thousand a share! That's a gift of ... five million bucks!'

'It's not a gift,' said Mort. 'You earned it. Friends are important. We know who our friends are. We like to reward them.'

'I can't accept it,' said Edgar. He was shaking. What was it? Fear or shame?

'Why not?' said Mort. 'You should feel good about accepting a token of appreciation from a friend. That's all it is.'

He crossed to the bar and poured two drinks. For Edgar a dry martini, for himself a bourbon and soda.

'To our new partner,' he said, raising his glass.

Edgar gulped down the drink. Between Bob Rosenfeld and Mort he was being torn apart.

'I can't take any more,' said Edgar, head in hands. 'I've had enough. I'm through.'

'What are you bellyaching for?' said Rosenfeld. 'Everything's going the way we planned it, isn't it?'

Edgar was subdued. He had lost his way. All that hate he had felt for Mort – where had it gone? He didn't know what he was doing any more, or why.

'So, what's the problem?'

'He's being so darned good to me. How can I do this to him?'

'Sure he's being good to you. With Mort everything is calculated. There's always a reason.'

'It's not like that.' Edgar flailed the air with his hands. 'We're friends. We go back a long way. For Chrissake, man . . . he's made me a partner.'

'Good timing,' said Rosenfeld caustically.

'He didn't have to do it. I feel badly about it.'

'He gave you shares?'

Edgar nodded wretchedly.

'What are they worth?'

'Five million bucks.'

Rosenfeld whistled.

'I wanted to give them back. He wouldn't let me. He made me take them. He forced me to take them.'

'If he forced you to take them, then it's not your responsibility,' said Rosenfeld reasonably. 'You tried. You did what you had to do.'

'What I have to do is get out of this mess. I can't live with myself. Whatever kind of a shit he was to me, I can't

535

go on playing this double game. You have to let me off the hook, Bob. I'll take whatever's coming to me, but I'll never give evidence against Mort.'

Bob Rosenfeld sighed. 'I see,' he said quietly. He had been waiting for this. It was not an unexpected development. Bob Rosenfeld was a fisherman. He knew about such things. There was that moment when the fish was there, apparently lifeless, ready to gaff, and then, just when you thought the battle was over, it came to life again, and the line spun out on the reel and your muscles took the strain. The battle had been prolonged, but there was no escape; the end result was always the same.

Edgar was not just hooked; he was hanging there, upside down on the quayside, only he didn't know it.

'I was talking to my boss,' said Rosenfeld.

His boss. Did Satan have a boss?

'I told him you might be having second thoughts. I guessed as much.'

Edgar raised his head, hoping to hear something good, something comforting.

'He feels you're committed. He says even if you pulled out now, he would have to use the information you already gave us and, of course, on top of that, you could still be indicted. I told him that wouldn't be fair, but he says if you refuse to cooperate . . .' Rosenfeld left the words hanging menacingly. 'Well, naturally, I tried to persuade him to see it your way, but he wouldn't.'

The truth was that they were badly disappointed with the information Edgar had given them so far. He knew less, far less, than they had hoped – too little to form the basis of an indictment. The case was going badly for the US Attorney's Office.

Edgar huddled miserably in his chair.

'Edgar,' said Rosenfeld consolingly, 'I never said it would be easy. You chose a hard road, but in your heart you must know it's the right one.'

'I don't know anything any more,' said Edgar.

'Don't weaken now,' said Rosenfeld. 'We need you more than ever. We have to move things along.'

'How do you mean?'

'We're going to wire you,' said Rosenfeld casually.

Edgar started to sweat. He felt it running down the inside of his arms and the back of his neck. 'No,' he said. 'I won't do it. Don't ask me to pull a stunt like that.'

Bob Rosenfeld's manner was sympathetic, but his eyes were merciless.

'Don't let it scare you, Edgar,' he said. 'It's no big deal. You and me – we're working together – that's all. You don't have to worry about a thing. Let me do the worrying.' His voice dropped. It was warm and caressing. 'I need you, Edgar. We all need you. Don't let us down now, not when we're so close.'

The words . . . was it the words or the manner of speaking? There was something about the insinuating way he presented things: unctuous, glib. Who did it remind Edgar of? Mort, of course. Who else? This guy was another Mort. They both pulled the same tricks. How could he trust them? Either of them? Kate had been right all along. What the hell did it matter who he worked for? There was only one guy worth saving: Edgar Proktor.

'I still don't understand why you can't leave those guys alone.' Daniel was nervous and upset and his father knew why. Still, it was hard to take criticism from his own son.

'Why do you love them so much?'

'I don't love them,' said Daniel indignantly. 'I just don't agree with the way you're handling the case. I don't happen to think it's fair.'

'You don't think it's fair.' Bob Rosenfeld repeated the words softly. There was a hint of scorn in his voice and a touch of menace, too.

'No, I don't,' said Daniel. 'All those press conferences you hold – the things you say about them.'

'Tell me, Daniel, what do you think is fair? You think cheating the government is fair? Stealing people's money –

is that fair? How about fraud? Tax evasion? Price-gouging? Forgery? Inventing phoney transactions? Milking illegal profits out of the country? Is that fair? Tell me. I'd really like to know what you consider fair.'

'A man's innocent until he's proven guilty,' said Daniel.

'So they tell me,' said Rosenfeld. 'They're guilty,' he added positively.

'Who says?'

'I do.'

Daniel shook his head disbelievingly. 'Who are you to say that? You're just one guy. You can't bypass the whole system.'

'I'm an Assistant United States Attorney.'

'You're not the judge. You're not the jury. Besides, you yourself told me that you didn't have enough evidence to indict them.'

'It's my job to find it.'

'It's your job to find the truth.'

Rosenfeld sighed. 'Look, Daniel, you're my son and I love you. I also happen to have a lot of respect for you, but you don't know the world like I do. You don't know people. You've always been sheltered – family life, school, college – they all put a fence round you. These men are like hungry wolves, greedy and dangerous. They circle the camp at night and stake out their prey. Decent people have a right to be protected.'

'That's all melodramatic bullshit,' said Daniel. 'These are just regular guys and you're trying to turn them into villains. I don't see that they've done anything so terrible. And maybe I do have a few things to learn about life, but I still know what a fair trial is. You have them guilty before they're even indicted. I never thought the day would come when I'd see my father presiding over a kangaroo court,' he said bitterly. 'Why don't you just take them out and shoot them?'

'I'm sorry if I'm ruining your love life,' said Bob Rosenfeld, and instantly regretted it.

'That was a cheap shot.'

'Yes, it was. I'm sorry.'

Daniel turned his back on his father. There were tears in his eyes. Bob Rosenfeld put his hand on his son's shoulder. 'You still have ideals. You still believe in people,' he said quietly. 'That's good.'

'And you don't?'

'I try,' said Rosenfeld. 'It's hard sometimes, but I try.'

'We're not talking ideals here. We're talking morality.'

'When you're dealing with criminals, morality's a luxury you can't afford.'

'Is that so? Then what's the difference between you and them?'

Now that, thought Bob Rosenfeld, was a good question.

* * *

'It's the best suite in the hotel,' said Sam, 'and I always think the Helmsley Palace is the grandest hotel in New York. Look, there's St Patrick's Cathedral down there. And there's Park Avenue and there's Fifth Avenue. There's Central Park.' He spread his arms wide. 'And how about this sitting room? It's as big as Mort's office. You like it?'

'We like it,' said Jane happily.

The baby was due in three weeks. Jane did not look that big. She had lied about the date to the airline in case they refused to take her. The trip to New York would do them good, she thought. Sam had to get away from the office and they needed to be together for a time. She had not moved in with him. He had offered it, but it was not what she wanted. If it happened – fine – but it had to be in a different way, for a different reason – not because of the baby.

'Poor Sam,' she said.

'Why poor Sam?'

'I don't know,' she said. 'You're so good. Another man would have yelled, or walked away, but you never did. No sooner did you get your divorce than you got this.' She patted her stomach.

539

'These things happen.'

She giggled. 'They do indeed.'

He was never quite certain how to take Jane. Some-times he had the impression she was laughing at him. It was almost as if everything he said she had heard before and nothing he did was surprising to her any more. She was as good-humoured as she had always been and fun to be with, but he had a feeling now that he was being patron-ized and tolerated, not, as he used to be, cherished. It occurred to him, naturally, that she had stopped loving him. Never, for an instant, did he imagine that she might have been deeply hurt by his cool reception of her pregnancy.

She tried not to acknowledge the truth to herself: that if Sam, by some miracle, could have made the foetus disappear, he would have been a happy man. Not that he approved of abortion. It was not a decision, in any event, that he could ever take himself, nor would he even have raised the subject. She sensed, nevertheless, reconciled to the baby as he seemed to be, that if she had once suggested the possibility, Sam would have jumped at it.

'A few days in New York will do us both a world of good,' he said, cheerfully. 'I'm not going anywhere near the office. We'll shop, take in a couple of theatres and relax. Oh, and I have to see Edward,' he added. 'He looks forward to my visits. He knows I'm here.'

'Of course.'

Of course. And Amy. What about Amy? How could it be, despite his vacillation and his weakness, that Jane still loved Sam? She hoped, desperately, that they could be happy together, but she often wondered about it. In a way, the baby had been a misfortune. She had been careless. But still, now that it was a fact and life had changed, he ought to accept it. He was compelled to.

'We'll get married,' he said firmly. 'I've thought about it plenty and I know it'll be good for both of us. It's the right thing to do.'

Good old Sam, she thought. The right thing to do. Always doing what was right, living his life looking over his shoulder, wondering what everyone else was thinking, adjusting his reactions, his thoughts, even, to suit the occasion and the audience. He was hooked on approval. Chameleon Sam. Put him on the grass and watch him turn green.

She had met Mort and Ruby. Everyone said they were sharp businessmen – crooks even, some said – but she admired them: they had guts; they stood up straight; they did what they wanted to, not what was expected of them. They might be wrong, but being wrong when everyone else so eagerly craved to be right was a refreshing change in this conformist world.

'We'll soon be married,' he said.

'We'll see.' She wondered if he was still in love with Amy and, if he was, if he was even aware of it.

'Like old times,' said Sam.

Not that it was. Not that anything ever was. In some ways, it might even have been better. Divorce had eased the tensions between them; they were still there, but the compulsion to please, to make the relationship work, had disappeared. Everything was more relaxed.

'I can't believe Edward's so tall.' Sam was feeling nostalgic. They had, after all, shared happy times together as well as sad.

As he sipped the rich, heavy Château Talbot, he eyed his ex-wife over the rim of the glass. She looked amazing. In this soft light, she could have been twenty-five. She was still a top model, still glamorous in her cool, uninvolved way, still clouded with that remoteness that had always teased and tantalized him. She was a marvellous-looking woman. He was still attracted to her.

He tried to imagine himself as a boyfriend of hers on their first date. It was not too difficult to do. How many boyfriends had there been in this room, he wondered. How many had sat in the armchair he was sitting in now and

541

sipped their drinks and sneaked lecherous sidelong glances at those glittering top-model legs? How many had shared her bed? Could it be that he was jealous of his ex? Ridiculous. He should not be thinking this way. It was time to go. Jane would be wondering where he was. She was probably in bed already.

'Edward was pleased to see me,' he said. That had surprised him. 'Maybe absence really does make the heart grow fonder.' Maybe it did something for the hormones, too.

'Of course he was,' she said. 'You're his father. He loves you.'

If only that was how it worked. He's my son, so he loves me ... You were my wife, but you never loved me ... How come? He had grown to accept it, however much it hurt and, as time passed, it hurt less and less, as he came to realize that Amy could never love anyone. She was not the kind of woman who needed to give herself. She enjoyed holding back. It was her way of asserting her own identity. But then – and this had never stopped tormenting him – what had happened with Siegfried Gerber? What the hell had happened with him? What was so different about that old man?

'I have to thank you,' he said. 'Some ex-wives poison their kids' minds – turn them against their fathers.'

'I would never do that,' she said, not protesting, just stating a fact.

'And you?' he said. 'How are you?'

'I'm great,' she said. 'As you see.'

Amy hid too much, everything important, in fact. What you saw was never that significant. It was what you didn't see that mattered.

'Were you pleased to see me?' Why the hell had he asked her that?

She nodded. 'I was surprised how much.'

'It's been a while,' he said.

'A long time.'

'Too long,' said Sam.

She poured him another glass of Château Talbot. The red wine was smooth and heady.

'I never knew you were such a connoisseur of wine,' he said. 'This is fabulous.'

'I'm not. I have this . . . friend. He knows about wine and things.'

He wondered what else he knew about, this . . . friend.

'It's strange,' he said, 'I seem to know you better now than when we were married.' Was that the Château Talbot talking, or had he really meant it?

Amy smiled a little sadly. 'I doubt we ever knew each other that well.'

'My fault. I should have worked harder at it.'

'Mine too,' she said.

'We could work at it now,' he said.

She stood and smoothed down her skirt. 'I don't think you should be here when Edward wakes up,' she said. 'He might not understand.'

She had always been so cool, so dispassionate. Now she clung to him, kissing his body hungrily, her fingers digging into his flesh as if she found the touch of him irresistible. But he sensed that it was the semblance of passion, not the reality.

'Is Jane in love with you?'

'I guess so.'

'Is she good in bed?'

'She's OK.' He kissed her body tenderly from her breasts down to her thighs. She lay there passively, her legs spread.

'Don't do that,' she said. 'Just put it in, Sam.'

He could have hit her. Instead, he raised himself up and, as she dutifully lifted her thighs, drove savagely into her. If he could have impaled her on the bed with his penis he would have done it. It was a sadistic fantasy; it lasted only a few seconds, like his desire. The warm fluid spurted out of him and he collapsed on his back, staring baffled and frustrated at the ceiling.

'Was that good for you, honey?' she asked him.

*

543

Jane was waiting for him.

Sam held up his hands defensively. 'Before you say something you're going to regret, let me just tell you I stayed at the apartment because Edward insisted. He went on pleading with me until I had to agree and by that time, it was too late to call you. I was afraid to wake you up. After all, you need your beauty sleep.'

It was a reasonable story, not great, but not bad either in the circumstances, which were not exactly favourable. For a few moments he thought he had got away with it. 'How's baby?' He grinned disarmingly.

'Baby,' she said, 'is fine. Just fine. Mother, on the other hand, is real sick – sick of you – you lying bastard. You can pack your bag and get the hell out of here. You can go shop with your ex and maybe take in a theatre or two.' She obviously relished flinging his words back in his face.

'Jane,' he pleaded, 'I know it looks bad, but do you really think I'd be stupid enough to . . .' He didn't have the courage to say it, so Jane helped him out.

'Screw your ex? While your pregnant mistress waits breathlessly in the hotel room for lover boy to show up? Yes, Sam, I do. I do think you'd be that stupid. And that cruel, too, you shit.' She started to cry. He tried to comfort her, but she pushed him away. 'I don't know what happened when they handed out feelings, but you were short-changed, Sam. You don't know what it is to feel. You don't know what it is to make a commitment. You always had someone to tell you how to do it, didn't you? You never knew how to do it yourself. Oh, you know how to screw. You're a good screw as screws go, but there's something missing in that chunky little body of yours. I don't know. Maybe it's me, but I just wish you had more . . .' She was searching for the right word . . . 'More heart.' She was crying again. He couldn't remember ever feeling so guilty and so ashamed.

'You've got it all wrong,' he said. 'I love you.'

'Why can't you at least be honest?' she said. 'I'm preg-

544

nant. Your ex was available and you needed a good fuck. Admit it. That kind of talk I can understand.'

'It wasn't like that.'

'Wasn't it?' she said, hopelessly. 'You mean you're still in love with her? Is that what you want to say?'

Sam shook his head. It was all too much for him. If only he could be free.

'It's time you met some young men,' said Ruby.

Ruth knew exactly what that meant. Her father would talk to her mother and they would both get busy. Soon there would be invitations to friends and acquaintances with suitable young bachelor sons and the Kings would be giving regular Sunday afternoon teas at which Ruth would be expected to display her many and varied charms and accomplishments.

Aside from her interest in Daniel, the whole performance was so embarrassing and primitive that the thought of submitting to it revolted her. She had seen it in action with several of her girlfriends. Most of them had reluctantly followed their parents' wishes and had sworn they would never inflict the same painful procedure on their children. But, on the whole, they had taken the view that the end justified the means. They had all seemed more than satisfied with the young men they got. By the time they arrived at the Chupah on their wedding day, all of them were convinced that they had freely selected their own husbands.

'You want to put a bottle on the roof, Pop?'

Ruby chuckled. If he did, he doubted it would stay up there for long. It was well known that the family was wealthy and that Ruth would, in time, be heiress to a substantial fortune. More importantly, she was an exceptional young woman of strong character, beautiful and intelligent. She was lively, open and direct. In a word, she was perfect.

'Pop,' said Ruth affectionately, 'I'm a woman now, not a child. I grew up. I've always done what you and Mom

545

told me, but this is different. I'll choose my husband myself.'

'Naturally you will,' said Ruby. 'Who else would choose him? All I ask is that you meet some young men from good families and then make your choice. What's wrong with that?'

'I don't want to get married yet. I'm too young. Anyway, I already met a young man from a good family,' she said.

'You met a young man whose father is trying to destroy me and my good name,' said Ruby angrily.

'That has nothing to do with Daniel.'

'You're a stubborn girl.' It was ironic that her independent spirit, the quality he most admired in her, was what caused him most pain in their relationship. Perhaps it was the same for all parents – how things were meant to be. You brought your kids up to stand on their own feet and, when they did just that, you tried to knock them down again.

'OK, Pop,' she said. 'I'll make a deal with you. I'll do what you want, but on one condition.'

'The condition?'

'When the time comes, you have to ask Daniel to tea as well.'

'Rosenfeld has something on you,' said Matthew Rowland. 'What exactly it is, I don't know, but he has something.'

Ruby was looking at him in disgust. 'Can I take your coat?' he said.

'No thanks,' said Rowland. 'I'm OK.'

Ruby jerked the camel's-hair coat off Matthew Rowland's shoulders and threw it triumphantly on a chair.

'You think he has hard evidence?' asked Mort.

The two aspects of his profession that most appealed to Matthew Rowland were money and the discomfiture of his clients. He saw men, celebrated and powerful, at their most vulnerable. The strongest characters, comfortable and unchallenged in their own environment, became uneasy, defensive and scared when they were entangled in the

546

web of the law. Matthew Rowland's quivering antennae monitored the vibrations of the doomed. The more afraid they were, the more they struggled; the more they struggled, the more he enjoyed it. Some he helped to escape, some he did not. One way or another, the pleasure and the reward were much the same.

'So he tells me. It could be bluff, but I've known the guy a long time. I believe him.'

'Maybe it's the Swiss records?'

'I don't think so,' said Ruby.

'I don't think so, either,' said Rowland. 'Rosenfeld made a strange remark. He said we shouldn't kid ourselves that he depended on records.'

'I wonder what he meant by that?'

'I've been in touch with Craig,' said Rowland. 'There's no change. The agreement you made stands.'

The agreement 'you' made, he had said. Rowland, despite everything Mort had told him, was certain that money was involved. Mort could hardly blame him.

'He's talking to a lot of companies who did business with us,' said Ruby thoughtfully.

'None we have to be concerned about,' said Mort. 'Sure, we bought and sold Domestic, but that's not a crime. No – Melvin was the only one we did daisy-chain transactions with.'

Mort and Ruby stared at each other. The cabal was operating.

'We have a mole,' said Ruby. 'Someone in the company.'

Mort nodded.

'It was always on the cards,' said Rowland. 'They've given immunity to a lot of guys in this office. You sure you know who your friends are?'

'Who knows that?' said Mort.

Rowland grinned slyly. 'It gets to be that the only guy you can trust is your lawyer.'

'So?' Ruby had seen 'camel's hair' to the elevator. 'It's Edgar isn't it?'

547

'I can't believe it,' said Mort.

'Yes, you can. You just don't want to.'

Mort looked at his brother without answering.

'What do we do?' Ruby lit a cheroot. He had given up cigarettes 'for health reasons'. He was on his tenth cheroot and it was barely eleven o'clock in the morning.

'I can't believe Edgar would talk to the Feds.'

'Immunity is hard to fight,' said Ruby.

'Remember what E.M. used to call me?'

'He called you a lot of things.'

' "Renegade". That's what he called me,' said Mort. 'The truth was, I was always up front with him, but this guy Edgar, he's lying to me, sticking the knife in my ribs. Why would he do that, Ruby?'

'Because he's weak. Because he's afraid. Because he's human.'

'I thought he was my friend,' said Mort. 'You want to know something? You want to know what I think, Ruby? I think I don't have any friends.'

'You have plenty of friends,' said Ruby reassuringly. 'Plenty. You're well liked.'

'Not one,' said Mort, ignoring him. 'I haven't given it the time, that's the problem. It takes time to cultivate friends. You have to do things for them. You have to give them presents, remember their birthdays – that sort of thing.'

'You remember birthdays,' said Ruby protectively. 'One thing you always remember is birthdays.'

'Sure I do,' said Mort. 'The business connections . . . It's not enough . . . I should start keeping a private diary with all the anniversaries and birthdays of people I know personally. Personally, Ruby. That's the key. Personal friendships are important, you know that? Friends don't just happen. You have to earn them. I'm not talking business friends, now. I mean personal friends. Those are the friends who count – the ones who can do you a lot of good or a lot of harm.'

Ruby nodded gloomily.

'I could have had a bunch of friends if I'd done more for them,' said Mort. 'No question about it.'

Ruby wanted to tell Mort that you only needed to care about people, not to take care of them, but there was no easy way to say it.

'What do we do about Edgar?' he asked instead.

'We can't be sure it's him. How can we be sure?'

'I'm sure,' said Ruby. 'What do we do about him?'

'How could he do this to me?' said Mort. 'How could he be so disloyal? After all I've done for him.'

The President of the Board of Deputies was apologetic. He was a good political man. He knew when to smile and when to be serious. Above all, he knew when to protect his back.

'After all, Ruby,' he said reasonably, 'it was me who proposed you. Don't forget that. And I do have something of a reputation to consider. Your resignation would be the decent way out.'

The self-righteous prig. Appearances. Always appearances. Who gave a shit about facts when rumours were flying? Who cared about friends when reputation was involved?

Ruby made his protest. 'We're talking unsubstantiated charges, snide insinuations fed to the press by cheap gossip writers who call themselves journalists. I'm not accountable to smear campaigns. I don't have to defend myself against crap like that.'

'Of course you don't,' said the president smoothly, 'but the Jewish community has a duty to protect its good name. You would be the first to acknowledge that,' he added smugly.

'And the Jewish community does that by stabbing me in the back?'

'There's no question of stabbing you in the back. We don't do things that way.'

'You sanctimonious prick!' said Ruby angrily. 'Like shit, you don't do things that way! You can't fire me. You're afraid I might sue you for victimization, discrimination and a few other things I could think of.'

'We're simply giving you the opportunity to do the right thing.'

'You know, my friend,' said Ruby with heavy irony, 'I'm glad you told me that, because if you hadn't – you know something? – I might not have guessed. So I have to thank you for doing me a favour. Well, do me another one. Deliver a message to the Board for me, so they know I truly understand what's in their hearts.'

The president looked suitably solemn. He was not a man to crow over his adversary in his moment of defeat.

'Tell them this,' said Ruby. 'Tell them I'll resign the day the President of the Board of Deputies fucks his wife on the Bimah. In front of the congregation mind you. Or, if he prefers it,' he added, 'someone else's wife. That might be more fun for him. Then, I'll resign,' said Ruby. 'As a matter of fact, it would definitely be worth it. Just think of the view I'd have.'

The President of the Board of Deputies drew himself up. 'I regret you should take it like this,' he said stiffly.

'I'll bet you do,' said Ruby. 'You can't throw me overboard and I won't jump.'

'What you don't understand is that I'm your friend.'

'Well, what do you know?' said Ruby.

'It's a real pleasure, Joe,' said Mort.

Joe Murphy did not look too happy. He had lost weight since Mort had last seen him. He walked with his head down, like a man with troubles. 'I wish I could say the same, Mort.'

'What's the problem?'

'I guess you know the Feds have been throwing subpoenas around.'

'I heard,' said Mort.

'Most of the guys in the trading department have been questioned – a lot of general crap, but mostly about our

550

dealings in Domestic, any information we might have about daisy chains, any suspicions about who in the industry was involved. All that shit.'

'They have nothing on Pacific Odyssey as far as I know,' said Mort. 'It's me they're after. Nothing for you to worry about.'

'That's the way I looked at it,' said Joe Murphy. 'What kept bugging me was why they never pulled me in for questioning. They called in everyone else except me.'

'Why worry? I'm sure the guys that work for you confirmed you weren't involved in the daisy chains.'

'That's what I thought until yesterday,' said Joe. 'Then, suddenly, they called me in and grilled me for six hours. Not about Domestic and daisy chains either. It was Rosenfeld and some big guy from the FBI.'

'Ed Goldwyn,' said Mort. 'He's smart. They both are.'

'Rosenfeld's suspicious,' said Joe. His hands were shaking. 'I don't understand why, but he's suspicious.'

'What of?'

'He figures that I . . .' Joe Murphy looked round the room nervously. 'This place isn't bugged, is it?'

Mort grinned. 'I doubt it, but anything's possible.' He handed Joe Murphy a memo pad. On it Joe wrote the words: 'He figures I took bribes.'

Mort looked at the pad, tore off the top sheet of paper and then, his face impassive, set it alight with the desk lighter, laid it in the ashtray and watched it burn. 'And did you?'

'Never in my life. Never. I never broke faith with the company. I never broke faith with myself.'

'Great. Then you're in the clear.'

'I'm not. That's just it. Someone talked about a fund. You remember the fund?'

Mort said nothing.

'I don't know who – maybe some guy in King Brothers talked to one of my guys – who the hell knows? Now they're saying I traded more crude with you than with all

551

the rest of the industry put together. They want me to explain it.'

'So explain. I had the crude. The rest of the industry didn't.'

'I tried to, but they won't buy that. They say I must have had a reason for doing so much business with you.'

'What do you want of me, Joe?' said Mort wearily.

'Tell them about the fund. Show them the books. Prove to them that I never had shares. They won't believe me, Mort. They won't believe me.'

'Get off my back, Joe. You think I don't have enough problems of my own?'

'All I need is audited accounts of the fund . . . something to show that I wasn't involved. Surely you can do that for me?'

'There – are – no – accounts,' said Mort. 'There was no audit. There was no fund. You know that.'

'What are you saying? Sure there was a fund. For God's sake, Mort, they're investigating my bank accounts. They're trying to freeze my assets. The company's hounding me. I'm desperate!'

'There's nothing I can do about it. These things happen. It'll blow over.'

'Is that all you have for me? Philosophy?'

'Joe. You never took from me. You never took from anybody. What's your problem?'

'My problem is that they've got me where I'm having to prove that I'm innocent. How do you do that, Mort? How do you do that? When your own friends and colleagues look at you in that special way, like they're convinced you're guilty? How do I prove I'm innocent?'

'You don't have to. A man's innocent until he's proven guilty.'

Joe laughed ironically. 'Not in this world. Not in this world, Mort. Maybe in the next.'

He stood up to go. 'I'm disappointed in you,' he said. 'I thought you took care of your friends.'

'I do,' said Mort. 'I remember who they are and what

they did for me. You could have helped me once, Joe. That's what I remember. Pacific Odyssey screwed me when they didn't have to. They blackmailed me. They forced me to take a huge loss on a contract when it should have been a bonanza for me. They tried to put me out on the street. And what did you do? Joe, my good friend? You sat there and nodded while your president took me apart.'

'I was against it,' Joe protested. 'I did everything I could to get you off the hook. What else could I do? I was helpless.'

'So am I, Joe,' said Mort. 'So am I.'

Matthew Rowland patted his stomach and hips. The unconscious gesture was ambiguous. It signalled complacency. The immaculate little man seemed entirely satisfied with himself and the way he looked. On the other hand, there was about it a hint of uncertainty, as if he had lost something, something valuable, a wallet perhaps. Or a court case. The tan camel's-hair coat rode his shoulders as smugly as ever, but all was not well beneath that silver grey coiffure.

'I guess maybe we should do something about Rosenfeld.'

Ruby gave Rowland his fish-eye look, blank and expressionless. He did not like him. He did not like his camel's-hair coat. He did not like the way he draped it over his shoulders – a coat should be worn or hung in the closet – he liked neither his fancy coiffure nor his manicured fingernails, nor the perfumed cloud of Aramis that enveloped him. Above all, he did not like Matthew Rowland.

'What did you have in mind?'

Rowland did not answer him directly. He addressed himself to Mort, sensing a more sympathetic audience.

'He's a terrier,' he said. 'He's got his teeth into you. He's not going to let go.'

'Then what are we paying you for?' Ruby asked sourly. A reasonable question, Mort thought.

Matthew Rowland patted himself. 'You're paying me to give you good advice.'

'So give it,' said Ruby, deftly removing the camel's hair and laying it on a sofa in the corner of the room.

Rowland sat in an armchair and studied his nails. 'You think the man has any weaknesses?'

'Who doesn't?' said Mort.

'Indeed,' said Matthew Rowland.

Ruby looked at his watch. 'I need to dictate some telexes before lunch,' he said, moving to the door of Mort's office.

'Stay,' said Mort.

Ruby sat down.

'How much do you reckon the guy takes home?' asked Rowland.

Mort thought for a moment. Ruby looked out of the window.

'Thirty-five, maybe forty thousand a year.'

'Incredible, isn't it?' Rowland said.

'What's incredible about it?' said Ruby.

'What's he do it for? He could make two, three times as much in private practice, maybe more. What's he do it for?'

'The experience?' Mort suggested.

'If he wants experience he should get out of the Justice Department and go find a job as an in-house lawyer. Think how much he'd make working for you guys. A lousy Assistant US Attorney. What's in it for him?'

'Not every lawyer has your preoccupation with money,' said Ruby.

'You don't say?' said Rowland, as if Ruby had announced that the earth was a triangle.

'You really don't know what's in it for him?' said Ruby.

'No I don't. Do you?'

'I think I do,' Ruby said. He considered how to put it so that the other two men would understand. 'Let's say that the guy believes in what he's doing.'

'Let's say that. He could believe in what he's doing for a hell of a lot more money.'

554

'He's following his master,' said Ruby.

'Master?' Mort was puzzled.

'Justice,' said Ruby. For some reason, he found it difficult to meet Mort's eyes.

Mort looked incredulous. 'You believe that horseshit?'

'What I believe doesn't matter.'

'I see,' said Mort. 'You believe it. Well, let me tell you something. I don't. I don't believe in justice if it allows the press to pillory a man. I don't believe in justice if it indicts and tries and convicts a man before he's even accused of anything. I don't believe in justice if it leaks lies to the press so that the case for the defence is destroyed before it ever goes to court. I don't believe in justice when it offers one guy immunity so it can make a scapegoat out of another. I don't believe in justice when it hounds a company because two guys have their name on the door. Justice! Justice sucks. Everything is a fix. Justice is a fix.'

Ruby clapped ironically. 'Great speech. And maybe you're right, but I'll tell you something. You may not like it, but that's how the system works.'

'Then the system sucks,' said Mort.

'Gentlemen,' said Matthew Rowland. *'Revenons à nos moutons.* Let's concentrate on the subject.'

'Rosenfeld,' said Mort.

'Right. My guess is that he's out to make a name for himself at the Justice Department so that one day he can go into private practice and clean up. I may be wrong, but that's how I see it.'

'Nothing wrong with that,' said Ruby.

'Nothing at all. And if I'm right . . .'

'Forget it,' said Ruby.

'Go on,' said Mort.

'If I'm right, we might, we might just be able to tempt him.'

Mort shook his head.

'You don't believe it?'

'No, I don't.'

'You don't think he'd take a million bucks?'

Ruby looked at his watch again. 'I don't and I'm getting tired of this – '

Matthew Rowland cut in. 'How about twenty million?'

Ruby turned away. Mort looked thoughtful.

'Or fifty?'

'For Chrissake,' said Ruby.

'How about a hundred million? A hundred million bucks? How about it?'

Mort and Ruby looked at each other.

'Well?' said Mort.

'Who would do it?'

'Rowland, I guess.'

'An indictment for attempted bribery of a Justice Department official on top of everything else? Jesus!'

'There are ways of doing such things, I believe.'

'I don't feel comfortable,' said Ruby.

'About Matthew Rowland?'

'About doing it at all.'

'You were in favour of the Domestic scheme.'

'This is different.'

'How different?'

'I don't know. In degree. In kind. Who the hell knows? It's different, that's all. It feels different.' Ruby stubbed out a cheroot and immediately lit another one. His hand was trembling. Mort had never seen Ruby's hand tremble before.

'We left the Garden of Eden,' said Mort. 'We're outcasts. No one's going to let us back in again.'

'I know it. Still . . .' Ruby was shaking his head.

'Let's put it this way. If someone told you that they could make the whole mess go away, disappear into thin air as if it never happened, so we could forget about it and go back to work, what would you say?'

'You're telling me you want to do this thing?'

Mort shook his head. 'I'm telling you nothing. I'm asking you.'

Ruby started laughing.

'What's so funny?'

'Three hundred million spermatozoa. Remember?'

Mort pulled a wry face. 'Things were different then.'

'They could be the same again.'

'They're never the same again.'

'If only we could do it some other way.'

'Some other way.' Mort crossed to the window. It was raining out there. He could not see Park Avenue. They were enveloped in clouds.

'There isn't any other goddam way,' he said.

Bob Rosenfeld had no problem recognizing extreme stress. He should know; he was a master at creating it. His instinct told him when a man was bearing his maximum load and how far he could carry it. Everyone had his breaking point, the point at which he could take no more. That was the moment when he stopped being useful.

'I have the feeling Edgar's about to crack,' he told Ed Goldwyn.

'What will happen, do you think?'

'He may have a breakdown. Could be he'll have an attack of conscience and tell Mort what he's been doing.'

'Why would he tell that bastard anything?'

'It's a love-hate relationship. You have to remember he feels guilty about what he's doing.'

'The guy's a wimp,' said Ed Goldwyn. 'He has no conscience and no guts.'

'No guts? Maybe not. No conscience. . . ?' Bob Rosenfeld pushed up his glasses and rubbed his eyelids with the tips of his fingers. 'It's a strange thing, conscience,' he said. 'Men will steal and murder and sleep peacefully. Then they'll torment themselves about a pet goldfish they forgot to feed.'

Ed Goldwyn lapsed into his customary state of brooding melancholia. It was tough for him to take lectures on conscience from Bob Rosenfeld. What did he know about conscience?

*

557

'Ed and I think it's time you took a rest.'

'What kind of rest?' said Edgar.

'A round-the-world cruise on the QE2, all expenses paid by the US Treasury,' said Ed Goldwyn gloomily.

'Funny,' said Edgar. 'I'd rather not, if you don't mind. I vomit easily.' He looked straight at Goldwyn as he said it.

'Take a pill,' said Ed Goldwyn.

'You can stop carrying the wire,' said Rosenfeld. 'We have enough tapes to digest for a while. You did a great job. We appreciate it.'

'That's right,' said Goldwyn. 'We appreciate it.'

'I've done a shit job,' said Edgar. 'I was going to tell you, anyway. The deal's off. I can't go through with it. I don't sleep nights.'

'Take a pill.' Goldwyn was in a real sour mood.

'Ed,' said Rosenfeld. 'The guy's trying to tell us something that's important to him. Enough with the pills.'

'What's done is done,' said Edgar, 'I can't change that, but I'm not helping you guys any more. You can't indict me now. I'm through.'

'I understand how you feel,' said Rosenfeld.

'Don't try to change my mind,' said Edgar.

'I wouldn't do that,' said Rosenfeld. 'You've helped us and we're grateful. It's over for you. We might need you for a couple of things later on,' he added casually, 'but we don't have to talk about that now.'

'What sort of things?' said Edgar apprehensively.

Bob Rosenfeld was moving files around his desk and Ed Goldwyn was looking at the wall about a foot away from Edgar's head.

'The grand jury,' said Rosenfeld.

'But we had an agreement,' said Edgar, his voice rising. 'You said . . . you said I wouldn't have to testify to the grand jury.' His head was hurting. That little pulse pounded in his neck. 'You told me I wouldn't be called as a witness.'

'No I did not,' said Rosenfeld. 'I said I would check with my boss.'

Edgar jumped up. His face was red and his eyes wild. For a moment he was out of control. He swept the files off Rosenfeld's desk, then he picked up the phone and threw it against the wall. 'You lying bastards! You lying – fucking bastards! You lousy crooks! You let me walk out of here thinking . . . You screwed me! Jesus Christ!' He fell back in his chair. The tears welled up in his eyes. His lips trembled.

'It wasn't legal,' said Ed Goldwyn. 'We found out it wasn't legal. This is the US Attorney's Office, Edgar. What do you want from us? We can't get involved in things that aren't legal, now can we?'

'We had an agreement,' said Edgar. He was crying now, not even bothering to wipe away the tears as they rolled down his face.

'I don't recall any agreement,' said Ed Goldwyn. 'What it seems we had was a misunderstanding.'

Edgar clenched his two fists. He wanted to punch that fat face so badly that he was groaning with the effort to control himself. Ed Goldwyn stared at him impassively, his eyes unwavering.

Edgar wiped his face and blew his nose loudly. 'You said . . .' He was hyperventilating, mouth open, gulping in air. 'You said we were working together. You said I should leave everything to you. That I didn't have a thing to worry about. You told me those things – and all the time . . .' He broke off, head bowed, arms hanging loosely between his legs. For a long time he sat there like that. No one said a word.

'It's a battlefield,' said Bob Rosenfeld in a low voice. 'A lousy battlefield. Some guys get hurt. I'm sorry, Edgar. That's how it is.'

'Joe Murphy on line three.'

'Hi, Joe. What's new?'

'I just wanted to say I'm sorry, Mort. I don't know what the hell got into me. I should never have come whining to you.'

'No problem, Joe.'

'You have enough on your mind.'

'You could say that.'

'It was right what you told me. It's my bag, not yours.'

'You need help? Money or anything?' said Mort.

'I don't need money,' Joe said. 'I never did. You know that.'

'Take care then.'

'You too, Mort.'

It was an odd call, he thought later. All the same, he respected Joe for making it. No doubt the guy was reassuring him that, whatever happened, he could handle it.

The fact that Edgar was drunk was, in itself, not at all surprising. To be crocked, however, at eleven in the morning was unusual, even for him. He wandered into Mort's office, swayed around aimlessly for a few moments and collapsed into an armchair in the far corner of the room, the furthest from Mort's desk that he could get.

'I'm smashed,' he announced.

Mort was busy. He had telexes to dictate and calls to make and he was hosting a lunch for bankers in his private dining room in an hour's time. Europe would be closing soon. It was not convenient for him to play psychiatrist to an alcoholic.

'Go drink some coffee, Edgar,' he said mildly.

'I already did.'

'Drink some more,' said Mort, a little less patiently. 'Maybe you should go home. Drinking in the office – it doesn't look so good. Know what I mean?'

Edgar eased himself out of the chair slowly, very slowly, and meandered across the room to Mort's desk. As he walked, he lurched first to one side, then the other. When he got to the desk he repositioned himself until he was exactly in the centre, facing Mort. He slipped his hand inside his trouser pocket. Mort instinctively flinched. For a wild moment he thought that Edgar was going to shoot him. Then he heard a voice – his own voice – saying, 'Drink some more. Maybe you should go home. Drinking in the office – it doesn't look so good. Know what I mean?'

For a second or two he stared blankly at Edgar.

'Know what I mean?' said Edgar and giggled. He took the mini tape recorder out of his pocket and put it on the desk. 'My cute little friend – a Nagra, they call it. A Nagra body recorder. What you do is strap it on your inside leg – just below your dick.'

Mort had never experienced the sensation before, but there it was in his stomach, the cramping hand of fear.

'The mike is tiny, tiny, tiny. You stick that between your tits. Very sensitive. Picks up every little thing. Burps, farts . . . Mortimer King.'

'How long?'

'Months,' said Edgar. 'Months and months and months and months.' He wandered back to the armchair in the far corner of the room and fell into it. 'And months,' he added.

'Why?'

'He told me I'd go to the pen if I didn't. See, I don't like the pen. Don't like it at all. They say the food is crap.' He smirked.

'I told you they had no evidence – not enough for an indictment.'

'They do now,' said Edgar. 'My little Nagra friend – he talked plenty. He talked real good.'

Mort was trying to think. He needed to be alone. 'I have some calls to make,' he said.

'Aren't you going to say anything?' said Edgar.

'What do you want me to say?'

'Aren't you going to ball me out, old friend, old buddy? I've been a bad boy.'

'Go get your absolution some place else,' said Mort.

Edgar looked puzzled. He picked up a *Time* magazine from the table by the armchair and flipped through it. Then he started to cry. He cried easily these days.

Mort touched the intercom. 'Call the driver and have him take Mr Proktor home,' he told his secretary.

'Goodbye, Edgar,' he said.

Edgar's eyes were red, his face wet. 'What do you mean, goodbye?'

'You're through.'

'For Chrissake, man, we have to talk. Talk to me.'

'I already did. You recorded it,' said Mort with grim humour. 'That's it. Finito!'

'Please, Mort,' Edgar pleaded, 'give me another chance. I'll make it up to you.'

'That's going to be tough, Edgar. What will you do? Bring me pastrami on rye in the pen?'

'I'll tell them the tapes were forged. I'll tell them anything you want. Don't fire me, Mort. I couldn't handle it.' He wiped his eyes with the back of his hand and swayed back to the desk again. 'I'm not asking for absolution. I need help.'

'Don't we all?' said Mort. 'The driver's waiting.'

'OK. So I'm through,' said Edgar, 'if that's what you want.' He waited for Mort to say something. 'I'm going,' he said. He stood there, swaying on his feet, as Mort thumbed through his telexes.

'I don't want a thing. No salary, no bonus. And as for the shares, you can have them back. I guess they're not worth a dime, anyway.'

'Like your friendship,' said Mort.

Edgar stood there, rocking from side to side, trying to focus his eyes. 'I used to be a nice guy,' he said. 'Didn't I? Before ... all this. Now look what they made me do.'

'No one made you do anything.'

'You should have let me marry Kate,' said Edgar. 'You should have let me, Mort. We could have been happy.'

'A man decides these things for himself,' said Mort contemptuously.

'Forgive me.'

562

Mort held up the mini tape recorder. 'Don't forget your friend,' he said.

Two days later Matthew Rowland was on the line.

'I need to know,' he said. 'I need to know if you want me to go ahead.'

'I'll get back to you.'

'Mort. Face it. You're in trouble. It's no use hiding your head in the sand like a goddam ostrich. It's time to make decisions.'

'Tex told us we weren't doing anything illegal.'

'You believe that?'

Mort did not know what he believed. Where did fraud and deception begin? Where did they end? Where was he now? In that shadowy no-man's-land between the legal and the illegal – or beyond? There had to be a way back – whatever he had told Ruby – a way back over the line they had crossed. The trouble was that no one wanted to let them find that way, not without indictments and court proceedings. And jail. Wasn't everyone allowed one mistake? It seemed not.

'We'll be OK. Everything's going to be OK. Melvin Craig will never talk and, as long as he's on our side, Rosenfeld doesn't have the evidence.'

'I hope you're right,' said Rowland.

'Why are you so negative suddenly? You've changed. I don't understand you.'

'Just being cautious.'

Mort chuckled. 'Cautious? You're proposing to bribe an Assistant US Attorney and you're just being cautious? I love it.'

'I intend asking him to sound out the US Attorney as well.'

Panic stabbed Mort's chest. 'For God's sake, man, I can't handle this. First it's the assistant. Now it's his boss. Who's it going to be tomorrow? The President?'

'What I'm saying is we have to know if O'Reilly would accept Rosenfeld's recommendation to drop the case – on the grounds of insufficient evidence, for example.'

'Do we really need this, Matthew?'

'It depends if you want to save your skin or not.'

Save his skin. What did a man have to do to save his skin? How many lines were there to cross? How many more lines? Where did it end? What had Edgar done? Betrayed his oldest friend. That was something Mort would never do. And yet the world judged that what Edgar had done was legal – even praiseworthy. But to bribe a Justice Department official . . . assuming he could be bribed . . .

'Do you, Mort? Do you? Because if you do, my advice is . . . you know what my advice is.'

Matthew Rowland's advice came expensive. In more ways than one.

Edgar walked into Queenie's on Union Street, San Francisco, and it was like no one had noticed that he had ever been away. They knew, of course, but they were too polite to mention it. It was assumed he was back for good. Who in their right mind would want to leave San Francisco and who, having left it, would not rush back there as fast as he could?

He drank the first three dry martinis quickly, then he leaned on the counter and looked around him. The decor of the bar was Victorian – fringed lamps, engraved mirrors and a large portrait of the formidable Queen herself, looking disapprovingly down on a bunch of characters who certainly would not have amused her.

'How you been?' asked Albert, the bartender. In Queenie's they asked questions like that, but a reply was not expected. If there was one thing no one wanted to know it was how you'd been.

'How you been?' said Edgar, respecting the ritual.

Albert nodded and gave the bar a perfunctory wipe. It looked like the same cloth the bartender was using ten years ago, when Edgar was last here.

That's what Edgar liked about Queenie's. It was social, yet at the same time anonymous. People didn't actually

564

talk to you. They talked to themselves. There were always two or three customers haranguing Albert, usually at the same time. Edgar had never seen this 'Albert' before. Every bartender at Queenie's for the last seventy-five years had been named Albert, presumably after the Prince Consort, and every Albert had possessed the same qualities. They had all been compulsive counter wipers and they all had a nice line in reactions – mostly one-word noises like a grunt or a 'huh'. Occasionally, they produced something more complex like 'you don't say?' or 'how about that?' or 'isn't that just the most?' You could pretty much tell what the drunk across the bar was saying by the expression on Albert's face. Of course, every now and then his concentration slipped and he cracked a big grin when some guy told him he had cancer, or his wife had just died, but it didn't happen too often. No one seemed to care much, anyway.

Edgar wandered from table to table exchanging cordial grunts and nods. Then he sat at the bar feeling free to talk to himself, to the guy sitting next to him, to Albert, to his reflection in the mirror behind the bar, or, for that matter, to Queen Victoria.

'I'm a drunk, but I'm harmless,' said Edgar. Her Majesty glared at him reproachfully.

Albert assumed a cautious expression, uncertain whether to smile, leer or look sympathetic.

'I love you, Kate!' said Edgar loudly. 'What's the big deal about a few drinks here and there?' Edgar looked round the room. No one seemed to be paying much attention. 'I love her!' he announced. For a moment, everyone stopped talking and there was scattered applause. An androgynous character at a window table smiled sweetly. 'I love you too, honey bun,' he said and patted his permed hair.

Queenie's was the end of the world. There was nowhere else to go. Like San Francisco itself, it was the pot of gold at the end of the rainbow. People came there expecting paradise.

'You think this is paradise?' Edgar asked Albert.

Albert looked vague. 'I've only been here two weeks.

You want a street map?' Edgar recalled that there was indeed a street named Paradise somewhere around.

'This ain't Paradise, honey bun,' said the man at the window table. 'This is Union Street.' He patted his hair again. 'I know you,' he said, with a cunning look in his eye. 'You're the Ayatollah Khomeini.'

'No, I'm not,' said Edgar.

'Oh no? Who are you then?'

'I'm Ludwig van Beethoven.'

Curly-top looked disappointed. 'You sure you ain't Khomeini?'

'If I was Khomeini,' said Edgar, 'I'd have a beard.'

There was a respectful silence in the room. Edgar had made a good point; it seemed unanswerable. The man at the window table was perplexed. Then he grinned. 'You could have shaved,' he said triumphantly.

'He fired me,' said Edgar. 'Threw me out. After ten years, the bastard threw me out, just because of a lousy Nagra. What was I supposed to do? Rosenfeld was blackmailing me. What could I do? Tell me that.'

The man at the window table raised a hand. 'You could have shaved,' he said.

'Who am I kidding?' said Edgar. 'I should have told Rosenfeld to shove it. I'm weak.'

'Aren't we all?' said Albert the bartender, and wiped the bar, nodding his head as if he knew all about life.

Edgar collected some quarters and called a girl he used to know. There was no reply. He sat at the bar for another couple of hours, calling her every few minutes. Finally, she answered.

'Jees, it's you! Call me tomorrow,' she said. 'I have company.'

'I have to see you now.'

'It's been ten years, Edgar,' she said. 'It's been ten years I haven't heard from you and you have to see me now.'

'That's right,' he said. 'I have to see you now. Don't hang up. Please don't hang up.'

There was a long silence at the other end.

'I love you, honey,' he said. 'Passionately.'

'You sonofabitch,' she said. 'Give me a couple of hours.'

The man at the window table stood up and pointed an accusing finger at Edgar. 'You ain't Beethoven,' he said derisively. 'You don't fool me. Not for a second you don't.'

'I got to confess it,' said Edgar. 'I'm the Ayatollah Khomeini.'

'What did I tell you,' said the victor exultantly, throwing his arms wide and appealing to the room. 'What did I say?'

As Edgar left, curly-top stood on the table and shouted at the top of his voice, 'Fuck you! You ain't Khomeini! You're Moses! I seen you in Macdonald's. You hear me?'

The Golden Gate Bridge was completed in 1937. Since then, seven hundred and sixty-two people had jumped off it. Twenty-three survived, most of them for a very short time. When you jump off the end of the world, it's a long way down. Edgar had thought about doing it a number of times. Now, here he was again, walking across the bridge to take a look – not that there was much to see. The fog was so thick it might almost have held him up if he had jumped. But it wouldn't. He knew that. What did it matter, anyhow? He wasn't going to jump. He knew that too. Tonight the fog horns intoned their melancholy dirge, as if the whole world were in mourning for him. Well, the mourning was premature.

Edgar needed to work things out. You couldn't work anything out if you were dead.

He walked back into town and hailed a cab by the Fine Arts' Museum. She had said a couple of hours. Great. The hell of it was, he'd forgotten where she lived. It was a long time ago. Everything was a long time ago.

He wandered around for an hour or so, then he caught a cab back to Queenie's. Curly-top, head on the table, was snoring loudly, and Albert, the bartender, was poring over a street map looking for Paradise.

*

It was only when Sam arrived at the Kantonsspital in Zurich that he remembered it was the same hospital Siegfried Gerber had died in all those years ago. He walked across to reception. He should have been happy, but all he could feel were the confused, bitter emotions of ten years ago: jealousy, resentment and self-pity. Why must Jane have her baby here? Her baby.

He remembered how he had followed Amy, how he had tormented himself, convinced that she was still in love with Gerber – if she were capable of loving anyone, that is. He remembered the tortured months that followed the morning he had walked in on them, how he had despised himself, how it had seemed to him that he was destined to accept perpetual humiliation. He had not even had the courage to leave. In the end, ironically, it had been Amy who had walked away from the marriage. Being here again – what a cruel sensation it was. As if time had not passed at all, as if it were that dreadful day and Siegfried Gerber were here, still dying in one of those chilly anonymous rooms, still his boss, still mocking him.

It was a girl.

'Isn't she gorgeous?' Jane was exhilarated, happier than she had ever been.

Sam picked up the bundle and looked down at the tiny wrinkled face. He felt nothing – nothing except shame that he could not feel what he should be feeling: pride, perhaps, love, happiness, all the normal emotions that a father was supposed to enjoy.

'She's beautiful,' he said.

'I'm so happy, Sam. I never felt like this before. Everything's going to be all right. I know it is.'

'I know it is too,' he lied.

Jane took the baby from him and cradled it. Suddenly, from one day to the next, she was a mother. She looked as if she had always been one. Sam felt excluded.

'We have to give her a name,' she said. 'What do you think of Melanie? I like it, but it seems a bit old-fashioned. I like Danielle, too.'

568

Sam hesitated. 'I thought we might call her . . . I thought . . . Laura,' he said. 'That is . . . if you don't mind.'

Jane was looking down proudly at her baby, but, as he spoke, the happiness died on her face and the light went out of her eyes. 'Laura,' she said, 'is no name for a child of mine.'

'It's my child too,' said Sam quietly.

'Yes, it is. It's our child. If we get married, it will be our marriage, our life. I don't think you know what that means, Sam – not yet. You want to live in the past? Well, that's fine. That's your problem, but don't ask me to live there with you.'

'I don't want to live in the past,' said Sam. 'I'm finished with it. The only thing that matters now is you and me. It was just an idea I had. To . . .'

'To what, Sam?'

'To give our child the name of someone I love.' His voice broke. 'Someone I loved.'

'That's right. Laura's dead.'

'Not for me, she isn't.'

'Nor is your marriage, is it?'

'That's not fair,' he said.

'You have to choose,' she said. 'No one can do it for you.'

Two weeks later Matthew Rowland still had not heard from Mort. He decided to give him a call.

'When can we meet?'

'How about next week? I'll call you.'

'How about today?'

'Today's busy.' He was lunching with a senator and he had to fly down to Houston in the afternoon.

'I have news.'

'What kind of news?'

'Good news.'

'Tell me.' Mort could do with some good news.

'The kind of news you give people face to face,' said Rowland.

'Oh,' said Mort.

569

'Two o'clock?'

He would have to cut short the lunch. 'Two o'clock then.' Reluctantly.

Matthew Rowland swept in, trailing the tan camel's hair and a waft of Aramis.

Mort was alone. He knew what his brother thought.

Rowland had something to tell him and he was making the most of it. Nothing, but nothing massaged his ego like a captive audience, and Mort, behind his desk, looked very captive. Matthew Rowland sat on the other side of the desk and leaned on it with one arm. Lawyer to client. Courtier to king. Mephistopheles to Faustus.

'Wow!' he said. 'Is that guy complicated.'

'What guy?' Mort asked. He knew very well what guy.

And Rowland knew that he knew. 'You want the details or you want the bottom line?'

The bottom line. That must be the last one you crossed, thought Mort, the River Styx that separated this world from the next. If you drifted across that, you were in hell.

'Give me the bottom line.'

'He'll do it.'

Mort did not know what to think. What should he be? Pleased? Shocked?

'I never gave you the green light,' he said coldly.

'You never gave me the red one either. Look, Mort. Nothing's set in concrete. All I did was sound him out. The discussion was extremely complex. The man has a conscience.'

'That's nice. Where does he keep it? In the deep-freeze?'

'He has some evidence, but he's no fool. In fact he's very smart. He agrees that their case is not strong enough to be sure of a conviction – maybe not even enough for an indictment. He accepts that all he can really do is make life uncomfortable for you and probably damage his own reputation in the process. He's very concerned about that. This is a real ambitious man. There's no room in his life for failure. He's not rich and the prospect of immense wealth without having to sell his soul to the devil – at least that's how I put it to him – is more than he can resist.'

Maybe Bob Rosenfeld would not be selling his soul to the devil, but what about Mortimer King? Mort felt himself being pulled gently over that line.

'He wants seventy-five up front. The rest when the case is dropped.'

Mort tried to look as though he were reading his telexes.

'I'm happy for you, Mort. I'm convinced this is the right thing to do.'

God in heaven. The right thing to do. Matthew Rowland knew the right thing to do. Matthew Rowland knew what was right and what was wrong. Only his right and wrong meant something different from Mort's. Saving your skin was the right thing to do. Anything else was wrong.

'I think you'll agree it would be a very satisfactory solution,' he said smugly, patting his hips and stomach. Even sitting down he was still wearing the camel's-hair coat draped over his shoulders.

Mort would have liked to wrap the sleeves around that plump neck and pull them tight.

He was silent for a few moments, thinking about Edgar. He had been worried about him, trying to remember what he had said to him when they had talked about the Domestic scam. Impossible to analyse every conversation Edgar must have recorded, but he was pretty sure that he had not said anything that would help the Justice Department's case, anything that would give them any more evidence than they already had. Anyway, taped evidence was always unsatisfactory. Juries hated it and judges were sceptical.

'It's a cheap solution.'

Cheap? Mort shook his head. 'The price is too high,' he said. It was what Joe Murphy had once told him.

'You're crazy. What's a hundred million to you guys? You're billionaires.'

'I wasn't thinking about money,' said Mort, looking at

571

Hades. He had paid his coin and Charon was rowing him across the Styx.

The way back. Would there ever be a way back now?

They told Sam and Jeffrey that their problems were over. There weren't going to be any indictments. Sam was happy and he asked no questions.

Jeffrey took the next flight to New York.

'How come?' he asked.

'Lack of evidence,' said Mort.

'They decided they had no case, that's all,' said Ruby.

Jeffrey nodded. If that was the way they wanted to play it, it was OK with him. It would not be the first time they had hidden the truth from him. Just as long as the case was dropped, nothing else mattered.

'You're quite sure?'

'Sure,' said Ruby.

'It's all over,' said Mort.

They looked like small boys caught in the act. What had they been up to? Those innocent, slightly self-satisfied expressions that he knew so well – what exactly did they signify? Whatever it was, it seemed that, indeed, it was business as usual. He was not obligated any more.

'In that case, I want you to know I'm resigning.'

It was probably the first time he had ever seen Mort look astonished. Ruby maintained his habitual antiseptic expression, his mouthwash special.

'You're what!' said Mort.

'I'm resigning,' said Jeffrey. 'Quitting, leaving, throwing in the towel. That's what I came here to tell you. It's not the kind of news you break to your partners on the phone.'

'It's not the kind of news you break to your partners at all,' said Mort.

'You've got to be joking,' said Ruby. 'Just when we're doing so great. You quitting? I can't believe it.'

'Think of the money you're making,' said Mort.

'I already did,' said Jeffrey. 'It's enough.'

'We need you, Jeffrey,' said Mort. 'It's not a good time

572

to go. Think it over. Give it a year or two. Then, if you still want to go, go with our blessing.'

'I'm sorry. I made up my mind.' He could feel the power of their opposition and their resentment. They were a formidable team to fight.

'Please, Jeffrey,' said Mort. 'One year. Give us one more year. That's all I ask.'

'And then another and another and another,' said Jeffrey, 'till one day I'll be trapped – like you are, Ruby. Then it'll be a life sentence.'

Ruby's pale features flushed bright red with anger. 'Trapped? Who's trapped? You're talking bullshit. I'm where I want to be.'

'Well, that's great,' said Jeffrey. 'I'm not.'

'I'm disappointed in you,' said Mort. 'I thought this was a lifetime partnership.'

'This is no time to abandon ship,' said Ruby.

Jeffrey rounded on him angrily. 'The ship isn't sinking and I'm not abandoning it. The way you two are heading, you'll soon own half the world. You can do it without me. You don't need me any more. You don't need anyone. I'm just an oil trader. I've done what I can for you. It's time to move on.'

'So that's what's bugging you,' said Mort. 'OK, we'll find a solution. Now I understand the problem. We'll do anything to make you happy. We'll divide the company in two. You run the trading, Ruby and I will take over expansion and acquisitions.'

'It's too late,' said Jeffrey.

'It's our company,' said Mort, spreading his arms. 'We've all benefited from it – you, me, Ruby, everyone.'

'I'm not denying it,' said Jeffrey.

Mort let his arms fall to his sides. 'Don't forget loyalty, Jeffrey. Doesn't the company deserve loyalty? Don't I?' he said . . . For Chrissake, where had those words surfaced from? They had come back to haunt him after all these years.

*

They lunched at Le Relais. Karl reserved the same table they occupied the last time they ate there.

'How long ago was it?' said Amy.

'I don't dare to think,' said Karl.

It was all the same: the noise, the bustle – even the menu, it seemed.

'Nothing's changed,' said Karl. 'Certainly not you.' He was not being gallant. It was true. She was amazing. He looked at their reflection in the gilt-framed mirror on the opposite wall. They were a handsome couple. She was a woman any man would be proud of. 'Last time we were here you walked out on me. Remember?'

'I remember.'

'You said I was programmed, afraid to do anything different, afraid to take risks.' Amy had forgotten, but Karl never would.

'I bought a farm,' he said. 'It's in the Engadine, not far from Zurich. Not big, but very pretty.'

'That's nice,' she said. 'I'm glad for you.'

'It's a great investment. Pays its own way. Right now I have a manager running things. I have fifty cows, a couple of bulls, chickens, ducks – oh yes and two rabbits – male and female,' he added grinning.

'You'll soon have a big family then,' said Amy.

Karl stirred his coffee thoughtfully. 'I've done well the last few years in King Brothers. I've saved more than I ever dreamed possible. What with my salary, bonuses and share options, I'm comfortable – not rich, you understand, but very comfortable. When I work the farm full time, I won't have to worry about money.'

'You're leaving King Brothers then?' said Amy. She was surprised. She had thought that business was his life.

'I've been in the oil business long enough. It's been good to me. But now I want to be a farmer. That's the real life. It's what my father was and his father, too.'

'If you're sure it's the right thing for you, then go for it,' said Amy. 'The world is full of people doing things they don't want to do.'

574

'I was talking to my bank manager the other day,' said Karl slowly. 'Right now, I reckon I'm worth nearly a million dollars. I could easily get a bank loan to buy an apartment house, and I could more than cover the interest with the rents and still have the capital appreciation. With that and the farm, why, I'll be secure for the rest of my life.'

Amy was digging her fingernails into the breadcrumbs on the tablecloth.

'Why are you telling me all this?' she said, suddenly alarmed.

He put his hand over hers. 'I think you know why,' he said gently.

'No, I don't,' she said. 'But whatever the reason, I wish you well. I never doubted that you'd make it.'

'I love you, Amy,' he said. 'I want to be with you – always. I know you have a lot going for you here in New York, but I can offer you a good life. We're perfect for each other. We'd be happy together.'

Amy's head was spinning. Leave New York? Give up her career and go live in some Swiss barn? She hated the country and she loathed farms. Jesus! Cows, bulls and rabbits. Think of the smell. The man was crazy, out of his mind. What did he think she was? She could just see herself up to the thighs in mud and chicken shit, washing his dirty underpants, ironing his shirts, cooking his dinner with a squalling baby in one hand and a pot of farmhouse stew in the other.

Karl was still dreaming. 'You told me I was afraid to cross the road. Well, maybe I was then. But not now. I'm giving up a good job with King Brothers to go out on my own. It's a risk, an adventure, and I want to share it with you.'

What could she say? To be anyone's wife would be bad enough, but Karl's wife? A farmer's wife? 'Karl, that's not for me. I'm not the marrying kind. I tried it once and it didn't work out.'

'If it's Edward you're worried about, I promise you . . .'

'It's not Edward. It's me. I'm sorry, Karl. I'm flattered you should want to marry me. Of course I am. You're a good man. You need someone to be a good wife to you and a good mother to your children. Someone level-headed and reliable.'

'You're the only woman who ever took me seriously. I need you,' said Karl.

'No, Karl,' she said, 'you don't. Imagine me a farmer's wife.' Suddenly, she could no longer control herself. She started to giggle.

Karl clenched his fists. She was laughing at him. 'Don't,' he said. 'Please don't do that.' It wasn't right. He had asked her to marry him and now he felt humiliated. She was mocking him. His head swam and he had to grip the edge of the table to stop himself from falling.

Jane was about to leave her room in the Kantonsspital when Sam appeared in the doorway.

'I've come to take you home.'

'I'm going back to my apartment,' she said. 'That's home for me.'

'I want you, Jane. I want my child.'

'She's not your child,' she said harshly.

Sam smiled. 'She's my child all right. How could she be anyone else's?'

'She's your child biologically, but that only gives you visiting rights. So visit. Just make sure you phone first.'

'It doesn't matter what we call her. I thought about it. What matters is us,' said Sam.

'Her name is Samantha,' said Jane.

Sam beamed. 'Thank you,' he said. 'I love it.'

'I thought you might.'

'Let's go home,' he said quietly.

'No, Sam, it's no good. Home is commitment. Home means being a husband and a father.' She picked up Samantha from the cot. 'I'd rather she had no father than a reluctant one.'

'She must have a father,' he said. 'We'll get married. You have to marry me.'

'That's where you're wrong, Sam,' said Jane. 'I don't have to do anything.'

'She wants Daniel to come to tea. We should say yes, Ruby. We promised. You know we did.'

Ruby was in no mood to be reminded of what he had said in a weak moment. 'No,' he said stubbornly.

Sarah looked so downcast that his heart went out to her. 'OK, let him come,' he said. 'It's no big deal – it's only tea.'

'She wants him to be the only guest and I told her "yes",' said Sarah.

'So, why ask me?' said Ruby angrily. 'If you told her "yes", why ask me?' How had he been manoeuvred into this situation?

'We have to handle it right, Ruby. If we don't, she'll leave home.'

'Then let her leave,' he shouted. 'Let her see what it's like out there, what it is to be on her own without parents to support her.'

Sarah smiled. 'We'll find her a husband to support her. That would be even better.'

'I'm with you,' said Ruby, 'just as long as his name isn't Daniel Rosenfeld.'

'What's so bad about Daniel? He's a decent boy, he's ambitious and he works. He doesn't do drugs. He doesn't drink. The boy's a *mensch*. Ruth likes him. What more do you want?'

'His father is an animal,' said Ruby venomously.

'Sometimes I don't understand you,' she said. 'You told me he's dropping the charges. That's like admitting he was wrong. Why do you still hate him so much?'

'I have my reasons,' said Ruby. 'Good reasons. The man's two-faced. He's not to be trusted. It's not the kind of family we should be associated with.'

Sarah sighed. She liked Daniel. She believed he would make a good husband for her Ruth, but it wasn't going to be easy.

*

The press had been quiet for some time now, as if the story were no longer good copy.

And then, one morning, there it was: an article in the *New York Times* headlined 'Kings dethroned!' All the old clichés were dragged out. King Brothers were the self-serving middlemen, the scavengers of the oil industry. Worse still, the article alleged that they were under investigation for some of the most serious offences ever perpetrated by white-collar criminals in the USA: fraud and tax evasion totalling hundreds of millions of dollars. There was a graph showing in detail how the Domestic scam worked and a full description of how the 'pot' operated, including three phoney transactions 'concluded' with Wald to milk illegal profits out of the country. The article ended by asserting that indictments against Mortimer and Reuben King were imminent and that if, as confidently predicted by the US Attorney's Office, they were convicted, sentences on the various counts could total three hundred years. It was a bombshell. Mort stormed into his office in a fury and called Matthew Rowland.

'You read the article?'

'I read it,' said Rowland. 'Relax. Everything's under control.'

'Get your ass over here,' said Mort tersely.

'You were supposed to be keeping the lid on this thing.' Mort was white with anger, controlling his rage, but close to exploding.

'I'm doing what I can. Like I said, everything's under control. It'll just take a little while for it to shake out.'

'The hell with shaking out. How can you let them print this garbage?'

'The press are hard to control. Impossible, in fact.'

'I want you to shut them up.'

'How do you propose I do that?'

'Sue them.'

'Right now, that would not be advisable. You're always

578

the one who wants to keep a low profile and I think you're absolutely right.'

'You call this article low profile? And what does Rosenfeld think he's doing? How can he allow these scum to say what they like?'

Matthew Rowland stroked his greying coiffure. 'I told you. Rosenfeld doesn't think he has a case.'

'It's time I saw some evidence of that,' said Mort angrily. 'Meanwhile, no more coverage in the press. See to it. I could kill that goddam reporter. Just when things were beginning to settle down. Now everyone in town has read those lies.'

'Who gives a damn?' said Rowland. 'No one takes that kind of stuff seriously any more.'

But Moses did. Rebecca found him lying across the breakfast table, still clutching the *New York Times*.

Mort and Ruby stood by his bedside in the intensive care unit. The old man was in a coma. He was breathing laboriously into the oxygen mask, making little moaning noises in the back of his throat, but his face, perhaps for the first time in his life, was calm and untroubled.

Mort wanted to touch his cheek, talk to him, reassure him, but he couldn't bring himself to do it. The habit of years could not be changed in a moment. It was too late.

'We should have warned him,' said Ruby. 'Explained things.'

'How could we ever explain?'

'I don't know,' said Ruby. 'All I know is we should have tried. This is our punishment. We thought we got away with it, but we didn't.'

'That's the way you want to see it,' said Mort. 'You want to feel guilty.'

'We are guilty,' said Ruby.

In the evening, Moses died. He just stopped breathing. One moment he was there, the next he was gone. He never seemed to regain consciousness. Once, he opened his eyes for a few moments and looked at his sons. They spoke to him, but they could not be sure that he had heard them. It was how it had always been.

They tore their clothes in ritual grief as is the Jewish custom and buried their father, throwing earth on the coffin until the grave was filled.

Then they went home to Rebecca and tried to comfort her during the Shiva, the seven-day period of mourning, but she looked at them with bewildered eyes and would not be comforted.

When Mort returned to his office, the first call he made was to Matthew Rowland. Rowland's secretary said he was unavailable, but when he pressed her, she admitted that her boss had not been in the office for several days – not, it turned out, since the day of his last meeting with Mort.

'Where is he?'

'He's out of town, Mr King.'

'Where can I reach him?'

'I really have no idea.'

Mort put the phone down. He was in turmoil. He sat at his desk and tried to think. What did it mean? He called a lawyer friend of his and asked him to phone the US Attorney's Office. 'You know Bob Rosenfeld, don't you?'

'Sure I know him. He's a good friend of mine.'

'Ask him when he's going to announce that he's dropped the investigation against us.'

'I heard nothing about it.'

'Do me a favour,' said Mort. 'Ask!'

While he was waiting for the man to call back, he told Ruby what he had done. They waited together for the call. In a few minutes, Mort's private line rang. He let it ring three times, then he picked it up and flipped on the speaker so Ruby could hear.

'I spoke to Bob Rosenfeld. He knows nothing about it. In fact, he laughed at me. He said it was his investigation, so he would be the first to know if it had been dropped. He's drafting a stream of indictments right now. That's what's taking the time, he said. There are so many of them. I guess it was wishful thinking on your part. I'm real sorry.'

'What does it mean?'

'It means Rowland lied to us,' said Ruby.

'Why would he do that?'

'You know better than I do.'

'I don't understand it,' said Mort. 'The guy's supposed to be a friend of mine.'

'What was it he said?' Ruby recalled. 'The only friend you have is your lawyer. Some friend.'

'He told me Rosenfeld had no case. Next thing he disappears.'

'The question is,' said Ruby, 'what did he disappear with?'

Two days later, the papers ran the full story. Matthew Rowland was a high-lifer. He had been in financial trouble for some time, using up his collateral and then his credit to try to put himself back on his feet. When that failed, he had played the foreign exchange markets and the Stock Exchange, but he was a tyro outside the legal profession and his desperate gambling had only made the mess worse. He was unable to meet his margin calls. His debts were massive. He had borrowed at high interest rates from some very tough characters and they were beginning to crowd him. For a time he had warded off disaster by borrowing from Peter to pay Paul, but in the end Peter and Paul crosschecked with each other and Matthew's luck had run out.

His personal life was largely to blame for his problems. The story behind the story was the oldest in the world. He had become infatuated with a hostess in Caesar's Palace, Las Vegas, when he was out there on a weekend gambling trip a couple of years back. She was twenty, a natural honey blonde, weighed a hundred and ten pounds and had slim, beautiful legs all the way up. Matthew's wife was fifty-two, had a pink rinse in her white hair, weighed a hundred and ninety pounds and her dumpy legs were bloated with blue varicose veins. It was no contest. It was also pathetic. He was terrified that he might lose the girl, so, of course, he had given her what she wanted. What she wanted most was jewellery and apparently she could be very grateful. Matthew Rowland had always made a bundle, but he had spent more bundles than he ever made. There was nothing in the bank or in a safety deposit box set aside for a rainy day. And when it rained on Matthew Rowland, it poured. There was nowhere for him to shelter, so he ran off to Europe – that's what they thought – and the natural honey blonde went back to hostessing. It was what she liked doing.

'I wonder if he took the camel's-hair coat with him,' said Mort.

'I wonder what else he took with him,' Ruby said slyly.

'Meaning?'

'You tell me.'

Mort looked thoughtfully at Ruby, his expression giving nothing away.

'He never talked to Rosenfeld, did he? It was all a con.'

'That's right. He told me Rosenfeld believed that he might have a weak case, but that he could make our life a misery for a long time to come. That's why Rowland said he wanted the hundred million – to bribe Rosenfeld to drop the case now. Seventy-five up front. The rest when the case was dropped.'

'Jees! You gave seventy-five million to that jerk and he stole it.'

Mort grinned almost sheepishly. 'I didn't give him a cent.'

It wasn't often that Ruby looked surprised. This was one of the rare occasions.

'But you said – '

'I didn't say anything. You assumed. I admit I thought about it. Who wouldn't? But I decided that was one line I was not going to cross.'

'I'm glad,' said Ruby. 'And not just because of the money.'

'Besides,' said Mort, 'those bastards will never get us. Not without Melvin Craig.'

Jeffrey called from London. 'I hear the investigation is still on after all,' he said.

'That's right,' said Mort.

'What happened? You told me they dropped it.'

'That's what we heard, but we were given some misleading information.'

'I hear Matthew Rowland skipped the country.'

'You hear a lot of things,' said Mort.

'You remember James Timba?'

'The Nigerian marketing manager?'

'That's him. The military wanted to make an example of someone – put on a big show to distract attention from the real criminals. So they tried him. He was sentenced to twenty-five years.'

'That's terrible.'

'They put him in Kiri Kiri in Apapa. They offered to reduce his sentence to five years if he paid everything back, the commissions and all that. God knows how he could do that. Most of the money wasn't even for him. It was for the big boys, the ones who'll never go to trial. It was all too much for him. He hanged himself yesterday.'

'Oh, God!'

'I liked the guy. He was a friend of mine. He had a great sense of humour.'

'There was no way you could help him,' said Mort.

'If I'd known what he was going through, I might have been able to do something.'

'You couldn't have done a thing. Not without involving the company.'

'That would never do, would it?'

'Don't blame yourself – it was one of those things.'

'Yes . . . one of those things.'

'He took from everyone. That's the way it goes. He knew what he was doing.'

'I wonder if any of us knows that,' said Jeffrey.

'When are you leaving?'

'I'm not. I'm withdrawing my resignation. What was it Ruby said? "This is no time to jump ship." '

'Thanks,' Mort said, 'I appreciate it. I can't tell you what this means to me.'

'This is a bad time for you.'

'You could say that,' said Mort laconically.

'It seems like everything is happening at once.'

'We'll handle it,' said Mort. 'Everything's going to be OK.'

Maybe it is, thought Jeffrey. Not for James Timba though.

'He wants to see you,' said Melvin Craig's lawyer.

'Why me? Why now?' said Mort. 'It's not a good time. Besides, I have to admit I hate the idea of going to see him in jail.'

Too close to home, the attorney thought. 'My recommendation is that you go see him – for your own sake.'

'What's it about?' said Mort.

'I can't say.'

Reluctant as he was, Mort had the feeling he had no choice in the matter. 'I'll see him tomorrow.'

Melvin Craig peered at Mort through the wire netting. He was thinner and paler than the last time they met, but otherwise he looked OK. There was something disturbing about his manner, though. He was uneasy and restless.

'I won't ask you how it is in here – I can guess.'

'No, you can't,' said Craig. 'I used to think they treated us white-collar guys better than the others – you know, like I never did armed robbery, or dealt drugs or killed anyone – but I tell you, man, they're after our blood. Don't let them put you in here. You hear what I'm saying?'

'I hear.'

Melvin Craig cracked his fingers viciously. 'I made you a promise,' he said.

'You did,' said Mort.

'Forget what I said,' Craig mumbled. 'I'm sorry.'

584

It was what Mort had feared. He wouldn't admit it to himself, but he had known the moment the attorney called.

'They kept on at me. Wouldn't leave me alone. Every week they made me a better offer if I cooperated.'

'Cooperated?'

'I told them I had records.'

'There aren't any records.'

'I kept my own. In a safety deposit box at the bank. I never told you about it. I never told anyone.'

'What is it you want of me?'

'What I want, you can't give me. You can't give me back a year of my life. That's what they're offering. They're after you, Mort. They're going to get you.'

'I'll kill you, you bastard!' Mort whispered the words so that no one else could hear, but they lost neither their intensity nor their venom. His green eyes were cold with rage. If the netting had not been between them, he would have put his hands round the other man's neck and strangled him.

'No you won't. Besides, you're too late. He already has the records.'

'God damn you!' Mort punched the wire netting with his fist. Craig flinched. He was scared. He had never seen Mort so angry.

'Cool it, man. You're out of control. I said I was sorry.'

'You think that's all it takes? All you have to do is say you're sorry and it makes up for everything? I don't buy that, Melvin. They might let you out of here, but that won't be the end of it.'

Time was up. As he left with the warden, Craig looked back. He was asking for forgiveness, but that was something he would never get from Mort.

Mort sat there staring blankly at the wire netting. For a moment, he imagined himself sitting behind it.

He shivered, wondering if that was the way it would be. His whole body felt cold. He realized suddenly that he was the only visitor still there. He was alone. The warden tapped him on the shoulder. He stood up and walked slowly away.

'You blame him?' said Ruby.

'The guy's a treacherous shit. He made me a promise, God damn it!'

'You know what, Mort? I'm beginning to be afraid. It feels like nowhere is safe any more. Nothing we do is working out. I'm scared.'

'Hell, Ruby, they have nothing on us. Not a thing. We'll fight it out. We'll beat the bastards.'

'I never thought it would come to this.'

'Who did?'

They were both thinking the same thoughts. All those years of struggle, hard work and achievement, all those dreams.

'We can't let the company go under,' said Mort. 'Whatever happens to us, we have to save King Brothers.'

'When the news gets out, there'll be a run on our assets. You know how over-leveraged we are. The company could go under unless . . .'

'Unless what?' said Mort eagerly.

'There's only one way I can think of to protect the company and that's – to sell it right now.'

'Sell King Brothers? Are you out of your mind?'

'Or merge it,' said Ruby slowly.

Mort put his head in his hands. 'I hear what you're saying, but how can I go to E.M. and eat humble pie? Besides, I'd have to tell him the whole story. He'd insist on massive provisions for fines and costs. I know the guy better than you do. He's a hard man. By the time he was through with me, the deal wouldn't be worth a dime.'

'If he's willing to consider a merger, then almost any deal is better than no deal. It's our last shot, Mort.'

Mort shook his head.

'Look, buster,' said Ruby, 'I hate to get heavy with you, but there's more to this than your pride, or your personal feud with E.M. We're talking life and death here. We have responsibilities, don't we? We have partners, employees. We can't just walk away from them. You know that. You're Mortimer King, remember?'

It was a long story and E.M. listened patiently. When Mort had finished, he had only one comment. 'I tried to warn you. You weren't listening.'

'The lawyers told us we were OK.'

'Since when do you listen to lawyers?'

'This is all hindsight, E.M. I guess you're right, but I have to find a solution. If I don't, it'll cost me blood. It may cost me the company,' he added in a low voice. It was a tough admission to have to make to his old rival.

'What's the alternative?'

'I want to merge King Brothers with the Oil Corporation like you once suggested. I don't know if you'd offer the same terms. They were more than generous. I'd listen to anything reasonable.'

'You think that merging with me would save King Brothers?'

'I know it would,' said Mort. 'Right now, the danger is the squeeze the Feds are putting on us. They're starting to freeze our assets. The next problem will be renewing the bank loans. If the banks pull out and there's a run on the company's assets by our creditors, we'll be forced to sell them and I don't know if we'll even be able to cover our debts, let alone pay any back taxes and fines the Feds might stick us with. If we merged with you, the banks would leave us alone. Our assets would be protected. I think the Feds might even drop the case.'

E.M. nodded. 'It's possible. Of course, your shares are not worth what they were.'

'I recognize that,' said Mort. 'Money isn't the problem. We'll work something out. You can have half the merged company and you can be the boss like you always wanted.'

E.M. could not conceal the gleam of triumph. 'You really want this deal badly.'

'It's the only way to save King Brothers. My feelings

587

don't count. I have to think of my partners and my employees.'

E.M. thought about it for a few moments. Then he shook his head. 'It's too late, Mort. I made you an offer a long time ago, an offer you couldn't refuse. That I was sure of. Only you, Mort – you refused it. You always were a stubborn bastard. It's too late. You've let things get out of hand. I'm too old. I'm getting tired. I have a hard enough time running my own operation, let alone yours as well. You know it's funny, Mort, there was a time when all I wanted to do was live long enough to see you go under. When you left me, it was like losing my own son. It hurt.'

'I know,' said Mort.

'Now?' E.M. shrugged. 'If I could help, I would. But I can't. I'm sorry. I owe you.'

'What do you owe me?' Mort asked.

'In a way,' said E.M., 'I blame myself for all this.'

'I don't understand,' said Mort. 'What's it to do with you?'

It was like pulling teeth. E.M. didn't want to talk, but he answered, in spite of himself. 'Jack Greenberg was the one who told Rosenfeld you were involved with Melvin Craig,' he said slowly.

Mort was dumbfounded. 'Why would he do a lousy thing like that?'

E.M. bowed his great head. Mort noticed the bald patch on the crown. When had that happened?

'Who knows why any of us does things?' E.M. muttered. 'Who knows? Jack is an animal – a sick animal driven out of the pack – that's what makes him so dangerous.'

'You knew about this,' said Mort, accusingly.

E.M. shook his head. 'I swear to you I knew nothing. I only found out later – of all people from my driver – that Jack had met an Assistant US Attorney. I guessed what had happened. When I asked Jack about it, he lied, like he always does, but in the end he admitted it. That's when I tried to warn you. I tried more than once.'

'How did Jack know that I was involved with Craig?'

'Craig came to me first and I turned him down. Jack sent him to you.'

'So if no one found out about the scheme he could always tip off the Feds.'

'I guess that was the plan.' E.M. began to pace restlessly round his office. Mort watched him. Still the Titan, but the giant was bowed now, his shoulders hunched, as if the burden of life was getting to be too heavy for him to carry.

'The bastard!' said Mort. 'The scheming, vindictive shit. All these years he's tried to destroy me. I never knew how close he came.'

'You still don't.' E.M. lowered his bulk into the safe haven of his high-backed chair. The chair looked bigger than Mort remembered it. Or could it be that E.M. had shrunk?

'Meaning?'

E.M. was playing with a silver paperknife on his desk. Absently, he turned the point towards himself.

'There's more to it.' He heaved himself up and started pacing again. He looked nervous. The Titan nervous?

'What do you mean there's more to it?' Mort persisted.

E.M. put his head in his hands. The words were muffled, but still clear enough for Mort to hear. 'You have to understand how I hated Jack for what he did to Rachel.'

'What are you saying? What has that got to do with anything?'

E.M. raised his head and, as he did so, the pitch of his voice began to climb higher, edged with hysteria. 'He seduced her. My Rachel. My only child. Made her have an abortion. It was murder. He murdered my grandchild! It was obscene. Wicked. Filthy.' As he looked at Mort, his eyes were pleading for understanding. 'I only wanted to scare him. Never in my life have I done anything like that before. Never. I was insane with rage. I was ashamed for my daughter and the way he had humiliated her. I hired two men to scare him. I swear to you that I gave them strict orders not even to touch him. No violence was to be used. All I wanted was for him to leave my daughter

589

alone. And those thugs . . .' E.M.'s mouth hung open. He was gulping for air now, his chest heaving. 'They beat him up. My God, if I had known I would never have . . .' He broke off and lowered his head into his hands again. 'Retribution,' he whispered. 'God has punished me. I will never have a grandchild now. Do you know what that means? Do you understand?'

'I understand,' said Mort quietly.

'How can you understand? You have no daughter.'

'No,' said Mort, 'I have no daughter.'

E.M. realized what he had said. 'I'm sorry. I didn't mean that. I . . .'

After a silence, Mort spoke. 'Hard to imagine,' he said. 'Hard to imagine what would happen if Jack ever found out that it was you who had him beaten up.'

'He did,' said E.M. 'But he found out too late.'

'Too late for what?'

E.M. almost whispered the words. 'Too late to stop you being shot.'

Mort's face showed no emotion. He was stunned. His ears had taken in the words, but his brain could not process them. Then, as he began, slowly, rationally, to comprehend what E.M. had said, he had to exercise all his massive self-control to restrain himself. The fact that Jack Greenberg was not present scarcely mattered. He came close to attacking the old man, and E.M. knew it. The Titan trembled.

'How do I know all this is true?' Mort asked in a low voice. But in his heart he knew it was.

'I wish it weren't.'

'How come you know so much?'

'I have connections.'

'Some connections.'

'He tried to save you. Remember that.'

'Big deal. I still got a bullet in the gut. The murdering bastard should be in jail.'

'For God's sake, Mort, drop it. Forget it. It all happened a long time ago and we're still suffering for it. All of us. Jack can't have kids. I'll never have grandchildren. You nearly died. And for what? Tell me that. What was it all for?'

Mort didn't know. He only knew who was responsible. That much was clear.

'The photographs,' said E.M. 'If not for those photographs . . .'

Mort was already at the door of E.M.'s office. He stopped short. 'Photographs? What photographs?'

'Some bastard sent me photographs of Rachel . . . My child . . . and Jack. They were disgusting. Obscene. Why would anyone take such things? Why would they send them to me? If I hadn't seen them, I swear to you all this would never have happened. It was Fate, Mort. Put yourself in my place. Try to understand.'

Mort rode the elevator down to the ground floor. He spun the glass doors and walked out onto Park Avenue. The sun was shining. The street was crowded. He waved away his driver. He had no idea where he was going, only that he had to be alone. He tried to work out who was innocent and who was guilty. He thought about all the other people on the street and, for the first time in his life, he envied them. At this moment, he would have changed places with anyone in the crowd, if only he could have started all over again.

A cold New York morning – one of those clear winter days when the sun shone and everyone remembered that winter did not last forever. Only it was January and spring still seemed far away.

Bob Rosenfeld was in the first car with two US Marshals. Ed Goldwyn followed in the next with another two. Six of them in all.

They stopped outside Kings' Tower and took the elevator to the fifty-fifth floor – the entrance to the executive offices.

Rosenfeld and Goldwyn pushed through the big glass doors. One of the marshals guarded the entrance. Another went round the back. They weren't taking any chances.

It was rare for an Assistant US Attorney to make his own arrest. But this was a special one. Bob Rosenfeld was giving himself a treat. Besides, Temp O'Reilly had made it more than clear. He wanted no slip-ups.

Rosenfeld had argued. It was too early. Not enough evidence yet. They would be out on bail in five minutes. O'Reilly wouldn't listen. He wanted an arrest. He needed results. The bastards were guilty. What else mattered?

Bob Rosenfeld and Ed Goldwyn ignored the girl at the executive reception desk. They waved their warrants and walked quickly down the corridor, trailed by the two big marshals with all their hip gear, including the handcuffs.

Rosenfeld was looking forward to the moment the hand-cuffs snapped on Mort's wrists.

Goldwyn and one marshal made for the anteroom to Ruby's office. Rosenfeld carried on to Mort's office.

He stopped in front of the secretary.

'I've come to see Mr King.' He handed her his card.

She looked up at Rosenfeld, then at the US Marshal.

'You have an appointment?'

'He'll see us. Just tell him we're here.'

'I'm sorry. He's at a board meeting.'

'When will he be back?'

'He didn't say.'

'We'll wait.'

Bob Rosenfeld took a seat. The marshal stood.

'I don't think he'll be back for a while,' said the secretary.

'Where is this board meeting?'

'In Wald,' she said.

'Wald? Did you say Wald?'

'That's right, Mr Rosenfeld. Wald, Switzerland.'

Rosenfeld sat motionless, tense, vigilant, appraising her with those cold eyes of his. Suddenly, his face flared red as if the welling rage he was fighting to contain had haemorrhaged. He stood up slowly, hesitated, and then abruptly turned away and limped down the corridor followed by the big marshal.

BOOK EIGHT

———◆◆◆———

The Well Runs Dry

Temp O'Reilly was angry. Not only did he call a press conference. He appeared on Channel Two.

'I challenge Mortimer and Reuben King to return to the United States and stand trial. If they're innocent, let them prove it. If their conscience is clear, let them demonstrate it in the courts. To shelter behind the legal ambiguities of an extradition treaty, to live as fugitives in another country, is not only cowardly, it encourages people to draw the obvious conclusion. That they are guilty as charged.'

He wound up with what sounded like a threat. 'They should not delude themselves that they can evade US justice indefinitely.'

The Swiss government took exception to the last remark, condemning it as a clumsy attempt to bully them into submission. They did not appreciate O'Reilly's 'cowboy' diplomacy. They issued a strong protest through their embassy in Washington.

As for the Swiss press, they were incensed. They condemned the US Attorney's Office for its 'gross interference in the internal affairs of another sovereign state'. In which view they were strongly supported by *Izvestia*. The subpoenaing of records held in Switzerland was scorned as a 'crude plot to compromise the neutrality of our country'.

Things were heating up. Depending on whether you sat in New York or Europe, there was talk of 'fugitive oil tycoons', 'Kings of corruption', or 'Federal bully boys' and 'kangaroo courts'.

Three weeks after Mort and Ruby fled to Switzerland,

the Federal indictments were issued ... seventy-eight pages of them, eighty-two counts.

Mortimer and Reuben King and King Brothers were jointly charged with criminal activities ranging from tax evasion to racketeering – the latter under legislation originally framed to combat the growing threat of the Mafia. The penalties under 'Rico' as it was known – Racketeering Influenced Corrupt Organizations – were draconian, enough to scare the most hardened of criminals.

'According to the lawyers, Rosenfeld has promised to drop "Rico" if we surrender to US Marshals,' said Mort.

Ruby was thinking that justice – like the press – made up the rules as it went along. The activities of its officials were self-serving. They had little to do with justice, even less with right and wrong.

'It's the Wild West,' said Mort.

'They have us guilty already,' Ruby agreed. 'What are we going to do?'

'Fight the bastards,' said Mort. 'What else is there to do?'

Yet another press conference. This time Rosenfeld. 'King Brothers has defrauded the US Treasury of hundreds of millions of dollars. Moreover, in order to conceal their illicit gains, they illegally transferred to their Swiss office in Wald at least three hundred million dollars in order to avoid payment of US taxes. Well, one of these days, they'll be getting a check from us ... a big one. I'd like to see their faces when that lands on their desk. And, make no mistake, ladies and gentlemen of the press, we intend to see that the check is paid in full.'

Bob Rosenfeld was not going to be a US Assistant Attorney forever. When he moved on, he was making sure as hell that he would be trailing clouds of glory.

'This is the biggest tax case in the history of the United States. We made it,' said Ruby. 'Finally, we're number one!'

The press was having a ball guessing what the jail sentences might be. Estimates ranged on up from a 'conservative' three hundred and fifty years for each King Brother.

'Don't worry about it,' said Ruby. 'With good behaviour, we'll be out in two hundred years.'

Mort was not amused. 'Those guys are the criminals – not us. They're manipulating the law. It's a vendetta. Where are the others who did what we did and more? I don't see their names on the indictment. What's so different about them?'

'They weren't number one,' said Ruby.

'They have the right friends,' said Mort bitterly.

'Guys in trouble,' said Ruby, 'don't have any friends, let alone the right ones.'

Another week. The United States government issued warrants for the arrest of Mortimer and Reuben King. Everyone knew, of course, that the warrants could not be served. But would the Swiss federal government in Bern hand over the two fugitives?

There was one glimmer of hope.

'Too bad that tax evasion is not an extraditable crime over there.' Rosenfeld was biting the quicks of his fingers. He hadn't done that since he was twelve.

'There aren't many crimes that are,' grumbled Ed Goldwyn. 'I checked. There's murder, rape, arson, forgery, armed robbery . . .'

'Forgery,' said Rosenfeld thoughtfully.

The Attorney's Office flew over a team of Justice Department officials to talk to the Swiss.

The leader of the Swiss team had to admit that they had a point.

'If the charge of forgery could be proved,' he said. 'Yes . . . I think we would extradite them.'

The head of the Justice Department team was ecstatic. He could smell fame and promotion.

'Give us the chance to prove it and we can wrap up this whole case.'

'To prove forgery you would, of course, have to put the two King brothers on trial.'

'No problem. Just hand them over and we'll do it.'

The other lawyer pondered. 'Of course, in order to put them on trial in the United States, they would have to leave Switzerland.'

'So?'

'In order to leave Switzerland, we would have to extradite them. Regrettably, none of the offences with which they have been charged are covered by our extradition treaty with you.'

The American lawyer put a hand to his forehead. 'Let me be sure I have this right,' he said. 'Forgery is an extraditable offence?'

'Correct.'

'But we have to prove forgery before you guys will extradite these crooks?'

'Before we extradite the King brothers – yes.'

'But we can't prove forgery unless we put them on trial in the USA?'

'Right.'

'And we can't put them on trial in the USA unless you agree to extradite them?'

'Exactly,' said the Swiss lawyer. He seemed delighted that the other man had so quickly grasped the argument.

The American lawyer smiled dementedly and began muttering. He took no further part in the discussions. When he was not muttering, he was glaring savagely at his Swiss counterpart, indulging in the fantasy that the man was strapped into an electric chair and he was throwing the switch, again and again.

Temp O'Reilly was getting desperate.

'We're screwing this up, Bob.' What he meant was that Bob Rosenfeld was screwing it up. Rosenfeld knew exactly what he was saying.

'First, we let them run off to Switzerland, now, we're

losing public opinion. Public opinion, Bob. We can't afford to lose the public.'

Bob Rosenfeld nodded. He knew all about public opinion. Didn't he work for Temp O'Reilly?

'These guys are guilty. If we let them go unpunished, we'll be sending a signal to Wall Street, to the oil industry, to big business – that this Justice Department does not care. That this Justice Department is powerless. That's no good, Bob. That's no good for justice, that's no good for law and order, that's no good for the administration we serve.'

And it sure as hell is no good for you and me. That was what Rosenfeld was thinking.

'Move it along, Bob. There's a lot at stake.'

There was indeed. Bob Rosenfeld's career included.

'What are we going to do ?' Ed Goldwyn was gloomier than ever. He looked worn out. His eyes were ringed with blue, his shirt round the armpits was stained with sweat, and he crossed and uncrossed his short legs incessantly as if there was no way and no place in the world to get comfortable.

'We make a deal.'

'For Mort and Ruby?'

'Never! For the company.'

'O'Reilly would go along with that?'

'O'Reilly wants progress. He wants something he can stand up and boast about. As long as he gets results, and it sounds good on Channel Two, he's happy.'

'You think Mort and Ruby will play ball? Give themselves up?'

'We don't give them any option. If they don't, they'll lose the company. We'll put the squeeze on them. What's the most important thing in their lives right now?'

'Staying out of the pen.'

'After that?'

'King Brothers.'

'It's going to be destroyed.' Bob Rosenfeld's expression

was sharp, his whole body tense, poised like a terrier at the entrance to a rabbit warren.

Ed Goldwyn's spine tingled. Rosenfeld was not a man he could ever warm to. Too hard, too dedicated, by far . . . a man to respect for his single-mindedness and his self-assurance, but cool, distant, unsociable . . . not one of the guys. In his own way, Goldwyn reflected, Bob Rosenfeld was a fanatic and fanatics were dangerous men. There was something chilling about his ruthless pursuit of lawbreakers, the weak and the flawed, as if they were his natural prey, and he the avenger by divine right.

Ironically, there was only one other man he could think of who possessed the same qualities, the same absolute confidence in his own judgement, the same sense of mission, the same ruthlessness.

Mortimer King.

'And who exactly is going to destroy it?'

Rosenfeld smiled that sardonic smile of his, with one side of the face. 'In the last few years, those guys have constructed the biggest pyramid outside of Egypt. They've built an empire with other people's money. They've bought the world with the help of the banks. That's how they turned themselves into a multi-billion-dollar corporation.'

'So?'

'If the banks have reason to be worried about their investment, they'll start to call in their loans. Once they do that, the whole goddam pyramid will fall apart.'

'Why would the banks do that? If King Brothers collapsed, they would never see their loans repaid.'

Rosenfeld nodded. The reasoning was logical. 'In theory, you're right. If the banks took the time to sit down calmly and work it out, they'd keep on rolling over their loans. My guess is they won't do that. When the panic hits, they'll be falling over themselves to get their money back.'

'Who's going to start the panic?'

Another sardonic grimace. 'Panics start easily.'

Ed Goldwyn turned his sad eyes on Rosenfeld. 'You have any idea how many people work for King Brothers?'

'Not exactly. Three, maybe four thousand.'

'If the company folds, they'll all be out of a job . . . every one of them.'

Bob Rosenfeld took off his glasses and started to clean them. 'Tough,' he said.

Ten days later, the Internal Revenue Service issued a jeopardy assessment and Bob Rosenfeld was in the Southern District Federal Court explaining to a sympathetic judge why, in the absence of the two fugitives in Switzerland, there was reason to doubt that the taxes and possible fines to be levied against King Brothers could ever be collected. In view of that, he asked the court to agree to the proposed assessment. The result would be the freezing of King Brothers' assets in the United States.

When the judge heard the amount of the assessment, his eyes popped.

'How can you possibly justify such a huge amount?' he asked.

Bob Rosenfeld spoke for thirty minutes, coolly, dispassionately, without rancour. When he sat down, the judge heard the indignant objections of the lawyer for the defence.

The next day, he gave his decision in favour of the jeopardy assessment – far, by far the biggest in history . . . one billion dollars.

Sam summed it up: 'We can pay the jeopardy assessment, but when we do, our remaining assets will be worth only somewhere between eight hundred million and a billion dollars.'

'What do the outstanding loans amount to?' asked Mort.

'Over a billion,' said Sam gloomily.

'That means we're bankrupt,' said Ruby. 'How can that be?'

'There must be some mistake,' said Mort.

'There's no mistake,' said Jeffrey. 'We went over the figures.'

'Some of the loans are recallable in the near future,' said Sam.

'Don't worry,' said Mort. 'I'll talk to the banks. They'll support us. They'd be crazy not to.'

They were besieged . . . fortress Wald. He looked out of the window. Everything he could see was neat, even the railway sidings. Everything was in its proper place, avoiding all extremes – picturesque snow-capped mountains, a lake as dark and deep as Switzerland itself. For some reason, he thought a lot about his father these days, Moses poised between life and death, drugged and imprisoned in the intensive care unit, lying in his oxygen tent, insulated from suffering and the experience of dying.

They had exchanged one prison for another. He felt constrained, by Switzerland, by his office. Sam had offered to surrender his own somewhat larger room, but Mort had refused. That was not his style. He had no desire to exercise power in insignificant ways. For the same reason, he always held doors open for others to walk ahead of him – even the least important of his employees. They respected his courtesy and wondered at his humility, but in truth it had nothing to do with either. It was just another way of massaging their egos, another manifestation of his need to control people.

It was early afternoon. The sky was overcast and the light dim and yellowish. It was starting to snow. The clouds were creeping lower, shrouding the forests on the crests of the hills, reaching grey fingers down to the lakeside villages. He switched on his desk lamp. Somewhere out there was the rest of the world. He would have to keep reminding himself of that.

'Everything's going to be OK,' he assured them confidently. 'I'll take care of the banks.'

The London office was in Mount Street, round the corner from the Connaught Hotel. The oil-trading room on the fourth floor was, during office hours, the noisiest and most active in the building, packed with traders sitting at banks of telephones, wheeling and dealing with New York, Zurich, Rio, Tel Aviv, Tokyo, Moscow – even with each other – shouting buy and sell orders across the floor, checking their positions, monitoring currencies and the price fluctuations of the oil market on their dim computer screens. Against one wall was a row of telexes – silent now – but during the day constantly hammering out messages to and from every continent.

Jeffrey and Sam sat there now in the stillness. Except for the two of them, the room was empty, the phones quiet. Only the screens flickered their unending flow of information . . . political developments in Washington and the Middle East . . . stock market and commodity reports . . . opening and closing prices of base and precious metals on world exchanges . . . currency parities reported by a dozen banks, changing every few seconds as each new deal was cut. In the corner, the Reuters news service machine chattered from time to time.

'What time is it?' said Sam. Something to say. Sam knew what time it was.

'Eight o'clock,' said Jeffrey.

One of the telexes started whirring. Jeffrey glanced at it in a disinterested sort of way. Slowly he wandered over to read the message.

'The Dow Jones is up five points.'

'That's nice,' said Sam. He moved across to the dispensing machine. 'Which one is coffee?'

'The one on the right,' said Jeffrey. 'It tastes like tea,' he added helpfully.

'How do you tell the difference?'

'The tea tastes like soap-powder,' said Jeffrey.

They sat at their desks, watched the screens and waited. New York's closing was two hours away. It would take time for the telex to reach them – the routine message renewing the loan, the first to come up for renewal since the jeopardy assessment. It would be good to know that a major New York bank was still supporting them. Worth staying late for. It would give them the needed shot in the arm. Mort and Ruby were sitting in the Wald office, waiting for Jeffrey's call. He was looking forward to giving them the first good news they had had for a very long time.

It was getting late – nearly nine p.m. Suddenly, the telex at the far end of the row was tapping out a message.

'For Chrissake, who is it?'

'It's Morgan. I know their answer back.'

Jeffrey rushed over and the two of them stood at the machine, waiting for the message to come through. It chattered for a few seconds and then stopped . . . in a minute or two it started up again. The keys were hammering out the text on the paper. Their eyes followed every word and their expressions showed that the news was bad.

'What does "for internal reasons" mean?' said Sam.

'It means they're too chicken to tell us the truth.'

'A hundred and twenty-five million dollars. Bad news.'

'When the other banks hear that a major loan has been called . . .' They looked at each other.

'Couldn't you talk to Morgan again?' said Sam.

'I already did – this morning.'

For the next hour, they played poker and idly watched as the screens pulsed their endless messages. The Dow Jones was closing down for the third day running. Sterling was weak. The dollar was strengthening against the Swiss franc and the German mark. Gold was up, coffee and cocoa down. There'd been an earthquake in the south of Turkey – thousands were homeless. Sugar was going through the roof and there was a famine in Ethiopia.

At twenty to ten, Bankers Trust came through and, fifteen minutes later, Chemical Bank. Both of them 'regretted'. No reasons given. They just regretted that the loans would not be renewed.

'Another three hundred and twenty-five million,' said Sam.

They phoned Mort and Ruby.

604

'Every one of those jerks said they expected to renew,' said Mort bitterly.

'Well, they didn't,' said Jeffrey.

'Try Tokyo,' Mort said.

'I already did.'

'Try Frankfurt and Zurich. I'll try Paris.'

'Mort,' said Jeffrey patiently. 'I tried the world. Not once, but several times. It's no good. The banks know what's going on. They're running scared.'

'Try Tokyo,' Mort insisted. 'Phone me when you've spoken to them and don't give them the idea that we're weak. Bargain on the rates. Hassle them. Give them a hard time. You understand?'

'Who gives a shit about rates? What we need is loans.'

Mort cut in. 'That's exactly the point. The banks think we're in deep trouble, that we need replacement loans, that we're dead if we don't get them. But we're not about to admit that. If we haggle on rates, they'll think we have options, and if there's competition, they'll feel a whole lot more comfortable about making us a loan.'

Jeffrey grinned. He never changed, did Mort . . . the eternal trader. He never gave up. There was something almost heroic about his refusal to acknowledge the truth. His battle would never be lost because it would never be over.

'I'll talk to Tokyo,' said Jeffrey quietly. 'I'll get back to you.'

'That's my boy,' said Mort.

It was so easy to earn Mort's approval, Jeffrey thought. All you had to do was agree with him.

The four partners sat down in Wald to discuss the situation and plan tactics.

'There's no need to panic just because a couple of banks call their loans. Who gives a damn, anyway?' Mort was trying to sound calm, but he was on edge and everyone knew it.

'No one's panicking,' said Jeffrey, 'but we have to face

the possibility that other loans could be called as they mature and the domino effect would be disastrous. You know how banks are. They act like sheep, rushing after anything that looks interesting and then scampering away in the opposite direction the moment they sense danger.'

It was true enough.

'Our financial position stinks,' said Sam. 'We're in a squeeze. Business in Europe is so-so, but in the States no one wants to know. We're nowhere near covering our overheads, let alone interest on the loans.'

'I've been going over the figures with Sam again,' said Jeffrey. 'They're worse than we thought. We have to shut down some offices and fire at least twenty per cent of our staff, overall. We're losing money every day and we can't borrow any more.'

Mort glared at Jeffrey and Jeffrey stared calmly back at him.

'I'm not firing anyone,' said Mort. 'I hired them. They're my responsibility. I'm not going to let them down.'

'You talk like you're God Almighty,' said Jeffrey angrily. 'Who gives a shit if you let them down or not? Face facts.'

'Why don't we all stay nice and calm and keep it polite,' said Sam.

Jeffrey looked at him disdainfully. 'Good old Sam,' he said. 'What the fuck does it matter if the ship's sinking? The important thing is for everyone to stay polite. Whatever we do, let's not say what we think. And heaven forbid we should actually face up to the truth.'

'There's no need to be offensive,' said Sam.

'What truth?' said Ruby. He had said very little the last few hours. He looked exhausted. His eyes, usually so bright and keen, were lustreless.

Jeffrey spoke slowly, beating the air with both hands for emphasis. 'We have to make a deal,' he said.

'What sort of deal?' said Mort suspiciously.

'A deal for King Brothers. We have to negotiate with

Rosenfeld. We should plead guilty to a few counts. Then we can start doing business again.'

'Why plead guilty?' said Mort.

'Because we are guilty. Or am I missing something?' said Jeffrey.

'We're not guilty of anything,' said Mort. 'It's been blown up out of all proportion.'

'Tell that to the lawyers,' said Jeffrey. 'We have to make a deal.'

'It won't work,' said Mort.

'Why not?' said Sam.

'Because they'll never agree to include Ruby and me in the deal,' said Mort. 'Whatever deal we make for King Brothers, we two would wind up in the pen.'

'Who knows?' said Jeffrey. 'Maybe it would only be for a few months. If you talked to them now, the lawyers could probably arrange for you to be in one of those special . . . places. I hear they're not too bad.'

'They call them Fed Clubs,' said Mort.

'Is that what they call them?' said Jeffrey. 'I never knew.'

'Why should you?' said Mort. 'You won't be in one, will you?'

'Would it help?' said Jeffrey.

'No,' said Mort, 'it wouldn't. But the fact is, you and Sam have nothing to lose.'

'No, that's right, Mort, we have nothing to lose,' said Jeffrey, with heavy irony. 'Only eleven years of our lives. Not to mention our shareholding in the company. I wonder what our shares would buy us now? A cheap day return to London?'

'At least you're free to go there,' said Mort. It was a less than gentle reminder. Mort and Ruby were not in jail, but they were still prisoners. There was an extradition treaty between the UK and the USA. If they went to London, they would be arrested and turned over to the Feds.

'No one asked you to mess with the DOE regulations,' said Jeffrey coldly.

'I didn't hear any loud protests,' said Mort.

'You didn't listen too carefully,' said Jeffrey. The two men glared at each other and Sam looked out of the window.

'No one asked you to run away to Switzerland either,' said Jeffrey.

'That's our affair,' said Ruby.

'OK, it's your affair. But when you refuse to negotiate for the company, then that's my affair and Sam's, too. What's more, it concerns everyone who works for King Brothers. They're the ones who are going to wind up on the streets.'

'I told you,' said Mort. 'No one gets fired.'

'There's no alternative,' said Jeffrey.

'I don't agree,' said Ruby.

'I don't give a shit whether you agree or disagree,' said Jeffrey hotly. 'Either you make a deal or I'm taking over the company.'

The silence was prolonged. Sam looked shocked. Mort and Ruby stared at Jeffrey, poker-faced. Finally, Mort spoke. 'Don't forget. We're majority shareholders. We won't let you.'

'Majority shareholders,' Jeffrey echoed. 'Majority share-holders who can't set foot out of Switzerland. You still have your titles, but that's all you've got. I'm closing down ten offices for a start and there's not a damn thing you can do to stop me.'

'I don't care to be threatened,' said Mort, 'especially by my partners.'

'Well, tough,' said Jeffrey.

'After all,' said Mort, 'this is our company. It belongs to all of us.'

'No,' said Jeffrey. 'It's your company. Yours and Ruby's. "In the last analysis". Remember? It always has been. That's the problem.'

Mort was trapped. If only he were back in New York. This damned claustrophobic office was getting to him. No, he had to admit – there was more to it than that. The world was closing in on him and Ruby. Fortress Wald no longer seemed as secure as it had only a few short weeks ago. He could feel power slipping through his fingers like sand.

'I started this company,' he said. 'I worked eleven years to make it number one in the world. No one's going to take it away from me. Not you. Not Rosenfeld. Not anyone.'

'There's only one chance to save it,' said Jeffrey. 'Tell the lawyers to make a deal.'

'If we made a deal for King Brothers, Ruby and I would be finished. We'd never be able to make a deal for ourselves. We'd have lost all our bargaining chips. We'd be fugitives for the rest of our lives. It's the one thing we can't do.'

'It's the only thing you can do,' said Jeffrey.

'You're making us scapegoats,' said Mort. 'If the company goes under, we'll be the ones to blame. That's it, isn't it?'

Jeffrey turned on his heel and walked out.

'Loyalty,' muttered Mort. 'No one understands the meaning of the word any more.'

The rented house in Wald was tiny. It looked like all the others on the hillside: grey concrete, streaked with rain, dark green shutters. For Julie, the one advantage it possessed was the tiny conservatory at the back where the previous tenants had grown orchids and where she now painted. She could not remember when painting had stopped being a pastime – an agreeable hobby – and become an absorbing passion. Not that she would ever admit to herself that she had made a commitment; one super-achiever in the family was already more than enough.

Almost without realizing it, Mort had grown accustomed to talking to Julie while she was standing in front of an easel. She could talk and paint at the same time without disturbing her concentration and he found her gentle abstraction soothing and, in a way, comforting. What he craved now, more than anything, was someone

609

to listen to him. It was a new and altogether satisfying experience for Julie.

'We shut down another three offices last week. One of them was Rio de Janeiro. You and I flew out there for the opening. Was it five years ago, or six. . . ?'

'I remember,' said Julie.

'Jeffrey and Sam think we should make a deal for the company. Ruby wants to go back to New York – give himself up. He has this overwhelming urge to atone. Me, I want to fight the bastards.'

Julie stepped back from the easel and narrowed her hazel eyes.

'Why are you doing that?'

'To get the perspective right,' she said.

That's what he needed to do, he reflected. If only he could step away from the whole goddam mess for a while and see it objectively. But no, it was impossible. He was too involved. He was not seeing anything clearly any more.

'You think I should give myself up?'

'You should do what you think is right.'

'For me? For the company? For you?'

'I don't come into it. I never tried to influence you. Whatever you decide is OK with me.' What she said was true – unhelpful, but true.

'I feel like I'm carrying those guys. I always have to be the strong one,' he said.

'Why?'

'Someone has to be.'

'Maybe the others don't have the same fear of weakness that you do,' she said. 'Anyway, strength is understanding. Like love. You're nothing if you don't understand.'

'Help me do that,' he said quietly.

She was touched. He had never depended on her for anything. Now it seemed, for the first time, that he did.

'I'm beginning to realize something,' said Mort. 'Life isn't worth a goddam if you don't get some satisfaction out of it. And you know what? Success has nothing to do

610

with it. Satisfaction is something inside you. It's either there, or it's not. My father was never satisfied. Whatever he did, it gave him no pleasure. Whatever I did was never good enough. I could always do better. I guess he was trying to programme me for success.'

'Your father was an embittered man,' said Julie. 'He needed your success to compensate for his failure. Surely you know that.'

'I'm just glad he's not alive to see this . . . this mess.'

'Why not?' said Julie. 'He might have learned something. Like you have.'

'I'm ashamed,' said Mort.

'What for?' said Julie.

'For involving you in scandal and disgrace.'

'Horseshit!' Julie put down her brush. 'You think I care what you did? You think I can't live with failure? You're the one who can't do that. I never needed your success, so why should your failure worry me? It would have meant so much more to me if you had said once – just once – that you – loved me, or even if you'd shown that you understood me.'

'Why this, suddenly? I thought we were OK.'

'OK is what we are,' she said, picking up the brush again. 'We could have been better than OK. We could have been a family. We could have been parents.' It was sad. Almost too sad to talk about.

'We could never have our own child.'

'You had yours,' she said bitterly. 'Why couldn't I have mine?' For a while she painted on and he sat there, fascinated, watching her. This was one place in her life he could never enter. It was like having a rival. Suddenly he knew how she must have felt about King Brothers.

'Leo promised me an exhibition in the summer,' she said casually.

'Leo,' he said dully. 'How's Leo?'

'He's OK,' she said. She stuck out the tip of her tongue when she was concentrating, painting the reflection of a tree in a lake.

611

Mort sensed that the reflection was the most important thing in her life right now. A brush, a canvas and a few oil colours – that was her world. She had made it her own and no one could take it away from her.

He had never envied anyone as much in his life.

Sarah cried when she read Ruth's letter, not because of the news it contained, not because Ruth and Daniel were living together, but because it was so full of happiness and love, love for her parents and love for Daniel. How Ruby would feel about it was another matter.

He read the letter, his face expressionless. When he had finished, he sat for a long time, staring into space. He was thinking about Ruth, remembering her as a child, experiencing the acute sadness of loss and an overwhelming sense that things might have gone better if he had handled them differently.

'What did I do wrong?' he asked Sarah helplessly.

'Nothing,' she said, 'except maybe . . .'

'Maybe what?'

'Sometimes you have to take people the way they are – accept them on their own terms. It's all she wants from us.'

'What she wants is to disgrace us. What she's doing is losing her self-respect,' said Ruby.

'Why don't you read what she says? Her self-respect is just fine. As for disgracing us . . .'

'Why don't you say it?' said Ruby. 'I'm the one who's done that.'

'That's not what I was going to say,' Sarah protested. 'No one's disgraced anybody. I'm proud of Ruth.'

'I'm ashamed of her,' said Ruby. 'She's made herself cheap. I never want to see her again.'

'They'll come round,' said Daniel reassuringly. He wished he felt as confident as he sounded.

'You think so?' said Ruth.

'When they see we're serious.'

'Pop knows we're serious. That's what worries him.'

Daniel put his arm round her. 'Why don't we just get married? What's the big deal? Your father will have to accept me then.'

Ruth was not so sure. 'You don't know him.'

'What's he got against me?'

'The case – and who knows what else? I guess he'd give any guy who wanted to marry me a hard time.'

'So, when do we get married?'

Ruth had asked herself the same question many times. 'When we have Pop's blessing,' she said quietly.

'You think he'll ever give us that?'

'I hope so,' she said. 'I want him to bless our marriage, Daniel. It's important to me.'

'And if he doesn't? What then?'

'I don't even want to think about it,' she said.

'Rosenfeld has offered us a deal,' said Mort, 'but only for the company.'

'What about us?' said Ruby.

Mort made a face. 'No deal. He wants us in jail.'

'Nice guy.'

'He's practically *mischpachah* – family. You could be in-laws soon.'

'What's that supposed to mean?' Suspiciously.

'I think we should meet him.'

'How can we do that? If we go back to the States, he'll have us arrested.'

'Invite him over here.'

'I don't want to see him.'

'Because of Ruth?'

'Because I don't want to see him. That's why.' Ruby had been very prickly since he heard that Ruth and Daniel were living together.

'It could be a smart move,' said Mort persistently. 'You could use the relationship.'

Ruby turned his back on Mort. He was angry. 'I want no part of it,' he said.

613

'If he agrees to come over, that would already be a hopeful sign.'

'You're grasping at straws.'

'What else have we got to grasp at?' said Mort.

The corner suite at the Baur au Lac overlooked the Lake of Zurich on one side and the canal on the other. Mort had selected the hotel because it was more central than the Dolder and, besides, inviting Rosenfeld there would some-how have contaminated the place. It had been the scene of triumphant meetings. Whatever this one turned out to be, it would certainly not be that.

It was hard to view this congenial, self-assured, apparently open and guileless man as the enemy. It was unreal, this meeting, as if it were being held in limbo – which, in a way, it was. Sitting there, looking out over the lake, they could have been on a ship. The wind gusted against the windows and the gulls shrieked mournfully.

'I appreciate your coming all this way.'

'No problem,' said Bob Rosenfeld. The very ordinariness of the guy was disturbing.

'My lawyers tell me that you and your assistants will be holding discussions with them while you're over here. I thought it would be good if we could meet – one on one – and maybe get to know each other a little.'

Mort was watching the other man carefully, trying to assess him, hoping to stimulate some meaningful reaction. There was none. Rosenfeld's eyes were sharp and steady behind the rimless glasses.

'I want you to believe that neither Ruby nor I ever intended to get ourselves into this mess. All we ever wanted to be was successful.'

Rosenfeld didn't even blink. 'We don't indict people for being successful,' he said.

'I'm not so sure about that,' said Mort. 'In any case, we're innocent.'

'The whole world is innocent,' said Rosenfeld.

Mort stood at the window looking down at the canal.

'We may have exploited some loopholes in the law, but we never broke it. Whatever we did was nothing more than many others have done – only maybe they were not quite as good at it.'

'We'll get round to the others,' said Rosenfeld drily. 'We try to accommodate all the criminals.'

'Is that how you see us?' said Mort. 'Criminals?'

Rosenfeld shrugged. 'What else? In my book a man who breaks the law is a criminal.'

Mort studied his hands. 'Let's assume, for a moment, that without intending to, we broke the law. Why should we be hounded? Threatened with hundreds of years in jail? Humiliated and disgraced? We're just ordinary guys trying to make a living. We never killed anyone. We never robbed anyone. We don't deal drugs. We don't run protection rackets. What in God's name have we done to deserve all this?'

'You broke the law,' said Rosenfeld.

'I never did,' said Mort angrily. He was trying desperately hard not to betray his impatience and resentment, but he was not doing too well.

Rosenfeld looked out across the Lake of Zurich, at the villas of the rich with their acres of lawns and marble statues, their private ports crammed with yachts and high-speed motor launches. It was not a world he knew, not his world.

'What is it you're asking me for?'

'I'm not asking you for anything.'

Bob Rosenfeld grinned sardonically. 'That's funny, Mort. It sure sounded like it.'

Mort wondered if he used his first name when he was talking about him. The implication of intimacy was ironic.

'OK, I'm asking for your understanding and sympathy. I'm asking you to think of me as Mortimer King the man, not as some kind of fantasy villain you dreamed up.'

'What I think of you is irrelevant,' said Rosenfeld. 'Let me tell you something. I've come across plenty of crooks in my time. Some of them I really liked. They had a darn

615

sight more to recommend them than a whole lot of honest guys I've met. What you don't understand is that there's nothing personal in this. I have a job to do, that's all.'

'What about compassion?' said Mort.

'It's not on the books. At least, if it is, I never found it.'

'I guess you didn't look too hard,' said Mort.

'Like I said, it's nothing personal,' said Rosenfeld. Suddenly, he grinned. It was an engaging grin, completely unexpected. Mort was encouraged to take the discussion a step further.

'Off the record,' he said, 'if the case went to court, and we were found guilty, what do you think it would cost the company?'

Rosenfeld hesitated. What the hell, he thought. Mort could never quote him. 'With fines, not less than five hundred million bucks,' he said.

'I'll settle for seven hundred and fifty million,' said Mort. 'We'll plead guilty to all charges . . . You drop Rico.'

'Sounds reasonable,' said Rosenfeld.

Mort's heart was hammering at his ribs. 'The lawyers can work out the details,' he said. 'Naturally,' he added casually – or he hoped it sounded casual – 'Ruby and I would be part of the settlement. No jail sentence.'

Rosenfeld shook his head. 'No deal. You stand trial or you plead guilty. Whichever way, you take what's coming.'

'Forget it,' said Mort. 'We'll never go to jail.'

Rosenfeld said nothing. For a long time, neither of them spoke.

'I have to tell you, I'm not accustomed to losing.'

'Then start practising,' said Rosenfeld.

'I guess you're an ambitious guy,' Mort said. 'You want to go places.'

Bob Rosenfeld stared at him, giving nothing away.

'You could be a wealthy man,' said Mort.

Still Rosenfeld said nothing.

'Is it really so important to you that Ruby and I spend a few years in the pen? Isn't it enough to nail the company and squeeze out the biggest settlement in history? Think of it, Bob. You'd be famous. The best law firms in the country would be falling over themselves to get you.'

'It's been tried,' said Rosenfeld quietly. 'It's been tried before, Mort. I'm not for sale.'

'You misunderstood me.'

'Sure I did.'

Mort had one last card to play. 'I hear your son Daniel and Ruby's daughter are living together,' said Mort.

'So?'

'You think they'll get married?'

'That's for them to decide.'

'That would make you and Ruby *mischpachah* – family.'

A slow smile spread over Bob Rosenfeld's face. 'Mort,' he said admiringly, 'I have to hand it to you. You're everything they say and more. Was this Ruby's idea?'

'Ruby was against my seeing you at all.'

'I respect him for that.'

'You don't know me,' said Mort angrily. 'You don't know anything about me. What you think you see is an ogre – a fiction invented by the press, by people who hate me, yes, and envy me.'

'I don't have to know you,' said Rosenfeld. 'I only have to know what you did. I hear good things about you, Mort. You're generous to your employees. You're well enough liked in business. You give a bundle to charity. It's all great what I hear, but so what? All that's between you and your Maker – not between you and me. I'm not your judge. I'm just a lawyer employed by the US government.'

'Oh no you're not,' said Mort. 'Whatever you say, you can make it tough for me or you can make it easy. You have the power to make a fair settlement, or pursue this witch hunt.'

Rosenfeld looked around the luxurious suite, at the ornate furniture, the gilt-framed pictures, the crystal wall lights, the huge TV set in the corner and the well-stocked bar. 'You want me to make things easy for you? Well, I'll tell you, Mort. I try not to allow personal feelings to influence my judgement, but I have to admit that guys like you, with all the advantages, all the money and all the power in the world – I don't think you guys deserve an easy ride – not from me, not for anyone. Life already gave it to you. You weren't brought up on the streets. You had decent parents who cared about you. You had a fine education and plenty of the good things of life. What's your excuse, Mort? The jails are full of guys with excuses, and I'll tell you, some of the excuses are pretty good ones. Life can be damn cruel. So what about you? Who turned you into a criminal? You know what I think? Nobody did. In your case, it was just greed, that's all, just good old basic greed. Whatever you made, it was never enough. Whatever success you had, some other guy had more and you envied him. You want it all and then some and you're not too particular how you get it. Just as long as you don't get found out. And, if you do, you can always bribe your way out of it. Isn't that right?'

'Are you accusing me of trying to bribe you?' said Mort.

'No, I'm not,' said Rosenfeld. 'You're too smart for that. But I heard what you told me, Mort, just like you intended me to hear it. Only I didn't react the way you wanted me to, so of course you never said it, or you never meant to say it the way it sounded, and if that's how it sounded then there was a misunderstanding. Right, Mort? Isn't that how it's supposed to work?'

'I don't know what the hell you're talking about,' said Mort icily.

Bob Rosenfeld stood up to go. His expression was telling Mort that they were further apart than ever. Rosenfeld was up there in the invulnerable Citadel of the Law looking down on Mort – just as Mort had always looked down on all the others.

'I'm asking you for the last time,' he said, 'can't we make a deal?' It was a final, hopeless plea by a man who did not know how to give up.

Rosenfeld shook his head despairingly. 'You don't get it, do you? You just don't understand.'

618

'I understand one thing. I understand that you and I are very much alike.'

'No, we're not – the things we want are very different.'

For a moment, Mort persuaded himself that he saw a gleam of light at the end of the tunnel.

'So tell me, Bob. What is it you want?' he said. 'Tell me.'

'That's easy,' said Bob Rosenfeld. 'I want you.'

The lawyers parleyed, but there was never any real hope of an outcome. King Brothers' lawyers insisted that Mort and Ruby's freedom had to be part of any deal. The lawyers from the US Attorney's Office were equally adamant that compromise was only possible on money; Mort and Ruby had to go to jail. Rosenfeld was eager to make a settlement for the company to avoid the time and expense of a trial, and to please his boss, but Mort would not hear of it.

Two days after the Federal lawyers flew back to the States, the Swiss authorities in Bern turned down the American government's request for the extradition of Mortimer and Reuben King. It was good news, but there was little else to celebrate. Every few days another loan was called and, as the squeeze on the company's assets tightened, they were obliged to shut down more and more offices. Sam and Jeffrey spent most of their time now flying round the world, closing doors and trying to find jobs for the staff they were compelled to fire. It was a depressing task, all the more so because there was no rational explanation they could give for the company's collapse. Were it not for Mort and Ruby's refusal to stand trial, there was no doubt that King Brothers could have been saved. No jeopardy assessment would have been levied. The company would not have been forced to raise a billion dollars in cash and the banks would not have called their loans.

'It's suicide,' said Jeffrey. 'It's like Mort and Ruby ordered us all to commit hara kiri.' He was wondering when they would have to shut down the Tokyo office. 'We're performing ritual sacrifice to save the skins of our senior partners.'

'Would you give yourself up if you were in their position?' Sam asked.

'I'm not,' said Jeffrey.

'Aren't you the lucky one?' said Sam.

One of the things Jack Greenberg lived for was to see his father-in-law dead. The sooner it happened, the better. It was an event he anticipated with the greatest pleasure.

It was a Friday afternoon in June and E.M. was in jovial mood as he always was last thing before the weekend. Jack himself never anticipated the weekend with any great delight. Too much of it was spent with his in-laws and no amount of chicken soup and matzoballs could compensate for the stunning boredom of an evening with the Meyers. No wonder that, by Sunday afternoon, Edmund Meyer could scarcely contain himself waiting till Monday morning.

E.M. summoned Jack to his office to discuss an oil products deal, but after a few moments he jumped to his feet and made for the door. 'I gotta go,' he said.

Jack chased after him down the corridor, the two of them still hotly arguing refining costs.

In the lavatory, E.M. made for the nearest cubicle and bolted the door.

Jack took a leak, washed his hands, combed his hair and chatted with E.M. to the accompaniment of the usual insanitary noises and smells. After a while, the old man was quiet; he was no longer responding to Jack's questions.

'E.M.? You OK?'

There was no reply.

Jack looked under the door of the cubicle. All he could see was a white bowl, the tips of a pair of shiny black shoes, rolled-down pants and blood-red suspenders.

He climbed onto the toilet seat of the next cubicle and looked down. E.M. was sitting on the toilet with his pants down, leaning against the wall, his neck twisted in an odd way. His eyes were staring straight ahead, anxious, clouded. He looked scared, and he was perspiring heavily.

Something he was trying to say – Jack could barely make out the words, but it was obvious that the old man was in serious trouble. He hauled himself up over the partition separating the two cubicles and dropped down beside E.M.

Now he could hear him clearly. 'Help me,' he was whispering.

'Long life!' said Jack. He considered his father-in-law. He was deliberating. It was a risk. If E.M. recovered . . . He dug into the old man's pocket for the bunch of keys he always carried around with him. Then he unbolted the cubicle door and closed it gently behind him. He walked back to E.M.'s office, taking care not to hurry, closed the door behind him and opened the wall safe. The files were there, thank God – the incriminating files E.M. had kept all these years, the only evidence anyone would ever have that Jack had stolen from the Oil Corporation. He locked the safe and walked out with the files under his arm.

'Where's E.M.?' he asked the secretary.

'In the toilet, I guess,' she said.

'I'll go look for him,' said Jack.

On his way, he locked the files in his office safe. Then he went back to the john and looked in the cubicle. E.M. was still sitting in the same position, his big head resting against the wall, eyes vacant, fixed, lips turning blue.

The Titan was dead.

Jack breathed a sigh of relief. 'When you gotta go, you gotta go,' he muttered.

He returned the keys to E.M.'s pocket and went to raise the alarm.

It was one of those perfectly composed early summer evenings in New York. The sun had slipped behind the Fifth Avenue skyscrapers and time seemed to stand still for a few moments, poised at the equilibrium of day and night. The shop lights flashed on in Madison Avenue and the sky turned indigo.

Outside Leo Stendel Fine Art at the corner of Seventy-Second and Madison, a few elegantly dressed ladies sipped champagne and listened to an earnest young man in a black leather jacket and yellow balloon pants explaining why Picasso was a Capitalist lackey and decadent hack.

Inside, the gallery was packed. It was a champagne cocktail party to celebrate the preview of Julie King's first exhibition and, already, it was a smash hit, exceeding even Leo's – and certainly Julie's – expectations. Within thirty minutes of the doors' opening, ninety per cent of the paintings had been sold.

Julie was surrounded by admirers – some who genuinely enjoyed the fifty or so canvases she had painted for the exhibition, others who were hovering in the hope that someone would explain what they meant.

She had not known whom to invite.

'That's easy,' Leo had said: 'A dash of people who know something about art. A squeeze of those who think they know. Then we top it up with money and give it a whirl. I call it the Madison Avenue cocktail. It never fails.'

And, indeed, he was proved right, yet again. The fact that Leo was convinced that his protégée had real talent was a bonus, but not, in itself, an essential ingredient.

'Honey,' a lady from Beverly Hills was telling Julie, 'you are so gifted. You should charge twice as much for your paintings. When I think what I pay my interior decorator . . .'

'Excuse me,' said another lady from the Deep South, 'I wouldn't want you to think I was being inquisitive or anything, but I just bought one of your paintings – that cute little red one over there. Tell me,' she whispered hoarsely in Julie's ear, 'how do you all get guys to pose in the nude for you?'

Julie looked puzzled. 'I don't do nudes.'

The Deep South was devastated. 'Oh, don't you, darling? Now that is a real shame. Just when I was thinking of taking up a new hobby. Men are so shy, poor dears,' she lamented. 'I can't imagine why. So few of them have anything to hide.'

'Congratulations,' said Leo affectionately. 'You're launched. They love you.'

'Leo, you rogue,' said Julie, 'if I hung some of my old shoes on the wall, you could sell them.'

'No doubt,' said Leo. 'Don't underestimate yourself though. The Leo Stendel seal of approval helps, it's true, but no amount of hype will sell paintings if they're not commercial.'

'So, that's what I am,' she said. 'Commercial.'

'What's wrong with commercial?' Leo put his hand gently on her shoulder. 'You have talent,' he said. 'How much more you have remains to be seen. Meanwhile, enjoy.'

Leo's assistant, Tina, came over. She had shiny black hair in a pudding-basin cut, brown eyes and a very intense manner. 'Leo,' she said, straightening his tie possessively, in a gesture intended to tell the world that she was sleeping with him, 'there's a real kooky guy over there in dark glasses and a beard who says he wants to buy a painting, but I've never seen him before.'

'Which painting?' said Julie.

'The self-portrait.'

'I was kind of hoping to keep that,' said Julie. 'I thought of giving it to Mort.'

'It's in the sale,' said Leo.

'I know it is. All the same . . .' said Julie.

'Go talk to the guy,' said Leo. 'Do what you think best.'

The man was standing in a corner of the Gallery, studying the painting. As she came up to him, he turned and removed the dark glasses. It was Mort. She burst out laughing. 'Where did you get that beard?'

'You dig?'

'Very sexy. What the hell are you doing here? How did you get into the country? How come they didn't arrest you? Are you out of your mind?' Suddenly she was anxious for him.

'Which question do you want me to answer first?' he said, grinning.

'How did you get in?'

'Private charter from the Caribbean. Florida has a bunch of private airstrips.'

She put her arms round his neck. 'I'm afraid,' she said. 'Someone will see you. So you're not. . . ?'

'Giving myself up? Not a chance,' he said.

'So why take such a dumb risk?'

'You think I'd miss my wife's first exhibition? Besides, I want to buy a painting – this one. It's you, isn't it?'

'Yes,' she said. 'I was keeping it for you.'

Mort nodded as he studied the painting. 'You look a bit hunted,' he said.

'You and me, both.'

'How much?'

'It's a present from your wife.'

He shook his head. 'No deal.'

'OK. It's thirty-five thousand dollars.'

Mort whistled. 'Not bad for starters,' he said. He wrote out the cheque and handed it to her. 'When can I have it?'

'I'll bring it over,' she said, 'with the original.'

'I have to go. I'm sorry.'

'Such a long trip for such a short visit,' she said gently.

'It was worth it.'

Julie kissed him almost shyly. 'I love you,' she said. The words just came out. In a way, they surprised her as much as they did him.

When Jack Greenberg walked into the library and saw Mort, his face turned pale.

'They told me it was Sergeant Doherty of the New York Police Department.'

'Would you have believed it if they told you it was Mortimer King?'

Jack relaxed a little. 'Probably not. Travelling incognito?'

'You could say that.'

'What brings you here?'

'Here, New York? Or here, your home?'

'Both.'

'Here, New York, to attend my wife's preview at the Leo Stendel Gallery.'

'I read about it. congratulations!'

'Here, your home, because you're someone I can trust.' Mort sipped his bourbon and soda. He had poured it himself, not bothering to wait for his host, Jack noted resentfully. The same old Mort. Still running the show.

'That's right, isn't it, Jack? I can trust you?'

'You know you can,' said Jack. He was feeling better. Obviously Mort had not found out about the 'contract' he had put out on him. It was a constant worry. Jack had been relieved when Mort had fled to Switzerland. He would feel a lot better when he was safely in the pen.

'I need your help,' said Mort.

Mortimer King needed his help. How times had changed.

'First I want your word that you won't talk about this – not to anyone. Not even Rachel.'

'You have it,' said Jack.

'By the way, where is Rachel?'

'She's at the hospital.'

'Something wrong?'

'Not exactly.' Jack chuckled. 'She's pregnant, would you believe?'

'But I thought . . .'

'That I was sterile? That's what the doctors told me. They said we would never have kids, but one of those new wonder drugs did the trick.'

'That's great,' said Mort.

'It's ironic,' said Jack. 'The old man died before we found out. He would have been a grandfather, after all. That's what he always wanted. I guess it wasn't meant to be.'

Somehow, Mort could feel no compassion for Edmund Meyer.

'It'll be great to have kids,' said Jack. 'You should try it.'

'I did,' said Mort.

Jack looked contrite. 'I forgot.'

'Tell me, Jack,' said Mort. 'Why do you hate me? You do, don't you?'

'How can you say that?' Jack protested. 'Why should I hate you? Matter of fact, I always liked you, always had the greatest admiration for you.'

'Then why did you try to destroy me?' said Mort.

Jack's face was ashen. The sweat bloomed on his forehead and upper lip and, for a second, he looked as though he were going to pass out. If Mort needed any confirmation of what E.M. had told him, he had it now.

'Destroy you?' Jack was fighting for breath. 'What the hell are you talking about?'

'You know what I mean,' said Mort calmly, deriving sadistic pleasure from Jack's torment. If he had ever felt a shred of respect for him, it would have been different, but Jack was not a man you could respect. Look at him now. He was trembling with fear; he was weak and gutless and Mort despised him more than ever.

'You did your best to destroy King Brothers,' he went on and was amused to see the look of relief smoothing out the tortured creases in Jack's face.

'King Brothers,' said Jack, still panting, but less agitated. 'That wasn't me. I told you before – it was E.M. I tried to stop him. I was on your side. The old man was obsessed. He thought he was the hand of God.'

'That's powerful,' said Mort drily.

'It sure is,' said Jack, breathing easily again. 'It'll beat you in an arm wrestle every time.'

'So, it was E.M.,' said Mort.

'It was always E.M.,' said Jack. 'Believe me.'

'And you really would help me?'

'Didn't I say so? What's the matter with you, Mort? You're paranoid. We go back a long way, you and me. Remember?' Smiling. Friendly, smiling Jack.

Mort appeared to hesitate. He crossed over to the bar and poured himself another bourbon . . . his bourbon, his bar, his world. But not for long, thought Jack.

'You understand that what I'm about to tell you is not to be repeated to anyone, not under any circumstances?'

'You already told me,' said Jack. 'Give me a break.'

Mort sipped his bourbon, enjoying the sharp tang at the back of his throat. 'The Feds are having a hard time putting a case together. They have King Brothers in a squeeze, but we're going to survive. Oh sure, they've scared a few guys into telling them some stories, but there's no hard evidence. How could there be,' he added, 'when we're innocent?'

'The whole industry knows that,' said Jack smoothly.

'I do have one problem though,' said Mort. 'There are some documents – mostly private papers, handwritten notes. They're here in my office. If the Feds got hold of them, they could be compromising – not for me, but for a few of my friends. Every company has a couple of skeletons in the closet. You know the kind of thing.'

'Don't I ever,' said Jack.

'I wouldn't want to create problems for my friends,' said Mort.

'I understand,' said Jack. 'Where are these papers?'

'They're in a suitcase in the bar of my office, behind a secret door. My secretary knows where it is, and she has the key. Can I tell her to expect your call?'

'Sure,' said Jack. 'What do you want me to do with the suitcase?'

'It's too dangerous to try to smuggle it out of the country. Besides, I wouldn't want you to take risks on my account. I just want you to check it at the parcel room in Grand Central Station and mail me the claims check.'

'Is that all?' said Jack. 'No problem.'

'I'll be grateful for your help,' said Mort.

'Think nothing of it,' said Jack.

There was not the slightest doubt in his mind whom the suitcase of papers would incriminate. Mort really must think him a gullible fool, but then he had always underestimated him. Careless of Mort to leave evidence like that behind. Obviously he never had the time to destroy it and

627

he was scared of being caught with it in his possession. He was not the sort of guy to take unnecessary risks.

He shook Mort's hand warmly as he left and squeezed his shoulder comfortingly in an intimate gesture of friendship. The great Mortimer King needed his help. Wasn't that something?

In a week, it would be Passover. Sarah was not looking forward to it. For her, Pesach was, above all, a family celebration and this year, it seemed, the family would not be complete. Saul would stay in Israel and Ruth would be in New York, presumably celebrating the two Seder nights with Daniel's parents.

For the first time ever, there would be no children to ask the traditional question: 'Why is this night different from all other nights?' There would be no one to hide the 'afikomen', the piece of matzo broken off and put aside at the beginning of the evening. Every year it was the same. Ruby would find an excuse to leave the room during the meal and, while he was out, Ruth and Saul would take the afikomen and hide it. Without it, the final blessing that ended the meal could not be recited. When the kids were younger, Ruby would pretend astonishment at its disappearance and great concern that there they all were, and there they would have to sit – all night if necessary – until the afikomen was found. Then the show would start. Ruby always hunted in the most unlikely places – under the front door mat, in the washing machine, in the dog's basket – much to the amusement of the kids – and, at last, red-faced, puffing and apparently frantic, he would surrender. He would tell the kids that if anyone happened to know where the afikomen was, it might just be worth a present.

The fact that everyone always knew where the afikomen was – in the centre drawer of the dresser under the paper napkins – was a secret only Ruby and Sarah shared. The kids would scream and shout and jump up and down, clapping their hands, as their silly, bewildered father opened one book after another and carefully shook the pages, searching for traces of the missing piece of matzo. Sometimes – and what a thrill and what a scare this was for Ruth and Saul – Ruby would put his hand on the dresser drawer and hesitate. But, somehow, he always changed his mind at the last minute, except one year, when he actually opened it and, as the two children sat at the table transfixed, hands over their mouths, not daring to breathe, he looked inside. Wonder of wonders. He didn't see it. And so it was that the afikomen was never found and the children never failed to get their presents. That was how it had always been; that was how it always should be on Seder nights.

As the children grew older, the game was still played – with less excitement and spontaneity perhaps – but with increasing warmth and affection, a symbol of the shared experience that bound them together and made them a family.

It was hard for Sarah to contemplate a Passover without her children. She was not, by nature, a person who indulged in nostalgic reminiscences; for her, tomorrow was more important than yesterday. Nevertheless, the thought of what the family had once been, and what they had now become, was infinitely painful for her. She was determined to try to bring about a reconciliation between Ruby and Ruth.

'If only Ruth could be here for Pesach,' she said.

Secretly, Ruby had been thinking the same.

'Let her come. Who's stopping her?'

'She'll want to bring Daniel, of course,' said Sarah.

Ruby said nothing.

'You should talk to her,' said Sarah. 'Phone her. Have a schmooz.'

'What's to talk about?'

'She's your daughter. She's in love. Let her get married.'

'Who's stopping her?'

'Without your blessing, she won't do it. You know that.'

'Without my blessing she won't get married, but she

629

still lives with him? What kind of daughter is that?'

'You leave her no choice,' said Sarah angrily.

Ruby stood there shaking his head.

'I would like us to be a family again,' said Sarah. 'Like we used to be.'

'Like we used to be . . .' Ruby mused. 'I can remember when a custom-made suit cost thirty dollars. I can remember New York without potholes. I can remember when my children did what I told them.'

'Please, Ruby,' she said. 'Phone her.'

Ruby looked at her for a moment with his impenetrable, deadpan expression. 'I can remember when you didn't nag me,' he said.

'Then you have an exceptional memory,' said Sarah.

Ruby shook his head. 'It's hard,' he said softly, as though to himself. 'Business is easy. You buy at five bucks and you sell at six. No one argues with the balance sheet. Being a parent, nothing's ever right. Nothing makes sense. There's no balance sheet.'

'Yes there is,' said Sarah. She took his hand. 'They want to come, Ruby.'

'Who says?'

'I do,' she said. 'If we ask them, they'll come.'

'So ask,' he said.

These days, Edgar was always drunk. Kate had not set eyes on him for months. Then suddenly, one day, there he was at the door of her apartment.

'It's me.'

'So I see.'

'May I come in?'

Kate stepped aside.

'So, what's the answer?' he said.

'The answer to what?'

'Will you or won't you marry me?'

'That was a while back,' said Kate.

'Was it? I hadn't noticed.'

'What brings you here?'

Edgar stretched out on the sofa. 'I was just flying by with the other lost boys. Thought I'd drop in.'

Kate laughed. 'You been eating right?'

'No, but I've been drinking real good.'

'I hear things are not so great at the office.'

'They've been better,' said Edgar. 'So I understand.'

'How do you mean – "so you understand"?'

'I don't work there any more.'

'Why not?'

'Mort fired me. He found out I was cooperating with the Feds.'

Kate didn't comment. She was not judgemental. 'Too bad,' was all she said.

'Oh, I don't know,' said Edgar. 'I guess I learned something. I learned you can't be everything to everyone. You can't please the world. I tried to please you, I tried to please Mort and, when it came to it, I tried to please the Feds. The only guy I never tried to please was Edgar Proktor. Little old Edgar. He lost out all the way down the line.'

'And I thought you were the boy who never grew up,' said Kate.

'I grew a couple of inches,' he said.

'You surely did.'

'It hurts to grow.'

'It was my fault,' she said.

'What was?'

'I set you a task,' she said. 'I had no right doing that. Like I was some fairy princess and you had to prove how brave and strong you were to win my hand.'

'Me, brave and strong?' Edgar laughed.

'I'm sorry,' she said. 'Really I am.'

'Does that mean you'll marry me?'

She shook her head sadly.

'What's wrong with me? I'm charming. I'm not bad looking. I have money. I'm a great lay.'

'I'd like to see more of you.'

'But not . . . marriage?'

'No,' she said, 'not marriage.'

'I guess not,' he said and hauled himself off the sofa.

'Why don't you go back to Mort?'

'Is this my ex talking?'

'The same.'

'I thought you hated his guts?'

'You have a couple of things to work out,' she said.

'You know, you're smart. I always said you were smart. You think he'd ever trust me again?'

'Probably not, but what the hell, he doesn't trust anyone, anyway.'

'The company's going down the drain,' said Edgar.

'So? It would be a nice gesture.'

'The rat climbing back on board,' said Edgar, grinning.

At the door, he said: 'I love you, Kate. What else can I tell you?'

That was the problem, she thought. She could have lived with almost anything – his lies, his infidelity, his drinking. But knowing he loved her – that was too great a burden to bear.

When Edgar got back to his apartment, he phoned Mort.

'I'll do anything,' he said. 'I'll make the coffee, I'll take round the mail.'

'Sorry, Edgar. It wouldn't work.'

'I'll even live in Wald if you want me to.'

'You don't owe me a thing. Don't do penance on my account. I'm not worth it.'

'I did wrong, Mort.'

'So? Who's judging you?'

'I am.'

'Edgar,' said Mort impatiently, 'go bleed somewhere else. I have my own problems. I can't solve yours as well.'

'I only want to help,' said Edgar.

'No you don't. You want a free ride. You want me to tell you what a great guy you are. You want another chance.'

'Is that too much to ask?'

'Maybe not,' said Mort. 'But it's more than I can give you.'

She wore a skirt that hugged her knees so tight it was hard for her to walk. But it did wonders for her wiggle. She had the shapeliest, most provocative little ass, and she wore a tartan bow in her golden hair. She looked young and fresh and innocent. Her lips pouted, pink and shiny, as if she were asking for it. Edgar felt the stirring between his legs. She was waiting in the Bistro Français for her boyfriend. He phoned to say he would be an hour late. He must have been crazy. Edgar sobered up and laid on the charm. The girl never had a chance. By the time her boyfriend showed up, she was back at Edgar's apartment.

'I want you to know, I don't normally pick up girls,' he said.

'Is that so?' she said. 'What do you pick up then?' She was a real cutie.

She had her clothes off before Edgar had removed his tie. She lay there on the bed watching him undress. To keep herself in the mood, she slipped her fingers between her thighs and massaged herself. She liked that a lot, judging from the little moaning noises she made.

'Hurry,' she begged, turning on her stomach and wriggling her butt at him. Edgar took one look at it, tore off his clothes and leapt on the bed. The moment before he landed, she rolled, as fast and agile as a squirrel. She pushed him down and sat astride him, teasing him, kneading his penis with the soft damp flesh between her muscular thighs.

'Honey,' he pleaded, 'be gentle. I'm a virgin!'

She giggled, rolled over and pulled him down on top of her, opening her knees wide and thrusting upwards with her thighs.

He slipped his fingers under that dream butt and drew her close.

*

633

After a while, he sat up and put his head in his hands.

'I can see you could be a lot of fun,' she said, sliding off the bed and putting on her clothes.

'I guess I had too much to drink,' he said.

'It's no big deal,' she said. 'My boyfriend will take care of me. He always takes care of me real good.'

'It's not you,' he said. 'I'd hate for you to think that. You're the greatest turn-on I ever saw.'

She snapped the cute little tartan bow on the back of her golden hair.

'See you around,' she said.

On the way out, she picked up an apple.

He called out: 'You may not believe this, but it's the first time it ever – '

The door slammed. It was too late. She had gone.

Well, there was always a first time. Funny, it was the only thing he had been completely sure that he could still do. What else was left? His marriage was down the tubes. His career – what fucking career? How about self-respect? Not too much of that left. He had always been an alcoholic, and a layabout. Now he was the guy who betrayed his friends.

No, there really wasn't too much anyone could say in his favour. Not any more. All the girls used to say that Edgar Proktor was the best screw in town. Used to say.

He started to laugh. The heck of it was, it wasn't funny.

It seemed to Jack Greenberg that everyone in the elevator was staring at him. He could feel the sweat beading on the inside of his collar, and he was suddenly aware that he was clutching the handle of the suitcase so tightly that his nails were digging into the flesh of his palm. 'Relax,' he muttered to himself. What was so unusual about a guy in an elevator carrying a suitcase?

The floors and walls of the towering entrance hall of Kings' Tower were clad in bronze-coloured marble. The place was an echo chamber, but he was convinced that his footsteps rang louder than anyone else's.

The suitcase was small. Why was it so goddam heavy? Papers. Papers were always heavy. Especially these. He must be nuts. Some risk he was taking. What would happen if the cops picked him up before he checked the case? What would the charges be? Conspiracy? Obstruction of justice? God knows what else. He would wind up in jail with Mort. Some prospect. Jack looked about him guiltily. He was scared. Not scared – terrified. Every step he took, he expected someone to challenge him. The security guard at the door looked at him oddly, advanced on him and held out his hand. Jesus Christ, this was it! His heart was racing. He felt faint and there was a sharp pain down the inside of his arm.

The man spun the revolving glass for him. Jack was so traumatized he could not open his mouth to thank him. His car was round the corner in a tow-away zone. It was too risky to use a driver.

In the street, he felt even more uncomfortable. How many guys carried suitcases down Park Avenue? Oh God! There was a cop standing by his limo. Take it easy, Jack. Take it nice and slow. He's there because it's a tow-away zone. He's not interested in the suitcase. Relax.

The cop stood there and watched him without a word as he heaved the suitcase into the trunk. 'Business trip,' said Jack, forcing a smile and wishing he had kept his mouth shut.

The cop said nothing – just looked at him.

Jack rushed round to the front of the limo. His hands were shaking so much that he had to rest them against the side of the car to steady them before he could insert the key in the lock. He dragged open the door and fell into the driver's seat. He sensed that the cop was still there, but he was too frightened to look. All he needed to do now was switch on the ignition and drive off.

But for Christ's sake, where was the key? He searched frantically in his pockets. The sweat was streaming down his face. He was almost crying with fear. What goddam luck. What the hell could he have done with it?

The cop was tapping on the electrically operated window. He tried to open it, but it wouldn't move. He tortured his finger on the button. If he didn't get some air soon, he would faint. He struggled with the door and opened it.

'Your key's in the door,' said the cop.

'What?' Blankly.

'The car key – you left it in the door.'

'Oh, Jesus! What a dumb jerk I am!'

He reached round to pull out the key, but it was not so easy. The cop was standing so close to the door that it was impossible to open it more than a few inches without hitting him and Jack was too scared to ask him to move. He had to contort his arm to get his hand out far enough; his wrist felt like it was going to break. He twisted his arm further round until it was on the point of dislocation and, with one final, agonized convulsion, closed two fingers on the key and pulled it out. He slammed the door shut, breathed deeply for a few seconds, inserted the key in the ignition and lowered the window.

'Thanks,' he said to the cop. 'Thanks a million.' He was pathetically grateful, not for the cop's help but because he had not been arrested. He looked up at the impassive face way above him, tormented his features into a smile and drove off.

There was nowhere to park outside Grand Central Station, so he left the car on the pavement. The important thing was to dump the suitcase as fast as possible. He had to stand in line for a few minutes, shifting impatiently from one foot to the other, but here, at least, he didn't feel out of place.

The moment the guy behind the counter took the case from him and gave him the baggage check was the greatest moment of his life. He began to breathe normally again. The pain in his arm disappeared.

There was a mail box in the station. He slipped the baggage check into the pre-addressed envelope and dropped it in. Mort would never know that he had sent it to the Feds. He would tell him the cops must have followed him

– searched the mail box. He did not even trouble to hurry out to the limo, expecting to get a ticket and not caring. He took his time. There was no ticket. It must be an omen. Things were looking up.

Bob Rosenfeld would get the baggage check the next day and, with it, all the evidence against Mortimer King that he needed. Mort would not be troubling Jack – or anyone else – for a long time to come.

Bob Rosenfeld leaned back in his chair and shook his head.

'It's incredible. Invoices, records, and a whole bunch of handwritten notes. It's all here.'

Ed Goldwyn was by nature suspicious. 'How do we know the stuff is for real?'

'Wait till you see it. I'm having the boys go over it. They'll report back to you in a day or two, but believe me, Ed, it's all the evidence we need. It's a gift from heaven.'

'Courtesy of the US Mail. Who sent us the baggage check?'

'We don't know. We have our suspicions, but we really don't know. This stuff has been lying around for a long time. Why it should only surface now is a mystery. Whoever sent it to us, he surely had his reasons, but whatever they are, he's wrapped up the case for us. There's no possible defence against all this. You'll see what I mean when you read it.'

'Someone didn't exactly love our friend.'

'You could say that,' said Bob Rosenfeld.

'What's in the suitcase?' asked Ruby.

'The complete dossier on Jack Greenberg. All the stuff I kept on him over the years – plus the records E.M. kept later. He was on to Jack, too. He knew what he was doing, but he could never bring himself to send his son-in-law to jail. Jack made a bad mistake. He behaved himself for a time – after I discovered what he was up to – but, being Jack, he couldn't resist. It wasn't long before he started milking the company again.'

637

'What will he do with the claims check?'

Mort spread his hands. 'That's his decision.'

'You think he'll mail it to you?'

'He said he would.'

'And if he does?'

'Then that will be the end of it.'

Ruby grinned slyly. 'You enjoy playing God, do you, Mort?'

'Who's playing God? I'm leaving it to Jack to decide his own fate. If he goes to jail, he'll have only himself to blame.'

'Will you be disappointed if he mails you the check?'

'Maybe. I guess I'd be surprised. Disappointed?' Mort picked up his telexes, patted them into a trim pile and laid them neatly on his desk. 'I might be at that. For all the dirty tricks, for all the times he tried to destroy us. For the time he tried to have me killed.'

'He did what!'

Mort told Ruby the story. Ruby's normally placid features were frozen in shock.

'I can't believe it. Why would he want to murder you?'

'E.M. had him beaten up. Jack was convinced it was me. I took the bullet for Edmund Meyer. Ironic, isn't it?'

'And you never said a word to me.'

'I only found out a few months ago. It was E.M. who told me. It was already history. There didn't seem to be any point in digging it up.'

Ruby sat there, unable to move, his brain trying hard to cope with the enormity of what Mort had told him. What had happened? Where had they all gone wrong? How had they lost control of their lives? It seemed like only yesterday that he had been just another regular guy, a struggling Midtown lawyer with no great prospects, but no great problems either. Now he carried burdens that he never dreamed existed before; burdens that others had loaded on him; envy, guilt and malice, and his own particular burden – ambition, the heaviest of all to bear.

*

Jack Greenberg was indignant and flustered. 'What is it with you guys? Did you have to pull me in for questioning with no warning, no explanation? Couldn't you at least have called me first? My staff think I'm some kind of criminal. I have to tell you this is no way to treat a respectable citizen. I warn you, I'll be talking to some very influential people about this.'

Bob Rosenfeld looked apologetic. 'We only want to ask you a couple of questions, Mr Greenberg.'

'Is it that urgent? Couldn't it have waited till I cleared my desk?'

'It's urgent,' said Rosenfeld patiently.

'So, what's it all about?'

The two men were watching Jack closely. Just for a moment, he felt apprehensive, but then the feeling passed.

'It's about this,' said Bob Rosenfeld. As he spoke, he produced an empty suitcase and dumped it, dramatically, on his desk.

Jack tried his best to hide his amazement, but he was no poker player. First he flushed red, then he turned pale and his eyes flicked uneasily. He was trying desperately to think, to control his reactions, but he was in shock. He had mailed the claims check anonymously. How else? There was no way they could have linked him with the suitcase unless, of course, he had been followed. That cop – could he have been suspicious? Phoned headquarters? Could they have put a tail on him? Surely not. Those things only happened in movies. Besides, they wouldn't have had the time. How could they? How could they have known? No. It was all impossible. All he had to do was tough it out.

'What is all this? What the heck is so urgent about a suitcase?' he asked.

'About a suitcase? Nothing. It's what was in it that interests me,' said Rosenfeld.

Jack was beginning to breathe easier. For some reason that he could not imagine, Rosenfeld suspected that he had mailed him the baggage check. He didn't like it, but

639

what could he do? One day Mort would find out what Jack had done to him. It was inevitable. By that time, he would either be safely in jail or still holed up in Switzerland. Either way, he would be no threat to Jack.

He decided to show his hand. 'I'll bet,' he said. 'I'll bet it interests you.' He grinned at Bob Rosenfeld conspiratorially.

He noticed the two men glance at each other. It may have been his imagination, but they seemed puzzled.

'I guess you know who sent you the claims check,' he said.

'Why don't you tell us?' said Rosenfeld.

'Look,' said Jack, 'you know, and I know you know. So let's stop playing games. I give you all the evidence you need and you treat me like I was a bagman for the Cosa Nostra. How about some good old-fashioned gratitude?'

Rosenfeld looked confused. 'Are you telling us you know what was in this suitcase?'

Jack winked. 'Aw, come on, boys. Of course I know. Who do you think mailed you the claims check?'

Neither of them said a word. They sat there, looking at him blankly.

'You two have got to be putting me on. OK, let's play it your way. You want me to tell you who mailed the claims check?'

'Tell us,' said Rosenfeld.

Jack grinned smugly. 'I did.'

Rosenfeld removed his glasses slowly, as if they were a barrier between hearing and comprehension.

'You! You mailed us the claims check?' he repeated incredulously.

'Sure I did,' said Jack. 'Who do you think sent it? Mort?'

It seemed as if Jack expected his joke to be appreciated, so Ed Goldwyn grinned wanly. 'May I ask you why you mailed it to us?' he said.

'Well, now,' said Jack, 'that's really my business, isn't it?'

'Sure it is,' said Goldwyn, humouring him, 'but we'd like you to tell us. If you wouldn't mind, that is.'

Jack hesitated. He wasn't sure he wanted to, but it was hard to resist talking. These two had a habit of leaving silence lying around like a baited trap. Besides, he realized now that telling them could prove to be a very satisfying experience.

'Mort and I go back a long way. It's an old story. I won't burden you with it, but that guy needs to control everyone around him – his friends and his enemies. Let's just say I don't happen to like being manipulated.'

Rosenfeld still looked blank. Jack wondered where he got his reputation for sharpness from. The guy's reactions were ponderously slow.

'The suitcase was in Mort's office,' he went on. 'It was hidden in a secret compartment. He'd collected all the incriminating evidence on the Domestic scam together in one place so he could destroy it, or smuggle it out of the country. But events moved too fast for him and he had to leave it behind when he ran off to Switzerland. Only his secretary knew about it. I guess he was afraid she would talk, or maybe that you'd search his office and find it – so he asked me to take care of it. That's Mort's way. He likes other people to do his dirty work for him.'

'Let me get this straight,' said Bob Rosenfeld. 'Mort asked you to pick up this suitcase from his office, check it in Grand Central Station and mail the claims check?'

'You got it,' said Jack.

'Who did he ask you to mail the claims check to?'

Jack grinned. 'To him, of course. Who else?'

The light dawned in Bob Rosenfeld's eyes. 'And instead of mailing it to him. . . ?'

'I mailed it to you. It seemed like a good idea,' said Jack.

'You decided to double-cross Mort,' said Ed Goldwyn.

'I decided to perform a public service,' said Jack, bridling.

'You did,' said Goldwyn. 'No doubt about it.'

'It's the most complete and incontestable dossier of theft, fraud and tax evasion over a number of years that I personally have ever seen,' said Bob Rosenfeld.

'I don't wish to sound vindictive,' said Jack, 'but for me,

the one thing that would ice the cake would be to see Mort's face when he hears about this. It's one hell of a shame that I'll have to miss that.'

'I see what you mean,' said Ed Goldwyn. 'It would be a real treat.'

'I can just see his expression now,' said Bob Rosenfeld.

Jack leaned back in his chair, clasped his hands behind his head and sighed a sigh of deep contentment. This was the ultimate. There could never be a better moment in his whole life. He was determined to relish it, to make the most of it. This was something he would always remember, something he was going to look back on, time and time again.

'You guys have no idea what this is going to do for me.' Smiling Jack.

'Oh but we do,' said Bob Rosenfeld.

'For the rest of my life,' said Jack dreamily.

'I wouldn't say the rest of your life,' said Bob Rosenfeld. 'It's not that bad.'

'I'd give it three to five,' said Ed Goldwyn.

Jack frowned. 'Three to five?'

'Years,' said Ed Goldwyn.

'In the pen,' said Bob Rosenfeld.

'What the hell are you talking about?'

Bob Rosenfeld explained and Ed Goldwyn read him his rights.

Someone had to fly to New York to pay off a hundred employees. The office was winding down, still holding on, but only just. If Jeffrey and Sam had had their way, the doors would be closed by now, but Mort and Ruby would not hear of it. They clung to their last fingerhold; they were not ready to surrender the headquarters of their crumbling empire.

Not a pleasant task, and yet Karl volunteered, with some enthusiasm, to go. Sam could not understand why, but he was happy to have a volunteer and he asked no questions. Jeffrey was tied up; he had his own problems in London.

642

Mort and Ruby, for obvious reasons, had to stay put. Karl could be trusted to handle things sympathetically and with discretion. That was the great thing about Karl. You could always rely on him to do the job properly.

He could not believe that she was nearly forty. It was impossible. Amy was the kind of woman who never appeared to age – she was how Karl had first seen her more than fifteen years ago, the way he would always see her. She had that timeless quality; she was so beautiful and so elusive. He wanted to hold her, to keep her forever, but trying to capture Amy was like attempting to catch a dragonfly. One moment it was hovering and shimmering near you, as if daring you to reach out for it, and then, as you stretched out your hand, it had gone.

'You look wonderful,' he said, 'so happy.'

'I am happy,' she said. 'I'm in love.'

He felt the stab of jealousy in his stomach.

Amy laughed. 'No. Not with a man. I'm in love with New York. The Big Apple. She's a temptress, that's for sure.'

So are you, he thought, but with a difference. Amy was not like the sirens who lured sailors to their deaths; she was herself a lost soul who needed help, someone to be loved and, above all, protected.

He sat in her apartment and watched, fascinated, as she arranged the long-stemmed roses he had brought her. The arrangement was spontaneous – disorderly even. You would never see anything like it in one of those smart florists on Fifth Avenue that displayed their flowers in arrangements of such exquisite symmetry and equilibrium. These roses could almost have arranged themselves. They were not trapped by sponge or wire; they were free. Like her.

'They're beautiful,' she said. 'Oh, I just noticed. The florist made a mistake. They only sent eleven.'

But it was no mistake. It was the way Karl had planned it.

The twelfth rose was delivered in person by the maître d'hotel of Le Relais.

Amy was clearly touched.

'This is so romantic,' she said.

Karl was delighted. He had been a little afraid that she would find the gesture ponderous, too carefully contrived perhaps, and, when he saw how she arranged his roses, he felt intuitively how different she was from him. Maybe he should have grabbed some flowers from a street stall on his way over to her apartment, but that was not the way he did things. So they were different. So what? It would be perfect. They would complement each other.

She invited him back to her apartment again after dinner, as he had known she would. They talked of fun things light-heartedly. Now was the time to tell her what was on his mind, to be serious. No woman had ever taken him seriously before. He loved her for that.

'It was ridiculous to expect you to settle down with a farmer. I must have been out of my mind. I see that now,' he said.

'A cognac?'

Karl shook his head with a slight frown. He hated to be interrupted and now it was so vital that she listen to him with her full attention.

'This is where you belong. New York. This is your scene. How could you ever be happy living in some Swiss village?'

She smiled and nodded, but was she really listening?

'Amy, I want to look after you.'

She started to speak, but he interrupted her. 'Wait. Let me finish. We can get married and live here – in New York, Amy. I've thought it all out. I have plenty of money saved. I told you that before. I could get a job with any one of a hundred companies – with my background and experience, they'll be queueing up for me. Or if not that, if you don't like the idea of your husband working for another company, I could start up my own little computer business, or even set up shop as an oil trader. I'll do

644

anything you want. What do you say, Amy? What do you say?'

Amy lay back in her chair and closed her eyes. She was slightly drunk and very tired. It had been a long day.

'Amy, what do you say?' he repeated. 'I asked you a question.'

'I know you did, darling,' she said. Oh God, what could she say that would convince him to go away and leave her alone? Hadn't he heard her right the first time? If only he could accept that they were friends – just friends. She had been concerned when she saw the roses. She should have known. She should have been more careful not to encourage him.

'Karl,' she said. 'I'm fond of you. I really am. I always will be. But that's it. I don't love you.'

'But I love you,' he said, as if that were all that mattered. 'We could be happy. I know we could.'

Jesus, she thought, what a broken record. To think she had once found the guy attractive.

'You're a good man, Karl, but you're not for me. Besides, I don't want to get married, not to anyone. I'm happy the way I am.' She slid one leg over the other, those long, glittering legs. How he wanted her.

'We were so good together,' he said softly.

'Sure we were,' she agreed. 'But what's the big deal? We had a few screws. We had fun. That's all there was to it.' It was cruel, but it seemed like the only way. She expected him to be shocked, but she was not prepared for the violence of his reaction. His mouth convulsed involuntarily. He shrank from her in revulsion and horror.

'You can say that after what we did together!'

'Sure I can,' she said. 'So we went to bed a couple of times. So what? Face it, Karl. I'm pushing forty and I'm divorced. I have needs like anyone else. What do you think I do with my free time? Play bingo?'

'And I thought it meant something to you. I thought you loved me.'

'I never told you I loved you,' she said coldly. 'Not once.'

645

'So for you I was just something to play with. The whole thing was a mockery.' He was angry now, angry and bitter.

'I never mocked you, Karl. I never did that.'

He did not hear her. 'I was just a Swiss peasant – a good fuck, but not to be taken seriously.'

Amy had heard enough of this maudlin crap. 'I'd say you were an OK fuck. As a matter of fact, you were pretty average as fucks go. Let me tell you, there are a lot of big pricks around town – they're a dime a dozen. I can take them or leave them. When I take them, I move right on to the next one. That's the way I am. That's the way I'll always be.'

Karl pressed his hands to his temples to deaden the pain, but it was no use. His head was bursting, the throbbing unbearable. And then, suddenly, in his torment, came a terrible calm. Everything was clear now. She hovered and shimmered and tempted you. How could he let her escape? Her neck was so small and delicate. He had to stop her from getting away, like the dragonfly. He reached out his hands to catch her . . .

But when he opened them again, she had gone.

The maid found them the next morning. Amy had been strangled and Karl lay on the floor at her feet. He had swallowed just enough of her sleeping pills to kill himself. That was the great thing about Karl. You could always rely on him to do the job properly.

The Haggadah lay open in front of Ruby. He made the blessing over the matzo, the unleavened bread, broke off a piece and put it on one side – the afikomen.

The glasses were filled with red wine. His family was gathered round him, Sarah facing him at the other end of the table, Saul on his right – he had come back from Israel when he heard that Ruth would be there – and on his left, Ruth and Daniel. There were also half a dozen close family friends.

The first night of Passover. Another Seder, another family gathering, another year. It was a happy occasion and, at the same time for Ruby, an ironic one. The story of the Children of Israel, freed from slavery in Egypt and led to the Promised Land, had always had a special meaning for Jews, many of whom could only dream of freedom, but, when they raised their glasses and drank the symbolic toast, 'Next Year in Jerusalem', they renewed their hope and their belief that one day the dream would come true. For some, these days, Jerusalem was as close as an airline ticket; for many, it was still light years away.

Now, for the first time, the toast saddened Ruby. Where could he go? Not Jerusalem. Not New York, either. He was an exile by choice, a prisoner with nowhere to run to. How long could he live like this?

Now and then he glanced across at Daniel. The boy had character. He knew how to conduct himself. He was not afraid of life. There was about him a sense of purpose and determination – the way he talked, the way he looked. He was a good boy. If only Ruby could forget who he was. At least now he knew that his father had not betrayed his profession. He was not a man who took bribes. Ruth could do worse, a lot worse.

They came to the end of the Passover story, refilled the glasses and prepared to sing the traditional songs that rounded off the evening. It was Ruby's custom to ask each of his guests to sing the first verse of a song. That way, everyone could participate in the giving of the Seder and sometimes the family would learn new melodies from their friends. There were always those too shy or too unmusical to accept his invitation. Tonight was one of those nights; it seemed no one wanted to sing solo.

'What about Daniel?' said Sarah.

'Why not?' said Ruby, looking embarrassed.

Daniel did not need to be asked twice. He had a fine voice – a strong and resonant bass. He sang not one, but three verses with complete composure and, as he sang, his voice grew louder and he seemed completely unaware of his audience. At the end of the third verse he suddenly realized that he was singing alone; he stopped and looked around him.

'Why isn't anyone singing?' he asked. 'Did I do something wrong?'

For a moment, there was silence. Ruth put her arm through his.

'No,' said Sarah, 'you did right.'

Then everyone started singing.

Ruby reached for the afikomen and looked surprised when he discovered that it was not where it was supposed to be.

'The afikomen is missing!' he announced dramatically. 'We can't finish the Seder. Does anyone know where it is?'

When no one answered him, he stood up and wandered round the room, eyeing possible hiding places, but the show was somehow unconvincing. There was a dresser here, much like the one in New York. For a moment he paused and looked down at the middle drawer.

'Aren't we all a little too old for this?' he said.

'I guess we are,' said Ruth.

Sarah looked at Ruby apprehensively, expecting him to open the drawer. He stood there, hesitating, his back turned to them. He was thinking that if he opened it and 'found' the afikomen, something important would have changed. Something fragile and precious that they had shared until this moment would be lost forever. But then, wasn't that life? Illusions were shattered every day. He opened the drawer and saw the afikomen lying there. Sarah held her breath.

'I don't see it,' he said, after a long moment, and shut the drawer. 'OK. If you tell me where it is, I'll give you kids a present. What is it you want, Saul?'

Saul said: 'I could use a car, Pop. I'm tired of hitching rides. There's a little Datsun I have my eye on.'

'You got it,' said Ruby.

'Gee, thanks, Pop.' Saul was ecstatic.

Ruby turned to Ruth. 'What about my daughter?'

648

She shook her head. 'Nothing, Pop. I don't need a thing.'

'There must be something,' said Ruby uncomfortably.

'Nothing,' she said.

'This is Seder night,' said Ruby. 'Tonight is different – special. There has to be something you want.'

Ruth looked directly at her father, challenging him with her eyes. 'I want your blessing, Pop. I want to marry Daniel.'

'Think of something else,' said Ruby.

'There is nothing else.'

Ruby walked over to the dresser again and stood there with his hand on the drawer. He was in torment.

Ruth came over to her father. 'Pop,' she said, 'Daniel and I are going to be married – with or without your blessing – but it's not the way I want it and it's not the way he wants it, either.' She put her arms round his neck. 'Hey,' she said quietly, so quietly that only he could hear, 'my name's Ruth. Remember me?'

Ruby put his arms round his daughter and hugged her. Then he held her at arm's length and looked at her proudly.

'You have my blessing,' he said.

Ruth jumped up and down with delight and kissed her father over and over again.

'It's enough now,' said Ruby. 'Will someone please tell me where the goddam afikomen is?'

'It's in the drawer, Pop,' she said. 'This one here. You were so warm, we were getting worried.'

Ruby looked at them all with mock astonishment. 'Well, wouldn't you know?' he said.

He took the afikomen from the drawer, broke it up and gave everyone round the table a piece. The Seder was over.

Jeffrey and Sam had decided it was time for Mort and Ruby to face facts. The four partners met in Mort's office in Wald. There was barely space for them all to squeeze into the tiny room. It was not exactly the Grand Hotel Dolder.

'You want bullshit or you want the truth?' said Jeffrey.

'Let's have it straight,' said Mort.

'We're finished.'

'Lighten up, Jeffrey. What kind of talk is that?'

'The kind you wanted. The truth.'

Ruby said: 'You were always a pessimist.'

'Screw you, Ruby,' said Jeffrey. 'We're finished and you know it. We were through the day the banks dumped us. You can't run a company on air, especially a company with our massive overheads.'

'I told you to go somewhere else for the loans,' said Mort. 'I thought it was all tied up. You were going to call me.'

'What was the point?' said Jeffrey wearily. 'We tried every major bank in the Western world – dozens of times. They all turned us down flat. A couple said they would reconsider if we settled the case with the Feds.'

'What do you want us to do?'

'Make a deal. Our position is hopeless.'

'A deal for the company only?' said Mort.

'It has to be,' said Jeffrey. 'There's no other deal possible.'

'We know that,' said Ruby. 'You'll be pleased to hear that Mort and I have decided to take our chances. The company must be saved.'

'I'm afraid it's too late for that,' said Jeffrey.

'What are you saying?' said Mort.

Jeffrey spoke slowly and with emphasis. He wanted his words to get through to them. 'Our assets were sold or mortgaged to pay the jeopardy assessment. Now our loans have been called. Business is dead. We have just enough to pay the tax bill and the fine – we think. But when we've done that, we're bankrupt.' He handed each of them a single sheet of paper covered with figures. 'There's the story. We've checked and rechecked it. I wish I could tell you something to make it look more cheerful, but I can't.'

The office was quiet. Mort and Ruby were studying the figures.

'If you and Sam are right, then what's the point of settling with Rosenfeld?' Mort thumped the desk to emphasize his words. 'Why in hell should the company plead guilty?'

'Because every day we open our doors, we're losing more than half a million dollars. You want me to figure out for you how long we can survive at this rate?'

'We can cut overheads,' said Ruby.

'We already did,' said Jeffrey. 'We closed down twenty-eight offices. We're winding down another fifteen. In a couple of months, we'll be left with London, New York and Wald and we won't have enough money in the kitty to pay our lawyers, let alone the tax bill. You want me to tell you what the damn lawyers cost us every day?'

'We'll find a way,' said Mort.

'Bullshit!' said Jeffrey. 'Why don't you face facts, you stubborn bastards?'

'What do you think, Sam?' said Mort.

Sam didn't think anything. It didn't matter any more. Nothing did since Amy's death. 'I don't know,' he said dully. 'There seems to be no way out.'

Mort wanted to get up and pace round the office, but there was no space. He was trapped. He raised his arms to shoulder level, held them there for an instant and let them fall back to his sides. Then he shook his head. He was damned if he was going to accept defeat.

'There's always a way out,' he said.

'Give us time,' said Ruby.

'It's not mine to give,' said Jeffrey. He was close to breaking point. How much more could he take? He hated them and he hated himself. 'It's the end,' he said. 'Don't you understand? Finale. Curtain down. Ragnerok. Doomsday. Twilight of the Gods. You get the general picture?'

'We get it,' said Mort.

'I'm going out for a haircut – while I can still afford it,' said Jeffrey and left them to think it over.

For a couple of hours, Ruby shut himself up in his office. When he came out, he went straight to Jeffrey.

'What would it take to keep us afloat for another year?' he asked.

'You're not making sense, Ruby. Why would we want to stay afloat when we're losing money?'

'It's more than just a company,' said Ruby. 'It's us. What we've put into it. We have to save it, Jeffrey. We have to.'

'Sometimes you have to let go,' said Jeffrey. 'Even you.'

'How much would it take?'

Jeffrey shrugged. 'Two hundred – three hundred million. I can't tell you exactly. We're bleeding all the time. There's nothing coming in.'

'We could turn that around. With more cash, we could do more business.'

'Maybe, but where's the cash?'

Ruby was thinking. 'Give me seven days. Please.'

Jeffrey threw up his hands in despair. 'You're just putting off the evil day. Meanwhile, we lose more money. What's the point?'

'The point? Does there always have to be a point, Jeffrey?'

'For me there does.'

Ruby lit a cheroot. 'The point is to keep going. Isn't that what life's all about?'

'Who the hell knows what life's all about?'

'I have to do it for Mort. Look what he's done for us.'

'Yes,' said Jeffrey. 'Look what he's done.'

'Give me a break,' said Ruby quietly. 'I have to give it a shot. I have to. If I don't come up with something in seven days, tell the lawyers to go ahead. They can make a settlement for the company and leave us out of it.'

'What about Mort?'

'I already talked to him. He agrees, but we want to make one last effort to save the company.'

'How are you going to do that?'

'I haven't the least idea,' said Ruby.

He shut himself in his office again, locked the door, told the switchboard not to put through any calls and gave his secretary instructions to protect him against all interruptions. At lunchtime, she knocked on his door with some cheese sandwiches and a cup of coffee. He glowered at her, took the tray through the half-open door and slammed it shut again.

He spent the first few hours eliminating ideas, one by one. They all involved attempts to corner one or other of the commodity markets, but he rejected every one of them for various reasons; either they were impracticable, or they would take too long to execute, or the potential profit was too small. Ruby had set himself a goal: to dream up a workable foolproof scheme for making three hundred million dollars in less than a week.

It was impossible, of course. A fantasy. No one could make that kind of money overnight. That's what made it exactly the kind of challenge Ruby relished. This would be the ultimate game. The equivalent would be sweeping the board in Monopoly – only this was for real. It was clear to him that to have the remotest chance of making such a huge amount of money, he would need to take risks, but, as in any trading operation, the risks involved had to be acceptable. He would have to gamble with every cent they could raise, but he could not afford to lose his stake.

By three in the afternoon, he had the germ of an idea. By five, he had developed it to the point where he was confident it could work. It was risky, but the risk was, indeed, an acceptable one and the potential reward colossal.

He spent another hour or two honing the scheme, checking the details. By seven, he was satisfied – more than that, he was exultant. If it worked, it would give them a few years to get their act together, pay off their debts and build up the business again. They could make a settlement for the company and he and Mort could tough it out indefinitely in Switzerland.

For the first time in months, he felt optimistic. This would be one for the record book. If he pulled it off, the world would remember Reuben King – no question of that.

*

Mort listened to Ruby with close attention. When he had finished, he was quiet for a long time.

'We never took risks like that before.'

'We never had to,' said Ruby.

'What's it for?'

'Can you think of any other way to save the company? You heard what Jeffrey said. When we've paid our debts and settled the fines, we'll be bankrupt – finished.'

'Why don't we just try and hang in there?'

'We daren't delay any longer. We're losing so much money, we soon won't have the means even to settle with the Feds. Besides, Mort, you see how it is. We can't do business with this thing hanging over us. No one wants to talk to us any more, let alone trade with us.'

'It's a hell of a gamble.'

'So is getting up in the morning,' said Ruby.

Mort walked over to the window and looked out . . . the railway sidings, the lake, the distant hills. It was so goddam calm and peaceful out there. If there was any neurosis, any turmoil in Switzerland, it was right here in their office. Well, at least he and Ruby knew they were living. He turned to his brother. 'You'll be needing a massive credit line.'

Ruby had been holding his breath, waiting for Mort to make up his mind. He let out a little sigh. 'Right,' he said.

'How big?'

'Ten billion dollars.'

Mort whistled. The lights were coming on along the sidings. Ten billion. A ten-billion line for just a week. Only six months ago one call would have done it. Now? What assets they still had were mortgaged. But not everyone knew that. Their financial scenario was complex. He might have to fudge a few facts, but, if he handled it discreetly, confidently, handled it as only he knew how to, he might just raise a twenty-fold line. That should do it. All or nothing. All the chips on one number, one man. Reuben King.

'You got it,' said Mort.

*

In the next two days, the activity in the office was frenetic. The place was full of workmen, breaking down the partitions between three offices, turning them into one large room and installing dozens of computers, telexes and telephones.

Soon the room began to look like an operations centre, or war room, which, in a way, it was. A dozen dealers would be sitting there, each one at his own desk in front of his own computer terminal, each with an assistant trader at his side, three outside phones and an internal link to Ruby whose desk was in the centre of the back row, where he could keep an eye on the whole scene. Dominating the room, two huge screens hung high, linked to every major news service in the world, relaying news flashes that could affect the markets.

Identical operations centres were being set up in New York, London and Tokyo, each one staffed by a dozen dealers and the same number of assistants.

In forty-eight hours, the frantic turmoil, the screaming and the shouting died down. The next twenty-four hours were spent testing equipment. There were computer snags to be smoothed out, communications problems to be overcome. It was a harrowing time. Ruby had given the engineers a deadline. He was working to one himself. Jeffrey had given him seven days. Only four were left.

At two p.m. on the fourth day, Ruby sat at his desk in the Wald operations centre and picked up the phone. He was about to talk to London, Tokyo and New York. His words would be relayed to all four offices and about a hundred dealers simultaneously.

'Good morning, New York. Good afternoon, London. Good evening, Tokyo. I chose this time so that we could all start off with a good night's sleep. We won't be getting too much of that for the next couple of days. Right now, it's two in the afternoon here in Wald, one in the afternoon in London, eight in the morning in New York and nine in the evening in Tokyo. Can everyone hear me?'

Each office confirmed, in turn, that they could.

'Good. What we're about to do is really very simple. We're going to manipulate the world's foreign exchange markets. In the process, I figure we'll make enough money to keep King Brothers operating and all you guys in work. It's our last chance – our only chance – and, believe me, we're going to make the most of it. Now you all know the scheme in outline – we've been through it a number of times. We have a foreign exchange line of ten billion – repeat ten billion dollars – and with that sort of money at our disposal, we should be able to move the market plenty.

'We're going to concentrate on one currency and, because the experts feel right now that it's the most volatile, I've selected the Japanese yen. Over the next few hours, we'll be spreading the rumour round the world that some very large and well-informed dealers are about to move in on the market and buy up the yen in huge quantities. It'll be done in such a way that the information can't be traced back to us. That initial and vital part of the operation has already started, and it's intended to soften up the market – prepare it for what's going to happen. It will almost certainly ensure that a lot of big punters – banks, mutual funds, corporations – will quickly jump onto the bandwagon and help us push the market up, once they see it moving. I expect the whole world to take a ride on our backs, so that the buying power of our ten billion dollars – already a huge sum – will be multiplied several times.

'Tomorrow morning at eight, when the market opens here in Switzerland, we'll move in on the yen. Pretty soon after, when the currency starts to take off, Tokyo will come in – then London. New York will stand by. It'll be only two in the morning in New York when we get busy here, so you guys over there will just have to be patient. We're going to create the impression that there are important buyers who have information about the yen that the market doesn't have – that they're ready to hold on to the currency indefinitely – that they're not going to dump it.

Otherwise, people will be afraid to buy. They'll suspect that the upward surge is some kind of hiccup or manipulation, and that the yen will drop as fast as it took off. New York will start buying as soon as they open. After that, we'll follow our plan. You know what this operation means to us. Let's make it a good one. Good luck to you all.'

At seven fifty-five the next morning, the operations centre in Wald was hushed. Every eye was focused on the screens.

In London, it was seven a.m.; in Tokyo, three p.m.; in New York, two a.m. The Tokyo market was quiet. Since its opening, the yen had moved down from 243.70/80 against the dollar to 243.35/45 and back up to 243.65/75, almost exactly where it started out the day. Dealing was thin. The few traders in the market had tested the water by selling the dollar, and then, when they encountered resistance, they took their profit. It was normal range trading on an uneventful day. Some would have made what, for most traders, would be considered good money – if they had bought and sold at the right time, of course. Timing is all and the risks are high. More money is lost on foreign exchange – Forex – than on any other commodity. It is no market for the faint-hearted. It is definitely not a market for anyone who cannot afford to lose.

The other three offices checked in.

'London standing by.' The guy had an Oxford accent. He sounded laid back. Ruby wondered how long that would last.

'Tokyo standing by.' This one sounded a little more excited.

'New York standing by.' The American sounded sleepy. At two a.m. who could blame him?

One minute to go. In one minute from now, the Swiss Forex market would open. Little did those guys know what was about to hit them. It was a Wednesday morning just like any other. Outside, the sun was shining.

657

The rates were static on the flickering screens. The yen was stable at 243.65/75. In Tokyo, you could sell the dollar for 243.65 yen or buy it for 243.75 – only no one was buying or selling right now.

So far, there had been no reaction to the rumour that there would soon be some big punters in the market, buying yen, selling dollars. The market had noted the rumour, but it had not acted on it.

Thirty seconds to go. Ruby lit a cheroot, drew on it and stubbed it out. The dealers were watching him curiously. He could imagine they were thinking that this guy was a real cool customer. For once, they would be wrong. Ruby felt the adrenalin pumping, and he was aware of a little flutter in his chest.

Fifteen seconds. Three dealers picked up their phones and started dialling: Crédit Suisse in Zurich, Swiss Bank Corporation in Geneva, Union Bank of Switzerland in Zurich.

In London and Tokyo, three dealers in each office were dialling the UK and Japanese banks.

In the first two hours, they sold five hundred million dollars against the yen. At first, the yen reacted sharply, then fell back on profit taking. The screens were showing 242.80/90.

A dealer shouted his latest trade.

'Twenty dollars at the "figure"!' The 'figure' was the exact round number – in this case 243.00 yen. He had sold twenty million dollars at that level.

Sitting next to Ruby was his Forex expert. 'The traders are sceptical. They don't believe we're in a bull market for yen. They think someone is driving down the dollar, setting a "Bear Trap" so they can move in later and pick up a nice profit.'

'What would you do?' said Ruby.

'I'd play the range,' said the dealer. 'Trade in and out.'

'I'm not interested. You can't make a killing playing the range.'

'You can if you take your time.'

'I don't have time.'

'Then we have to convince the market we're serious,' the dealer said. 'How far do you want to push the yen?'

'I'll be satisfied with fifteen or twenty big ones. Anything below 230.'

The dealer looked at him as if he were crazy. 'There's no way you can do that,' he said.

'You want to bet?' said Ruby.

The screens were flickering busily. Dealers shouted the levels at which prices were offered and traded. They were still selling in lots of ten and twenty million dollars, but the market was moving against them. The yen was weakening.

'243.10/20!'

'243.20/30!'

The Forex expert was nervous. 'We can't buck the market. 242.80 is an important chart point and when it held, dealers rushed in and took profit.'

Ruby pressed the intercom. 'OK,' he said, 'let's not fight it. Let's back off for a while till the yen selling eases off. Then we'll move in again.' He was talking to all four offices. The dealers yawned, stretched and relaxed. For a while, the room was quiet.

Tokyo came through on the intercom. 'We close in five minutes.'

'OK, goodnight, Tokyo,' Ruby acknowledged.

At 243.50/60 the screens stopped flickering. The yen was almost back to its opening level of the morning. It hovered there for thirty minutes. It was eleven a.m. Swiss time, ten a.m. London time, six p.m. Tokyo time and five a.m. in New York.

Ruby flipped the intercom and gave his instructions. The Forex expert shook his head, indicating his disapproval. Ruby ignored him.

At five past eleven, twelve dealers in Wald and twelve dealers in London entered the market simultaneously. The noise was unbelievable. They screamed down the phones at dealers in Crédit Suisse, UBS, SBS and Volksbank in Switzerland, Barclay's, Lloyd's, Chemical and the rest in London. The assistants noted the trades as they were called. They bought yen, sold dollars in lots of forty to fifty million dollars at a time. Ruby was turning the screw, piling on the pressure. The market had moved up fast and drifted all the way back. Now, it was looking for a signal which way to go and, this time, he wanted to be sure that the signal was clear.

The screens were going crazy. The huge dollar selling was pushing up the German mark and the Swiss franc too, and the sterling dollar exchange rate – 'cable', as they call it – was picking up as the dollar dropped. The yen was taking off. Above the uproar, the dealers called the prices off the screens and from the phones, one phone clamped to each ear.

'242.70/80!'

'242.40/50!'

'242.10/the figure!'

They were down to another key chart point. The Forex expert was watching the screen in front of him intently.

'241.70/80!'

Clean through the chart point in a few seconds. No problem at all. Ruby sat back with a huge smile.

'We're on our way,' he said.

At one forty-five Swiss time, the yen was 240.20/30 – three and a half big ones against the dollar in less than five hours. In fifteen minutes, New York would open. A lot of people would be in shock when they saw how much the dollar had fallen. Most of the action had been in selling dollars against yen, but there had been substantial copycat trading against the dollar – in German marks especially. The mark had already strengthened from 2.68 to 2.66. It was a clear indication that their own buying – which was restricted to yen – had persuaded others to jump on the bandwagon. Things were developing exactly as Ruby had hoped they would.

At five minutes to two he was on the intercom again.

'We started out great! The market is in shock. They know the yen is strongly bid, but no one knows why. They'll be scrambling for explanations and they won't find any. Rumours will be flying around, but nothing of substance. It's inevitable that, after a while, some dealers will be looking for reasons to test the yen on the downside. That's when we move in again. We're going to buck the trend and this time we'll raise the stakes even higher. We can't afford to let the yen fall back again.'

As expected, New York opened quietly. Dealers reported that the market was indeed stunned. Traders kicked themselves for missing the biggest market swing in over a year, although no one could explain why it had happened. For a couple of hours dealing was aimless – up and down – minimal range trading with no direction. Then, just as Ruby had predicted, the market began, tentatively, to test the downside of the yen.

'240.55/65!'

'240.75/85!'

'240.90/the figure!'

It was not an especially important chart point, but the round numbers always had some psychological significance and Ruby was not prepared to take the risk of the yen weakening further. If it did, it might be tough to hold. Trading was light and nervous. Now was the time to move back in before the downtrend gathered momentum.

'Now!' he shouted into the intercom.

Thirty-six dealers in three countries went into action simultaneously. The decibel sound level in the room reflected the concentrated, frenzied activity. The dealers yelled the prices, screaming the deals to their assistants, and the assistants shouted them back, just to be sure that the trades were correctly recorded.

Within seconds, the yen was on its way up again and the dollar was tumbling.

'240.50/60!'
'240.25/35!'
'239.80/90!'

The yen eased smoothly through the 'figure' and was soon heading towards the 239 level.

But the Forex expert was looking increasingly troubled.

'What's your problem?' said Ruby, none too gently. The man knew his stuff – he knew a whole lot more about Forex than Ruby would ever know – but he was a technician with neither imagination nor flair and, what was worse, he was a negative bastard. 'Two thirty-nine is a major support level,' he said.

'We've been through a few already,' said Ruby, his eyes fixed on the screen in front of him. The noise and activity were still unabated, but he noticed that the yen's surge was slowing down.

'239.55/65!'
'239.50/60!'
'239.50/60!'
'239.60/70!'

The yen was sticking – even edging up a fraction. What was happening? By now, they had committed a large slice of their credit line. They were eating into it fast, dealing in trades of up to a hundred million dollars. The yen should be taking off. It was not. Something was wrong.

Beside him, the Forex expert slammed down the phone. 'The central banks are intervening,' he said.

Ruby could have sworn he caught a fleeting look of complacency on the guy's face. If Ruby refused to do it his way, what could he expect but trouble? And trouble was what he had warned Ruby he would get.

'Which banks?'

'The Bank of England, the Federal Reserve, the Bundesbank, the Bank of Tokyo, the Swiss National.'

'All of them?'

'All of them.' Again, just that hint of satisfaction. 'They're in together buying the dollar. It's coordinated action.'

'What amounts?'

'The amounts are small,' the dealer admitted, 'but it's a warning.'

Ruby pondered. Naturally, he had foreseen the possibility. The question was, how serious were the central banks? In theory, their liquidity was almost unlimited – they could certainly overwhelm him if they wanted to – but it would cost them dearly and central banks normally acted with great discretion. They liked to wave the big stick; that was usually warning enough. The mere threat of central bank intervention – even a few calls around the world asking for prices – was often enough to stabilize markets. Clearly, it was not in the interest of either Germany or Japan for their currencies to rocket into the stratosphere. A significantly stronger mark and yen would make their exports more expensive and that was the last thing either country needed right now. As for the Bank of England, it was no doubt cooperating in an effort to stabilize the Forex market.

To take on the central banks you had to be either gutsy or just plain dumb. The room was quieter now. Ruby had suspended buying for the last few minutes. The dealers' calls came in intermittently and the screens were pulsating less frenziedly.

'239.80/90!'

'240/the figure!'

The market hung poised – trading was very thin. There was a feeling of expectancy in the room. No one knew quite what was coming.

'What happened to the central banks?' asked Ruby.

The dealer picked up the phone.

While the man was talking to his contacts in Europe and the Far East, Ruby worked out the next stage of the operation. He had already made up his mind to test the resolve of the central banks. He had no other choice.

'It looks like they're out of the market,' said the dealer.

'You sure they were ever in?'

The dealer hesitated. 'It's not clear,' he admitted. 'They asked for prices – that much is sure.'

Ruby nodded and set his mouth in a determined line. It was the old dodge. They had waved the stick to frighten away buyers. He found it more than significant that they had made no serious attempt to sell the yen and support the dollar. Well, he was not easily frightened. The dreaded mystique of the cold-eyed omniscient central bankers patting the keys of their computers and deciding the fates of markets with a couple of phone calls – that was for the faint of heart. He did not buy that. Mostly these guys didn't know what the hell they were doing and, as for deciding the fate of markets, well, he would see about that. Ruby had always been ready to take on the world; he had never had much time for bureaucracy. A few lousy gnomes were not about to scare him.

It was nearly five p.m. In less than five minutes, the Swiss Forex market would shut down. He decided to close it with a bang.

The dealers attacked the market again – small deals, ten to twenty million dollar shots – but, every now and then, at a signal from Ruby, one of them hit the market with a hundred million dollar slug. The tactics worked. The yen started on up again. There was no central bank intervention. They had a clear run.

'239.45/55!'
'239.20/30!'
'238.90/the figure!'
'238.70/80!'

The dollar fell faster and faster as the yen climbed, slicing through one chart point after another. The dealers screamed and waved their arms. The sweat poured off them. Their damp shirts clung to their backs. Their faces were flushed, their eyes unfocused and expressionless as if they were drugged. In a way, they were. This was the ultimate high, the 'fix' of a lifetime.

At five p.m. exactly, the last deal was cut and, suddenly, the phones were silent in the Wald operations centre. The yen stood at 236.30/40 to the dollar. More than seven big numbers down on the day.

The dealers lay back in their chairs, eyes closed, exhausted, physically and mentally drained, unable even to speak.

London traded on for the last hour and, by close of business, had pushed the dollar down even further. The yen closed in Europe at 235.70/80.

Ruby sent most of the dealers home and stayed on with a skeleton night staff. It was vital that the day shift got a good night's sleep. They would be needed in the morning.

New York still had another five hours left to trade. It was Ruby's strategy to hold the yen at its present level and even, if necessary, to let it slide a point or two. He preferred to give the market time to breathe; he had no wish to tempt the fates. The prospect of a full-scale battle with the central banks did not alarm him, but why involve them if it was not necessary? Better to create a sense of stability, to let everyone get used to the new level. It would be that much easier to administer the *coup de grâce*. Ruby was flexible, always adaptable, ready to react to any unexpected development, but still operating to a basic plan.

And the plan was working just fine. By New York's close, the yen was 236.10/20. He had committed very little more of the line and the yen had held, slipping only an insignificant forty 'pips'. Ruby still had more than three billion dollars of his line in reserve to play with. He intended to commit it all in the overnight market. It would be too dangerous to wait for Europe's opening to try to push the yen higher. The less time he gave the media, the central banks and the traders to think about what was happening, the better. He intended to be in and out before the market knew what had hit it.

He was hungry now. He ate three corned beef sandwiches with hemischer cucumbers and drank a couple of Amstel Lights. This was the quiet time of the Forex market between New York's closing and Tokyo's opening, the time when traders counted their profits or licked their

665

wounds, the time when nothing much could be done except reflect on the day's successes or failures and try to figure out what the overnight market would bring – how those guys out there in the Far East would react to the events of the day in Europe and New York. It was peace in war, like standing on the steps of a church, like sanctuary. It was a void between worlds.

If you were really hooked – and many Forex punters were – you would start trading again at around midnight and maybe leave instructions to call you through the night if the market moved significantly either way. If you were not, you left your orders – buy or sell, take profit or stop loss – and went to the theatre, or out to a restaurant or, like most people, dozed in front of the TV and staggered unsteadily to bed.

Ruby set the alarm on his pocket calculator and fell asleep in his chair. He had the knack of sleeping wherever and whenever he chose.

An hour later, at midnight, he woke to the beeps of the tiny computer. New Zealand had been open for two hours already. Australia was just opening. Down there it was eight in the morning. Neither market was normally that active in this no-man's-land of time before Tokyo's opening, but they sometimes gave an indication of a trend that the Tokyo market would follow. Tonight, there was no trend. The market was 'gapping'.

Ruby asked one of the dealers to get him a price.

'235.60/236.10!' the dealer called across.

That meant that the thin market was uncertain of itself and it would be unwise to trade. If you sold dollars, you would get only 235.60 yen which was way below the level at New York's closing. They were bullish for yen. It looked like they were assuming down under that the trend would continue – for what that was worth. He continued to monitor the market through the dealers, but there was no action to speak of – either in Australia or New Zealand. They were waiting for Tokyo to open.

*

666

At one a.m., Swiss time, Tokyo opened. After such a spectacular rise in so short a time, the logical expectation in the Far East might well have been a dramatic sell-off of the yen. However, an hour or two before the opening, Ruby had seen to it that traders and the inter-bank market generally were inundated with calls from New York, Zurich, Frankfurt, Paris, London, Kuwait and Hong Kong, preparing dealers for massive yen-buying interest. It was crucial that both banks and dealers be convinced that, though the market was heavily long of yen, no one was interested in selling.

The result was that at Tokyo's opening, things remained quiet. Dealers advised their clients to be cautious and await developments. For a couple of hours, Ruby let the market feed on 'buy' enquiries. The longer he could delay the last big push, the better. It must happen fast to achieve maximum effect. His resources were not unlimited.

By noon, Tokyo time – five a.m. Swiss time – the yen was drifting again. It was a sign that the market could no longer be supported by rumours alone. If something were not done soon, the sell-off would begin. It was time for action.

Tokyo began buying a few minutes past midday, gently at first and then, as the market gathered speed, increasing the size of each buy order. They were trading in lots of twenty to fifty million dollars and that was more than enough to move the yen further on up. The market had been primed, expecting buyers to move in, and, when they did, a number of big punters waiting on the sidelines moved in with them. Two American corporations had left 'buy' orders for the yen if it broke the 234 chart point. The amounts were colossal – two billion dollars each. A rush of mutual fund dealers and corporate traders followed and, at one thirty, there was a massive buy order of yen from Bahrain – three billion dollars. The yen jumped from 233.10/20 to 231.80/90.

It was six-thirty in the morning in Wald. In half an hour, dawn would break. The room was lit only by the lamps on the dealers' desks and the dim green glow from the screens. There was scarcely a sound. It was hard to imagine the pandemonium, the noise and excitement in the Tokyo office, but the screens told the story. A small cheer went up from the night staff in Wald as the yen sliced through the 231 barrier. Ruby grinned and picked up the phone to talk to Tokyo.

At ten minutes to five p.m. Tokyo time, the yen stood at 227.20/30, a dramatic increase of more than sixteen big ones since Europe's opening the previous day – for the second time running, the biggest move in the market that anyone could remember.

It was nearly ten in the morning in Wald. Tokyo closed at five without any further change in the level of the yen.

Now, it was all up to Europe. Today would determine whether the operation was a success or not.

Ruby allowed himself a few moments to recheck his strategy. His dealers had sold the dollar massively short against the yen – a total of ten billion dollars – and, of that huge amount, about seventy per cent had been sold at the higher levels, between 243.80 and 235.80 and about thirty per cent at levels between 235.80 and 227.30. Ruby calculated that, if he could buy back the full ten billion dollars at the current dollar/yen level, the company would make seven hundred million dollars! But that was clearly only a theoretical calculation. The dollar would start to move up as he bought it back and the yen would weaken, so he would have to cover in his short dollar position fast. The trick would be to move the market as little as possible and, to do that, he would have to spread the dollar buying around the world and limit, as far as he could, the size of individual buy orders. The fewer waves he made, the better.

So far, so good. By eleven a.m., they had bought back just over five hundred million dollars against the yen and netted a profit of thirty-two million dollars. The yen had crept back up to 229.60/70. The market was calm and inter-bank dealers, encouraged by calls from Europe and the Middle East organized by Ruby, reported only a slight technical correction in what was still an overwhelmingly bull market for the yen.

Ruby's eyes were red and sore. They had hardly left the screen since the operation began, more than twenty-four hours ago.

Next to him, the Forex expert was satisfied. 'Looking good,' he said.

Ruby said nothing. He was thinking only one word: chickens. This time, he was not going to count them before his eggs hatched.

As the yen dipped, they had to move cautiously to avoid pushing it down too fast. The rate of buying back slowed down. By one in the afternoon, the currency stood at 231.80/90. They had repurchased another half a billion dollars and the accumulated profit was now fifty-seven million dollars.

Things were moving along, but too slowly for Ruby's liking. Very soon, the market would wake up to the fact that there were no more buyers around for the yen and, when that happened, it could take a nosedive.

Ruby gave instructions to the dealers in Wald and London, and also New York which would open in thirty minutes, to begin some selective, high-profile selling of the dollar, at the same time as the main dollar-buying operation continued quietly. He was deliberately sending out confused signals. It would be disastrous if traders got the idea that all the action was in one direction, that the market had turned around for good.

As he hoped, this had the effect of slowing down the yen's slide. A few minutes later, it stood at 232.30/40, but they had only been able to repurchase another hundred million dollars.

At two p.m. precisely, one of the big overhead screens pulsed out a news flash. Mr Volcker, chairman of the Fed, had issued a statement at New York's opening to the effect that the dollar was oversold and should shortly return to more normal levels. The announcement was timed have

669

maximum impact on the market. At first there was no reaction, but then, as the implication of Volcker's statement became clear to traders, the yen's slide began to pick up speed.

The dealers called the prices.

'232.80/90!'

'232.90/the figure!'

'233.20/30!'

The Forex expert sitting next to Ruby was biting his nails nervously.

'233.30/70!'

'That's a wrong call!' Ruby shouted across the room to the dealer.

'233.40/90!' A call by a dealer on the other side of the room.

'What's happening?' Ruby asked the expert.

'The market's "gapping".'

'That's impossible,' said Ruby. 'I thought that only happened in the overnight market when trading is thin.'

'Not necessarily. It can happen any time dealers are unsure of the direction of the market.' He stopped and pointed at the screen. 'The dollar's picking up fast.' He was on the phone in a flash.

Ruby began to feel uneasy. Something was going on that he did not understand.

'234.10/20!'

The gapping had stopped. For a while, the market had hesitated. Now the dollar was taking off. The yen was under pressure.

'They say a Middle East punter just bought two billion dollars against the yen.' The dealer was worried. He kept his voice down. He didn't want the whole room to hear. He was on two phones at once. 'The Federal Reserve is in buying dollars.'

'The Bank of Japan is selling yen!' a dealer shouted.

'The Bank of England is in!'

Ruby had to make a decision fast – either wait and let the market run out of steam, hoping that the yen would stabilize – or jump in now and take whatever profit he could before it was too late.

He shouted into the intercom. 'Let's go! Sell the yen! Fifty and hundred million dollar trades!'

It was a mistake. The yen plummeted. In thirty minutes it was back to 238.50/60. They had repurchased another billion dollars and their profit was now a hundred million, but they still had nearly seven billion dollars to buy back. It was obvious that if the yen continued to fall at the present rate, the profit would be far less than Ruby had hoped for. Still, one way or another, a hundred million dollars would certainly help.

By four in the afternoon, the market was red hot. It seemed like the whole world was buying dollars. It was on its way back to its former level – and fast. Buyers from across Europe and North and South America, buyers from the Middle East, buyers from behind the Iron Curtain, private and corporate buyers, inter-bank traders, mutual funds, pension funds, brokers and punters – all of them screaming down phones, all of them dumping yen, German marks, Swiss francs, selling anything they could lay their hands on, just as long as they bought dollars.

It was bedlam in the Wald operations centre. The dealers were jumping up and down, screaming down their phones, yelling at each other. Time was running out on them. It was tough to find anyone ready to sell the dollar. The whole world wanted to buy. The banks had a real problem laying off their customers' orders. No one wanted to risk getting stuck with any position, certainly not a dollar short. Even the biggest banks, the Forex giants: Citibank and Chemical, Chase and Morgan, Barclay's, Lloyd's, Midland and the rest – even they were scared to hold positions. The market fluctuations of the last forty-eight hours had been too violent and too inexplicable. Now was the time to lay off positions and be satisfied with turning over a commission. Who knew what the next few minutes would bring, let alone the next few hours?

'243.70/80!'

671

It was exactly four-thirty in the afternoon, Swiss time. Thirty minutes to closing. The yen had skidded down to the level at which they had started buying the previous day, and they had still not been able to sell out their yen position – not by a long way. They were sitting on a short position of four billion dollars at levels between 238.70 and 243.80. So far, they had made a hundred and thirty million dollars on the liquidated short position, but, even at the current yen/dollar parity, they had already lost forty million dollars on the uncovered position – the dollars that they had not been able to buy back. That meant a net profit of ninety million dollars. So far.

But the market was not stopping there. The yen slide had turned into a rout. The dumping continued at the same frenetic speed. Another twenty minutes to go before the Swiss market closed. London would still be trading for nearly an hour and a half. New York had most of the day left to trade.

'We have to unload the position,' urged the expert. 'This is a massacre. The yen could drop another ten big ones. We'll be killed.'

Ruby was smoking feverishly. His hands were trembling. He had lost control and, with it, his cool. He was caught in his own bear trap. He had tried to dupe the market and the market was taking its revenge. He had raised a monster.

He picked up the phone to talk to Mort.

'What's happening, for Chrissake?'

Ruby told him.

'What's the downside risk?'

'Hard to say,' said Ruby. 'But all my instincts tell me to hold on. The yen has to recover.'

Mort was not too sure about Ruby's instincts right now. The pressure seemed to be getting to him.

'It's too risky,' he said grimly. 'You have to cover, even if it means covering at a loss.'

Ruby just nodded without saying a word, and put down the phone. It was what he had expected Mort to say.

Two hours later, they were out of their position. The yen had broken 245. And it was still dropping.

Ruby made the final calculations. Overall, they had lost twenty-three million dollars. He rested his elbows on the desk, covered his face with his hands and swayed from side to side in despair.

The dealers stood up and stretched, they switched off their computers. One by one, the screens went blank. It had been a long vigil.

The expert was the first to leave. He walked out without a word.

One of the dealers came over to Ruby. 'I'm sorry it didn't work out,' he said, 'but I have to tell you, it was the most fun I ever had!'

On the way out, a couple more dealers patted Ruby on the shoulder consolingly. The rest of them left quietly with their heads down.

Ruby stayed there alone at his desk until it was dark.

*   *   *

The news of Amy's murder had overwhelmed Sam. It was too much for him to grasp. He had shut himself in Laura's bedroom and wept. So confused were his emotions that he was not even sure for whom he was grieving – Amy, Laura, or himself.

He had never stopped loving Amy – not for a moment. He had never cut the cord, never lost his dependence on her. Their divorce had nothing to do with it. Married or not, he had leaned on her, fed on her strength and her independent spirit. For Sam, rational behaviour had always been an obsession; it was the only way he could handle his life, but what fascinated him, what had drawn him to Amy and held him enthralled, despite everything, was her waywardness, her capricious fascination with the irrational. Some would regard it as weakness. Sam saw it as strength. She had been resolute in her refusal to be shackled by life; she had allowed nothing and no one to possess her. That was what he so admired in her. It was how he would have liked to be himself.

As for Karl – how to understand – how to forgive him? What a fool. What a pitiful wretch. To think that she and Karl had been lovers. It was the one thing that hurt more than anything – his wife and Karl, honest, faithful Karl, good old reliable Karl. They had betrayed him – the two people he loved most in the world.

God, what a mess. He pitied Karl and hated him at the same time. But it was all pointless now. The poor bastard had committed suicide. There was nothing he could do for him any more. Nothing anyone could do. He had destroyed himself. No, that wasn't true. Amy had destroyed him.

For the time being, Amy's parents were taking care of Edward. Sam would bring him back to Switzerland just as soon as he could. Meanwhile, what about Jane? He would have to think carefully about her, decide what it was he really wanted.

It was twelve years since he had walked in on Siegfried Gerber and Amy. They were both dead now. It was all impossible to take in. What had he done to deserve all this? Surely some malign fate was working against him. He could remember how it was to be content – happy even. Maybe that was it. He had been too happy. He had climbed too high up the ladder. That was why the company was doomed. They had been too successful. It was never good to climb too high. Someone or something was always waiting to bring you down. The camera was always watching you.

Laura had been so brave. She had experienced so little of life and known so much. Everything of hers was still in its place, just as it had been that terrible day he flew back from Luanda. Amy never entered this room after Laura died – not once. She had let her go. She had given her daughter her freedom, as she now had hers.

But Sam had not. It was not something he was capable of doing. How many times had he picked up the drawing of the man and the little girl hand in hand? How many times had he fallen asleep clutching it? Dreamed that he was flying in the sky with Laura and felt the warm touch of her hand in his? It always seemed so real – as real as life itself, more real, in fact. He could feel it now. He could swear that Laura's hand was in his. No, he would never let it go.

'I'll be out of a job soon, but who cares? I have some money saved and I'm thinking of starting up on my own as an oil consultant.'

'Great,' said Jane.

'Edward needs a mother. Samantha needs a father.'

'Let me see if I'm hearing you correctly,' said Jane. 'You want to marry me to give the kids parents? Legal parents?'

'I want to marry you. Period,' said Sam. He had started badly. He could see that.

'Why?'

'We have a stable relationship. We respect each other. We're comfortable with each other. These things are important.'

'Sure they're important, but they're not everything.'

'I know that. Of course I do. Look, Jane, what was missing from me was commitment. I refused to face up to my obligations. You always said that and you were right. Now I have that commitment.'

'Well, I hope you'll both be very happy,' she said.

'What do you mean?'

'I'm saying goodbye, Sam.'

'What did I say? I love you. That's all I said.'

'No, Sam. That's what you didn't say.'

'But I need you. I can't live without you.'

'What you need, Sam, is a mother ... and I can live without you.'

'What about Samantha?'

'She's our kid. You can see her whenever you like. That's not going to change. It's me that's changed. I've gotten used to my freedom and I'm not going to give it up for anything less than the best. And you, Sam, let's face it, are not the best.'

It could have been Amy talking. He felt like a small boy. 'Jane, you're angry. You're not yourself. You're not thinking straight.'

She pushed him to the door.

'I wasn't going to tell you, Sam, but I have a lover,' she said. 'No obligations, no commitments. He's unstable as hell and he doesn't respect anyone or anything, but boy, can he hump!'

Sam was horrified. 'That's disgusting.'

'I know,' Jane said blissfully. 'But it sure as hell is fun!'

The next time Jeffrey saw his father, he had aged. Suddenly. Was that how people got old – from one day to the next? He was stooping. When had he ever stooped? Surely he had never stooped before? His eyes were no longer focused on anything in particular, unless on some distant horizon that Jeffrey could not see. There was, too, something different about the expression in his eyes. What was it? A certain resignation, perhaps? As if the debate had been wound up and the votes counted and, yes, something else, a hint of bewilderment, as if life had, after all, been too difficult to comprehend, too confusing to come to terms with.

The affectation of unconcern, the deliberate obtuseness, the contrariness – all these had disappeared. There was no more mockery, no more banter. It was as if the veneer that had protected their mutual esteem, not hidden it, had, from one day to the next, been summarily stripped away. They had seen each other through a glass, darkly, and now, at last, they were face to face.

'Why don't you come and see me any more?' The voice was querulous.

Jeffrey's spirits sank. 'I was here yesterday, Father.'

'Nonsense.'

'You said you were feeling fine.'

'That wasn't me. That was someone else,' his father said positively.

Jeffrey tried to cheer up the old man but it was useless. 'Everything's great,' he said. 'There's nothing to worry about.'

The newly anxious eyes focused on him for a moment. 'Do you ever worry, my boy?'

'Sometimes.'

'What about?'

'About the kids. About what I'm going to do tomorrow. About making a living. About the Bomb. What do you worry about, Father?'

'About the greenfly mostly. They killed the roses this year. There was too much rain.'

'It's not important.'

'What's the point of worrying about important things? There's nothing you can do about them.'

'What's the point of worrying at all?'

'That's easy to say. You don't have greenfly.'

'I don't have a job, either.'

'You can always start again.'

He could always start again. That was true enough. Something his father could not do. So that was what was occupying the old man's thoughts. No longer was he walking the earth with confidence. The ground was starting to move, throwing him off balance. Long ago, Jeffrey had bought him a new pair of gardening gloves, but his father had never used them. His hands were inflamed and ulcerated, scratched by rose thorns, the skin worn thin by the years, as it is with old people. The sores would never heal now.

'Why don't you wear the gloves I bought you?'

'I don't want to spoil them,' his father said.

Where would he use them if not here? When – if not now? 'Gloves I can always buy for you,' he said. 'Hands are more difficult.'

The old man grinned wickedly, a gleam and a glint of what he once was.

677

'How are pork bellies?'

'They could be better,' said Jeffrey.

'They tell me I need a pacemaker.'

'You already have one,' said Jeffrey patiently. 'They fitted it in 1970.'

'You don't say!'

'Maybe you need a checkup?'

'What's the use? The doctors pull you around, subject you to the most diabolical and degrading tests. And then what do they tell you? They tell you you're old. I know that already.'

'You're in pretty good shape considering.'

'Considering . . .' Jeffrey's father looked at his son affectionately. 'Yes, I'm in pretty good shape, considering. So are you, Jeffrey.' He was mocking him. The old bastard. 'Do you remember your mother?' he asked suddenly.

'I remember her.'

'It's been a good life.'

'Don't give up,' said Jeffrey. 'For God's sake, don't ever give up.' He was surprised how passionate his feelings were. 'You have to keep fighting.'

'Why would I give up? Someone has to look after the roses,' his father said.

It was raining – a steady winter drizzle. You could smell the grass. Somewhere out there a blackbird was singing. The old man tottered into the garden, more sideways than forwards. Jeffrey remembered when he used to walk upright, proudly, putting the earth firmly in its place.

He needed to be alone. It was only a few days to Christmas. On an impulse, he drove to the West End, parked off St James's and wandered down Piccadilly. The rain had stopped. It was a cold, sunny afternoon. High up, the sky was trimmed with ribbons of white cloud in a herring-bone pattern. The street was almost deserted. Most people, it seemed, had already done their Christmas shopping.

Outside the Royal Academy, a Salvation Army band was playing 'The Holly and the Ivy'. He crossed the road and put a fiver in the box.

'God bless you!' said the Salvation Army sergeant with feeling. 'Merry Christmas and a Happy New Year!'

It was, thought Jeffrey, astonishing what you could still get for a fiver.

The band started to play 'Good King Wenceslas' and, treading purposefully in their master's steps, moved up Piccadilly towards Hyde Park Corner.

Somehow or other, life went on. Suddenly, for no reason that he could think of, he felt better.

He went home and wound the clocks: the mahogany *grande sonnerie* in the drawing room, the long-case William and Mary.

'It's not Friday,' said Caroline.

'I know,' said Jeffrey. 'It's Wednesday. I'm feeling spontaneous.'

'But you always wind the clocks on Friday. Something's wrong.'

'You know that this one was made in 1700? William of Orange was on the throne of England, and Handel was a teenager.'

'You never wind the clocks on Wednesday.' She couldn't get over it. Suddenly: 'Whatever happened to Victoria?'

He finished winding the William and Mary, lowered the hood, dropped the winding handle into the case and locked it. She had never mentioned Victoria. He had no idea she even knew. He ought to say: 'Victoria? Who's Victoria?' But he didn't. Instead, he said: 'Can you imagine? This clock has been around for three hundred years and it's still going. Incredible.'

'Isn't it,' she said.

'Incredible how stupid and blind a man can be, not seeing what's there in front of his nose, taking the important things in his life for granted.'

'Important things?'

'You. The kids.'

679

She nodded. 'So Victoria. . . ?'

'Was nothing. Is nothing. I'm ashamed. Forgive me.'

'A mid-life crisis?'

'Aren't I a bit young for a mid-life crisis?'

Caroline smiled. 'You mean I still have that to look forward to?'

'They don't make them like you any more,' he said.

'Well, thanks.'

'Like these clocks. They're marvellous. I love them. They'll still be here when I'm dead and gone.'

'Oh, so that's what it's all about. Survival?' she said. 'You admire things that survive.'

'Like King Brothers,' he said ironically.

'What will you do?'

'Get another job. It shouldn't be a problem. I'm quite famous, you know.'

Caroline put her arms round him. 'You'll stay till the bitter end?'

'Bitter indeed,' he said.

'Why blame yourself?'

'Who said I did?'

'Don't you?'

He thought about it. 'We're all involved,' he said. 'None of us can walk away and say that he didn't know what was going on. No one can feel good about it.'

'You're getting older,' she said. 'That's all it is. You're thinking about all the things you've got to lose.'

Jeffrey shook his head, looking through the window at the bleak winter garden. 'I'm thinking about what might have been,' he said.

Bob Rosenfeld had decided a long time ago that he could not indict Joe Murphy. Sure, he had sold huge quantities of Domestic crude oil to Mortimer King, but there was no proof that he had known what King Brothers was doing with it. If he could have proved what he once suspected – that Joe had taken bribes from Mort – now that would have been something else. He tried to put a case together,

680

but there was no case. He could not indict him for a very simple reason. Joe Murphy was innocent.

But such fine distinctions as guilt or innocence did not, it seemed, trouble Pacific Odyssey. For twenty years, Joe Murphy had wielded unique power for a chief buyer, the kind of power that comes from being right most of the time, the kind that makes other men envious. Naturally, he had made enemies in his own company, especially of those who could never make a decision to buy or sell, those who knew only how to intrigue, to manipulate, to whisper in the right ear.

The senior vice-president was thirty-five – twenty-two years younger than Joe. 'We're promoting you to vice-president, Joe. Congratulations!'

'I don't want to be a vice-president,' said Joe. 'I'm happy where I am.'

'You'll be getting a bigger office. I've arranged for you to have a corner office on the fifth floor. It's one of the biggest we have.'

The fifth floor was where they dumped the trash – the deadbeats they didn't know what to do with. It was no-man's-land between the trenches. They shelled you from both sides. The next move was a one-way ticket out the front door.

'Tell me,' said Joe, 'what will I be doing?'

The vice-president hesitated. 'You'll be in charge of regional planning.'

'What kind of planning is that?'

'Long-term.'

'What regions?'

The VP was getting impatient. 'Joe, if you want to talk details, see the guys in your department. They'll fill you in.'

'I'd rather stay where I am,' said Joe stubbornly.

The VP bit his lip. 'Take it, Joe. As a friend, I'm advising you. Know what I mean?'

Joe took it.

He occupied his new office for six weeks and then someone remembered he was there and moved him to the fourth floor so that he could be 'nearer central regional planning'. Joe enquired about that department too, but no one seemed to know what or where it was. For the first time in over thirty years he was without a secretary. They assured him that it was only a temporary situation – until they found a girl of the 'right calibre'.

Joe asked to see the president. There was a time when the president consulted him before he took a leak.

'He's busy right now,' said the VP. 'Just hang in there, Joe.'

Joe hung in as long as he could, and then some. Then, one day, he handed in his resignation.

'Honest to God, Joe, I wasn't looking for this,' said the VP. 'I really hoped you'd be more adaptable.'

'It's tough to adapt to humiliation,' said Joe.

'That's not fair,' the vice-president protested. 'Times change. We have to change with them.'

'Is that what we have to do?' said Joe. 'I didn't know.'

It was Joe Murphy's son who called Mort to give him the news. 'He took some sleepers – a whole lot. Not quite enough to kill him, though.'

'Thank God!' said Mort.

'They tell me people do that when they need help. A cry for help . . . that's what they said it was.'

'Tell me what I can do,' said Mort. 'I'll do anything you ask. Anything.'

'I spoke to him when he came round. He said he was sorry. Imagine. Him apologizing to me.'

'How is he now?'

'I went home for a couple of hours to get some rest and he had this stroke. This massive stroke. I should have stayed.'

'Oh God! Don't tell me,' said Mort.

'It happened this morning. I thought you'd like to know. You were a friend of his.'

'That's right,' said Mort. 'I was a friend of his.'

*

682

The bottle of bourbon on his desk was almost empty. The office was in darkness. All you could see through the window were some dim lights along the railway sidings.

Poor Joe. He had never taken bribes. He was an honest man. There were not too many of those. But where had it got him? Joe always needed to be the good guy. Well, that was a goddam tough thing to be. Impossible. In this world anyway. Everything's a sham. Life's a sham. The fund was a sham. Even Joe's suicide was a sham. He had not wanted to die. Poor Joe. Poor goddam Joe.

He finished the bottle. If only he had known that Joe was going to have such a tough time. His own company had turned on him. They were the ones that killed him. They took his job, then his self-respect. No one could have done anything about it. If only Joe had phoned him, asked for his help.

But then the truth was he had phoned. When was it? A long time ago. He was trying to remember what he had told him the last time they spoke. 'If you need any cash, call me.' Something like that. Whatever Joe had needed it was not cash. What he really wanted was understanding and Mort had none of that to give him.

It was so goddam final – death. He would have helped. Of course he would. If only he could talk to Joe and explain things, but the bastard had walked out on life. It was a cruel, cowardly thing to do. Whoever learned anything by killing themselves? He had walked out on his wife, his son and his friends. He was a selfish, vindictive shit.

He wanted to shout at Joe, but he wasn't there to shout at. He wasn't anywhere he could be reached. He picked up the empty whisky bottle and threw it at the wall with all his strength. 'Fucking unicorn!' he muttered. Then he laid his head on the yellow copies and passed out.

Bob Rosenfeld's prediction that King Brothers would be destroyed had been all too accurate. By early summer, Jeffrey had closed the doors on the London office for the last time. What was left of the company was being run out of Wald and New York.

The settlement with the US Attorney's Office had left the company on the verge of bankruptcy, with few assets. The huge office on Park Avenue, once the flagship of the mighty corporation and the biggest money earner, could no longer generate enough business to pay its overheads. They were negotiating the sale of Kings' Tower. The company's days were numbered. It was a matter of time – and not much time at that.

'It costs us a hundred thousand dollars every day we open the doors. No one's doing any business. It really is the end,' said Jeffrey sadly.

'You want to close New York?' said Mort.

'I have no choice.'

'Do what you have to,' Mort said. 'Shouldn't we ask Ruby?'

'Ruby's in Disneyland. He's not sure whether he's Mickey Mouse or Snow White and the Seven Dwarfs.'

'Poor Ruby.'

'He doesn't know what's happening any more,' Jeffrey said. 'He's spaced out on Valium, or whatever it is he's into.'

'Ruby always thought he could beat the world by being smart.'

'Didn't we all?'

'It's tougher for him. It's like he was happily playing an electronic war game and suddenly the damn machine blew up in his face.'

'That's Ruby all right.'

'What will you do?' said Mort.

'Something on my own. I couldn't go back to working for Shell – or anyone.'

Mort pulled a face. 'The problem with you, Jeffrey . . . you were never hungry enough.'

Jeffrey grinned. 'Maybe you're right at that.'

'Forgive me,' said Mort.

'Who am I to forgive? We were all in it.'

'The best team in the world. That's what we had,' said Mort proudly.

'And the best company.'

'I wanted to make you a rich man.'

'What would I have done with it? I have too many bloody clocks already.'

'I hear they sentenced Jack Greenberg,' Mort said.

'His kid will be three when he gets out.'

'Jack deserves it,' said Mort.

'Not everyone gets what he deserves.'

'Meaning me?'

'Meaning all of us.'

'You have another problem, Jeffrey. You think too much.'

'It's been . . .' Jeffrey swallowed hard. For once, he was lost for words.

'Hasn't it just?' said Mort.

One day, Ruby seemed fine, the next, he did not know what was going on. Most of the time he sat around smiling, like a bewildered cherub. Sarah had a tough time waking him in the morning.

'Why don't you get up?'

He looked at her, wondering why she was asking him dumb questions.

'It's a beautiful day. It's pointless to stay in bed.'

Ruby blinked, not understanding. He thought it was pointless getting up.

And so Sarah took to giving him his daily dose of Valium and pointing him in the direction of the office. The driver made sure he got there safely.

Ruby kept his secretary busy sending telexes to offices that no longer existed, for the attention of people who had long since been fired. Mort hadn't the heart to say anything to his brother. When Ruby was ready to face the truth he would do it himself, without anyone's help.

The day came when Ruby pushed aside the Valium. For a week, he was morose and irritable, refusing to talk to anyone, rejecting all Sarah's attempts to reach him, leaving early for the office – sometimes before dawn – wandering the corridors looking for a secretary to dictate to at six a.m.

'What the hell's going on? I've been at the office three hours already and there's no one to take dictation. I don't get any goddam replies to my telexes. No one works any more. No wonder the company's in trouble.'

Ruby had been wearing the same crumpled grey pants and the same filthy shirt – black with cheroot ash – for over a week now. He had not shaved for a month and he never combed his hair. He looked and smelled like a hobo. Mort, as neat and controlled as he had always been, tried to feel compassion for Ruby, but it was hard. Such pity as he felt was laced with disdain.

'You should take some time off,' he suggested.

Ruby shouted at his brother – something he had never done before. 'How can I take time off when there's so much work to be done? Someone has to run the company. Someone has to care.'

'I care,' said Mort.

'Oh, yes. You care. But what about the others? What about all those guys we turned into millionaires and now they can't even reply to my telexes? We spoiled them, that's what we did. We were too good to them. No one wants to work any more. They don't have the motivation.'

'They're not there any more,' said Mort gently. 'They're gone, Ruby. We paid them off. The company's finished.'

Ruby swayed on his feet as if Mort had hit him. Then he drew himself up and looked scornfully at his brother. 'I have work to do,' he said.

Then came Saturday. Every Saturday morning Ruby went to the synagogue near his apartment. That was where he should have been now.

He phoned Mort from the office. Mort was still in bed – it was six in the morning.

'I've been sitting here for an hour, Mort. You're not going

to believe this. There's no one in the office. What in hell is happening?'

'It's six in the morning, Ruby.'

'Someone has to open up.'

'It's also Shabbath.'

'Look, don't give me jokes,' said Ruby. 'It's Monday. I know it's Monday. I looked at the calendar.'

Mort was at the office in fifteen minutes. Ruby was sitting at his desk, staring at the wall. 'What is it?' he said. 'What's wrong with me?'

'I'll take you home.'

'I'm not well, am I?'

'You're overtired, that's all. It's nothing.'

'I'll never see Park Avenue again.'

'Sure you will.'

'I don't know who I am any more,' said Ruby. 'This isn't me.'

'Sure it is,' said Mort. 'The same old Ruby.'

'I'm leaving. I'm tired. You hold the fort. Monday's a busy day.'

'I'll hold the fort,' said Mort.

The doctors kept Ruby sedated for a week. When Mort visited him in the hospital, he was pale and thin. He had lost twenty pounds. The circle of white above his left ear was bigger, much bigger. His hair was fringed with grey.

'I made a fool of myself, didn't I?'

'You could never do that.'

'How do I look?'

Mort sat on the bed. 'You look great.'

'Liar.'

'OK, you look like shit. It's time you came back to the office,' Mort said.

'I always thought it was a game. It wasn't a game, was it?'

'No,' said Mort. 'It wasn't a game.'

'When did it get to be so goddam serious?'

'Everything's going to be OK,' said Mort.

'You always say that, don't you?' Ruby looked at his brother affectionately. 'You said that the night they shot you.'

'When are you coming back to the office? We need you.'

'After all we did. We built up the best darn company in the world. Now what's left? What's left, Mort? What's it all about? Tell me that. It beats me. All that struggle. . . .'

Mort's green eyes glowed. 'It's about life. It's about being someone, trying to live with yourself. It's about having a laugh, keeping your tits up, having something to get out of bed for. It's about self-respect. Maybe it's about leaving something behind for people to remember. What can I tell you? Sure it's a goddam struggle. Maybe that's what it's about. Maybe that's all there is to it.'

'I have bad dreams. You ever have bad dreams?'

'Never.'

'Lying here, I have time to think. Conscience. It's like a nagging tooth. Doesn't your conscience bother you sometimes? The things we did?'

Mort shook his head. 'I have my own ideas about what's right and wrong. I don't lose any sleep worrying about the things we did. You ever think what conscience is? It's the fear of a day of reckoning. That's all it is.'

'You remember the night you were shot? I asked you if you were afraid. You said, "If you're afraid, you don't win, you don't lose. You're nothing." '

'I remember.'

Ruby lay back on the pillow and stared at the ceiling. 'You were right. We were winning. Now, we're losing. But one thing – we've never been afraid. Have we, Mort?'

'Never. We're still in there trading punches.'

Ruby chuckled.

'Your secretary sends her love.'

Ruby made a face. 'How is she?'

'You know how she is. She's repulsive,' said Mort.

'Damn right,' said Ruby and began to laugh. Mort too. They laughed like they used to laugh when times were better. They laughed until the tears ran down their cheeks and they had to hold their sides to prevent the muscles cramping.

'Oh, my God!' Ruby groaned. 'Jesus, that felt great!'

'We had good times,' said Mort.

'Yeah, we had some good times.'

'So, when are you coming back to the office?'

Ruby made a fist and punched his brother gently on the arm. He could feel the strong uncompromising muscles. There was something solid and reassuring about Mort, even when he was down – a sense that he would never change, never be defeated, that one day he would bounce back again. The man was altogether admirable and courageous in Ruby's eyes and he would never understand why the rest of the world didn't see him the same way.

'I'm tired,' he said, 'physically, mentally, every way.'

'Don't give up,' said Mort.

Mort never gave up. Ruby had gone as far as he could. For him, the struggle was over. But Mort, he would never stop fighting.

'I'll make it up to you, Ruby. I'll make you a multi-millionaire, just like I promised . . . one of these days.'

Ruby grinned at Mort. 'One of these days. . . .'

'You miss New York, Ruby?'

'Miss New York? Why should I? I mean, look what we have here. Peace and quiet. Fresh air. No traffic jams. No potholes. Miss New York? Here you can walk the streets without getting yourself mugged. You feel secure. Everything's clean and tidy. Everyone's polite and reasonable. Who needs all that noise and pollution? You freeze to death in the winter and you suffocate in the summer.' He lay there, shaking his head. 'Miss New York? Hell no!'

Mort grinned. 'I miss it too.'

'I want to go home,' said Ruby.

'I'll call Sarah. She'll pick you up.'

Ruby shook his head. 'I don't mean Switzerland. That's just where I live right now. I mean New York. It's where I belong. I want to go home.'

*

Rebecca flew over to try to persuade Mort to give himself up. As long as he remained in Switzerland, Ruby would stay with him out of loyalty.

For her, the issues were not complicated. 'You have to come back. If you're innocent, you can clear your names.'

'We're condemned already,' said Mort.

'Then pay your debt and start over. You agree, Ruby?'

'I'll do whatever Mort does.'

Mort turned his back on them. 'You want me to be the Judas goat? Well, that's not my style. I'm not one of the world's victims. I'm not surrendering to a lynch mob.'

'I'm only asking you to do what's right.'

'Forgive me, Mom, but who are you to say what's right? If I'm guilty, then what about all the others? Why should I be the one to pay?'

'They say you broke the law,' she said.

'The law,' Mort echoed. 'You show me a businessman or a politician who never broke the law. Show me a guy who never cheated on his taxes. Then, maybe, they can put me in the pen.'

'I'd rather live with the shame of having two sons in jail than see them fugitives for the rest of their lives.'

'You wouldn't be the one doing time, would you?' said Mort.

'Mort, I'm sorry,' Ruby said quietly. ' I'm with Mom. I've fought the system long enough. I can't fight it any more.'

'You going to let them hang a leper's bell on you?'

'I don't have your strength. I thought I did, but I don't.'

Rebecca shook her head. 'Is that what you call it? Strength? I call it stubbornness. You're like your father, Mort. You're never satisfied. Whatever we gave you, it was never enough. What is it you want from life?'

'Everything.'

'That's too much.'

'One thing I learned,' said Mort. 'If you ask for too little, what you get is nothing.'

*

690

Four United States Marshals were waiting for them at Kennedy. Also the press, photographers and representatives of three television networks.

Also Bob Rosenfeld, upright citizen, Korean veteran.

When they got off the plane, the marshals couldn't get anywhere near the two brothers. They were celebrities. The TV cameramen thrust the bulging eye lenses inches from their faces. The reporters yelled questions:

'Are you pleading guilty, Mort?'

'Was the "pot" really your idea, Ruby?'

'Where's Matthew Rowland?'

'What happened to Kings' Tower?'

'How d'you feel about jail, Mort?'

The four marshals fought their way through to Mort and Ruby and dragged them back through the mob. Two police cars were parked on the edge of the tarmac. It took a few minutes to reach them. Ruby lost his hat in the mêlée and Mort's jacket was ripped.

As the car holding the two brothers drove off, the marshal sitting between them in the back seat arrested Mort and Ruby. Then they were handcuffed.

As the cuffs snapped on his wrists, Mort said: 'I didn't come back to the USA to try and escape. Is this really necessary?'

'I'm afraid so,' said Rosenfeld. He was enjoying his moment of triumph and he was not trying too hard to disguise it. 'I never thought you'd give yourself up,' he told Mort. 'Ruby, yes, but not you. I'm glad you had the sense to do it. For your sake.'

Mort looked at him. 'Go fuck yourself,' he said.

Rosenfeld's eyes glinted angrily behind the rimless glasses. 'Let me tell you, Mort,' he said. 'You may think you're something special, but to me you're just a crook – just another crook getting what's coming to him, and, believe me, whatever it takes, I'll see that you get it.'

Ruby sat in the back seat, saying nothing. The big marshal sat between them staring straight ahead. Another one drove. Rosenfeld was in the passenger's seat, his tense, alert, terrier's head twisted round to face them.

'Whatever it takes? You said it, Rosenfeld. Whatever lies, whatever dirty tricks. What are you going to do? Fix the evidence? Pay off the jury? Talk to the judge?'

'No, Mort. I'm only going to do my job.'

'You're getting off on this, you little bastard.'

'Most guys in your situation would try to be polite.'

They had handcuffed his wrists behind him, just to make it a little more awkward. Otherwise he might have hit Rosenfeld.

Instead, he leaned back in the seat and controlled himself. Like he always did.

'I'm not most guys,' he said.

'No,' said Rosenfeld thoughtfully. 'That you're not. All this, Mort, it's not my doing. It's how it is, the handcuffs and all that stuff. I'm sorry. It's the system.'

'Tell me about it,' said Mort.

'You already found out. It's the thing you can never beat.'

'You can sure as hell keep trying,' said Mort.

The car drew up outside the Metropolitan Correctional Center on St Andrew's Plaza.

Bob Rosenfeld watched the marshals lead Mort and Ruby away into the building. That guy Mort. He was a real pain. One thing for sure, though. He had balls.

Six days before the trial, Ruth and Daniel were married. It was a small affair. Only the two families were there. After the ceremony, Ruby kissed the bride and shook his son-in-law's hand.

Daniel hesitated. 'We never had time to talk. I just want you to know, I think this . . . the case and all . . . it's shit. I really admire you and Mort. That guy's a genius.'

Something in his eyes . . . the expression. Was it like his father's? No. Jesus! It was Mort! His eyes. The same look in them, intense, glowing, rapacious.

'Just keep your nose clean, Daniel,' he said.

'You really made them sit up and take notice. That's what I'd like to do. I'm going into business. You'll be proud of me.'

'Stay legal, Daniel. Whatever you do, stay legal.'

'Sure, sure. Why not? But I'm going to make it big.'

Ruby nodded. 'Good luck to you,' he said. 'You take care of my daughter.'

'Wait and see. She'll be the richest girl in New York,' said Daniel. 'One of these days. . . .'

One of these days . . . where had Ruby heard that before?

Bob Rosenfeld came over to say goodbye. He shook hands with Ruby. 'If there's anything I can do,' he said.

'No, really. You did more than enough already,' said Ruby.

'I hoped we could put that behind us,' said Rosenfeld.

Neither man could think of anything else to say.

'You have a beautiful daughter – a fine girl,' said Rosenfeld at last, awkwardly. 'I'm proud to have her as a daughter-in-law.' The man was sincere. Why did Ruby feel he was being patronized?

'Daniel's a good boy,' he said.

'He's a lucky guy. Lucky to get Ruth,' said Rosenfeld, shifting on his stiff leg.

Ruby smiled. 'I hear jail's not all it's cracked up to be.'

'I wanted to tell you,' said Rosenfeld, uncomfortably. 'I mean I know this may not be the place or the time, but where you're going . . . What I mean is if the case goes against you . . . well, Danbury, Connecticut, it's not like a real jail. You might be pleasantly surprised. I did what I could.'

'They call it a Fed Club,' said Ruby. 'You see, I'm an expert already.'

'Time passes,' said Rosenfeld.

'So I hear,' said Ruby. He took a long look at Rosenfeld. 'Tell me something,' he said. 'Did it ever occur to you that we might not be guilty?'

Bob Rosenfeld smiled with one side of his face. 'No,' he said. 'Never. Not for one moment.'

'That's what I thought,' said Ruby.

There didn't seem to be anything else to say. As they were standing there wondering how to say goodbye, Mort came over.

'Good luck to you both,' said Rosenfeld and walked away.

'The guy's a jerk,' said Mort.

'I think he was trying to be nice.'

'I liked him better the way he was before,' said Mort.

The lawyer's name was Nash. Mort had never heard of him. Supposedly, the matter was urgent and confidential. Since he had nothing better to do, he had his secretary show him in.

'I know you're a busy man, Mr King,' said Nash. That was how he started. Ironic. Busy? Who was he kidding? Busy waiting to be tried? Busy waiting to go to jail?

'I'll be brief,' said the lawyer. 'I represent the estate of the late Edmund Meyer. As you surely know, Mr Meyer was a very wealthy man.'

'Sure I do. What's that to do with me?'

'A substantial part of his considerable estate consists of his shares in the Oil Corporation.' Nash coughed, the way discreet lawyers do, and extracted a letter from his briefcase. He handed it to Mort.

'Mr Meyer has left you his total shareholding in the Oil Corporation.'

Mort sat up sharply. 'Say that again!'

'Mr Meyer has left you the Oil Corporation.'

Mort jumped out of his chair and paced round the room. 'That's the craziest thing I ever heard. Why would he leave me the corporation? It was his baby. His life's work. Besides, he hated me.'

'You're quite wrong, Mr King. Mr Meyer had great respect for you.'

'But his family? What about his family? His wife? His daughter? His grandchild?'

'They have all been generously provided for. It was Mr Meyer's wish that his company remain in strong capable hands. It was, as you say, his life's work and he was deeply concerned that it should not die with him. The family are well aware of his feelings. They will not contest the will.'

Mort was dazed. 'How can I possibly accept this – this gift? It wouldn't be right. Besides, who knows? I may be out of action for a while. I can't run the biggest trading corporation in the world from jail.'

'Mr Meyer foresaw that possibility. Naturally, he didn't expect to die so soon, but he made provision for a team of his top executives plus a first-class independent board of directors to run the company until you are . . . available again. Mr King, I can assure you that the Oil Corporation will remain a healthy company until your return to active business life.'

And meanwhile, Mort was thinking excitedly, he could still take the major policy decisions – even if he were in jail. Jesus, what an opportunity! It was a dream come true!

Suddenly, he realized that he was still holding the envelope. He tore it open. Inside was a sheet of the Oil Corporation's letterhead on which E.M. had scrawled: 'Finally an offer even you can't refuse.'

He sat down heavily, staring at the lawyer.

'I don't believe this,' he said. 'It's incredible!'

'Mr Meyer was an incredible man,' said Nash. 'A giant among men.'

'You can say that again.'

'I'll have the transfer papers drawn up.'

Mort nodded absently. Edmund Meyer was paying him the supreme compliment, a last salute to the son he wanted to make his own. . . . Or was he? The root of Mort's motivation had always been the desire to be number one. Nothing else would do. And what was E.M. really telling him? He was telling him from the grave what he had told him so many times when he was alive, that he would never be number one, that he would always walk in the shadow of the old Titan, that, without him, he was nothing.

It was a master stroke – E.M.'s final play. After all these years of doing it his way, he would wind up doing it E.M.'s way.

'It's an unbelievable gesture,' he said. 'An amazingly generous gift.'

'When can I see you again?'

Mort did not seem to be listening. The lawyer coughed. 'Mr King?'

He started. 'I'm sorry. Yes?'

'If I draw up the papers today, can we sign them in my office tomorrow?'

Mort was laughing. The lawyer looked startled.

'The bastard!' said Mort, still laughing. 'The cunning bastard!'

'Excuse me?' said Nash, confused.

'No, Mr Nash,' said Mort. 'Don't trouble to draw up the papers. I won't sign them. Not tomorrow. Not any day.'

'I don't follow you, Mr King.'

'It's simple. You can keep the Oil Corporation. Give it to the family. Sell it. Burn it. Do what you like with it. I don't want it.'

'Mr King,' the lawyer said, not believing his ears, 'do you know what you're doing? You're turning down a unique gift – the number one oil-trading corporation in the world!'

'Yes, Mr Nash, I know exactly what I'm doing. You tell Mr Meyer he may be number one right now, but one of these days I'll knock him off his perch – only it's going to take a little longer than I planned.'

'What are you saying? Mr Meyer is dead.'

But Mort knew differently. E.M. was still here, still towering over him. Brobdingnagian in Lilliput.

*　　*　　*

The reporter stood by the window that spanned one side of Mort's office.

'It's a long way down. It sure is a long way down.'

The symbolism of the banal observation pleased him. He made a note on his pad.

Jeffrey winced. It started coming back to him . . . the pain and the thrill. The sun dipped behind the skyscrapers and a myriad windows glowed red. The office was protected — and not just from the pollution of noise. It was a world apart, apparently untouched by the frantic struggle for existence that overwhelmed most people. It was like being in a capsule, a bronze-tinted, padded capsule, remote and privileged.

Lying around the enormous room were stacks of wooden crates, all shapes and sizes, like so many coffins crammed with the bones of a dead company — files and computers, desks, tables, chairs, lamps, sculptures and paintings. Only the one high-backed chair and the huge glass-topped desk stood there uncrated.

The reporter raised an eyebrow.

'Mort didn't want them sold. They'll be stored, waiting for him.'

'They could be waiting a long time.'

'It's your article,' said Jeffrey brusquely. 'You write it.'

They ended where they had begun: at the fiftieth-floor entrance lobby. It was gigantic.

'I have to tell you,' the reporter said, 'this place blows my mind. I mean, look at this lobby, man. It's Rockefeller Center!'

'It's big,' said Jeffrey.

'Didn't this building used to be the Glass Tower?'

'It did.'

'I remember the story. How he bought it. Wasn't that something? That was really something.'

He pointed to a large bronze plaque on the wall, a sculpture in high relief of an oil derrick in operation, topped by a crown.

'King Brothers. They surely were the kings. No question.'

Jeffrey said nothing.

'Why?' the reporter asked.

'Why what?'

'Why did they do it? They had everything.'

'Everything was not enough for them,' Jeffrey said.

The reporter shook his head and looked at him as if he were crazy.

On the great glass doors of the entrance lobby, deeply etched and filled in gold, were the locations of the company's offices: fifty of them, the eyes and ears of the organization, Amsterdam to Zurich, twenty-five on each door.

The reporter put on his reading glasses and peered closely at the names of the gold-filled offices, as if, somehow, they might hold the key to the mystery. He caressed Paris lightly with the tips of his fingers, a curious, almost devotional gesture, like that of a pilgrim at a shrine.

'I think you're getting the idea,' said Jeffrey drily.

They pushed their way through. Behind them, the heavy glass door swung slowly back on its hinges, hesitated for a moment, poised, as though reluctant to surrender the last inch, and then, with an arid whirring sound, closed with a terminal click.

They rode down in the elevator. It was Saturday. The vast street-level entrance lobby of Kings' Tower was deserted except for a couple of cleaners wet-mopping the marble floor.

They strolled across to the Park Avenue entrance, their footsteps echoing off the floor and walls.

'It's tough,' said the reporter. 'It's tough writing about criminals these days. It used to be easy. There was a time you could tell them apart from the good guys. They looked different, they talked different, they acted different. Now they look just like you and me.'

'Very like,' said Jeffrey.

'Of course, I know these guys cheated on their taxes.'

'You don't know. You don't know anything. You're like the rest of the world. You've condemned them before the trial.'

The reporter nodded. 'It makes you wonder who the real criminals are.'

'They're the ones who don't get caught,' said Jeffrey.

The man wheezed with laughter. 'I sure wish I could write that.'

'Why don't you?' said Jeffrey. 'It's the truth.'

'I try to write a good column, Mr Lewis,' the reporter said. 'One that the average guy enjoys reading. Truth doesn't sell too well.' He held out a limp hand. Jeffrey ignored it.

The reporter grinned apologetically. 'Just as long as it makes a good story,' he said.

'Sure,' said Jeffrey and took the outstretched hand. The guy was only doing his job – giving his readers what they wanted.

As he walked aimlessly up Park Avenue, Jeffrey looked around him at faces in the crowd and wondered about them. Who were they? What did they do? How many times a day did they cheat each other, or the system? They were all out there on the street – the lawyers, the bankers, the realtors, the brokers, the journalists, the surgeons, the socialites, the politicians, all of them making their daily compromises, small or great, spewing their plausible self-serving lies to their kids, their friends, their wives, living the daily pretence, until the pretence became reality, until the story had been told so many times that no one – least of all themselves – could distinguish it any more from the truth.

He thought about the US Attorney's Office, too, and how what mattered to them was their kind of truth – results, indictments, convictions.

It seemed that what you did was not important. It was what you were seen to be doing that counted. You could do what you liked, just as long as you stayed out of trouble. Ironically, the ones who did were the harshest judges, as if keeping your nose clean were a moral imperative, deserving admiration, sanctioning hypocrisy.

Yes they were all involved, thought Jeffrey. If there was any truth, it was that: the lawyers who advised and betrayed them; the politicians who courted them when times were good and deserted them when the going got rough; the friends who shunned them; and the judges who condemned.

That was how it had always been, how it always would be. There were no innocents. They were all guilty. The guiltiest of all was the system – the monster they themselves had created. The system. The system judged and the system condemned. It condemned you to be rich, famous and powerful, to be, in a word, successful. If you were not successful, you were nothing. If you were too successful, you became a target.

And the monster had to be fed from time to time. It demanded its regular victims, its plump sacrificial offerings. How, or why, it hardly mattered. Just as long as it made a good story.

He hailed a cab. The driver scowled at him through the bullet-proof plexi-glass that divided them.

'Where you heading, bud?' he said morosely.

Jeffrey grinned wryly. 'Who knows?' he said. 'Why don't you just keep on going.'

When it came right down to it, Ruby was right. What else was there to do?

*   *   *

The trial was held in the United States District Court for the Southern District of New York. On the forty-ninth day of the trial the jury was instructed by the judge and retired to the jury room.

Four days later, at eleven in the morning, there was a knock on the courtroom door. The judge was in his chambers. The jury was still out. The clerk of the court announced that the jury had reached a verdict. The court was packed. Near the front were the reporters. Outside the courtroom, seemingly relaxed, but ready to jump when

700

the doors opened, were the press photographers and the TV cameramen. This one was big, the biggest ever of its kind.

Mort and Ruby sat with their counsels. Ruby was pale. Mort's cat-green eyes were unusually bright, focused unblinking on the anteroom door that the judge would come through. He came in fast, his black robe floating behind him, as though he could not wait to wrap up this case and get on to the next one.

He called the court to order, which was a formality. It was so quiet that you could hear a reporter breathing at the back of the room. He had a touch of asthma.

'Bring in the jury!'

As the jury filed in, Mort looked at them. In their hands . . . Never before had anyone had that power over him, the power to determine if he was guilty or innocent, the power to decide how he was to pass the next few years of his life. It was a new experience. Whatever happened, he would never be the same man again.

'Mr Foreman, has the jury reached a verdict?'

'It has, Your Honour.'

'What is the jury's verdict on Count One?'

'What is the jury's verdict on Count Eighty-two?'

'Not guilty.'

The court was in uproar. This time the judge's call to order was no formality. It took a while before he could make himself heard.

'The jury has rendered its verdict and found the defendants not guilty on all counts.'

On the steps of the United States Court House a man with grey hair hanging down to his shoulders and dressed in a long white robe pushed through the crowds of spectators and media representatives and screamed at them.

'The Day of Judgement has come! The sinners must be punished! The people shall be free! We shall cast you aside and God will forgive us our sins for your sake!'

The police closed round Mort and Ruby to protect them.

'Let me talk to him,' said Ruby. He pushed through the police. The man in the robe thrust out his lips contemptuously and muttered angrily.

'Who are you?' said Ruby.

'I am the voice of the people! Know me, sinner, and tremble!'

'I'm trembling,' said Ruby. 'Is this some kind of gag? Someone send you?'

'God sent me! He sent me to judge you!'

'They already did that,' said Ruby. 'They found us not guilty.'

'Watch out!' Mort warned him. 'He's crazy. He might have a gun.'

'Who are you calling crazy? I am the voice of the people! I am the instrument of God! You are the crazy ones! You are filth! You are unclean! You pollute the earth! You shall be slaughtered and fed to the vultures! Mankind must be purged or we shall all die!'

Clearly the man was deranged. There was no sense in talking any further. As they turned away and moved on down the steps, he followed them, still raging and screaming abuse.

'You shit! You obscenities! Fuck you! You shameless, fucking shitbags! Die! You are the guilty ones! Guilty! Guilty! Guilty!'

Ruby turned sharply, almost stumbling on the steps. 'They found us not guilty!' he shouted. 'They found us not guilty! Read the papers!'

Mort put out a hand to steady his brother. 'The hell with him. He's a nut. Forget it. Let's go.'

But Ruby just kept shaking his fist and shouting over and over again.

'They found us not guilty! They found us not guilty!'

The floor of Ruby's midtown office was stacked with files. So was the desk. And the windowsills. Through the open

702